LIES AND CONSEQUENCES

Also in the Series

West Country Tales

A Rooftop View
A Marriage of Inconvenience
Looking for Henry
Godmother's Footsteps
Haste to the Wedding
Stormclouds
Things that Go Bump in the Night
A Different View
Winds of Change
Time to Say Goodbye
Full Circle

Also by Jane Hatton
A Dream of Dragons

LIES AND CONSEQUENCES

Jane Hatton

British Library Cataloguing in Publication Data
A catalogue record for this book is available from the British Library

ISBN 978-1-8380372-2-2

Cover design by Amolibros, Milverton, Somerset
www.amolibros.com
This book production has been managed by Amolibros
Printed and bound by Lightning Source worldwide

About the author

Jane Hatton was a child during World War II, and grew up in the unpermissive fifties, when career options for women were largely confined to Secretary, Nurse, Teacher, Physiotherapist. She opted for the first, thinking the skills required would be useful in her preferred career as a writer, but has also worked in hotels, as a sailing instructor, in a craft workshop and as a cookery demonstrator – a remarkably unstructured career – while continuing to write whenever there was a spare moment: sometimes there were not many! She has had two children's books published in the mainstream (a while ago now), followed by three novels in the genre of "literary fiction", plus The One Too Awful to Mention – which we don't mention – and has also independently published a long series about the Nankervis family and their friends and relations, all set in various areas of the West Country. Apart  from writing, her interests include sailing, painting – including at one time scenery for the local pantomime – archaeology, photography and cooking. She lives in Cornwall, on her own these days, with a small black cat for company and a background of family and friends.

I

There's nothing in the whole world so hard to bear as injustice.

Cressida thought the words sounded terribly impressive, and she didn't particularly care that they weren't original – or even, in the context in which she thought them, appropriate. In her mind, it *had* been unjust, there was no possible doubt about that. She was the injured one, and they had turned her away without a second thought, because *he* –

She stopped that thought abruptly. Her talent for self-dramatisation had never managed completely to rationalise the harsh events of her recent life: there were some scenes that couldn't be re-written, some dark places that wouldn't bear close inspection. She consoled herself with the simplistic, if dramatic, statement that they were too terrible, therefore she mustn't let herself think about them. She imagined herself as the tragic heroine of one of the paperback romances that formed her favourite reading. Beautiful, of course, that went without saying, and somehow tragic, with a dreadful secret in her past that she would never tell. *Could* never tell, she liked that better. There was no need to dwell on it in too much detail, and the romanticised version helped to blot out the real truth. Truth and Cress had never been on very friendly terms. A wonderful imagination, her mother had said, teasing. A shocking liar, had said her classmates at school, less forgivingly. Don't think about it. Concentrate on the story.

There's nothing in the whole world so hard to bear as injustice.

Somehow, this time the truism was less comforting, probably there were a lot of things that were harder to bear. Cress stirred uneasily and the entrance to one of those dark places gaped at her invitingly. She shut her mind. If the words had become disturbing, then she mustn't think them. Everyone kept telling her that she mustn't think so much about unpleasant things, as if simply not thinking about them would make them go away.

They had told her to pull herself together, she reminded herself in disgust. Pick up the pieces, they had said encouragingly. But there were simply too many pieces to pick up, they must see that. This, Cress found an easier thought because there was a certain amount of truth in it; none of them had known quite what to do, what to say, and in a rare moment of complete honesty, Cress could see their problem. But that didn't excuse how they had chosen to deal with it.

Take Allison, for instance. Seven years her senior, a worldly young woman, an air hostess or whatever she called herself – cabin crew or something – with a flat of her own near Gatwick, fully in command of an independent life that Cress suspected the family knew very little about. She envied Allison, but that was one thing. It was quite another for her to be so pleased with life and with herself, and she had no right to be so unfairly critical. She couldn't know how her more sensitive sister felt, she was hard.

'If you had any decency at all, you would stop whining and be pleased,' she had said, her brown eyes snapping indignantly. 'You let him take all the blame – you're even beginning to believe your own l – '

Allison had never finished that sentence, because Mum interrupted her, cutting her short with a warning lift of her hand, and a look had flashed between them, so quickly that Cress had nearly missed it, and had been unable to interpret it. If any of them came near to understanding, of course, it would be Mum. *Poor baby duckling,* she had used to say, when Cress had wept for some childish upset that either of her sisters would have shrugged off. *She's born with no oil on her feathers, we must look after her.*

But that was a long time ago.

Without realising it, Cress wriggled in her seat, uncomfortable. She had never been good at reality. *I thought it was true,* she told herself, knowing that she had not. She let her thoughts run free again, touching up memory to make it acceptable. If she did anything else, she would start to be frightened again, and that wouldn't do.

Cressida bent forward so that her hair, the long, black glossy hair that Mike had loved to brush for her in those lost days so far, now, beyond recall, fell forward to hide her face like a curtain. Her voice was taut with the effort to control it.

'I told you,' she said, in desperation. 'And I told him, too – I can't ever bear to see, or speak to him again – never, never! Please...'

But there, the scene went a bit wrong, because what Allison had actually said at that point was, 'Selfish little pig!' and Mum had given her a sorrowful look and said, 'But Cress, my poor baby, it's his home too. You can't make us turn him away. We must all try and put it behind us. We have to, you must see that, or it's going to be…' She had let her voice tail off, and then said, under her breath as if she didn't want Cress to hear her, 'impossible.'

That would take some editing. She tried anyway.

Put it behind them! The shock of their betrayal went deep, like an arrow into living flesh. The pain of it took her breath, made her answer almost without thinking, 'All right then, I won't make you turn him away. I'll go!'

'I'll go to Gran, then,' had been her actual words, spoken sulkily, but they lacked nobility, so she re-wrote them now. She hadn't needed to defend her determination very hard. None of them, not even Mum, had made a serious attempt to prevent her, and she had packed her bag, slammed the door behind her with childish defiance, and walked off into the blue… well, to catch the bus to the station, actually, but that wasn't terribly romantic so she re-wrote that, too.

'Let us know when you get there,' had been Allison's parting shot, but she was still angry and her voice had held neither warmth nor caring, and that, there was no need to re-write. It was true. Mum had kissed her, but it was just an ordinary kiss.

'Perhaps it's all for the best for now,' she had said. 'Take care, darling, remember we all love you.'

Dad had simply filled in the background, looking desperately unhappy. But no, they had none of them reached out to stop her. None of them. Not one. And none of them had offered to run her to the station, either, which she had resented. It wouldn't have hurt them!

And so she had gone out into the world, alone, where she had no friends now, no refuge waiting for her. Gone without a word, to make what she could of a life that she no longer valued — to make what she could of life without Mike, while in the home that had been hers since childhood, they prepared a welcome for his ki —

No.

Even Cress couldn't go that far.

Yet.

She could, of course, have done exactly what she had said she would do, and gone to her maternal grandmother, Gran would have been pleased to see her, spoiled her and made much of her — but she, too, had a different slant on events that she would have tried to put forward, as Cress well knew. So, she had got on the train at Launceston, yes, but when it reached St. Austell she had stayed on it. She was still on it, now.

As the long track to the far south west rolled under the wheels of the train, Cress sat in her seat, consciously clamped in misery. She had never really intended to go to Gran, or for that matter anywhere, she had simply been putting pressure on the family. She had gone to the station more than half-expecting that Dad would come rushing after her in the truck, and when he hadn't, she had got on the train simply because there was nothing else to do.

When she didn't turn up at Gran's, they would all be worried. The thought gave her a strange satisfaction. So, let them worry, was her unspoken thought. Let them be sorry! Then she bit her lip, suddenly uncomfortable and for a second, genuine tears pricked behind her eyes. There was nothing at the end of her journey, and they had made it impossible for her to go back.

A faint, a very faint surge of indignation pierced the sticky tide of her self-pity. After all that had happened, after all that she had been through, the family had withdrawn their support and given it to him. They couldn't seriously expect her to face him. They simply couldn't!

They didn't, remarked her better self, unexpectedly, and with unusual and unwelcome objectivity. They won't make you meet him at all. Not ever again, if you don't want to. But they won't shut him out, either, and they won't admit your right to expect them to. And how are you so different, anyway? If you weren't at this moment sitting in this train and going away, he would have nobody to turn to and that, as you know perfectly well, is *why* they didn't stop you. Not because they don't love you. Because they love you both.

And you've had your share.

She considered this proposition for a mile or two, liking its overtones of high-minded sacrifice, but the part didn't suit her temperament. It required her to be positive and self-reliant, two things at which she had never been good. She dismissed the novel idea and immediately forgot it, thinking instead, *But how could they love him, how can they be so cruel to me, after what he put us all through, what he did?* The tears rolled down again. It'll serve him right, when I don't turn up at Gran's. They'll hate him then.

For I have no haven, she thought, dramatically, abruptly changing pitch. *I have none at all. There isn't a haven in the whole wide world, in the universe,* where you can hide from your memories. And while I can remember him, he isn't wholly dead, nor all that happy time we had together.

That was true. She smiled at the secret thought, hugging it to her as if it was a precious thing, and the woman in the opposite seat, who had been about to ask her if she was all right and offer her sympathy and a cup of tea from her flask, suddenly changed her mind.

The train stopped at Truro, another town with which she was familiar, but she didn't get off. She couldn't, she could *not!* For once, she couldn't analyse why – the conceptions of self-blame or personal guilt had no place in her interpretation of events, even in her beloved romances it existed only when wrongly assumed – but her instincts told her that the one place that she was never willingly going to want to visit again was the Helford River, she shuddered away from the mere thought of it. Anyway, she had no way to get there, she had never gone by train.

And there was nothing for her there, either, not any more.

Never again, never. The hanging woods, the sparkling water, the picture-book village with its shining white inn on the foreshore, the boats, the friendly faces… gone, all gone. Blown away in the explosion that had wrecked her world and left her in this miserable nowhere, where life could never be the same. Would she ever be able to be whole again, to live again?

…would he?

She couldn't recall his face clearly; which seemed odd when she had known him all her life. His photograph had been taken from the table in the lounge two years ago, of course, and put in a drawer where she needn't see it. Mum had cried when she put it away. She hadn't known that Cress had seen her.

The train gave a jerk and started on its way again, and Cress went with it. It was stopping at every station now, but she didn't leave her seat. The woman opposite got off at Hayle, relieved to do so for some reason that she couldn't explain, but Cress sat where she was, paralysed with self-pity, and let the train take her where it would. St. Erbyn and the shining, irretrievable past were well behind her. Ahead, the end of the land, *the end of the world, oblivion.*

But however easy it had become to shut out unwanted faces, unwanted memories had proved a different problem. She would never, for instance, forget Mike's funeral – *Oh Mike, my dearest, how could I ever forget that day we said our last, long, goodbye?* In the real world, in which she still had a toehold, she was conscious of a faint resentment that his name had been *Mike,* it struck a discordant note. He should have been called something more romantic, like Luke, or Damien maybe. She frowned, but only for a moment before returning to the long procession, herself weeping behind the coffin, her eyes reddened and her nose swollen and sore, supported on Dad's arm, and the tears running down his face, too. For some reason it wasn't possible to fantasise the sting out of that, it remained uncomfortably real and genuinely, deeply painful.

As did the trial.

There were tears there, too. Mum sniffing into her handkerchief, Dad looking so white and ghastly that she had really wondered if he was going to faint, and then herself... *cool and self-controlled against the hysteria of the others, as she stood in the witness box and told how she had had to go away — to run away, if they wanted to put it like that, because loving someone wasn't enough and she had needed to find herself — as a person, as an artist.* She had given up art school to marry Mike.

... and because she had so selfishly gone away, the man that she had loved was dead and in his grave, and how could she ever forgive herself?

That had the ring of truth, of genuine tragedy, she told herself. The fact that her modest talent demonstrably didn't justify it, she ignored, using it for an excuse had meant she hadn't needed to be too specific about the events that had led up to her flight. She had run, and Mike had followed, and met his death in doing so, those were the facts. Her fault, her tragedy... *tears, tears, tears.*

Counsel for the defence had called her a spoiled, immature child. Her eyes had met... well, *his,* across the courtroom and her own had filled, against her wish. His had remained steady, thoughtful rather than anything else What was going on in his head behind that steady look was beyond her comprehension or imagining, but she thought that he had been afraid, and so he should have been. Even so, he hadn't given her away, perhaps because he knew that he wouldn't be believed, and it would stand against him. A thrill of shocked dismay ran through her, and she hurriedly quelled that line of thought. After that had come the verdict, the judge passing sentence — but there was no need to remember all that. It was rather sordid and uncomfortable. Cress and reality weren't on very good terms: what she had — inadvertently, she assured herself — done, frightened her if she thought about it too hard. She preferred to nurture her deep and lasting grief, to feed her sense of personal tragedy, all the more poignant since she had become gradually aware…

Her heart leaped, rising like a singing bird, all unaware that she stood on shifting ground that could drop her through, if she wasn't careful, into unknown and dangerous territory. She had discovered something in those days that she couldn't do without, and so – she didn't. It had never occurred to her that the night she had reached out in her misery and guilt and despair and imagined she truly felt his arms come around her had been a turning point that might be that of no return.

Mike, Mike, our love so strong, so deep that it can span the great river, rise out of the grave, warm me with just an echo of what we lost, just enough to make things bearable. Give me time, oh my love, my darling. I can stand without you, I will, I promise, I will let you go. I can rebuild my life, I can come to terms with tragedy. I'm trying, I really am – I love you – I need you – stay a little while, just a little while.

But the rebuilding foundations were only fragile, even with this help. It had taken one telephone call to destroy them.

One telephone call, to say that he was coming home.

Just one telephone call to shatter the illusion of regained peace, and send her, raw and shaken as if it had all happened yesterday, out into an uncaring world, away from love and comfort, catapulted on the elastic of her own divided and outraged loyalties, with no place where she could hide. The fact that the instincts that had sent her flying had been genuine only confused her. She found the colours of the real tragedy too garish, preferring the delicate pastels of her own illusions. So –

They had been cruel to make her go.

She had almost thought there, *let* her go. She pulled herself up abruptly, but the thought once given expression was as slimy and insidious as creeping oil.

After two whole years? The question slid into her head, coloured with incredulity. Years that had been easier by far for her than for him, so far as material things went. Years full of love and sympathy and kindness. He had had none of these.

He had what he deserved.

The train rattled on over points, coming into St. Erth now. It would run out of line soon, and she would have to get out. Penzance, she supposed. Well, why not? It was as good as anywhere, when you were so unhappy that everywhere looked the same.

Perhaps it had been time she left. Cress stirred uneasily again, as so often in the past afraid of looking facts in the face, even in the privacy of her own mind. Home was home, she didn't want to feel that she didn't belong any more in the semi-detached villa that her father had rented for them in Launceston only last year, or in the rambling house in St. Austell where she had grown up. The only thing was, it was so very difficult to think back to the time before she married Mike. Four years that had, all unknowingly, comprised a lifetime. Before that, there was being a child, school, college, friends and a loving family, but the gulf was too wide, too deep, it felt like a different life. Then Mike. *Then tragedy.*

It took two years, they had told her – everyone had told her. At least two years after you lost someone, before you could begin to live again. Her two years had run their course, but she was different, wasn't she? More sensitive, and anyway, Mike had been… but she couldn't even think the M-word. Instead, she felt thankfulness, and absolution from whatever it was her head was trying to tell her. *Because if getting over it meant letting Mike go, putting her love behind her, then a hundred years wouldn't be long enough. And if that was wrong, then she would just have to be wrong.*

Penzance was the terminus. Cress took her suitcase and left the train. Nobody had asked to see her ticket, nobody seemed to want her to pay an excess. She left the platform and walked out into the sunlit station yard.

She had no idea of where she wished to go. The bus station was next to the railway station, she went there and as the Trelewan bus was waiting, she climbed onto it.

The bus pulled out into the late-afternoon traffic and Cress began to consider seriously, for the first time, exactly what she was going to do. On her left, as they rumbled along, the sea sparkled cheerfully in the late evening sunshine, to her right, shops and cafes were beginning to stir to the approach of Easter. Perhaps, Cress thought, she could find work in the town. Mum had been saying for some time that it might help her to get herself a little job, had even asked her if she wanted to go back to college to finish her course – but going back was beyond imagination. *Nobody had ever yet succeeded in going back.* Cress thought in clichés quite a lot of the time. She never questioned whether they were true. It was enough that they were familiar.

So, a job? That would be a positive step. She didn't need it in order to live, thanks to the wonders of Life Insurance and her parents' help, but perhaps she did in order to live fully.

She considered this revolutionary idea as the bus travelled through Penzance to Newlyn, past the busy harbour and up the hill into open countryside, but reality had become tangled with fantasy again, and after the first surprise at having thought of it at all, she didn't consider it as a genuine option. It became an element in the story she made up about herself.

At least, if she worked she would have less time for thinking. She let her thoughts run on, speculating. She would be good at her job – whatever it was – but remote, and somehow unattainable. Her workmates would whisper about her. There was a shadowy boss in the fantasy somewhere, not a bit like Mike of course, perhaps the rugged, dark womaniser in *A Lover for Ruby* – his name had been Rafe she recalled, but of course it had been he, not Ruby, who had the secret sorrow.

The houses had been long left behind now, and the bus was bowling along a twisty road going ever westwards. Fields with cows and a stone circle, also with cows, a hill, a dip, another hill. Glimpses of sea sparkling to her left, and a junction on the right with a signpost reading TRELEWAN 1½, but the bus kept straight on. The switchback road narrowed, curled downhill, crossed a bridge over a shallow stream and wound upwards again across a green expanse of farmland before plunging gently downhill into trees. There was a gate across a driveway with the name THE QUOIT carved into it, and a glimpse of a grey house among leaves. An optimistic early-season sign swinging from the branch of a convenient tree read BED & BREAKFAST and VACANCIES in roughly painted black lettering. On impulse, Cress left her seat and made her way forward along the bus, leaning towards the driver's ear.

'Can you drop me off somewhere along here?'

It was a country bus, with country habits. She stood by the roadside with her holdall at her feet and watched it drive away, and then, picking up the bag and slinging it over her shoulder, she began to walk back towards the wood.

It was very quiet, very still, under the spreading branches, just beginning to fur over with green ready for spring. The rhododendrons that almost hid the house from the road rattled their leaves, and on her left, a copse of pussy willows was powdered with its fluffy blooms. She wasn't sure after all if she was ready for so much isolation… peace, quiet, trees, the stirring little wind among the leaves… *time would stand still here, unlimited*

Tragedy for those at home had two faces. Not simply the abruptly, shockingly bereaved daughter, but the son too.

Cress stopped abruptly on the verge.

I can't. If I'm alone, I won't be alone. They will sit on either side of me, Mike and him, and if I call there won't be anyone to hear and help me, their ghosts will rend me apart, the dead and the living.

The low sun shone out of the pale, April sky, the wind ruffled green shoots in the broken stone wall beside her, beyond the concealing bushes the grey house waited, square and quiet. The gate, not quite closed, moved gently in the light wind, creaking on its hinges.

The quoit. The burial place. The place, perhaps, to bury the past.

And if she could still not confront what she had done – no! – what had happened to her, squarely in the face, or manage the whirl of devastating emotion that had sent her rushing out into the world only this morning, then at least here it wouldn't confront her every hour of the day, and time, that greatest of all healers, could do his work. From this quiet place, she could go forward. Never go back. *She had said that herself. She should have added, long, long ago, never stand still.*

Mike would be there to help her. She felt his love reaching out to her as a warmth that shamed the spring sunshine.

Cress walked forward along the verge, and opened the gate.

The house was built of granite, square, grey and uncompromising amid its concealing rhododendrons and camellias. The camellias were in bloom already, snow white and vibrant, vivid crimson, and on a rough little lawn to the side, a hutch and a wired-in run housed a family of black and white rabbits. The place didn't look particularly prosperous, in fact it had a run-down air that Cress hadn't expected, and the bushes so close to the windows made it dark, but the room to which she was shown was clean and freshly painted, and at least it was somewhere to be. Everyone had to be somewhere.

The owner, or at least, the woman of the house, was young, not so very much older than Cress herself, a dark, Irish beauty in tight, faded jeans and a torn shirt, who introduced herself as Kate – short for Caitlin, she said, but nobody called her that. She had a forceful, rather scornful way with her, but perhaps it was just her manner. Cress, left alone in her room, went to the windowsill and sat down, leaning her forehead against the window frame. She had been treated with the gentleness due to an invalid rather than the bereaved for so long now that Kate's brusque welcome had left her feeling bruised. To Kate, she was simply a visitor. Her name had meant nothing. Nobody but herself, now, cared at all. Yesterday's news. Mike had died at twenty-eight and already become yesterday's news. She drooped.

Her window looked out over the lawn, with distant glimpses of sea over the rhododendrons. As she sat there, feeling isolated in her self-imposed perpetual misery, a man came out of the bushes and began to walk towards the house. He was tall, thin almost to the point of emaciation, with unkempt brown hair and a close, stubbly beard. He walked with a purposeful stride, and as he walked he yelled,

'Kate! Katie! Where the shit are you, Katie?'

A voice called back from somewhere below, but to Cress it was just a mumble. The man passed from her sight, and she heard laughter. People, living their lives together. A shiver ran over her skin. Her loneliness pressed on her.

The lawn was empty now except for the rabbits, hopping and nibbling in their run. Cress got stiffly to her feet, threw her bag on the bed, and began to unpack, throwing clothes and books onto the bed until she came to the bottom. Mike's photograph lay there, under her white woolly jumper, safe in its silver frame. She picked it up and held it in her hands, letting the sense of her own isolation pour round her, enfold her. The pain of her own emotion choked in her throat.

Mike. Dear, kindly, loving Mike, companion of so few short years of perfect happiness, so cruelly ended. Her conscience, which still retained a spark of life, gave a small twinge. It hadn't been perfect happiness, that was the whole point – but, she told herself hurriedly, that had only been on the surface. *Underneath* it had been perfect. It was her own need for her art that had caused the pressure, that was it. Her conscience, shrugging its shoulders, fell silent. She looked down at Mike's lean, intelligent face with its narrow, mobile mouth and the thin hawk nose, and the frame of exuberantly curly fair hair so different from her own, straight and dark, falling nearly to her waist. The photographer hadn't quite caught the look in his eyes… grey eyes, quietly smiling, deep, warm. Of all things, she had most loved his eyes.

Conscience stirred again, memories rose unwanted to the surface. The last time he had looked at her with those eyes, it had been with hurt, anger, distress… scorn. *Not with that loving smile that had turned her heart over and made her blood run like fire through her veins. Oh Mike, Mike, how can I ever say goodbye? If I had known, if I had only known, how short our time would be I would never, never, have wasted a moment of it.*

There was a brief knock on the door, and Kate came in holding a hot-water bottle.

'I thought you might like to borrow this,' she said, holding it out, limp and flat. 'There's no radiators in this house, but the water in the tap is sizzling hot, thank God, with the stove downstairs. If your feet are warm it never seems so bad, somehow.'

Cress had been so far away with her fantasies that it took her a moment to come back. She stood there with the photograph in its silver frame pressed against her heart, and her eyes dark pools of tragedy.

'Good God!' said Kate, appalled. 'What on earth is the matter?'

The tears that Cress so often shed stung yet again behind her eyes now. She swallowed. *Red-eyed at Mike's funeral, red-eyed through the awful weeks and months that had followed,* come down to crying over a pink hot-water bottle and the kindness of a stranger. Fantasy and unacceptable reality grated painfully where they came too close and touched. She couldn't face it.

'So kind – ' she said, with a tight throat.

Kate dropped the hot-water bottle onto the bed.

'What you need is a nice cup of tea,' she said, briskly. 'I've just made one for Charlie, I'll bring one up for you.'

'Charlie?' queried Cress. 'Oh yes – your husband. I saw him outside, I think.'

'Oh, we aren't married,' said Kate, and grinned at her. 'Marriage is strictly for the birds.' Her eye fell on Cress's wedding ring, circling the third finger of the hand that held the photograph, and she hurriedly back-tracked. 'It's all right for some, I suppose.'

'It was all right for me,' said Cress, rather too defiantly. She put the picture down on the dressing table, arranging it carefully so that she could see it from the bed. Kate watched her with a sardonic gleam in her eyes.

'They're none of them worth tearing yourself to bits for,' she suggested. 'Gone off, has he?'

'He's dead,' said Cress.

'Oh!' Kate looked momentarily taken aback. 'I'm so sorry – I didn't realise.'

'Yes,' said Cress. *She stood for a moment, looking down at Mike's loved face that would never smile at her again, and added the terrible, the unforgivable thing.* 'He was murdered,' she said.

Kate went downstairs to the kitchen in a thoughtful mood.

'We've got ourselves a real weirdo this time,' she said. Charlie was sitting at the kitchen table with his mug of tea and the paper. He looked up.

'What, the PG?'

'Yes.' Kate picked up the teapot from the edge of the stove and stood holding it. 'She's been telling me her husband was murdered.' Her voice, rich as cream and soft as velvet, thrilled on the words.

'But that's terrible.'

'Yes, it is.' Kate gave a sigh, and hooked a spare mug towards her by its handle. The tea gurgled into it, hot and black, just the way Charlie liked it. 'Somehow, she makes it sound like something out of one of those tacky little romances. She had a pile of them on the bed. She almost made me feel it wasn't true.'

'Perhaps it wasn't.' Charlie wasn't that interested. His attention began to stray back to the sports page.

'I think it was. You didn't see her face.' The top of the milk bottle had left her fingers greasy. Kate licked them thoughtfully. 'The awful thing is, I think she's looking to me for sympathy.'

'Is that so difficult to give?' He had almost stopped listening.

'And a mother-figure to lean on and dry her tears,' said Kate, caustically. Charlie gave a great bellow of laughter.

'You?'

'Not if I can help it.' Kate picked up the mug and the bag of sugar and made for the door. 'If she wants a shoulder to cry on, she's come to the wrong shop. I'm dreadfully sorry for her, if it's true, but I can't stand wet women. Will crying bring him back?'

She walked briskly out of the door and Charlie turned back to his newspaper with a smile. Kate's heart, he knew, was a lot softer than she made out – but other people's tragedies were their own affair. He poured himself another mug of tea, absently, with his eyes on the rugby results.

★

If Kate had no intentions of being a substitute-mother figure, she was at least kind in her way. Cress came downstairs later on, composed and calm, and asked if she might use the telephone.

'There isn't one,' said Kate, cheerfully. 'They cut us off. There's a box up by the crossroads, it's only a few minutes walk – while it's still there.'

'And meals,' said Cress. 'You only do bed and breakfast, don't you?'

Cress had never been practical, it had been a contributory factor in her own personal tragedy had she but realised it, and her lack of practicality was all too obvious. She was one of those women, Kate thought in irritation, who needed to be looked after every minute of the day.

'I can do you an evening meal if you like, but it'll be whatever we have, and you'll have to eat it with us,' she said, knowing it was against her better judgement but, in the face of this helplessness, unable to help herself. 'And not every night, mind. We aren't always here.'

'Is there somewhere in the village where I can eat?'

'There's the pub. It's a bit of a walk in the dark, though.'

Cress's chin jerked up as if Kate had hit her.

'I don't like pubs much anyway,' she said.

'Please yourself.' Kate shrugged. 'It'll have to be Penzance then. There's nowhere else.'

'Are there buses?'

Kate looked at her in despair.

'Haven't you any transport of your own?'

'No.'

'Then why pick on somewhere like this, right out in the sticks?' asked Kate, she thought reasonably. Cress's face crumpled.

'I needed to be alone,' she said, dramatically. Kate laughed, but kindly.

'Well, you'll certainly be that here! All right, I suppose I can hire you my bike when I don't need it – it isn't much, mind, but it'll get you around. But the phone box is only a short walk, you can find that all right on foot. It's usually working out of season.'

She gave Cress directions and shut the door on her, raising her eyes expressively to heaven, although there was nobody to see her. Charlie had said that their guest might be in shock still, and perhaps he was right. But if anyone murdered Charlie, she thought vaguely, she wouldn't sit around under the rhododendrons wringing her hands. She would get out there and murder *them*!

Outside, the bright evening sun had long ago faded into twilight, clouds had begun to build up behind the trees and the wind was rising. It was only April, after all. Cress walked along the deserted road, her feet crunching on small stones, enjoying the loneliness now of the place, that was so different from the unrecognised loneliness of her spirit. Things didn't look too bad from here. You could – you had to – get over the death of a loved one eventually, she had been constantly told so although there were no signs of it yet, and of course Mike was still near. For other tragedies, it was different.

The phone box showed as a glow of light ahead of her, and her footsteps began to slow. She had left it too late, she realised. He would be there. There wasn't the remotest chance that he would be the one to answer the telephone, but he would be in the same house where her own voice would be speaking… why, oh why, the real Cress asked unexpectedly, was this hurdle being so much more difficult to surmount than the fact of death, which was so utterly final and awful? She need never see him, need never speak to him again, there was no need to cringe at the thought that he might, however distantly, hear her voice speaking to someone else. Probably, he wouldn't even be within earshot. *It was all that they could give each other now, total withdrawal. He had no apology, she no forgiveness. Stalemate. She was glad for it, if it kept them apart.* Her moment of honesty was over. Whatever the truth that lay behind it, she wouldn't find it now. If guilt wasn't a concept she understood; if her lies had taken her a step too far, she would never admit it simply because the results had been too far-reaching. It had all run away with her. It was still running now.

She stood outside the phone box on the damp grass verge for some time, wishing that she didn't have to open the door and go in, reaching after the idea of herself that was so much easier to live with than the uncomfortably torn, dutiful daughter, who knew somewhere inside her that she had no right to worry everybody so. But it was no use, even her fantasies allowed that you could not demand – but she preferred the word *need* herself – the last reserves of sympathy from people who loved you and then suddenly walk out and not even let them know that you were safe without putting yourself in the wrong. Being in the wrong wasn't Cress's favourite place. Steeling herself, she went into the booth and dialled the number of her home.

Allison answered. It would be Allison.

'Hullo Cress,' she said. 'Are you OK? Where are you?' She wouldn't give Cress the satisfaction of knowing how much she had worried them all, walking out like that and never turning up at Gran's. Her voice was so cool that Cress felt physically chilled by it.

'Down somewhere near Land's End,' Cress said. 'I'm in a B&B for a few days. The people are very nice, it'll be quite fun for a change, I'm going to enjoy it. I thought it was time I stood on my own feet.' Allison couldn't see her, but she lifted her chin bravely.

Pause.

'You sound better,' said Allison. She relented a little. 'Happier. I'm sorry if I was horrible, Cress. Mum says I was. I didn't mean to be.' A discerning ear might have thought that she sounded rehearsed, but Cress, whose whole life, to quite a considerable depth, had always been rehearsed, wasn't critical. She spoke her own line:

CRESSIDA (*with generous forgiveness*) 'I know I've been being a drag. I'm sorry too. Is everything all right at home?'

She hadn't meant to ask that. She hadn't meant to say anything that would admit, even to herself, that there was a chance that everything wasn't all right, that the quiet home she had left was likely to be the scene of terrible emotional devastation. They weren't, after all, emotional people.

'Oh, fine,' said Allison, and it was impossible to tell from her voice if she was speaking the truth or not.

One had to go through the motions. Civilisation demanded it, and she had begun this, not Allison. Cress swallowed.

'So he got back safely?'

Allison made a small sound that down a telephone wire could have been taken for a laugh, a sob, or even a hiccup.

'Of course,' she said, and added, unasked and unwanted, 'He might never have been away. We all behaved perfectly, and it's all been quite easy.'

So he wasn't within earshot. Cress was glad.

'Oh – good,' she said.

Over the distance, her voice sounded so detached and complacent that Allison was swept by an awful impulse to add, *we've all been acting our socks off, and Dad is shut in his office and Mum is crying in the washing-up, and it's all a million times worse than a self-centred little bitch like you could ever dream!* She bit it back with an effort. Time might show Cress where she had erred, people had already tried and failed. No point in starting it all over again.

'Well, I'm glad you're settled happily, even if you didn't think to tell us what you were planning,' she said, instead, trying to keep the sting out of her voice. 'Have a nice time. Be sure and send us a postcard.' No. She wasn't being sarcastic, was she?

'Give Mum and Dad my love,' said Cress.

'I will.' For what it's worth.

'Goodnight, then.'

End of conversation. Cress put down the receiver and stepped out into the cool, windy night. It was a relief to have that over.

She walked back to The Quoit. The house was warm and welcoming as she went in through the door, with a rich smell of frying onions thick in the air. Charlie poked his head through a door at the end of the small hall.

'Grub up,' he said cheerfully. 'We were just waiting for you to come in.'

That first meal they had together was impersonal. They talked of ordinary, everyday things, the erratic bus service and whether Cress could eat macaroni cheese (she couldn't, ugh!), things of that kind, and after it, Kate refused an offer of help with the washing-up. Feeling vaguely dismissed, Cress made her way back up to her room and lay on her bed with a book.

Lovely, after all, to be quite on her own, she told herself.

The book was a light romance of the most superficial kind, perfect holiday reading. Cress, who had what her sisters considered an unnatural passion for such things, tried to become interested in the doings of the pretty blonde heroine and the tough, on the whole rather arrogant and unreasonable hero, but found that for once they were failing to hold her attention. Usually, she could lose herself in the doings of the repetitive and stereotyped pair, but tonight her head was playing tricks on her. For one thing, the hero was dark (they generally were) and her imagination, which was normally equal to anything, couldn't seem to hold his image steady. He would come glowering onto the scene, six-foot-plus of unreconstructed alpha male, and before he had taken three paces into the story there would be nothing left of his creator's intentions but the colour of his hair. His piercing blue eyes, that wreaked such havoc on the heroine's susceptible little heart, would have become hazel, alight with laughter, and his rather-too-long, luxuriant and wavy hair would be close and fine, and — regrettably — starting to recede a little on the temples. His grim (but devastatingly attractive, of course) lips would soften and betray evidence of a lively sense of humour that the script hadn't written for him, and his impressive height and lean, rangy body would be impossible to visualise. It was infuriating.

And it hurt a lot more than she cared for.

Cress laid down the book and stared across the room at Mike, smiling at her from the dressing table.

Mike, Mike, Mike. Mike, I love you – I loved you. No, I love you. I love you still. Whatever I do, wherever I go, whoever I meet, your corner of my heart is always warm for you.

Mike, my friend. Mike, my love. Mike, my husband. Mike who died and left my life a wasteland.

Mike who died, and not in an accident or an illness, or any half-way bearable thing, but at the hands of my own brother, whom I once loved too… and who was freed from prison this morning on parole after serving just two-thirds of a three-year prison sentence for manslaughter.

Oh God, why can't I cry any more?

Why is it that he, who is alive, is more dead to me than you, who are truly dead and in the grave?

My husband. My brother.

And my tears.

She lay on her bed in the lamp lit room with the book face-down on her lap and grieved, torn between what was true and what she would have liked to be true, but at that moment and in that place, with Kate and Charlie laughing in the room below, and the rabbits sleeping in their hutch under the window, she was still redeemable. She had only to reach out and take the reality – the casual friendships, the new life, the wider horizons that beckoned within her grasp and she could still be safe.

She had only to turn her back on her dangerous fantasy and tell the truth.

II

Charlie was a real artist, not an amateur. Not a terribly successful one, he went in for what Kate described as *original concepts*, with a humorous quirk of an eyebrow that expressed at one and the same time exasperation, despair, and a great deal of warm affection. Not love – or at least, not what Cress considered to be love. She didn't admire him, and neither did she cherish him. She didn't always even cook his meals. But she lived with him and laughed with him, and glowed a little more when he was there, teasing him by telling him that his work wasn't so much Brit Art as brat art, with no capitals and giggling and leaping to the other side of the table when he plunged at her, growling.

Cress had, whatever her protestations, really given no thought to going back to her painting, but when they learned that she had done two years at art school, both Kate and Charlie suggested that she should do some sketching.

'Get out onto the cliffs in the sunshine,' said Kate. 'The fresh air will do you good, you need some roses in your cheeks.' She never referred to Cress's problems, but she was tacitly kinder than she had been at first, trying to bring her out of herself and, maybe too obviously, not to be over-critical. Charlie was different.

He looked at Cress's sketches with a critical eye.

'Not bad, for someone who's been to art school,' he said. He had never been near such a place himself. 'Get yourself some paints and things, and you can work them up in my studio if you like.'

His studio was a tumbledown stone shed beyond the rhododendrons, in which he daubed, hammered and generally created curious, almost three-dimensional artefacts, half picture, half sculpture, with the support of an Arts Council grant. He didn't use oil paints, but sample pots of ordinary household enamels, and his confidence in his own ability was such that he was occasionally able to convince other people and sell one of them. Kate eked out their slender means picking daffodils and potatoes in season, and doing bed and breakfast for passing tourists. Kate had an honours degree in history and an agile, clever brain, and had told Cress in one of her more expansive moments that she found the world a terrifying place. The village referred to them, Cress had discovered, as *that wild, feckless pair of drop-outs up on the cliff*, and looked at them askance, but they believed in themselves and worked hard, and the description was unfair.

Perhaps Charlie's invitation had been a mistake. Kate certainly thought it had been, for April slipped into May, May into June, and Cress was still at The Quoit, easing into a niche that she hollowed out for herself like, Kate thought cynically, a maggot in an apple. She wished that the rather childish and immature girl would move on, or return to her home that was surely not too far away, but she paid her rent regularly and they did need the money. But taking her in, Kate decided, had probably been the wrong thing to do. Trying to be honest, she decided that it wasn't anything to do with Charlie, particularly, but very definitely to do with Cress herself. And it was unusual, and for some reason worrying, to find a native Cornish girl as one of their guests, and she wondered about it when she had time.

Working with Charlie in the same environment, Cress naturally came to know him well. He was a tough cynic with a soft underbelly of easy sentiment, and bitter about the artistic world in which he worked.

'It's not what you do in this life that counts, it's who you are,' he said, one day, when one of the more prestigious local art galleries had, yet again, turned down two of his works offered for one of their regular exhibitions. 'And it's not simply professional, it's a social thing. Look at this village, and take a case in point.' He jabbed the end of his brush in her direction to emphasise his words. 'Here's Kate and me, living in a rented house. Here's me, painting. We've been here four years now and never asked anything of anyone, and yet when we go up to the pub of an evening, they still treat us as if we were outsiders. Why? Because Kate is Irish and I'm from Surrey!'

Cress giggled. *Surrey* made her think of afternoon tea on the lawn and tennis parties, maybe, not Charlie.

'What're you laughing at?' asked Charlie, suspiciously, but Cress wouldn't tell him.

'Go on,' she said.

Charlie dipped his brush into red paint without bothering to clean out the previous blue, and slapped the resulting dirty purple streaks onto a piece of hardboard.

'All right,' he said. 'So, out on the other side of the village, there's two people, just like us – he paints, God knows what she does. They live just as feckless a life as we do, and they haven't been here half as long, and what do we find? Everyone in the village treats them like long-lost friends, and why?' He paused rhetorically, and Cress said dutifully, 'Why, then?'

Charlie said, explosively, 'Because he's bloody Cornish, that's why! You Cornish are as clannish as the Scots, and as exclusive as the bloody royal family! And that isn't all!' His brush went indignantly, *slap, slap, slap,* across the board. 'I've been painting more than ten years now.' *Slap, slap, slap.* 'I've worked my bloody arse off, trying to say something that those morons out there will listen to, and I can't so much as get a picture hung in a piddling bloody local art gallery! But him! What does he get offered? Not just the bloody Arts Guild, or some warehouse gallery on the fringe, the Ladbourne Gallery, no less! London, West End, bloody champagne parties!'

Cress knew the Ladbourne Gallery by repute from her art school days, and was impressed.

'He must be good,' she said.

'He may be,' said Charlie, with deep scorn. 'I doubt it, but he may be. But I bloody hope he goes flat on his bloody face!'

'Don't you like him?' asked Cress, after a cautious pause.

'I don't know him,' said Charlie. 'I don't know him, but I know who he bloody is, and that's what gets under my skin! Oliver bloody Nankervis, that's who, and if he was anyone else he'd be having his bloody exhibition at the Cosgrove Gallery in the town here, like the rest of us poor bloody struggling painters!'

It was only when he was painting that Charlie's conversation became quite so sanguinary. Normally the mildest of men, with a brush in his hand he became a raging iconoclast. Kate said tolerantly that it released his libido, and Cress didn't know what she meant.

'Oliver Nankervis that sailed round the world?' she asked, surprised.

'The very bloody same!' said Charlie. He painted for a moment or two in silence, and then said, with a characteristic swing to the other side of the fence. 'Of course, you can't be too down on the man. If he'd turned his bloody hand to anything but painting I'd have said he deserved all the success he could get. It can't be much fun to be a cripple, after the things he's done.'

Cress's mother had once worked for the social services. She said, repressively, 'They prefer to be called disabled.'

'They can call it what they bloody like,' said Charlie, carefully.

Kate appeared in the doorway with a tray bearing mugs of tea.

'Charlie ranting again, is he?' she asked, tolerantly. 'What is it this time, the parish council, the Government, or the Arts Guild?'

'Oliver bloody Nankervis,' said Cress, with a flash of rare humour, and Kate grinned.

'Oh, him. Well, it's always galling to see someone succeeding where you haven't quite managed to.'

Charlie didn't so much put down his brush as fling it from him. It narrowly missed Cress and splattered into the corner of the studio.

'He hasn't succeeded yet! We'll see what he's made of come next year!'

Kate put down the tray and sat on the edge of Charlie's workbench, pushing aside a stack of offcuts mixed with wood shavings in order to do so.

'You don't seriously think he won't, do you?' she asked.

Charlie seized his mug and drank thirstily and noisily.

'All right then, so his mother is bloody famous as a sculptor – '

' – tress,' Kate interrupted.

'As a bloody sculptor, I said,' said Charlie. 'But he's not chosen to sculpt that I ever heard. And his bloody father uses his bloody commuter belt to hold up his bloody pin-striped trousers –'

Kate giggled, provocative, brilliant as a peony against the dirty white wall.

'Char-*lie*! And what does your father do?'

Oh well…' Charlie turned a dull red and rubbed the back of his neck. Kate said, to Cress,

'He's a consultant surgeon. He can't understand Charlie, but when he has time to remember, he's quite proud of him because of that grant. If only he knew!'

'Knew what?' demanded Charlie, but Kate sipped her tea and flashed her marvellous Irish blue eyes at him over the rim of her mug, and he looked sheepish.

Cress liked to hear them talk together, tossing the subject of their conversation around like a ball, teasing and insulting each other. She didn't understand them, but she found them exciting. Their talk, the way they lived, the things they did, were so different from her own life. When they were around, the memory of Mike began to fade and she thought that at long last she was living for herself. She wasn't aware, and neither were they, that instead of living through Mike, or before that through the brother whom she had worshipped from her cradle, she was beginning to live through Charlie. That she was the kind of woman who could only live fully through a man, who needed a man, who would take her colours from the object of her desire like a chameleon hiding on a leaf. Because of this chameleon quality, which unconsciously burnished his own idea of himself, Charlie at first found her delightful, but Kate, equally unconsciously, increasingly feeling a threat, held her at arm's length, and tolerated her, no more.

Cress extended her stay yet again, and Kate let her because paying guests weren't actually thick on the ground in a tumbledown place such as theirs, but she was beginning to wonder if she hadn't let practical cupidity outweigh her judgement. The *maison à trois* had begun to be too much of an accepted thing.

'She'll go home soon, and then you'll have your studio to yourself,' she said, one evening as she and Charlie sat by the stove after Cress had gone up to bed.

'I don't know that she will,' said Charlie, frowning. 'She won't talk about home, she won't come through with anything about herself.'

'Won't she?' Kate raised her beautiful eyebrows disbelievingly. 'She looks to me the kind that longs to tell you her life story at the drop of a hat. Are you sure you've given her the opportunity?'

'We mostly talk about painting,' said Charlie. Kate laughed. She made herself more comfortable on the sagging old sofa, lying back and resting her feet in his lap.

'You mean, you mostly talk about Charlie Price, and she lets you,' she said. Charlie stroked the soles of her feet with his finger, his eyes bright.

'You never listen anyway. She's a harmless enough little thing, why do you want her gone?'

'I don't know,' said Kate, who genuinely didn't. She frowned. 'She troubles me.'

'Oh, come now!'

'Don't do that! It tickles.' She withdrew her feet, toes curled, and sat on them instead, settling into the angle made by the corner of the sofa with the fluid ease of a cat.

'She's had a rotten time,' said Charlie.

'If the little she told me is actually true,' said Kate.

'She wouldn't make up a thing like that.'

'Yes, but *murder*!'

'You read about it every day in the newspaper.'

'But we didn't,' said Kate. 'We didn't see it on the telly, we didn't read it in the *Western Morning News* – surely we'd have remembered, if we had? We'd have remembered the name as soon as she said.'

'So what are you suggesting?'

'Ask her,' said Kate. 'She'll perhaps talk to you more easily than she does to me. She seems to like you better. You ask her.'

'When I get the chance,' agreed Charlie. He wasn't much interested in Cress, except as she reflected himself. He lunged forward and caught Kate by the shoulders, tumbling her over into his arms. She struggled, laughing, the curling black ringlets of her hair falling round their faces like a silken curtain.

'Charlie, no – not in front of the cat! Charlie!' They were both laughing now. Charlie gave a growl, biting at her ear.

'Come here, you luscious Irish colleen, and let me show you a thing or two – ' He stopped abruptly, and released his hold, and Kate, flushed and startled, slipped off his lap onto the floor.

'I'm sorry,' said Cress, at the door. 'I left my book down here.' She walked across to the table and picked it up, and Charlie and Kate watched her, all three of them equally embarrassed. The journey back to the kitchen door felt like ten miles. 'Goodnight,' said Cress.

''night, Cress,' said Charlie.

The door closed softly behind her.

Kate got to her feet, and stood there buttoning her shirt with her face the colour of a poppy.

'I've had enough of this!' she said. 'We can't even be private in our own house now! She'll have to go.'

'Come on Katie, we've had PGs before,' said Charlie, placatingly. Kate frowned at him, angry at his taking sides against her, as it seemed to her.

'They've never set foot in this room before. We should never have let her get so intimate with us. It never works.'

'Katie!' He reached up and pulled her down beside him again. She sat, unrelaxed, on the very edge of the cushions. 'Katie, it's not that simple. She needs us. She's just been brutally widowed, how can we send her away?'

'Why did she have to come here?' countered Kate, angrily.

'She had to go somewhere, I suppose.'

Kate dropped her burning face into her hands, so that Charlie couldn't see it, ashamed of herself, of her own lack of charity.

'I don't want her here any more.'

'I'll talk to her,' said Charlie. 'I'll talk to her tomorrow, see how the land lies. I promise.'

'I'm going to bed,' said Kate. She stood up abruptly and went to the door.

'I'll be up in a minute.'

'Don't bother,' said Kate. 'I'm not in the mood any more. And you remember, you promised.' She slammed out.

'I'll remember,' said Charlie, to the closed door.

But he didn't.

Cress heard their angry voices, and she heard the slam of the door and Kate's feet running on the wooden stairs. She sat on the bed and felt miserable. She didn't care about Kate, Kate could take care of herself, but Charlie... *so sweet, so vulnerable, so much in need of love.* She could see his face now, red and embarrassed, looking at her apologetically over the back of the sofa. Poor Charlie, Kate was far too strong for him, she ate him alive.

'Mike?' she said, tentatively. She didn't feel him constantly beside her, but she knew that he wasn't far away, watching over her. Sometimes, she would talk to him, and feel the comfort of his unspoken replies. 'Mike?'

She reached out her hand, as if to a living entity.

'You do like him, Mike, don't you – Charlie? He's such a lamb. All that shouting and swearing... like a naughty little boy. It doesn't mean anything, it's just bravado. Underneath he's just a little lost child.'

The house was silent now, Kate had flounced into her bedroom and gone to ground, and Charlie hadn't come upstairs. Well, he wouldn't, would he? He must feel terrible, if he felt about her the way she was beginning to feel about him, the way she thought he must do. He could talk to her, confide in her – with Kate it was always fighting and skirmishes, excited spark-striking that surely agonised the artist's soul in him that must long for peace.

'It's going to be all right, Mike,' she said, to the watchful spirit that she felt so near to her. 'They're not married, or anything. She doesn't want to be his wife, she doesn't love him or anything. She's very hard, really.'

She waited, and in the silence she thought that she felt approval. She smiled, a tight, private smile.

'He's so kind to me,' she said. 'He's just like you, before everything went so wrong. Did you bring me to him, Mike? Did you?' She caught her breath, as a new idea struck her. '*Is* he you, Mike? Is that how you stay so near?' She stretched out her arms, reaching for something only she could see, and gave a little laugh. Pleased with herself, and with life, she rolled into bed and slept. Kate, in the next room, lay awake, alone in the big double bed, uneasily conscious of a feeling about the house that she couldn't account for, and downstairs in the kitchen, Charlie, curled up uncomfortably on the sofa, slept in all his clothes with the cat tucked in behind his knees.

'Is there really a quoit?' asked Cress. 'I've walked all round, and I've never found one.'

'Sort of.' Kate rubbed her nose and looked thoughtful. 'There was at one time, but the farmers took the stones, a long time ago now, and used them to prop up their walls.'

Charlie grinned at her, bright-eyed. She loved Charlie with the sort of love that one keeps for the unobtainable, and for Kate, who stood in the way of their happiness, she told herself that she had great pity. She returned Charlie's grin, and he said, 'It's terrible bad luck to disturb those old graves. There are awful stories about what happened to the farmers afterwards, but of course, it was done then.'

'What sort of stories?' asked Cress, breathlessly. Kate and Charlie exchanged a glance, pregnant with meaning.

'Oh, I don't know that we should tell you,' said Kate. 'I mean — some of them are *really* awful. Like the one about — no, I can't say it!'

'Ill luck dogged their footsteps from that day on,' said Charlie, in a sepulchral voice. 'Their crops failed, and they had strange illnesses, and their cows walked over the cliffs. Their chickens hatched out with three legs. Everyone said that they were natural misfortunes, but... well, I wouldn't like to give an opinion.'

'You're teasing me,' Cress accused. Kate shook her head.

'Would we, now? I'm Irish, I wouldn't joke about such things. There are forces in this world that we know nothing about, and the Old Ones knew a thing or two.'

Cress didn't know whether to take them seriously or if they were pulling her leg. She looked from one to the other, doubtfully.

'I never know if you two are serious or not,' she accused.

Kate leaned her elbows on the table and rested her chin on her hands. Her face, thus framed by her fingers, was serious enough, apart from a lurking spark at the back of her eyes.

'One farmer got frightened, and put one of the upright stones back again,' she said. 'He couldn't make it stand, of course, but he laid it down where the grave had been. They say today that if you go there you can work magic on that stone, so long as you know the right words. Black magic… there's no white magic up there.'

'Does anyone know the words?' asked Cress. Kate shook her head.

'Some of the old crones in the village, maybe. Soon, though, it will all be forgotten and the blackness will be trapped there – for ever.' She broke off, and spoke in quite a different voice. 'It's a horrid place. Don't go there.'

Charlie shouted with laughter.

'Which particular old crone had you in mind?' he demanded. 'I'm sure the senior citizens of Trelewan would simply dote on your description! And as for you, Cressida Stanley! What do you intend to do? Go up there casting spells?'

Cress blushed, and Kate went off into a fit of giggles.

'Trust you to make a joke of everything, Charlie!' But she went on giggling just the same, Cress noticed. She asked,

'Where is it? The stone, I mean. Is it near?'

'Just up on that rise you can see against the sky as you walk down the road,' said Kate. 'You can see the sea from there, and right across to the village church the other way. Nobody ever goes there.' She sounded surprised as she spoke, as well she might after all the tall tales she and Charlie had been telling. She even wondered, for a second, if they had all been tales after all, for the remains of the quoit were certainly there. She had seen them herself, and it was quite true that nobody went there. Then again, why should they?

'I might walk up there and have a look,' said Cress, but she had formulated no ideas. She seldom did so, preferring to let events guide her rather than the other way around.

'Well, wear trousers,' Charlie advised. 'It's all gorse and brambles up there.'

'Except in the very centre, of course,' added Kate, in a gloomy voice that she rather spoiled by giggling again. 'Around the stone, nothing ever grows – no gorse, no brambles, no flowers, nothing but grass. It can't. The powers of darkness are too strong for it.'

'Grass, of course, as everyone knows, is the Devil's own,' said Charlie, and they both went off into fits of laughter, before Charlie got up and said that he was going back to work, and if they wanted to make up fairy stories all morning that was their affair.

The summer waxed hot and sunny, other PGs came and went, if only sporadically, but Cress was happy at The Quoit, and her imaginary Mike merged himself more and more, it seemed to her, with the more volatile character of Charlie, so that the two of them often seemed to her like one now. She felt secure, thought that it would be nice to stay here always, make it her home. There was a small hotel just down the road where she could get work to placate Kate, and there was Charlie and the studio. She suggested to them that she should rent their room on a more permanent basis.

'I've got to live somewhere,' she said. 'I don't want to go back – I *can't* go back.'

It wasn't strictly true, for he had long ago left the house in Launceston and returned to his own place. His visit had lasted, she knew, not the couple of weeks her mother had urged on him, but a brief and disastrous few days, and ended in a blazing row. Allison had told her so much at the time, but hadn't specified what the row was about. He had stormed out, she had said briefly, and they hadn't seen him and hardly heard from him since. Cress found the thought that he must be so much closer to her creepy, but with the stubborn determination of the normally weak-willed, she had no intentions of leaving.

Kate looked at her from under her eyelashes, and said nothing. She and Charlie had had a very satisfactory talk about Cress – and about other things – and she did feel sorry for the poor little thing. She left it to Charlie to make the decision as to whether she stayed, knowing that her own view was tainted by prejudice. Cress, after all, had done them no actual harm and the money came in handy. The summer tourists hadn't gone for Charlie's particular art form – unsurprisingly.

'I don't see why not,' said Charlie. 'Do you, Kate? Perhaps she could give you a hand in the house, and we could reduce the rent.'

Kate had long marked Cress down for a feckless dreamer who wouldn't know dust if it choked her, and she needed the money more, Charlie was a fool with money. She shook her head.

'Oh, that isn't necessary. I don't need help. Maybe until the season ends…'

Both Charlie and Cress took this for tacit agreement.

'That's fixed, then,' said Charlie, and Cress thanked them prettily.

She did have pretty ways, thought Kate later. She had pretty ways and a taking little face, and those eyes of hers, those dark brown peat-pools of drama and distress, they could wring a heart of stone. She was more considerate about the house these days, too, and she kept Charlie out of mischief and safely applied to his work for once. Why then this continuing sense of uneasiness? She had always had it, right from the start, and she had no idea *why*. She herself and Charlie were secure in each other, there was no threat there, and Cress, so recently and terribly bereaved, was still obviously grieving for her late husband. Kate gave herself a shake; he looked nice anyway, worth a tear or two. Kate wasn't going to criticise her for that, she could be emotional herself. All things considered, she thought, reluctantly, that Cress was being rather courageous.

So what was it? This sense of something askew, out of balance, that niggled at the back of her mind and made her uncomfortable, what was the cause of it? Was it simply her imagination? Surely she wasn't going to turn into one of those jealous, possessive harpies who thought they owned a man body and soul?

Well, she could be as jealous as anyone else with due cause, but here – here there was no cause. That Cress admired Charlie she was well aware, but she didn't begrudge her that. What Cress did was immaterial, it was Charlie's reactions that mattered.

She worried at the problem like a terrier with a rat, but got no further. Eventually she told herself to stop being neurotic, and thrust it firmly out of her mind.

Well, to the back of her mind, anyway.

Cress had steadied up a little for a while, the necessity to maintain her position at The Quoit keeping her grounded, but now that the immediate future was comfortably settled, she began to fantasise more often, to live the dream-life of one of her favourite heroines, to lose touch with her soul. *They couldn't go on like this,* she told herself. *Already it was August, and they seemed to have settled into a routine now, where Charlie spent his days with her and his nights with Kate. Her part-time job at the hotel had failed to come between them.* She spent her evenings alone, of course, up in her room as often as not. After that one occasion she had hesitated to intrude on her hosts again without invitation. She was a little afraid of Kate, to be truthful, and she thought that Charlie might be too. At the very least, she wasn't certain that he would champion her against Kate's strong will. In spite of their new arrangement, she thought that when the summer was over, Kate would almost certainly send her away. She had already said, once or twice, how much she and Charlie enjoyed the winter when they were free and on their own.

Charlie had never mentioned the word *love. She had read it in his eyes, heard it in his voice, felt it in his touch as he deliberately brushed close to her when they were together in the studio. She hadn't heard him put it into words.* She wished that he would, if he would only do so they could go away together and leave the house to Kate. Kate had no need for Charlie. She loved to be wild and free and uncommitted, on her own; she never sought his company as Cress did. *Poor Charlie, he must have been so lonely before she, Cress, arrived in his life. They needed each other, two refugees from the storm. He would paint wonderful pictures when he was secure in her love, everyone would hail him as a genius and herself as his muse... and only she herself would know the truth.*

Not realising it, Cress began to let her guard down, as fantasy once more began to be more real than reality. Charlie, wrapped in his own preoccupation, failed to notice, but Kate, relieved, she found, to have something on which to hang her prejudice, noticed it at once. By the time September came, she had no illusions. She knew a great deal more about love than Cress did, quite enough to read the look in those great, expressive, pansy-dark eyes. It had all gone far enough.

'It's no good, Charlie,' she said. 'I'm as sorry for her as you are, but she's got to go.'

'Why must she?' asked Charlie. He had got used to Cress around the place, and he was no more immune to not-so-subtle flattery than anyone else. 'I thought she was good company for you.'

'For me?' Kate stared at him. 'I never see her, except at meals. Oh Charlie, you must have realised! She's got a full-scale crush on you.'

Charlie stared at her. His astonishment was so obvious that it disarmed her.

'Oh Charlie, you are a fool!' said Kate.

They discussed it as they lay entwined in bed that night.

'I don't blame her, of course,' said Kate, nuzzling his neck. 'I love you myself. But for her own sake, she must go.'

'I never realised,' said Charlie, conscience-stricken. 'Poor little bugger, I just thought she was unhappy.'

'She was – very unhappy.' Kate was suddenly still, shaken with pity. 'Poor kid, she needed us, I know, but we can't help her any more. Not with this thing. She must go before she gets hurt again. It's only transitional,' she added, more to convince herself than anything.

'Where can she go, if she won't go back to her folks? – and she won't, from what little she says, they seem to have upset her somehow.'

'Why does she say so little?' Kate wondered momentarily, but dismissed the speculation as no business of theirs. 'She's in her twenties, Charlie, she must be – she isn't a child. She can't expect strangers to be responsible for her. If she won't go home, she must look out for herself.'

Charlie, and Kate too if she was honest, was obscurely aware that what Kate had just said wasn't entirely true. Cress *was* a child, in some undefined way. She certainly wasn't one of those who found looking out for themselves easy. Particularly not under the circumstances.

'She's that sort of woman,' said Kate, worriedly. 'I imagine that her family made a pet of her, and her husband spoiled her – and now you, too. She sort of invites it, sitting there all helpless and soft, like a kitten in the rain.'

Charlie ignored this as coming too close to home. He said, in the darkness, 'If she won't go to her family, for whatever reason, and her husband is dead, where will she go? What will she do?'

'Oh God!' said Kate, suddenly coming out with what had been bothering her for a while now. 'We should have done it months ago – we should never have let her stay after that first couple of weeks – she talks to her husband's picture when she's alone in that room, did you realise? I've heard her… at first, I thought it was the radio, but she hasn't got a radio. Charlie…'

'I talk to myself, too,' said Charlie, bracingly. 'It's a sign of great intelligence. Come on, Kate, pull yourself together! If there's nowhere else for her to go, she must go back to her own folks. There's no other way. Perhaps I should take her back – explain things, what do you think?' Kate said nothing, and he went on. 'I shall be quite glad to have my studio to myself again, actually. Bless the child, she means well, but she does trivialise.'

'I'd have had her out of here long ago, if you'd said that before,' said Kate, and he was glad to hear the more usual robust note back in her voice. He laughed, and kissed her.

'I manage to ignore her most of the time. Let it all go past me. I'm sorry for her, if you must know.'

'You always say that artists are above such things,' Kate accused.

'Yeah… but she gets to you. Even artists can't turn their backs on bloody stark tragedy, can they?'

'We've given her almost six months,' said Kate. 'Surely, we must have taken her over the worst.' She sounded troubled, but Charlie was tired. He kissed her.

'Stop worrying, woman. It isn't our problem, you said it yourself.'

Charlie slept then. Whatever had to be done, he wouldn't be the one to have to do it. Kate lay in his arms in the darkness and listened to his breathing as he slept.

I won't be responsible for her, she thought angrily, aware that she already was. Why should I? Charlie is right, we must take her back to her people, it's their affair, not ours. They should never have let her go off on her own after all she must have been through, I don't care what happened. It was cruel of them. It's their fault. She must tell us where they are, who they are, and she must go back. She doesn't really love Charlie, she's made him into a substitute for her husband, or something –

And then, for some reason, she was scared, covered suddenly in a skim of sweat that broke on her skin in the cool night. It was a long time before she closed her eyes.

III

At four o'clock in the morning, Charlie got up and began to dress. Kate, who had lain awake most of the night worrying, sat up.

'Charlie Price, where do you think you're going?'

'To London,' said Charlie. 'Got any money, love? Just for the train fare?'

Kate threw back the bedclothes indignantly.

'Sod you, Charlie, you're doing this on purpose! No, I haven't any money, and if I had, I wouldn't give it to you.'

Charlie looked at her long, bare legs with absent-minded admiration.

'You must, Katie. It's important.'

'Too right, it is! You're doing it just so that you can escape any unpleasantness that might be going, and don't you try to kid me!'

'Unpleasantness?' He sounded as if he had never heard the word, let alone knew what it meant. 'Oh – you mean Cress. There won't be any *unpleasantness*, Katie love, and anyway, you don't want me there. I just need to get away, you know me – touch base, see a few people – *you* know!'

Kate padded barefoot across the room and opened the top drawer of the chest, feeling around under her clothes.

'Why is it suddenly so important to go dashing off to London?' she wanted to know. 'Look that's all I've got, can you manage on that?'

He took the slim roll of notes and riffled through it.

'It won't pay for the train. I'll have to hitch, that means I won't be back until tomorrow.'

'You wouldn't be anyway. I know you.' She climbed back into bed and drew the blankets up to her chin. 'What are you up to, if you're not running out on me?'

'I wouldn't do that.' But he looked shifty, and she didn't quite believe him.

'*Charlie!*'

'Oh all right, if you will have it. I want to hear what the word is.'

'Word? *What* bloody word?'

'On Oliver Nankervis. I want to know… well, what there is to know. If he's for real.'

'The exhibition isn't until next year!'

'Someone will know. Katie darling – ' He stooped to give her a swift kiss. 'I just want to hear the talk.'

'Wouldn't it be simpler just to go and see for yourself?' asked Kate, curiously, not that Charlie had ever done anything the simple way. 'He only lives the other side of the village, for God's sake!'

'No, I can't do that.'

'Why not?' Kate grumbled. 'I never knew you for a celebrity hound, Charlie Price, what's got into you?'

'You haven't heard the whispers I've heard. See you tomorrow, sometime.'

'I'd better!' Kate called after him, without hope. She knew Charlie pretty well by this time. 'You're not leaving me with all the mess, don't think it!' But he was already gone. She lay down and pulled the pillow round to make herself more comfortable. 'Have a nice trip,' she said, drowsily.

Cress was surprised to come down to breakfast and find Charlie gone.

'He never said anything yesterday about going away,' she said. Kate shrugged.

'That's Charlie. Here today, over the moon next Wednesday. He never changes.'

'But he'll be back tomorrow?'

'He said so, for what that's worth. Last time he did this, he was gone for a month.'

Cress looked aghast.

'But did you know where he was?'

'Sort of.' Kate saw Cress's appalled face and laughed. 'I don't own him, you know. You can't own people.'

'If you're married –'

'We're not,' Kate pointed out.

She hadn't meant to say anything to Cress until Charlie came back, even if it took until Christmas – which was a possibility. But it wouldn't be an easy subject to broach, and Cress had never before given even such a slender opening as this. Kate said, carefully, 'You never talk much about your marriage. Were you happy?'

'Of course!' cried Cress, with such immediate indignation that Kate was at once suspicious. She twiddled with a fork on the scrubbed wooden table.

'I only ask, because people who have had happy marriages usually like talking about them. You don't.'

Cress sat very still, looking down at her hands, startled for a moment into down-to-earth real life.

'I can't talk about it. I feel so bad.' It was true enough. Not about her marriage itself, particularly, but all the buried guilt that went with it. She felt sometimes that it was bound on her back, a burden to carry with her wherever she went, even though she didn't recognise it for what it was and named it easily, *grief*. Kate sensed a truth there somewhere, and her ready sympathy that had all her life taken her from crisis to crisis – from Charlie to Cress, if you liked to look at it that way – promptly rose to the surface. In any case, if they were ever to be rid of Cress, they had to know.

'It helps sometimes to talk. If you want to, I'll listen.'

Cress said, slowly, 'He was at school with my brother. I've only got one brother, and two sisters. Marianne – but we always call her Anna – she married a Swiss who works in computers, and lives abroad. Allison is an air hostess, she has a flat in London. They're all much older than me.' She gave Kate a sly look. 'And anyway, it was different. I was adopted. My mother had a baby that died when it was born, and I was instead. My father was a famous actor.' She looked at Kate sideways again to see how she was taking this, and when Kate said nothing, went on. 'He was killed in a car crash, and my mother died in childbirth when she heard the news. So Mum and Dad took me, because they had no baby, and I had no parents and it seemed the right thing at the time. But I never fitted in.' She squared her shoulders and lifted her chin a little. 'It's not been easy for me. We don't have anything in common.'

Kate listened to all this with a certain scepticism, not altogether believing it, but accepting that Cress probably needed to work up to the present through all this unlikely-sounding family background. She put down the fork and prepared to pay proper attention.

'Dad is a builder, and Grandad is a builder,' said Cress, which Kate thought sounded more probable. 'You can see why it was hard, with my background. Grandad started as a labourer, but he worked up to be one of the most respected workmen in the town. He's very proud of that. And that Dad has done the same.' She stopped, and to get her started again, Kate asked,

'What town?'

'St. Austell.'

After a long pause, during which Cress did nothing but stare, and Kate had time to wonder if she realised about the care usually taken to match children with adoptive parents, or ever considered that the child of a famous actor would hardly end up adopted by a Cornish builder and his wife – adopted at all – Kate said conversationally, 'And is your brother following the family tradition?'

'He started to,' said Cress. 'He didn't like it much and he gave up, almost straight away. Dad was dreadfully upset. It was awful.'

She contemplated the awfulness of it privately for a minute or two, but Kate found that her sympathies were more with the brother than the older generations. Parents who expected their children to be a continuation of themselves, to further their own ambitions, were a pain, she considered. People were individuals. She didn't know what Cress's brother had to do with anything, but she sympathised anyway.

'So, what did he do?' she asked.

'He went away,' said Cress, unhelpfully. She was at the centre of her own world, other people's lives would never interest her as much as her own. 'He was abroad a lot – that's how Anna came to meet Kurt, of course.' Really? 'It means that the firm will come to an end when Dad retires, unless Allison marries someone who wants to take it on…' She trailed off vaguely, and Kate, realising that she was going to get no further along this road, said briskly, 'Or you. You're young and attractive, you could find yourself some likely lad and put the whole miserable business behind you, you know.'

'Never,' said Cress, with finality. 'What Mike and I had was special… different. I couldn't want anyone else. Not ever.' She spoke with too much emphasis.

Charlie? Kate wondered and the hairs rose on her arms for no explainable reason. How did she rationalise her infatuation with him? Or was she, as Kate had long suspected, wholly self-deceiving about just about everything? She looked at Cress, so vulnerable in her grief and her youth. Poor child. She was pliant and fragile as a winter twig, that would bend and bend and then break. She could be very close to breaking. Kate saw her tragedy as harsh and recent, and knew an impulse to reach out and offer shelter from life's storms. She was furious with the unknown family, with Dad and Grandad, Anna and Kurt and Allison, the so-far nameless brother, and at the same time angry at her own weakness. How could they be so cruel as to leave this silly little twit to fend for herself? To dump her on other people whose business it wasn't? She wasn't sure she believed all that about adoption – in fact, she was pretty sure she didn't believe a word – or air hostesses and Swiss brothers-in-law come to that, but even if it was true it wasn't an excuse.

'So tell me about your husband,' she prompted. 'He was your brother's friend, you said.'

'Yes – no. They knew each other from school, but Mike was younger. We met at a party, I didn't take much notice of him at first, I was at art school and busy, and everything was fun – *you* know.' She sounded, and looked more animated, and as thinking of those past days brightened her eyes and made her smile, Kate caught a glimpse of the girl she had been then. Very young, naïve, full of fun, enjoying what must have surely been her teenage years just like any other girl. Poor Cress.

'Anyway,' Cress said, 'We fell in love after a bit and got engaged, and then when I was nineteen, we got married and went to live in Liskeard. Mike had a good job, we had a dear little house on a nice estate, and friends, and everything was lovely.'

That sounded as if it might be true, but nineteen! thought Kate, good God, what were your parents thinking of? You must have been far too young for marriage at nineteen. If you ask me, you're too young now!

'So, when did it start to go sour on you?' she asked, because all of a sudden it was obvious it had. She wasn't sure why, some wistfulness in Cress's tone, perhaps. But Cress looked indignant.

'It didn't! I never stopped loving him.'

Her phrasing was uncomfortably explicit, but Kate knew she would get nowhere if she destroyed the child's precious illusions. She was thinking of her as a child, she realised. A rather tiresome one. She said, cautiously, 'You can love people and still find them exasperating. Look at me and Charlie.'

Cress seized on the lifeline with relief.

'Of course you can, and that was exactly it. He seemed to want to carry on just as he had before – going out with his friends to the pub in the evenings and leaving me with the telly. It wasn't fair, and we were always arguing about it. He wouldn't see it – '

'Couldn't you have gone too?'

'They played *snooker*,' said Cress, distastefully. 'He knew I thought it was boring, but he still went. Every week, always. Anyway, it was a bloke thing.'

'I expect he *didn't* think it was boring,' Kate suggested. 'Anyway, surely it wasn't every *night*?'

'Every Friday. I had to sit at home on my own and watch the telly. I was all on my own, and he was always back late.'

Kate thought the unknown Mike's behaviour reasonable enough; couples didn't have to be joined at the hip, that was a recipe for disaster in her experience. More, she found herself thinking that if she had been in his place, confronted with a whining wife who wanted to keep him always at her side, she wouldn't have gone home at all. Had he had a Friday night bit on the side? she wondered with interest. Cress's next words dispelled this idea.

'They used to go on to each other's houses after, and drink coffee. They never came to ours, though. The other wives used to tell me what fun they had, laughing and talking.'

Kate's sympathy changed sides again.

'Men can be thoughtless pigs,' she said. Cress nodded.

'He didn't understand,' she said. 'I got so lonely. I was too far away from Mum and Dad to go home, or anything, and if I did Mum would only say that that was being married for you. Sometimes, I'd borrow Gran's car and go down and see my brother, just for the day. In those days...' She slowed, and broke off. Tears filled her brown eyes, and Kate was conscious of impatience with her. What a watering can!

'In those days?' she prompted, after a pause which she suspected, perhaps wrongly, was consciously dramatic. Listening to Cress was like being on the dodgems at the fair, she decided. You never knew quite where you were. Cress gave herself a shake, like a dog coming out of the water. She said, 'In those days he was the only one on my side. He'd listen to me, when he had the time. I wish I'd realised why...' Another flicker of the eyes to see how Kate was taking it, but this time, it wasn't possible even to guess at what the lie might be, she simply knew, by this time, that it had to be there. Cress was setting a scene – *another* scene.

In the silence which followed, that Kate found obscurely pathetic, it was so still that the sound of the coal settling in the stove made them both jump. Kate, interested now in spite of herself by the drama being unfolded, wondered cynically if big brother's tolerance might have been simply because he was the only one without a ringside seat. She said, 'Then what happened?'

'He began – Mike did – to be away on business overnight. He got promotion, and it meant going up to London to visit Head Office and things. I thought I might be less lonely if I had a little baby to keep me company. All my friends had babies, and after all we had been married for two whole years. People were beginning to ask questions, and anyway, isn't that what you get married for?'

Kate didn't think so, but she knew better than to say it. Instead, she found herself thinking, ah, enter the totty.

'And he wouldn't?'

'He said he didn't want a baby. Why did he marry me if he was just going to leave me to sit in the house on my own? I asked him that, and he couldn't answer. We loved each other so much, but we had drifted desperately, dreadfully far apart. I didn't know what to do.'

She might have loved Mike, although Kate wouldn't have put money on it. Mike didn't sound as if he had loved her much. By this time, it was all reminding her of nothing so much as a dose of soap on the telly.

'In the end,' said Cress, in a small, still voice, 'one of my friends told me that he was seeing someone else.' Bull's-eye! 'I packed my case and I got on the bus and I went home.' *It was summertime, a lovely, golden day, but in my heart it rained all the way.* She hesitated, feeling the poignancy of the unspoken phrase.

The commonplace little tragedy was coming to its dreadful climax. Kate didn't prompt this time, but sat waiting, letting Cress choose her own pace.

'He came after me,' said Cress. 'I never thought he would, but he did. He came after me and shouted and stormed, and wouldn't listen to anyone.'

'Why?' asked Kate. 'I mean, why did he shout?'

Cress looked at her as if she was mad.

'Because he loved me, of course.'

Of course. Well, anyone who believed in that by this time probably believed in Father Christmas too. The question remained, however. Mike Stanley quite obviously hadn't cared a toss for his silly little wife by this point – so *why* had he shouted? Because she had driven him right over the edge? Possible. But Cress was speaking again.

'He and Dad shouted at each other, and I couldn't bear it, it made me cry! Mum rang my brother and told him to come home. She thought Mike might listen to him. They went out into the garden and – ' She broke off, swallowing visibly, Kate saw her throat move and found it in her heart to be very sorry for her. She obviously hadn't a clue what any of it had been about, when anyone listening to her could have written the book, and a sad, predictable little book it would be, too.

Or no… maybe not. Cress was speaking again. Her eyes had shifted away from Kate, in a way that Kate was beginning to distrust.

'I didn't realise… I always thought of him as my brother… but of course, he's no relation really. And he was in love with me, and so… so…' She pressed the heels of her hands into her eyes and bowed her head. 'Oh, I *wish* I'd known!' Oh dear, thought Kate, cynically. How poignant! That flicker of the eyes earlier, when big brother had re-entered the story, made a brief, fleeting picture in her head. She said, 'So what happened?' and tried to keep her scepticism out of her voice.

'We heard them shouting. He and Dad – and Granddad – all have very quick, noisy tempers, but we never thought…' Her voice, muffled by her smothering palms, wrung out the last dregs of disaster. 'He killed him,' she said. 'He took him by the shoulders and bashed and bashed and bashed him against Mum's rockery, until he died.'

Kate's mouth dropped open. The ending had taken her by surprise, it had an unfinished feel about it.

'But –' she said. Cress began to cry. Kate said, pertinently, 'Did you see him do it?'

Cress shook her head, gulping down her sobs.

'No!' She spoke quickly – too quickly? 'We would have stopped him, of course.'

Of course.

'So what…?' Kate began to ask, but stopped, shaking her head. Cress said, 'There were two girls in the garden next door. They heard the shouting and climbed a tree to see what was going on, *they* saw it. The first we knew was… was…' She pushed the heels of her hands hard against her eyes. 'He came in,' she said. 'He came in from outside and he just stood there, and he said, *I think I've killed him,* just like that, like it didn't even matter.

Like *I've put the cat out*, or something. And I *loved him*!' She began to cry, in earnest now, but Kate found herself not at all sure if she was talking about her brother or the deceased Mike, or where truth ended or if it even began. The characters in the sorry little tale had thoroughly caught her interest now. Whatever the rights and wrongs, what a carry on! She borrowed a word from Cress's vocabulary, *awful*! About the feelings of the unfortunate family, if any of it *did* happen to be true, she found that she preferred not to think.

She would have let it go at that point, thinking that she had heard enough, but Cress had got into her stride now. She continued of her own accord.

'We went out into the garden,' she said. 'Mike was lying there by the rockery, and he looked quite all right, but he was breathing funny… sort of snoring – and there was a patch on the back of his head that was all soft, like an egg when you hit it with a spoon. And then he just gave a sort of rattle and stopped breathing, and Dad went indoors and rang the police. And I knew then… just like that, how much I *really* loved Mike, in spite of everything, and my heart broke.'

It should have been immensely moving, but Kate found herself shifting uncomfortably on her chair. Cress had almost seemed to… well, to be *enjoying* that last bit. Kate was left wondering if Cress had made it up afterwards, and hated herself for it. Cress raised a tear-drenched face from her hands.

'They had to arrest him, of course,' she said. 'He was let out on bail to begin with, but of course, he couldn't come back home. He went to Granddad's, they made it a condition, they wouldn't let him go back to St. Erbyn. Then there was the inquest and they said it was murder, and so he went to prison until the assizes. The trial was in Bodmin, and I had to give evidence, but his counsel was very clever and made out it was only manslaughter. He got three years, and they took him away and locked him up.' She sounded so bitter, and her mouth had taken such a hard, downward turn, that she suddenly looked ten years older. Spite and resentment looked out of her eyes. 'They should have thrown away the key,' she said. 'He killed someone, and they hardly punished him at all. My husband was *dead*! You'd think it didn't matter.'

So at bottom, at least, there were real facts; that had the unmistakeable ring of rather unpleasant truth. But how much, and where was the join?

'Perhaps it was an accident,' said Kate, too startled to think of anything else, and Cress said,

'No,' and her face was suddenly ugly.

Kate hated to hear about living things being shut up. Her rabbits enjoyed the freedom of the house and garden when she was around to keep them safe from foxes and wandering dogs, although they also had a run the size of a billiard table. She could never have kept a cage bird, or a hamster. Cress had made her brother — surely a loving brother to defend her so fiercely if not precisely "in love" with her — so real to her that it was if someone she knew had been shut away. She knew St. Erbyn well. It was a beautiful place, right on the Helford River, so beautiful that summer visitors flocked to look at it. To exchange that for a prison yard... to Kate, it was simply unthinkable.

'You mustn't be vindictive,' she said. She wouldn't have said it if Cress hadn't looked that look. Grief, she could understand, and bitterness too, but spite didn't seem to her to be a relevant emotion in the circumstances.

'Why shouldn't I be *vindictive*?' said Cress, almost spitting the word. 'He killed my husband, he ruined my life, he left me a widow at twenty-one — my life ended when he killed Mike. *Mine!*'

'Don't be so silly,' said Kate, sensing imminent hysteria. 'Of course it didn't! It's a dreadful thing, to be sure, but you're young, you'll put it behind you in time. You *must* put it behind you.'

'I can't,' said Cress.

She sat there looking so stony, so cold, that Kate was revolted — and alarmed. Reluctantly, she got up and went to her, putting her arms round her, letting her natural warmth rule the more cautious promptings of her head.

'Come on, darling. You can't alter it by wishing, the only thing you'll alter that way is your own sweet self. All right, it's early days, it's not been long. But give it time, let it work itself out. Cry, my darling, cry about it, and then go home to your mum and dad where you belong.' *Please!*

She was rocking Cress in her arms like a child, talking for the sake of it, appalled as much by what she sensed as what she had been told. She wasn't given to being fanciful, but she was sensitive. What she sensed was black and unnatural. She'll give us the poltergeists, the poor child, she thought confusedly, and for all her pity she wanted Cress gone — gone now, at once, before Charlie came home.

'I can't go home,' said Cress, in a tight voice. 'You don't understand. They turned me away. I can't go back.'

'*They turned you away?*' echoed Kate, in disbelief. 'No, but surely, and after all you'd been through – and here's us thinking all along it was your own brave heart that brought you.'

Cress stirred, and detached herself from Kate's arms. Her chin lifted a little, she had liked that bit about *your own brave heart*, and toyed with it for a moment before settling on strict, if slightly biased, truth.

'You see, he was coming back,' she said. 'They let him go, and he was coming back. I couldn't be there when he came, but still they let him come. I had nowhere to go, but they made me – because I'm only adopted, you see. Yes, that's why! That's how I came here.' She gave Kate a defiant look.

'They let him go?' Kate echoed, blankly. 'How do you mean, they let him go? Did he appeal, then?'

'He wouldn't appeal,' said Cress, with a firm shake of her head. 'Would you believe it that the lawyers wanted him to? They knew he murdered Mike, he didn't even deny it, but they said it could be made to be an accident and they wanted *to get him off*, can you imagine that? I cried and cried, and he said he wouldn't do it.'

You little bitch! thought Kate, quite suddenly, and to her own surprise. You vindictive little vixen, you, and now let's get to the bottom of things, for I'm sure we've not heard the whole truth yet, or any of it maybe!

'Then why did they let him go?' she asked, reasonably. Cress looked at her in surprise.

'On parole, of course. He'd done two years, so they paroled him and put him on probation instead and he came home, and I was sent away – and after all that, he made a row and walked out and they never – they *never* said they wanted me to come back. Oh Kate, what shall I do? What will become of me?'

Kate's mind had started reeling.

'You mean,' she said, ignoring this and doing a quick sum in her head, 'that all this happened more than *two years ago?*'

'Well, of course it did.' Cress looked surprised that she had even asked. 'You must have heard about it – everyone did. Mum and Dad had to move, they couldn't face the neighbours, it was in the paper and everything, and –'

'I never heard of it,' said Kate, and immediately she had spoken, realised that she very well might have. Cress had never mentioned her brother's

name, and perhaps her husband, as the victim, had been only a bit-player
– *his brother-in-law*, or something. There was so much doom and gloom in
the newspapers, nobody could remember it all and in that context, two
years was ages.

'They had to go away, where nobody knew them, and it wasn't easy. Dad
wanted to stick it out, but I couldn't go on living in that house, I couldn't!'

There was a whole world of difference between a bereaved and –
possibly – grief-stricken, certainly shocked, child-widow, going bravely
out into the world hard on the heels of tragedy, while her family stood by
and let her, and that same widow, two years after the event, being forced
out, as Kate was now certain she had been, by nothing more than her own
unforgiving bitterness. Yes, she could see that Cress might have a problem
with her brother's return, but the story was nothing if not confused as she
told it, with its mixture of murder, manslaughter, incest, rejection and true
love. Manslaughter wasn't deliberate, anyway, she had always understood it
to be the difference between pure accident and accident due to negligence
and the brother's counsel obviously agreed. The brother himself must have
felt terrible, and he had served his time – thanks to Cress. Surely it was
overdue – more than overdue – for Cress to pull herself together and get
on with her life, learn to view it as a shared tragedy. Had she hung on her
family the way she hung on Charlie and herself? If so, they must have been
glad of a way out. The picture she suddenly had, of Cress crying and crying
to get her own way, revolted her anew. Whatever her unfortunate brother
might have done, and Kate wouldn't have liked to be the judge of that,
her family had acted, in Kate's view, rightly. She no longer even believed
that they had in any way turned Cress away. She had, quite simply, walked
in an attack of spleen, Kate was by this time sure of it. Mum and Dad
and all the rest of them must have been in a real dilemma – particularly
if, as Kate was inclined to believe, Cress had been disenchanted with her
marriage before the fuss even began. But then, Kate didn't like Cress, and
she was fairly certain, too, that while the bones of the story might have
been sound, the flesh was so much silly rubbish.

'*I, I, I!*' she said indignantly, before she could stop herself. 'You mean
that for two years, you've trailed around trading on everyone's sympathy,
making up stories to make yourself feel better, making Charlie and me
sorry for you, making your poor family carry you? For *two years?*'

The change in Cress's expression was so fleeting that Kate nearly missed it. She realised that she had struck a chord somewhere, but before she had time to home in on the impression, 'I can't manage without Mike,' Cress cried, childishly, and Kate stared at her.

'Are you crazy? You're the one who walked, remember! Good God, how much do you expect? How much are they – are *we* – to give you? Life, is it? A woman of any backbone would have got out there and taken a slap back at fate for all it sent her long since! Have you no spine – have you no pride?'

Cress looked at her, sensing the withdrawal of sympathy, not understanding why. She was the tragic widow with the murderer for a brother, wasn't she? Surely *Kate* couldn't be on his side, too?

'You won't send me away,' she pleaded. 'You can't do that, you can't!' She looked up into Kate's scornful face, and was uncomfortably reminded, suddenly, of Allison. She began to cry again. 'I can't face being alone, not yet, don't send me away. Charlie won't let you, anyway.'

Kate's mind was still working, analysing, speculating, trying to sort it all out. If they had wanted the brother to appeal, there must have been good grounds for it, so what *was* the truth, exactly? The mention of Charlie interrupted her thoughts and sent her off at a tangent.

'Charlie!' she exclaimed.

'We need each other – '

'Charlie needs you like he needs a cold in the nose,' Kate told her. She had almost said *a hole in the head*, but stopped herself on the brink. Cress might be a tiresome little brat, but she didn't deserve that, exactly. 'Come on, grow up! Be thankful for what you've got. You're young and healthy, you're independent, and at least you don't have to live with the thought that you killed someone you liked –' She broke off, knowing that it was useless, that Cress was incapable of being independent, and Cress went on crying. Kate thought that she was deliberately working herself up and despised her for it, thinking despairingly that Cress's technique must have placed impossible strains on her unfortunate family, but after a while Cress began to say things that frightened her. Her eyes had gone blank, she spoke in a little-girl voice that made Kate's flesh creep.

'Mike doesn't want you to send me away. He wants Charlie to help me, he told me so! He's sorry he was cruel, he wants to make it up to me.'

Kate's heart gave a sudden hard thump under her ribs. She said, more bracingly than she felt, 'You're talking nonsense!' and Cress cried again, talking in a wild way that made Kate wish that The Quoit wasn't quite so far from its nearest neighbours.

'Ever since he died, he's kept close to me, he's looked after me. He chose Charlie, he brought me here, you can't stop us loving each other, Kate! It's not as if *you* were his wife or anything, he's not tied to you, you keep on saying so.'

It was one aspect of being a common-law wife that had never occurred to Kate. No legal protection, for what that was ever worth, against home-wreckers, against silly little fools like this, who still thought, after all that she *said* had happened to her, that it was the piece of paper that made the bond, and how wrong, how very wrong, she was! Scared, threatened, and angry because she felt she had been emotionally used, Kate lost her temper.

'I never heard such rubbish in my life!' she said. 'Grow up, and stop whingeing and don't be so wet! All right, so you've taken some knocks, but so have we all — you have no right, *no right at all, do you hear me?* — just because you set your brother up as the killer of a husband you'd had enough of anyway, to come round here making up stories about Charlie!' And where had that gem of insight come from? Kate, shaken more than she would admit by her own words, continued more calmly, but only with a conscious effort. 'All right, we're not married, but so what? There's more love between us, Mrs. Michael Stanley, than you ever dreamed of between you and the unfortunate man who was fool enough to marry you, and more than you'll ever understand, too. Get on your own feet, and get from under ours — take a look at yourself before it's too late, or where do you think it will end? You're not even sorry for him — for either of them, only for yourself!' Her patience, such as it was, slipped, Cress wasn't even listening! She just sat there, weeping. 'And get out of my kitchen before I shake you, if you can't stop that silly snivelling!'

Cress had stumbled to her feet, and now she ran round behind the table. She stood there, gripping its edge and staring at Kate with her mouth open.

'I didn't set him up, I didn't! You don't know what you're saying! I loved him, how could I — '

'Because you never think, that's how!' snapped Kate, hardly listening, knowing that Cress had nearly brainwashed her and hating herself for it. 'You drift about at the beck and call of some oozy primeval instinct deep in what you call your brain, and you never stop to consider anybody's interests but your own! You let Charlie alone before you drive him crazy, you're ruining his work and you've outstayed your welcome!'

'I'm not ruining his work! He's never worked so hard, *you* said so!'

'I'm talking about quality, not quantity!'

'You're jealous!' cried Cress, beside herself. 'You know he loves me, and you're jealous!' She turned and ran as Kate came leaping over the table at her, too incensed to waste time going round it. She ran out into the flagged hall and towards the front door, and as she ran, she heard the kitchen door slam behind her on the wings of a fine Irish fury.

Kate sat down abruptly on the chair that Cress had so hurriedly vacated, and found that she was trembling. With anger, she thought, but she wasn't as sure as she should have been. Silly little bitch! Whining and whingeing as if the whole world, anybody but herself, had to be responsible for what had happened, for her welfare! Talking like one of those trashy novels she was always reading... and weaving into it that horrible, unreal thread of haunted superstition that never came out of any novel. You couldn't act a thing like that if you didn't feel it, even if your putative father was the greatest actor in the whole world, which Kate didn't buy, not for a minute – talking to her dead husband, listening to his advice... it was creepy. Kate had herself known people who had believed that they felt the near presence of a loved one soon after death, and on balance, believed them, but never, ever, anyone who took it that far. It was sick.

Nor would she have thought that someone so self-centred would feel things that deeply. Cress had pretty manners and a sweet face, on the surface anyway, but they were about her only positive attributes. She was weak, she was the sort of woman that you would expect to drift away from her husband's funeral in a cloud of black chiffon and drift in the same way into the arms of another man, another protector. She might – indeed, she almost certainly did – fantasise about her own misfortunes, but it was something that she would very soon trade for reality – and unless she married a saint, another marriage in which she would be disappointed. There were women like her in every walk of life.

But for a woman – any woman – to talk of her dead – her murdered – husband in the way that Cress had done, there had to be something very deeply wrong indeed.

And what else had she said? Kate reached after an impression, caught it, sat very still.

I loved him. She had said that twice, with no ambiguity.

Cress only meant she loved her brother as a brother, she didn't mean…?

Hell knows no fury like a woman scorned.

I'm only adopted. Was that true, or more rubbish?

Now who was fantasising?

Kate sat at the table for a long time while her thoughts reorganised themselves, and then she became aware that the house was very quiet, with an empty stillness that meant she was alone in it. She wondered where Cress would have gone, uneasily now. Perhaps she had been a bit outspoken. She suspected that she might have been guilty of that same heedlessness of which she had accused Cress, she had opened her mouth and let the words say themselves. She hadn't considered at all what effect her words might have on Cress, so swift had she been in defence of Charlie.

In the protection of her own interests.

What *had* she said, exactly? She wished she could be sure. She had a horrid suspicion that she had accused Cress of being responsible both for her husband's untimely end and for her brother's involvement in it, and only supposing it was true… and it could be true. She was that silly, she could have done it quite unintentionally, and if she had, and if what she, Kate, had said had made her face it… what would she do? She was so unstable, the answer had to be, just about *anything*!

The cliffs round here were tall, the sea surged around the rocks beneath, cruelly, greedily. In her mind, she saw Cress running, running, onto the cliff path, running to the edge, slipping, falling, sucked in by the hungry sea as she crashed to her death.

No. She was being ridiculous. Cress's brother was a bad-tempered bully who had let his temper get away with him, just as she was a silly, immature little fool. The whole tragic family was probably moronic, if the truth were known, from Grandad downwards.

Kate got to her feet and went slowly upstairs. The best room, the one which looked out to the sea, was the one Cress rented. She went into it and leaned out of the window. She could see the sea, and the rim of the cliff over the tops of the rhododendrons, but she couldn't see anybody moving there. The lawn below was deserted except for the rabbits, hopping about.

'Cress!' she called. 'Cress, are you out there?'

The sunlit world outside was placid and uninhabited. If Cress was within earshot, she was lying low. Kate brought her head back in and looked at the room.

Who was she, anyway, where did she come from? Whatever Cress said about the publicity at the time, she still didn't recollect ever having heard of a Cressida Stanley, and if Charlie had ever read anything about it, it would have gone over his head like nearly everything else. Her family's name, of course, would be different anyway. But she would have to go home, she wasn't fit to be on her own, they must take her in and look after her. She needed help, that was all too obvious – psychiatric help, Kate suspected. If she wouldn't go on her own, they must come and fetch her. But for that, she had to know who they were.

On the surface, at least, the room held no clues. It wasn't very tidy. There was powdered green eye-shadow all over the shabby dressing-table, and the bed wasn't made, and everything that Cress had touched during the last twenty-four hours or so seemed to be lying where she had dropped it. She was a slutty piece, thought Kate, despising her. If this was a sample of her housekeeping, her house must have been a tip, and no wonder her husband hadn't wanted to take his friends home! She picked up a couple of paperback books that were lying on the floor, shook their pages into order and smoothed out a couple of bent corners. *Passionate Stranger* and *Escape to Love*. One of them, she saw, had a heroine called Velvet and a hero called Storm. Such stories were all very well as escapism, Kate supposed, although she didn't read them herself, but surely to goodness nobody thought life was really like that? Nobody but Cress, that is, silly little idiot. If that was the sort of thing she believed in, her marriage hadn't just been a dreary mess, it had been a catastrophe! Men weren't heroes – or at least, they weren't consistently heroic. Oliver Nankervis for instance, whom Charlie had gone rushing off to find out about, had the reputation of a hero, but from what Kate had heard from her friend Maggie Soames, who knew him and his wife quite well, living with him was like a three-ring circus. Unlike Michael Stanley, he had survived a murderous attack, mob violence in his case, and now had to learn to live with the results and was finding it uphill work. His wife too, no doubt, although Maggie hadn't said so. Cress should be thankful for small mercies. Death wasn't the worst that could happen to a man.

The books had Cress's name written in them, *Cressida Stanley*, as if anyone would want to borrow, still less to keep, such tripe, but it wasn't her married name that Kate was looking for. Her dressing-table drawers were a tangled muddle of garments, clean and dirty all jumbled together without care, and mixed with another half-dozen well-thumbed romances. There were yet more tossed under the bed, but nowhere was there any clue as to who Cress had been before her marriage. Kate didn't even know where her family lived, the only place mentioned had been St. Austell, and Cress's tears had flooded them out from there.

And St. Erbyn. The brother lived – had lived? – in St. Erbyn.

Along with several hundred other people. Anyway, he would be the last person to approach. And Cress had never mentioned his Christian name, leave alone his surname, nor even what he did there.

If Cress had deliberately meant to cover her tracks, she couldn't have done it better, in fact she probably wouldn't have done it as well. There were many things in the room that spoke to what she was, but none at all that told who she was. Kate gave it up. She would have to be made to tell them, just as soon as Charlie came home.

In the meantime, what should she do?

She had no real desire to find Cress, she didn't want to speak to her, she didn't want to have to listen to her. On the other hand, neither did she feel that she should leave her on her own. If Cress was upset, it was her fault, and she was quite capable of letting her empty little head dictate her actions and doing something altogether daft. Kate, who by this time, not only disliked her but feared her, knew that she would have to look for her. However silly nature had made her, she was still sick, of that Kate was beginning to be certain, and whatever the real truth, she had had a bitter experience, even if it had been long enough ago for any normal person to have made an effort to put it behind them by this time. Cress simply wasn't normal, and that was that.

Kate spent most of the day searching the cliffs and the woods, but she didn't find Cress. She sat alone in the house that evening, sick at heart and ashamed of her own part in events, and wished that Charlie would come home.

IV

In the morning, Cress still hadn't come back. Kate searched the woods again with no success, and then walked over the fields to the village to see if she had taken refuge with someone there. It was very much a last resort. She was sure now that Cress must have fallen, or jumped, from the cliff, for if she was still alive why had she not, at the very least, returned for her things? She had run out into the bright morning wearing nothing but a summer dress and sandals, with no money, no coat. Run, run, run. Run rabbit, run. That was what she was, silly creature – a rabbit. You couldn't be angry with a rabbit, soft, harmless little things that they were… but a *crazy* rabbit? Kate imagined one of her own rabbits maddened and tearing with its long yellow incisors and curved, steely claws, beside itself. It might not be fatal, but it wouldn't be funny, and of course it might poison you and send you mad, too. She shivered, although the sun was warm.

She asked in the shop first if they had seen Cress, perhaps catching the bus yesterday, or even walking, but Jim and Sally Tregillis were busy at this time of year. If Cress had passed through the village they hadn't noticed her. Nor had the old men who sat and dreamed, day in, day out, in the sunshine on the seat by the bus stop.

There were so few places where she could have gone, and although she might have had a pound or so tucked in her pocket, Kate supposed, it would certainly not have been any more, it wouldn't have got her very far. And it was all too likely that wherever she had gone, she had been looking for a prop, a sympathiser, someone who would take her in and listen to her troubles. She might run, but she would probably run true to form.

Where would she run? Think, think, who did she know?

Hardly anyone, was the answer to that. Just herself and Charlie, and one or two of their friends, but those only very casually. Apart from the house and her job, she had no life outside the pages of her romances.

Her job! Of course! Why hadn't she thought of that before? Of course, Cress would have run to Mrs. Roberts at the hotel, and they would have given her a bed there. Mrs. Roberts didn't like Kate and Charlie, she wouldn't have bothered to tell them if Cress had told her that Kate had driven her out, it would be just what she would expect of them. Relieved, Kate almost ran the half mile along the road and turned up the short drive to the hotel.

Mrs. Roberts hadn't seen Cress at all. She had thought, when she saw Kate, that perhaps Cress was ill and had sent a message. She knew there was no telephone at The Quoit.

'I haven't seen her at all,' she said, sniffing. 'Not yesterday, not today, and very inconvenient it's been. We're full right up, and extra work we don't need.'

'I'm so sorry,' said Kate, as if it was her fault, as in a way it was.

'Well, come to that she's not much loss,' said Mrs. Roberts. 'She's a feckless creature that's not even been taught to make a bed properly, but an extra pair of hands for all that.'

'If she does turn up, can you let me know somehow?' Kate asked.

'*If* she turns up, I'll send her straight back with a flea in her ear, more than that I won't promise,' said Mrs. Roberts, tossing her head. 'We've enough to do without sending people running messages all over the parish.' She was already closing the door, too busy even to be normally curious. Kate walked slowly home.

Cress was still not back. It was no good hesitating any longer, if she couldn't put the responsibility into the hands of those to whom it rightly belonged, she would have to take it herself. Cress was a missing person. She had been missing for twenty-four hours. If she had done anything stupid, it might already be too late, but missing persons were the province of the police. Kate walked up to the crossroads and rang them.

*

Charlie came home just before midnight the following night, having been gone three days. Kate was sitting on the kitchen sofa, bunched up and hugging her knees when she heard the front door go. She leapt to her feet and ran to the kitchen door, flinging it open.

'Cress! Oh, thank goodness – *Charlie!*'

She ran to him, holding out her arms, and he walked straight into them. They held each other close for a long moment, each feeling the other's need, at one.

'What's the matter, my darling?' asked Kate.

'Oh God,' said Charlie, on a groan. 'I wish I'd never gone. I wish I'd never listened to you. I wish I'd stayed at home.' He walked down the hall with his arm around her shoulders, his fingers dug into her arm. Kate was puzzled.

'What did I say?' She was used to Charlie's occasional crises, but not usually over a few pictures for an exhibition – and somebody else's pictures at that, that he hadn't even seen.

But now, it appeared that he had seen them.

'I didn't go to London. I did what you said, and went to see him, one artist to another… oh yes, I went, and I wish I never had – I wish I'd never been born – I wish – oh shit!'

It was by this time obvious to Kate that Charlie had been on quite a considerable bender since his visit to Oliver Nankervis, which she did hope hadn't taken place at five in the morning, you never knew with Charlie. She couldn't see why he had been so particularly upset, but she knew from experience that if Charlie had something on his mind he would very soon make sure that it was on hers as well, and she was right. He flung himself down on the sofa with another terrible groan, and cried aloud, 'I'll never be an artist! I might as well make a bonfire of my infantile daubs and use my brushes to paint the house! I'm useless – without virtue – Charlie the charlatan, Kate, and I never knew it before!'

'His pictures are that good?' Kate ventured, after a moment.

'They were –' Charlie broke off, made an extravagant gesture with his arms, and began again. 'God, Kate, you should have come too! Light – beautiful, shining light – the bastard paints light, Katie, he paints bloody light! He makes it glitter and gleam and dazzle off water like bloody diamonds, it gets in your bloody eyes and makes you blink! I've painted and worked my fingers to the bloody bone for ten bloody years, and it's me that's the bloody beginner, not him. Not *him*, oh God, he must have been bloody born with it!' He writhed against the cushions, tearing his hair, acting out his despair at his own inadequacy. 'Oh God, Katie, Oh God, if I could only paint like that, I'd gladly be a cripple the rest of my days, I'd give anything but my hands and my eyes '

If what Maggie had told them was true, Oliver Nankervis had come very close to doing exactly that. Kate said, trying to bring Charlie back from the depths, 'So you met him. So, does *he* think it was worth it?'

'I met him, and I don't know what he thinks. I only know what I think. Katie, beautiful Katie – my God, isn't that a bloody song?' He hummed a phrase and then burst into verse, raucously. '*Oh Katie, be-ewtiful Katie, I'll be waiting at the k-k-k-kitchen door!*'

Kate looked at him with an experienced eye.

'What are you on, Charlie?' she asked.

'Only a little sniff, Katie, not even a snort – just a little sniff, a valedictory bloody little sniff for Charlie Price, artist – ex-artist. Charlie the charlatan, Charlie the failure – come and hold me Katie, be-ewtiful Katie, and let me weep on your beautiful breast.'

She cradled his head against her, containing the force of his furious self-knowledge in the circle of her arms. He was over-reacting, she knew it, he knew it. Charlie was no genius, maybe, but he was good. He had vision and he had integrity: it wasn't what he had, but what he hadn't, that tormented him now. Paradoxically, if he had not had talent himself, sufficient for most men, he wouldn't have known or even cared what Oliver Nankervis had that he did not. The noise might be childish, but the feeling behind it was deep, genuine and adult. She understood, and because she was Kate and knew his weaknesses, she was strong for him. However he had spent the past three days, and knowing him as she did she had no illusions as to that whatever he told her, she would still protect him and love him.

After a while she said, because she could keep it to herself no longer, 'Cress has run away.'

'Cress?' He looked at her blankly, returning from his pre-occupation with himself only with reluctance. 'She won't have gone far. Katie –' He reached for her, but she drew back a little.

'She's been gone more than forty-eight hours.'

'So long as she paid before she left –'

'She didn't *leave*, Charlie. She *ran away*.'

Charlie had no room in his mind for anything but his own problems. He got to his feet, lurching a little, and went towards the door.

'She'll come back. I'm going to the studio.'

'I tried to talk –' Kate began to tell him, but the door was already swinging open on an empty hall. He had ranted, he had wept, and now he would come to terms with himself, but for that he needed solitude. She let him go.

Charlie walked through the rhododendrons, a path so familiar that even in the darkness he didn't trip or stumble, or even think about it. If he had taken in what Kate had said about Cress, he had already forgotten it. He suffered the torments of a creator who knows himself fallible, and although the agony would only last a short time, for that short time it would resemble the tortures of the damned.

He pushed open the door of the studio, surprised and displeased to find that it wasn't locked. But then, what did it matter? There was nothing in here of any value. The pretty pictures that little Cress had painted, and his own rubbish, that was all. He switched on the light, and Cress, behind the workbench, stiffened with fear.

Kate – Kate, or the police. She had sent for the police, Cress had seen them come from where she stood concealed in the rhododendrons, and go away again. But perhaps they had come back, searching, searching – she screwed herself into a tight ball, as if by doing so she could make herself invisible.

She heard Charlie's footsteps as he walked across the floor, and the rattle and clang of a paint can as it flew across the room. He had kicked it deliberately, but she wasn't to know that. Some of the paint spattered on the floor almost under her nose, red as blood and as sticky.

There was the sound of someone fumbling among the tools on the workbench, and then an oath, and a screwdriver dropped onto her hand, rolled, and lay on the floor beside her. She heard Charlie – she realised it must be Charlie now – pick up something and saw his feet on her own level under the bench, and she was about to get up and run to him when he began to behave very strangely indeed.

Something crashed down onto the top of the workbench, heavy and hard, and then Charlie began to hit it, rhythmically and with violence, and as he hit, he spoke, slurring the words between his teeth, the emphasis falling on the beat of his hammer blows.

'I *hate* you, Oliver Nankervis, I *hate* you, I *hate* you! Why should *you* have what *I* would give my *eyes* for? To *he* that *hath* it *shall* be *given*, and where under *heaven* is the justice in *that?*' Then, at a faster pace, he went on, hitting out, his words becoming almost a votive chant. '*Hate, hate, hate, hate, hate –*'

Cress got slowly to her feet. She stood behind the bench, her eyes like saucers, and watched Charlie beating one of his own works viciously to death, only it wasn't Charlie that she saw. And then he saw her, too, and his hand that held the hammer dropped to his side and he stared at her as if she was a ghost.

'Oh, Mike —' said Cress, in a broken little voice, and ran round the bench to fling her arms around him. 'Oh Mike, you've come! Take me away from here, take me away, please!'

Charlie made no attempt to take her into his own arms, but he let the hammer fall to the ground.

'Cress?' He sounded like a man wakened from sleep, dazed and confused.

'Take me away, Mike, take me away from here. I love you Mike, I love you, I love you!'

Charlie was hardly listening. He said, 'Yesterday, I looked on genius such as I would give the world to possess, and today there is no love in me.'

She didn't understand his extravagant speaking, for all that she dramatised herself. She said, 'Kate said such cruel things, you never heard such things. She hates me and I can't stay here, I can't! She said *I* killed you, Mike, darling Mike —'

She was clinging to him, letting her knees go limp so that he was forced to take her by the elbows to avoid being pulled over. He lifted her back onto her feet, not gently.

'Shut up, Cress, you know that's rubbish!' The necessity to concentrate on her distress rather than his own made him furious. The studio was his own sanctuary, even Kate knew when to come and when to go. He knew that Cress must have witnessed his private exorcism, and at that moment he hated her.

'Don't be angry with me, *please!*' she cried. 'Please don't be angry, when you love me!'

'I love you?' said Charlie, blankly.

'It's all right,' said Kate, tartly, from the door. 'You're living inside the covers of a paperback novelette. You'll get used to it. I've been doing it for three days now, should you care about that.'

'You're unjust!' cried Cress, on a sob.

'Don't whimper!' Kate snapped. 'Where have you been, you stupid, silly woman? Don't you know that I've been half out of my mind, worrying that you'd gone over the cliff or something equally stupid?' She was as furious as Charlie, not only because of the fright Cress had given her, but for her intrusion on Charlie at a time when even she herself would not have gone near him. She saw his face, blank with shock and white with fatigue, and she plucked Cress out of his arms like a puppy, by the scruff of her pretty neck, and deposited her onto a handy chair.

The broken picture lay in splinters of wood and jags of rusty nail on the bench. Kate looked at it with pity, and then at Charlie.

'Come on, love,' she said tenderly.

He took her then, and held her close, mumbling into her hair, cupping her shoulder blades in his two hands. It sounded to Cress as if he wept, but surely that couldn't be so.

'Fine and true and rapier bright,' he said, and Cress didn't know what he could be talking about. 'A living flame that never burned for me. Katie – Katie –'

He slid down until he was on his knees, with his arms still round her. She bent and stroked his hair. Neither of them remembered Cress.

'It's all right, my love, my Charlie, it's all right.'

'I invited him here,' said Charlie, muffled, into her thighs. 'You'll like his wife, she's fey as you are.'

'And shall I like him?' asked Kate.

'Oh yes. The very stuff of heroes, and the bringer of light… Katie…'

Cress had read enough about love, however debased, to know it when she saw it so clearly presented before her eyes. She had eaten little in the past two days, just a few biscuits she had found in the studio, she was hungry and weary, even a little fevered. Her sight was clear, clearer than ever before. She saw two kinds of love. The love of a man for a woman, and the love of a man for the embodiment of his own values and ideals, but only one of them did she understand.

Mike loved Kate, and Oliver Nankervis, whoever he was, had made him cry like a little child.

There is a saying about the last straw, the one that breaks the back of the camel. The last unbearable pressure, whether self-inflicted or the work of fate, that breaks a human being.

Cress stood up and walked out of the studio, and neither Kate nor Charlie noticed her go.

She ran like a wild thing through the night, winged feet and flying hair, a spirit without feeling, a dead thing that yet moved. She ran and ran until the brambles caught at her ankles, and the rising ground made her stumble and fall, and then she scrambled to her feet and pushed on and up.

On the top of the rise there was only grass, the gorse and brambles ringing a circular clearing, nibbled by rabbits, a green, untrodden carpet. To her left, the flat sea lay like a sheet of steel under the moon, on her right, the ground fell away, back towards the road.

In the centre of the clearing lay a great stone, like a gravestone, broad and flat and smooth. Cress knelt on the green carpet and ran her fingers over it, feeling its cool smoothness under her hands, feeling its strength. Close to her, so close that she knew that she would see him if she looked up, she felt the presence of her dead.

'Mike?' she said, softly. 'Mike?'

The night breeze stirred her hair like the touch of a spirit hand. She smiled to feel it. Kate hadn't held him, then. The bond was unbreakable after all.

'There can never be anyone but you,' she said, into the listening darkness. 'Never, never, never.' She repeated it like a mantra. 'Never, never, never.' The words had the very feel of magic, and she chanted them yet again. 'Never, never, never.'

It came to her then, in the whispering depths of the night, that it was true after all, Mike had died brutally, tragically, so that only his spirit remained, and Charlie had rejected that and condemned it to drifting for ever on the wind. So, she was alone but not alone. She heard the whisper in her head, soft and clear.

Avenge me, Cressida. Avenge me. He took my life and yet he lives.

'I'll kill him,' said Cressida.

Her name hissed through the grasses.

Cresssida... Cressssida....

The stone under her fingers felt alive, warm, as if her pulsebeat was its own. She heard the voice on the sighing little wind.

Being alone is worse than dying. Leave him alone, Cressida, Cresssida. Let his spirit bleed as yours will bleed, every bitter day of a long, long life. Kill the woman, Cresssida... let the man live and suffer.

'But there is no woman,' said Cressida, and the sigh of the wind answered her.

V

February of the following year, and a very nasty day.

The snow poured silently down, thick and clogging as swansdown, from a sky the colour of an uncleared grate, blanketing the wide moorland with a cloak of nondescript, featureless white. The wind, that blew in heavy gusts across the open countryside, periodically caught and shook the little car, swerving it across the road, wheels skidding, bouncing and crunching against the drifts of snow to right and left. Already, the brief winter afternoon was closing in towards an early dusk.

It was a long, long way to the Helford River yet, but only a short, short way, if she wasn't careful, to an unpleasantly premature eternity.

Debbie dragged her thoughts resolutely away from this dangerous ground. There was no mileage in looking on the black side, even if she had been caught for the biggest mug this side of Exeter. It was she who had decided to ignore the weather forecasts, she who had talked airily about global warming and the unlikelihood of being caught in a blizzard in what was, literally, the present climate. Also, on the credit side – if there was a credit side – even if she had been caught unawares by a white-out, the moor wasn't exactly uninhabited. Anyone would give her shelter on a day like this, surely, and even if she didn't see a house right at this moment, if she could keep going she would eventually find one. She might even run right out of this horrible weather, which according to her car radio was largely confined to the moor, and once she had done that she had every chance of making it safely to her destination. There was absolutely nothing to sweat about.

It would, however, have been more comforting if there had been even one other car on the road. Either they were all hidden in the drifts, or other motorists had more faith in weather forecasts. More sense, in fact, tell it like it is, Deb. The terrible sense of isolation was, arguably, worse than the weather conditions. She could be alone in the world.

The CD player momentarily ceased belting out cheerful pop music, and the car radio cut in, crackling and sizzling with atmospherics. A distorted voice that sounded not unlike Donald Duck informed her that freak snowstorms in the West Country were making conditions hazardous to traffic, and that the main A30 across Bodmin Moor was blocked. Motorists, said the gabbling voice, snug and secure in its warm broadcasting studio, were advised to stay at home.

Thanks a million, Auntie Beeb! thought Debbie, with indignation directed unfairly against the owner of the bodiless, distorted voice. So now she had to worry, not only about whether the snow would continue, or if the night would find her snowed up by the roadside, and whether anyone would worry about her and send out search parties, but also over whether the A30 was blocked behind her, or ahead of her. It might have helped if she had had even the faintest idea of exactly where she was.

She hadn't so far admitted to herself that she was frightened, it was easier to keep the baying black monster of fear at a distance if she didn't look at it. The bright music, the concentration required to keep the car on the road, her deliberately detached admiration for the beauty of the falling snow, all these superficialities had helped to keep optimism alive and flourishing, and fear firmly in its place. Donald Duck, with a few well-chosen words, had changed all that. Debbie's heart began to pound, and she found that her hands were slipping on the steering wheel. In spite of the biting cold, she broke out into a hot and uncomfortable sweat all over.

The snow continued to fall, thick and cloying and inexorable. The little yellow Volkswagen struggled gamely on, slipping and slithering, now sticking with wildly revving engine, now lurching forward over hidden obstacles that for all she knew, Debbie thought with graveyard humour, were the bodies of buried motorists who had left their cars to look for shelter, frozen and hard under the white covering, and all the time the light faded in the leaden bowl of the sky. If she survived, she told herself, she would really be able to call herself a driver – and then immediately wished she had chosen another word than *survived*. Or *if*, now she came to think about it.

Impossible that the snow was getting thicker, it was already, surely, as thick as snow could be, but the area of windscreen cleared by the labouring wipers was definitely becoming smaller, wedges of impacted snow firmly stuck round the edges. Gusts of wind, tearing across the open moorland, sent the car shuddering and slithering again on the treacherous surface of the road. It was becoming difficult to see at all.

It was by this time obvious, even to an incurable optimist such as Debbie, that she was shortly going to be forced to stop. If she stopped from choice now, and got out to clear the windscreen, she might travel far enough to find a house before it silted up again. The payment for this chance would be the loss of heat from the car and from her own body, and the certainty that she would get wet in the falling snow. If there was then no convenient house to be found, these things would materially affect her chance of lasting out until rescue came. On the other hand, if she simply stuck to the wheel and went on until she had to stop, she would conserve heat and body warmth, stay dry, and – possibly – reduce her chance of finding a refuge.

On balance, that chance was already negligible. The snow cut visibility practically to nothing, she could easily have passed any number of farms and cottages and never seen them at all. Rightly or wrongly, Debbie decided to opt for maximum warmth and dry clothes. She struggled on through the white, whirling dusk.

Maximum warmth was a laugh, too. She was by this time frozen to the ends of her toes, in spite of the heater.

If she stopped and left the engine running to keep the heater going, she would stand an excellent chance of dying from carbon-monoxide poisoning. The query in that case became, which took longest, asphyxia or hypothermia? Both sounded fairly conclusive. Nice long, impressive-sounding, stupid things to die of.

These thoughts, and others equally cheerless, she pushed firmly out of her mind – or at least, into the very back of it where she could ignore them for the moment. She had already decided to go on for as long as she could, so no useful purpose was going to be served by changing her mind or compromising. There probably wasn't a right thing to do in any case, it was all down to chance – fate – kismet – whatever you liked to call it. She had to concentrate on driving to the best of her suddenly inadequate-seeming ability, and thereafter keep her head at all costs. Panic could turn out as big a killer as either cold or poison gas.

The car gave a bigger lurch than it had given yet, and a wall of solid white appeared at the nearside window. Debbie, who could have sworn that she was keeping to the road, realised with a shock that went right down to her toenails that, in spite of the care she had thought she was taking, she had driven onto the verge, and in her consternation she swung the wheel and over-compensated. The Golf bounced, skidded, slithered sideways down the road. Through the restricted windscreen she saw ahead of her another white wall – far too close –

Oh God! She wasn't any longer *on* the A30, so the position of the blockage had become immaterial. One worry out of the way, anyway, but what on earth was she going to do now, slithering sideways-on down what seemed to be a fairly narrow lane to God-knows-where? She had no idea how long she had been driving down it, or at what point she had come onto it. She made the discovery that fear wasn't just in the mind, fear was a devastating physical pain sweeping in electrified waves along the complicated net of her nervous system, forcing sickness into her throat and blurring her sight. Her hands were shaking out of control, her grip of the wheel lost. Her stomach churned.

Only for a second, thank goodness, but long enough. The impetus of the skid helped her to straighten up in the confined space between the stone hedges, and still shaking, Debbie eased the car cautiously down the lane. Impossible to turn anyway, and lanes led somewhere, often to farms. She must cling to that. At the end of this one would be a friendly farmhouse, warmth, hot tea, food, people, a leaping fire in a wide hearth, security, telephone, dog on the rug, all the fixings. She thought about that security, and thus insulated, managed another hundred yards. The end was sudden and predictable. Round a bend, snow, drifted by the wind and lodged between the hedges on either side of the narrow lane, formed an impassable barrier. Debbie slithered into it before she could stop, and there she was.

She reached out automatically and switched off the engine. Into the quiet, the CD crooned seductively that it loved her only, always, never to part. The song was as old as the hills, and Debbie felt the same. She turned that off, too.

An eerie, wind-torn silence descended, with a heaviness that could almost be felt. Debbie put her cold hands into the pockets of her warm coat and took stock of her situation, a little shakily, but mercifully without that agonising web of Panic fear. What was done, was done.

It was a comfortless exercise. She was sitting in the car looking at a snowdrift, and not even she knew where. Not safely on the main road, where she should have been, where friendly rescue teams could find her;

stuck in a narrow lane apparently to nowhere that was rapidly filling with snow. Her assets were dry clothes, a bottle or water and a bar of chocolate, her company a radio and CD player that would last exactly so long as the car battery, or the fuel if she chose the asphyxiation option, and no longer. Her prospects… well, *gloomy* seemed as good a description as any.

How airtight was a car? If you could asphyxiate from carbon-monoxide poisoning in one, could you also suffocate from lack of oxygen? If, for instance, you had to spend a day or so in a snowdrift? Debbie didn't know. She lowered the nearside window a cautious inch, it was possibly better to play it safe. A cold draught cut across the top of her head and ruffled her blonde hair, the cost of fresh air might be a bit high. She closed the window almost shut again and went on thinking. There wasn't much else to do.

A day or so… well, that was just a thought plucked out of the air. It might not be as long as that, hooray for global warming after all! And this was Cornwall, supposed to be ten degrees warmer than the rest of the country, or so she had been told, although there wasn't much evidence for it right now. It would thaw quickly. Well, wouldn't it?

She didn't know that, either.

Debbie felt the first wave of returning panic quiver along her nerves. The wind howled over the tops of the hedges and caressed the roof of the car, died, moaned gently with returning vigour and died again.

'*… the bad weather sweeping south west England,*' announced a distant voice, tiny but clear through the open crack of the window, '*shows no signs at present of easing…*' and was drowned out by a renewed blast of wind, snow and bitter cold.

Debbie sat transfixed in her seat. Her eyes went involuntarily to her own radio, but of course she had switched that off. Unlit and uncommunicative, it had nothing to add.

Not her radio then, so it must be somebody else's. And close. Before she had thought it out, Debbie had opened the door of the car and tumbled out into the snow.

She slammed the door behind her and listened, with the wind tearing at her hair and clothes and icy snow driving into her face and down her neck. Huddled there in her coat, she could hear nothing. It occurred to her, too late, that what she had heard could simply be another trapped motorist, but at least they could huddle together for warmth, she supposed.

Or an abandoned car. Abandoned by someone who had got out to prospect for human life, leaving the radio on to help him find his way back… and never done so. That was a sobering thought, one that she wished she hadn't had.

A heavy gust of wind, roaring over the hedges, blew a hole in the swirling snowflakes, lifted them, whirled them away dancing in a fantastic cloud, and through the thinning veil she saw a light. Quite close, the solid orange oblong of an uncurtained window, shining like a lighthouse through the flurried early dusk. The sudden wave of relief was as undermining in its way as panic. As the snow came down again and hid the welcome light, Debbie stumbled in the direction in which she had seen it, and against all the odds found the solid feel of a gate under her groping hands. The snow was so deep she had to climb over it.

The window belonged to a cottage, tucked under the lee of the moor and close to the road. Through the window, she could see a tiny lamp lit room, comfortable chintz-covered armchair and a sagging sofa, a fire glowing away to ashes in a hearth stacked to one side with fresh logs, and a table spread with books and papers on which sat an oil lamp and a portable radio, chattering and singing away to itself, and clearly audible from here through a gap in the top of the sash. The front door, firmly closed, was within a few steps of the gate. Debbie lifted the knocker and hammered on it.

Only the moaning of the wind answered her, and a renewed burst of music from the crack at the top of the window.

She rapped again, harder, and the wind mocked at her in reply.

The lamp was lit, the radio playing, the house couldn't be empty. It was possible, of course, that whoever lived here was at the back and hadn't heard her knock above the sound of the gale. Perhaps they were deaf, whoever they were? The door wouldn't open; Debbie fought her way through the deep snow and some thick, wet bushes, keeping close to the cottage wall where it hadn't drifted so deeply, came to the corner of the house and turned towards the rear. If she couldn't make anyone hear, she resolved, she would climb in through that window somehow… but somebody, surely, must be at home. She really wanted somebody, never mind whom.

The side wall of the cottage led her to a tiny yard, enclosed by a wall and a couple of small outbuildings. The back door, as firmly closed as the front, opened into it with snow drifted against its green-painted surface, so nobody had been out of it for a while. There was no knocker here, but

Debbie hammered on it with her fists and without success, and then in final desperation, tried the latch.

This door opened easily under her hand, spilling snow through into a narrow, stone-flagged passage with doors to right and left. Both were open, one poured out light and music across the flagged passageway, and the other, a black rectangle in the white wall, gave away no secrets. At the far end of the passage, the front door presented a blank expanse of polished wood and the negative evidence of a shot bolt. There was no movement, no sound but the radio and the wind, an eerie atmosphere of desertion, but there was also the warm smell of coffee, underlaid with lavender wax.

'Hullo?' called Debbie, but nobody answered.

She stepped inside and pushed the door to against the wind and cold, a pool of melting snow lay on the flags around her feet. She could hear the wind battering the solid wood like some wild banshee desperate to get in. Even the stone walls of the little house seemed to shake with the furious buffeting. She drew her coat more closely round her and shivered, more in retrospect than anything, for the quiet house felt warm after the freezing world outside.

She called again, but tentatively for she was beginning to be sure that the little house was empty. Her mind began to make disturbing pictures, the owner, perhaps, had gone outside for something, slipped and been covered in snow. The body would be found, decomposing, when it melted… she knew an impulse to rush out and dig in the drifts, but recognised it as foolish. If that had happened, it had been a long time since. There had been no mark on the chilly surface of the drifted snow.

In any case, from a purely practical angle, why should anyone go outside? There was fuel in the hearth, she had seen it, oil in the lamp. No, they were asleep, that was it, having an afternoon nap upstairs and when they – whoever *they* might be – woke up, they would be very surprised to see her, and they could laugh about it together, and congratulate each other that she wasn't an axe murderer.

Meanwhile, she couldn't stand here all evening. To say that the passage was warmer than the outside world wasn't giving it high praise after all, and on a night like this, nobody, surely would begrudge it if she intruded further. Nervously, feeling absurdly like a burglar about to be caught in the act, she stepped to the warmly lit doorway and looked inside.

The room was tiny and crowded, but friendly, the glowing ashes in the hearth giving out a faint residual warmth. A pen with its top off was laid ready to write beside the papers on the table. There was a laptop computer with a blank screen, and she could see some tax tables in among the muddle. Bor*ing!* She left the table alone and looked around her. Nobody asleep in the armchair, as she had half-expected, but in the far corner of the room another door, painted white to match the walls, had almost escaped her attention. She tiptoed across and opened it, and found a narrow box staircase leading upwards.

She knew what all this reminded her of. *Goldilocks and the Three Bears.*

Who's been sleeping in my bed?

'Hullo?' she called, again, and her voice echoed back from the chilly darkness above.

Nobody, then?

A wave of cold air had come into the room from the stairs, she closed the door and took another, more thoughtful look around her. The fire, she reckoned, might blaze up again with a log on it, wood fires were very good tempered, and since she was here she might as well attend to it. Nobody would want it to go out tonight. She took a log and threw it onto the embers and turned to pick up the lamp. She would go upstairs and wake whoever must surely be sleeping up there, but first of all she would check the other room downstairs, which must be the kitchen, where come to think of it, evidence of the laptop notwithstanding, she would quite possibly find some dear old silver-surfer dozing in a rocker beside an old Cornish slab. The smell of coffee was permeating the entire house, whoever lived here couldn't be far away.

Her mind, in spite of an attempt to prevent it, added laconically, *alive or dead,* and the softly lit room was suddenly less cosy.

Lamp in hand, she went back into the passage and crossed to the opposite door. Electric light switches, she noted automatically, and clicked one up and down. Nothing. The power was off, hence the lamp. How long for?

Don't try to answer that.

She stepped through the door.

The light shone on a compact kitchen, a little larger than the sitting-room, original wooden cupboards lovingly restored, table and three chairs pushed against the wall, a sink with a few plates and a mug draining beside it. Not a Cornish slab, but even better: an old Rayburn sitting warm and comforting against an outside wall, with an old-fashioned coffee percolator, battered but obviously still serviceable, spluttering gently on the simmering plate. Unduly strong, her mind registered, the splashes that leapt in the glass top were literally black, as if it had been percolating overlong.

… and a fourth chair, overturned beneath a high cupboard that was open, and beneath the swinging door, the occupant of the cottage in an untidy heap on the floor.

Debbie put the lamp down on the table with hands that weren't quite as steady as they might have been. She stood for a moment or two, summoning courage, and then stepped forward and bent over the still figure, dreading what she would find, her irresponsible subconscious muttering on yet again about bodies.

Little old ladies were the bodies that one usually found in lonely cottages, she had always understood, possibly with ranks of starving cats mourning hungrily alongside, but this one was male, and far from elderly. He couldn't be much above thirty; jeans, sweatshirt and trainers, like a million other young men. Gypsy dark, with short, fine hair receding a little at the temples, his swarthy skin an unhealthy greyish-yellow, deeply unconscious. But not dead. She was almost certain that he wasn't dead. She knelt beside him on the stone floor, feeling his wrist for a pulse, and to her relief it was there, fluttering and unsteady, but unmistakeable. In spite of the warmth from the Rayburn, his hand was freezing cold. She sat back on her heels and considered. Faced with something definite to do, her fears and fantasies packed their bags and slunk off.

Debbie knew a lot more about the care of the injured than she wished to think about, even if only at second hand, for her own brother had spent almost a year in a spinal injuries unit. She knew all about warmth and careful handling, levels of consciousness and freedom from anxiety. But Oliver's terrifyingly extensive injuries had been diagnosed by experts, she had only been an onlooker after the event. Here, she was starting from scratch.

Anxiety she could discount for the moment; he was so deeply unconscious that he had no responses at all, but for the rest she had no idea if he had suffered serious injury, and even less how to find out. There was no blood that she could see, and that was as far as her emergency first-aid knowledge went. She knew that it would be wrong to try to move him without knowing more – a thought that was immediately followed by the realisation that she would be lucky to be able to do so. Her discovery was a sturdy specimen, of only average height, but squarely and solidly built and with the regrettable beginnings of a beer gut. He must, she thought uneasily, have gone down with the impact of an elephant.

He was lying on his right side, which was a bonus for in that position he was unlikely to choke, or anything terrifying of that kind, but he was so cold. His hands and face were like ice, so the first thing must be to get him warm again. Slipping off her own coat, she tucked it round him and got to her feet. There would be blankets upstairs, maybe even a hot-water bottle, so upstairs she would go. When she had done all she could to warm him she could take stock of the situation again – although she was already dismally aware that anything she did while he was still unconscious, and possibly even after he came round – if he did – would be in the realms of guesswork, with a faint seasoning of common-sense. Which, brought down to basics, was probably nothing at all. Nothing at all seemed a useless thing to do in an emergency.

Better nothing at all than the wrong thing. If the person who found Oliver had done the wrong thing, or anything other than run for help, he would have been totally paralysed, or more probably dead, and that was something that taught an unforgettable lesson.

Upstairs, there were two bedrooms, or possibly one and a half, Debbie thought as she peeped into the tiny second one, and a minute shower room. The bed in the larger room was made up, she stripped off a duvet and a blanket and gathered up the pillows, failed to find a hot-water bottle in the shower room, and returned to the kitchen as quickly as possible, where her involuntary host still lay where she had left him, dead to the world and intensely vulnerable, totally at the mercy of her ignorance.

She removed her coat and replaced it with the pilfered bedclothes, tucking them as closely round him as she could without moving him, and slid the flattest pillow very carefully between his cheek and the cold tiles. He could have fractured his skull, quite easily. He wasn't dead now, but he could die...

Whatever shall I do if he dies? If I'm shut in this house for days, perhaps, with his body? In this warm kitchen?

She pushed the macabre thought out of her mind and got up from the floor.

There was nothing more that she could do for him for the moment, she might as well look after herself. She took the percolator, which had almost boiled dry, from the stove and refilled it, replacing it on the boiling plate. It must have been simmering away there for simply ages, which was rather a daunting thought. She looked at the bundled figure on the floor for a moment, biting her lip, and then picked up the lamp and went back into the other room. There might be a telephone.

There was. There was a mobile in among the papers on the table. It registered no signal, so either the battery was flat, or the cottage was in a no-signal area. Terrific! Her own mobile, as she had realised the minute the snow began to fall, was sitting on the table in her London flat. She tried anyway, but it was useless. The thing was as dead as… no Deb, let's not do the *dead* word.

So, no telephone. He didn't need a blizzard to cut him off from the company of his fellow men. She stood in the crowded little room and faced her predicament squarely.

She was cut off from all communication with the outside world, snowed up in an isolated cottage with a man who might be dying, who must at the very least have been unconscious for some time, who could be seriously injured. She could be stuck here for days. The best that could be said was that she was better off than she would have been snowed up in the car. She had fuel – at least for the moment, and presumably if he lived here he had a fuel store: it would be outside in the snow somewhere, but it must surely stop snowing soon. This was Cornwall. It never snowed in Cornwall. She supposed that there was food in the house, and oil for the lamps – and the last item she had better check on now, for if this lamp had been burning for as long as the coffee had been percolating, which was a reasonable assumption, she was likely to find herself in the dark soon, and it would be a long night if she had to spend it with an unseen, unknown man perhaps dying in the dark beside her. It would be bad enough if she could see him.

Debbie went back, reluctantly, to the kitchen, carrying the lamp with her. Florence Nightingale – or maybe not. The immortal Flo would have known what to do.

The owner of her sanctuary hadn't moved, but she thought that he looked less deathly. His pulse was still weak and she hoped that it was steadier, but she could pinch his cheek and brush her fingers against his eyelashes without getting any reaction at all, so he was still pretty far gone.

She stepped carefully round him, stumbling over a powerful torch rolled onto the floor as she did so, peering into all the cupboards she could reach without treading on him, and was rewarded with the discovery of a stack of tinned foods and packets, a can of paraffin, some matches, and better yet than these, another lamp ready filled and trimmed, standing on the window sill. The torch, when she tried it, was dead, but she had seen a spare battery beside the paraffin can. The tiny fridge on the worktop contained milk, cheese, butter, and a loaf of bread wrapped in foil. Decent bread too, a plump, crusty loaf that almost looked as if it had never seen the inside of a supermarket. There was something bloody in a basin, too, covered in cling wrap, and a couple of six-packs of beer, one of them reduced to a four-pack. Vegetables in the drawer. Eggs in a bowl on the side, apples in another. Starvation wasn't an option then. She took the half-empty bottle of milk and using the mug from the draining board, poured herself a mug of coffee.

She had turned off the radio when she went to look for a telephone, and the house was extraordinarily quiet. Outside, chaos and darkness were doing their best, but within the thick stone walls of the cottage was a sheltering haven from the storm. Minute noises: the shift of coal deep inside the stove, the *gloop* of the percolator on the simmering plate, the soft hiss of the lamp, her own breathing. His breathing too, she supposed, but he was being very quiet there on the floor. She thought that she had heard or read somewhere that people with serious head injuries breathed stertorously, or even snored, and drew comfort from the recollection. Just so long as he *was* breathing –

Sudden panic, far worse than the panic in the car, swept over her in a tidal wave as her overstretched nerves recoiled on her. She was on her knees beside him in a flash, bending close, listening

He was breathing. Evenly, deeply, like a man asleep. When she touched him this time, his eyebrows twitched together and his mouth tightened, and then relaxed again. Feeling for his pulse, she found it steady and strong and his hand was warm in her own. Very soon he was going to wake up, and whatever injury he had suffered, she was certain now that it wouldn't turn out to be a skull fracture. Just so long as all those books she had read had known what they were talking about.

She knelt up and groped on the table for her hurriedly deposited mug of coffee, and settled down where she could watch him properly, beside him on the floor with her back against the table leg.

The coffee was vile, over stewed and bitter but hot and comforting too. She sipped it, looking down at his shuttered face. He was pale still, but not the deathly pallor of her arrival; a dark man, nice-looking only in an ordinary way; strong eyebrows, long eyelashes, a stubborn, blunt-featured face but with a pleasant mouth that saved him from the classification *thug*. She imagined him awake, talking to her, his eyes open and aware – grey eyes, or blue, black, brown, green – and then his eyelashes flickered and lifted drowsily, and they were golden-green, a true hazel. They stayed open, looking blankly at her knees for a moment or two, and closed again as if wearily. She didn't think he had realised that there was anybody there. She reached up to place her empty mug on the table, and went on waiting.

A few minutes ticked by quietly, and then he stirred, rolled over onto his back with a groan that curdled the blood in her veins, and looked her squarely in the face.

'Proper job!' he murmured distantly. 'A punk angel!' and began to retch alarmingly.

'No!' cried Debbie, scrambling untidily to her feet. 'Don't – you can't – ' But obviously, he could. There was a plastic washing-up bowl in the sink, she seized it hurriedly and was back on the floor in a shower of teaspoons before the worst had happened, and there followed an unpleasant interval during which she had time to reflect nostalgically on the pleasures of being snowed up in a car on her own. It could only happen to her, she thought resentfully, cradling the head of a total stranger in her supporting arms. On television, or in a sloppy novel, the girl who found a man – but of course, it ought to be a devastatingly handsome man – lying unconscious in an isolated cottage thereafter enjoyed a romantic interval. She ended up holding a basin. Reality did have a way of being the kiss of death to romance, she had noticed it before.

The horrid upheaval seemed to be over, at least for now. He lay with his head in her lap, sheet-white and sweating profusely, but he was still conscious. She put the bowl down on the floor, as far away from her as possible, and he stirred as she moved, looking up at her, frowning.

'Where've you sprung from, my bird?' he asked, weakly, but with interest. A pleasant voice, but with a definite local accent. A native, then, not a so-called Emmet like herself.

'My car's stuck in a drift, outside,' Debbie told him. 'Your door was unlocked, I just walked in when I couldn't make anyone hear. I found you lying on the floor.'

'Oh.' His eyes closed for a moment, and a spasm of pain twisted his mouth and sent a tingle of alarm along her nerves. 'I fell off'n the chair...' he said, tentatively, and drew an unsteady breath. 'Look, whoever you are, can you find the brandy? It's in the cupboard in t'other room.'

'I'm not sure that's a good idea – '

'You think it's a better one, I just lie on the floor, skrift up?' he enquired, through gritted teeth. 'Just fetch it like a good girl, and think about'n later.'

She looked at him, and at the sweat running off his forehead into the damp tangle of his hair, and felt the weight of her own total lack of any sensible knowledge weighing on her like the sins of the world. Eight top of the range GCSEs and three spectacularly good A-levels, and what use were they?

'You might have some internal injury,' she said. Her brother had had internal injuries, massive internal injuries. Horrid spectres gibbered in the corners of the room. She knew too little, and at the same time, too much. She felt sick. His voice, in contrast, was coolly assessing, as aware of the dangers as she was but more pragmatic.

'I haven't got no internal injury. I fell off the chair and hit on my elbow, and I think I've smashed'n to pieces, but I can't stay on the floor all night. If I'm to get up, I need help – your help – and a good, stiff, drink. You must help me. I can't do nothing without you, I've tried. I just pass out again.'

Their eyes locked for a moment, hers storm-grey and frightened, his gold, and clouded with pain. The blizzard still raged outside, louder and more boisterous than ever, and there was nobody else within call. He was quite right, he couldn't stay on the floor, in spite of the blankets the draught from the door could be lethal. Among the rapidly growing ranks of her own inadequacies was an ignorance of how to treat hypothermia – there it was again – so best not to invite it in the first place. Debbie laid him gently back on the stone floor and fetched the brandy and two glasses without further argument, and they gained a bit of Dutch courage together.

She had managed, with his painful co-operation, to prop him up against the cupboard, but his usable left hand was shaking so much that the brandy leapt in the glass. He looked terrible.

'I'm still not sure that moving you is a good idea,' she said, suddenly assailed by doubts once more.

'I'm not sold on it neither, but can you think of anything better?' His teeth were chattering, and the sweat on his skin gleamed in the lamplight. He was badly shaken up, she suddenly realised, and the knowledge made her pull herself together.

It would have to be the sofa by the fire, she decided. There wasn't the remotest chance that she could get him upstairs to bed properly, and it was warmer down here, anyway. And if he had to be moved, the quicker and shorter the distance the better it would be. But if he really had smashed his elbow – and he was in the best position to know that – then it wasn't going to be as simple as he was trying to make out. Someone – herself – would have to think of some way of immobilising it while the transfer across the passage took place. A broken elbow wouldn't paralyse his entire nervous system like a broken back could do, but it could seriously impair the use of his arm, and that would be bad enough. She poured him another stiff brandy and went upstairs to see what she could find to help them.

There was little to be found in the bathroom. Sticking plaster, a small tube of antiseptic cream, a burn spray and a packet of Paracetamol tablets. She pocketed the Paracetamol, but the situation was way beyond the scope of sticking plaster, she left that. The airing cupboard was more helpful, apart from the hot water tank, it also contained a small supply of clean linen. Surprised at her own resourcefulness, Debbie helped herself to a pillow case to use for a sling. Messing about with broken bones was something she didn't intend to try, so there was not, she thought without regret, the smallest need to start ripping up sheets like a heroine in historical fiction. Pushing her faltering courage back up to the sticking point, she returned downstairs.

In the warm, fire lit downstairs room, she paused. It was impossible not to think about possibilities. Suppose, in her ignorance, she was helping him to do something terminally silly. Suppose he had more than a shattered elbow… suppose she crippled him for life? She knew something about that sort of thing, and she wouldn't wish it on a dog.

And suppose, she told herself briskly, that you don't help him, and he tries to do it on his own? He looks quite capable of it, and then he could fall and make things a hundred times worse for himself. You don't really think you could stop him trying, do you?

No, she didn't. He had that stubborn, determined look to him, there was no mistaking it. She returned to the kitchen with her pillowcase and found that in her absence he had fainted again, slumped against the woodwork and looking long overdue for the mortuary.

It had its compensations. She could see to his arm without subjecting him to unimaginable agonies that would have been pretty bad for both of them. Remembering that it was best to immobilise a broken joint entirely, she ripped the pilfered pillowcase into long strips with the aid of a kitchen knife and, using the sturdy framework of his ribcage as a splint, bound his right arm firmly to his body. Her heart was in her mouth all the time she did so, and when she had done, she had a quick check over the rest of him. It began to dawn on her that it must have been in a dead faint that she had first found him, for there was only a small bruise on his temple, not nearly enough to knock him out cold. When he had said that he landed on his elbow, he had apparently been speaking the exact truth.

It must be horribly painful, and she was sorry to have to bring him round, but it had to be done. Cold water and more brandy did the job, in true story-book style, but that was the easy bit. The transfer to the other room was more like a horror movie.

In terms of actual distance, it was only a few yards, for the cottage was tiny. In terms of time, it stretched into eternity. In spite of the cushioning effect of three brandies, albeit smallish ones, he was sobbing with pain before he was even on his feet, and he was so giddy and unsteady after his long faint that Debbie was virtually supporting his entire weight on her own shoulders. She dragged one of the kitchen chairs with them so that she could ease him onto it when it became too much for her, and they managed somehow. It took them a nightmare ten minutes.

He sank thankfully down onto the sofa, speaking rather unevenly and looking like death.

'Sorry bird, I feel rough as rats.'

'Lie down properly,' said Debbie. 'I'll fetch the blankets.'

'Don' start fussing, please!'

It seemed an inappropriate remark from someone who was bathed in sweat and shaking, with his lip bleeding where he had bitten it to stop himself screaming with the pain. Debbie was fairly well frightened by this time. She snapped at him, angrily, 'Don't be so *stupid*! You're in shock, if you make yourself really ill, what do you think I'm going to be able to do? Just lie down and don't be so… so…' She bit her own lip. There had to be a phrase to cover the present circumstances. She finished, '*bloody difficult!*' with a depth of feeling that astonished both of them.

He looked up at her, obviously considering what to say next. What he saw was a slim, angry blonde girl with a spiky halo of bleached and shaggy hair, modern as tomorrow, exotic as a sunbird and as startlingly beautiful. Unusual eyes too, of a dark, stormy grey, fringed with unlikely black lashes and cleverly made-up to turn heads, warm-tinted skin that had been in the sun, a determined mouth with much sweetness about the lips… angel, if he was lucky, maybe. Punk, nothing so *passée*, but it only a needed a ring through her nose to complete a definitive picture, and she had, he noticed, two studs in one ear and a fine silver ring in the other. He wondered what colouring nature had given her, and then realised that he was deliberately shutting off. She was all that he had right now. Best not to antagonise her. He lay down obediently, and once there he was glad he had done as she said, for the normally stable walls of the room began to spin round in a very strange way, and the beautiful face above him was apparently receding to the end of a long, dark tunnel.

'Sorry,' he said, hearing his own voice from a point way up in the sky somewhere. 'I'm going to throw up again —'

'You can't!' cried Debbie, and made a dive for the kitchen and the bowl.

No, it wasn't in the least romantic.

VI

Outside, the blizzard still raged. Debbie, crossing to the window to close the shutters against the tumultuous night, peered out into the wild darkness through a window-pane splattered with snowflakes. There was very little to be seen beyond falling snow and the dim, white hump of the hedge. Drifts lay thickly against the walls of the house, it was a bleak and disturbing prospect.

A voice from the direction of the sofa recalled her attention.

'That coffee smells good,' he remarked. Debbie turned and looked at him. He sounded horribly shaky still, but tucked under the warm blankets he had at least lost some of the alarming grey tinge.

'It isn't, it's pretty disgusting,' she said. 'Anyway, you'll be sick again.'

'No, I promise. That's jus' trying to move — that's why they say *a sickening pain*, I suppose. I never knew it was true, did you?'

Debbie knew that it was, she had met the phenomenon before. Her look became more speculative, as yet again she weighed the pros and cons of their situation. One should, she knew, be wary of giving nourishment to victims of accidents, but since there seemed to be no chance of any proper medical attention for hours yet, if not days, she felt the rules could — should, in fact — be ignored. A warm drink was probably the best thing for him, if he could keep it down. Shock, she seemed to recall being told, deprived the body of essential fluids, which needed to be replaced quickly. She should have thought of it for herself.

'I'll fetch you some,' she said. 'Can you drink it with sugar? I think you should.' If only to disguise the flavour.

'Always do.' He sounded exhausted. Her heart gave an uneasy thump.

As she reheated the coffee yet again, Debbie considered what the next stage should be. They had weathered phase one without actual disaster, but things were going to get worse, not better, before they were in touch with the outside world again. The thought was daunting. Isolated cottages, like yachts, should be fitted with radio transmitters. *Mayday, mayday, mayday.* What wouldn't she give...?

Was there, perhaps, something else she should be doing? She had only his word for it that he had broken his elbow, but he seemed sure enough and there wasn't a lot of point, really, in looking to check, she wouldn't know what to do about it and she would only hurt him. He had endured enough pain for the moment. Rightly or wrongly, instinct told her to leave well alone, but there was, she fully realised, a time limit. Her subconscious mind, always an unruly member, muttered about septicæmia; on a more conscious level, she knew that neglect could give rise to complications, and that as time went on Paracetamol was going to be of very little use. They were both of them in for a rather sticky time.

Unless, of course, she suddenly thought, it wasn't an isolated cottage at all. She hadn't seen another building, but at the precise time she hadn't exactly been looking. At the thought that there might be human life within a hundred yards or so, her heart lifted. Then dropped again. Surely, he would have mentioned it?

He hadn't said very much at all.

She returned to the other room with a steaming mug in each hand, and pulled a small stool over to where he could reach it easily. Settling herself in the armchair, she said,

'Do you have neighbours?'

'Neighbours?' He sounded bewildered.

'You know, people who live near.' People who might help, but she didn't add that. He said, 'There's a farm down the lane – 'bout half a mile. Nothing nearer.'

Half a mile didn't sound far, but in the dark and the storm and the snow it might as well be a hundred miles. Forget that, then, for now. Maybe in the morning.

'What are we going to do?' asked Debbie.

He looked back at her, as aware as she was of the size and extent of their problem. His eyes looked enormous and there was a skim of sweat on his forehead to which his hair was sticking spikily.

'Have any options, do us?' he asked, quietly.

'Well, no. I suppose we haven't. But –'

'I think,' he said, speaking carefully, 'I'd sooner not talk about it – or even think about it – least until I need. You just do your own thing, do you mind?'

His position, of course, was a lot worse than her own. Debbie sympathised, but found his attitude unhelpful. She sighed inwardly.

'Anyway, we seem to have plenty of food.'

'So long's you can find the tin-opener.' He gave a forced laugh, mainly for her benefit she decided, and went on. 'So what're you doing here anyways? Not that I aren't glad to see you, but it seems a funny place for you to be, particularly as you don't seem to know where 'tis. The lane only goes to the farm, and it's a bad time to pick to explore the countryside.'

He was talking for the sake of it, she realised, not really interested. She said, neutrally, 'I was on my way to the Helford, and I got caught by the blizzard. I got off the road somehow, but I don't know when. It was… scary.' Understatement of the year. He looked at her with sympathy.

'I c'n imagine. Anyway, you aren't all that far off the main road.'

It wasn't the only thing that was scary. Nightmare licked its lips in the shadows, and Debbie took a firmer grip on her mug, and on her imagination. He stirred uncomfortably, catching his breath.

'Since we got to know each other intimately, perhaps we ought to introduce ourselves. I'm Mawgan.' Debbie heard this as "Morgan", and took it for a surname. It didn't sound particularly Cornish. Welsh, perhaps. But –

'Intimately?' she asked, blankly.

'Well, yes. Did you think you already knew the worst? Apart from that I'd probably better not, I don't think I can get off'n this sofa. I wouldn't get upstairs to the bathroom. So I'm a bit at your mercy.' He tried to laugh, but it wasn't a good effort.

'Oh God!' exclaimed Debbie, and gave a horrified giggle that was pure nerves. Brought face to face with the gritty facts of life, not for the first time in the last crowded hour she thought with fleeting longing of a nice comfortable snowdrift on the A30. She wondered which of them was more to be pitied. To avoid the subject until she had to face it, she said, 'My name is Deborah Nankervis, and I'll settle for Debbie, or Deb.'

'That's Cornish.'

'Nankervis? Yes, I know, but we only found out quite recently. Well, I suppose my father knew, but he didn't say. I always had a romantic idea that it was Greek, or Turkish, or something.'

'How exotic! So you're an emmet in spite of the name?'

''fraid so. What an awful fate for you! Delivered to the mercy of an emmet!'

'Trussed and bound, too,' remarked Morgan. He smiled. She wished he hadn't, she didn't want to like him too much, in case... she closed her eyes, opened them again on a pause to find him staring sightlessly into the fire. She swallowed, hard. It was all very well for him, Debbie thought, he couldn't do anything but take what fate and herself chose to hand to him. For her, it was slightly different.

'Look, Mr. Morgan – ' she began. He looked at her, startled.

'Who?'

Intimacy had to be kept on a manageable level. He was too young and too nice for any other course. She didn't dare, as things were, to get too close to him.

'Mr. Morgan,' she repeated, firmly, and perhaps he understood, for he didn't do anything more than grin at her. She went on. 'It's no good sitting here making trivial conversation. We're in trouble, you and I, and I... oh God, I don't know what to do!' She was horrified at the sound of her voice. Like a child, crying for help. She thought she heard a dangerous echo of tears at the back there somewhere, too, how shame-making! Morgan closed his eyes, all amusement gone.

'Don' you say that, Miss Deborah, please. Me neither.'

There was no reply to that. A silence fell between them, broken only by the continuing howl of the wind and the crash of heavy gusts that seemed to be shaking the cottage to its sturdy foundations. The shutters, closed now against the night, rattled like castanets, and up on the roof somewhere Debbie thought that she heard a tile move. She looked across at Morgan and her heart smote her. He looked scared.

'It's all right,' she said, and to her credit kept her voice steady and light. 'Don't worry about it. I'll manage, I'll think of something. It's going to be all right.'

He didn't answer her, and after a while she thought that he was asleep, or had maybe fainted again. Better that way, probably. He must be in appalling pain, for all he hadn't complained. She curled her feet into the chair and stared into the glowing fire, and her own eyelids began to droop heavily in spite of everything. She jerked awake, but shock, fright and weariness were too strong for her. Her head dropped onto the arm of the chair and worn out, scared, and weighted down by sudden and unacceptable responsibility though she was, she slept like a child.

She awoke some time later with an appalling crick in her neck, and found that the lamp had burned out, the fire had burned low, and the world seemed enfolded in an uncanny silence. For a moment she couldn't think what was different, but suddenly it dawned on her. The gale had dropped. There was no more rattling and buffeting, no more wild moaning in the chimney. The embers burned clearly with a steady glow, and no smoke came gusting out into the room. She sat up and peered into the gloom.

There was enough light still left in the fireglow to show her that Morgan lay as she had last seen him, an unmoving hump under the duvet. She lowered her feet to the rug and uncurled the rest of herself painfully, cramped from her long sleep, and as quietly as she could put two logs from the hearth onto the smouldering remains in the grate, and looked at him again. No sign that she had disturbed him. She got carefully to her feet and crossed the room, gently unlatching the shutters and peering out into the night.

'Has it stopped snowing?' asked Morgan, and she nearly jumped out of her skin.

'I thought you were asleep,' she accused.

'Chance'd be a fine thing. Wind dropped 'bout an hour gone, has the snow stopped?'

Debbie looked out onto the quiet, white blanket that smothered the tiny front garden and took all identifying shape from bushes and walls. There was a hump to one side that looked almost like a car, it wasn't hers, so it must be his. Nothing moved, a cold starlight struck an answering glitter from frosty crystals on gate and hedge. Through the gap that framed the gateway she could see the lane, heaped and deserted and unmarked by track of man, beast or tyre.

'Yes,' she said. 'It's stopped. I think it's freezing.'

She heard him grunt painfully as he tried to shift his position on the sofa.

'That's all we need.'

She closed the shutters again.

'The weather can change so quickly down here. It may be thawing by tomorrow. Anyway, when it's daylight I might be able to get down to the farm and get help,' she said.

'Well, we'll see,' he said, and she knew that he didn't want her to try. He was afraid – for her, yes, but mainly for himself. Of being left on his own. She didn't blame him. She wondered, and knew that he must have already wondered, what would have happened to him if she hadn't got lost in the blizzard. Presumably he would have been found in the end, but even if he had survived the cold it wouldn't have been very pleasant for him. She came back to the fire.

'I'll go and fetch the other lamp from the kitchen,' she said. 'Then, I suppose we ought to have something to eat. Are you hungry?'

'Not much.' Not at all.

'You should be. After your performance earlier, you must be totally empty.'

'Ugh, don' remind me!'

Debbie went out into the kitchen. She wasn't very hungry either, but they must eat something. She made omelettes, about the peak of her cooking skills, cut some slices off the crusty loaf and carried this into the other room on a tray with some more coffee – fresh, this time – and a couple of apples.

Over the food, they talked. Casually, on any subject but that of the dilemma in which they found themselves. He asked her what she had been planning to do by the Helford River in the middle of winter.

'I was on my way to visit some friends. They're starting a sailing school down there, and they want me to help them. We were going to talk about it.' She paused. 'You're not eating anything.'

'I aren't hungry. And I'm dreadfully right-handed.'

Debbie cut his omelette into neat squares and went on talking, anything to take his mind off things. He did, she noticed out of the corner of her eye, eat about three mouthfuls.

'Lesley was left this house by an aunt. It's big – she used to do bed and breakfast in it, and she turned the garage into a holiday let too. They were going to sell it, but then Tim was made redundant, so they decided to pack up and come down here and make it work for them instead.'

'Why a sailing school? Why not straight B&B? It's a national pastime in Cornwall.'

'Tim wanted to do something for himself. He had quite a good golden handshake, and he's always loved boats. That's how I know him, we used to sail together. He only married Les last year, I don't know her so well.'

He gave her a weary, shadowy look that she didn't quite understand.

'Good luck to him, then. Where do you all come from?'

'Dorset. Well, I work in London at the moment, and I have a flat there, but I was born in Embridge, and that's where Tim worked and where we used to sail together.'

'South coast jet set, then?' He smiled at her, faintly.

'If you like to put it that way.' She returned him a demure, dimpled smile, and he was glad to see that, as he intended, she was regaining her balance. She looked jet set, somehow – and she looked tough, too, as if she knew her way around. She was going to need to, he thought, and found the thought depressing. The pain in his arm jagged at him insistently.

Debbie had finished her supper and set the plate aside.

'What do you do?' she asked. 'Are you a writer, or something?'

'Whatever made you think that? Do I look like one?'

'I've no idea,' said Debbie. 'Do they look like anything in particular? The ones I've met are just like you and me – not that that amounts to many. I suppose it was this cottage – it's the sort of place I always imagine writers living in.'

'I don't live in it.'

'You don't? But –'

'It's a holiday cottage.'

'Funny time for a holiday.'

'Yes.' He laid down his fork. 'I'm sorry, Deborah, that was a perfectly good omelette, but I can't.'

Debbie took the plate from him and put it on the floor with her own.

'You'll feel better in the morning,' she said, knowing it to be untrue but unable to face the fact for either of them. 'I expect it's still the shock. You were saying?'

'No I wasn't.'

'You were saying why you were here.'

'Was I? Oh.' He wasn't going to tell her, she saw, but couldn't resist one last try, it was surely not a great secret, after all.

'Of course, you don't have to tell me if you don't want to.'

'No. I don't.' He looked at her, frowning. 'Sorry, that was rude. Tell me about this sailing school instead, you qualified to teach in one?'

He wasn't really interested, she thought, but he needed something to distract him, and Tim and Lesley would do as well as anything else.

'You need RYA certificates and things, but that isn't a problem. I've been in and out of boats since I was a child. As a matter of fact, I'm doing my Yachtmaster at Easter, only I need to do a First-Aid course first.' She paused, and they exchanged a wry smile. He made no comment, but the unspoken words hung in the air between them. Instead, he said, 'I didn't never think of sailing as something as you learn in a school.'

'You can learn anything in a school these days. People – some people anyway, like that sort of holiday, either for themselves or for their children, it's a wonderful way of keeping teenagers out of mischief, for instance. And if there's nobody around where you live to teach you, where else do you go? I think it's a very good thing.'

'You didn't learn in no school, I know.'

'Well no, I didn't. My brother taught me, against strong opposition from my parents – well, my mother anyway.'

'Why, did she think as he'd drown you?'

'I honestly don't know. I think it was just because it was Oliver. Everything he did was always wrong, as far back as I remember.' She seemed to feel that this statement needed some explanation, for she went on. 'He isn't her son, and my sister isn't Dad's daughter. Our family is a bit of a muddle.'

'So where do you come in?'

'Me? Oh, I have a foot in both camps.'

'It's different, anyway.'

'Oh yes, it's different.' It was her turn for staring into the fire now, absently, as if her thoughts were miles away, as maybe they were. 'If it had worked, it might even have been rather fun. It does work for some people.'

'But not for your family?'

She shook her head, almost imperceptibly.

'We were never really a family. I used to try and make believe we were when I was little, because I wanted a proper family, but wanting doesn't make things so.' She fell silent, and he lay and watched her for a while, with the orange light from the flames making shadows and hollows of the planes of her face. She was beautiful to look at, in her own extravagant way, but she had the air of someone who was entirely uncommitted to anyone or anything. Not spoiled and selfish, so much as individual. He was grateful for it, she was less likely to go to pieces in what might lie ahead of them if she had no sense of involvement.

The snowed-in cottage was uncannily quiet, smothered and insulated from the world outside. Debbie said, almost as if she wasn't really talking to him, 'I loved Oliver, when I was little, with a sort of doggy devotion that took no account of anything else, and I used to think that Mum was a pig to him. Now I'm older, of course, I can see her side, because he was a pig to her as well. She's proud of her position in the town, she enjoys being top of the heap. She's a pillar of the local church and does lots for charity and she likes people to look to her for an example. That's how she is. Oliver was never respectable at all. He rode a big bike and hung out with dangerous friends and he was always in trouble – not quietly in trouble, really flamboyantly in trouble. Thumbing his nose at her and her standards, all the time.'

'And are you respectable?' asked Morgan, with gentle interest.

'You're laughing at me.' She turned and grinned at him, friendly in the firelight. 'Do I look respectable?'

'Not in the least. You look like your brother's sister to me – a scatty young care-for-nobody.'

'You're absolutely right, of course.' She was laughing at him, enchanting, and he thought, unaware of it. He thought of another little sister, one who had had her faith in a loved older brother rudely overturned, and hoped for her sake that Debbie's was made of sterner stuff. She seemed to enjoy talking about him, but he needn't listen, he supposed... he wished that she would talk about something else.

'When I got older, of course, he wasn't home that much. He didn't live at home from the time I was about ten, but he had a job at one time doing sea trials for the shipyard further round the harbour, and he used to ship me as crew. That was a fantastic year! And a couple of times I sailed with him to the Med, delivering yachts for people, but he decided to stay out there in the end, and I couldn't, because I was under age and Mum and Dad wouldn't let me.'

'I'm surprised they let you go at all.'

'Dad said it would do me good, so long as they were yachts belonging to people we knew. He was a professional skipper – Oliver was, not Dad – when he wasn't just beachcombing or diving.' She broke off abruptly.

Something stirred in the back of his mind, elusive and gone as swiftly as it had come. He felt terrible. Sick again, and freezing cold, shivery. This wasn't funny.

Debbie had stopped talking and was gathering up the plates.

'I'm going to get some more coffee. Do you want some?'

'No.'

'OK.' She left the room, taking the lamp with her, and he was left with the firelight. Bless her, she wasn't going to fuss after all. Probably she valued her own integrity too highly to violate another person's. Not that he had much left. Thank God for her, Deborah the parallel line who would never converge uninvited.

He wasn't even thinking about her brother then, or about anything other than his own pain and the unnamed things that lurked in the shadowy corners of the familiar room, and the two names clicked together in his subconscious like a docking spaceship.

Deborah Nankervis and her brother, Oliver. Oliver Nankervis.

He knew now exactly what sort of a brother she had, the influence that had given her such confident individuality, and if he was lucky, such flawless courage. The discovery gave him no satisfaction. Although he knew that she must have had cause to weep, it would never have been for shame. If she ever recognised him for what he was in the same way, she would look after him, no doubt, but she would justly despise him.

Little sisters… his own, or Oliver Nankervis's. He was burning now, where he had been cold, he wanted to call for her but couldn't remember her name. He said, 'Cress…' but it came out as a whisper that didn't even cross the room.

It was a long night. Debbie, having already slept for two hours, wasn't particularly tired, and found the armchair unaccommodating. Morgan's suggestion that she go and sleep upstairs, she rejected on the grounds that he might need her in the night, but sitting in the dark was boring. She ended up back in the kitchen with the lamp, sitting on a wooden chair with her elbows on the table, reading the only book that she could find in the place, an advanced modern novel of almost unbelievable complexity that at least had the virtue of keeping her mind off her problems. She wondered if that was why Morgan was reading it, too; she had a feeling that he had left a great deal unsaid.

At midnight, stiff and restless, she got off her chair and went to the back door to peer out into the yard. The air was crisp, cold and clear, underfoot the snow crunched like sugar, frozen solid. No thaw, but at least while it went on freezing, probably no more snow. She stood there breathing the frosty air, wondering if Tim and Lesley were worrying about her non-arrival and had alerted her family, or if they assumed that she had stopped safely in some overnight accommodation when the blizzard came. Yet another problem to which there was no solution. She closed the door on the sparkling night, turned out the lamp in the kitchen and tiptoed back into the front room.

Morgan slept. He was really asleep this time, a shallow sleep that barely held the barriers against pain, but sleep nonetheless. Angry at her own ignorance, Debbie climbed back into her armchair, wriggled herself into a comfortable position, and hauled the blanket she had filched from the second bedroom round her shoulders for extra warmth. Resolutely, she closed her eyes. There was nothing to be done. Time to sleep too.

She did sleep, for a little while, but was woken in the early hours by Morgan calling out urgently – not specifically for herself, but for someone, she thought. Some girl, his wife – she really didn't know. She struggled from the depths of sleep to administer a drink of water, more Paracetamol, reassurance. He had slept, yes, but badly, and dreamed the depths of hell. On waking he was confused with pain and the sight of a stranger. She sat beside him until he had calmed down, and rose in the cold, crisp dawn to have a hot shower and another mug of strong coffee. She felt as if she hadn't slept at all.

There was a packet of oatmeal in the cupboard. Debbie, more familiar with the proprietary brands of quick porridge, followed the instructions printed on it with care and prepared a panful as a warming start to the day, and while it simmered gently on the hob, poured another mug of coffee and carried it back into the other room. Morgan, heavy-eyed and pale, greeted her with a wavering smile.

'Did I make a nuisance of myself in the night? I'm sorry.'

'Don't you remember?' asked Debbie.

'Not really. Just hearing your voice, I think.'

'How do you feel this morning?'

She looked, and sounded, as exotic and self-contained as ever, he had no idea of the alarm signals that were racing along her nerves and thanked God for her, forgetting the crack in her armour that she had shown the previous evening. He needed her just the way he saw her now.

'I think it hurts more, but I feel less shaken up. But....' He tailed off what he had been going to say, made an expressive face at her, and said instead, 'Are there any of those Paracetamol things left?'

'A couple.' Debbie tipped them out and handed them to him. 'I think there's some in my suitcase, I'll see if I can get into my car when we've had breakfast.'

'There's a shovel beside the stove. Poor Deborah, you are having to work hard, aren't you?'

'Talking of the stove, said Debbie. 'It's awfully low this morning, should I do something about it?'

'Damn, I should have thought. I hope it's not gone out, then we will be in trouble.'

'I don't think it has, quite,' offered Debbie. 'Anyway, there's a microwave, I saw it.'

'Er...' he said, and met her eyes with a laugh in his own. She blushed, and he grinned at her. 'Amazing how you come to take things for granted, i'n't it?' he said. 'Do you know what to do with a solid fuel stove?'

'You'll have to give me a crash course while we have breakfast, because the answer to that is *no*.' But she smiled at him as if she didn't mind, the same deceptively demure smile as before, that made deep dimples at the corners of her mouth and reached her eyes only as a watchfulness that was interested but not intimate. He thought that she was lovely.

After breakfast, Debbie set about the chores for the day. Making up the boiler entailed digging a path to the coal shed and a lot of riddling and fiddling with the stove itself, but she must have got it more or less right for after a while, the temperature gradually began to rise again. Saved at the eleventh hour – and then she wished she hadn't thought that. She fetched in a fresh stack of logs that she found beside the coal, and then, taking the shovel, set out to dig her way down to the gate. Her car wasn't completely smothered rather to her surprise, the stone hedge had protected it, and a brisk ten minutes digging enabled her to reach the back. It took longer to unfreeze the lock, but it was pleasant to have access to a change of clothes.

That was all that was pleasant, though. The lane, she discovered to her alarm, was virtually impassable. Even with the shovel, there was no way she could dig along it for half a mile, and although Morgan had told her that the main road was closer, according to the radio it was still blocked, and anyway, she didn't feel that it was fair to him to leave the cottage unless she was certain of getting back. If she fell herself, out on the icy, snowbound lane… her blood chilled at the idea. She looked out across the white, frozen snowfield around them, but nothing stirred. She could see no sign of human habitation, just miles and miles of flat, untrodden snow. They could be alone in the world. She went slowly back indoors.

Morgan, who had taken a running start at the day, had flagged considerably by lunchtime. He looked exhausted and there were beads of sweat on his forehead again, and on his upper lip. The contrast of grey skin and dark, overnight stubble was disquieting. He lay under the blankets and looked ill and had completely run out of small talk. Debbie, removing an untouched mug of soup to the kitchen, made the rather daunting discovery that she had, so far, barely tapped the wells of anxiety, and hard on that discovery came another. As she washed the dishes she contemplated the knowledge that her anxiety wasn't simply because his condition was obviously deteriorating, but because from being a stranger who needed help, he had become Morgan. A friend, in a way. You could be coolly impersonal – up to a point – over a stranger. It was different with a friend. To say the least.

Through all that long day, there was no sight or sound of another human being, and the cottage lay isolated in its swansdown feathering of snowdrifts, until just before four o'clock, when Debbie, sitting staring at the fire with her back against the sofa and Morgan, she suspected, sliding into a fever behind her, heard the sound of an engine. For a moment, she didn't recognise what it was, and then as she understood, she ran for the back door and out into the yard.

The helicopter passed overhead, quite close and low, and Debbie jumped up and down waving her arms, yelling uselessly at the top of her voice. It might have seen her, it might not. Presumably patrolling for stranded motorists and people in trouble, the chances were that it had. Her abandoned car, after all, was a nice conspicuous sunflower yellow. But chances weren't good enough.

Relieved at having something sensible to do at last, and wishing that she had thought of it sooner, Debbie set about positive action. Fetching her coat and boots, she laboriously lugged baskets of logs into the field behind the cottage until she had a big pile, and set to work. It was heavy work in the deep snow, and she was soaked and exhausted before she had finished, and it was dark too, too late for it to be any help to them today.

But if anyone came over in the morning they couldn't avoid seeing her message, laid out on the white snow like black paint on a signboard.

HELP, she had written, and having done all that she could, struggled wearily back to the cottage and the things that she could do nothing about.

VII

The second helicopter flew overhead in a cold dawn, waking Debbie from a shallow sleep, but it flew on without any sign that it had seen her desperate message, and Morgan was obviously worse. No good trying to avoid the truth any longer, he had done more than simply break a bone, and that would have been plenty bad enough. She suspected that he must have a complicated fracture at the very least, probably with internal bleeding; he was in terrible pain by this time, and hardly seemed to know what was happening. Sometimes, she thought that he was actually delirious, then the next moment he would say something so sensible and ordinary that she thought it must be her nerves playing up. Once, he turned to her and said, with a depth of urgent conviction that astonished her, 'It was an accident – I swear it was an accident.'

'Of course it was,' said Debbie, soothingly, but a second later found herself wondering if either of them had really understood what he was talking about. She wiped the sweat from his face with a towel, and took his free hand gently between both her own.

'Come on, don't go to pieces now. Someone will be here to help us soon.'

'You must believe me,' he insisted. 'It was an accident. I never meant it.'

'Of course you didn't.' Oh, help me somebody, this sort of thing isn't my scene at all. Somebody come, somebody come soon.

She sat beside him for most of the morning, he only wanted to drink, glass after glass of cold water, and seemed to her to wander in and out of lucidity, so that her own appetite for lunch was non-existent. This was nightmare in three-dimensional reality, beside which the problems of the last forty or so hours seemed ridiculously trivial. She had been able to care for him while he had been calm and conscious, she had even begun to congratulate herself on her competence at one point. If he became really ill and unable to help her, she knew that she would have no idea what to do. His attitude had bolstered her confidence, as much for his own sake as for hers. She hadn't realised quite how much, and was ashamed at how heavily she had leaned on him. Without the prop of his courage, she had doubts of the quality of her own.

He seemed to have drifted away now into a half-sleep from which it was difficult to rouse him, his eyes half-closed and heavy and languorous with fever. She realised that there was something she should have steeled herself to do right at the start, and because they were both afraid of it, hadn't done. Better late than never. She went into the kitchen and fetched the kitchen scissors.

She cut away the sleeve of his sweatshirt and of the shirt underneath it with infinite care, he stirred and moaned under her touch but didn't wake, proving conclusively and alarmingly that he wasn't truly asleep. With thumping heart and fingers that weren't quite steady, she bared the damage to the light of day.

The very first thing she saw was that she had been wrong from the beginning, there was blood, not a lot, thank goodness, but enough to stick his shirt to the wound, and the horrible spectres of septicæmia and gangrene immediately raised their gruesome heads and gibbered at her. She fetched hot water and soaked the shirt gently away, and her stomach turned over at what she found. It was a mess. Black with bruising – she hoped very much that it was bruising – with splinters of bone and oozing yellow pus showing through a crust of dried and blackened blood, and all badly swollen right down to his fingers. She thought, cold with shock, that her lack of courage had cost him his arm, at the very least, and had to fight back great waves of nausea that threatened to overcome her.

There was nothing in the house that would help, except for the small tube of antiseptic cream that she had found in the bathroom. She cleaned the horrid mess with a feather touch and squeezed the cream over it, covering it with a strip torn from yet another clean pillowcase, and while she did it she committed to memory an important lesson. Never pretend unpleasantness doesn't exist, for it will only become more unpleasant. There was nothing that she could have done to reduce the fracture – there was still nothing she could do – but she should have known about the broken skin, and she might have done something about the perfectly hideous swelling. She wasn't, after all, exactly short of ice. She could try now, but she had left it rather late.

She emptied the bloody water down the sink and made an ice-pack from the plastic bag from round the bread and some icicles from the roof of the shed, and wrapped it in another pillowcase, but by this time it was a bit like trying to mend a burst dam with chewing gum. She was bitterly ashamed of herself. She, of all people, knew what disablement did to its victims, she should have done everything she could think of, and then thought of more, long since, instead of soothing herself with comforting platitudes, ducking and diving away from trouble.

Come to think of it, it was a bit of a thing of hers, ducking and diving away from trouble. She had done it with her home life, with Oliver, with her private life, with just about everything. Pick up the carpet, sweep it all out of sight, don't get involved.

She was involved now. If he ended up mutilated by the loss of his right arm – Morgan, who was *dreadfully right-handed* – she would have it on her conscience for the rest of her life. Perhaps she couldn't have done anything useful, but she could at least have tried.

The day crawled on as if it intended to do so for ever. Debbie sat beside Morgan, who was by this time unmistakeably delirious, not knowing what to do, or worse, what she shouldn't do, and hoping for a miracle. One minute he would be icy cold, shivering with chattering teeth, and the next burning hot, trying to fling the duvet off, with no idea of what he was doing or who she was, looking at her with brilliant, unrecognising eyes smudged with black in a grey face. His colour appalled her, bringing back as it did memories of her brother Oliver, smashed up and desperately ill, hovering on the very edge of death. Moreover, he was very strong. She knew that if he made a really determined effort to fight her off, she would have her work cut out to prevent him. She had no idea what he did for a living, but from his muscular development he could have been a docker.

The light was beginning to fade in the windows before she heard a noise in the lane outside. A heavy engine, throbbing like a giant's pulse, working its way closer. Morgan was quiet for the moment, his face pale and sunken against the tumbled pillows. Debbie left him and ran to the front door, unbolting it and dragging it open. A pile of snow came in, uninvited, and spread itself across the flags, but she didn't even notice. Stumbling through, she stood on the garden path and saw, in the lane, the most beautiful sight on earth. A tractor with a snow plough attached coming up from the direction of the farm, with a large and friendly farmer perched aloft, muffled to the ears and waving to her.

'Hullo, my lover, is all right with you?' he called.

'Get an ambulance, quickly,' said Debbie, and to her own surprise and horror, burst into tears, there in the snowy garden and under the astonished eyes of a complete stranger.

He was very good, that farmer. He came in, took a look at Morgan, and asked a couple of questions in a Cornish accent so strong that it was nearly a foreign language. Then he was gone back out to his tractor, talking urgently on a mobile phone, while Debbie sat down in the armchair and snivelled helplessly into the final remains of the second pillowcase. She couldn't seem to stop. She was sitting there still when the Air Ambulance came, and took the whole mess right out of her hands.

She was sitting there too when the police arrived, from the opposite direction, alerted by her message in the snow, but by that time, Morgan had been taken away, a stranger going out of her life as dramatically as he had entered it. As if on cue, the eaves of the cottage had begun to drip and the clear sky was clouding over. The thaw was on its way.

She had asked the helicopter crew where they would take Morgan, and they had said, to Truro, and she would be able to follow on soon. The A30 was open, they assured her, and then they were gone. The farmer, who had stayed with her, patted her shoulder.

'He'll be all right. The likes of him don't kill easy,' he comforted her. 'We'll soon have you out of here. Don't cry my bird, it's all over.'

Unreasonable therefore, and how stupid, to half-wish that it wasn't all over. Debbie gave her reddened eyelids a last scrub with the drenched pillowcase and began to gather the disrupted threads of her life together again.

'How do I get my car out?' she asked, and that was the moment when the police arrived.

She spent the night in Bodmin, where she slept in a comfortable bed and dreamed gruesomely that she was hacking at Morgan's arms and legs with a breadknife, he was still very much on her mind. In the morning, she telephoned the hospital in Truro and tried to find out how he was, but they told her, although kindly, that if she wasn't a relative they couldn't tell her anything. The man whom she had helped was comfortable, he would be all right, she had been very brave and there was no need to worry. She believed none of it, but there was nothing she could do. She wasn't even certain that they knew who she was asking about.

By lunchtime, once more at the wheel of her cheerful, if slightly dented, yellow car, she was dropping down through a wood covered with the lightest possible powdering of snow already washing away in fine, damp rain, descending a series of hairpin bends that would take her to the waterside village of St. Erbyn, on the south bank of the Helford River.

Lesley Howells had inherited a large, square, granite house right beside the river, with a long jetty reaching out to the water across a stony foreshore and a dry boathouse tucked under trees to one side. Her uncle, long deceased, had been a lover of boats, and her aunt had spent her entire married life urging him to be practical. On his death, it was discovered that his hobby had taken all his money, and so his current beloved boat had gone, the boathouse had fallen into disuse and then into disrepair, and his widow had turned the house into a guesthouse. She had prospered. In time, the large double garage beside the drive had become a holiday letting unit, and only her own untimely death had prevented the boathouse under the trees from sharing the same fate. Lesley and her new husband, Tim, had planned to sell the place, for it was far too big and too far from their south coast home to be of any use to them, but Tim's redundancy had altered their plans. Suddenly finding themselves released from the treadmill, they had launched out into a serious of ambitious schemes as insubstantial and delightful as daydreams generally are. Cornwall, the guesthouse, the river… it had to be a gift from the gods.

Debbie had been there on one other occasion, back in September when Lesley had first come down to view her inheritance, and discuss with her aunt's lawyer how she would make use of it. They had driven down together, and Debbie had taken the opportunity of slipping down to Trelewan near Land's End, where her brother and his wife were temporarily living, thus combining helping Lesley out with her own affairs. That had been just after Tim's redundancy, and she had only seen the outside that time, when she had taken Lesley out to meet the lawyer, but she had no trouble finding her way back. She drove through a narrow and hazardous village street lined with pretty cottages straight out of a picture book, and past a prosperous looking pub right by the foreshore. At the top of springs, the tide must come right up to the retaining wall that bounded its forecourt, and the road ran across the shingle on a concrete causeway before curving up a shallow hill on the far side. Seagulls Guest House was on the left, tucked in among shrubs and low trees, with a gleam of water showing through the bare winter bushes behind it. Debbie pulled up on the drive, and Lesley came running out and round to the car door, wrenching it open.

'Deb! We were so worried about you! Were you all right? We were so relieved when you phoned last night!'

'I got snowed up in a cottage without a telephone,' said Debbie. That nightmare seemed already so far in the past that it was, in very truth, the stuff of dreams. Reality was the grey glitter of water under the rain, the solid stone house, Lesley's warm and welcoming hug. It was good to be back in the real world once more.

'Come inside,' said Lesley, dragging at her arm. 'It's freezing out here. Lunch is all ready, and Tim will bring your case.'

It was warm in the hall, and Tim, tall, fair and spectacled, was coming through a door behind the stairs to greet her.

'So you had a bit of an exciting trip did you, young Debbie?' he asked, with a friendly grin. She had known Tim for always, they had grown up together although he was a couple of years senior to her. They had sailed together, danced together, laughed and quarrelled together, even at one point contemplated officially becoming a couple. It had come to nothing. Tim had met Lesley, a farmer's daughter knowing less than nothing about boats and fallen deeply in love, and Debbie had entered into a passionate affair with a man she had met in London. She had regrets about that, but none about Tim. He was in many ways more like a brother to her than her own, rather older, half-brother. A girl didn't want to fall in love with her brother. She rejoiced with him at his marriage, grieved with him over his redundancy, was pleased for both of them over the unexpected legacy, and quietly relieved that things had fallen out as they had. She was a little wary of close relationships, of whatever kind. She had, in fact, very little experience of them, and feared them as one fears the unknown, although she would have denied it if anyone had told her so. It was one of the reasons, had she but known it, why her passionate affair had ended in disaster. Tim's invitation to be part of his new enterprise had come at exactly the right time for her. She returned his welcoming grin.

'Peary's voyage to the North Pole had nothing on it,' she said. 'Now then, you two, what's this all about?'

Over lunch, which they ate in the kitchen with a warm Aga close beside them, they told her. At length, individually and together, interrupting each other and bubbling over with enthusiasm.

'It's a gift,' said Lesley, which could be taken literally. 'It's made for us! There's already bookings coming in for the season from adverts Auntie had out last year, and I love cooking and things like that, and Auntie's cleaner has already said she'll come and give us a hand – '

'The boathouse is enormous,' Tim interrupted her, his eyes gleaming with enthusiasm behind his thick glasses. 'I don't know what Les's uncle drove, but it'd house the QE II! I know where I can pick up a Wayfarer or two, dirt cheap, old boats but sound, perfect for teaching, my redundancy money will cover the cost easily. You and I can give sailing lessons, and in time we can turn it into a residential sailing school, but of course it will pay us to teach other people too –'

'– bed and breakfast and evening meal, we thought,' said Lesley. 'Nothing fancy, just a good set meal – good home cooking, if they want posh stuff they can go down the road to the pub –'

'What, for a luxury chicken-in-a-basket?' asked Debbie, giggling.

'You've got to be joking!' Tim grinned at her again. His grin seemed to be a fairly permanent feature, which was a lot better than the down-in-the-mouth gloom of their last meeting. 'Except for the bars, it's closed until next month for staff holidays and redecoration, but our little pub is a bit of a gourmet's delight. Super restaurant, fantastic food, big reputation – they aim at the yachting crowd, of course, that's where the money lies, but people come from pretty well everywhere to eat their chicken-in-a-basket at the Fish, I can tell you.'

'We had a meal there to celebrate my birthday,' said Lesley. 'It cost us an arm and a leg, but it was worth every penny! Anyway, we couldn't eat anything else for days, so it was an economy really. But they won't be competing with us – '

Debbie interrupted with a splutter of laughter, and Lesley looked at her, surprised.

'What did I say?'

Tim had already forgotten the Fisherman's Arms, and was back riding his own hobby horse.

'You and I can give lessons to the guests, a carefully graded one week or two week course, and I've got a friend who'll come down for the summer and do the casuals. We can give lectures too –'

'– a nice homely atmosphere, so that it's like having friends to stay. We can have time to get to know them. It won't be at all elaborate, but very cosy and easy-going –'

'– and we thought we'd apply for a licence, and have a little bar,' said Tim, changing tracks abruptly. 'Somewhere where the guests can sit in the evening, and we can all exchange sailing yarns and make a good atmosphere, like a really small and intimate sailing club, and perhaps they can buy wine to go with Les's wonderful home cooking.'

'We can coin it in the summer months,' said Lesley, happily. 'And then, in the winter we can sit back and enjoy living in this lovely place. What do you think?'

'I can do maintenance work then, and Les can help if she likes,' said Tim. 'You too, I suppose, although we can't pay you in the winter, although I expect we can feed you and you'll still have accommodation. We've got to be sensible.'

It sounded anything but sensible to Debbie, but she liked living dangerously, and a substantial trust fund cushioned her existence in any case. The prospect of giving up her secure job with its good prospects and incidental lively social scene, weighed very lightly in the balance against such an exciting proposition. She had never been much for security anyway, in that respect she had learned a lot from her footloose brother's example.

'It sounds brilliant,' she said. 'How many people can you take, Les?'

'There's eight letting bedrooms,' said Lesley. 'Three family rooms, and the rest doubles. We thought we could all live in the self-catering unit where the garage used to be – '

'– we can manage sixteen pupils at a time, you and I in two Wayfarers doing morning and afternoon shifts –'

'– I'll show you after lunch, it's a bit basic, but we'll be too busy to mind much, and over here most evenings anyway –'

'– we shall have to keep a spare in case of accidents, and one for the casual lessons, of course.'

'Are you going to hire out boats to people who want to sail them for themselves?' asked Debbie, and they fell to discussing it while Lesley made tea to round off the meal. They were pleased with themselves and with their plans, it looked simple and fun, the perfect way to earn a living.

'Of course,' said Lesley, blithely unaware of pitfalls, 'it won't be an easy life in the summer, but we won't mind that. We'll be working together, after all.'

They discussed it almost non-stop for the rest of Debbie's visit. Walking through the dripping woods, sitting round the warm Aga with bowls of soup at lunch time, in the bar of the Fisherman's Arms in the evening, when they woke in the morning and when they went to bed at night. They planned and replanned, and even when they tried they couldn't really think of any snags.

'We'll each be doing what we like doing,' said Lesley, happily. 'I love cooking and looking after people, and Tim will be happy with his boats – and I expect the guests might help a bit too, make their own beds and things. It'll be part of the fun.'

'Like an adventure holiday,' said Tim, who saw nothing incongruous in expecting paying guests to make their own beds. 'Can you get your certificates in time, Deb?'

'Any time, it's only a formality. What about you?'

'I've applied, and Steve – that's my friend – he's got his already. Yachts and dinghies –'

'Yachts!' said Debbie, laughing at him.

'In time, maybe,' said Tim. 'We can charter, do cruising holidays round the coast –'

'Here, here – hold on!' cried Lesley. 'Let's walk before we run, shall we?'

They all laughed, euphoric with their own dreams.

Most evenings, they spent in the bar of the pub down the road, making a couple of beers each go as far as possible and building fantastic castles in the air. Debbie, who could have easily stood an extra round and hardly noticed it, knew Tim well enough not to suggest it, and kept to the pattern set by her friends, it didn't bother her if she didn't drink. The barman came to know them, he set up their order as soon as they appeared in the doorway after the second night, and the locals looked on them with indulgent smiles.

Lesley and Tim, impervious to remarks about emmets, had rapidly made themselves at home, Debbie discovered. As Lesley pointed out, local goodwill was important to the success of their plan. Their affairs were discussed in detail in the public bar, the lounge bar, the village shop and the parish council meetings and, said Lesley, probably in the pulpit too, but she hadn't actually heard that. It would be too much to say that the village was solidly on their side, but there was little overt criticism, and a definite feeling that most people were content to bide their time and see what happened.

'Regular nine-day-wonder, it is,' said one local farmer to Debbie, in the bar one night. The villagers hadn't quite decided how they viewed Debbie yet. Her name was in her favour, her appearance and her vowels against her. As with the sailing school, they withheld judgement.

'Oh no,' said Debbie. 'You wait and see, it'll happen all right.'

He looked at her over the rim of his glass.

'Mrs. Latter never had no ba-ar?' He drew the word out into two syllables, as a question. Debbie laughed.

'You don't really need one for family parties.'

'Them sailing folk won't be supping their beer in the Fish, then? He won't like that.'

'I expect they will now and then. They'll like to get out sometimes, I expect.'

'And Mrs. Howells, will she buy her goods locally, or from the supermarket, like?'

'What did Mrs. Latter do?' asked Debbie, diplomatically, but he wouldn't be drawn.

This conversation was fairly typical of the village attitude; wary, not criticising openly but ready to do so if given the opportunity. They didn't, Debbie concluded, really like outsiders setting up in business on their patch, and they would take offence if any trade thus generated went elsewhere. She mentioned this to Lesley.

'Oh, I mean to buy locally,' said Lesley, immediately. 'New laid eggs and farm butter, farm-cured bacon if we can get it, and I plan to make all our bread. It'll be part of the image.'

It sounded wonderful.

At the end of her unavoidably shortened visit, Debbie left for home, delighted with the imminent change in her prospects and ready to make the most of it. As she drove back up the hairpin bends, the Cornish winter weather had pulled itself together. It was cold, but clear and sunny, with not a snowflake in sight. It seemed a lifetime since her experiences up on the moor, but she hadn't completely forgotten them, and had a stop in mind before she headed off for London.

Like telephoning, it didn't prove simple. The Royal Cornwall hospital in Truro at first denied any knowledge of a Mr. Morgan with a smashed elbow, but when Debbie recounted the circumstances of his admission, they sent her up to an orthopaedic ward. Here, she told her tale again to a brisk nurse at the desk.

'Oh yes, I know who you mean,' she said. 'You can come in this afternoon to see him, visiting is from two o'clock.'

Debbie explained that she was on her way to London.

'And I would really like to see him,' she said. 'After what happened… well, I'd like to see for myself that he's OK.'

The nurse looked down her nose, which was nicely designed for the job.

'Mr. Angwin has been very ill.' She pronounced the unfamiliar name in the Cornish fashion, An*gwin*, with a hard 'g' and the emphasis on the second syllable, as in Debbie's own Nan*kerv*is.

'Mr. Who?' asked Debbie, surprised, but was ignored.

'You can have ten minutes, under the circumstances, but don't make a habit of it.' The nurse was on the march, and Debbie ran to keep up.

'I don't want any Mr. Angwin. His name was —'

'Here you are.' They had stopped outside the door to a side ward. 'Ten minutes, no more.' She smiled unexpectedly, and before Debbie could protest again, opened the door. 'A visitor for you, Mr. Angwin.' The door closed behind her.

Debbie was left there, contemplating Mr. Angwin with disapprobation. He looked better, she was happy to see, and he still had his arm. He smiled at her.

'Well, if it isn't the disco kid!'

'Why,' said Debbie, coldly, 'did you tell me your name was Morgan?'

'Because it is,' he told her.

'They've just told me out there that it's An-*gwin*.'

'Ah. Well, it's not my fault if you chose to take it as a surname, is it? Mawgan, spelt M A W G A N, that's me. Mum has fancy ideas about names. You should hear what my sisters are called.'

'She was way off beam when she named you,' said Debbie. 'You're no saint, I know!'

He looked at her oddly, but answered with lazy ease, 'Oh, she dug it up somewhere and landed it on me. Way too late to change now, I'm stuck with it.'

'Are you all right?' asked Debbie, since that was why she had come – wasn't it? 'I haven't been able to get you out of my mind all week.' That wasn't quite true, but it was true enough that the recollection of him had haunted her in the night occasionally. 'When I saw what a mess you'd made of your elbow, I was petrified. It was –' She broke off, unable to contemplate even the memory without squeamishness. He smiled at her.

'I'm fine – or at least, so they tell me. The first few days weren't much fun, but since they gave me a new joint a couple of days back, hell has gone back into its box. Skewered like a kebab, and that'll teach me to climb on wobbly chairs.'

Debbie thought that his voice sounded less amused than the words, and he still had a way to go before he actually looked well. She answered him lightly. 'There are better ways of getting plastered, certainly.'

'You can say that again!'

'What were you doing on that chair, anyway?'

'I wanted to check the trip switch. I'd have felt a bit of a fool if that was all it was, and the power on all the time.'

'I can see that. Pity, though.' She smiled at him, not knowing quite what to say next.

The conversation foundered there, and Debbie had time to be glad that she wasn't still responsible for him. Into the pause, he said, 'Did you get your job?'

'Oh yes.' Debbie seized on the change of subject with relief. 'It's all set, we get launched in the spring. A residential sailing school, Les will run the domestic side, and Tim and me and a friend of his will teach.'

He said nothing for a moment or two, looking at her thoughtfully – assessingly, she thought. She looked as if she had been poured into her jeans, and the loose, baggy sweatshirt she wore over them was a brilliant cerise and showed her collar bones. This time she had three silver rings in one ear, and an enormous hoop in the other. The pale, streaked hair must have cost a fortune to bleach and style. With her name and antecedents, and her looks, she had to be an invaluable asset to a sailing school. He mentally saluted Tim Howells on his business acumen.

'Well, good luck to you, Deborah,' he said. 'You deserve it. I'm told I owe you quite a lot.'

'Me? But I did everything wrong!'

'Not quite everything. I still have an arm, don't I? And it still works, too. *Will* work, anyway.'

'I felt so stupid.'

'Me too. See you at First Aid classes next winter?'

Debbie laughed. He was going to be fine, and the nightmare was beginning to fade at last.

'Lightning never strikes the same place twice.'

'Don't believe it. I bet it does!'

'Just keep off chairs,' Debbie advised.

She left soon after, mindful of her promise to be only ten minutes, and went back outside to get into her car and drive away. He was going to be fine, and she could forget the whole uncomfortable episode and look forward to a future that had suddenly taken on all the exuberant colours of a rainbow.

She couldn't imagine why she should feel so terribly flat.

VIII

When Cress left West Penwith, she didn't return home, or at least, not immediately. They didn't want her there, she told herself defiantly. She took herself and her woes to her grandmother – not to her father's parents, who were down-to-earth Cornish folk, tough-minded and unsentimental as he was himself, and who had taken sides against her from the first by allowing *him* into their home; their sensible advice that it was no good crying over spilt milk – *spilt milk!* – wasn't what she wanted to hear, certainly not after Kate's sweeping castigation of her behaviour. Her mother's mother, a strong-minded woman, long widowed, who believed wholeheartedly that her youngest grandchild was far more sinned against than sinning, was much more to her taste. Cress could behave very prettily when she wanted something and what she wanted was sanctuary. There would be no talk of phantom lovers and murder at her grandmother's house.

She stayed with her Gran for much of the winter, spoiled and cosseted and made much of, nursing a sense of undirected spite and grievance that ate into her like acid, and causing a further rift in her already deeply riven family by telling the harrowing tale of how she had been turned out of her home to make room for her husband's murderer, and forced to spend the summer in digs with a bullying and vindictive landlady who hated her. She had convinced herself, by this time, that that is what had really happened, and Gran was duly shocked, making firm representations to her daughter Cally, and to her bewildered and angry son-in-law, Pip Angwin, that it was unfair to be so hard on poor little Cressida. Even if their marriage had been failing, Michael Stanley *had* been her husband! A coolness sprang up where there had been none before, and Grandad, facing out the family's shame in the family home by the builders' yard in St. Austell, opined that it was a bad business that was never over and done with.

So she drifted, cold and impersonal as the snow up on the moor, her emotions frozen into ice by a slowly growing conviction that she was alone in the world with her grief. Nobody remembered any more, or if they did, they didn't care. So far as Mike was concerned, the page had been turned. If it hadn't been for the unseen warmth of his spirit beside her, she thought that she would have ended it all then, but she had promised him restitution… vengeance. She knew that she must keep her promise before she could join him, or his blood would cry aloud from the stones for ever.

'Poor little girl,' said Gran, with a sentimental sigh. 'She's taking it hard still, it grieves me to see her breaking her heart so.'

'My baby was always too soft-hearted for her own good,' said Cally, but without the partisan warmth that her mother would have liked to hear. 'She needs looking after, she's always needed more care than the others.' She knew that was true, had always been true, but she was beginning to worry about *why* it was true, or even if, however unconsciously, they had all tried to abnegate responsibility by marrying her off so young. The idea was horrifying. She couldn't bring herself to voice her fears to her mother, however. She mentioned them – or some of them – to Allison instead, a frown between her eyebrows. Allison, however, had little patience with her sister's histrionics, through which she thought she saw with the friendly detachment of a sibling.

'She's a spoilt little brat in the sulks,' she said, firmly. 'I was sorry for her when it first happened, but is this to go on for ever? It was rotten luck for Mike, but *she* had long ago fallen out of love with him – if she was ever *in* it.' She was about to add that it had been even worse luck for Mawgan, but her mother was already speaking, immediately on the defensive.

'You and Anna were always different,' said Cally, still worried. She would have liked Anna to be called by her full name of Marianne, but had given in to family pressure long ago. Allison shook her head, rejecting a suggestion that she wasn't about to discuss with her mother.

'She should get off her tight little arse and try to put it all in the past,' she said, resenting being called *hard*, even by inference. Cally said, tartly, 'If that's the language you learn among all those pilots, you had better come back home and help your dad in the office!' She resented Allison's job as cabin crew, feeling that, like Mawgan and Anna before her, she had grown away from her roots. Allison, who knew that as a girl, there was no future for her with her father, and who didn't want a dead-end job as an office dogsbody working for family, felt the ongoing resentment and reacted too strongly.

'She's selfish,' she said. 'She's like a leech. She sucks people dry – look what she did to Mawgan!'

Cally would have liked to retort, what *she's* done to *him*? but was too honest. At the end of her weekend home, Allison got into her little sports car with the argument still unresolved and drove away. When Cally repeated the conversation to her husband, Pip looked shifty and wouldn't be pushed into taking sides. Pip hated the whole thing, and agreed with his daughter that it was time they were all allowed to put it behind them. Then, perhaps, they could all go home.

'Don't bother me when I'm tired,' he said.

The phone call came early the following evening.

'Is our whole life to be spent dreading the sound of the damned telephone?' demanded Pip, furiously, when he saw Cally's frightened face. 'What is it this time? Not reported to his probation officer, or is there worse to hear?'

Cally shrivelled inwardly, wishing back the past when the family had been at ease with itself. She hated being at odds with Pip, and these days, she almost always was.

'Mawgan's had an accident,' she said. 'He's in the hospital, in Truro. It happened in the snow.'

'And I suppose we can expect more newspaper stories, digging up the dirt all over again!' Pip exclaimed, unreasonably. 'Are we never to be allowed to live it down? All I ever asked for was a son to work beside me, and what did I get? A poncy chef, dragging my name through the mud at every turn!'

Cally wouldn't have that.

'An accident is an accident. And he's quite badly hurt.'

'Driving like a lunatic again, I suppose,' said Pip, dismissively. Wild horses wouldn't have made him tell Cally about the jab of concern that went through him at the thought of his son, badly hurt. The only way he could deal with the family's problems these days seemed to be anger. You couldn't choose between your children, so to be angry with them all impartially was the easiest way. He was a man who found anger easy, but there was no weight behind it. As he had always thought, there was no weight behind his son's anger, either. He said, with gruff dismissal, 'I've to be down that way tomorrow, I'll call in if I've the time.'

'Pip –' began Cally, but he was already stomping across the hallway to the door, on his way out to the pub.

Mawgan's accident became the talk of the family. Poor Mawgan was going to lose his arm, said Gran, surely anyone could sympathise with that. Cress only looked at her with dark, tragic eyes. She thought it quite likely that he had fallen on purpose to get their sympathy back from her, and it would serve him right if he had to pay for it. In the end, even Gran lost patience with her, and told her to stop her play-acting in uncomfortably forthright tones that were most unlike her, and made Cress cry.

Mawgan didn't lose his right arm, and he came home to convalesce because there really wasn't anywhere else for him to go, since Nan had that stroke over all the unpleasantness, and Grandad had his hands full without another invalid to look after. He had been home for just three days, as pale and silent as the snow that could have been the death of him, when Cress rang.

'I want to come home,' she said, catching her breath on sobs. 'I'm catching the morning train. Gran's being horrid to me!'

A windy March brought with it blue skies, scattered with torn shreds of cloud, a feel of dampness and growing things, and great curved, prickly humps of golden-yellow gorse. It was the daffodil-picking season, but a sense of the sap rising in dry wood and new life astir in the countryside sent Kate out onto the cliffs whenever she could spare the time, walking for miles to sit in sheltered corners and look out over the sea, tossing, tossing in a welter of creamy white foam on the black rocks. She loved the wildness, and the loneliness, and the screaming cries of the nesting gulls awakened something in her that rose, airborne, to join with them. It was on one of these walks that she ran into Chel. She was on her way home along the coast path, and came round a bluff of rock and found herself nose-to-nose with her. There was nowhere to go to avoid each other, so they both had to stop.

'Isn't it a lovely day?' said Kate, as to a passing stranger. She would have smiled and stepped back to allow Chel to pass, but Chel didn't move. She simply stood there, her reddish gold hair blowing into a halo in the wind, and said, 'You're Kate, aren't you? We just came to visit you and Charlie, but only he was there.'

Kate recognised her, she had seen her occasionally in the Cornish Arms in the village.

'You're Oliver Nankervis's wife,' she said.

'Yes. I don't think we've met, though, have we? Until now, I mean.'

Kate shook her head.

'But we would have, if you had come when Charlie asked you.'

'Oh well,' said Chel. Her name was Cheryl, but nobody ever called her by it these days. 'Oliver ran into Charlie at the pub last night, and because we're moving on, and Charlie asked him again… well, we came now, instead.'

'Come back to the house,' Kate invited. 'I'll make some tea. If Charlie is holding forth, we've all the time in the world.' And Chel turned round and they walked back together.

'Why are you going?' asked Kate, as they walked. 'I thought you lived in that place out on the Sennen road – the one with the ghost in the attic.' Chel laughed.

'We only rented that house, the owner is selling it, so we haven't any choice, really. We're going to spend a month or two in a friend's villa out in Greece, then I suppose we'll have to have a serious look around.' She spoke light-heartedly, as if it was unimportant, and her carefree attitude struck a chord with Kate, who looked at life in a similar way. Perhaps, she thought, it went with living with artists. She said, 'Why *didn't* you come, last summer?'

'Oh…' Chel tweaked at a piece of new bracken as they passed it, curling and uncurling the delicate, pale green frond in her fingers, concentrating on that rather than what she had to say. 'It was a casual invitation… if you're in the sort of situation that Oliver was then, you need to be very sure of your ground before you accept casual invitations.'

'Because he's famous?' asked Kate, and Chel said, simply, 'Because he's disabled.'

The whole country must know the story, the brave young man who made a record-breaking circuit of the globe to raise money for a spinal injuries unit in his home town, and then only a couple of years later, ended up in it himself. The free-as-air adventurer who was, in some sense, forever caged. She flinched away from the sympathy that was surely coming. Kate said, 'That's silly.'

Chel took a breath, treading carefully.

'I agree, but it's true. Don't they call it the Does-he-take-sugar Syndrome?'

'Does it make things very difficult?'

'It made them embarrassing,' said Chel. 'And funny, sometimes – but Oliver didn't always laugh. It's different now.'

'That's good, then.'

Kate's lack of either pity or overt curiosity was restful, and Chel found herself relaxing. Shame, to have found so congenial an acquaintance just as they were leaving, but that was the way it went. They walked on together, and came to a rise in the ground. Kate held back, slowing, and Chel stopped a few paces ahead of her.

'Aren't you coming?'

'Not that way. Let's go down to the road.'

Chel came back a few paces along the path.

'What's the matter? What's up there?'

Kate hadn't expected to be seen through so easily. She spoke airily. 'Oh, nothing really. Just some old quoit. Not even that, any more. Most of it's been taken and made into barns.'

'It sounds interesting.'

'It isn't. It's rather boring, really.'

They looked at each other, deadlocked, and Kate shifted her feet uncomfortably. The quoit always made her feel this way now, which was odd, for it never had before. It held memories that she would sooner forget, and that was all it was, of course. It reminded her of an incident – several incidents, by association – of which she was not proud.

'I'm going up there, anyway,' said Chel, with sudden decision, and turned towards the rise.

'It's easier if you go down – ' Kate broke off, and then shrugged her shoulders. Her new friend would think that she was a complete fool if she wasn't careful, and that would be a pity. Kate thought that she was probably one of those rare people to whom one didn't have to explain anything anyway, so she could just walk past very quickly, and that would be that. No questions.

They pushed their way through the gorse and brambles, and stood on the circle of green grass. Chel walked across it and hesitated by the fallen stone. Her face was thoughtful.

'There's nothing here, you know. Why does it bother you so much?'

OK, questions then. Kate had paused on the far side, she said, 'These old burial grounds are weird.'

'Some of them are.' Chel looked down at the great slab at her feet, and then at Kate. 'This one isn't. It's so negative, I'd doubt if it was ever a burial place at all if you hadn't told me.'

'We made up silly stories about it, and someone believed them,' said Kate, shamefacedly. Chel said nothing, and Kate added, 'It was… it got to be… unpleasant.'

Chel had climbed on top of the slab the better to admire the view. A silence fell between them, in which the whisper of the wind and the surge of the sea at the foot of the nearby cliffs sounded unnaturally loud.

'You don't have to tell me if you don't want to,' said Chel, to break an awkward pause, and Kate said, 'There isn't really anything much to tell.'

She obviously didn't want to dwell on it. Chel jumped down onto the grass again, dismissing the subject, since Kate didn't want to discuss it. 'Come on,' she said. 'Let's go, if you dislike it so much.'

'You must think I'm stupid,' said Kate, and Chel said, 'No.'

They walked in companionable silence back to the house. There was a strange car parked outside it, a smart convertible deserted on the weedy gravel, but no other sign of human life.

'They're still in the studio,' said Kate, shaking her head. 'Come on in, and I'll put the kettle on, I don't expect they even know we're back — let alone care, if they're talking painting. Was Charlie in a good mood? He can be a real bastard.'

'Makes two of them,' said Chel, following her into the kitchen. 'They seemed to be getting on all right when I left them. In fact, that's why I thought I'd go for a walk. They'd forgotten I was there, I think.' Kate, her back to her, bit her lip. The quarrel that she and Charlie had had on that terrible, never-to-be-forgotten night before she had put Cress and her luggage out onto the road hadn't ever really gone away, and in a very real way, Oliver Nankervis was part of it. It was like a damper on their relationship, draining the light from it — well, Oliver Nankervis was supposed to be the light merchant, perhaps he would put some of it back. Something was going to have to, and whether he knew it or not, he owed her.

Chel was unusually silent for her. She sat down at the kitchen table and watched Kate putting the kettle on without speaking, and then she suddenly said, 'There are some other pictures there that aren't Charlie's, aren't there? Are they yours?'

Kate froze. She had forgotten them entirely. She said, 'No.' It had sounded too abrupt. She added. 'We had a PG here last year who did them. Charlie let her use the studio.'

'They're pretty,' said Chel, and as a painter's wife, she didn't necessarily mean to be complimentary, but it was difficult to be sure. 'Why didn't she take them with her?'

Kate turned to face her.

'Why do you ask?' she countered.

Chel didn't answer for a moment or two. She looked at her hands, which lay clasped together on the table in front of her.

'Charlie and Oliver were talking painting,' she said. 'It was boring, to tell you the truth. I was bored, anyway. Charlie said to have a look around, and so I did. I found all those pictures shoved down behind the bench. They didn't look like Charlie's, and I pulled them out just from curiosity. I'm glad they aren't yours,' she ended, unexpectedly.

Kate pulled out another chair and sat down.

'Why do you say that?'

Chel shivered, an involuntary action that Kate found strangely disturbing. She said, 'What happened to her?'

'Now look,' said Kate, after a pause in which she had time to think a number of things, all disquieting. 'What did those pictures…' She tailed off. She remembered another odd thing that Chel had said, about the quoit. 'You had better come clean with me,' she said. Chel met her eyes.

'I will if you will – but I don't think you will.'

'I will,' said Kate, thinking. 'I'm almost certain I will. But you go first.'

'It's difficult to explain,' said Chel. 'In fact, I don't even want to explain it.'

'You're a psychometrist,' said Kate, helping her out. Chel stared at her.

'God, I do hope not! Why do you say that?'

'That's what they're called – people who can tell things about the owners of things. When they hold them – like you did, didn't you?'

The suggestion had been made before, not seriously, Chel hoped. By Oliver, as a matter of fact, on an occasion when his sister Debbie had got lost in a snowstorm earlier that year. She had denied it then, and she denied it now.

'Oh no, I'm sure it wasn't like that… but I've had one or two odd experiences, and it can be really weird… and now you think *I'm* really weird, don't you? You'd better say, if so, because I'm not going on if you don't believe me.'

'I believe you,' Kate said. Chel hesitated, but only for a moment.

'Those pictures,' she said. 'They were all shoved out of sight and covered in dust and spiders. I took them out and looked at them, and first off I thought, *how charming*, and I wondered why they were there, and then… it's quite hard to explain, actually. I got a feeling… I mean a physical feeling, as if the hairs on my arms had all stood on end, you know? And suddenly the pictures weren't charming at all, they were terribly, terribly unhappy, and I just dropped them. It was stupid, but I was trying to wipe them off my hands on a bit of rag, and… well, if I'm honest, they'd scared me. I was scared for the person who did them, and that's why I said I was glad it wasn't you. Who was she, do you know anything about her?'

Too much was the answer there.

'She stayed with us,' said Kate, slowly. 'I mean *stayed* with us, she was like *The Man Who Came to Dinner*. About a year ago, I suppose it must have been, she suddenly appeared on our doorstep. It was right at the beginning of the season, I'd just hung the sign out to catch the Easter trade – you remember, Easter was early last year. We can't afford to miss money if it passes the gate, you know.'

'And?' prompted Chel, after a pause during which Kate frowned at some memory of her own and said nothing.

'She was an odd little thing,' said Kate, at last. 'Local – well, Cornish anyway, which was unusual for a start. She spoke prettily though, no real accent, and she had great dark eyes in a little white face, and black hair all down her back. She must have been in her early twenties, I suppose, because we found out later that she had been married nearly four years ago – five, by this time, I suppose – but she looked, and behaved come to that, like a child. I thought at first she must have run away from home, and as it happens, she very nearly had.'

'And?' said Chel, again.

'It was a tragic, messy story. She had her head stuffed full of silly romantic stories, and she had tried to make the unfortunate man she married fit into them, instead of getting to grips with things as they are. Of course, the whole thing had gone pear-shaped, and there was one of those great big family rifts that never heal, only this one was worse than usual. Her husband had been a friend of her brother's, they had a fight because she said that he – her husband – did this, that and the other thing and had another woman – I don't think she really knew, someone had just told her, that was the grottiest part of it. I think myself he was just an ordinary man driven beyond bearing it by having to perpetually live up to Storm.'

'*Who?*'

'Oh, he was the hero of some sloppy book she was reading, you know the kind. Black and bad-tempered, great big macho, devastatingly handsome brute who sweeps women off their feet and makes them grovel at his. I should think they'd be quite impossible around the house, but I suppose they do to dream about if you've nothing better to do. But she had a husband that she kept insisting she loved – I couldn't get my head round her, to be truthful.'

'I take it, the husband had left her?'

'Very thoroughly. Her brother killed him.'

'God! How awful!'

'Well yes, we thought that at first. She told us that she was a widow and her husband had been murdered, the very first night she was here. We felt very sorry for her, anyone would. She never spoke about it after that, and we imagined that it was very fresh and raw and recent. We thought how brave she was to get out there and try and put her life together again so soon, and how horrible her family was being to make her. Charlie let her paint in his studio and I bore with her silliness, and she stayed here in the end the best part of six months. I thought we were helping her, and that she'd go away and pick up her own life again when the winter came, so I put up with her.'

'And she didn't go away?'

'No,' said Kate. 'No. She fell in love with Charlie. No – that's not quite true. She somehow superimposed her dead husband onto Charlie. She… she began to get really creepy to have about the place, and I told Charlie that she must go home, back to her own people. She hadn't been like that when she came… she was quite sweet, in a feckless sort of way. She was sick though, and getting sicker… and we had no idea who she was.'

'She must have had a name,' objected Chel.

'Cressida Stanley. If it was hers, who the hell knows? Does it mean anything to you?'

Chel shook her head.

'I've never heard the name. But then, I've had a lot on my plate these last two or three years, and I probably wouldn't remember anyway.'

'It didn't mean anything to us, either. I asked her in the end, exactly what happened – I thought – I think I thought – that it would make her feel better if she told me instead of brooding about it, and she might go away then. Well, she did tell me.'

'And?'

Kate shivered. She could see Cress now, in her mind's eye, sitting in that very chair where Chel now sat, pouring out all that self-seeking grievance, going on and on, *I.. .I... I...*

'It all happened more than two years ago – nearly three, by this time, I suppose,' she said. 'And yes, it was a terrible thing as she told it, and if she had made any effort to put it behind her and get on with living, I would still have felt really sorry for her – but she hadn't. She'd sat around for two years, hugging it to her like a... a gruesome sort of teddy bear! She'd got so that she thought it excused her anything. She thought that people – her unfortunate family, me, Charlie – should give her everything she wanted, should cosset her and look after her and carry her about for evermore. It was her own brother who was tried for murder, but they reduced it to manslaughter and only sent him to prison for three years, and they didn't do that on a sympathy vote, now did they? She walked out of her home – his home too, his family too – because they paroled him and he was going to go there. She wanted him put away for ever – I think she even wouldn't have minded seeing him hanged if they still did that, God help her – and I can see that she wouldn't want to stay at home if he was there, but it was the way she put it, as if he wasn't a person any more. She told us they sent her away and she had nowhere to go, when she had the whole world, and everybody's sympathy, surely, and what did he have?'

'He'd killed her husband,' said Chel, but doubtfully.

'He'd loved her, and spoiled her, and listened to her whingeing, and she knew he had a quick temper because she told me so – she set him up, and whether she did it on purpose or whether she didn't, the result was the same. She made him angry enough on her behalf to kill, but when he'd done it, she didn't want to know – that's if what she said was even true! The whole thing was such a mess that his solicitor thought there was grounds for an appeal, but she washed *that* away with her tears of self-pity! She wanted to forget him, because she knew if he was guilty, then she was guilty, and she wanted everyone else to shut him out too, because if they did she could justify herself to herself. She was a taker –

she took and took, from her husband, her family, us, but most of all from her unfortunate brother – and she hadn't even the grace to admit it! And as for telling the truth about it, I don't think she could have done it if she tried! I'm very sure she lied to me.'

Chel said, quietly, as if it mattered, 'Where did she go, when she left here?'

'I don't know. She made a scene, and Charlie… well, she tried to make a scene when we had troubles of own, and when we didn't take any notice of her she was piqued and ran away. She'd got to the stage when she thought she was the most important thing in the world. She ran off to that place… the old quoit, you know, where I didn't want to go. She went up there with her head full of some silly tale we made up to tease her, and tried to cast spells, or something, it was foul. I went out to look for her, and she was lying on the stone hugging it as if it was alive, and talking… oh God, I've never told even Charlie this. She was talking to it, acting as if it *was* her husband, and I can tell you, I was really scared. I brought her home, I thought she was right out of it, you know? Off her head, but when she saw Charlie she started ranting and screaming… I threw her out. I couldn't deal with it. I packed her things the next morning, and I put her case on the step, and I pushed her out after it, and she picked it up and went, and we've never seen her again, but nothing's gone right since that night. It's as if she was standing between us all the time.'

Chel said nothing, and after a moment, Kate said, 'The dreadful thing about it is, I think that when she came here, we could have helped her. I think she really was – belatedly – trying to pull herself together. If we'd asked her then, and not left it to fester… we weren't really that interested, to tell the truth. We should have been.'

'No,' said Chel. 'No, that isn't so. You mustn't think like that. If she chose to keep it to herself, then she had a perfect right. You couldn't know she was obsessed. How could you?'

'If we had bothered to find out – '

'Look,' said Chel. 'I've had troubles enough in my life, but I don't want people questioning me about it. I don't want *you* questioning me about it. Think about it.'

'It isn't my business, unless you want to tell me.'

'Exactly. And the same goes for Cressida Stanley. I assume that you know most of it anyhow, because of all the publicity, and you were entitled to believe that she did that, too. She had no grounds for feeling slighted by you, and none at all for expecting you to carry her.'

'I still can't help wishing that we had tried.'

'I expect she went home,' said Chel, but uncertainly. 'They'll look after her there.'

'And if she'd worn her welcome out there like she did here? They'd had her weeping round their necks for two years already, remember.'

'But it's their problem. It isn't yours.'

'Well, yes, maybe… but I think sometimes, like in the middle of the night when I can't sleep, or when I'm alone in the house because Charlie's gone to the pub – I think I ought to find out who they are and make sure.' Kate shivered again. 'There was something… at the end, there was something dark about her. I was afraid. I think that's why I sent her away, and nothing to do with Charlie at all.'

'What were you afraid of?' asked Chel.

'I wish I knew.'

It was Chel who shivered this time. She said, 'She painted those pretty pictures with hate in her heart. I felt it.'

'She *must* have gone home,' said Kate.

The kettle boiled, hissing over onto the hotplate, and she got up to make the tea. Chel said, 'She's gone from here, anyway. You mustn't let her become an obsession of your own. Burn those pictures and forget her, it really would be best.'

'Do you think so?'

'I know so. She's out of your life and she sounds the kind who will always find someone to cling to. Now, bring that tea, and I'll introduce you to Oliver, for I don't think Charlie will, from what I saw.'

Kate giggled, picking up the tray to take it to the studio.

'*Does he take sugar?*' she asked, wickedly, and Chel grinned.

'He'll tell you that for himself,' she said.

They left the house and went along the path to the studio, and Kate, having at last got her troubles into the open, felt released, and happier than she had done for months.

It was Chel, strangely, who couldn't rid herself of the surely irrational idea that Cressida Stanley had left Kate's life only to enter her own.

Irrational, yes… but the idea lingered and shadowed the bright spring afternoon, and she was less good company than usual.

IX

May was well advanced before Debbie had worked out her notice, settled her affairs in London, and was free to return to Cornwall to join her friends, so that by the time she was once again crossing Bodmin Moor, it was ablaze with gorse, dancing with lambs, green with new growing things. It was hard to imagine the blizzard, and the eerily deserted, snowbound road that now hummed with traffic. She drove past the end of the lane that led to the cottage and wondered, not for the first time, how she had come to go down it in the first place. Lucky for Mawgan Angwin that she had. She wondered where he was now, but knew that she would be unlikely ever to meet him again. That chapter of her life had ended, lingering on only as a brief, slightly unpleasant memory, and on the whole it was probably best to let it go.

She approached St. Erbyn some time later with an unexpected sense of homecoming, descending through the hanging wood with pleased anticipation. Through the trees, in almost full leaf now, she caught glimpses of sparkling water, moored boats, life and movement, quite different from the empty, wind-whipped grey of her earlier visit. In the village itself, cottage gardens glowed with colour and Bed & Breakfast signs hung creaking in the warm light wind. The windows of the Fisherman's Arms were open, curtains bulging gently in the stirring air, and the main door and the door to the bars both stood welcomingly wide. One or two people sat outside in the sunshine, at slatted wooden tables set under bright umbrellas advertising beer. As Debbie drove across the narrow causeway, everything looked busy and friendly, and smelled evocatively of low tide – seaweed and mud.

Lesley greeted her with a smile and hot coffee, but it seemed to Debbie that the bright enthusiasm of three months ago had tarnished a little, the smile held a reservation. Lesley's normally round and smiling face had a slightly drawn look about the eyes, and her welcome seemed a little forced. Debbie wondered if her friend was finding guesthouse life less easy than she had expected. She thought that Lesley had put on a bit of weight, too, from plump and cuddly, she had let herself get dangerously close to fat, which was a shame. They sat in the kitchen amid preparations for dinner.

'Tim and Roger are down with the boats,' said Lesley, her sun-brown fingers curled around her mug and her mind obviously mainly on the evening meal. 'Checking things over before the next lot of guests arrive, they say – it happens every Saturday, and they never seem to think that I might like some help in the house.'

'That's men for you,' suggested Debbie cautiously, and added, 'Who's Roger?'

'Your fellow hired help,' said Lesley. 'You'll like him – if Oliver hasn't spoiled you for life, that is.' There was an unexpected sour note in her voice that made Debbie look at her in surprise.

'Whatever do you mean?'

Lesley looked at her, blank-faced.

'Oh… you expect too much – or something,' she said.

Well, perhaps that was true – if it was Lesley's business – Oliver was a hard act to follow, but it was no reason for Lesley's peculiar look, almost of dislike although that had to be her imagination, surely. Debbie said, 'I thought his name was Steve.'

Lesley shrugged, as if she didn't care very much.

'Steve changed his mind and didn't come after all. It wasn't so easy to find someone, actually, because it had to be a person with all the right certificates, but someone put us onto Roger in the end. Only, because he's not a friend we can take advantage of, we have to pay him a proper wage, which is a pity, particularly at the moment, when there aren't that many people around.'

'But apart from that, how's it going?' asked Debbie, skirting what she instinctively felt might be dangerous ground. 'Did you hit any other snags? I never thought you'd get it all together to open in time for Easter, to be truthful, what with all the red tape and planning and things.'

'Oh well,' said Lesley, wrinkling her nose distastefully. 'Only one snag that really mattered. We didn't get a licence. Mine Host at the Fish put the mockers on it, and Tim was simply furious.'

'Well, that's only a small thing,' suggested Debbie, but Lesley disagreed.

'It spoils the whole thing. Tim wanted a proper sailing school, and if they had all been able to drink here in the evening it would have kept everyone together, and we'd have maybe got it off the ground. As it is, one lot goes out to the Fish, someone else goes out because *they've* gone out, everyone scatters and we lose them. It's just a holiday with sailing on the side, and they don't take it seriously. They enjoy themselves, of course, but it isn't the way we planned it.'

'Was it that important to the Fish? I would have thought they did all right without worrying about the tiny bit of trade you'd take away from them.'

'You'd have thought so,' said Lesley, moodily. 'I can't see anything we could do affecting their business in the least, the place is always packed out at weekends even this early in the year, and in the summer it'll be worse. But he's a moody bastard, him down there. Every Eden has its serpent.' She sighed, and her eyes strayed away to an open recipe book on the table. Debbie said, 'I thought he seemed rather nice.'

'Who?' asked Lesley. She looked surprised.

'The landlord of the Fish.'

'You haven't met him, have you? He was away living it up in the sun, in Tenerife or somewhere, when you were here in the winter.'

'I thought that was the landlord behind the bar.'

'No, that was Tommy. The fat one, you mean? Tommy, he's just the barman, he's OK.'

'Even so,' said Debbie, 'I don't see that it need make that much difference. If you get in a few cans of beer from the supermarket, Tim can organise the odd evening, and people are bound to want to go out sometimes.'

'Oh well…' said Lesley, listlessly. 'He rather fancied himself as Mine Host himself, I think — and he's right, in a way, if you think about it. It would have made the business quite different… still, perhaps when the Fish finds we aren't hurting them, we can apply again. It would have brought in a bit of extra cash, but not enough to make much difference. Cash,' she added, 'is a bit tight. We've had to borrow from the bank against the deeds, and we have to pay the interest, we had to have money for all sorts of things we hadn't expected. Public liability insurance, gear and spares for the boats, life jackets, and estate duty on the value of the business or something, which we hadn't even thought about. If this thing falls flat on its face, it's the dole queue for us, legacy or no legacy.' She put her mug down and got to her feet. 'Finished? Come on then, and I'll show you the changes we've made, and then we'll go and find Tim and Roger and make them take us down the road for a drink. There's nobody due to arrive until late this afternoon, and it's over an hour to closing time. You'll like Roger, he's nice.'

She had said that twice. Matchmaking, Lesley? Oh, I do hope not! Debbie put down her mug and followed her out of the room.

There weren't many alterations, but Lesley brightened a little as she showed Debbie round. The house seemed more alive, as if the people coming and going had woken it from sleep, the rooms were less impersonal now that they were being lived in.

'We all muck in together in the holiday flat outside,' said Lesley. 'It's a bit cosy, but we all get on so it isn't too bad. There's only two bedrooms, so Roger has the sofa, it makes into a bed so he doesn't mind... and this is Tim's lecture room, it used to be the TV lounge.' To Debbie, it still looked like the TV lounge, but she thought she wouldn't say so. It was here, Lesley went on, that Tim had planned to have his forbidden bar, but decent people proposed and the criminal population, it seemed, disposed and that was that.

'Criminal?' enquired Debbie, looking out of a window that overlooked the sloping lawn and the river. Through the trees beyond the lawn, she could catch tantalising glimpses of nautical activity, and she wasn't much interested in domestic affairs. It was time, she thought, to join Tim and Roger.

'The serpent at the Fish,' said Lesley, zoologically. 'He's on probation, or something. He killed his brother-in-law.'

It was sufficiently startling as a statement to reclaim Debbie's attention pretty smartish.

'What did you say?' she asked, in disbelief.

'Well,' said Lesley, reddening a little. 'I suppose that wasn't quite fair. He got three years or something for manslaughter, but he got parole after two. I don't know the ins and outs, but you can ask Mrs. Tregear — she's the cleaning woman — if you want the details. He's a pretty smooth operator, as we know to our cost, and the village don't like him much even though he's Cornish, and one of them, so allow for a little prejudice. Only a little,' she added.

'Perhaps it was an accident,' said Debbie, and wondered as she spoke why the simple phrase should strike a familiar chord.

'Fatal accidents that involve a third party are awfully difficult to believe in,' said Lesley. 'Unless it's a motor accident, I suppose, and it wasn't.'

Debbie, who didn't necessarily agree one-hundred per-cent, recognised prejudice, as advertised, when she saw it, and didn't waste her breath. The landlord of the Fisherman's Arms, on current form, didn't need her to defend him.

They left the house and crossed the lawn to the river, where a flight of stone steps led down to the shingle. On the foreshore beyond the trees, they found four smartly turned out Wayfarers, and two less than smart men. Tim and Roger, checking things over.

Roger saw them first and looked up, waving a lazy arm. He was, Debbie noted with interest, a pleasant young man of around Tim's age – twenty-six – with tightly curled, light brown hair and innocent blue eyes like a baby's. His arms and his bare back rippled with well-developed muscles, and he looked at Debbie with the same interest she was according him. Each was pleased with what they saw, recognising that they were bound to see a great deal of each other in the months to come and assessing the possibilities.

Introductions over, Tim took Debbie's arm and led her over to the boats.

'Not bad, are they?' he said, with proprietorial pride. 'Not new, of course, but Roger and I have done a lot of work on them, and they look pretty good, don't you think?'

'Spent a lot of money we hadn't got, too,' Lesley muttered, in the background.

'I think they look terrific,' said Debbie, pretending for now that she hadn't heard her, and added that she was sorry to hear about the licence. Tim snorted, enraged.

'Bloody Angwin! Bloody monopolist, if you want my opinion!'

'Mention of Angwin,' drawled Roger, lazily propping himself against the foredeck of one of the boats, 'is liable to send Tim's blood pressure soaring. If there was somewhere other than the Fish to drink, he'd drink there – but teetotalism doesn't recommend itself as a sensible alternative.'

Names are funny things. Debbie had had a mental picture of the landlord of the Fish, in line with popular television's idea of a smooth operator. At the mention of the name *Angwin*, this picture suddenly became an older version of her own acquaintance of the same name. Her question was purely instinctive, she hadn't realised she was going to ask it until it was out.

'Does he have a son?' she heard herself asking. A stupid question, for there must be many Angwins in Cornwall, it was a Cornish name after all.

'So far as I'm aware, he doesn't even have a wife,' said Tim, and added, scathingly, 'Which is fortunate for the wife he doesn't have.' Lesley grinned.

'Why, were you fancying a spot of cradle-snatching?' she asked mischievously, and to her annoyance, Debbie felt her colour rising.

'Why cradle-snatching?' she asked, too defensively. Lesley's grin broadened.

'You haven't seen Angwin,' she said, obscurely. Roger looked at his watch and reached for his discarded shirt.

'And judging by the position of the sun over the mainmast, it's high time she did,' he said. 'We're wasting valuable drinking time.'

They walked to the pub. It was only a few hundred yards down a gentle slope, Lesley and Tim walked on ahead and Debbie followed with Roger. As they progressed thus towards the causeway he told her, in his gentle, mannered drawl, exactly what Tim thought of the as yet unknown Angwin, and why.

'Tim had some ideas about expanding, in time,' he said. 'Not just a simple sailing school, but a sort of mini-marina, where he could have his own complex, hire out boats and give sailing lessons, do minor repairs for yachtsmen, have a little shop for stores — the village store here is fairly basic, and not necessarily the kind of stuff yachtsmen want — a chandlery, a cafe for light lunches and things — nothing that would compete seriously with the Fish, he made that quite clear. Heavens, they talked it over down there enough, everyone knew what he had in mind, Angwin as well as anybody.'

'It sounds terribly ambitious,' said Debbie, putting in a quick hop to keep up with him.

'It needs to be,' said Roger. 'Tim has to look to the future. It sounds a great idea to run this place as a sailing school, but the outgoings are tremendous. Have you seen the size of their bank loan, for a start?'

Debbie said that she hadn't, and wondered privately that Roger had, but Tim and Lesley had always been very open about their affairs — too open, in some ways.

'Astronomical! And the guesthouse doesn't really warrant it on its own.

It was different for Auntie, she owned it unencumbered. They're both quite mad, of course, they should have sold the place right at the start.'

'Who wants to be sane all the time?' enquired Debbie.

'True enough.' He paused, and after a minute, Debbie prompted,

'Go on about Tim's great plan, then.'

'It's not a bad plan if it was rationalised just a little, but the trouble is it needs capital,' said Roger, considering. 'They've encumbered the house to the hilt to pay the estate duty and equip the sailing school, and they can't possibly borrow any more. They got caught with negative equity in their own house, which didn't help. Without capital, the whole idea is a dead duck, and the only way they can get that is to earn it. Tim thinks – rightly, maybe, I don't know – that Angwin having blocked his licence, has strangled the whole thing before it's even got off the ground. He'll never lift it above the level of a guesthouse with a bit of fun on the side, not from a cold start like this. He feels the whole venture is stillborn. Lesley and Tim,' said Roger, swishing at the surrounding greenery with a casual hand, 'are a pair of dreamers. They aren't *practical* at all. Angwin is very practical indeed, and moreover, he's a realist and a bit of a swine as well. He runs circles round them. And I, for one, would have been careful how I trusted my tender little budding ambitions to his ears, but perhaps I shouldn't say that.'

'Poor Tim,' said Debbie, sorry for her friends.

'He should play in his own league,' said Roger.

The sunlit foreshore opened up ahead of them at the end of the tunnel of trees. Debbie slowed down, and Roger stopped.

'What's the matter?'

'Tim can be a bit of a swine, too, on his day. I know him.'

'True,' said Roger. 'But then, can't we all? But you're right, of course, Tim set Angwin up too. He had spilled all his dreams and plans out to the whole village – I don't know that they necessarily agreed with them, but when Angwin knocked them on the head, they were quite happy to pretend that they did. Public opinion frowns on Angwin. He's stepped out of line, as I expect Lesley has told you. Anyway, when the licence was turned down on his objection – if that was the only reason, and maybe it wasn't – Tim tackled him about it – publicly, according to Lesley, in the bar at the Fish, which was hardly a good place when you think about it. He said what he thought of Angwin's business methods, and Angwin said some pretty direct things in return, and the locals all sat on the sidelines and took notes. Tim had them all solidly behind him at that point, or thought he had at least, and from all accounts he let it go to his head, and Angwin has apparently never heard of sarcasm. It must have been an epic confrontation.'

It was what he left unsaid that told Debbie the most. Tim himself, she knew, had a nice line in sarcasm. She began to be sorry for the unknown Angwin.

'So, what happened?' she asked. Roger took her arm and moved her forward again.

'Come on, or they'll have drunk all the beer.'

They fell into step side by side.

'Sarcasm is a good weapon, in its place,' said Roger, thoughtfully. 'Against Angwin, it's a bit like using a bug spray against a machine gun. Angwin is a good, solid performer with a machine gun. Exit Tim, discomfited, amidst growls of supportive disapproval from the locals. Only thirst got him back inside the place – that, and the knowledge that Angwin had done himself no good by it.'

Lesley and Tim had reached the Fisherman's Arms considerably before Debbie and Roger, since they hadn't dawdled along the way, and had secured the reversion of one of the umbrella-clad tables. Lesley had swept the clutter of empty glasses and crisp packets left by the previous tenants into an untidy heap and sunk into a chair.

'It may be only May, but it's as hot as midsummer,' she was complaining, as Debbie and Roger joined them.

'Jog off some of those extra pounds, and you won't feel it so much,' said Roger, crudely Debbie thought, but Lesley didn't seem to mind. She merely said,

'You're obsessed with jogging. Is somebody going to buy me a drink? I've earned it.'

'Deb,' Tim said, 'what'll it be?'

He and Roger went inside to get the drinks, and Debbie sat down beside Lesley.

'You didn't tell me Tim had actually had a row with this Angwin,' she said.

'Dwelling on unpleasantness simply depresses me,' said Lesley, moodily. 'I love Tim, but he can be so stupid!'

Debbie recalled a hard-learned lesson.

'It's no good pretending it didn't happen. He's practically your next-door neighbour, and however you look at it, he must carry a certain amount of clout.'

'What do you expect me to do about it?' Lesley demanded, indignantly. 'Beg his pardon? No chance!'

'But if you have to live with him – '

'Don't worry, it's all terribly civilised,' said Lesley, and Debbie heard a note of bitterness behind the easy words. 'If we have to live with Angwin, he has to live with the village. It's our only card, but so far it seems to be the ace of trumps. Angwin's on eggshells – I'd almost be sorry for him, if I thought for a moment that he cared.'

Tim and Roger reappeared, carrying drinks.

'Getting pretty busy in there,' said Tim, seating himself beside Lesley and throwing a casual but affectionate arm around her plump shoulders. 'Beginning to look as if there's really going to be a season after all. I was beginning to wonder, myself.'

Roger sat down opposite to Debbie.

'Don't start grumbling,' he advised. 'People mean business, for us as well as Angwin. It's a short season when it comes, it can't start too early.'

'Our bookings aren't bad,' said Tim.

'Catering's a dead duck in this country,' said Roger dogmatically, he seemed fond of the phrase. 'It's only people who can offer an exceptional service – like this place – that make any money at it.'

'We shall provide an exceptional service of our own,' said Lesley, quietly. Roger looked at her with a sort of hopeless warmth.

'Oh really, Lesley!' he said, and left it at that.

Tim began to discuss the bookings for the season, and the way that things had gone so far, which didn't sound like guaranteed success to Debbie, but perhaps she was tired, she decided. Lesley had fallen into a dream about meals, and listening to Tim and Roger talking, Debbie began to feel herself being drawn in, becoming part of a team. The sun beat down warmly, people in bright summery clothes strolled along the shingly foreshore, children paddled at the water's edge. It was sunlit, peaceful and lovely.

A man came out of the pub and began clearing glasses from the tables with a practised hand, paused when he came to their own, took a second look, and then quietly reached past Debbie's shoulder to gather up the empties.

'Well, hullo,' said a familiar voice. 'It's The Angel Deborah. I thought you'd never get here.'

The next few moments were crowded. For one reason and another, all four of the group round the table were staring; Lesley, Tim and Roger at Debbie, and Debbie at the man who had spoken, and now stood there entirely at his ease, balancing his tray of glasses and with a sunny smile on his face. Of the four of them, Debbie was possibly the most surprised.

She had met Mawgan Angwin at a distinct disadvantage. Nobody is at their best lying unconscious on the floor, nor yet when suffering from shock, pain or fright, still less all three together. She hadn't realised that he wasn't merely ordinary-looking, as she had thought on their first meeting, but wickedly attractive. Looking at him now, in the full glory of his health and strength, loaded with enough mischief for a whole cageful of monkeys, she thought that she must have been blind. No, he wasn't eye-catchingly handsome in the sense that her brother Oliver was, he still looked like a good-natured thug – but there was a vivid and obvious intelligence living behind his pleasant, seemingly open and friendly face, if you were foolish enough to discount a watchful look in the eyes, and an overdose of easy charm that had been totally extinguished under stress. She saw at once why he got on Tim's nerves.

Her second impression was less happy. A hurried and hasty mental review of the various confidences that had passed between them, together with his opening remark, made it abundantly clear that he had known perfectly well all along that Tim and Lesley had to be the friends she had told him about. Why she should feel that this made his advertised conduct perfidious, Debbie wasn't sure. She only knew that it did.

She became aware that everyone was waiting for her to say something.

'Oh!' she managed, and then added, weakly, 'Hullo.'

He grinned at her. She thought that he was enjoying the situation; scoring off Tim, a spy in the enemy camp, a misplaced sense of humour, any or all of these things, she didn't know. A tide of colour rushed up her face. It wasn't only his present treachery that was robbing her of words, it was past memories. He burned brightly enough to light up a dark room, and while he had lain helpless on the sofa she had done things for him… she didn't consider herself either naïve or inexperienced, but she knew that she had gone as scarlet as a lobster dipped in boiling water. She covered her burning cheeks with her hands.

Roger looked at her with a measuring eye, and said, with an underlying amusement that didn't have to be involved, 'Bit warm, are we, Debbie?'

Debbie was wishing that the ground would open and swallow her up, she hadn't thought that people really did that, but now she knew. She said, trying not to sound strangled, and idiotically, as she realised as soon as she spoke, 'What are you doing here?' and could have died on the spot. The treacherous Angwin gave her a slightly malicious smile, and scooped the last of the screwed-up crisp packets onto his tray.

'I live here,' he told her gently, and to her great relief, moved away. A silence fell. Lesley broke it.

'Explain,' she said, coldly.

'When I got snowed up, you remember,' Debbie said, for of course she had told them all about it at the time, 'it was him.'

Lesley and Tim stared at her. Roger, who hadn't heard the story, looked a question.

'But – ' Lesley began, and stopped. It was quite possible to see her mentally equating the *Morgan* of Debbie's winter adventure with the Mawgan Angwin of their own acquaintance.

'He was in Marbella, or San Marino or somewhere,' objected Tim.

'He came back late, and he'd had some kind of accident,' said Lesley, thoughtfully. 'He kept out of everyone's way and hardly came into the bar at all. Less even than usual.'

'If he's on probation, can he go abroad? That's a thought.'

They both looked at Debbie censoriously.

'He was up on Bodmin Moor,' said Debbie. 'I can't help it if he let you think he was somewhere else, he was lying.' She felt as if they thought it was somehow her fault, and added, defensively, 'And anyway, even if I'd known, it wouldn't have made a scrap of difference. He hadn't done anything then, and I couldn't have left him on the floor even if he had – could I?'

'He'd knocked off his brother-in-law,' said Lesley, and then fortunately saw the funny side and laughed. 'Poor old Deb – expecting to be shot at dawn!'

Memory flashed for the second time, stilled, focussed, took on a new colour. The bright scene faded, Debbie saw only a desperately sick man reiterating urgently, *It was an accident, I swear it!* Her companion from the cottage on the moor had spent two years in prison. She didn't think that it would have agreed with him. She recalled the prompt arrival of the police, and something the farmer had said to her, and was conscious of an unexplained and horrid sense of desolation.

'How did he do it?' she heard herself asking, and then added, 'You told me he wasn't married,' almost accusingly.

'He isn't — he doesn't seem to be, anyway,' said Lesley. 'You can have a brother-in-law without marrying anyone.'

'Just so long as the brother-in-law has married someone,' said Roger, deftly unscrambling this elliptical statement, but he didn't need to. Debbie was already aware that Mawgan Angwin hadn't been an only child.

'And I don't know,' said Lesley, answering the original question. Debbie sipped her drink, wondering and finding no help in it.

There was no time, said Lesley firmly, to sit and hold post-mortems, particularly when none of them knew what they were talking about. Angwin was a blight, full stop, and at home the vegetables needed peeling, and if anyone said the words *final checks* again, well, two could play at manslaughter just as easily as one.

They left without seeing Mawgan again, to Debbie's private relief, and returned to the house. Tim, magnanimous to the last, said that although there was a little work left to be done on the boats, he and Roger could manage if Debbie liked to help Lesley.

'That told you,' said Lesley, waspishly, as the two of them went back into the kitchen. 'Women to the galley, leave the real work to the men! Sometimes, I really hate Tim!'

It seemed a long way from the optimistic plans of the winter. Debbie said, 'I suppose it's all new to you both, it'll probably get easier.' She resented her cool banishment to the domestic chores, for it was work she wouldn't have taken on for Tim or anybody else, and he knew it, but making an issue of it could wait. Lesley looked as if she hardly needed encouraging to blow her top completely.

'Huh!' she said now, with such a determined toss of her head that Debbie put down the vegetable knife she was inexpertly plying among the carrots and said, 'How about, we take a quiet sit down and you tell me all about it over a glass of cooking sherry?'

'What cooking sherry?' Lesley demanded, suddenly and inexplicably furious. 'We can't afford cooking sherry! I'd love some cooking sherry right now, bottles and bottles of it, and I hate Tim and I hate this place, and I hate everything –' She dropped the pan she was holding with a clang and put her hands to her face. 'I'm sorry, and I didn't mean it.'

Debbie drew out a chair from the kitchen table and pushed her down onto it.

'Sit,' she said. 'Now, tell me.'

Lesley told her. It all came out in a long tirade with no recognisable punctuation marks, as if had been bottled up for some time.

'He just messes about with his beastly boats we've had builders and bills and bloody Angwin and things and all he's done is pottered with his pots of paints and things being nice to people and doing things he enjoys while I've cooked and swept and shopped and stitched and struggled and worried – who does he think I am, the genie of the lamp –?' She broke off to take a necessary breath and began to cry. Debbie handed her a roll of kitchen paper and silently waited for more. That there was more was obvious. After a moment, Lesley said more calmly, 'He's done his bit and I've done mine, and I know that's what we arranged, but we never knew what it was going to be like. He likes sailing, it's a game to him, he enjoys himself and he's got Roger to help him, and now you, you can't really call it work.'

'You've got Mrs. Tregear,' ventured Debbie. Lesley said, 'Yes, I have, but she isn't here all the time, and anyway, she isn't what you'd describe as a friend. I can't talk with her the way I can to you, or like Tim talks to Roger, so it isn't the same thing. And although I don't mind housework, in fact I used to quite like it, this isn't housework, it's slave labour.' Her voice was breaking dangerously again. 'I try to tell Tim that it isn't fair, but he doesn't want to know and just says it's what we agreed, and it's true, it is, only I thought he was at least going to do the accounts and things, and –' She broke off abruptly as the door from the yard opened and Roger came through. He stopped on the threshold, warily, as if, Debbie thought, he had played this scene before.

'Tim said, what about a cup of tea,' he said hesitantly, retreating a stealthy step back towards the door. 'He'll be up in a minute.'

'Good,' said Debbie, getting briskly to her feet. 'Then he can make it. Don't go, Roger – look, there's all these carrots to peel.'

Roger hesitated, and Debbie picked up the knife and slapped it into his hand. He looked at it helplessly.

128

'There's the sink,' she pointed out, and went towards the door into the hall.

'Where are you going?' asked Roger. 'Look, I thought this was your job – '

'Well, you thought wrong then.' Debbie had her hand on the doorhandle. 'You and Tim can have tea, if you care to make it, but Les and I are tired, and we want something stronger. I'm going out to buy a bottle.'

'He'll be closed by now,' said Roger. 'And the village shop hasn't a licence.'

'So bloody what? He owes me a favour. At least one.'

'I haven't time to sit around drinking,' Lesley wailed, as if they were contemplating a full-scale orgy.

'Yes you have, you've got Roger to help you, and Tim says it's tea break time anyway,' said Debbie. 'It's time to call an emergency general meeting if you ask me, and I'm not doing it over a cup of tea, so pull yourself together, Les darling, having the vapours never achieved anything. Not, at least, if you go on having them too long,' she added, as an afterthought.

Roger rocked shiftily from one foot to the other.

'What do I say to Tim?' he asked. 'After all, he employs me to help with the boats.'

'Me, too,' said Debbie, finally, and slammed out through the door.

She was angry as she walked down the hill, angry with Tim and angry, too, with Lesley. She hadn't intended, and didn't want, to find herself in the middle of a marital row over the chores, and she had no intentions of being used as a solution to the problem – and she suspected that Tim had thoughts along those lines. Her indignation smothered, for a short distance, a deeper and more tangled emotional reaction, but nobody was more aware than she that worse crises had been weathered on strong tea and mutual understanding, and that alcohol wasn't a pre-requisite for the solving of problems. She realised long before she reached the Fish that she had followed a gut instinct that she didn't think she fully understood, and that its roots went a lot deeper than the events of the past half hour.

Never sweep unpleasantness under the carpet. Awful complications could result therefrom, and some of them needed to be faced right now.

The Fish, when she reached it, presented an appearance of afternoon siesta, no crises, domestic or otherwise, troubled its well-organised calm. Debbie, going in through the main entrance, stood in a cool, polished hall and listened to peace. A weary little voice at the back of her mind, that had driven a long way and not been offered lunch on arrival, mentioned caustically that this was the difference between being professional and the amateur shambles up the road. She pressed a bell that invited her to PLEASE RING FOR ATTENTION, and waited.

He came himself, from a passage leading to the back of the house, cool, competent and glowingly attractive, his shirt sleeves rolled up above the elbow and revealing fresh and ugly scars, crude purple lines against his brown skin that brought back the very chill of snow.

'Why, hullo Deborah,' he said. 'This is a surprise.' He followed the direction of her eyes and grinned. 'Sorry, I was just unblocking a drain. Some things about catering are very fundamental.'

'So I've just found out,' said Debbie. 'How is it – your elbow?'

'Good as new.' He dismissed the subject and went on. 'What can I do for you?'

He was less like Morgan from the cottage, in close-up, than she would have believed possible. Perhaps it was because of the things she now knew about him, although she hoped not. Debbie said, 'I don't suppose you could sell me a bottle of wine, could you?'

He looked at her steadily, thoughtfully, unrolling his shirtsleeves down over the scars as he did so.

'The bar's closed, and so is the restaurant.'

'I know,' said Debbie. 'I wouldn't ask, but it's an emergency.'

He raised his eyebrows in enquiry, but Debbie had no intention of explaining. You didn't sell your own side to the enemy, whatever your private feelings might be.

'It doesn't matter if you don't want to,' she said. He took her by the arm and spun her round.

'Come into the restaurant, Deborah, we can't talk here.'

The restaurant, which didn't seem to be directly part of the pub, was uncannily quiet, the tablecloths crisp and white, the glass and cutlery sparkling, and not a soul in sight. Mawgan leaned against the counter of a small but well-stocked bar against the rear wall, and looked at her, speaking deliberately,

'Do your friends know as you've come down here? I'm not their favourite person, you know – they think I'm a mannerless yob on probation.'

Debbie met his eyes without faltering.

'What they think is up to them,' she said, and he let out a breath that she realised he had been holding.

'You know, then. I thought they'd've told you.'

'So what?' asked Debbie. 'I've often felt like bumping off my own brother-in-law, come to that.'

It was a mistake, and she knew it before she had finished saying it. She couldn't imagine what perverse instinct had prompted her.

'Yes, but I did 'n,' he said, and turned abruptly away to a wine rack behind the bar. 'Red or white?' He didn't wait for her reply, but lifted down a bottle of red, and placed it on the bar top between them. 'There you are, Deborah. Take it away.'

She didn't touch it. Her eyes met his miserably.

'I'm sorry. That was a really stupid thing to say.'

'Don't we all say 'em?'

'*That* stupid?'

'Even worse, some of us. Don't look so tragic – if prison does nothing else, at least it blunts your finer feelings.'

There was no answer to that, at least not one that she felt it was safe to make.

'How much do I owe you?' she asked, feeling in the pocket of her jeans for the money.

'You don't. The boot is on the other foot.'

'But – '

He picked up the bottle himself and placed it in her hands, clasping her fingers around the neck.

'There. You needn't tell your friends it was a present, and then it won't choke them. Cheer up, Deborah, and smile! In fact, from what I saw at lunchtime, you'd be better with two – that won't go far between you all.'

He took a second one down and held it out to her. She took it, having as she saw it no option, thanked him and left, with an obscure and miserable feeling of having started down a wide and open road leading to some pleasant place, and then found it was a dead end after all.

The wine, she found as she carried it home, wasn't the cheap and cheerful red plonk that she would have probably picked out herself – should he have such a thing, of course – but an Australian Cabernet Sauvignon with a modest pedigree. She would have a fine old time explaining it.

Fortunately, Lesley was still so upset that explanations were needless, she wouldn't have noticed if she had been given fifty-year-old vintage port. Tim had come in from the foreshore and was defending his position by the simple technique of trying to put her in the wrong.

'All right, I'm sorry,' he was saying, his back propped against the sink and his face as red as a turkey's. 'I'm sorry, I'm a pig if you say so, I'll admit it if it makes you feel better. But there's no need to develop a martyr complex, is there? We're trying to run a sailing school here, after all, not the St. Erbyn Hilton!'

'Oh Tim, don't be so *bloody* human!' snapped Debbie, driven suddenly beyond endurance by the whole inexplicably dreary day. 'Try a little martyrdom yourself for once, and see how it feels for a change!'

'Oh don't, don't!' moaned Lesley, in the middle.

Roger, imperturbable as ever, busied himself with the corkscrew and poured wine. He lifted his glass and sipped with appreciation, viewing the combatants consideringly.

'How about a truce?' he suggested. 'I propose a cease-fire and a few summit talks. Let's look at this thing objectively.'

Three very un-objective pairs of eyes fixed themselves fiercely on him.

'As I see it,' he continued, unruffled, 'there is something to be said on both sides. We all intend to work hard, and there is, of course, plenty of work to be done. The difference seems to be that we three are going to enjoy ourselves with our share, people to be with, each other for company, whereas Les is all alone with Mrs. Tregear and the kitchen sink. On balance, I know which I prefer.'

Nobody was quite sure if he was referring to the division of labour or to Mrs. Tregear and the kitchen sink. This kept Lesley and Debbie momentarily silent while they thought about it, and Tim jumped in, singing the old song.

'It's what we planned,' he argued. 'Deb knows, she was here. And if we don't maintain the boats properly, there'll be an accident, and then we're all in trouble.'

'We've hardly begun and we're rowing about it!' lamented Lesley, tragically.

'Just don't think I'm going to spend any time in the kitchen that you two don't,' said Debbie. They glared at each other.

'Then what do you suggest?' demanded Tim. 'That we pack the whole idea in? You can't have it both ways.'

'Well, I don't see why not,' said Roger, carefully. 'We don't do lunches, after all, so there's no reason why we can't give Les a hand with the preparations for dinner in our lunch hour. I don't mind, if you two don't.'

Debbie was calming down, although she was unaware that there was any reason other than the obvious one for her flying off the handle in the first place. She said, 'On a fortnight's course, I really don't see why boat maintenance can't be the last lesson. Then you can take a whole day and have plenty of help, and have time on Saturday to lend a hand with the change-over. It would be logical.'

Tim didn't want to be lumbered with the domestic chores, and looked mutinous.

'It's not that simple.'

'Why not?' demanded Lesley, springing to the attack. 'You just tell me, why not?'

'It's not my department –' began Tim, and Debbie and Roger spoke in a chorus.

'It isn't ours, either!'

'Oh, none of you need help if you don't want to!' said Lesley, on a wail, and began to cry again. It was so unlike Lesley to cry at all, let alone twice in one afternoon, that Debbie stared at her, and Tim said, 'Oh God!' in a long-suffering voice, and went to her and took her in his arms. 'Lesley my darling, I'm a swine. I'm lower than Angwin, and that's low! I'm sorry, of course we'll all lend a hand when we can, and you can have Mrs. T in the evenings too, if you want. And this wine, Deb, is ambrosial. What did my fellow swine down the road sting you for it?'

'A fair price,' said Debbie, non-committally, salving her conscience for the white lie with the reflection that forty-eight hours intensive care, however inexpert, must surely be a fair exchange for two bottles of even a rather good wine.

'First fair thing he's done in his life, then,' said Tim, and buried his face in the curls at his wife's neck. 'Stop crying, Lesley my darling, for the bell has just rung.'

'I look a mess!' cried Lesley, and Debbie said,

'I'll go.'

She didn't think, as she went out into the hall, that the discussion had solved anything at all. Words were only words, and while Roger had meant to be co-operative, she thought that Tim hadn't, he was only paying lip-service to the proposal because Lesley had cried and he didn't like seeing her cry. Something was sadly amiss with the perfect way to earn a living.

An uneasy and resentful presentiment that she was going to be dragged in and forced to become involved took hold of her. She even wished, in the time it took her to join the new arrivals, that she had never agreed to come.

Restitution and vengeance were just words, really. On some deep level, almost buried, Cress was still aware of that. She could curl up in bed at night and discuss them with Mike, in long conversations that mainly took place inside her head – she wouldn't speak aloud where Allison might hear, and Allison seemed to be home a lot these days. Allison would say she was loopy, and she wasn't. *It was quite natural, after all that they had meant to each other, the way they had loved each other, that Mike would stay near to her. They had been so close that they had merged their spirits into one, and now that his body was ashes in the wind, his spirit couldn't leave hers even if it would.*

She could skip restitution and vengeance, she supposed, and try sleeping pills instead. Gin and sleeping pills, she had seen that on the telly. That girl in the soap had recovered, of course; she, Cress, wouldn't, and nor would she want to, life on her own was too empty, not worth the bother, too tiring… all sorts of things that she could never cope with. She would be found… *still and lifeless, the white quilt on which she lay no whiter than her skin, dark lashes like fans against her pale cheeks…* . No – that somehow implied that her eyes were in a funny place. Cress frowned. They would be sorry, anyway. She would make them be.

You don't want to do that. It might have been the voice of common sense that spoke, but Cress didn't recognise it if so. She sat up on the bed, staring. She hadn't thought that thought for herself.

'Mike?' It came out as a whisper in the dark room. She imagined that he moved towards her through the shadows, and she let out a long breath, like a sigh. Reality faded… she forgot all about Allison.

'You talk in your sleep,' Allison informed her at breakfast time.

Answering Allison was useless. She was totally unfeeling. Cress gave her a shadowy look from beneath her eyelashes and said nothing.

'Oh God!' exclaimed Allison, unimpressed. 'Why don't you stop mooning around the place and get yourself a job? There must be hundreds of things you could do in the summer, if only you'd get out and try!'

'Let the child alone, Allison, do,' said Cally, coming in with the toast in a rack. Cress picked at a slice. Her face had gone vacant, as if nobody lived behind it any more. Allison watched her and felt uncomfortable. Cress was really getting very odd, why was it only she that seemed able to see it? Because she wasn't at home all the time, or because she really was hard and unfeeling, as people – like Gran and Cress – kept telling her? Fortunate somebody in the family was, somebody had needed to keep trailing over to Exeter to visit the prison hadn't they? She remembered how awful those visits had been. She reached for the toast and began buttering a slice, swiftly and efficiently as she did most things. Cress had made hers into a pile of crumbs and was pushing it around her plate, giving a very good impression of the village idiot.

There was nothing that she could do for him here but mourn, and perhaps they were right, the mourning time was over. The sleeping pills would have to wait, there was work to be done first, work that could only be done if she steeled herself to return to the golden days of the past... to the river.

But she couldn't get a job in St. Erbyn, everybody knew her there, *he* knew her. To her family's surprise – and relief, to be truthful – she found a summer job at the Blue Crab Cafe in Falmouth, and Grandad looked around and found her a bed-sit. Everyone seemed pleased with her. If they wondered that she had chosen Falmouth, they didn't show it, perhaps they thought she meant to make her peace with him, to kiss and make up. They were so wrong, in that case.

The cook at the Blue Crab was fat and talkative, and thought that Cress was really genteel, poor little thing. She had a truly awful son who had received most of his sketchy education at a detention centre for young offenders, and who worked at the cafe as washer-up. But you couldn't tell people like that your secret sorrows. Cress drifted around the tables in an ineffective sort of way with plates of sausages and beans and glasses of coke for the tourists, and wondered what Mike would like her to do next.

Poetic justice was all very well, but you couldn't destroy a woman who didn't exist.

X

It took only a few days for it to begin to be obvious that a policy of non-involvement was going to be difficult to pursue. Debbie found this tiresome. She preferred to live her life separately, preserving her own identity, an attitude that stemmed in the first place from the childish adoration of a brother whose growing-up years had been unhappy and rebellious. She had started by copying Oliver without even realising it, but she had ended by understanding him. Like her brother before her, she was popular, fun to be with, a focus for incident and excitement, and like him she kept an invisible barrier between herself and intimacy. Oliver, in the end, had made a remarkably successful marriage, suffered immense personal loss, and gone a long way towards breaking down the barrier. Debbie, who had lived with a man who said he loved her and found it a disaster, couldn't, this time, understand him at all.

It wasn't that she was unfeeling. She was very fond of Tim and liked Lesley, and she had been perfectly happy to come to Cornwall to help them get started with their sailing school. She wasn't at all happy to find herself dragged headlong into their personal problems, she had lived with too many of these from her childhood.

That there were real problems became apparent almost at once.

At this time, it happened that the rooms at Seagulls were almost fully occupied, partly with bookings held over from the previous ownership, partly with students for Tim's sailing course.

'They seem to mix fairly well, that's one mercy,' said Tim. 'And that couple who came with two teenagers are thinking of having a bit of instruction from Roger.' He sounded jubilant, the success of his venture was very important to him. If the guests wanted to sail, he was prepared to love them whatever they did. Lesley, however, looked glum.

'The elderly couple in No. 5 complained that we'd let the place get rowdy,' she said. 'They've been coming here practically since the flood, but they said they won't be coming again.'

'Oh well,' said Tim, dismissing it as unimportant. 'We don't need their sort. They don't fit in, anyway.'

'They talk,' said Lesley.

'Don't listen,' advised Tim blithely, and Lesley didn't say, as she could have done, that the talk wasn't to her but to other guests, that people were amazingly suggestible, and that the consequences rebounded not on Tim, who was out on the water doing what he loved to do best, but on herself, who was readily available to receive complaints.

Neither Debbie nor Roger took much notice of discussions of this kind – if discussion it could be called. They both of them appreciated that Tim wanted a young and lively atmosphere, and that staid and elderly couples who went birdwatching and enjoyed a quiet day's fishing would be happier somewhere else. It was less easy to ignore the fact that the working lives of the four of them were falling into two distinct categories.

Lesley's original complaint that Tim did nothing but enjoy himself was obviously not entirely true. Tim worked very hard, as did both Debbie and Roger. There was plenty of hard work involved in instruction, and in seeing that the four boats were always in tip-top order, and there were enough customers around, both resident and casual, to keep the three of them constantly busy. Tim was absolutely right when he said that it was necessary not only to be competent and safety-conscious, but to be seen to be so at every turn. The instructors must always be available, smiling and ready to help. It was, however, very easy to smile when the sun shone and the water sparkled with thousands of points of light like diamonds, and everyone was keen to learn and have a good time.

Back at the house, Lesley and Mrs. Tregear made beds, swept and cleaned, and prepared meals. Lesley, too, dealt with the business side of things; as Tim pointed out – again, quite rightly – she was on the spot to answer the telephone, and there to deal with reps and bookings and send replies to letters, and while she was there anyway it was only reasonable that she should deal with the accounts too. It was her inheritance, after all, he said – with truth, yes, but too often. Where he failed disastrously in understanding was in not realising that she didn't particularly enjoy these things. Lesley was a country girl, not necessarily naïve, but shy with people. She might have enjoyed it more if instead of Mrs. Tregear, she had had a friend such as Debbie to help her, for she wasn't by any means stupid. But being left on her own with what she considered the responsible side of things, while the other three very obviously had great fun together, was making her bitter. She had hoped that Debbie might be an ally, might give her a hand. Her disappointment at Debbie's failure to do so was a constant reproach in the background that Debbie felt to be unjust. She had taken on a job teaching sailing, she had not contracted to be a chambermaid, waitress, or kitchen assistant.

Because Lesley wasn't enjoying herself as the others were, she had less energy than they did. The work she was doing was both physically tiring and mentally unstimulating, and she knew nothing about sailing.

'We're all going down to the Fish this evening when dinner's over,' said Tim. 'The whole crowd of us – well, not those two in No. 5, miserable old bats, but everyone else.'

'We can't leave them on their own,' was Lesley's instant reaction.

'Why not? They'll be all right. They shut themselves up in their room every night anyway.'

'I think I'll stay, though,' said Lesley. 'It seems rude just to leave them, and someone must answer the phone.'

'Please yourself,' said Tim.

He and Debbie and Roger spent the evening in the lounge bar of the Fish, entertaining their students with highly-embroidered tales of their sailing exploits, and when they got home, some time after closing time, Lesley had gone to bed. Tim didn't seem bothered by this, but Debbie, her conscience pricking her a little, had a distinct feeling that he should have been. Although it was true when Tim said that Lesley could have come with them if she had wanted, it was at the same time not true, if she could only pinpoint why.

On another occasion, Tim did persuade his wife to accompany them. She sat quietly in a corner for most of the evening, saying little and looking almost as if she was going to fall asleep at any moment, and when they got home they had a row.

'You could at least have pretended that you were enjoying yourself,' Tim said, accusingly.

'I wasn't,' said Lesley. 'I didn't want to go in the first place. I'm tired.'

'Well, so are we all, a drink and a bit of fun should have cheered you up.'

'What fun?' asked Lesley. 'You all sat and talked about nothing but boats. Everyone ignored me. I was bored.'

'You needn't have looked it quite so thoroughly,' snapped Tim.

Roger took Debbie's arm and drew her aside.

'How about a romantic walk in the moonlight?'

It was quiet and cool down by the water. The shingle on the foreshore crunched under their feet as they walked, above their heads the stars shone in a vast immensity of space. There was a moon, not full but enough to see by. Roger tried to put his arm round Debbie's shoulders, but she was as allergic to casual fondling as a cat. She walked a little away from him, and alone.

'It's a lovely night,' said Roger.

'Beautiful.'

'Do you know anything about the stars?'

'A little. Oliver taught me.'

Roger glanced at her in the dimness.

'That's the first time I've heard you mention his name. Why don't you boast about him a little? Tim would like it if you did.'

'Tim may get his publicity elsewhere.'

'I would have thought you would be proud of him.'

'I am,' said Debbie.

'Why, then?'

They walked a little way in silence. They were level with the Fish by this time, the last customers were just leaving from the restaurant and the bars were closed up and dark. Upstairs, a light shone in an end window. Debbie looked at it thoughtfully, wondering. She had seen very little of Mawgan since the day she had arrived; the restaurant was open in the evening and he was, she assumed, occupied with that, for he was only ever in the bar then on Sundays, when the restaurant opened at lunchtime instead. At lunchtime on other days, when she supposed that he might be around more often, they were generally at home peeling potatoes for Lesley. There was no reason why it should niggle at her the way that it did. They were the most casual acquaintances, and there would be hell to pay, both back at home and here at work if they were ever to become anything else – which was unlikely when, apart from other considerations, they inhabited different worlds.

'Well?' prompted Roger, and she remembered that he had asked her a question to which she had yet to reply.

'Firstly, I suppose, because I'm me, what I may owe to him is private between us. If the students knew who I was, they might – they would – link us together and change towards me.'

'Would that be bad?'

'Yes. I think so.'

'Please yourself,' said Roger. 'And secondly?'

'Secondly?'

'You said *firstly*, so secondly must follow as the night, the day.'

He heard her sigh, the faintest breath in the quiet night.

'Secondly, then, when people ask about Oliver it isn't, these days, because of the brave thing that he did.'

'I'm sure it is. It's why I would ask.'

'And the next thing you'd ask is how he can come to terms, after that, with being disabled.'

'Isn't that natural?'

'It's his business.'

'From the little I know, he's come to terms with it with the same courage that took him round the world. Aren't you proud of that?'

'Of course I am.'

Roger said, quietly,

'You mustn't let him overshadow you all your life, Deb.'

'He doesn't,' said Debbie.

Roger said nothing for a while, and when he did speak again it was about something quite different.

'What are we going to do about Lesley and Tim?'

Debbie was surprised.

'Do we have to do anything?'

'I think we do,' said Roger. 'They're friends of yours, don't you want to help them?'

Roger barely knew them. Debbie felt criticised.

'At the moment, they're both so convinced they're in the right that they're unhelpable.'

'They're drifting apart, very rapidly. Can't you see it?'

'It's all new, and they've a lot to worry about.'

The river, lapping against the shingle, made a soft sucking sound. Roger said, 'Tim was a friend of yours before he knew Lesley, he tells me.'

Debbie stopped walking.

'What are you trying to say?'

Roger stopped too, and faced her.

'That Lesley is letting herself go downhill, that Tim neglects her, and that you're a very attractive girl. Doesn't all that sound to you like a recipe for disaster?'

'Lesley isn't so stupid,' said Debbie, with less conviction than she would have liked.

'Anyone can be stupid when they're under pressure,' Roger told her. 'Do you want Lesley to hate you? She already resents you – he did nothing but talk about you before you arrived, and now she gets the housework while you go off with her husband and enjoy yourself. She probably thinks he only married her because you wouldn't have him by this time.'

'Oh *shit!*' said Debbie, fiercely.

They began to walk slowly back towards the boathouse. Just that one light burned in the Fish now, dimly, behind a wide open, uncurtained window. An owl was hunting in the woods behind the village, his call, muted by distance, was eerie.

'How come you notice something like that, and I don't?' demanded Debbie resentfully.

'I have a ringside seat,' said Roger. 'I can watch you and Tim together all day. You treat him as if he was your brother, and that can be heady stuff from a girl like you. You can treat me like a brother any time you want.'

'Lesley surely doesn't think I encourage him.'

'Not at present, no.'

'They're not going to drag me into their quarrels. I'll go first!'

'That would be a really helpful thing to do,' commented Roger, dryly.

She felt that she was being unfairly blackmailed, and was angry. Her anger found its expression in an impatient toss of her head.

'You can't make one of a team and still be entirely an individual,' said Roger, which was perceptive of him. She began to think that she had underestimated him.

'All right,' she said. 'So what do you suggest?'

It was Roger's turn to sigh.

'If we weren't fools, we'd both go. As it is, I suppose we shall have to peel more vegetables.'

If they had to do it, they had to do it. Debbie said, resignedly, 'You're really getting very handy with that paring knife.'

'Tim could do the Cash & Carry trip if he doesn't want to do domestic work. Perhaps she could go with him sometimes.'

They were nearly at the little holiday unit by this time. The light burned in the kitchen behind the glass outside door, but the rest of the place was in darkness.

'They've gone to bed,' said Debbie, relieved.

They paused in the kitchen before parting to go to their own beds.

'You wouldn't care to behave like a sex-object and be kissed goodnight?' enquired Roger, with an enquiring lift to his brows.

'I don't feel in the least kissable,' Debbie told him.

'One of these fine days, something is going to batter down the walls and let the world in,' he warned her. 'Goodnight, Deb.'

'Goodnight.'

But the world had been in, she reminded herself as she undressed. The world had been in, and had been driven out, and the defences repaired behind it. People from disrupted homes tended to repeat the pattern. She had certainly done so. And nobody looking at Lesley and Tim would find them a recommendation for love and marriage. Roger could find himself a sex-object, if he wanted one, but as for herself, she wanted no part of it.

Her last thought before she fell asleep was that, unfeminine or no, the thing she hated most in the whole world was housework, and cooking followed it a close second.

And yet, it was over the housework that Debbie came to learn a bit more about the landlord of the Fish, for if she had not reluctantly volunteered to help Lesley on Saturday mornings, she wouldn't have seen very much of Mrs. Tregear.

Mrs. Tregear came in every day but Sunday to *do the rough*, as she described it herself. Doing the rough included scrubbing the kitchen floor, cleaning the stove, keeping the bathrooms and the downstairs cloakroom in shining order, and helping with the upstairs rooms. She also came in the evenings these days to wash up, but it was in the mornings that she had a free rein to gossip. She was a terrific worker, but an even more terrific gossip, and Debbie, busy changing beds while Mrs. Tregear polished and dusted and cleaned washbasins, received the full brunt of her cheerful chat.

Mrs. Tregear had no inhibitions about discussing her employers' affairs. Their doings, in fact, formed the backbone of village gossip, together with the more shameful doings of Mawgan Angwin, and where the two touched there was a positive eruption of delicious scandal.

'Of course, you'll have heard about Mr. Howells' big row with Mr. Angwin from the Fish,' she said, busily polishing taps. The village all referred to him in this formal way. Debbie found it the rather sad measure of their unfriendliness towards him.

'Oh, I wouldn't call it a row,' she said now, mendaciously. She had by this time heard a little more about it from Lesley, and if Lesley was to be believed, Mawgan had rather let himself go. Tim, too, presumably, but Lesley was less forthcoming about that side of it. Mrs. Tregear sniffed, pointedly.

'I don't know what you would like to call it, then,' she said. 'Now, there's one that does all right for himself, Satan looks after his own they say and there's the living proof. Mr. Howells hasn't any call to take too much notice of what such as he says, you can tell him that from me. There's none in St. Erbyn has any love for that Angwin.'

'Has he had the Fish long?' asked Debbie, against her better judgement.

'Five or six years, if you count his little holiday.' Mrs. Tregear wasn't without her own brand of humour. 'He's done a wonderful lot with that old place, I'll give him that, but ambition is all very well in its way, there's no need to trample on others on your way to the top, and that's what I say. A shame it was, the way he treated Mr. and Mrs. Howells, and seeing who he is them justices should have known better.'

On balance, Debbie thought she had to agree with this, but then, she didn't know Mawgan's side of the argument and neither, she assumed, did Mrs. Tregear. Feeling that she might be venturing into overfalls, she tried to change course.

'Did you know Mrs. Latter, who was here before?'

'Oh yes, everybody knew Mrs. L! I worked for her until she died, many's the time I've cleaned this same basin.' Heavy breathing filled a gap in the conversation as Mrs. Tregear got onto her knees to polish the pedestal. 'My daughter works down at the Fish. I don't like it for her, things being the way that they are, but a job is a job these days. If Mrs. Howells found she needed someone extra, I'm sure she'd be glad to leave. Mr. Angwin's not an easy one to work for, very particular and a hard way with words if things are a bit rushed, as if we don't all get behind sometimes! Cheek, if you ask me, you'd think he'd be glad to sing small after what he did, but no, not him.'

'I suppose you can't run a business properly *pianissimo*,' said Debbie, but satire was as much wasted on Mrs. Tregear as it was on Mawgan himself.

'After all that's happened, he shouldn't go around whistling as if the heavens never fell on him,' she said, firmly. 'It's neither right nor nice. And as for criticising them as has led decent, God-fearing lives and never raised a hand in anger — well!'

'Oh well,' said Debbie, uncomfortably. She shook the duvet into place on the bed. 'I've finished in here now, Mrs. Tregear, I'll get on and do number seven.'

She went into the next room, putting herself out of temptation's way. She would dearly have liked to know a little more about Mawgan Angwin's fall from grace, but she disliked the idea of gossiping about him behind his back. She was still having the greatest difficulty in reconciling the things she had learned since she came to St. Erbyn with her original concept of him. She wondered a lot as she pummelled pillows and fought with the duvet covers just what were the rights and wrongs of it all.

Killing someone, however accidentally, really did go beyond the definition of pure carelessness. Perhaps it had been a motor accident, although Lesley hadn't sounded as if she thought so. But then, Lesley was prejudiced, and with reason if rumour didn't lie.

It was a hefty sentence, these days, for a death resulting from an accident. Three years. Two years in prison and a third out on parole, on his best behaviour. A yob on probation, as he had said, that was how most would see him. Except that "yob" was a bad description.

She went on wondering.

Debbie managed to keep a jump ahead of Mrs. Tregear for a room or two, which seemed to be the best way of preventing further revelations, but they met again when Lesley called up the stairs to say that there was a cup of tea in the kitchen. Lesley had no particular feelings one way or the other about gossip, she was glad to talk to anyone and made no attempt to prevent Mrs. Tregear from saying whatever she liked, and since the affairs of the Fish were at the top of the local gossip table, they were very soon served up with the tea. Lesley listened, and Debbie had to listen too.

'There was a manager in while he was the guest of the Queen,' said Mrs. Tregear, savouring the phrase. 'A nice man, he was, but he left when Mr. Angwin was let out on parole. Didn't like it for his wife, he said. Mind you, the place wasn't the same with Mr. Baines there, but then, who needs all these frills and furbelows with their food? Plain meat and two veg is good enough for ordinary folk, and not at thirty or forty pounds the throw, neither!'

'Wow!' said Debbie, looking impressed as she was obviously supposed to, although being familiar with London prices she actually thought it sounded remarkably reasonable.

'That's what you can easy pay for a meal down there, so my daughter tells me,' said Mrs. Tregear. 'For one person, that is, mind you, and then there's the wine on top of that – not just a murderer, a robber too, I told her!'

Debbie found this funny, which perhaps she shouldn't have, but Mawgan had never struck her as either of those things. She drank some tea to cover a smile, and Lesley said, listlessly, 'Success always seems to go to the wrong people.'

'And you never spoke a truer word, Mrs. Howells!' Mrs. Tregear launched off onto a new tack. 'Not that any of us begrudges a man success as he's worked for – we all wished him well when he first come here with that friend of his, and him not even an incomer but Cornish born and bred, and not so far from here neither. I'll admit it, when we read what he done in the papers we couldn't none of us believe it, and when that Coroner said as it was murder – well! But that, they say, it wasn't, and when he come home there wasn't a decent-thinking man nor woman in the village as didn't feel as he'd paid for what he done, and should be helped put it behind him. We thought he'd be a bit down, like, but not him! Just drove up one day as if he'd been no further than Helston, walked in the place and carried on as if nothing had happened. Killed his own kin and come home laughing – it didn't go down well in the village, I can tell you! Never a sign of repentance, and him raised good Chapel too – bouncier than ever if anything, you'd think he hadn't an ounce of shame in him! And that poor little sister of his a widow in her weeds!'

This was too much even for Lesley, who choked into her tea and had to be thumped on the back. She put down her mug and got to her feet.

'I'm going to spend half an hour in the office, Deb,' she said. 'When Tim comes back, tell him where I am. I've some work to catch up on.'

The laughter had died from her face, and as she left the kitchen Debbie watched her go with a frown. Roger had succeeded in making her feel guilty about Lesley – needlessly, surely, for she hadn't done anything – and she thought that Lesley had something more than usual on her mind. She followed her to the tiny office very soon, therefore, and found her sitting at the desk staring at the reservations book with a hopeless expression on her face. She looked up as Debbie came in, and said without preamble.

'It isn't going to work, Deb.'

'What isn't?' asked Debbie.

'This – any of it. Tim thinks it's paradise on earth, but it isn't. Look at the bookings – July and August aren't too bad, I suppose, but look at this month! After that last burst, there's almost nothing. We can't manage on eight weeks' trade, Deb, it's impossible. We were reckoning on three times that. And Tim wants all his sailing money to go back into that side of the business, he wants more boats. *More boats!* It's as if we were running two separate businesses, his and mine!' She buried her face momentarily in her hands, and then peered out at Debbie between them. She sounded scared.

Debbie turned the book round so that she could see it properly and studied it.

'I see what you mean. One couple on the eighteenth – is that *all* for that week?'

'You can see that it is. I suppose Tim may get the odd casual, but it won't help much.'

Debbie bit her little finger, thoughtfully.

'You could advertise a bit more.'

'Advertising eats money – if it's to do any good, anyway. And the overheads on this place are enormous, money seems to run out like water. It frightens me Deb, and Tim spends all day on the river, and then goes out drinking every evening, buys rounds for everyone, as if he thinks the Lord will send ravens, or something. He seems to forget *they* should be paying *us*! What shall I do?'

So quickly had dreams become nightmares.

'Help me,' said Lesley. Her eyes were full of pleading, huge, tired eyes that had once sparkled with fun. Debbie could think of nothing sensible to say.

'How can I? I'd like to, Les, but I know nothing about catering – or your private affairs, or anything.'

'Our *private* affairs can be summed up in one word,' said Lesley, caustically. 'Disastrous!'

'Tim doesn't mean it,' said Debbie, helplessly.

'Oh, I know you can't teach sailing without sailing yourself, and I know that someone has to entertain the guests. Only those are things he enjoys. I know I said I've no violent objections to housework, but nobody actually enjoys it on this scale, do they?'

It was old ground, and there were no answers, they already knew that.

'We all help where we can.'

'You and Roger do,' conceded Lesley. 'Tim only came to the Cash & Carry with me because it was Roger who suggested it. He wouldn't have if I'd asked him.'

'You don't know that.'

'I do know that. Tim's idea of helping me is to generously suggest I employ someone else – as if we can even afford it! Anyway, it isn't the point. You know it isn't, if you think about it.' She paused. 'I'm not totally selfish, Deb, I don't expect everyone to run around helping me when they've things of their own to do, and I've Mrs. Tregear, it's… I don't know how to explain what it is without sounding petty.'

'Try,' said Debbie.

Lesley looked down at her hands as they rested on the upside-down book. She thought that she probably would sound petty, and that Debbie would despise her for it. Debbie was so superbly confident. She had no worries, she was well cushioned against life's blows. The thought sneaked into Lesley's mind, treacherously, that Debbie could afford to put money into the business to help them, but she dismissed it. You couldn't ask that of friends, not when the business was teetering on the edge of catastrophe.

'Last week,' she said. 'All those people… you three made friends with them. You were out on the water with them all day, you knew their first names and what they did, and they knew you and liked you – respected you. You could all do something they wanted to be able to do. They thought I was the hired help. Tim didn't even bother to introduce me.'

Debbie was silent. There was nothing to be said because it was true, and she and Roger were to blame too.

'I don't know anything about the things you all talked about,' Lesley went on. 'I don't know a thing about boats, I expect they found me dull, anyway. I expect they all do, none of them ever says much to me. I'd sooner stay at home, even if it means that I sit on my own, worrying – and Tim lets me, Deb. Nearly all last week, he let me.'

'But that cuts both ways. If you say that to him, he'll say you could have come if you'd wanted, and he did ask you. And you could take an interest in the boats, and learn something to talk about.'

'If we'd had a licence, it would have been different.'

'I don't see how. We'd still have been talking about the same things. People – most of them anyway – come here to learn about sailing. Of course they want to talk about it.'

'But I could have come and gone if I'd been bored, and still been part of it. I could have knitted, or read, or helped behind the bar. People always chat up barmaids. At the Fish, all I can do is sit and feel out of things.'

Debbie made a helpless gesture with her hands, and Lesley said, 'I'm not trying to be awkward, honestly. I just don't seem to fit in.'

She sounded depressed, and Debbie, unable to find any comfort to offer her, left her to her problems and went down on to the foreshore, where she sat on the jetty and thought, not about Lesley and Tim and their troubles, but about Mawgan Angwin and his. There was small choice in rotten apples after all, and both sets of problems seemed equally insoluble.

At least she wouldn't be dragged into Mawgan's, he was very well able to take care of himself.

Life was probably more comfortable if you didn't let yourself like anybody. Liking people brought them too close to you, and people too close to you were always a nuisance. Parents – friends – sisters – even the agony of her dearly-loved brother wouldn't have been such agony for her if she hadn't cared so much for him.

I wish I could be detached and aloof, and simply not care, thought Debbie, people's problems are so messy, and completely failed to recognise that the wish was the first step along the opposite path.

Lesley's burst of confidences in the office preyed on Debbie's mind and on her conscience, until in the end she felt forced to say something about it. The chance came on the following Saturday, when they had only a small change-over, and Tim decided that there was time, for once, to go for what he termed a personal sail. Roger was in charge of the casual trade, weekends brought business, but they could steal a boat for once. There was nothing left to do in the house.

'Would you like to come out with me, Deb? It's a great day for a sail.'

Debbie hesitated, Roger's remarks as well as Lesley's uncomfortably in her mind. She wasn't conceited, she hoped, but she wasn't stupid either.

'Why not take Lesley?'

'She wouldn't want to come. She'll have things to do.'

'She might let them wait for once. You could help her later.'

Tim scowled.

'Oh no, we're not back at that again!' he groaned.

'Come off it, Tim! I only suggested you took your own wife sailing.'

'She won't come. She never does.'

'When did you last ask her?'

'I've asked her plenty of times. Even before we were married, she never would.'

Debbie sighed with exasperation, not sure which of the two of them, Tim or Lesley, was trying the hardest to make difficulties.

'It was a bit different, wasn't it, when you left her ashore at the sailing club with all your friends, and went racing?'

Tim knew a tight corner when he saw one.

'I'll ask her,' he said. 'I'll ask her – I promise.'

He did ask her. He said, 'Les, Deb thought you might like to come sailing with me this afternoon, instead of her. Would you?'

'No thank you,' said Lesley. 'I've too much to do.'

End of conversation. Debbie, despairing of them both, went to fetch her life-jacket.

It was a beautiful afternoon. The tide was well in and they sailed up river as far as Polwheveral Creek and then back again to the mouth of the river. The water was blue under the early summer sky, glittering with reflected sunlight and warm and silky to trail the fingers in on the lazy reach home over the start of the ebb. Debbie, lolling on the centre thwart relaxed and at peace with the world, ventured a remark.

'If we bought some beer,' she suggested, 'we wouldn't have to go down to the Fish in the evening.'

'We couldn't re-sell it,' objected Tim.

'Who'd know?'

'I wouldn't trust Angwin not to guess.'

'He wouldn't care if he did,' said Debbie.

'Want a bet?'

'All right then,' said Debbie, recognising unreasoning prejudice. 'Get it from the supermarket, then he won't even know. Or suggest that they go down and buy their own and bring it back, nobody can possibly object to that. We can all go, and bring back supplies and drink them in the lounge.'

'Where's the point? I don't like Angwin, but he runs a good pub. There's more atmosphere there than there is at home.'

'There's no atmosphere at all at home,' pointed out Debbie. 'We haven't tried to create one.' Not the right sort, anyway, she mentally added. Tim said, argumentatively, 'We can't make an atmosphere without proper facilities.'

'It's a nice enough house.'

'It's a dry house,' said Tim. 'We can't even serve wine with Lesley's admirable cooking.'

'We could suggest that people provide their own.'

'Bloody Angwin!' said Tim, not for the first time. 'How could my having a licence have hurt him?'

It was a question that Debbie had asked herself, and more than once. She found it difficult equating such pettiness with her friend at the cottage – but then, that had been an abnormal situation. People, she had noticed before, were different against a different background, and there was obviously a lot more than she knew to know about Mawgan anyway.

The sailing school came into view round the curve of the cliff, and Debbie remembered something she had noticed several times now, and wanted to investigate. There was still enough water in the river, she calculated. She pointed it out to Tim.

'See that creek there? What's up there, does it go anywhere?'

'Just one or two houses,' said Tim. 'Do you want to have a look? They're rather nice.' He altered course slightly. 'They had boats laid up there last winter, but it dries out about two hours before low water.'

The boat sailed gently onward, and the creek opened up ahead of them, a quiet stretch of water that lapped against a high revetment, with a narrow walkway along the bottom and steps leading up at intervals. There were rings set into the walkway, and one or two small boats tied up. One yacht, with lines laid out astern. Above, a row of houses, waterside dwellings in a variety of styles, all fairly old. One or two of them had dates set in the wall above the door, Debbie read 1897, 1903, 1911... what a wonderful place to have a house! She said so.

'What a gorgeous place to live! Do any of them ever come up for sale?'

'They must do sometimes, but not very often I should think. Probably when people die and get carried out feet first, it looks that sort of place. Why, do you want one?'

'I wish!' said Debbie. 'No, I was thinking of Chel and Oliver.'

'I thought they were living in Greece now.'

'Yes, but not permanently. They're just idling around in somebody's villa, passing the time.' The boat sailed on, barely rippling the water under the shelter of overhanging trees on the bank opposite to the houses. There was the sound of birds singing, and a gull flew by, low on the water. 'Look,' said Debbie, pointing ahead. 'Swans!'

'We're going to run out of water in a minute,' said Tim. 'Going about – ' There was a moment of action, then they were sailing back towards the river. 'Ask Mrs. Tregear,' he suggested. 'She knows everything. But hasn't Oliver started painting, or something? Won't he want a studio?'

'He can put up a shed, I suppose,' said Debbie. 'I don't know – perhaps it's a silly idea.'

'Knowing your family, he'll run a mile from the idea of having you so close,' said Tim.

'Maybe.' They slid out of the shelter of the creek, and the boat heeled gently, feeling the wind again. Debbie shifted position to balance it. 'I will ask though, that's a good idea. You never know.'

St. Erbyn came back into view, a cluster of grey and colour-washed cottages climbing the hill towards the trees, with the Fisherman's Arms white as salt in the sunshine drowsing on the foreshore to the left of the picture. Closer to them, their own jetty ran out into the water with a small figure in a bright blue dress sitting on the end.

'There's Lesley,' said Debbie. Tim grunted, gybed without warning, and bore away for the short run in.

'I thought she was oh, so terribly busy, looking after about four people,' he muttered, almost inaudibly. Debbie bit her lip, exasperated.

'Don't be like that, Tim.'

'Perhaps,' said Tim, suavely, 'we should employ chambermaids and waitresses, as well as Mrs. Tregear.'

Debbie felt her patience slip. It had been a pleasant afternoon, but the nearer they came to the shore, the more she felt all the old grievances sitting there waiting for them like so many unfed stray cats.

'I'm surprised you don't get on better with poor Angwin,' she said, waspishly. 'Going on your estimate of him, you should have a lot in common!'

'Pigswill of the world, unite?'

'You're not being fair. To Lesley, I mean.'

'Lost the knack of it,' said Tim. 'Sorry.'

'She's drawn the short straw, and you know it.'

'She volunteered for it. I even recall her saying that she was going to enjoy it. It's a bit late to start crying about it now.'

'She had no idea what it would really be like,' said Debbie, adding shrewdly, 'and neither had you.'

'Never answer the unanswerable,' said Tim, as if to himself. He asked, 'All right, what do you want me to do?'

Debbie wanted to inform him that he shouldn't need telling, but she had the sense to see that it wouldn't help. She said, instead, 'Stop criticising her so much and introduce her to people as your wife when she fights her way out of the kitchen,' and was satisfied to see a tide of bright colour wash over his face.

Lesley walked back along the jetty and came down on the foreshore with a launching trolley, meeting them as the bow grounded on the shingle and Debbie leapt out to hold the boat. There was a strange, almost excited look on her face.

'An odd thing happened while you were out,' she said, as she helped to haul the boat up the shingle. 'Some people came in off the road and wanted to know if we had any rooms vacant.'

'That doesn't sound very odd to me,' said Tim. 'We let rooms for a living, there's a sign outside that says so, if you remember.'

Lesley gave him an old-fashioned look almost of dislike, and Debbie said, hastily, 'What were they like?'

'Foreigners – Swedes, I think. There were two of them, but actually, there's four, when they come. But...' She seemed oddly reluctant to continue.

'But what?' asked Tim impatiently, and Lesley said, 'They're staying at the Fish.'

Both Tim and Debbie stared at her.

'Then why do they want to come here?' asked Tim, understandably bewildered.

'They don't like it, apparently. They say it's noisy, and the landlord was rude to them, and they're not a bit comfortable. And their old father has a drink problem, and staying in the Fish doesn't help.'

'It wouldn't, of course,' said Debbie, with a grin. Tim said, 'He'll have a drink problem here, too. Don't we all?'

It was obvious that the prospect of doing Angwin in the eye to the tune of four lost guests was putting him in a good mood. There was a sparkle in his eye that had been missing for some days.

'I thought we might as well take them,' said Lesley. 'If they don't come here, they'll only go somewhere else and we could use the money. Did I do the right thing?'

'I should think so!' Tim grinned happily. 'I'd love to be a fly on the wall when Angwin finds out where they've gone!'

'He'd swat you,' said Lesley. She smiled at him, and he smiled back.

Some time later, Debbie was stopped on her way through the hall by a handsome, middle-aged man with a quiet manner, who asked in a strong foreign accent,

'I wish to speak with Mrs. Howells, is this possible, please? Or Mr. Howells, it does not matter. Can you tell me where I find them?'

Lesley was up to her eyes in dinner, Tim was down in the boathouse with Roger, clearing up.

'Perhaps I can help,' suggested Debbie.

'It is about my father.' He leaned forward, putting his face close to hers. 'I wish to speak about my father. It is in confidence, you understand this?'

'Of course,' said Debbie, mystified.

'He has the problem. With the drink, you understand. He likes to drink but he has a heart, and his doctor says he must not drink. My mother, too. They must not drink.'

He must not drink, she must not drink, they must not drink. It sounded like one of those interminable French verbs people had once been made to learn at school. Debbie was tempted to say that they would have their work cut out to drink here, but thought she had better not.

'That's no problem,' she said. 'This is a dry house.'

'A what?' He stared at her in bewilderment. Debbie tried to explain.

'We don't have a licence. We can only sell soft drinks, and tea and coffee. We can't sell alcohol, we're not allowed.'

She thought he looked startled as much as anything, and decided that he, too, had a drink problem now. That of where it was going to come from.

'No alcohol at all?' he asked, as if he could hardly believe it, and Debbie said, finally, 'None. Unless you buy it and bring it in for yourselves.'

'That will be all right, then,' he said, uncertainly, and Debbie left him to his dismay and went down to the kitchen to recount this story to Roger and Lesley. With so few people in, Mrs. Tregear wasn't here tonight, she had been given the evening off. They all giggled over it, unaware in their innocence that perhaps it wasn't all that funny. Tim laughed too, when he came in and they told him.

In deference to Debbie's remarks that afternoon, Tim took Roger down to the Fish while the guests were dining and brought back a few cans of beer and lager and a bottle of gin. Debbie wondered a little what effect this action might have on their latest house guests, but in the event they all disappeared to their rooms very shortly after dinner was over. The remainder of the guests, and Lesley, Tim, Debbie and Roger, foregathered in the lounge, talked until the moon was high in the heavens, and broke up to go to bed with no sense of impending doom, after an evening that everyone had enjoyed. It had lacked the conviviality of an evening spent down at the Fish, but it had been pleasant, and hopefully might have set some kind of pattern for the coming week. Tim, gathering up empties after the guests had retired to their rooms, voiced what all the others were thinking, and not saying for fear of starting him off again.

'If it wasn't for Angwin, it would have worked out a treat,' he said.

'It will work very well as things are,' said Lesley, who had enjoyed herself, more at ease in her own house.

Tim was in a benign mood from the presence of the four pirated guests.

'We'll do it again,' he said. 'It made a change.'

Debbie picked up the tray of empty glasses and went out into the hall, where she was surprised to find an old gentleman in a dressing-gown coming down the stairs. He was huge, well over six feet tall and broad as the Albert Memorial, with scanty grey hair decorating a bullet head set on a neck like a Sumo wrestler's, and little bright eyes peering out on either side of a large purple nose, pitted like a Seville orange and bulbous as a Chianti bottle. His drink problem needed no PR work, it advertised itself. He swept regally downward, and stopped when he reached the hall.

'My wife must have a drink,' he announced. 'Without a drink, she cannot sleep.'

Debbie offered cocoa, her head tilted back uncomfortably to address this mountain on legs. His face turned a shade darker.

'A drink, I said. Champagne. She must have champagne. You have champagne?'

His breath hit her like a blast from a distillery. Debbie, beginning to be mildly alarmed, noticed that he swayed a little on his feet and took a cautious step backwards, if he collapsed on her, she thought she might be flattened.

'I'm so sorry,' she said, for the second time that day. 'This is a dry house. I can get your wife a hot drink if she'd like one.'

'She does not wish a hot drink,' he said majestically, leaning close and blasting her with such intoxicating fumes that she imagined her head swam. 'She is thirsty. A hot drink – no!' He made an abrupt, flat gesture with his hand.

'I'm sorry,' said Debbie, again. 'There's only squash, coca cola, or juice.'

'I saw beer earlier. Beer would be good.'

'I'm sorry,' she repeated. 'It belonged to the other guests, and they drank it.'

'They have beer, and my wife cannot?' he roared, and swayed towards her once more. She stepped back again. An unworthy suspicion had just entered her head, which she had no intention of sharing with Tim and Lesley. Was it remotely possible that the Svensen family hadn't left the Fish of their own volition? She acquitted Mawgan of sending them here deliberately, but she couldn't see him taking any backchat from drunken Swedes at midnight. At least, not more than once.

'Just the things I said,' she said, firmly. 'If you want beer you must ask your son to buy it for you.' Let him deal with his own drunken father, she thought grimly. Colossus muttered angrily, and his eyes snapped at her, jewel-bright and furious.'

'Squash!' he growled. 'All right, if that is all there is, it must be squash. But I am not pleased, my wife will not be pleased. You may bring this squash at once so that my wife may drink. I wait upstairs.' He turned, and with a majesty only slightly marred by his unsteady tread, began to climb the stairs once more.

'What was all that about?' asked Tim, when Debbie came into the kitchen. She recounted the tale of the thirsty wife.

'You might have come to help,' she added. Tim grinned.

'We thought you were doing very nicely on your own,' he said. 'What was the problem?'

'He was as pissed as a newt,' said Debbie, shortly.

'He can't have been,' said Roger.

'Well, he was. If someone had lighted a match, the whole place would have gone up in flames!'

Roger assumed a thoughtful expression.

'I thought their cases seemed a bit heavy when I brought them in,' he said.

Lesley had prepared a jug of orange squash, heavily laced with ice, and put it on a tray with two glasses.

'Here you are, this will cool him down a bit.'

Debbie thought that Tim or Roger might like to take it upstairs instead of her, but they declined the treat.

'He's expecting you,' said Tim. 'Always give the punters what they expect.'

'His wife wouldn't like it,' was Roger's excuse. Lesley just grinned, they all thought it was very funny.

The elder Mrs. Svenson was lying with her face turned to the wall when Debbie got upstairs, and appeared to be in some sort of stupor, and the atmosphere in the bedroom was on a par with the bar at the Fish on a busy evening. Debbie handed over the orange squash to a towering, glowering Swede and made her way over to the staff quarters in a thoughtful mood.

Tomorrow, she thought, might prove interesting, it would certainly be different from usual. She began to appreciate Lesley's point of view.

XI

The younger Mr. Svensen caught Lesley in the hall after breakfast, and apologised on behalf of his father.

'I have spoken with him, he is sorry,' he said. 'I take the whisky that he hid in his room, it will not happen again I promise you. My wife and I wish to go out today, Mrs. Howells, may we leave my parents here in your care? We will collect them at lunch time, but this morning my wife wishes to shop. They will sit in the sun and be no trouble.'

'What could I say?' said Lesley, relating this to the others in the kitchen. 'I couldn't very well say, get out of here and take them with you. Anyway, perhaps it was an isolated incident, we don't know.'

'Father's a crafty sod,' said Roger, appreciatively. 'Good luck to the old soak, I say!'

The elder Mr. and Mrs. Svensen sat on the terrace outside the lounge during the morning, and drank orange squash. Sunday was Mrs. Tregear's day off, but Lesley kept a close eye on them as far as she could, and she was almost certain that it was orange squash.

'But I can't be *absolutely* sure,' she said, when the others came indoors to help with the lunchtime shift at the sink. 'They seemed to be enjoying it rather… they had a little jug…'

'Have they said anything?' asked Tim. 'They look very peaceful out there.'

'I went out and chatted to them earlier,' said Lesley. 'Just for a minute. He's an interesting man, he was captain of a sail training ship before he retired. I told him about Oliver, Deb, he was impressed, but he doesn't have a high opinion of Wayfarers.'

'That maybe explains the nose,' said Roger, grinning.

'And the drink problem,' suggested Tim. 'Blasting round the horn on a square-rigger – pow!'

Debbie's unworthy suspicion of the night before was growing into a certainty. With the growth of suspicion there grew, side by side, a sneaking idea that they were in shoal water, quite probably with reefs ahead.

'Perhaps we ought to encourage them to go,' she said.

From the expressions on the faces of Tim and Lesley, she realised that this thought had already occurred to them. She enlarged on the theme.

'I'm not at all sure they ought to drink themselves senseless on unlicensed premises. Anyway, they're a terrible responsibility. Their son has gone out, and they're not supposed to drink at all. What do we do if they drop dead, plastered, and he comes back and accuses us of killing them?' The part of Sweeny Todd wouldn't suit Tim. Mawgan had at least refrained from bumping off his customers.

'How do you ask a guest to go?' asked Tim, doubtfully. 'If they've done nothing? After all, we're not absolutely sure about the drink this time, are we?'

Debbie didn't know the answers to any of these questions, and neither did Lesley or Roger.

'Oh well,' said Lesley, hopefully. 'They're being very good now. Let's let them alone.'

'I think Deb and Roger had better look after the students this afternoon,' said Tim. 'I'll stay ashore. You can manage, can't you Deb? There's only the four of them.'

Lesley's face reflected her pleasure in this suggestion, but unfortunately, before it could be put into practice, the younger Svensens returned. They were not going out again, they said, they would sit in the garden while their parents rested, and they proceeded to do just that.

'They drank orange squash, too,' said Lesley, uneasily when the others returned from the river. 'They're up in their rooms now. They want dinner there, I didn't know what to say.'

'Parents too?' asked Debbie, determined to carry no more trays to drunken ship's captains.

'All of them. It's a bit odd, isn't it?'

Roger strolled in from the garden, returning from his usual pre-dinner jog.

'I hate to depress you,' he said. 'I passed their car as I came in – the Swedes' car. I just thought I'd have a look, it wasn't locked. The boot is wall-to-wall gin bottles.'

'Oh *God!*' cried Lesley, and dropped the basket of rolls she was holding.

Certainty finally solidified. Debbie wondered whether it was funny or disastrous. It would depend a lot on what happened next, she decided.

'They can't come to much harm in bed,' said Roger, comfortingly, and strolled off to shower and change before becoming a waiter.

'Whatever are we going to do?' demanded Lesley, gathering up the scattered rolls. 'We've got the worst of the season to come yet, is everyone going to be like this?'

'I hardly think so.' Debbie rescued a roll that had gone under the table and returned it to the basket. 'You haven't had any alcoholics before, have you?'

'Some of them have been a bit difficult,' said Lesley. She looked at the rolls in the basket. 'These are all we have. Do you think anyone will notice?'

'They won't know, if you don't tell them,' Debbie pointed out.

'I bet *Angwin* wouldn't serve them.'

'The difference there is that Angwin wouldn't have dropped them in the first place. Cheer up, Les, for goodness sake. Worse things happen at sea!'

'Yes – on square-riggers!' said Lesley, bitterly.

Dinner was only marred by the fact that when Debbie took the tray up to the younger Svensens, she found them otherwise engaged.

'They said *come in* when I knocked,' she said, scarlet to the tips of her ears. 'I don't consider myself as narrow-minded, but really, I thought for a moment there they were going to suggest three-in-a-bed!'

Tim and Roger thought that this was the funniest thing of all, but Lesley was reaching the end of her tolerance.

'They'll have to go,' she said. 'It's no good, we can't keep them. We shall never know what they're going to do next.'

'Oh come on Les, they've not done any harm yet,' said Tim. She looked at him scornfully.

'Do we wait until they have, is that what you're suggesting? They're all drunk as skunks! All that gin!'

'I never heard of gin being used as an aphrodisiac before,' mused Roger. 'It always works just the opposite for me. You can't just tip them out, Lesley, that idea's a dead duck. They'd sue you, or something.'

'I'm not sure that they would – or could,' said Debbie.

'Oh, you know everything!' said Lesley, unreasonably. 'Ask your friend Angwin, why don't you? He looks as if he enjoys a good laugh!' She stopped speaking abruptly, and a curious look came over her face. Her eyes swivelled round to Debbie, circular with speculation, and her mouth opened and firmly shut again.

'I'll see to the coffee,' said Debbie, hurriedly.

'I'll help you,' said Lesley.

Over the tray of cups in the lounge, they faced each other.

'He wouldn't, would he?' Lesley muttered, under cover of the conversation among the other guests. Debbie didn't pretend to misunderstand her.

'No, he wouldn't,' she said. 'I'd put money on it.'

'He always strikes me as a bit of a tease,' said Lesley.

'I'm sure you're wrong.'

'They did come here from the Fish.'

'I know they did,' said Debbie. 'I think he got rid of them somehow – but I can't believe he sent them here. They just came of their own accord.'

'What do we do?' asked Lesley, appalled.

'I don't know,' said Debbie, and added, slowly, 'but I might know a man who does.'

Their eyes met conspiratorially.

'You wouldn't!' said Lesley.

'Why not? It seems to me the obvious thing to do.'

'You must never let Tim know.'

'God, no!' Debbie shuddered at the idea.

After the guests were settled with their coffee, Debbie said she thought it would be nice if Tim and Roger cleared the tables for once, and that stacking the washing-up machine was hardly rocket science. She and Lesley, she said, would go down to the Fish for the beer, they needed some air. Tim looked as if he would have liked to argue, but Roger only grinned good-naturedly, and said, 'Don't forget to bring enough back for the Svensens.'

Leaving the house was almost like escaping from it; behind the brightly lit windows trouble lurked like an unexploded bomb. They hurried down the hill together, giggling like schoolgirls released from school.

'Just don't bring me into it,' begged Lesley. 'Tim would never forgive me. I'll get the beer and wait outside for you, and you'll have to go into the restaurant and ask for him. He's never in the bar in the evening.'

'It's Sunday,' said Debbie. 'The restaurant'll be closed, he could be anywhere.'

Lesley stopped.

'I never thought of that. Well, you go into the restaurant part where the locals can't spy on you, and I'll ask Tommy if he can get Angwin to join you – oh God, I hope he's not gone out or something.'

'This is ridiculous!' said Debbie, not sure whether to laugh or not.

'You must, Deb. The Tregear clan are everywhere!'

For some reason, this struck both of them as exquisitely funny, and they arrived at the door to the bar in fits of laughter. The Fish was crowded, the patrons of the two bars spilling out onto the forecourt. The people sitting about at the tables looked at them indulgently, two pretty blondes having a good time. Debbie pulled herself together – well, more or less together. She saluted, smartly.

'Good luck, Captain Howells, sir. I'm going over the top now!'

Lesley went into the bar, still laughing, and Debbie went round to the residents' and restaurant entrance. As she approached it, slowly because the nearer she came to her goal, the more outrageous her behaviour seemed to become, she noticed something that she must have seen many times over the door to the bars and never before fully registered.

*THOMAS THOMAS, Licensed to Sell Alcoholic Liquor
for Consumption On or Off the Premises.*

Tommy was the Licensee. Not Mawgan. Of course, he would have to be, Mawgan was a convicted criminal, technically still serving a sentence. Laughter vanished as swiftly as if someone had thrown a switch.

'*Oh shit!*' said Debbie, under her breath, and went inside.

In the hall, she hesitated. There was nobody around; the shutter was down over the reception window, although beyond the foot of the stairs that rose to the landing above, she could see an open lounge area where a couple of people were sitting reading newspapers. Overnight guests, she supposed, replacements for the terrible Svensens. Otherwise, the place was utterly deserted. After a moment, she reached out and tentatively touched the bell beside the reception window.

'Can I help you, Deborah?' asked Mawgan, behind her, and she swung round to find him coming down the stairs.

'They rang through from the bar to say you were here,' he said, reaching the bottom. 'What's up now?'

'I was looking for you,' said Debbie, wondering why it was that she always opened her mouth and said something stupid when she came near him. He grinned at her.

'Yes, I worked out that much. Any particular reason?'

'Of course. I know it's probably an imposition on your night off, but can you spare a moment?'

'Night off is good! What's one of them? It'll have to be a very short moment, I'm meant to be in the bar, so is it private, or can we talk here?'

'Private would be good. I mean, I don't want to shout about it.'

Mawgan said, 'Come in the office then.' He opened a door on the left beyond reception and switched on the light. '*Come into my parlour, said the spider to the fly*. Sit down. Now, what's the problem?'

Debbie sat. It was a very different kind of office from Lesley's cubbyhole up the road, being much given over to computers and fax machines. Poor Lesley wouldn't know where to begin here, she and modern technology had only a nodding acquaintance – which, now she came to think about it, made it doubly unfair that Tim wouldn't – didn't anyway – help her.

'You're busy,' she said. 'I'm sorry, I shouldn't have come when the bar was open.'

'The place won't fall apart if I turn my back a minute.' He perched on the edge of a large desk. 'Or, heads will roll if it does. So? What is it?'

'It's about some Swedes,' said Debbie, and looked straight at him. He stared at her, and she watched an unholy glee deepen in his eyes.

'Swedes? Oops! I don't suppose you need telling how to cook 'em, so it must be – has to be – the Svensen family.'

'It's not funny,' said Debbie.

'Oh, yes it is! You've no idea how funny! Did they go from me to your two little innocent friends? No wonder Mrs. Howells has that hunted look!'

'Mawgan, please be serious,' begged Debbie. 'You must realise that only the direst emergency would have made Lesley let me come to you for advice.'

'What've they done? Set fire to the place? It wouldn't never surprise me.'

Debbie told him about the orange squash – or not, maybe – and about the wall-to-wall gin bottles, and he was unimpressed.

'They aren't trying. Haven't they thrown nothing yet?'

'*Mawgan!*' exclaimed Debbie. 'I told you, I'm here asking for help.'

'Can't Howells solve his own problems?'

The joke was suddenly over. Debbie looked at him.

'He doesn't know I'm here.'

'I didn't suppose so. I'm surprised his wife let you. Did she tell you what he said to me?'

'No,' said Debbie. 'Well… not exactly. She told me what you said to him.'

'Oh.' Very non-committal.

'Was he very rude?' asked Debbie, nervously.

'Yes, very. I did'n' like it, in my own bar, in front of my own customers. Do you blame me?'

'He was upset,' said Debbie, thinking how awkward it was to be on both sides at once.

'So, what'd I do that was so dreadful? He's a grown-up, he can't expect to have everything his own way.'

'You didn't have to topple his ivory tower quite so brutally.'

'Did I? I hadn't realised.'

'If you had – '

'I'd've done it just the same. I'm in business – I can't afford to be sentimental.'

'But why?' asked Debbie. 'What possible difference would it make to you if he had a licence? Be honest – it wouldn't make any at all!'

'That's not quite true. If I try'n explain it you, will you promise not to go biting me – at least until I'm done?'

Debbie promised.

'But make it good,' she advised. 'I like Tim and Lesley. You've spoiled their party.'

'Babes in the wood, they are,' said Mawgan, and it might have sounded condescending, but didn't. 'That's the whole point, Deborah. They've got a nice property along there, in a prime waterside position, and they've got a load of over-ambitious ideas to go with it, and as far as I can see, no capital behind them. If they got an on-licence as they wanted, of course it wouldn't have made no difference to me because there's no chance they'll take things any further, in spite of all their fine plans. What would have made a difference is the all too obvious fact that at the end of this season, or possibly at the end of next if they've a kind-hearted bank manager, they're going to go bust. When they sell up, as they will, the person who buys them out – with an existing on-licence, if they'd got it, and who-knows-what planning permits by then – might well be the sort of person who would try to set up in direct competition with me – I don't mean the pub, but the restaurant, and the way things are, the planners might very well go for it. In this small village, there's not room for two of us. So hard luck, Tim and Lesley, and all right, I used them to create a precedent. I'm sorry, but that's how it goes. You look after number one in this life, if you're sensible, for you can bet your sweet life, nobody else is going to.'

Debbie looked at him as if she had never seen him before, and the hazel eyes under the strong black brows looked back at her, unsmiling.

'That told me,' she said.

'You asked, I thought.'

The discussion seemed to have reached an abrupt end. Debbie, suddenly confronted with something that she should have seen from the start, could find nothing sensible to say. A smooth operator. A professional. An intelligent man who had been humiliated in his own place and in public by an ignorant amateur, and an emmet at that. So much for Tim! Nobody could reasonably expect any help under this roof for the problems of Seagulls, they would have to sort them out for themselves as best they could.

'Now we've got the lecture out the way, let's take a look at your Swedish problem,' said Mawgan. 'The answer's very simple, and Howells will just have to steel himself to do it. They're only casuals, there's no contract. Show 'em what the door's for.'

'You make it sound so easy,' said Debbie, when she had got her breath back.

'But it is easy. If you don't want to tell it like it really is, tell them you're terribly sorry, but the rooms are taken. They'll go, don't worry – they must be used to it by now.'

'They'll see we're green, it sticks out a mile. Suppose they won't go? Suppose they sue us?'

'They didn't book a set stay, did they? Pay a deposit?'

'No. At least, I don't think so.'

'Then you've got no problem. Even if they had, I could provide you with any number of witnesses to tell what they did here. It'll be all right, I promise you.' He studied her worried face for a moment. 'Don't you lose no sleep over it, Deborah. People like that don't often cause trouble – not that sort of trouble. There are people that do, but maybe you won't be unlucky enough to meet them — and if you do, and if you can't handle it, you come straight here to me.'

Debbie stared at him.

'You're very magnanimous.'

'My bird, I can afford to be. And tell Mrs. Howells I'm sorry, if I thought they'd go in her direction, I would've rung and warned her — and in future, if I throw out a bad egg, I always will. And now, much as I like your company, I must go.' He stood up, and Debbie rose with him. For a moment, he hesitated.

'Do they give you remission for good behaviour up there? They give it me.'

Debbie wasn't certain if she was meant to laugh or not. She covered her uncertainty with a thoughtful look.

'There's only the four of us, but I suppose we shall have to have time off sometimes. We haven't discussed it yet.'

'You should complain to your shop steward,' Mawgan advised. 'You always get time off in a halfway decent job. Well, when they let you out, if they ever do, you let me know — that's if you've nothing better on, of course.'

'I'd like that,' said Debbie, startled. 'But supposing you're busy?'

'Then you can help me. But don't let Howells know, I don't want to be afraid to go out in the dark!'

Lesley and Debbie walked back up the hill together clutching their cans of beer, and Debbie retailed the generously offered advice on how to deal with Swedes pickled in spirits, together with Mawgan's final message about bad eggs. Lesley listened in silence, and then said, 'I suppose you got to know him pretty well when you were snowed up together.'

'Sort of,' said Debbie. 'He was too ill for most of the time. It didn't make for intimacy — not that kind, anyway.'

'He's a terribly attractive man. Tim says he's a gypsy, and he wouldn't trust him a yard.'

'I'm very fond of Tim, but he can say some awfully stupid things.'

'Don't I know it!' said Lesley, with feeling. She hesitated, and then said, 'He won't accept how ignorant we are, Deb. Catering is a jungle, I never realised how many innocent-looking people have such Jekyll-and-Hyde personalities. We're so inexperienced we're like children playing a game, and there's your friend Angwin just down the road, knowing the whole thing from A to Z, so what does Tim go and do? He falls out with him, and he couldn't have found anything more stupid, or less helpful, to do if he'd sat down and planned it!'

Debbie thought that this was a little unjust, after all the first blow had been struck by Mawgan himself in the cause of self-interest.

'Tim couldn't know he was a friend of mine,' she objected. 'I didn't myself, until I saw him here.'

'It doesn't alter the result,' said Lesley.

They walked on a yard or two in silence.

'If Tim had taken defeat gracefully, we could have picked his brains when things went wrong,' said Lesley. 'If we had someone to advise us, we might just avoid going under. Just someone to talk things over with would help… anything would help.'

Debbie hesitated. She hadn't told Lesley everything that Mawgan had said, apart from the obvious omission, because she wasn't at all sure that it was fair. But Lesley was in dire need of help, and it wasn't going to come from anywhere else. And Roger had made her feel guilty about Lesley. She said, 'He said – Mawgan said – that if we had any more trouble we couldn't handle, we were to go straight to him.'

Lesley stopped in her tracks. She peered at Debbie in the darkness under the trees.

'You're joking!'

Debbie took her arm and moved her on.

'Why should I be joking? He thinks he owes me something.'

'He does,' said Lesley, with conviction. 'If you hadn't chanced along, what would have happened to him when the stove went out? From what you told us, he was far too badly hurt, and very quickly too ill, to do anything sensible – hypothermia, shock, thirst, gangrene or starvation – which would have got him first, do you think? I reckon they were queuing up in roughly that order.'

In all her mental reviewing of her two days on Bodmin Moor, Debbie had never given this a thought. Warmth had been so much a part of the episode that she had taken it for granted, she was, she realised now, the only one who had. For the first time it dawned on her that without her, the much-vilified Angwin would quite possibly not have been around to upset Tim, and it wasn't a good thought. She was silent.

'But that's all very well,' Lesley went on. 'He doesn't owe me anything at all. You might have saved his life a thousand times over, but how can I take our problems to him? Tim loathes his guts, and I shouldn't think he likes Tim all that much better – he can't!' She swallowed. 'I couldn't... I just couldn't, Deb – lay all Tim's frailties and... and ignorance in front of Angwin!'

'I don't think anyone was suggesting that *you* did,' said Debbie, considering this. 'Obviously you couldn't, not under the circumstances. But if we get any more problems like the Swedes, what's to stop me going and asking him what to do? He knows you're amateurs already, that can't hurt Tim. You needn't even know about it if it makes you feel better, I can just repeat what he tells me as if it was my own idea.'

'It seems dreadfully deceitful,' said Lesley, with longing.

'Mmm, isn't it? But it's my conscience, not yours, that will suffer. How can you stop me, short of locking me up?'

Lesley laughed, and Debbie heard the relief in the sound.

'You'll get a terrible reputation for infallibility!'

'I can live with that.' Debbie paused. 'Whatever's that noise?'

They had turned the corner into the drive and the house lay before them. Through the open windows drifted the sound of violent shouting, interspersed with crashing and screaming, and what sounded like splintering wood. Debbie and Lesley took to their heels and ran.

Indoors, the noise was deafening. Whatever was going on was taking place upstairs, and Roger and Tim stood in the hall looking upwards, their faces a study in suspended horror. Somebody – several somebodies from the sound of it – appeared to be having a violent argument, made all the more disturbing by the fact that the whole thing was being conducted in a foreign language. The thud and, Tim insisted afterwards, the whistle of flying objects made an interesting counterpoint to the main theme. Obviously, the Swedes were doing their thing, and the fire doors weren't doing much to muffle the fact.

'Well, do something!' cried Lesley, running into the hall and scattering beer cans around her like windfalls. 'Stop them, don't just stand there!'

'What do you suggest we do?' asked Roger, pitching his voice above the din. 'I'm paid as a sailing instructor, not a bouncer, and I'm having nothing to do with a drunken brawl! I'm already being a waiter and an assistant cook, and if you think I'm going to risk life and limb up there, I can tell you now that idea's a –'

'Don't tell me!' interrupted Lesley, sweepingly. 'A dead duck! And I thought you were a friend!'

'I am,' said Roger. 'Only I prefer being a live friend to a dead one.'

'Tim!'

Tim looked sheepish.

'Well, Roger's got a point, you know. They sound pretty violent to me. It might be a mistake to interfere.'

'Then send for the police!' Lesley cried. 'What about our other guests?' She glanced towards the lounge door, which mercifully was closed, and lowered her voice to a conspiratorial whisper. 'You must do something, Tim! You're supposed to be in charge.'

'Listen,' said Tim. 'They've stopped.'

An extra loud crash had been succeeded by a sudden silence.

'That sounded like a chair,' said Debbie, uneasily. 'Perhaps they've killed each other.'

A door slammed upstairs and somebody ran along the landing, shouting something incomprehensible in a tear-choked female voice. A second door slammed, cutting off the sound. A silence fell, broken only by the thud of some object hitting a closed door. The four in the hall looked at each other.

'They'll have to go,' said Lesley briskly, avoiding Debbie's eye. 'They didn't book any particular stay – we must tell them tomorrow that the rooms are taken. They can't argue with that.'

Tim stared at her.

'That's brilliant!' he said admiringly. 'You can do it first thing after breakfast. With luck, they'll be so subdued after this little lot, they won't even argue.'

'*I* can do it?' said Lesley. Tim went red.

'All right, we'll both do it.'

Roger was going round the floor, gathering up beer cans.

'With the hangovers they'll have, they may not even hear,' he said. 'Come on, I think I've got them all now. Let's go and work up hangovers of our own.'

The rest of the guests tried to pretend that nothing out of the ordinary had taken place, but the drama had taken its toll, and there was no enthusiasm for burning the midnight oil tonight. Everyone said goodnight early, and retired to their various rooms.

Debbie lay awake for a long time. There had been more to the evening's events than she had told Lesley, and she needed to think – and seriously, for the implications couldn't be taken lightly. She thought back to the scene in Mawgan's office, his quite undeserved kindness and the unexpected invitation that had followed it. Obviously, her disastrous attack of foot-in-mouth on the day of her arrival had been forgiven, diplomatic relations were resumed. The question was, how far, if anywhere at all, did he want to go and was she prepared to go?

She liked him. She had been aware for some time that she liked him very much, but it was no more than liking at present. There would be no harm done if she simply ignored the invitation and kept their acquaintance – it was no more – on its present level. Attraction was something that faded quite easily if it had no fuel to make it burn, and if she wanted a romantic summer, there was always Roger. With Roger, there would be no strings attached, and she didn't want strings.

With Mawgan Angwin, there might well be strings.

He was older than she was. She thought that he might turn out to be older than Oliver, who was eight years her senior. He didn't have the appearance of a confirmed bachelor on the make, he looked like the makings of a reliable husband, and that was a scene for which she hadn't studied the lines. She had a presentiment that her personality and her aims in life would slot into his like the pieces of a well-made jigsaw puzzle, and it was a possibility that in the particular circumstances required very careful consideration.

She had tried a serious affair, and it had been the most unhappy time of her life so far. Perhaps it was true what Lesley said, that Oliver, with his idealistic concept of personal freedom and his uncaged, adventurous spirit, had spoiled her for other men. Her lover had tried to possess her body and soul and make her over to his own specifications and she had fought him every inch of the way. He hadn't wanted her as she was, but as he thought she ought to be, and looking at the marriages of her friends – even of her parents – she was afraid that most men did. The fact that she had also come to believe that money, too, entered into the equation had simply been the final straw.

But Oliver wasn't like that. Oliver, like herself, wanted neither to possess nor to be possessed, and yet she knew that he had found great happiness in his marriage to Chel.

Hold on, she was getting a bit ahead of the game here. For all she knew,

Mawgan was simply lonely, and she was the one person who would still speak to him.

It needed thinking about, even so. He had stood trial for murder even if he had only gone to prison for manslaughter, he was now on probation. She could be putting herself at risk, and even if she wasn't, those around her might still think, with some justification, that she was.

You could detach yourself as far as possible from your family, but you couldn't make them go away. Her father, her mother, her sister, her brother... the words made a jingle in her head. What would they make of the news that she was even just going out with a man who had been in prison for manslaughter? There had been enough of a furore over Robin, and he had been so eligible as to make you sick!. A lot of the blame for her going to live with him instead of marrying him had been laid, by example, at Oliver's door. She didn't want that to happen again. She hadn't taken sides in the continuing running battle that her mother had always had with Oliver, but she knew that in the end it had split the family apart and administered the *coup de grâce* to her parents' marriage, which even a fool would see now was all over bar the shouting. She was quite likely, in the present family climate, to find herself an outcast, and she could say that she wouldn't care, but it might be a different proposition if it actually happened.

Outcast, she would be in the wilderness with Oliver, and she quite honestly had no idea what his reactions would be. He hadn't approved of her living with Robin either, but then he hadn't liked Robin; so far as living with people went he was in no position to criticise, having, quite apart from previous liaisons, run off with Chel first and married her afterwards. She respected his opinion as she didn't necessarily wholly respect her mother's, and she wouldn't be happy falling out with her father, either. Or with her sister Susan, tiresome though she could be. It was annoying to discover, after years of independence, that she was still stuck fast in the family web.

Or was she? Unless you were totally selfish, and she didn't think that she was, it was natural to consider how your actions would affect other people. It was a different matter if you let other people affect your actions. If she ever found a man prepared to give her the same thing that Oliver and Chel gave to each other, be he Mawgan or anyone else, the family could go chase themselves.

Why did he have to have gone to prison? It made what should have been a simple decision – to accept an invitation or to ignore it – quite unnecessarily complicated. It enjoined on her the duty to look ahead to consequences that might never happen.

Debbie tossed over onto her other side and gave her pillow a vicious punch, trying to make herself comfortable, and resolutely shut her eyes. She would sleep now, and in the morning the problem would quite possibly have solved itself. Problems did that, quite often.

It wasn't only the family, bother them. There was Tim as well. If he found that she was seeing the hated Angwin, he would probably indulge in a little manslaughter himself.

Her eyes opened again onto the dark room.

Tim was a friend, not a keeper of public morals. He had no right to dictate to her.

Tim was a friend, and she probably ought not to deceive him, or to go against his known wishes when she was not only under his roof, but in his employ. On the other hand, the thought of *telling* him made her shudder.

Night was a bad time for thinking.

She did fall asleep in the end, and the last, irreverent thought that whispered in her head was that her mother, an upright moralist of rather rigid and narrow-minded Christian convictions, would have a fit at the bare thought of being threatened with a possible son-in-law who was not only an ex-convict, but kept a pub, and to top it all, spoke with a Cornish accent.

Only much later did she recall, with bitterness and grief, that she had thought it was funny.

The following morning Tim, all unknowing, put Angwin's sensible advice into operation, and the Svensens packed up and left, leaving behind them a vague impression of gentle charm, which could only be explained by the fact that sober, they were perfectly normal, even rather pleasant people, whatever they might be under the influence of large quantities of gin. They also left behind them a total of nine empty gin bottles and six empty whisky bottles, which it was surely impossible that they had consumed just during their short, eventful stay. Wasn't it?

Their departure left a contented peace behind it, which Mrs. Tregear, in all innocence, put to flight with a hatchet.

Unfortunately, so far as gossip was concerned, the affairs of Mawgan

Angwin and the Fish remained firmly at number one in the charts. Although generally speaking it was only Lesley who became involved in it, on this particular morning not only had sailing school business been delayed by the need to rid the house of unwelcome invaders, but they had all wakened to a thick and clinging mist and no wind. The students had seized the opportunity to spend the morning in Falmouth looking at the shops and the castle, and it was therefore all four of the resident staff, plus Mrs. Tregear, who met around the kitchen table at eleven.

It must have been the shortest coffee break on record.

It was inevitable that their recently departed guests should form the main subject of conversation. For one thing, Mrs. Tregear had gathered all the empties into the laundry basket and brought them downstairs, where they sat mutely inviting comment beside the back door.

'Thank goodness they've gone,' said Lesley, who felt in spite of the mist as if the sun was shining from a perfect blue heaven.

'Your brainwave was a killer,' said Tim, with satisfaction. 'They hadn't a leg to stand on.' He ruffled her hair affectionately. 'Clever little thing, aren't you? Anyone would think you had been born to this lark!'

Mrs. Tregear had no inhibitions about entering into conversation with her employers as an equal, which was fair enough since Debbie and Roger didn't have any either. She seized on this opening with glee.

'My daughter was talking about them when she came home for her tea Saturday night,' she said. 'She said they carried on terrible down at the Fish, and do you know what she told me?' She paused for an answer and Debbie had time to think *Oh no!* and Lesley had time to turn pale, before she continued with the air of one imparting really exciting news.

'They didn't leave the Fish because they didn't like it, like they told Mrs. Howells they did. Mr. Angwin sent them packing!'

The resulting silence could be felt. Thinking perhaps that her revelation had fallen rather flat, Mrs. Tregear innocently followed bad with worse.

'They got drunk and broke the place up, just like they done upstairs, and he upped and told them he needed the rooms. Only they made a lot of unpleasantness, my daughter said, because he added the damage to the bill. There was some high words...' Her voice died away, it was obvious that her story, although it had made an impression, had made an impression of the wrong kind. Tim had gone white to the lips.

'Angwin!' he said, in a furious undervoice. 'Bloody Angwin again!'

He rose to his feet and his voice rose with him, in a sweeping, passionate cadence. '*Bloody Angwin sent those wreckers here to my wife?*'

Bad enough, thought Debbie confusedly, but not the worst. She scrambled to her feet beside him and put her hand on his arm.

'No Tim, I'm sure he didn't.'

Tim, oblivious to the fact that if Mawgan Angwin's business could be the subject of village gossip, so too could his own, was beyond reason. His words cut like a whip across a stunned and seemingly endless pause.

'By God, I'll get the bastard for this!'

'Oh, Mr. Howells!' piped Mrs. Tregear, alarmed at the drama she hadn't meant to precipitate. 'Do be careful! Remember he's a killer!'

Tim's fist crashed down on the kitchen table, making the mugs rattle together.

'That does it!' he exclaimed, and stormed out of the room.

Lesley burst into tears.

Mrs. Tregear, all fussy kindness, rushed to console her and Debbie and Roger exchanged glances.

'Should I go after him, do you think?' asked Roger, uneasily.

'Let him alone, I should,' said Debbie. 'It's no use trying to talk to him while he's in that mood, he'd only yell at you too.'

'What made him go up like that, anyway?' asked Roger, under his breath, so that Lesley and Mrs. Tregear didn't hear him. 'I mean, I've seen him being a Grade A pig, as can't we all be, and I've heard about him searing holes in Angwin, but I've never known him go off like a bloody bomb before!'

'Perhaps,' said Debbie, tartly, for the implications of the little scene were just beginning to dawn on her, 'he feels that he has a monopoly in making his own wife miserable.'

In the event, the advice to leave Tim alone was needless, he had disappeared. He didn't return at lunch time, although the mist was clearing nicely, and it was left to Debbie and Roger to conduct the afternoon's sailing programme on their own. It was only when they came ashore that Debbie, stowing the sailbags under cover for the night, found him in the boathouse. He was sitting on a pile of life-jackets, sunk in gloom.

'Hullo,' said Debbie, cautiously. She knew he hadn't been there earlier. 'Where have you been?'

'For a long walk,' said Tim, moodily. He stretched out his long legs and stared at his feet, his eyes miserable behind the magnifying lenses of his glasses. 'Did I make too much of an ass of myself, Debbie?'

'You did, rather,' said Debbie, seeing no point in telling comforting untruths, and in any case less than pleased with him. 'And you made Lesley cry.'

'Again,' said Tim, so that she wished that she had left that last bit out. 'I seem to have a gift for it. What am I doing wrong, my old friend? Can you tell me?'

Debbie resisted an unworthy impulse to reply, *everything*.

'I expect it's the strain of running your own business when you aren't used to it,' she offered.

'I always seem to end up picking on Les,' said Tim, and Debbie said nothing.

A shaft of sunlight, peering dustily through a grimy window, fell across the toe of his shoe, he seemed to find it fascinating.

'Everything's going wrong,' he said. 'It's all that bloody Angwin's fault.'

'No.' Debbie, recalling generosity, felt driven to protest. 'No, you can't blame Mawgan – honestly, you can't, Tim.'

He sniffed.

'*Mawgan* now, is it?'

'Oh, don't be so dumb!' exclaimed Debbie. 'I spent two days snowed up with him, remember? And with nobody else to talk to. What do you expect me to call him – bloody Angwin?'

Tim had the grace to blush, and muttered something that she could take as an apology if she so wished.

'He's entitled to watch his own interests, as he sees them,' continued Debbie. 'You would, after all. He hasn't forfeited any basic human rights by going to prison. And he may have sent those Swedes packing, but he didn't send them here. What do you take him for? He isn't going to bother trying to score off you, why should he? It wouldn't gain him anything to be so petty, and you flatter yourself if you even think there's a need!'

Tim kicked at the trailing lace of a life-jacket, squirming it around the floor like a worm.

'All right, so I lost my temper. I'm sorry.'

'A bit late to be sorry,' suggested Debbie.

'Debbie – look, just give over, will you? You know how I feel about Angwin. I'm sorry if he's a friend of yours, but there it is, he isn't a friend of mine. You may acquit him of malice if you like, but I don't have to share your opinion.'

'Fair enough, but was there any need to sound off like that, back there in the kitchen?'

'About getting back at him, do you mean? I told you, I lost my temper – how could I do it, anyway?'

'I think you may find that you already have,' said Debbie. A throbbing rage against him made her voice come out hard and tight, unlike itself. Tim looked at her, bewildered.

'How? I never touched him!'

'What makes you think,' said Debbie, between her teeth, 'that Mrs. Tregear doesn't gossip to her daughter just the way her daughter gossips to her?'

It took a moment or two for this to sink in, then Tim said,

'Oh, shit!'

'Exactly,' said Debbie, angrily. 'You should have thought. It was a rotten thing to do.'

'I'm sorry,' said Tim, defensively. 'It seems I never do think, doesn't it?'

'You said that, not me,' said Debbie bitterly. Tim got to his feet.

'I think we had better call time on this rather unproductive discussion, don't you?'

'No.' Debbie caught at his sleeve, holding him back. 'No Tim, you can't just walk away as if it never happened. You must undo it.'

'Undo it?' He stared at her. 'How? Go around the village with a placard saying ANGWIN IS INNOCENT, I DONE 'IM WRONG? I could make a matching sticker for the car while I'm about it. Don't be so daft – it would only make things a hundred times worse!'

'You could say you spoke without thinking in the heat of the moment if anyone mentions it to you.'

'All right – if they do, I will. Satisfied?'

Debbie was far from satisfied, but she saw as clearly as Tim did that it would have to do.

'Thank you. And we'll agree to differ over what we think of him.'

'What does that mean? It sounded loaded,' said Tim, suspiciously and accurately.

'It means that whatever you choose to think of him, to me he's a friend.'

'Bloody hell, Deb – come on –' protested Tim.

'You shut up!' said Debbie. 'If there was someone who disliked you and I happened to know them, would you expect me to cut *you* dead?'

Tim gave her a dark look.

'I suppose I have nothing to say to what you do away from here, but don't you ever dare to bring your *friend* to my house.'

'What makes you think he'd come?' riposted Debbie.

Roger's shadow fell across the pool of sunlight from the window, as he came to the doorway of the boathouse.

'You two can be heard halfway to Helford,' he remarked. 'Brawling again? Cool it, both of you. Brawling is a dead duck at the best of times, how about a little pulling together for a change?'

'The only way I want to pull Tim,' said Debbie, 'is to pieces!' She caught sight of Tim's face and suddenly burst out laughing, relieved to feel the tension breaking. If the laughter had a slightly hysterical ring, neither of the men appeared to notice.

'That's better,' said Roger. 'Look here, I've had an idea. It's only just after four, Lesley won't have started cooking yet. Let's all abandon ship and go and have a Chinese somewhere. I've sounded the others out, they think it's a great idea. What about you two?'

Debbie and Tim exchanged rather shamefaced glances.

'It sounds great,' Debbie agreed, and Tim said,

'I'll go and tell Lesley before she gets carried away with the casserole.'

The incident was over, and both of them were greatly relieved – but it did occur to Debbie, following the chattering group of students up the lawn, to wonder what would happen if Tim ever thought back over his morning's work and remembered how Mawgan Angwin was reputed to have rid his house of gin-swilling Swedes. She sincerely hoped that he never would.

XII

For a while, it began to seem that the temperamental outbursts of late May and early June had faded with the bluebells that carpeted the woods, and it even seemed that some of the cards were beginning to be dealt from the top, rather than the bottom of the pack. Debbie had a word with Mrs. Tregear about the houses along the creek, and learned something that interested her greatly. One evening, she put through a call to Chel's mobile, at present with her in the Saronic Gulf.

'Hi, Chel,' she said, when her sister-in-law answered.

'Debbie! Hullo, this is a surprise!'

'A nice one, I hope,' said Debbie. 'Listen Chel — I won't run up a bill on this one, but are you still looking for a house?'

'Why? Do you know of one?'

Debbie smiled to herself, it was a nice change to have good news for somebody.

'Actually, yes. It's not on the market yet, but it will be soon, and it looks like the sort of thing you might like — that is, if you don't mind living on my doorstep. Oliver might object, of course.'

'Oliver might surprise you, these days. Where is it? What's it like?'

'I'd say it was perfect.' Debbie described the creek, and went on, 'The house at the end nearest the river is the one that might be for sale, I only know because our cleaner mentioned it, but listen, it's perfect for you. It's quite old — they all are — three bedrooms — well, more like two-and-a-half — and all the rest of it, a terraced garden at the back and a little patch of lawn opposite, on the creek side of the lane. But the crunch line is this, there's a garage and workshop adjoining, and up above it — guess what — is a studio! Quite big, according to Mrs. Tregear, with a balcony overlooking the creek. It used to belong to a real artist, although the present owners use it as a playroom for their grandchildren.'

'It sounds too good to be true,' said Chel, which Debbie had to admit, it did. 'Why are they selling, if it's so perfect?'

'Too much for them, they're going to live near their daughter in Surrey – they just want one more summer there for the grandchildren, and then there's vacant possession in about September – if you got in quick, they'd probably make a private sale to someone who was prepared to wait, and it might cost you a bit less. I thought I'd let you know quickly in case you were interested...?' She let her voice rise in a question mark, and there was a long pause, while she had time to imagine Chel's face.

'You'd better speak to Oliver,' said Chel.

Oliver was monosyllabic on phones, particularly mobiles, but he listened to what Debbie had to say with interest.

'It's time we came back anyway,' he said, when she had gone through it all again. 'Make a few enquiries, can you Deb? We'll be in touch as soon as we're home.'

'What did they say?' asked Tim, when Debbie came back into the lounge. 'Here – have a beer.'

Debbie took the offered can and pulled the ring with a pop.

'They said, we're on our way home,' she said. 'Not that they actually have a home at the moment, so I don't know what they plan to do when they get here.' The beer frothed into the glass. 'It would be great if they did buy it.' If they could afford it, she wasn't really sure about that. Oliver, unlike herself and her sister Susan, had no trust fund, which was his own choice, he preferred to be beholden to nobody. He did, however, as she knew, have a handsome insurance settlement from being disabled, which had been called, she remembered, rather optimistically *compensation*. She had no idea what he expected to gain from his latest pursuit of painting.

'Do you think he'd give classes in navigation?' asked Tim, hopefully, but Debbie shook her head.

'Pigs might fly, Tim. I'm afraid that idea is a dead duck, so it won't.'

Roger grinned at her, recognising the dig at himself, but made no comment.

There was nothing immediate to be done about the house, although Debbie intended to scrape acquaintance with the owners at the earliest opportunity and see how the land lay. Meanwhile, the second week of June, as Lesley had predicted, brought an almost empty house, but a sudden rush of long overdue goodwill, probably, Debbie thought unkindly, because the results of Tim's last outburst had even frightened himself. Lesley, more at peace with herself for knowing that she was no longer alone in the world with her problems, suggested that while it was so quiet, they might take it in turns to have some time off, and they drew lots to see who would take the first day. Debbie won.

'What will you do with it?' asked Tim, with friendly interest. 'Go and check up on that house for Oliver?'

A good question. She ought to do that, of course, she had promised that she would, but…

'I haven't really decided,' she said.

'Take a boat, if you want,' offered Tim, but Debbie said that she thought she would like a change. She had almost decided what she would do, but she had no intention of telling Tim or Lesley, and certainly not Roger.

She hadn't spoken to Mawgan since the Swedish incident, now, she hoped, forgotten and in the past, although she had seen him occasionally when they had been down to the Fish for a rare lunchtime drink. He looked much as usual, casual, light-hearted even, talking to his customers with his easy charm and smiling at Debbie when their eyes met. She was aware, however, as with Mrs. Tregear around none of them could fail to be, that Tim's outburst had borne its own unfortunate fruit, and that one or two of his regulars had taken to drinking at the pub in Helford. She was sorry for it, it was a poor return for his help, but it was true that it was easier to inflict harm than to mend it, and the Fish, with the growing influx of summer visitors, couldn't be said to be suffering. Public opinion was fickle, good or bad. The winter would probably find the breakaway group back in their nearest bar. Tim, she knew, had kept his word, but the main result of that had been to earn him an undeserved reputation for generosity, which shamed him as much as it enraged her. Tim was still the much-abused underdog, Mawgan still the man who had come home laughing instead of suitably chastened.

It was, in some strange way, Mawgan's battered reputation that had given the boost to Tim's. If Mawgan had never been in prison, Debbie was fairly certain that, if the village had taken sides at all, they would have backed one of their own. The Cornish were nothing if not loyal to each other and they would have closed ranks. It was a curious paradox, and an unfair one, that things had gone the way that they had.

She thought about this as she walked down the shallow hill after a late breakfast, and entering the hall of the Fish for the third time, found a girl sitting behind the reception desk, typing something into a computer.

Mr. Angwin had just gone out, she said in reply to Debbie's enquiry. He had gone to Falmouth, she went on, when questioned, and would probably not be back until this afternoon. Could she do anything? Debbie said thank you, but no, and more disappointed than she had thought she would be, for of course she had considered the possibility that he might not be there, said that she might drop back later. She left by the front door, conscious of two curious eyes following her, and hoped devoutly that they weren't Tregear eyes. Thinking about Lesley's belief in a Tregear spy system, and feeling laughter bubbling up, she stepped out into the sunshine again without looking where she was going, and was all but run down by a white Volvo estate coming down the narrow, briar-hung lane that led to the inn's back premises and car park.

'It's much too fine a day for suicide,' said Mawgan, when he had recovered from the shock. 'Come to Falmouth with me, instead.'

Debbie got into the car, and the interrupted trip to Falmouth was resumed.

'Out on parole?' he asked her, cheerfully. 'Good feeling, isn't it?'

Not for the first time, Debbie was stuck for a reply, but this time she thought she caught a touch of bravado behind the words.

'We're not all that busy at the moment,' she said, vaguely.

'June's always a funny month. Things'll get going in a week or so, don't worry.'

Lesley was still fretting about the bookings. Debbie watched the countryside spinning past the windows and was unaware of how informative her silence was.

'Were you going to Falmouth for any particular reason?' she asked.

'To see my solicitor and pick up a couple of things on the trading estate at Budock. I'll meet you for lunch though, if you can keep yourself happy until then.' He paused for a moment, and then continued smoothly, 'Your friend Howells trying to get me lynched, is he?'

'Oh!' said Debbie. She felt herself blush, although she had no reason. 'He was upset,' she added lamely. 'He didn't realise what he was saying.'

'And does he now realise what he said?'

'Yes,' said Debbie, and was relieved, in the context of Mawgan's solicitor, when he laughed.

180

'Bugger, weren't it? By the way, I hear your haul was bigger'n mine.'

'What?' asked Debbie, staring.

'I only had eleven empty bottles.'

She enjoyed herself in Falmouth, strolling around the town and poking into odd little shops down side-streets, and at a quarter to one, when she had arranged to meet Mawgan, she went down to the quayside and leaned on the rails that bounded the edge of the car park, almost under the windows of the Blue Crab Café, watching the yachts at their moorings and the big ships in the docks. Mawgan had said he would find her anywhere along the waterside, and he did.

'The jumping off point for faraway places,' he said quietly, materialising like a genie against the rail beside her. 'Don't you find ports – of any kind – some exciting? I do.'

'You never told me that you were an adventurer as well as an entrepreneur,' said Debbie, idly. 'Do you hanker for faraway places, then?'

'Sometimes.'

'But surely, you wouldn't want to abandon the Fish?'

'There's times I'd cheerfully do what your brother did, and pray as I sank on the way round.' Pause. 'Probably would too, come to think on it.'

'Oh, come on – ' exclaimed Debbie. She turned to look at him, perturbed, but he was laughing at her. It slid through her mind, so swiftly that it was hardly even a thought, that there was more than one form of personal loss, and that for Mawgan there would be no sun-soaked Saronic Gulf shining under a Mediterranean sun, but it was so quick that it left no lasting impression behind it. She found herself returning the smile, which was infectious, and laughing with him.

'Shall us go and find some lunch, then?' he suggested.

She gestured to the café windows above the car park behind them.

'In there? It's not quite the Fish, but it may not be too bad.'

He looked at the place almost as if he was shocked to see it there.

'I sh'd think not! That dive!'

Debbie grinned at him.

'How élitist of you! You should try how the other half lives occasionally.'

'But not there, thank you.' He grinned back at her buoyantly, and an odd feeling that she had said the wrong thing again swiftly evaporated. He linked his arm through hers and they strolled away.

Over lunch, his wit and intelligence sparkled for her like sunlight on water, shallow and bubbling as a stream over stones. They ate curried prawns and drank cider from the cask in a pub whose ceiling was beamed, and black with age, and Debbie became more and more involved by the minute, and failed to take note of even one danger signal. She knew only that she had seldom enjoyed herself more. Worldly-wise she had learned to be, but even so, an unsuspectedly cosmopolitan thirty-plus could, and did, make rings round her. They sat long over their lunch, and after, he drove her home to the Fish making a brief stop at the trading estate on the way, kissed her soundly, and tipped her out onto the causeway to allow him, he said, to get back to work, he had wasted half the afternoon already.

She walked up the hill unaware that life could never be the same again, and found the house eerily deserted. Tim and Roger were out on the water, Lesley was nowhere to be seen. She wandered down to the water's edge, and she could see two of the Wayfarers in the distance, in the open waters at the mouth of the river, but Lesley wasn't sunning herself on the foreshore as she had half expected. She turned and began to walk up the lawn again, and was suddenly assailed by the oddest feeling that she was being watched.

She paused and looked around her, but there was nobody to be seen.

'Lesley?' she called, tentatively. The wind sighed in the trees and the water bubbled over the mud at her back. There was nothing else, no other sound, but the uncomfortable feeling of not being alone persisted. She looked back towards the river, but there was nobody there either.

It must be in her imagination. She gave herself a shake and walked on up the lawn to the house. She wasn't used to being alone here, that was the trouble. She went indoors, and the feeling immediately left her. She thought no more about it.

Debbie had a swim in the river, followed it with a shower, and was about to make herself a cup of tea to drink in solitary peace on the terrace when the telephone rang. She was on her way up from the kitchen to answer it when it stopped abruptly, and a moment later, to her surprise, she heard Lesley calling.

'Debbie? Deb, are you in?'

Debbie put her head out of the kitchen door.

'Yes. Are you?'

'Where were you? I didn't hear you come in, there's a call for you waiting in the office. Angwin.'

'Angwin?' echoed Debbie, in surprise. 'What's he want? I've only just left him.'

'You could try asking him,' suggested Lesley, with the merest flicker of her eyelashes betraying her surprise. Debbie went into the office. Mawgan was dicing with death here, she thought irreverently, she must give him her mobile number.

'Deborah?' His voice came lilting down the wire, light and unconcerned. 'I was missing you. Fancy dinner, or did you eat too much lunch?'

'No, I didn't eat too much lunch, and I'd love dinner. When?'

'Half-past nine suit you, or is that too late?'

'Half-past nine sounds incredibly civilised.'

'Good, I'll see you then. Can you find your own way? If I came up for you, your boss might lie in wait with a shotgun.'

'I think I might manage – I can always bring a compass,' said Debbie, smiling to herself.

'See you later, then.' He rang off and she went back to the kitchen.

'Lucky you,' said Lesley wistfully, when she heard. 'We had a meal at the Fish once – before World War III broke out, naturally. It was on my birthday, didn't we tell you? It's lingered in my memory ever since.' She looked discontentedly at her own preparations for the evening meal. 'Steak and kidney pie and beans just isn't the same.'

'That Angwin never takes a thing seriously!' said Debbie, lifting two mugs down from the shelf.

'Want a bet?' asked Lesley, unnaturally serious herself all of a sudden.

'He makes stupid jokes about prisons, and leaves me sitting there with my mouth open.'

'Does he, indeed,' said Lesley, dryly. 'And do you laugh?'

'Actually, I don't think it's particularly funny.'

'If you want my opinion, which I don't suppose you do, Angwin doesn't find much at all particularly funny right now – and if you want to know why I think so,' Lesley added, 'well, it takes one to know one.'

Debbie was in no mood for conundrums.

'What do you think I should wear?' she said.

She was wined and dined at the Fish on pickled salmon, guinea fowl *en cocotte* with a mouth-watering selection of fresh vegetables on the side, and a totally mind-blowing *crème de menthe* and chocolate mousse, accompanied by wines as appropriate and followed by Gaelic coffee, and was escorted to her gate, feeling somewhat overfed and mildly intoxicated, shortly after midnight. She slept badly and had weird dreams, but told Lesley in the morning that it had been well worth it.

After that, the rest of the week fell flat for some reason. The few guests that they had in the house were happier sitting in the lounge with coffee than in the bar of the Fish with a beer, and it all seemed rather dull. Roger and Tim had each had a day off, but Lesley said that she couldn't very well, because of cooking the meals, but she was having an easy week and she honestly didn't mind, what would she do on her own? After all, she quite often went out anyway for the business. Tim, Debbie noticed with irritation, allowed all this to pass. If he had made the slightest protest, she thought she might even have offered to cook her one dinner-party dish – *Coq au Vin à la Debbie* – and made Roger help her so that Tim and Lesley could go out together, but for her to suggest it unprompted would, she instinctively felt, have been a mistake that Lesley might not have forgiven easily.

It was towards the end of that week that they began unexpectedly to pick up passing trade, some of whom even became sold on the idea of a bit of sailing. It was only a gentle trickle, but it lifted everyone's spirits a notch further, and it was quite by chance that Roger discovered that most of it had come by way of the Fish. Fortunately, he had the sense to keep his discovery to himself until he had Debbie and Lesley alone, and when he broke the news to them he was completely astonished when Lesley sat down and burst into tears, which was becoming an all-too-frequent habit that she seemed unable to control.

'Oh, damn!' she said furiously, scrubbing at her eyes with a tissue. 'Why am I so *stupid*?'

'I don't know,' said Debbie, whom tears tended to make uncomfortable. 'Why are you?'

'We've been so horrible to him,' sniffed Lesley, which she, at least, had not been.

'He wouldn't thank you for crying over him,' Debbie pointed out.

'How did you find out?' Lesley asked Roger, choking back a sob.

'I heard them talking on the terrace,' said Roger. 'Angwin's full up – he's only got a few letting rooms anyway – they went in off the road and he sent them on up here. It must have been Angwin himself, nobody else down there answers to that description.'

'What description?' asked Debbie, curiously.

'*A dusky charmer from Italy.*'

'*Italy?*'

'More likely to be Spain,' said Roger. 'There's supposed to be a lot of Spanish blood mixed into the Cornish, particularly as you go further west. From marauding pirates, mostly.'

This seemed appropriate enough and Debbie didn't argue with it. In fact, she rather liked the idea, and added it to her mental file on Mawgan. By this time, although she had no idea of it, she was well on the way to being not just hopelessly involved but very much in love, but it was only in the very, very darkest recesses of her subconscious that the seed planted by Lesley was struggling to put out roots. On the surface, she was only aware that she enjoyed his company and was glad, in spite of the childish behaviour of Tim and Lesley, that she had come to Cornwall. It was so amazingly easy to put the prison sentence out of her mind whenever she was near him.

'If he carries on, we might even weather the season,' said Lesley, with longing in her voice. 'I feel so much safer since you had that talk with him, Deb – ' She remembered Roger, and looked guilty. Roger eyed her meditatively.

'Do I detect murmurings of mutiny in the fo'c'sle?' he queried, with interest.

'No,' said Lesley, firmly. 'We simply decided, Debbie and me, that we were safer on the right side of Angwin than on the wrong side, and see how right we were.'

'Mmm,' said Roger. 'Well, watch him, that's all. Angwin may be a lot of things, but I doubt if purely altruistic is among them.'

Debbie gave him an indignant look, but he refused to enlarge on this statement and merely smiled enigmatically before wandering off, with a remark about whipping the end of a mainsheet.

Altruistic or not, the situation couldn't be allowed to go unrecognised, and appreciation must be shown, Lesley insisted. She couldn't show it herself for obvious political reasons, but Debbie seemed to be getting away with things so far, so she would have to do it instead. Debbie, by no means averse to the idea, said that she would.

She slipped down to the Fish after breakfast, while the few students were assembling for Tim's pre-sailing homily, and was lucky enough to catch Mawgan in his office with columns of figures all over one of his computer screens.

'Casting up accounts, I see,' said Debbie, and he picked up on the sub-text immediately, in the way that made him so good as a companion. His answering grin was brimming with mischief.

'You should be thankful,' he pointed out. 'Nobody knows better'n you what I can cast up on my day. What's up? More problems?'

'Not this time – or only the problem of how Lesley can say thank you without being seen to do it,' said Debbie. 'You've been very kind, and she wants you to know she appreciates it.'

'After the first input she had off of me, I'm glad she feels so forgiving.'

'If anyone is being forgiving under the circumstances, it isn't Lesley, it's you,' said Debbie.

'Oh, me!' he said, with a sudden flash of moodiness. 'I live on Prozac. You'd be amazed.'

For a second, Debbie wondered if she actually believed that, but then he looked up with the laugh back in his eyes and she suspected that he had been teasing her again.

'Time for a coffee?' he asked, and when Debbie said that she wouldn't mind a quick one, he passed the request to the girl who was once more in reception and invited her to sit down. Tipping his chair back idly, he fiddled with the mouse on his desk and gave her a steady look that made the colour, inexplicably, rise into her face, making her wish that she was less fair-skinned. She hurriedly reverted to the reason for her visit.

'Lesley wanted you to know she feels better knowing that you're there if she needs help. Ignorance is scaring – as don't we know ourselves.'

'You and me, as I remember it, didn't invite the exposure of our ignorance, we had it forced on us.'

'In a way, so did Lesley and Tim. It's not a good world to live in when you're a skilled technician with a brand-new wife to support, and you've suddenly lost your job and it isn't even your fault. You could remember that.'

'I'm sorry,' he said, after a pause.

The arrival of the coffee made it unnecessary for Debbie to add anything to this, but when they were alone again he went on. 'Tell me, Deborah – not that it's none of my business – why didn't they sell that house and invest the money? It could've set 'em up for life, unemployment or not.'

Debbie thought about it.

'It would, of course,' she agreed. 'But it wasn't just a question of money. I don't suppose you've ever been on the dole, but suddenly to find yourself there out of the blue can't be much fun. It's a matter of self-respect, I think. Tim – and Lesley, too – they didn't want to just take a hand-out and be set up for life, they wanted to show what they could do and prove that they were still of some value in the world. Tim, particularly, since the money would have been Lesley's. You can't blame them.'

'What they're doing is to show what they can't do,' Mawgan pointed out.

'They'll learn quickly enough,' said Debbie. 'They've learned quite a lot already. And Tim may be, but Lesley isn't, too proud to pick your brains. But you know that anyway, don't you?'

'I suppose, if I hadn't, I wouldn't've been stupid enough to say what I did to you.'

'You weren't stupid. You were amazingly generous.'

'And stupid too. It's only spinning out the agony, the end of that story is already written.'

'With your advice – '

'Oh, I can advise them – if they ask, and if Howells never finds out. I can't help 'em, that's a different can of worms altogether. Help is something that Howells won't ask for, and I'm not sure that I'd give it anyway.'

'Would give – not could give?'

'Where's the difference?'

Debbie thought that there was quite a lot of difference, but didn't press the point. They were back in no-man's-land again.

'I don't want them to go bust,' she said.

'I don't *want* them to either, don't think that, please. It just so happens that the writing is on the wall, and you – or me, for that matter – can't do nothing about it. Go bust or bust up or both – it happens to a lot of small caterers these days. Not necessarily just the small people, come to think of it. Catering is a bloody battlefield, Deborah, littered with casualties. Lost hopes, shattered dreams, broken marriages, you see them all in this game. Too many people see it as an ideal existence, and it isn't, it's a hard job of work like any other, and worse than a lot of them, and it takes years of experience to learn it properly, just like anything else worth doing.'

'Broken marriages?' queried Debbie uneasily, and met his eyes. He wasn't laughing.

'My solicitor once told me that he saw more hoteliers go through the divorce court because one or other of them was always too tired for sex than for any other reason,' he said. 'That, Deborah, is only one reason why I say I was stupid. I might've been kinder to go on laughing at you, that evening. The sooner it's over, the less the damage. Howells may have a real reason to hate me 'fore he's through.' He saw that Debbie was looking horrified and smiled. 'Listen to us! Sorry, Deborah, VAT returns always spoil my day.'

'Is that what you're up to?' Debbie sipped her coffee and returned the smile with sparkling eyes. She looked very attractive sitting there. The sun had kissed her fair skin to a warm gold that was sensational with her hair, fairer than ever now from the sun, so she had to be a natural blonde after all. He had once wondered about that, he recalled, and there was the answer. The black-lashed, blue-grey eyes were beautiful. He wished that things were other than they were with a fierce and quite useless longing and asked himself, not for the first time, what on earth he thought he was doing?

'If you hate it so much, you should keep a girl,' Debbie was saying, and he laughed aloud.

'What a fantastic idea! You applying for the position?'

Debbie felt herself go hot all over and wondered at herself, for teasing of this kind generally ran off her like water from a duck's back – a dead duck or a live one, she thought irrelevantly.

'Fool!' she exclaimed. 'I meant an office girl.'

'Oh. I thought for a moment you meant something different, what a shame.' He grinned at her. 'Well, I do, as you must've noticed – but I prefer to keep my financial affairs as my own business.'

Recalling how information went round the village like wildfire, Debbie decided that she didn't blame him, but a wayward thought, as delicate as a butterfly and as difficult to pin down, flitted through the ill-regulated back of her mind. Was Mawgan Angwin, entrepreneur and self-confessed adventurer, one hundred per-cent honest? She found that she wouldn't care to put money on it either way, and the discovery was vaguely disquieting.

'You need some help, though,' she said. 'You seem to work every hour of the day and half the night as well – there must be somebody around that you can trust, who could take some of the load.'

'Stops me from thinking,' said Mawgan, dismissively.

There wasn't time to linger over the coffee, Mawgan was busy and Debbie had to get back to Seagulls before Tim had time to wonder where she was. She walked back up the hill in a pensive mood. That was three times now that she had been kissed goodbye. Not passionately, to be fair, but certainly warmly. If he had been other than he was, she could have believed herself to be on the verge of that appallingly-named modern phenomenon, the meaningful relationship, but as things were, she couldn't be sure. She hadn't, so far, plumbed any real depths in him, and that was undeniable.

Or had she? This morning had been a little different, surely. The tiny seed at the back of her mind stirred and put out a tentative leaf.

She thought that she would go with the tide for a while; let nature take its course. There was plenty of time yet for the whole thing to fizzle out, and no harm done.

One thing, he was a lot older than Robin, and so was likely to be more objective. If it came to anything, it might be fun – while it lasted. When she was with him, everything looked brighter and more interesting, which was strange when you remembered that he was only a small-town Cornishman and she had lived for years in a London-based social whirl – or even a south coast jet set. She smiled at a memory.

The clock on the village church was striking ten. Debbie began to run.

After that conversation with Mawgan, Debbie, in spite of her avowed policy of non-involvement, began to pay closer attention to her friends. That Tim and Lesley were growing further and further apart was undeniable. Although the sailing school wasn't yet really busy, even with help from the Fish, it was seldom that the two of them seemed to spend any time together. Days spent on the water, evenings spent in the Fish or even talking sailing over a beer in their own lounge, these shut Lesley off from the rest of the group. She had no knowledge of sailing and apparently little desire to learn, nor did Tim encourage her to do so. She spent her time in the house, gossiping with Mrs Tregear about domestic affairs and things that had happened in the village, and in the evenings, even if she sat among the rest of them, it was quietly and with very little to say. Often, nowadays, she went to bed early whether they had all stayed in the lounge or not. After the early outbursts, she made no complaints, to Debbie or anyone else, but looking at her carefully in the light of her newly acquired knowledge, Debbie thought that her face was settling into lines not so much of unhappiness as of bitterness. The fun was dying out of her day by day.

Tim, on the other hand, seemed to be perfectly happy with his lot. He didn't appear to notice whether Lesley was present or not, and had long since ceased to ask her to join him either in one of the Wayfarers or down at the Fish, even if opportunity arose. It was impossible to say that this wasn't partly Lesley's fault, but Tim made no effort, either, to interest himself in her affairs even where they touched on his own. It seemed to Debbie to be a miserable deadlock, almost, she caught herself thinking, as if Tim resented that the house and all it contained belonged to Lesley and only the four boats to him – and some of the money for those had been borrowed against Lesley's inheritance. All pretence at partnership seemed to have evaporated. Lesley had been right – His and Hers. Never the twain shall meet.

She comforted herself with the thought that they would have the chance to grow together again during the long winter, but Mawgan's words kept leaping out at her at unexpected moments, haunting her.

Lost hopes, shattered dreams, broken marriages…

Tim's over-ambitious dream for the future had been the first to shatter, ruthlessly put down in infancy by Mawgan himself. A lot more, it now appeared, had shattered with it. It had subtly changed Tim, disappointment had brought with it disillusionment, and a hard wariness that came very close to a self-interest to match Mawgan's own… but Mawgan wasn't a married man. Debbie wondered if he realised what he had done to Tim, and if that was why he was falling over backwards to accommodate Lesley now.

She still couldn't make anything sensible of Mawgan. He sought her company, he kissed her frequently and with considerable warmth, and he made no secret of the fact that he found her attractive and amusing, but at the same time she was finding it increasingly difficult either to take him seriously, or to see him whole. It was almost as if he didn't want her to. He appeared to saunter through life thumbing his nose at criticism and personal unpopularity alike, he made jokes about the humiliating position in which his own actions had placed him, he had displayed for all to see a shameless self-interest – and he went out of his way to see that Lesley, and indirectly Tim, too, had informed advice and practical help whenever it was asked on their behalf, and sometimes when it wasn't. She had toyed with one reason for this, and of course it might be, as Lesley had said, because he thought he owed his life to Debbie herself, but somehow, in the face of Tim's behaviour, this seemed to constitute a thin excuse, very much overstating Tim's importance to her. It was as if he was a person in two distinct halves, so diametrically opposed in character that they were quite irreconcilable.

One thing, though, she was becoming certain about. Whatever might be the truth, she couldn't bring herself to believe that he had really killed somebody deliberately. Although in her more logical moments she knew that it had to be true in some degree, her mind rejected it utterly. She wondered a great deal about what had actually taken place, but there was no way of finding out, of course. She could hardly ask Mrs Tregear, even if Mrs T actually knew, and she certainly couldn't ask Mawgan, he hadn't permitted that much intimacy. He was all light-hearted charm, sunlight playing on shallow water with all the depths hidden in shadow.

She tried to put it out of her mind and concentrate on the job in hand. There was no other way. One of the jobs in hand, of course, was the house by the creek, and she walked up there one morning to see how the land lay. The elderly couple living there had done so for a long time, and were therefore not surprised that their unspoken intentions had passed, by a process not unlike osmosis, into the pool of village knowledge.

'It's those Tregears, of course,' Mrs Horsefall sighed. 'One of them does our garden, it's like employing the CIA.'

'One of them works for us, too,' said Debbie.

'Explains it, then,' said Mr Horsefall, philosophically. 'So come in, young lady, and let's talk.'

The result of that talk was that Oliver and Chel drove over from St. Ives, where they were camping in somebody's studio for the moment, on a Sunday afternoon in order to have a look at the place. They met Debbie, by arrangement, for a bar lunch at the Fish, and not entirely to her surprise, Tim and Roger and most of the current crop of students turned up there too. It was Oliver that was the attraction, she knew, and hoped that he wouldn't mind, but she did wonder what Lesley was going to say. Tim and Roger were supposed to be on vegetable fatigue. She mentioned it.

'Oh, she said it was only salad and jacket spuds tonight, and didn't matter,' said Tim, easily.

'Then wouldn't she have liked to come too, just for once?'

'Someone has to stay and answer the phone.'

Debbie caught Roger's eye and hurriedly looked away, and before he could work round close to her in order to speak into her ear, Chel and Oliver arrived, coming through the pub from the car park and out by the main entrance. She stared.

The last time she had seen Oliver, he had been on crutches, admittedly that was now some months ago but nobody had mentioned that times had changed. Now, he walked without even a stick, maybe a little awkwardly if you knew what to look for, but nothing that would stand out in a crowd. Both he and Chel looked brown and fit and very pleased with themselves. Their months in Greece had obviously done them both a great deal of good.

Debbie performed introductions. Tim knew Oliver already, of course, although they hadn't met for several years, but he had never met Chel and it was impossible to ignore the rest of the crowd either. They settled naturally into a group, and Tim positioned himself behind Debbie's chair in a proprietorial way that earned him, Debbie thought, a very strange look from her sister-in-law. She raised her eyebrows at Chel, but only got a smile in return.

'So, what do you think of the show so far?' she asked, gesturing towards the river.

'Seems like a pleasant enough place,' said Chel, cautiously. Tim leaned more heavily, breathing on Debbie's neck.

'Oh, it is – give or take the odd bastard.'

'Like it might be you, sweetheart?' riposted Debbie, provoked, and again got that strange look from Chel. Gossip, of course, wasn't endemic only to St. Erbyn. Quite a lot of it went on in Embridge too, but what had she done that could have got back there, and from there to St. Ives? She tried to catch Oliver's eye to get some reaction from him, too, but Oliver was too wily. He was talking to Roger and a couple of the students and taking no notice – apparently. It would have surprised Debbie a great deal had she known that Chel and Oliver's arrival back in England had been greeted by a letter from Susan, relaying the information that Lesley had reported to her mother and her mother had reported to *their* mother that Tim was becoming far too interested in Debbie, and Susan had from that deduced that her sister wasn't discouraging him, and would Oliver please go and sort her out – a vain hope, as Susan must have known when she wrote. Nothing happened during that lunch to change the picture. Mawgan's restaurant was open for lunch on Sundays and closed in the evening instead, and he wasn't in evidence. If he had been, Debbie wondered in her ignorance, what would Chel and Oliver have made of him?

The days went by. Debbie was still seeing a certain amount of Mawgan, in spite of the fact that the season was beginning to gain momentum now, for the Fish and at last for the sailing school too. They met in his bar very occasionally, at lunch time and on Sunday evenings, and he always had a smile and a word for her whether Tim was there or not. On the rare occasions when she was free in the afternoon she sometimes walked down the hill and dropped into the Fish to see if he was there, for early afternoon, she had discovered, was the best time to catch him with a few minutes to spare. He always welcomed her, always kissed her, never let her come within touching distance of February's intimacy, sliding through her fingers like sand or the sunlit water to which she had likened him. He would talk to her on these occasions on almost any subject that she chose, but only once did she ever get him to talk about himself.

As she already knew, he opened his restaurant for lunch on Sunday instead of in the evening, and one Sunday at the beginning of July, he rang her on her mobile during the afternoon and asked her if she would care to go out somewhere when she had finished work for the day. Debbie thought that this was a very good idea. Roger was due to give a lecture on the theory of sailing tonight, and she had by this time heard it five times. It never varied by so much as a word, she wouldn't miss anything, nor yet be missed.

'I'd love to,' she said. 'Did you have anywhere particular in mind?'

'Do you have any ideas?'

'I've not had the chance to go anywhere much since I got here. Take me somewhere very Cornish, away from the river.'

She left to walk down to the Fish shortly after eight, leaving the students gathering in the lounge with Tim and Roger, and Lesley, the new, self-contained, hard-eyed Lesley, pottering around in the kitchen. She had almost given up on Lesley and Tim now, you had to be a pretty dedicated do-gooder to help two people who so determinedly rejected all help, and her interest in the first place had been fairly peripheral. Perhaps their marriage would crash, but although it would be a pity, it wouldn't be

the first marriage ever to do so, and there was nothing that she or anyone
else but themselves could do about it. She hadn't exactly forgotten what
Roger had said when she first arrived on the scene, but it had certainly
gone into the very back of her mind.

It was pleasant to be out of doors in the cool of the evening, and as she
went down the gentle hill, she was looking forward to the coming drive
out, although she had still not clearly analysed just why being with Mawgan
gave her such pleasure. The passion that she had felt for Robin had been a
swift but transient burning that had consumed itself as it burned to ashes,
and because it had hurt her pride so deeply she had thought that it had
to be the real thing. It was love of quite a different kind that was stealing
up on her now, so gently that she didn't recognise its face.

That something really was stealing up on her, she became slowly aware.
She stopped abruptly under the trees, listening. This wasn't the first time
that she had thought herself being watched or followed, she realised, but
as before she could hear nothing, see nothing. Imagination – her nerves
must be going to pieces in sympathy with Lesley's, she was getting as
jumpy as a cat.

But no – she was sure she had heard it, that footfall on the gravel at
the side of the road that had echoed her own.

'Is anyone there?' she called. It wasn't in her nature to be unduly
nervous, but a slight curve in the leafy lane cut her off from any sight
of either Seagulls or the Fish. There was nobody in sight, and nobody
answered her call. She walked on down the road with a brisker step than
previously, and was unexpectedly relieved when she reached the causeway.

How completely idiotic!

Mawgan came to meet her as she appeared, informal and relaxed on
this rare evening off, taking her arm and kissing her lightly, as elusive as
ever and apparently as uninvolved as she mistakenly considered herself to
be. They smiled at each other with a warmth that would have deceived
nobody but themselves had anyone been watching, and strolled away up
the lane towards the back of the inn and his car.

Cress had been looking at the girl by the railings for some time before
anything happened. She had noticed her because she was so beautiful; slim,
blonde, her fresh young skin sun-tanned like that of the girl in the book
she had pushed into the pocket of her jacket, now hanging back there in

the kitchen, ready to read in her lunch hour. She was striking and very much of the moment, people turned to take a second look at her as they passed – the men, particularly. She was everything that Cress had dreamed of being and never dared to be. And she was alone, which was strange. She didn't look the sort of girl who would ever be alone.

'Come on, Cress, look, those people are waiting!' Susie, the head waitress, looked at her in irritation as she ran past with her hands full of plates. Cress was pretty hopeless really, she thought, she wouldn't last long if Mrs Bennetts hadn't taken a fancy to her. It meant that other people had to do twice as much work while Cress stared out of the window like one of those zombies from Haiti she had seen on the telly. 'Get moving!' she said, but good-naturedly enough.

Cress moved reluctantly away from the window and took the customers' order, but before long she found an excuse to drift back. The beautiful girl was still there. She was leaning on the rails and looking at the boats, and now there was a man walking purposefully towards her. Her heart missed a beat. It could be *him*, except that no girl who looked like that would need to be waiting for a murderer.

The man walked up to the rails and stood beside the girl, he had his back to the cafe windows. The wind ruffled his short hair. He looked pleased with himself, even from this angle.

'Miss – hi, miss! Can we have a bit of ketchup?'

Cress drifted sideways towards the service table, where the bottles of vinegar and the little sachets of sauce and mayonnaise were ranged in neat ranks. She picked up a couple of sachets of sauce without looking and carried them to the table, her eyes still on the window.

'Ketchup, I said,' said the customer. 'This is brown sauce.'

Susie made a tutting noise, grabbed the right sachets and took them over.

'Oh Cress, do wake up!' she said, and to the customer, 'Sorry, sir.' She gave Cress an exasperated poke, and Cress pushed her hand away without taking any notice.

It *was* him. He had turned now, and he and the girl were looking at each other. You couldn't mistake your own brother even if you hadn't seen him for nearly three years. The girl was looking at him with her head tilted back, and even from this distance you could see that she was enjoying herself. They were laughing. How could he laugh? He had no right to behave like an ordinary person and go out with a girl like that!

The customers were staring at her curiously, and Susie was pulling at her arm. She began to feel very strange indeed.

It was true, then, what Mike had told her. There was a girl. There was this lovely, long-limbed, golden creature to help him to forget what he had done, to make him put the little sister he had wronged, the little sister who had loved him so much, right out of his mind, behind him. And if that was so... if that was so, her promise held good. For Mike, and for herself, too.

Kill the woman, let the man live...

There was a strange ringing noise in her ears, and Susie's persistent voice had begun to echo as if they were both in a tunnel, with Susie at the far end. The darkness rushed at her with a sound of many wings beating, and Cress fell forward in a dead faint right across the table, all among the beefburgers, chips and peas, and slid to the floor in a shower of plates, checked tablecloth and ketchup. It was the most exciting thing that had happened in the Blue Crab all season.

Mrs Bennetts' truly awful son, Gary, was the one detailed to take her back to her bedsit because everybody else was too busy. He looked at her curiously as he drove along in the van that belonged to the café, and tried to question her, but she was in too much of a daze to answer. They had all been very kind, but she wasn't going to tell them anything.

Who was that girl? She had to find out. If she hadn't fainted like that she could have run out of the café and followed them, but she had missed her chance of that. Perhaps she lived in Falmouth, or perhaps she was a St. Erbyn girl, or perhaps she was just a visitor and meant nothing at all.

What shall I do, Mike? You tell me, you help me. You must help me, I can't do this on my own.

He came, as he always did. She felt the pressure against her arm as he sat beside her. She had lost the trail this end, she must pick it up at the other of course. She should have thought of that for herself. She looked at Gary.

'My brother lives in St. Erbyn,' she said, in a pathetic little-girl voice. 'I'd like to go there. Would you take me, Gary? Please?'

She was a pretty little thing, and Gary wasn't averse to a bit of skiving off work. It was quite a distance but, he justified it to himself, she was better with her family if she wasn't well, wasn't she? He drove her there, and because Debbie and Mawgan had stopped for lunch, and then on the trading estate, she got there first.

She asked Gary to drop her at the top of the steep little street, and when she had seen him drive away, walked down towards the water, as she had done so many times before. Nobody recognised her as Mawgan Angwin's tragically widowed little sister, nobody here now had known her that well. She was waiting up the little lane by the Fish when the car came back, she saw them kiss, she saw the beautiful girl walking away up the lane. When Mawgan had driven past her place of concealment and was out of the way, she followed her.

After that, she went to St. Erbyn whenever she could, walking with her head down and her eyes hidden behind sunglasses, disguised. She couldn't ask anyone about the girl, for who was there to ask, and how could she frame the questions anyway? She simply watched, and sometimes followed, and what she saw was love growing quietly between two people as the summer days went past. *But he didn't deserve it, he couldn't have it, it wasn't for non-people like him!*

She followed the girl down to the Fish one summer evening, and saw them meet on the causeway as if they were already lovers. She didn't want to kill that lovely blonde girl, Cress thought, but why should he have such a beautiful companion to smile into his eyes in that heart–snatching way, when Mike was dead and would never smile again?

Perhaps it would be possible to make her go away, and to make anyone else who looked at him like that go away too, to leave him in the wilderness, hated by everyone as he so richly deserved. It would be justice, a sort of death in life. It ought to be easy enough: she couldn't possibly know what he was.

And when she had done that – it seemed to her a quick and easy thing to do – then she would punish that artist, Oliver Nankervis, who had made Mike cry. It was all she remembered about him now, that he had made Mike, who was always so strong and confident, weep like a little child, but he wouldn't be hard to find. He was famous. Famous people couldn't hide from punishment, everybody knew where they lived. In her own mind, Mike and Charlie had become so intermixed that she no longer knew where one ended and the other began. She looked quiet and pretty and mouse-like, and nobody looking at her could have told that she was dangerous.

Under the sheltering leaves, she reached for the hand of the man that only she could see, and felt it touch her own. She would start the search for Oliver Nankervis at the weekend, then she would be ready when his turn came. She would go to Trelewan again, and start there. Her shadowy companion nodded his approval.

It would all be over with the summer, and then she could lay the burden down. At the end of the summer, she could leave…

XIII

Mawgan and Debbie went to Coverack, where they walked along the beach in the warm summer dusk with the calm sea whispering along the shingle to their left and the village to their right, and Debbie sensed an off-duty relaxation in him that she had never felt before. He worked very hard – she had frequently thought, unreasonably hard. The pursuit of material success should leave some time for leisure, surely, it shouldn't be an end in itself. She hadn't quite got the picture yet, but it was taking shape slowly – too slowly. She slid her hand through his arm and felt his other hand cover her own warmly.

'Happy?' he asked her.

'Mmm, yes.' Debbie looked out over the tranquil sea, and back at the companionable twinkling lights in the cottages, and felt at peace with the world. 'It's good to get away. I enjoy what I'm doing, but with so many other personalities all asserting themselves all over the place, I never feel completely… well, myself, I suppose. We live too close together.' Except for those of us who are beginning to live too far apart, but she couldn't say that aloud.

Lesley and Tim didn't have enough time to be themselves. And Mawgan. Did he? Perhaps that was all his trouble. That simple?

'You work too hard,' she said, putting the thought into words. 'You should get away from it more often. Don't you find it difficult in the summer, running the place on your own?'

'On my own?' She heard the laugh in his voice. 'Deborah dear, I employ a second chef and a housekeeper, a barman and a restaurant manager, and God knows how many lesser fry. That's hardly being on my own.'

'Employees are rather different,' said Debbie, unanswerably. 'Have you never thought of taking a partner, or even simply just someone to share some of the responsibility? You look tired to the bone sometimes.'

'Do I?' He sounded amused, if anything, and her own solicitude had surprised her, too. 'No Deborah, if you do everything yourself, there's only you to let you down. I think it's better that way.'

She wondered from that, and from his tone, which was odd, if he had ever had a partner, but what she actually said was, 'How did you ever get into catering? Were you born into the trade?'

He laughed, and she felt some unexplained tension easing.

'Far from it. My father's a builder, and my grandfather a builder before him, and I was meant to be a builder too.'

'So what went wrong?' asked Debbie, curiously – more curiously than he could guess, for her father was a solicitor, and her grandfather was a solicitor before him, and Oliver was meant to be a solicitor too. Some hopes!

'I di'n't like the idea, that's what went wrong. I always knew what I wanted, and it weren't bricks and mortar and drains and plumbing and all the rest of it. I just weren't into drains. Dad di'n't go down without a struggle, but he couldn't force me. Which isn't to say that he di'n't try.' He sounded as if the recollection had no thorns to hurt, and she was emboldened to ask,

'Tell me about it.'

'I left school at sixteen to start in the business from the bottom. I learned bricklaying and plumbing, and all sorts of other skills that have come in pretty useful since – and went off on day release to classes that were meant to be about building and things, and learned catering and kitchen management, cooking, and all the other things as I needed to know. When I had all the proper qualifications, I gave Dad back his job, got my cards and a good telling off, and went abroad.'

'Why abroad? Was Dad that bad?' He and Oliver would have a lot to talk about – if they ever met. It all sounded so very familiar.

He gave an appreciative chuckle, but said, 'More money, more fun – and more prestige, on the whole. Catering is still a bit of a poor relation in this country. I was a night porter in Marseilles for 'bout ten minutes, while I looked around, after that a kitchen porter in Amsterdam, then a commis-chef, a sous-chef in Brussels, and then a head chef in Lausanne. Later, I worked as head chef in a restaurant in Milan, that was a great job, I nearly stayed there, but –'

'I beg your pardon?' interrupted a startled Debbie. 'You're a *chef*?'

He looked at her in surprise.

200

'Well, yes. Why does that surprise you? You must've known.'

'No,' said Debbie. It felt strange. She thought about it. 'I don't think Tim and Lesley do, either.' Too wrapped up in their own affairs and in their private feud to care. 'So *that's* why we never see you around when the restaurant is open. I thought you just ran it…' Her voice tailed off, helplessly.

'I can't believe you didn't know,' said Mawgan, and she sensed the amusement in him although he kept his voice solemn. She shook her head in amazement.

'I never even gave it a thought, how awful of me! Did you cook that wonderful meal I ate the other night?'

'Some of it. Not all of it, obviously, since I was sitting there with you.'

'So that's why we ate so very late.' Debbie mused on this for a minute, and then laughed. 'Well, you have surprised me! Do you do that often?'

'What, entertain young girls to dinner? No, not very. Not at all. It mostly wouldn't work out like that anyway. That night was a lucky one, we had a last-minute cancellation. Normally we wouldn't finish cooking that early.'

They walked a little way in silence. Finally, Debbie said, 'Do you have any more like that up your sleeve? When did you come back to England?'

He laughed, quietly.

'About six years ago. I worked in a hotel in Bristol for a while, but it wasn't all that much of a job, and then I came up on the Pools – yeah.' He caught her eye and grinned. 'Full of surprises, me. We had a syndicate at work – it weren't a huge sum, mind, but enough. That's when we bought the Fish. It was pretty seedy and run-down, it took a couple of years to bring it up to scratch – and yes, I did have a partner then, he ran the pub and I ran the restaurant, and his wife was the housekeeper. He packed it in when…' He faltered, but only for a moment, and went on with apparent unconcern, 'when I went to prison. He put the place in the hands of a manager, but he was a bit of a disaster. He kicked him out before I got back and a stop-gap put in to keep the show running, and then I've spent the last year bringing it back up to scratch on my own, but lost reputations are hard going to get back. Satisfied?'

'So you had to buy your partner out?'

'I didn't have no choice, so yes. It could've been worse, at least I was the major shareholder.'

'Eeuch!' said Debbie, expressively. 'You haven't had it easy, then. But an interesting life, anyway.' If there were strange gaps in that tale, she was too enthralled to spot them.

'Oh, very. And varied.'

Very varied. Prison on top of all that.

'Do you speak all those languages, too?' asked Debbie, curiously.

'French and Italian – not brilliantly, but enough to get by. Like plumbing, it can come in handy. I never really got to grips with German.'

'French and Italian with a Cornish accent?'

'So they tell me.'

Debbie giggled appreciatively.

'And is your father proud of you now?'

It slipped out before she had thought, a desperate relapse into foot-in-mouth disease. The shadow of the prison walls seemed to fall across their path to Debbie's fanciful mind, but Mawgan answered her lightly, as if it didn't really matter.

'No, Deborah, he isn't. He still feels that only a screaming queen would go in for cooking and work in a kitchen, and he still thinks I should've been a big macho builder and taken over when he retires – if he ever does, that is. I don't see it myself.'

'Haven't you a brother to take over instead of you?'

'No, my bird, I haven't.'

Nobody had ever called her *my burrd* before she met Mawgan, or called her anything, come to think, with quite that affectionate caress in his voice. Startled yet again, she felt a faint, premonitory tingle run across her skin, a lifting excitement that she almost recognised for what it was, and then lost again. The spectre of Robin stood at her elbow, and behind him, Exeter prison – if that was where Mawgan had been, she hardly liked to ask – bulked as big as the Taj Mahal.

'Are your family local?' she asked, idly, remembering something that Mrs. Tregear had once said.

'I was born and brought up in St. Austell,' he replied, 'so not that local, no.' The answer sounded dismissive, she had a feeling that it wasn't strictly the answer to her question, and that she had trespassed too close to some private place – of pain or humiliation, or simply of disappointment, there was no way of telling.

Sand and shingle crunched under their feet in the still evening. The sea whispered beside them. It was turning chilly.

'How about a drink in someone else's pub?' suggested Mawgan.

'That works for me,' said Debbie, agreeably.

They altered course towards a flight of steps leading up to the road.

'Mawgan,' said Debbie, on a sudden impulse, 'why are you so very generous towards Tim and Lesley? Tim's done nothing to earn it.'

He had detached her hand from his arm and put the arm around her shoulders instead. His left arm, she had noticed once or twice before that he had a tendency to use the left in preference to the right that was undoubtedly of recent date. She had wondered if it was from habit or necessity, and she had plenty of time to wonder again now, as she waited for his reply.

'That's a good question,' he said at last.

'That's why I asked it.'

There was another long pause, and then Mawgan said, 'I s'pose I feel a bit guilty.'

'Whatever for?' asked Debbie, surprised.

'Oh... what you said. Ivory towers aren't made of strong stuff, if you smash them down they can't be rebuilt. I know that... I used my marked talent for demolition on Howells' tower, and I can see it's made his wife unhappy and him bitter and resentful. And...' His voice slowed and stopped entirely.

'And?' prompted Debbie, after a moment, but introspection seemed to have taken itself off during the pause, and he laughed.

'And I know that I'd do it again if I had to – if he gave me cause.'

'Conscience money then, sort of?'

'Oh Deborah,' he said. 'They're friends of yours. Howells might not believe it, but I should like to be wrong and see him succeed.'

'But not at your expense, is what you're saying?'

'If he leaves me alone, I only wish him well.'

Debbie's understanding of Tim was as faulty as her present understanding of Mawgan, and she didn't make the reply that perhaps she should have done.

'You're too forbearing,' was what she said.

'I don't think that's the word you want,' he replied, and by that time they had reached the road level and were among people again, not isolated with the sea and sand and shingle. Debbie was still trying to decide exactly what he had meant when they reached the bright and welcoming doorway of the Paris Hotel.

So she had been right in her unlikely guess, he was sorry that he had knocked down Tim's impractical castle in Spain. She could explain, she supposed, that it had been at best a pipe-dream, but he knew that already, and anyway, it wasn't really the point. Tim and Lesley had believed in it, and it had for a short time given them a great deal of happiness, both in itself and in each other.

Mawgan must have seen a dream of his own turn sour. At least one.

He came over to her now with a beer for himself and a glass of wine for her, and the rest of the evening ran on pleasant but predictable lines, with no further surprises. Debbie found it unusual to be with a man who obviously held her in great affection but made no overtly sexual demands, and once or twice, found herself wondering why this was. She wouldn't have minded, she realised. She enjoyed being kissed by him, and she had liked the feel of his arm around her as they walked, but sometimes he felt like her brother, he kept his hands to himself so assiduously. Since she placed no confidence in his father's estimate of him, and didn't believe that his father really could either, it left a very large question mark hanging in the air. It couldn't be that he simply didn't fancy her, because he wouldn't bother to ask her to go out with him if that was the case.

Big mystery.

'What are you thinking, Deborah?' he asked, looking at her curiously. Debbie felt herself blush.

'Nothing – just thoughts. You know…'

She was relieved when he laughed and didn't pursue it.

'Another one? Then we must be going, while I'm still sober enough to get away with it. I can't afford to be stopped by the fuzz.'

He dropped her off at the gate of Seagulls later that night, and she ran up the drive with the touch of his lips on hers as a warmth in her immediate memory, and walked abruptly into one of the more obvious complications of her growing friendship.

Roger's lecture was long over. The students, together with Roger and Tim, were sitting over drinks in the main lounge, still discussing technical points that had arisen during the evening, absorbed in their common interest. Lesley wasn't there, she had presumably already gone to bed. Debbie peered into the kitchen to make sure that she hadn't been left to provide the household with hot drinks single-handed, but finding it in darkness and deserted, went into the lounge to join the others.

'Oh, back at last, are we?' Tim greeted her. He sounded sarcastic, Debbie thought, not at all his usual friendly self, and she wondered a little. His eyes were bright behind his glasses. She decided that it was safest to take the remark at its face value.

'As you see, yes.'

'Have a beer,' said Roger, reaching for a can. 'Or, no.' He gave it an experimental shake. 'We seem to have drunk it all. Sorry.'

'I didn't want one anyway,' said Debbie. 'I've been drinking wine all evening. It wouldn't mix too well.'

'Did you have a good time?' asked one of the students, conversationally.

'Yes thanks.' Debbie had one cautious eye on Tim. A fair amount of the vanished beer seemed to have flowed in his direction, he wasn't exactly drunk, but he was over-excited and, she suspected, upset about something. Lesley probably, and she felt irritation with them both. She hoped that the subject of her evening out might now be allowed to drop, but the girl who had spoken to her before smiled at her in a friendly fashion, and asked, 'Boyfriend?'

Before Debbie could answer this perfectly reasonable question, Tim cut in from his position leaning against the mantelpiece. 'Oh, Deb prefers the company of cut-throats and murderers to ours. You have to make allowances.'

Debbie gasped.

'Tim!' she exclaimed, indignantly, and Roger said, too quickly, laughing, 'Can you blame her? I mean, look at us, and there was that lecture too! But actually, I don't think that it was anyone worse than the landlord of the local pub, am I right, Deb?' It was a neat cover-up that should have worked, but Tim spoilt it.

'That's what I said.'

The students looked as if they weren't sure whether they should laugh too or not, and one of them said, 'Do I scent a mystery? Come on, you've got to tell us now – what's Debbie been up to?'

'I admire his nerve in what he charges for a pint, but surely that doesn't make him a murderer,' added one of the men, laughing.

'Done time for it,' said Tim, at the same moment as Debbie said, 'Of course not!'

They looked at each other, Debbie with rising fury, Tim with a cool insolence that was new, and a challenge in his eyes that she would sooner not have met. Not tonight, at least, and not in front of everyone.

'Look,' said Roger, pacifically, 'it's old history, don't dig it all up, Tim. It's a dead duck. It's time we all turned in, we've a hard day's sailing ahead of us tomorrow.'

One or two of the students took the hint and began to drift away, saying goodnight as they went, but unfortunately some of the others were more tenacious. A couple of bright-eyed girls seated together on the window seat pressed for more details. They didn't, Debbie realised, have the least idea of the seriousness of it all, and thought it was some kind of joke, but she hated them for it just the same – not so much on Mawgan's behalf, strangely, for presumably he had prepared his own defences long since, but on Tim's. Tim was making himself look mean and small, even if his listeners didn't recognise it. She wished he would stop.

'So what did he do?' one of the girls was demanding. 'You can't go this far and not tell us – really!'

'Look we really shouldn't be talking about it,' said Debbie, on a note of desperation. 'It isn't our business.'

'You seem to be making it yours,' said Tim, silkily, and went on with hardly a pause. 'Anyway, it's hardly a big secret when everyone knows. Our local publican got himself involved in a murder case.'

'Manslaughter!' said Debbie, swiftly. It hardly helped, as she immediately realised.

'You mean, he *really* killed somebody?' The girl leaned forward in her chair, eyes like saucers, and several of the others looked pardonably startled.

'By accident,' said Debbie. Tim raised his eyebrows.

'Bashing somebody over the head with a large rock doesn't sound very accidental to me,' he said.

Debbie choked on a startled cry, and one of the students exclaimed, 'He didn't!'

'According to the locals here, he did,' said Tim. 'I don't know how much you can believe of what you hear, mind you.'

It was a bit late for that. Debbie began to hate him.

'But – ' The girl who had first spoken was looking straight at her, round-eyed with half-alarmed, half-pleased speculation. 'Debbie, is it safe to go out with someone like that?'

'I'm still here,' Debbie managed, trying to make light of it. She thought her voice sounded different – strained. She cleared her throat.

'Well, I don't think that you should! A man who could do a thing like that… well, he might do *anything!*'

'Tim's exaggerating,' said Debbie, trying to strike a note of amusement, as if it really was some kind of joke, and failing dismally. She gave Roger an agonised look. He got to his feet and began gathering up the empty cans and glasses.

'Gossip, gossip, gossip, like a load of old tabbies, you lot! It's a good story to us, but it's pretty damn serious for him. I know none of you will say anything outside these four walls, but maybe best we should mention it. You might have heard something in the village, and really, it's all a load of balls. He wouldn't be here if it wasn't.'

It was clever of Roger to turn it round that way, but kinder to Tim than to Mawgan. Debbie felt a twist of misery deep inside her that took the edge off her pleasure in her evening out. This sort of thing must be what Mawgan lived with. He didn't seem to let it bother him unduly, but he could hardly like it. The pain she felt on his behalf was actually physical.

The students had taken the hint at last and were gathering up their belongings preparatory to going up to their rooms. One of the girls said, with an enjoyable shudder, 'Well, I'm glad that you did tell us. I shall take care not to be out alone after dark!'

She was enjoying making her own flesh creep, not meaning to be taken too seriously, but as she spoke, Tim seemed to realise exactly what he had done. He went suddenly scarlet and turned away to help Roger with the empties. The party began to break up, until only Debbie, Roger and Tim were left. The room seemed suddenly very quiet. Roger picked up the tray and looked from Debbie to Tim.

'I think I'll turn in too,' he said. 'Goodnight.'

The door closed behind him. Debbie went over to the window and stood looking out over the moonlit garden, startled to find how coldly angry she really was. She had difficulty in keeping her voice level.

'I hope you're proud of yourself,' she said.

Tim stood irresolutely by the door.

'Roger's right. It's time we called it a day.'

Debbie turned to look at him.

'Not for a minute. Tim, what's the matter with you? We've been through all this once already, you must – you really must – mind what you say.'

Tim met her eyes.

'Have I said anything tonight that isn't true?'

'True or not, you shouldn't have said it.'

'If I hadn't, they would only have heard it somewhere else. Did you know that I've already had one lot of guests – that family who were one of Lesley's aunt's bookings – complain to me that it was hardly a safe place to encourage people to bring their children?'

'For God's sake, Tim, he's not a *pædophile*!'

Tim ignored this.

'They criticised me for not telling them, Deb. Not *warning* them. They took the kiddies down to the Fish to have a Coke outside in the sunshine, they told me, and had the poor little innocents served by a murderer.'

'It was manslaughter.'

'Only by a whisker, Deb. Don't you *know* what he did?'

Debbie shook her head, miserably.

'Jesus Christ!' said Tim, throwing up his hands. 'You are something else, do you know that? Well, I'll tell you now! He lost his cool, Deb, and hammered his unfortunate brother-in-law with a chunk of rockery stone. There's no room for argument about it. There were two witnesses.'

'I don't believe you.' Her voice sounded suddenly hoarse.

'Well, you may. And did you know that dear Mrs T has suggested to us that we should stop you from seeing him? *Really not safe, Mr. Howells, and all the village talking about it*! I'm seriously wondering if I should send you home.'

'You can't,' said Debbie. 'You're not my keeper.'

'I realise that.' Tim looked serious. All the excitement had died out of him, he was himself again. 'I'm aware that you couldn't be made to go, and that you're safer where we know what you're doing – but if anything happens to you, Deb, how do you think we're going to feel, explaining to your parents – to Oliver?'

'I'm perfectly safe, and Oliver isn't that stupid. Mawgan wouldn't hurt me – he wouldn't hurt anyone.'

'How can you possibly say that?' Tim stared at her, hopelessly. 'I don't think you've been listening. He's been in prison, he's only out on parole if you want to speak the brutal truth. However you may feel, can you blame me for feeling responsible? I brought you here.'

'You can salve your conscience with the recollection that I already knew him when I arrived,' said Debbie, furiously. 'I've been of age for years, you don't have to feel responsible, nobody does! It's my business, not yours!'

'I ought to write to your father.'

'Do that, if you want to cause a huge family row,' Debbie invited him, cordially.

'Debbie – Debbie, is he worth it?'

Debbie's thoughts flew instantly to the cottage in the snow, and the endless forty-eight hours when she and Mawgan had been alone, cut off from the world with only each other to rely on. The picture, as it always did, blotted out the present truth. The one was something she knew of her own knowledge, the other simply hearsay. Her trust in Mawgan might be unfounded, but it was absolute.

'Whether he's worth it or not is hardly anything to do with you, and anyway, it isn't the point,' she told him. 'Whatever he's done, he didn't do it to *you*, and you have no right to damage his reputation – or his business!'

'I can do no more damage to either than he has already done for himself.'

'You managed it before,' said Debbie.

'And I've said I'm sorry, and I've tried to put it right.'

'You never said you were sorry to him.'

'He damages my business simply by being there – and he hasn't said he's sorry to me, either.'

'Tim, don't be such a wanker! He's entitled to live somewhere – and he was here first! You didn't have to open a sailing school on his doorstep.'

'I wasn't intending his pub to play such a large part in our lives.'

'If you really believe he might assault your students, it was very irresponsible of you to come here in the first place!'

'I don't believe it.'

'Then what has this been all about?' Debbie shouted at him, enraged.

'Oh Debbie,' said Tim. 'Don't be so dumb. I can look after myself, Angwin doesn't scare me and he's hardly likely to injure casual visitors, damn it, they're his livelihood. But you... you're different. I can see that he might be attractive to women in a swarthy kind of way, even if Lesley hadn't told me so – but Deb, he's got a nasty, vicious, out-of-control temper on him, and I don't think you quite realise it.'

It didn't match with courage, with kindness or with generosity.

'A Cornish nasty, instead of a Cornish pasty?' snapped Debbie, defensively, throwing her remaining caution to the winds. 'I won't believe it!'

'You won't believe it, well how nice! Well, keep out of rockeries, my girl, or you may find you have to believe it.'

A feeling that Tim had somehow managed to turn what was initially his fault into hers sent self-control flying out of the window. Debbie rounded on him.

'Nasty, vicious tempers show in the face, and you watch it, Tim Howells, because it's what's beginning to show in yours!' She drew an unsteady breath, because she hadn't meant to say exactly that. 'I'm sorry. Shall we go to bed?'

'I think we'd better,' said Tim, shortly. He went over to the door and stood with his hand ready on the light switch, waiting for her. His face was set in lines of rigid disapproval, and Debbie walked past him with her nose in the air, seething. Friendship, of however long-standing, wouldn't survive very much more of this kind of thing. She had never thought that Tim could be such a two-faced git!

They walked over to the staff quarters together after they had locked up, but of speech between them there was none. Once inside, Tim marched across the kitchen and through the door of the room he shared with Lesley without even bothering to say goodnight, and Debbie made no attempt to prevent him. She had felt relaxed and happy, at peace with all the world, when Mawgan had kissed her at the gate, now she felt like a cat with its fur brushed up the wrong way. She went into her own room, and without bothering to put on the light, sat down on the edge of her bed and fumed, her thoughts chasing round and round in a jumble of unpleasantness that sent sleep flying into all the distant corners of the room.

Tim, kind, easy-going Tim, whom she had known for years, was changing under her eyes into a bad-tempered bully with no sense of justice, either towards his wife or to others about him. Lesley, sweet, competent, unruffled Lesley was taking on the character of a discontented drudge. Each of them, in their own way, was passing the blame on to Mawgan rather than apportioning it between themselves. Debbie didn't see how having their own licence would have altered everything, and she didn't seriously think that they did any more, it was the old, old story of the scapegoat. They couldn't go on like this without disaster. They weren't, according to Mawgan, even being original. And Mawgan was too vulnerable to be used as a scapegoat anyway.

It was division that was building up the pressures, but how to make them see it? Division, and Lesley's ignorance of sailing that she was too proud to admit in front of the students, Tim's stubbornness that wouldn't allow him to adapt his original plans to leave room for his wife. That, and the fact that neither of them knew how to deal with people on a business footing, either their own guests whom they persisted in treating as friends, and tonight had illustrated the fundamental mistake in that, or Mrs Tregear, or even Roger and herself, still less the slick professionalism of the Fish itself. It was perfectly true what Tim had said, the Fish did play a big part in their lives. And as the season progressed, and the numbers of their guests became greater, so the Fish would become more important still. It was so close, for one thing. People whose holidays were disciplined by tuition during the day quite naturally liked to get out in the evening. Younger people, as most of their students were, as come to that she was herself, wanted other people and laughter and talk, some local colour and a drink among friends in a convivial atmosphere, all things that the Fish could provide. Even if Lesley and Tim had achieved their cherished bar, things wouldn't have been very much different. Professional jealousy was helping to curdle the milk of human kindness in Tim's veins, whatever other causes there might be.

There was no doubt at all about Mawgan's professionalism. If she had ever had any illusions on that score they had been dispelled tonight. He had worked his way around Europe, it now appeared, with but one end in view, to have his own restaurant – possibly more than one, which was a new thought – and there was no doubt at all, either, that he was more than a match for Tim and Lesley. If he ever happened to feel like it, it would probably not be beyond him to put them out of business entirely, so it was fortunate that he appeared, so far, to want them to stay in. She hadn't yet had time to come to terms with the astonishment she had felt on learning that he was a fully trained chef and not just someone who owned a pub with a restaurant attached. She had for some reason never thought of his being so very highly qualified, equating him more with themselves, but obviously with more experience.

He had accepted her estimate of himself as an entrepreneur and an adventurer, it seemed that it was to be taken seriously. She had thought it to be a bit of a joke. Her mistake.

Had she made any other mistakes?

She went on thinking, and a sense of discomfort grew in her, as much with herself as anything.

It was unfortunate that Tim had said what he did in the first place, but Debbie, however reluctantly, had to accept that some of what he had subsequently said might have some justification. From Tim's point of view, she was taking a risk, if Mawgan had really done what he was supposed to have done – and Tim obviously believed that he had. The fact that she herself found it impossible to believe a word of it became, considered in that context, totally irrelevant. It must also be uncomfortable for Tim and Lesley to have Mrs T throwing out dark hints and warnings, and she didn't herself relish the news that the village was talking about her. The fact that she was of age, as she had pointed out, and quite unrelated to either Tim or Lesley as she hadn't pointed out, didn't really make it any less their business. If people were warning them she was putting herself at risk, and they believed it… well, they were supposed to be her good friends, after all. If there was anything else behind Tim's outburst, she chose not to recognise it.

'Oh shit!' said Debbie, aloud. Divided loyalties were the worst kind of dilemma.

Lesley was glad enough of Mawgan's advice. She had called him generous, admitted openly that he was a godsend to her and that she needed the knowledge that he was there in the background to manage at all. Could she, at the same time, believe that he was the next worst thing to a murderer?

She had to start with. It had become expedient to smother that belief, but was it still there underneath? Had she and Tim been talking about it, quarrelling maybe, and could that be what was at the back of tonight's nasty little scene?

She contemplated in a daunted silence the possibility that things had got to such a pitch between Lesley and Tim that Lesley would prefer that she herself should continue to go out with a man convicted of a most unlikely-sounding manslaughter rather than go without the help she didn't get from her own husband. This pitfall was one with spikes at the bottom, not necessarily for herself, but for Lesley. She had no belief that Mawgan would use violence on her, but under the circumstances, what would Tim do to Lesley if he ever found out?

This thought led onwards to what was, for her, the darker side of the coin. However protective he felt, Tim really shouldn't say things like that about Mawgan in front of other people. He didn't know any of those present tonight personally, he didn't know if, or even how, they would repeat what he had said. If anything got back to the Fish, via Mrs T or by any other route, she didn't think that Mawgan would take it so well a second time. She had no idea what he would do, but she was quite sure that whatever it was, Tim wouldn't like it, and that it would make things a hundred times more complicated for herself, and even more for Lesley. And for Mawgan? That, she didn't know.

So much for non-involvement. It appeared that it was also a non-event.

There was no point in thinking about it, she would go to bed and to sleep, and perhaps in the morning the whole thing would have blown over. She didn't think it would have, but there was no harm in hoping. She got to her feet and switched on the light, and saw for the first time that there was a folded piece of paper lying on her pillow.

She picked it up without any feeling of impending threat, thinking if she thought about it at all that it would be some message from Lesley, a phone call or something equally trivial. It looked that kind of thing, written on the torn-off back of an envelope. She unfolded it without presentiment, and looked at it.

It was written crudely in capital letters with no punctuation marks, using what she thought might have been a lip-liner pencil. The words, red and ragged, danced before her eyes.

IF YOU GO OUT WITH MURDERERS YOU DESERVE WHATS COMING TO YOU YOU FILTHY WHORE

XIV

Debbie's first reaction was to feel contaminated. She dropped the piece of paper as if it had bitten her and stood there, looking at it lying on the quilt, with a sensation that her flesh was humping along her bones like a flock of caterpillars. It wasn't that its phrasing was particularly foul, she had heard a great deal worse than that in her time – it was the thought that some person unknown had taken the trouble to direct such unnecessary venom against her, and had invaded her space in order to deposit it.

It was several moments before common-sense took over. She wasn't so stupid as not to realise that the world was far from being peopled by angels. There must be someone, even in so idyllically pretty a place as St. Erbyn, who was sick enough to direct spite against Mawgan for what he had done, and also against her for being seen, apparently, to condone it. If she asked him – which she had no intention of doing – she would very likely find that anonymous letters of this kind were no surprise to him. The thought sickened her as the letter itself had not. She picked it up with the tips of her fingers, took it into the bathroom, and was about to flush it down the pan in the classic manner when she thought better of it. She thought coolly, standing there with the letter in her hand, that there might be others. If so, nobody need think that she was going to sit down under them. She folded it carefully, putting a sheet of toilet paper, which seemed to her a most suitable covering, over the lettering so that it didn't smudge, and put it away in the drawer of her dressing table.

So one way and another, it was hardly surprising that she didn't sleep particularly well. The anonymous letter apart, she found it difficult to stop thinking about rockeries and the implications thereof, and wondering, against her will, if she was being wise to trust Mawgan so implicitly. She needed to know exactly what had happened, and it wasn't any more simply idle curiosity. If someone told her, fair enough, but she knew that the only person she could honestly ask was Mawgan, and that was impossible.

Trust… it sounded so easy when you said the word quickly.

She tossed and turned, and rose in the morning heavy-eyed and short-tempered, to face another jolly day on the river.

After breakfast, for which she had very little appetite, she asked Lesley if she had heard anything after she had gone to bed the previous night. Tim and Roger had finished and gone to organise their day's work, and she and Lesley were dawdling over a last cup of coffee.

'Heard anything?' asked Lesley, blankly. So blankly, in fact, that it occurred to Debbie, fleetingly but for the first time, that maybe *Lesley*…? But no, that was pure paranoia, Lesley surely needed the friendship to continue.

'What do you mean?' Lesley went on. 'I heard you come back around ten o'clock, that's all.'

Debbie hadn't returned until almost midnight. She said, 'Oh,' and left it at that, still uncomfortably uncertain what to think.

Anyone could have seen her leave, could have watched Lesley go over to the staff quarters, have seen her light go out and waited their chance… but they would have had to be studying her very closely, know where she went and with whom, where she worked, where she slept. She remembered the feeling she had had of being followed in the lane, and the recollection was unpleasant. But was it also *unreasonable*?

'I think we ought to have some extra keys cut and lock the staff flat when we're not there,' she said. 'Anyone could get in.'

'There's nothing there worth pinching,' said Lesley. 'What's the matter with you this morning?'

It wasn't what people might take, but what they might leave… if locks would even help.

'I didn't sleep all that well,' said Debbie. She got to her feet, yawning ostentatiously. 'I'd better get off and join the others. See you at lunch time, Les.' She left the kitchen in haste so obvious that Lesley watched her go in astonishment.

People see what they want to see. What Lesley saw was Debbie hurrying to get away to rejoin Tim. She had no idea, because she had taken herself off immediately after dinner, where Debbie had been last evening. She had even less idea of Debbie's suspicions or their cause, she simply knew that something was wrong. It came into her head, not for the first time, that she knew what that something might be. She got to her feet and began gathering the debris from breakfast together onto the draining board. Exhaustion, both mental and physical, dragged at her.

The briefing session was just coming to an end as Debbie came into the study, and Tim was winding up.

'… and if all that goes to plan, we should be ashore in nice time for a drink before lunch to put the strength back into you.'

'Down at the Cut-throat's Arms?' asked one of the young men, grinning.

'At the Fish, yes,' said Tim repressively, but after his outburst of the evening before none of the present company was likely to take much notice of a tone of voice. Unfair to blame them, it was Tim's own fault. They were strangers.

'Will he be there?' asked one of the girls, and gave a delicious little shiver. 'I've never met a murderer. What's he like, Debbie?'

One of the older men, who had perhaps given more thought to the events of the previous night, said, 'If he's a friend of Debbie's, he'll be OK.'

Debbie threw him a grateful look and avoided Tim's eye. Completely sober this morning, he fully realised what he had done. He had apologised at breakfast, and with luck that was the end of it, but Debbie realised that it was going to be very hard to damp down the high spirits of some of the members of their group, and to keep a proper curb on what was said. Tim had cut the ground from under his own feet, and it was still possible that he had also started the clock on a time-bomb. She wished that they hadn't established a new habit of finishing the morning session at mid-day and going with the students down to the Fish for a drink before leaving them there to have a quick sandwich lunch and slipping back to deal with their own domestic chores. Tim had been pleased when he had formulated the plan, today, she wished very much that it had never entered his head. It had seemed like a great idea at the time.

She did not – she most desperately did not – wish to be involved in another row between Tim and Mawgan. There was no room for misunderstandings in the delicately balanced friendship that lay between herself and the landlord of the Fish, and in spite of his own admission, she didn't think that prison had blunted his finer feelings one bit. Tough, he certainly was, and prison no doubt had something to do with it: insensitive, no.

The morning's session went well, a figure eight course sailed in the open water opposite the sailing school, in a brisk breeze that gave the students plenty to think about and left them pleased with their own prowess. The three boats that had been out came ashore at a quarter to twelve and the whole crowd made its way in a laughing, chattering group down to the Fish. Lesley, a little to everyone's surprise, had elected to come too. Dinner was only pasties and salad, she said, there was nothing much to be done about it until later on. She had begun to cut corners with the catering lately, a certain proportion of frozen vegetables and baker's goods had begun to replace the fresh produce and home cooking of the early days.

The breeze was not only brisk, but rather chilly today, and the sun kept clouding over. It hadn't mattered out on the water but it wasn't good weather for sitting outside. The party went into the lounge bar, which was already reasonably full, and squeezed itself into a space by the window that was just being vacated. Debbie, after a quick look round, saw with an unfamiliar sinking feeling that Mawgan himself was behind the bar for once, and Tommy presumably in the public bar that was favourite with the locals. He was more frequently there at lunch time since the pub had become busier, but she had rather hoped that today would be either the rare exception or his turn in the other bar. Both he and the young barmaid were fully occupied with other customers, and he hadn't noticed her come in specifically, although he was no doubt aware of the group itself. It always gave her a strange feeling to watch him at work, his life style was so very different to her own. Even more different than she had imagined, after what she had learned last night. *Chef…* that's who he was. If they could have afforded to eat in the restaurant, or been less involved in their own affairs, they would no doubt have realised that long ago.

Tim and Roger were collecting orders, Debbie asked for a half of lager and then winced, as Tim cut unceremoniously across something that Lesley was saying to ask her companion what she would like. The girl looked startled, and said a lime-top, thank you. Tim, ignoring his wife, went on round the circle, and it was left to Roger to ask Lesley what she wanted. Debbie didn't think Tim had done it on purpose, but it was unfortunate all the same. Lesley, who had been making some sort of effort to be part of the group, retreated into glum silence, and the talk left general subjects and drifted back to sailing.

Roger and Tim had gone over to the bar, and Mawgan, realising when he saw them that Debbie must be there too, sent her a smile across the width of the room that made her heart unexpectedly turn right over. She returned it warmly.

One of the girls broke off what she was saying and, intercepting the smile, said, 'Wow! Is that him, Debbie? Incredibly sexy!' admiringly.

Debbie admitted that it was and tried to swing the conversation back to matters arising from this morning's lesson, but without success. Lesley didn't help her, and Roger and Tim were still at the bar. Disaster gathered momentum.

'But he's simply *gorgeous*!' cried the girl who had first spoken. 'Nobody told us he was like that!' Her eyes gleamed, Debbie thought, acquisitively. Well, she was welcome to try.

'Why isn't he married?' asked one of the others. 'What's the matter with the Cornish girls to let that get away?'

Debbie had wondered that herself before last night, but now she knew. He had never been in one place for long enough before he came to St. Erbyn, and he worked very unsocial hours. She didn't say so now.

'An ex-con isn't every young girl's dream,' suggested one of the bright young men who had made up Tim's crew for the morning. 'Particularly one who's done his time for bumping people off, I should think.'

'It was manslaughter, not mass murder,' muttered Debbie, under her breath. She hated to hear Mawgan referred to as if he was some kind of hired assassin. 'Look, fair play – don't talk about it here, please.'

'But surely, everyone must know,' said the bright young man. 'Or was it just a hoax? Come on, Deb, confess! He never killed anyone at all, did he?'

They were all looking at her now, beginning to tease and laugh, relieved to have found such a simple solution. There was only one way to stop them that she could see. Debbie got to her feet and walked away without even an *Excuse me.* In the silence that followed her departure, she heard a girl's voice, rising with disastrous clarity above the noise in the bar.

'Oh goodness, I thought it was a joke! Did he really bash somebody's head in?'

Outside, it had begun to rain. Debbie leaned against the wall of the inn and felt the drops falling against her face, and wondered how she could possibly have been so gauche. It wasn't a bit like her to be heavy-handed, she who prided herself on her streetwise poise. They had meant no harm – none of them had meant any harm – and they had teased her in good faith, she should have laughed back, and it would all have been over by now. She felt shaken, and rather sick. They had all thought it was a joke because they knew that Tim had drunk a little too much last night, and if she hadn't been so clumsy, they would have gone on thinking so, and that would have been the end of it. They none of them would remember exactly what had been said, they had most of them been in much the same state as Tim. They were mainly only young, like herself and Tim, Lesley and Roger... another lesson. Keep an eye on your guests' alcohol intake, and how could you do that anyway?

Everyone in the bar must have heard that short but disastrous speech. Mawgan must have heard it too. Whatever the rest of the people might have made of it, he would have known exactly what to think.

'Debbie?'

She turned her head. Roger had come out of the bar and now stood beside her.

'Debbie, they really did think it was some kind of in-joke. They're sorry. Won't you come back inside?'

'No,' said Debbie.

'Angwin didn't move a muscle, you know. I was standing right by him, I'm not sure he even heard. It's all right.'

Oh, he had heard, no doubt of that, but of course, he wouldn't react. He must have schooled himself not to do so long ago.

'Don't be too sure,' said Debbie, and failed to recognise her own voice.

'You'll get wet,' said Roger. 'And you're making them all feel uncomfortable. Come on, Deb.'

The punters must come first. Debbie felt none too good herself.

'All right, I'll be there in a minute,' she said. She stared hard at the now choppy grey waters of the river, willing herself not to cry – she, Debbie Nankervis, who never cried – in front of Roger. The boats in the little anchorage were beginning to dance, pulling on their anchor chains, the water slapping under their curving sides and throwing up little spurts of spray. She concentrated on them and the tears slowly backed off. Roger, she thought, had gone, but she didn't turn her head to see. She wished that she could be alone for ever.

'Are you all right?' asked Mawgan.

Debbie jumped. He was standing a little to her right, and she hadn't seen him come so he couldn't have come through the bar, or round from the restaurant entrance. There must be a back way. Her mind played with these irrelevancies, and her mouth opened of itself and said,

'I tried to stop them.'

'Yes,' said Mawgan. 'I supposed you must have.'

'I never started it,' said Debbie, swallowing hard, for the tears hadn't gone quite far enough. 'They thought it was a joke, teasing me – I know none of them would have done it, if they'd thought… if they'd thought…'

'Look, Deborah.' He took a step towards her and put his arms round her shoulders, comfortingly. 'You mustn't let it churn you up like this. What did it matter anyway? Nobody knew what she was talking about, except the ones who knew already.'

He had never held her quite like this before. Not casual at all. Not, strictly speaking, lovingly either. She might have wondered if she wanted it to be if her thoughts had been less occupied.

'You knew,' she said, with her face hidden in the front of his shirt.

'So what? It's not exactly news to me, neither.'

'But you must mind.'

'How can I mind? I brought it on myself. Anyway, it's something I've got to live with, and I'd be a fool if I hadn't learned, wouldn't I?'

'Have you learned?' asked Debbie, without moving. He took one arm away in order to tilt her chin up towards him. Incredibly, he was smiling at her – almost laughing at her. It struck her as all wrong even while she was relieved to see it. She managed to return the smile.

'That's better,' said Mawgan. 'Now then, tell me how this – joke, began.'

He hadn't been hurt – maybe – but he was very angry. She felt the anger like a wedge between them, although his continuing embrace absolved her, at least, from blame. She thought of Tim in the lounge last night, excited and spiteful, and of Mawgan painfully rebuilding his damaged business stone by stone after his world had crashed in ruins. She knew that of all things she must be careful, because Tim was out of his class and in the wrong, and in spite of everything, her friend of long standing.

'When I got home last night,' she said, unevenly, 'they all wanted to know where I'd been and what I'd been up to. They were teasing me.' She stopped, and Mawgan waited, unhelpfully silent. He was no longer smiling. She had to say it, or he would rend Tim, metaphorically at least, limb from limb, but the words stuck in her throat. 'Tim told them… because it was a natural opportunity and he'd had come-backs from people who thought he should have told them, and he thought…' She ran out of words, and ended pleadingly, 'They all thought it was a joke, none of them took it seriously. It was me, just now, that made them believe it. Not Tim.'

There was a long silence after she had spoken. Mawgan still had his arms around her, but he was no longer with her in spirit, his eyes had an inward look. No sudden burst of fury, as she had half expected. Deliberate calculation.

'He mustn't do it, you know,' said Mawgan, quietly. 'I'm sorry if he finds me an embarrassment, but he must deal with it as it comes up, not wholesale like that. Really.'

'I know,' said Debbie, miserably.

'It's not the first time, neither,' said Mawgan.

'No.'

'I can't let it go a second time.' Oddly, her pleading seemed to have found an echo in his voice, too.

'No,' said Debbie, again. 'What will you do?'

'Tell him not to?'

It sounded so simple. Debbie felt her hands, which were at present flat against his chest, begin to shake. She stopped them with an effort. She tried to imagine the scene, and failed.

'How?' she asked.

'Don't Deborah – please.' He had felt the shake, and his hands moved from her shoulders to cover hers. 'I'm not going looking for a fight, don't look so scared. But I've got to shut him up, you must see that. I was just beginning to live it down when he came along.'

It made a change to be able to say, 'Yes.'

His mood seemed to have swung back again as swiftly as it had darkened before. He drew her towards him and kissed her, and the laugh was back in his voice.

'Don't look so tragic, it i'n't the end of the world. I've lived through it all before, the heat's gone out of it. Come indoors again out the rain, and forget it.'

And anyone who would believe that, Debbie thought as she obediently preceded him through the door back into the bar, would believe anything, but at least he had taken it fairly calmly. At least he hadn't said the obvious thing, *perhaps we should stop seeing each other.*

Relief that it was all going to pass off so quietly swamped anything else that she perhaps should have wondered about. She rejoined her friends, and Mawgan went back behind the bar, and it seemed as if the whole incident was magically forgotten. Only Tim seemed unnaturally quiet, and Lesley had become totally silent and withdrawn. The look that she occasionally gave her husband was extremely difficult to interpret. Lesley thought that her foundations had been blown away and she would, of course, blame Tim. Debbie wished that it was possible to reassure her, but in the crowded pub it couldn't be done. Another deadlock. Life was suddenly full of them.

At least this one was breakable. Debbie managed to drop behind Tim and Roger beside Lesley as they made their way up the hill, leaving the students lunching in the bar.

'It's all right,' she said. 'He isn't going to make a fuss.'

Lesley looked, if anything, more dispirited than ever at the news.

'He has every right,' she said.

A curious answer, even if a true one. Debbie tried again.

'He said he wasn't looking for a fight.'

Lesley spoke soberly. 'Tim could do him a lot of harm if he goes on like that – and every week, Deb! People like these, just joking about it, they don't matter… at least, yes they do, but they won't do any deliberate damage. But we'll be lucky if we go through the season and never get a stinker – a spiteful person, or just someone who likes to make mischief – and it's not fair. He's had a year to start putting it behind him. Tim mustn't… mustn't…' She stopped.

'Tim's unhappy,' said Debbie, excusingly. She didn't feel like excusing him, but it would help nobody if Lesley used the incident to feed her own growing resentment.

'Why should Tim be unhappy?' asked Lesley, in a tight little voice. 'Everything is going his way.'

Debbie didn't know why she had said that at all. She hadn't consciously thought it. She abandoned that line of argument, and said, instead, 'Anyway, Mawgan is only going to ask him not to do it, nothing more.' Mawgan hadn't actually used the word "ask", but Debbie hadn't the heart to be strictly honest.

Lesley laughed, but didn't sound amused.

'I thought you just said he wasn't looking for a fight?'

'That's what he told me.'

There was a silence for a moment, and then Lesley said, uncertainly,

'Debbie, don't you ever wonder why he should be so nice to us – not just you, which would be easily explained, but me? And Tim – everything he does for me is for Tim, too. Haven't you ever asked yourself why?'

Debbie said, slowly because she hadn't yet worked that one out to her own satisfaction, and didn't wholly believe in Mawgan's glib explanation, 'He's a nice man....'

'He's ruthless and ambitious and self-involved,' said Lesley, scathingly. 'He isn't *nice,* Deb, and you know it. So come on, tell me why?'

'I don't know, then,' said Debbie.

'Then perhaps you should give it some thought,' said Lesley, and after a pause, added, less firmly, 'What exactly is he going to do? Did he give you any idea?'

'I don't know that, either,' said Debbie.

In fact, it looked for a day or two as if the answer to that was going to be, nothing at all. The students had stopped teasing Debbie, a little shamefacedly, Tim had added nothing to what he had already said, Lesley had calmed down. Mawgan, when she saw him, treated Debbie as he had always done. The whole thing seemed to have fizzled out like a damp firework, and life, which had gone over something of a bump, settled back to normal.

But on Saturday, Tim came into the kitchen during the students' breakfast, white to the lips and holding a sheet of paper rather as if it was a snake that had bitten him. Lesley, busy at the stove, and Debbie, lining up plates of bacon and racks of toast for the dining-room, had scant time for him at first, but something in his manner very shortly altered that. He was tense to the point of explosion, utterly oblivious to anything but the thing that was foremost in his mind. Lesley put down her frying pan, and Debbie stopped making toast.

'What's the matter?' asked Debbie. The first disquieting thought that went through her mind was that Tim, too, had received an anonymous letter, but it turned out to be worse than that.

'This came in the post!' Tim flung the paper down on the table between Lesley and Debbie, and whatever else it was, it certainly wasn't anonymous. Mystified, and more than a little alarmed, they bent over it together. Lesley's mind had gone immediately to trouble with guests, Debbie's second thought had been of Mawgan.

Debbie was right.

It bore the name and address of a firm of solicitors in Falmouth, and it requested Mr. Howells, in no uncertain terms, to be careful in what manner he discussed the affairs of their client, Mr. Mawgan Angwin of the Fisherman's Arms in St. Erbyn. It pointed out, austerely, that the line to be drawn between the truth and slander was a very narrow one, and unless and until Mr. Howells was certain of his facts, he would be well advised to keep silent. It mentioned unpleasant words such as *malicious intent*, and it ended by expressing their client's reluctance to take the matter further, and with a gentle intimation that the writer was sure such a course wouldn't be necessary. Altogether, it was a beast of a letter, and the more so since it was wholly deserved.

'How dare he, how *dare* he?' raged Tim. 'I didn't slander him – slander means it isn't true – and I wasn't being malicious! Damn it all, if he can protect himself at my expense, can't I do the same?'

'It's not the same,' said Debbie, uncomfortably.

'It bloody well wasn't slander!' stormed Tim.

'But it bloody well was malice!' retorted Lesley.

They glared at each other, and in the silence that followed, Debbie had time to wonder, much as Tim had wondered, why the word *slander* should have come into it at all. The only answer that she could come up with was that, however Mawgan's unfortunate brother-in-law had met his end, it hadn't been precisely from being bashed over the head with a rock. She didn't make the mistake of reading too much into this, however. The law, as she well knew, was great on nit-picking in defence of the indefensible. Her own father was a master of the art, come to that.

Tim had stopped eye-balling his wife, he had turned from white to red, and snatched up the letter, and for an instant it looked as if he was going to march straight out of the room, as he had done on another never-to-be-forgotten occasion, but he didn't. Instead, he ignored Lesley and swung round on Debbie.

'And what do you propose to do, after this?' he demanded.

'Me? Do?' asked Debbie, taken aback.

'Yes, do! It's your swanning around in the company of murderers that's got me into this mess!'

'Tim, that's not true,' exclaimed Lesley, before Debbie had found breath to speak.

'Bloody Angwin!' said Tim, viciously. 'It seems he can do what he likes round here, and my own friends – my own wife, even – will be on his side! Well, it's nice to know where I stand!'

'You called him down, in front of everyone,' said Debbie. 'It wasn't fair – how could he defend himself directly, he wasn't even there when it began! And later, it would only have made it worse for him, not for you.'

'He let you get away with it once,' said Lesley. 'Is he to do it for ever?'

Tim stood perfectly still, only his eyes going from one to the other of them as they spoke, and when they had finished, he turned abruptly on his heel and strode out of the kitchen. Lesley and Debbie, as if by some unspoken agreement, went instantly and uncomfortably back to their work. There seemed nothing to be said, and at least frying eggs and the making of pots of tea and coffee occupied their hands, if not their minds.

The line to be drawn between the truth and slander is a very narrow one.

So what, then, was the truth?

That Saturday, after its appalling start, wasn't one of the most successful of the season. Tim was sulking, and Debbie seemed away on a different planet half the time. When the boat hire finished business for the day, Roger was glad to get out on his evening jog, away from the place. It had sounded as if it was going to be such a perfect job for the summer, but he thought as he jogged his way along his usual route up the hill that he might not stay once August was over. Tim was all right, he knew his stuff and was pleasant enough to work with, but his wife was a pain, and Debbie Nankervis had proved a disappointment. When he had first seen her, he had thought that his luck was in, but that had been short-lived. He had known it for a dead duck the moment that Angwin had walked out of his pub and staked his claim for all to see. He had wondered since, with slightly sardonic amusement, how long it would be before bright, sophisticated Deb realised what Angwin was up to. He had her by the short and curlies, all right, and if it hadn't been so inherently disastrous, he thought that he might have found it amusing. It was another good reason for leaving, really. It was all nothing to do with him.

As he reached the top of the hill, there was a girl sitting on a stile. As he passed her, she said, 'Hi, there,' and he stopped, jogging on the spot, to return the greeting.

'It's a nice evening for a run,' she said, and smiled at him. She was pretty, he noted appreciatively, not as pretty as Deb but not at all bad. Dark brown eyes, and dark hair falling to her waist, a round little face with a full, pouting mouth, a pretty figure. He thought for a moment that he knew her from somewhere, but decided afterwards that it was a fleeting expression that reminded him of someone – if only he could remember who.

'Great,' he agreed, jogging up and down, and grinned at her. 'Care to join me?'

Her smile was friendly, and she had a pretty laugh to go with it.

'You work down at that sailing school, don't you?' she said. 'I've seen you there.'

'You should have come and had a lesson from me,' said Roger. She shook her head.

'I'm frightened of the water. I can't swim.'

'You could soon learn. I'll teach you, if you like.'

She said, 'One of the instructors down there is a girl, isn't she?'

'If she isn't, she's hidden it well,' said Roger. He had stopped jogging on the spot, and was now rising up and down on his toes.

'It seems a funny thing for a girl to do. It's more for a man, isn't it?'

'Oh, Debbie knows a thing or two,' said Roger. He began to wish he hadn't stopped, although he wasn't certain why. She was pretty and friendly – but he had a sudden, rather horrible feeling that if she turned round, she would have no back to her. She was cardboard. He thought that he would go on.

'Well, I must be on my way,' he said. 'Jog, jog, jog along the high road, and all that. See you around.' He started off again, with a casual wave that she didn't return, and when he came back, twenty minutes later, the cardboard girl had gone.

226

XV

Although she had only met her a couple of times, Kate had found that she missed Chel when she and Oliver left Trelewan for the Saronic Gulf. She had little chance to make close friends, living so far out of the village and having to work so hard, and with Chel she had felt an instant rapport which she knew could have grown into a real friendship given the chance. Postcards reaching Trelewan from Ayios Giorgos simply were not the same. And Chel had understood what she meant about Cress, too, and had given her sensible advice, which was more than Charlie ever did. Charlie seemed to want to pretend that the whole thing had never happened these days.

In fact, Kate had so far managed to follow Chel's advice pretty well, the more easily since the school holidays began to bring a thin, but steady stream of overnight guests to the Quoit, and her relationship with Charlie had greatly improved. For this last, she suspected that she had Oliver to thank. Charlie had decided to carry his method a stage further and become a wholly three-dimensional artist, and Kate thought that Oliver's influence had to be behind his decision, the change had come too swiftly on cue after his visit. Charlie had bought himself a lot of tools, and a lathe that had been very expensive, although second hand, and converted his studio into a sawdusty waste, but he was happy again. He was happier than he had been for months, and to see him happy she was prepared to put up with any amount of room changes and sandy children running everywhere, and in order to finance his new career, had begun to write articles on living the good life in Cornwall, which she sold to a women's magazine. They didn't pay particularly well, and she was aware that most of what was in them was sentimental and misleading, but if that was what the readers wanted, and if they paid for Charlie's lathe, Kate wasn't going to argue. Life was good again, and what else mattered?

That is, it was good until the day she walked up on the cliffs and this time, ran straight into not Chel, but Cress.

She hardly thought about Cress these days. She couldn't have said if it was telling Chel about her that had exorcised her memory, or the fact that Charlie, positive and re-directed, had returned to his old self – or if he had returned to his old self because his workshop now held no traces of that unhappy little ghost. It was a chicken-and-egg situation, she decided, strolling along the coast path. The sun was warm on her skin, the sea glittered like a mirror that stretched to the horizon and beyond, and Cress, thank goodness, had gone right out of their lives and no point in thinking about her. Chel and Oliver were back in Cornwall at last: even if St. Ives was a bit of a trek they would probably see them again, which was another plus point in a sunlit landscape. She tilted her face up towards the sun as she thought this – and there was Cress on the hillside above her.

She knew that it was Cress even at this distance, she would never forget that flowing dark hair and the slim little body as long as she lived, even if until that moment she had thought that she could. It was only when she saw her that she realised that the unrightness of her had hung around like a persistent smell and she hadn't forgotten it so much as ignored it. She felt all the hairs rising on her arms as if she was still some jungle animal, and her immediate instinct, which she followed, was to steal out of sight.

Once round the bend in the coast path, reason returned. She had no idea why Cress might have come back, but she had a perfect right to be here if she wanted, it was a public place. It was, Kate decided, the shock of finding that she was still so close. She had thought that she had gone home to her folks. Then she had a nastier thought and decided that perhaps it was time she went back to The Quoit, she didn't really think that Cress would try to see Charlie again, after the way they had parted company, but the idea was there in her mind. She trusted Charlie absolutely, at least, where Cress was concerned she did, but Cress had put his work out of gear for months last time, and Charlie's work was important – if not to the world, certainly to Charlie and therefore to herself. She turned round, trying not to feel it was with reluctance, and began to retrace her steps.

It was a burning hot day, but on the coast path there was a pleasant breeze blowing. Kate walked along enjoying the coolness of it and feeling a little silly now, for of course Cress would have gone by this time anyway – and then, as if she was truly a ghost to haunt them, she saw her again.

She was walking a little ahead, her head bent and apparently doing something with her hands, twisting them, Kate thought, and she seemed to be talking — to herself? Kate hadn't forgotten the night that she had caught Cress talking to her dead husband up by the stone. Her flesh began to creep, and she had to call herself severely to task. Cress was only a poor little widowed thing who couldn't cope with life, she wasn't actually *evil*, surely! Personal dislike could be carried too far.

Cress wasn't walking as fast as Kate was. Her legs were not so long, and she wasn't as strong as Kate. Kate slowed down, stopped, in order not to catch up with her. Stopping gave her an opportunity to think more clearly.

Cress was sick in her mind. She had been, last year, and she looked no different today, in fact from this distance she looked worse. She hadn't gone home, she was still hanging around in the region of that wretched stone. Kate couldn't know that she had come to seek out Oliver and failed to find him because he had moved on, and so had come up here where Mike was so close to seek counsel of him, but she had wished many times that she and Charlie hadn't teased Cress and made up that ridiculous story — to please her, she remembered. They had done it to please her. It seemed incredible. There was nobody with her now, and having flung her out of the house in the way that they had — she had — Kate couldn't help feeling responsible. It was none of her business, but she knew that she ought to check — check that Cress had touched base with her people, and that someone was looking after her and knew where she was. She needed looking after. If nobody looked after her she would think that her husband was doing so again, perhaps she had never ceased to think it. If anything awful happened because she was alone, then Kate knew that, however she felt about Cress, she would never forgive herself.

Cress had stopped and was looking up towards the rise in the ground where the old quoit had stood. She had flung back her head as if she was seeing something other than the gorse-covered slope, and liked whatever it was that she saw. On impulse, Kate hurried forward.

'Hullo, Cress,' she said.

Cress turned. Her eyes didn't see Kate, they saw a stranger. She said, in a cool little voice,

'Good afternoon.'

It was ridiculous, but Kate thought that she wasn't there at all.

She still had no idea what Cress's maiden name had been. She had only a very few useful facts to go on. She had a rough date, which might enable her to find something in an old newspaper if all else failed, she had the name Michael Stanley, and she had the information that father and grandfather were builders, well known in St. Austell but moved away some time in the last two or three years. Of those three pieces of information, she decided that the last presented the best chance of finding out more, somebody in business couldn't afford to disappear completely. She looked in on Charlie, who was busy and didn't notice, and then took her bicycle up to the village to consult with Yellow Pages in the post office.

There were quite a few builders in St. Austell, and it didn't really matter which of them she tried, it was a long shot anyway. She chose one at random, changed a pound for small change at the counter, and cycled back to the phone box near the Quoit.

A man answered at the third ring, in a leisurely Cornish voice. Kate said, at her most persuasive, 'I wonder if you can help me. I'm trying to trace the builder who built my extension a few years ago, and I know it's stupid, but I've forgotten his name.'

'Where would that be to, then?' he asked, and Kate quickly made up a likely-sounding address out of her head. There was a ruminative silence at the other end of the phone.

'I 'a'n't never heard of that,' he said. 'It wasn't we did that.'

'No no, I know it wasn't,' said Kate. 'The firm moved away, I think — they went somewhere else in Cornwall, there was a bit of family trouble, I believe…?' She let her voice rise into a question.

'Ah,' said the voice, and fell silent again, thinking it out. He knew who she was talking about, Kate realised. He was just working out whether or not to tell her. Finally, he said, 'You mean Garfie Angwin's boy, that's who you do mean. Went up Launceston way, two, three years back.'

It had to be right.

'That's the name!' cried Kate, delightedly. 'How kind of you! I don't suppose you have an address for him?'

'Naw…' He made it into a long-drawn-out sound. 'Naw, I don't. He didn't leave no address, but he'll be in the book, I don't doubt.'

He wasn't. Kate tried directory enquiry, but there was no Angwin, Garfie — or Garfield, she assumed — or any other, listed under builders in the Launceston area. She considered repeating her experiment, but decided it would have to be a very last resort: she would probably not be so lucky a second time. At least she had a name now, so she rode back to the post office and tried a different approach. In the private subscribers section of the general directory there were a disconcerting number of Angwins, but none of them as far east as Launceston. He would be ex-directory, she thought, hiding the family's shame. Poor man. Launceston was a biggish place to hide in, maybe that was why he chose it.

Cress had impressed her with that family shame so strongly that it never occurred to her to double check to see if there was a builder called Angwin still listed in Yellow Pages. Reading the telephone directory at the best of times can make the brain start shutting down, and of course, she had already been through the Yellow Pages once, so she totally missed G. Angwin & Son of St. Austell. Kate would never have made a private detective.

St. Erbyn, she thought instead, unlike Launceston, was small. A swift trawl through the private section failed to bring an Angwin to light there, but she was luckier in the trade section. *Angwin M.G.* appeared to own, or manage at least, the local pub and restaurant, the Fisherman's Arms. Could he be Cress's brother? If he wasn't, he could probably point her in the right direction.

Kate had her own ideas about Cress's brother. She didn't kid herself that he was more sinned against than sinning, but she did think that Cress hadn't given her a full tale. She would never have sought him out, still less mentioned Cress's name to him, if she hadn't thought it was urgent. She couldn't get out of her head the picture of Cress's face, gentle and enquiring, not knowing her at all, with that empty look behind the eyes. She couldn't shed her own sense of responsibility. If he didn't want to know himself, which was more than probable, he would at least tell her where to find the rest of the family. Surely, he would do that.

St. Erbyn wasn't the easiest place to reach on the bus from Penzance, but it was one of those places to which tour operators sent coaches on day trips during the summer. The coaches left in the morning and did a trip around Gweek and Helford, taking in a couple of gardens and ending up in St. Erbyn in the afternoon for a cream tea. The coach parties had tea organised for them at the Kosy Kafé at the top of the hill, but Kate skipped that and walked straight down the village street to the pub. Only residents' cars, those of people staying in guest houses, and deliveries were allowed down the street between June and September. It was very pleasant and peaceful, but Kate felt neither. She was beginning to wish she hadn't come – no, be fair, she had never wanted to come in the first place – but it would be an awful waste of money to turn back after getting this far. She had come all this way because she knew that Cress needed help, and she couldn't go back without making an attempt, at least, to get it for her. She wished now that she had taken the easier option of phoning, but it would have been too easy for him to refuse to tell her anything, or worse, to hang up on her. At least face to face he would have to give her his attention. And if he was himself the man she sought, couldn't exactly hurt her, could he?

He hadn't done Cress and her husband any good…

The street led down to the water, and the pub straddled a causeway across the shingle. The road went on up the hill on the far side, Kate saw, and knew an unworthy impulse to keep on walking. It was a well-kept pub, quite large for such a small place, oldish, with a slightly more recent two-storey extension, quite possibly a residential conversion, on the side towards the village, that now housed a restaurant. Not by any means a café, still less a "kafé" or a place where you could take the kids for a burger at lunchtime. It didn't open, according to the sign outside, until half-past seven in the evening. Posh job, then. Maybe she was barking up the wrong tree, Kate thought, with relief. Cress's brother wouldn't have anything to do with a place like this, and it wasn't his name over the door, either. She took a deep breath. Ask then. One Angwin would surely know of another in a small place like this.

But the moment she saw him, she knew that she had hit the jackpot first time round, and her heart sank – unreasonably, for hadn't she been looking for him? The family resemblance was quite strong, as Roger had more subconsciously noticed, dispelling immediately any lingering doubts she had felt about Cress's claim to be adopted, although he didn't have Cress's tragic dark eyes but eyes of a sunlit hazel. He was a real person too, not a ghost. She immediately recognised the swift, shallow charm and the far more vivid intelligence that underlay it, and Cress had prepared her for neither of them. Confronted with such a finished performer, Kate found her errand almost impossible to broach. Her preconceived notions shattered like a dish hitting the kitchen floor, pieces flew everywhere.

'I'm really sorry to bother you,' she said. 'I didn't know who else to come to… I'm really worried about your sister.'

He looked at her, coolly. He knew exactly who she meant, she was sure of it, but what he said was, 'I've three sisters.'

Awkward cuss, then. Well, could she blame him? Kate said, 'Cress.'

Cool became freezing.

'We don't have nothing to say to each other.'

He wasn't as smooth and prettily-spoken as Cress, he had a rough Cornish edge to him. Moreover, she was trespassing, and he was resenting it. She said, 'No, but listen. She lived in our house for six months last year, and she was...' She paused. She really should have thought this out a bit more. If Cress was mentally ill, he was at least partly responsible. It made it an impossible thing to say, particularly here in this public place with people passing to and fro through the hallway. 'Couldn't we go somewhere more private?' she asked.

'I don't think so. My sister was what?'

'We thought she was ill,' said Kate, taking a run at it. 'She was dreadfully emotional... odd, even. When she went, we thought that she had gone home. I saw her a few days ago and she looked awful. I just wanted to make sure... that someone was keeping an eye on her.'

She should have told him the rest, but she couldn't. Couldn't admit that she had dumped Cress and her suitcase on the doorstep in the middle of the night, and slammed the door on her distress. Couldn't tell him about that unpleasantness up by the stone. He had an impermeable granite surface, from which all her concern slid like rain down glass.

When he answered, which was only after a pause, he sounded utterly uninterested, but she wasn't certain that was the truth.

'So far's I know, my sister has a job in a snack bar in Falmouth and goes home regular. I don't see her, but that's what I'm told.'

'I'm sorry,' said Kate. 'I shouldn't have come.' He thought that she had made an excuse out of curiosity, she knew it. She felt worse by the minute.

'I'm sorry I can't be more helpful.' He was already turning to go. Kate said, 'You don't know which snack bar?'

'I believe it's called the Blue Lobster, something of that kind.' His tone dismissed it as negligible, having seen his own establishment, Kate couldn't feel surprise.

'Thank you,' said Kate.

He hesitated then, perhaps feeling that she deserved more from him after her concern.

'I can ring my sister and check up, if you think I should, I suppose.'
The term *my sister* dismissed Cress as if she too was dead – as to him,
perhaps she was.

'I think you should,' said Kate. 'Tell her… just tell her that you saw
Kate, that's me, and that I was worried about Cress. That I think someone
should be with her.'

'You can't force company on people if they don't want none of it,' he
suggested.

'You can if they're ill.'

'I'll speak to Allison,' he said. Kate thought that he probably would,
maybe not today, or even tomorrow, but sometime, when occasion arose.
The interview was over, she walked back up the hill to the Kosy Kafé
and treated herself to a scalding hot potful of very strong tea under the
painted eyes of the olde-tyme Cornish smugglers daubed inappropriately
all over the walls. She wished that she had left well alone.

She cadged a lift into Falmouth with her friend Maggie a few days
later – something that she normally avoided doing, not just because she
didn't like to keep asking favours, but also because Maggie, who had six
badly-behaved children, had no control at all over her offspring, who were
all noisy and rude, apart from the baby, who was the noisiest of the lot to
make up for his lack of deliberate rudeness.

The Blue Lobster turned out to be the Blue Crab, and Cress certainly
worked there, although Susie might have selected a different job description.
Trim and composed in a blue-and-white checked overall, with her hair
twisted up into a knot on top of her head, she looked no more than
normally vague, a totally different person from the distraught waif up on
the cliff, and she recognised Kate at once. She seemed to have forgotten
the circumstances of their last real meeting, or at least forgiven it. She
asked after Charlie, and brought Kate's coffee, slopping it into the saucer
as she put the cup down. The same old slatternly Cress, then. One of the
world's losers, maybe, but nothing to shout about. Kate felt extremely
foolish and wished that she had never gone near St. Erbyn.

The only thing that did surprise her, but she didn't think it was that
important, was that Cress should have settled down to live comparatively
close to the brother who had killed her husband, when she had the whole
of Cornwall to choose from.

★

It was too much to expect that Debbie's activities would go completely undetected. Yachting is a fairly small world even these days, and both the Helford River and her home town were popular yachting venues. The growing reputation of the Fish, too, was against her.

'I've got the most peculiar letter here from Susan,' said Oliver.

'What, another one?' Chel was in a hurry, for she had a job these days in the craft shop underneath their borrowed studio. She wasn't in the mood for Susan, with whom she only intermittently got on. 'What's she want this time?'

'I'm not really sure. She goes rambling on and on about Deb, and never gets to the point. Here, you'd better read it for yourself.' He held it out to her, but Chel was already on the move to the sink.

'I haven't the time, you tell me for once while I clear up, or I'll be late. What's Deb been doing this time? Is she still on the home-wrecking trail?'

But Oliver looked puzzled.

'If she is, Susan doesn't say so. She says that Colonel Marriner and his wife – they're some rather boring friends of my father's – sailed into the Helford River and put into St. Erbyn to have a meal at a rather good restaurant they have there – that must be the pub we went to for lunch, it certainly wasn't that caff up the hill – and they ran into her. They went home and said she was going about with some undesirable, and getting herself talked about. I don't see what it's got to do with me.'

That was typically Oliver, Chel reflected, squeezing washing-up liquid into the bowl. She said, 'Do you want your sister going about with undesirables, then?'

Oliver took no notice of this, but continued to study his stepsister's letter with knitted brows.

'Bollocks!' he said, in patent disbelief.

'Bollocks to what?'

'According to Mrs. Marriner, Deb is altogether too friendly with a man who's been to prison for killing his brother-in-law. It doesn't sound very likely, does it?'

'I would have thought Deb had too much sense. It sounds like another scare to me.'

'The family think I should go and talk to her about it, you'd think they'd have learned from the last time. They've got a nerve!'

'Why?' asked Chel. The plates rattled onto the draining board. 'You're about the only one of them she might listen to. Will you?'

'Will I what?' He was reading the letter through again, only half-listening to her. It had to be a first, he generally didn't read Susan's letters at all, Chel had to do it. She sighed.

'Speak to her, you moron!'

'No, why should I? She didn't side with them against me when I was going around with an undesirable.' He smiled at her, but Chel didn't laugh. She had that horrible feeling that she sometimes had as if she had walked into a spider's web. She said, 'I wasn't *homicidal*, Oliver! Don't you feel that you might have an interest in your sister going about with a man who murders his brothers-in-law? He might have a "thing" about them.'

That hadn't been it. The feeling was still there, but no stronger, so she wasn't even warm. She dropped a fork on the floor, and bent to pick it up. Oliver, who never admitted to feeling things like that – warnings, spirits, whatever you liked to call them – only laughed.

'He might at least have enough blood in his veins to see Tim Howells off.'

'It's not the blood in his veins I'm worrying about, it's the blood in yours.'

Oliver looked at her thoughtfully; he knew that something was bothering her, and he also knew that she wasn't going to tell him what it was. He thought he didn't believe in clairvoyance, but the very fact that Chel always denied it in herself lent weight to its possible reality.

'If Debbie wants to discuss it with us, she knows where to find us. And if she doesn't, she won't anyway.'

'You can't be happy about it,' objected Chel.

Oliver considered this.

'No,' he said. 'No, I'm not. Not if it's true, at least, but I know the Marriners, and you don't. But I don't own Deb, and neither does anyone else.'

'Your family has a very barren way of expressing affection.'

'Debbie is nearly twenty-five. That's hardly in the nursery.'

'And how would you feel if he kills her, too?'

'Don't be silly,' said Oliver, dismissively. Chel put the last mug onto the draining board and dried her hands on the towel. She wished she hadn't made that last remark. For that time, she knew, she had come uncomfortably close to… well, what? She didn't know enough about the situation to begin to guess.

'Oh well,' said Oliver, screwing up Susan's letter and pitching it in the general direction of the bin. 'We'll be living there quite soon. We can see for ourselves then.'

That's too late.

'Perhaps we could drive over and see her one evening,' said Chel, but Oliver, she knew, was too busy preparing for his coming exhibition, and probably wouldn't go. He had moved away now, his mind already on the day's work, and it was time she went downstairs.

As she went, she found herself trying to project a clear, white ring of protection around her sister-in-law, and wondered, in amazement, where that idea had come from.

Debbie's one postal offering that morning had been not very much better than Oliver's. Not an anonymous letter, this time, but almost as bad, a letter from an old boyfriend. It was of the *I thought you ought to know* variety, and rather upsetting.

I've been a bit exercised in my mind lately, he had written, which was, in Debbie's view, dork-speak for *I thought I'd shift this problem from my shoulders onto yours.* She was right. He went on: *As I think you know, the firm that I represent is responsible for marketing those new flats down by the marina.* Oh yes, Debbie recalled, he's become an estate agent. Big deal. She read on. *I don't know if I should be telling you this, but I've been thinking it over and I think you have a right to know.* Bad news then. Nobody ever felt you had a right to know something good. *It isn't really my business, and if anyone ever knows I passed it on, I should get the old S A C K, so keep it to yourself, won't you? Only, your father came over when the Channel House complex went onto the market, and he had a look around the show flat. Well, the long and the short of it is, he's bought it, lock stock and barrel. Furnishings and everything. We're not supposed to give out information of this kind, and he isn't living in it or anything, but I thought you ought to know.* Oh yes, that old chestnut, there it was! *I know that your mother and father have rather an uneasy relationship from our days together, and I just thought well, forewarned is forearmed. It may be nothing at all, of course, but I couldn't reconcile it with my conscience, after what we meant to each other, to keep it a secret from you.* Why, what had they meant to each other? Not a lot, as Debbie remembered it. She sighed, and dropped the letter onto the table.

So what was she supposed to do? She already knew that her mother and father were on borrowed time, everybody who knew them must know. Some major row last year with Oliver had been the start of it, but they had papered over those cracks, she had thought. Now, it appeared that they hadn't. She hadn't thought that she was that worried about the prospect, but now it had come suddenly closer, she found that she was. She didn't want her home broken up, particularly right now; she needed to know it was there, a secure rock in a great ocean of unanswered questions. She made a face, and picking up the letter again, folded it and put it back in its envelope.

'Bad news?' asked Lesley, on the other side of the table.

'Not good, anyway.'

'Me, neither.' Lesley held out the bank statement. 'Just look at this! We're full up now, and *still* going from bad to worse! Unless we can get rid of the loan, we'll never get out of the spiral!'

Debbie wasn't in the mood for other people's troubles.

'Perhaps you should burn the place down, and start again,' she suggested, moodily. Tim, pouring coffee at the stove, gave a snort of laughter.

'That's a bit extreme,' he said. He came over to the table and sat down, looking at Debbie. 'I don't suppose you'd like to take a share in the place, would you Deb? I was thinking, you know – if we *could* get rid of the loan payments we might have a chance, and then, if we did have to sell, you'd still get your money back.' He smiled at her, persuasively. Debbie picked up her mug and drank, to give herself time to think. Think, that is, not so much what she should do as what she should say. What she should do was perfectly clear in her mind, Mawgan could exterminate half the population of Cornwall but he was no fool. She would still trust his business acumen to the hilt.

'I don't think my trustees would let me,' she said. 'Sorry, Tim.'

'You could try them,' persisted Tim. 'We could draw up a business plan and work out a scheme that would give you an income, maybe.'

'If you're giving me an income, you might as well keep the present loan,' Debbie pointed out.

'It wouldn't be as much as that.'

'Don't you believe it. You don't know my trustees.' She knew perfectly well that her trustees would release capital for a sensible business venture on request, and no strings attached, but not *this* business venture and, she realised, for more than one reason. Not only was it not, in Mawgan's trusted view, financially viable as it stood, but it would include Tim and… and she had had enough of being a buffer state between them. Roger, too, she rather thought. Without Roger, who had become, almost unnoticed a major bulwark of the business, it would all gurgle down the plughole without a chance of stopping it. Nevertheless, Tim's disappointed face made her feel mean. He covered it with a joke, but it wasn't a very good one.

'Right then, it's an arson job for the insurance.' He looked up as Roger came in through the door. 'Know how to make a Molotov cocktail, Rog?'

'You can find out on the internet, I believe,' said Roger, unperturbed. 'Is there any coffee left?'

'On the stove.' The presence of Roger had brought the discussion to an end. Debbie was glad of it. She was very sorry indeed for Lesley and Tim, but it was probably true that the sooner they crashed, the better their chance of surviving as a couple. If they hadn't gone too far already. She got to her feet, wanting to change the subject beyond hope of revival, and to get out of the kitchen too. 'I'll go and check how they're doing in the dining-room. Mrs T will be down in a minute, anyway.' The door swung to behind her. Tim looked apologetically at Lesley, who was looking at him with a scornful expression on her face.

'Well, it was worth a try,' he defended himself.

'Was it?' Lesley got to her feet. 'I'll go and give Deb a hand with the clearing. If you've got time to sit and drink coffee, perhaps you could see to that lock on the bathroom door upstairs, it's still sticking.'

When the door closed behind her, too, Tim exchanged a glance with Roger, and raised his eyes to the ceiling.

'Women!' he said, and held out his mug. 'Pour us another, Rog, there's a good chap.'

Cress liked to imagine herself as tragic and self-contained, going on her own dark way alone, but in fact she was very much the type of woman that Kate had her down as. She couldn't stand unsupported. Sooner or later she automatically looked around for a shoulder to cry on and a man to look after her. In Falmouth, she hadn't far to look.

She had managed to rationalise Kate's visit and fit it into her fantasy, Kate was spying on her because Charlie/Mike had never stopped thinking about her. She had wondered if she dared to go and see Charlie, because it had gradually begun to dawn on her that she was going to need help on more than the astral plane if she was going to avenge him, in his proper character as Mike. It was logical that Mike's carnate form should help her... but she didn't quite have the courage to go back to The Quoit to see him.

It wasn't on this earthly plane that they were destined to meet again. Outside influences were too strong, that arrogant Irish beauty with her possessiveness and her scornful face would work to keep them away from each other. Her own, more gentle, nature couldn't compete. Kate was like a river that flowed between them, unfathomable and swift-running, holding them apart. There was no bridge that she could build to cross the river.

And anyway, it was part of the pattern that there should always be the Other Woman. The eternal triangle that should have been a straight, unswerving line between two people. She hadn't envisaged what might happen to Charlie when she had achieved her revenge and Mike had taken her to himself. Possibly she imagined that he would physically disintegrate, as if he had never been there at all.

So she opened her heart to Mrs. Bennetts, Susie and Gary in the shabby kitchen of the Blue Crab, while she and Susie cleaned the fryer and Gary pushed an unsavoury-looking mop around the floor. The story had been steadily improving with repetition from the start: she herself became more deeply wronged, and Mike, far from coming after her in sheer exasperation to try to sort things out tidily, as he had done, now realised, when he came home from the arms of his scheming mistress whose name, of course, was by this time Kate, to find his wife gone, that he loved only her, and drove after her on a sweeping wave of sentimental romance, repentance, and imminent loss. By this time, her brother, who had at the time been merely slightly partisan in her favour and a lot more irritated with her, was rapidly becoming an ogre acceptable only in the pages of the more sensational tabloids. The word *incest* hung unspoken in the air, and not for the first time. It was not – after the first shock it had never been, in Cress's mind – brotherly defence of herself that had caused a tragic accident, but jealousy of Mike that had been the springboard for deliberate murder, and the colours she used for this picture were brighter after time. And of course, if she was adopted it was perfectly understandable, she told herself hurriedly, and possibly even a little guiltily. She had no recollection of when the story had diverged from the truth, or even any real idea that it had done so.

Their natural horror was gratifying. Mrs. Bennetts had always thought Cress a sad little creature that needed looking after, and she threw up her hands in a most satisfying way. Susie said admiringly that it was just like *Eastenders*, wasn't it, and why hadn't Cress told them before? Gary wondered how much the life insurance had been worth and looked at Cress with more interest than he had previously shown.

'I had enough money,' she had said, listlessly. 'There was even a clause in the policy that said I got extra if he didn't die from natural causes, but what does that matter, if he isn't here any more? Life's just… empty, really.'

'What happened to your brother?' asked Susie, avidly curious. Cress shrugged.

'Nothing very much,' she said. 'He was in prison for a bit. What's that, in exchange for a man's life?' She wept a little, because it was really very sad, and the women comforted her.

'You should of sued him,' said Susie, who was a keen advocate of people standing up for their rights. Cress made a disclaiming gesture with her hand. She had never thought of it for herself, and nobody had suggested it. It was a bit late now, even if it had ever been an option. They mistook the gesture for a magnanimity that the brute hadn't deserved, and a compassion for the rest of her family that was touching. They shook their heads over it all.

'You sit down here, and I'll make us all a nice cup o' tea,' said Mrs. Bennetts.

'I'll finish that fryer for you,' said Gary.

She remembered that he had been kind the day she had had that spectacular faint in the middle of the café. He wasn't so awful, after all – a bit flash-looking, but he might know ways that she wouldn't even think of to get back at people. Her tragic expression gave way to speculation as she looked at him. Susie said, 'You'll find yourself another fella one day, don't you worry.'

Mrs. Bennetts nodded approvingly.

'Pretty little thing like you, you won't have far to look.' She smiled at Gary with motherly pride. 'Bit o' money too, and no kids to get in the way. You see, it'll all work out right.'

She was a bit dim, Gary thought, but the money was a great temptation, and after all, some girls thought being married made a man more attractive, not less, always allowing it wasn't them he was married to. He waited a day or two, being attentive to Cress and helping her with her share of the clearing up when they closed at five o'clock, and then he said, 'How about a date, then?'

Cress had already decided that, when he asked her, she would say yes. She thought that it was her tragic story and her bravery and her pretty face that attracted him, she hadn't thought about the money at all, but if she had it wouldn't have made any difference. He was another tool that Mike had sent her. He looked perfect for the job. Everything was running so smoothly it must surely be meant to happen.

'That'd be nice,' she said.

Gary was quite a character. He went with a rowdy gang, and he had helped in the odd robbery and pinched a car or two to go joy-riding. He didn't think Cress would like to know things like that, even though her own brother had been in the slammer for a lot worse, so who was she to turn up her nose? He took her to the pictures, and for a fish-and-chip supper afterwards, and walked her home to her digs. They parted with no more than a chaste kiss on her cheek.

'Silly little cow,' thought Gary to himself, as he walked away. He was already bored with her, but his mother had always said that money didn't come easy. Everybody said it.

Because she was obsessed with the idea, he very soon realised that she both resented and hated her brother. He owned a posh pub down by the Helford River – *owned* it, didn't just run it for a brewery, it was his. He had a girlfriend who drove her own car and wore expensive clothes and lived a glamorous and interesting life.

'Rich?' asked Gary, with interest.

Cress didn't know, but said yes anyway.

'He's got everything, and I've got nothing!' said Cress, tragically. He kissed her – on the lips by this time, but really, for a girl who had been married she was unbelievably prissy. He liked a bit more spice to his relationships, a bit of fun and a little bit of sex – but not too little a bit, of course. This sexless girl with her one-track mind was *boring, boring, boring.* He felt a sudden impulse to liven things up a bit.

'Get rid of her,' he suggested. She stared at him, her mouth stupidly open. Really, she was so dumb it was painful.

'How?' she asked, with an avidity that surprised him. Her face was suddenly eager, alive. He wasn't to know that she had taken his words as a sign.

'Easy enough,' he said. 'A few letters – don't sign 'em, or anything silly like that, just let her know what's what.'

'I think she already knows,' said Cress. She didn't admit that she had already written one letter, sort of, because it had only been on impulse, and she had been rather ashamed of it after she had done it, it seemed cheap somehow. She was even more ashamed of the fact that she was going to do it again, or why had she bothered to find out the blonde girl's name, or part of it at least? She hadn't liked to ask too obviously. Gary snorted.

'Silly bitch! Then we'll ginger 'er up a bit. I know how ter do it. I've got friends as'll help. It might take a bit o' time to organise, what do you say?'

'What sort of thing?' asked Cress.

'Something as'll make her sit up and take notice,' said Gary. He didn't like anything he knew about Cress's brother, it would be fun to make him jump a bit. He grinned at Cress. His teeth were very big and white.

'You keep needling 'er,' he advised. 'Leave it to me. We'll frighten 'er so as she runs home to Mummy and Daddy faster'n you can see 'er go.' He put his arm round her. She was about as responsive as a statue in the park. 'You just wait and see what Gary can do,' he said. He thought that she might press him for more information, and even kick a bit when she knew what was in his mind, but she didn't. Instead, she stopped outside a shop they were passing, and said on some impulse that he didn't pretend or wish to understand, 'I want to buy a postcard – that one.'

He looked at it with a grin.

'For the posh chick? Hey, nice one – you're not so dumb, are you?'

Not so dumb as you think me, Cress thought. All right, Gary, crucify him – if you can!

XVI

The card had been typed, and was addressed simply *Debbie*, care of the sailing school. Tim, handing it out with the rest of the mail, remarked, 'Some daft student or other who's managed to forget your name! That'll teach you to be such a dark horse, Deb.'

Debbie took the postcard and looked at it, crunching a spare piece of toast that she held in the other hand.

'I like to be loved for myself alone,' she said, indistinctly. The message was short, also typed. It read simply, *You need to watch yourself in places like this!* There was no proper signature, only a squiggle that could have been anything. She turned it over, and abruptly choked. Roger patted her on the back.

It was a pretty card. A photograph of part of a famous garden, a rugged looking rockery in full bloom. Still coughing, she turned it back to look at the postmark. Cornwall, but she supposed she could have guessed that anyway.

It was upsetting, but it didn't give her the same crawling distaste as the scrawled note had done. If being bombarded with anonymous letters was the price she was being asked to pay for Mawgan, she was beginning to see that she must pay it, or perhaps she was just getting hardened. You could get used to anything. She had begun to get letters from home that left a lot to be desired, too, about *getting herself talked about,* and *undesirable acquaintances,* which were quite as bad as either of these, anyway. She slipped the card into the back pocket of her jeans, casually, as if it didn't matter.

'What's on today, then,' enquired Tim, pushing his own mail aside. 'Me for the Cash & Carry, I suppose, do you want Roger for anything before he goes down to the boats?'

'If you could both move those extra beds into the right rooms, I'd be glad,' said Lesley. 'And when you come back, can you fix that lock on the bathroom door? I have told you about it before.'

Tim looked down his nose, ignoring his own shortcomings to focus on hers.

'This bed-shifting thing is getting beyond a joke. Can't you work the bookings out better?'

If Lesley had been thinking, she wouldn't have bothered to explain, she would simply have said, *no*. As it was, she went into a long and unnecessary dissertation on people who wanted twin beds and people who wanted doubles, and the difference between three or four young men or girls sharing a room, and a family with young children that her late aunt had booked in. Tim yawned.

'We don't want the families anyway. All along, they've been the ones to cause trouble.'

'We took on the bookings with the house,' Lesley argued, glaring at him.

It was true about the trouble. The rowdy, high-spirited younger crowd who in the main formed the sailing students were a nuisance to the parents of young children, who complained about the noise after the children had gone to bed. The parents and children were a restraint on the students that prevented them from having enjoyable late-night parties in the lounge when they got back from the Fish. It wasn't true that it was necessarily the families that caused the trouble. It was the families that mentioned it. The students tended to accept it as just one of those things, and make no real attempt to moderate the noise they made.

Roger said, peaceably, 'You can weed them out next year. The first season was bound to be a bit of a muddle under the circumstances.'

'You can't explain that to guests,' argued Tim. 'It's been a bloody nuisance, all along.'

Lesley turned back to the stove.

'If you think you can manage so much better, you do it,' she invited. 'I've yet to see you even take an interest, except to complain! And don't forget about that lock again, someone else got trapped in there last night. It sometimes sticks and only works from the outside, you have to shove the key under the door to somebody else, and there isn't always anybody there.'

'Oh, stop nagging about the bloody lock!' said Tim. 'I'll do it when I have time, I've told you.'

'Well, mind you do.' Lesley swept the dishes on the kitchen table into a pile. 'Now get out of my way, if you don't mind, all of you. I've got work to do if you haven't!'

It wasn't a total change-over today; because of the inherited reservations and their own inexperience, the bookings were staggered throughout the season, which was something that made life easier for Lesley and harder for Tim now that they were fully booked all the way through until September. It meant that with only two instructors, he had difficulty in arranging tuition on different levels, and he had had to withdraw Roger from the casual trade except at weekends. It was losing them money, he said, and he blamed Lesley for it.

'She could have managed better than this,' he grumbled to Debbie, flicking over the pages of his diary. 'Look at this lot, it's practically unworkable! What with that, and all this domestic help we're expected to provide as if that was the most important thing in the world –' He broke off.

'Did you talk it over with Lesley to begin with?' asked Debbie, pertinently, but Tim only snorted.

'We can't go on like this. I tell you what, Deb, I've been thinking. We can't afford another full-time instructor *and* more domestic help, but we might be able to afford one more person. I was thinking, if you helped Les in the house in the mornings, and then me in the afternoon with the boats, I can probably pick up a university student with the right bits of paper to do the full-time instructing.'

Debbie stared at him.

'What?'

'Well, you wouldn't mind, would you?' asked Tim, reddening a little.

'Yes, I would! And if you do any such thing, I shall leave!'

'Come on, Deb – I'd never get a bloke who'd agree to make the beds. That's women's work!'

'Then find a woman to do it,' suggested Debbie. 'I didn't come down here to make beds and clean up after people, Tim Howells, and that's flat!'

'I thought you were our friend. You can see Lesley is in a state.'

'Then you help her!' retorted Debbie. 'Saturday morning I can just about stand, but that's it, don't push your luck! And now I'm going to help your wife.' She left him to his ill-humour and took herself indignantly upstairs to the beds and Mrs Tregear. She was beginning to hate Saturdays with a deadly hatred that she felt sure was corroding her soul, and this was proving to be a particularly awful one. But perhaps it would improve later.

It didn't. It got worse.

Because there was no sailing instruction on Saturdays unless people booked it separately, those guests who were staying on a second week usually went out for the day. On this particular Saturday, after a bit of furniture-removing upstairs, Tim departed in the car to the Cash & Carry and on one or two other errands, and Roger went down to the jetty to attend to hire customers. Lesley and Debbie had shared an early lunch when Mrs Tregear left at mid-day, and now Lesley was doing the accounts in the office and waiting for expected arrivals, leaving Debbie pottering around the kitchen making a trifle for dinner. It wasn't the way she would have chosen to spend a fine Saturday afternoon, but it was a full house all the time now and Lesley had to have a bit of time for the day-to-day running of the business and Saturday seemed to be the only available space in the schedule, unless, of course, she was going to work in the evenings while everyone else went off and enjoyed themselves. The fact that Tim could quite easily have helped her on the odd evening, while Roger and Debbie went down to the Fish with the students and he and Lesley came on together later, was never mentioned between them.

Debbie thought, not for the first time lately, that she had had about enough. It was no fun any more, with Lesley and Tim perpetually at each other's throats, and now Tim busily thrusting what he considered to be women's work in her direction. She wondered if she could stick it out until the end of the season, knowing that she didn't really want to go back to London, and certainly not to go home to Embridge and her mother. She gave the custard in the saucepan she was stirring an indignant poke at the thought of Tim's cheek this morning. If he wasn't such an old friend, she would have been very tempted to ask Mawgan if he could find her a job down at the Fish. She had taken her turn working behind the bar in the sailing club at home, she wasn't green, and it would give the village something new to gossip about. And if Tim was under the impression that her cooking was going to add prestige to his establishment, he had another think coming, she had to be the world's worst cook.

Perhaps she should just settle down and marry a chef.

The thought came at her out of the blue, but before she had a chance to consider it seriously, the kitchen door was flung open and Lesley came in. That she was upset, was immediately obvious. Debbie pulled the custard pan to one side of the hotplate; her custard could easily go lumpy even if she was concentrating on it.

'What's happened, Les?'

'The Arnotts – you know, that family we had booked into No. 6, with those bunk beds Tim was making all the fuss about. They've just arrived.'

'And?'

'They say they aren't going to stay.' Lesley looked close to tears. 'They came into the house and asked to see the room without even unloading their luggage, and then they said it was unfit for a family of squatters and they wanted their deposit back. They've just had a week in a place up in North Cornwall that had every facility in the book, and according to them, this is disgusting by comparison!'

And that was before they even saw the custard. Debbie looked at her friend in a wild surmise.

'But they can't do that. Can they? They booked it.'

Lesley was crashing around the kitchen, filling a kettle and rattling cups onto a tray.

'I said, why didn't they have a sit down and a cup of tea and think about it, but I know they're going to go. And they were here for a fortnight, Deb, and that's an awful lot of money when there's four of them.'

Debbie said, uncertainly, 'They'll change their minds I expect, when they've had a bit of a rest. They'll just be tired, I expect.'

Lesley shook her head.

'They said the room was dirty, and it isn't true Deb, it isn't! There's a tiny piece of wallpaper off where that tiresome Barker child kept picking at it, that's all! They can't possibly expect us to re-paper the rooms every time we change round!'

Debbie had come to believe that people could expect anything, but it was no time to say so.

'Well, it certainly isn't dirty,' she said. 'Mrs T may have her faults, but not doing her job properly isn't one of them.'

'What shall we do?' asked Lesley, miserably. 'Give him his money? Tim will be furious, and we can't afford to lose the booking, we just can't, Deb! We're right on the edge of bankruptcy as it is.' She was crying now in earnest. Debbie reached for a teapot and began to make the tea.

'Go to the office and sit down,' she said. 'Pull yourself together, Les. I'll take this to the Arnotts, and then I'll be with you. In the lounge, are they?'

Lesley sniffed, and said something that could be taken as an affirmative if Debbie wished.

'Then you keep right away from them. I won't be a minute.'

The Arnotts were sitting in the lounge, two adults and two sulky-looking children, saying nothing either to each other or to Debbie. She left the tray with them and went to the office. Lesley was still weeping, silently and with her whole heart in it. Debbie looked at her in despair.

'Oh Les, don't cry,' she said. 'Dry your eyes, while I consult the oracle.' She picked up the telephone, and entered the number, pressing the keys as if she hated them. God, life could be a bitch! And people, come to that!

'I did warn you,' said Mawgan, unhelpfully, when she told him what had happened. Debbie was annoyed with him, she wasn't having a good day already, she didn't need him joining in.

'There's no need to say that as if it was our fault! That room is perfect – the whole house is spotless. Mrs Tregear may be a fiendish old gossip, but she works like an angel. And Lesley is crying.'

'Where's Howells to?' asked Mawgan. 'How come he's always somewhere else when anything goes wrong?'

'He's gone out for the business,' said Debbie, crossly. Tim hadn't been gone all that long, he wouldn't be back for ages yet.

'Stop snarling at me,' said Mawgan, mildly. 'Calm down. And listen.'

'I'm listening.'

'This may sound an odd question, but have they, by any chance, already been somewhere else before they came to you?'

'Are you psychic?' asked Debbie.

'No. Just old in the ways of sin. What you have there, Deborah my bird, is the rare but curious second-week's-holiday syndrome. I don't suppose they said where they'd been, did they?'

'I didn't speak to them. Lesley did. Does it matter?'

'Not really, but it can sometimes be interesting to check back. What they've almost certainly done is to overspend. They can't afford you no more, Deborah, and they're trying to give you the run-around. Or maybe, they've fallen out with each other, but it comes to the same thing in the end.'

'Oh no!' cried Debbie. Lesley raised her head in alarm, her eyes swimming.

'Well, it's a guess, but *oh yes,* probably. You're quite sure that your own feet are planted on rock? No dust, no earwigs, no cobwebs or cockroaches?'

'Don't be insulting! Mrs T and Lesley too, would die first!'

'Just checking. Now listen carefully, this is what you must do.'

Debbie listened, scrawling down the information on the desk jotter as she did so.

'You make out an account for two-thirds of the value of their booking, the third you knock off is for the food they aren't going to eat, OK? Got that? Now, you deduct from that total the deposit that they've already paid, and you present them with the result, saying that you'll do your best to re-let the rooms and you'll be in touch with them again at the end of their booked stay, and if necessary send them a rebate. In your particular case, of course, you must also take into account any tuition fees, to which the same applies, except that you presumably won't make any allowances. You tell them that this amended account must be settled on the spot now, and that any attempt to stop the payment will end in the hands of your solicitor. Now, did you get all that?'

'Yes,' said Debbie, scribbling busily. 'What do we do if they won't play ball?'

'They haven't an option, that's the law – as much for their protection as for yours. In theory, I suppose, under these circumstances there's possibly no obligation on your part even to try to re-let the rooms, but I wouldn't like to put it to the test.'

'Suppose they say they're going to sue Tim and Lesley?'

'Make a rude gesture and say goodbye. But get the money first.'

'This time, it doesn't even *sound* easy,' said Debbie, nervously.

'Well, they might make themselves unpleasant, but they can't get out of it – just so long as you don't let them bully you. When's Howells back?'

'He's not been gone that long – he won't be back for ages, he's got to go to Penryn for some englefield clips on the way back.'

'What on earth are englefield clips?' asked Mawgan. 'No – don't waste time telling me, I'm up to my eyes in it too. And good luck.'

'Thank you.' Debbie replaced the phone, and turned to Lesley. 'Right, are you sitting comfortably?' She took a breath, and picked up the jotter. 'Then I'll begin…'

Lesley showed a marked lack of enthusiasm for the programme.

'There's going to be a row, I know it, and I hate rows,' she said unhappily.

'I'd do it for you if I could,' said Debbie, sympathising with her for once. 'But I'm only the hired help, and they must realise it.'

Lesley had pulled the invoice book towards her and picked up a pen.

'Perhaps we can talk them out of it,' she said, without much hope. Debbie didn't think much of this idea.

'Argument would be undignified,' she suggested. 'And anyway, imagine what it would be like if you happened to succeed! They'd spend the whole time sniffing about looking for trouble!'

Lesley agreed, but still without enthusiasm. She began to make out the account with much tapping on a calculator. Debbie went over to the window and stared out in a reverie which was broken by the sudden ring of the bell. Lesley jumped nervously.

'Oh God, not somebody else arriving before we've got rid of them!' she cried shrilly. 'Witnesses, we really don't need!'

'I'll go and get them upstairs very quickly,' said Debbie, heading for the door.

'Oh hurry!' pleaded Lesley. 'I can't face those Arnotts alone, I just can't –'

Debbie went out into the hall and found Mawgan standing there.

'I thought Mrs Howells might need some back-up,' he said.

Debbie could have flung her arms round him, but didn't think that it was quite the time.

'Come in,' she said. 'She's just totting up the bill.'

'I just hope you're right about Howells,' said Mawgan, following her to the office. 'I can't help thinking, if he arrived in the middle, Mrs. Howells would throw herself under a bus.'

Debbie opened the office door.

'Look who I found,' she said, and Lesley took one glance and burst into tears again. Mawgan gave her a grave look but made no comment, and Debbie picked up the completed account and handed it to him for checking without asking Lesley, regardless of the, for the moment irrelevant, fact that by doing so she could be said to be handing secrets to the enemy.

'You wouldn't like to give it to them, I don't suppose?' said Lesley, scrubbing at her eyes with a tissue. He didn't reply, running his thumb down the column of figures, and before she could repeat the request there was a knock on the door. Debbie opened it and Mr Arnott stood on the threshold, with his wife peering anxiously over his shoulder. Neither of them looked entirely at ease, but they were putting on a good show.

'I've come to settle up for the tea,' said Mr Arnott. 'And then, we'd like to be on our way, if you would be good enough to prepare a cheque.

My wife and I have discussed it, but we don't feel prepared to change our minds.' At that point, his eye fell on Mawgan, idling about on the far side of the desk with the bill folded casually between his fingers and an interested look on his face, and Debbie had a fleeting impression that he was sorry to see him. 'Mr Howells?' he asked, stiffly, and Mawgan replied, misleadingly, instantly, and without shame, I understand you feel you've got a complaint.'

'Yes.' He glanced uneasily at Lesley, sniffing into her tissue. 'The accommodation isn't what we were led to expect. The room is shabby, and the place generally is really not very clean. You must admit that.'

Lesley and Debbie he had marked down for a couple of tenderfeet from the very first. The putative Mr Howells, he was about to discover, was a horse of a very different colour.

'Oh, I don't think, you know, that you'd find any as would agree with you,' said Mawgan, smiling. *The smile on the face of the tiger,* thought Debbie, fascinated, and he was being very careful about final consonants, which he often wasn't. Mr Arnott seemed to have slightly diminished in size, like a balloon that gently deflates with a tiny pinprick, but his wife jumped in with a disdainful sniff.

'Why, the wallpaper is peeling off the wall!' she exclaimed. 'And the garden, just look at it! All those bushes, growing all over the place, quite unpruned!'

Gardening, apart from occasionally mowing the lawn, which Roger had taken on, didn't rate high on the list of jobs to be done at Seagulls. But anyway, Debbie thought, you couldn't *stop* bushes from growing, could you? She wondered how Mawgan would parry that one, but he was far too wily to chase red herrings like these and get embroiled in arguments, and behaved as if Mrs Arnott hadn't spoken. His manner became so pleasant that Mrs Arnott looked positively bewildered. He went on talking as if she had never interrupted, with a gentle and devastating charm that had her gasping as if for air.

'I been hearing how much you enjoyed your last week's holiday in North Cornwall, Mrs Arnott,' he said. Mrs Arnott, no able conspirator, went bright scarlet, and Mr Arnott opened his mouth and closed it again. Mawgan held out the bill, suddenly as cool as ice and as slippery, the charm switched off as if it had been a light.

'Your account, Mr – ' He glanced at the piece of paper, although he had already seen it, and finished with telling effect, 'er, *Arnott.*'

Ouch! thought Debbie, and winced for Mr Arnott.

Mr Arnott exploded into rage, but there was an undertone of bluster by this time.

'My what? I'll tell you now, Howells – '

'No,' cut in Mawgan, swiftly, but still pleasantly enough. 'I'll tell *you,* Mr Arnott. I appreciate your problem, never think I don't, but it's not mine, and I don't mean to make it mine. You've upset Mrs Howells quite unnecessarily, and I suggest that you listen very careful to what I'm going to say.'

Mr Arnott listened. Indeed, words seemed to have deserted him. Mawgan, having already rehearsed his own speech once to Debbie, spoke for a few minutes with great fluency. At the close, Mr Arnott scrawled a black and angry cheque, which, Debbie noticed, Mawgan checked very carefully, going so far as to ask to see Mr Arnott's credit card and to make a note of the number. Mr Arnott positively snatched his receipt, and turned to go.

'We'll see what *my* solicitor has to say about this!' he said furiously. 'And *I* won't forget that you upset *my* wife, either.'

They left without making further trouble, but angrily.

A good, solid performer with a machine gun. Well, she had been told. Debbie watched Mawgan crossing the hall on his way back from seeing the Arnotts off the premises, and remarked,

'Goodness, do they all form fours and march up and down there at the Fish? I bet nobody dares to complain of so much as the coffee is cold!'

'If they did, and it was, I sh'd be next complaining,' said Mawgan, simply. 'It never is.'

Lesley lifted a tear-stained face, ignoring this potted lesson in catering management.

'They're going to make trouble, I just know it!'

'I think they'll try, yes. Just stick to your guns and find a good solicitor.' Mawgan looked at her thoughtfully. 'Mrs Howells, the world is full of bullies. You mustn't let them down you so easily.'

'How can I thank you?' asked Lesley, helplessly.

'By keeping it dark from your scary husband.' He hesitated, began to say something and stopped. 'Goodbye, Mrs Howells. And remember, never trust the man who won't unload his luggage.'

Debbie walked with him back to his car.

'You're an incredible person,' she told him.

'If being the biggest sucker in Cornwall is incredible, I agree,' he said. 'Goodbye, Deborah.'

A swift kiss, the slam of the car door, and he was away down the drive in a shower of loose gravel. As he drove out, two more cars drove in – fortunately not Tim – and Debbie had to put the whole, rather upsetting interlude behind her.

When she eventually got back to the kitchen and the trifle, she found that the custard had burnt black onto the bottom of the forgotten saucepan. Muttering darkly to herself, she started all over again.

When Tim heard a suitably edited version of the afternoon's events, he was pleased with Lesley, but they left their mark, even so. It had taken yet another strip from the gilt that was steadily peeling from their gingerbread. Although the Arnotts didn't stop the cheque, they did write a rather nasty letter threatening to report Seagulls to the Health & Safety inspector, which Mawgan advised Debbie to throw into File 13.

'File 13?'

'The bin, Deborah. If they meant it, they'd have already done it and not given you any warning neither. Just bin it and forget it. Or maybe you'd better just stick it away somewhere, but that's the end of it, promise.'

He was right, as it turned out, but even so, the incident had left behind it a bitter taste that wouldn't go away. It was all very well for Mawgan to point out, as he did, that if your reputation was part of your livelihood, a good solicitor was – had to be – the first line of defence. The mere fact that they had almost needed one to deal with one lot of guests indefinably spoilt their relationship with all the others. They would never again be quite so free and easy.

The initial deception that had seemed so simple and sensible and had now become so important was beginning to create as many problems as it solved. Debbie had a feeling, strong but unspecific, that on the last occasion it had gone a step too far, and she was beginning to be haunted too by the idea that one day they would reach out for Mawgan and find him not there, and themselves in a real mess. So far they had been lucky, but he wasn't imprisoned within the walls of the Fish, and it would be infantile to suppose that he never went out anywhere. With the turnover of business from his restaurant alone he must, for a start, make fairly frequent sorties in search of supplies, and if the standard of the food at the Fish was anything to go by, they wouldn't take the form of a quick dash to the Cash & Carry. Moreover, if something went wrong when he was busy in the restaurant kitchen, it wouldn't only be the chicken that was well stuffed. Between this, and the constant unpleasant anticipation that each day's post now brought with it, her own nerves were beginning to shake under the strain.

By this time, the only one of the four of them who appeared unperturbed was Roger, jogging his way up and down the lanes morning and evening, and describing every forlorn hope, however unsuitably, as a dead duck. Roger, of course, wasn't in quite the same position as Debbie. His loyalties were more to the job, not specifically to Lesley or Tim, and when he left at the close of the season, if he stayed that long, it would be as carelessly as he had arrived. He had begun to describe the place as *Fawlty Towers* and Lesley and Tim were not amused.

Debbie saw much less of Mawgan these days, too. The pressures were building up at the Fish as well as up the hill at Seagulls, his bars and restaurant were filled to overflowing during their opening hours, and all his letting bedrooms taken. When she did see him, it depressed her a little to find that even he was showing a few cracks. Not to his customers, before whom he remained light-hearted, confident and in control, but sometimes with her, on the increasingly rare occasions when they could meet to talk.

On one particular day, when she had raced up to the post office at the top of the village after coming ashore from sailing for some stamps for the office, she saw him playing ducks and drakes on the foreshore outside the Fish, with another man standing beside him watching, hands in pockets. Whatever they were discussing, it didn't please Mawgan, who looked both stormy and frustrated. As she came back down the hill with her stamps, the stranger was just saying goodbye. He turned and walked up towards her, a kindly, middle-aged man with friendly eyes, and they exchanged a greeting and a few words about the lovely weather as they passed. Debbie hesitated for a moment when he had passed by. Mawgan hadn't turned round, he didn't seem even to have seen her. He had sent a flat stone whizzing an incredible distance across the water and was watching it hopping and skidding towards the rows of moored yachts with a scowl that seemed to Debbie to bode no good to anyone. She decided that on the whole it might be wisest to just walk quietly past, but as she drew level with him he called to her.

'Deborah?'

Debbie paused. He hadn't looked round, so he must have seen her as she came along the road. She stepped off the causeway and crossed the shingle towards him.

'Hullo. Playing truant?'

He laughed, but without mirth.

'Something like that, I suppose. Did you see that man?'

'Yes,' said Debbie, cautiously.

'My probation officer. A conscientious and painfully tactful do-gooder. He makes excuses to come out here because he likes the place – he thinks nobody knows who he is. God, I wish he wouldn't, I hate his guts! Can't wait to see the last of him!'

Debbie wanted to ask, when will that be? but decided not to. Instead, she said, 'I haven't seen you for a while. Have you been very busy? We've been in over our heads!'

'That's August for you. Be thankful.' He stopped throwing stones and turned to look at her directly for the first time. 'All well up there? I don't seem to've had no frantic phone calls lately.'

'We do cotton on, eventually,' said Debbie.

'The first, and most important, thing to learn,' he said sombrely, 'is to lose your faith in human nature.'

'Yes, well, I think you taught them that one yourself,' said Debbie.

'True, bird. I'm the world's expert, as you may have noticed.'

'Oh, don't!' cried Debbie, hating his tone.

'Don't what?'

'Be so bitter. What's the matter with you this afternoon?'

'*Laugh, and the world laughs with you, weep, and you weep alone,*' quoted Mawgan, mockingly.

'What are you weeping about, particularly?'

'Bleeding hell!' he said, with sudden and startling violence, for he wasn't a man who habitually swore. 'I killed a friend. Will nobody let me try an' forget it?'

Debbie was silent, her lack of years and experience betraying her. She knew an impulse that astonished her to gather him into her arms and offer comfort, but could hardly do so under the windows of the Fish. Moreover,

256

she thought that he might throw her into the river if she did. Fortunately, he seemed to realise himself that he had created an impossible situation, the tension in his face unravelled as rapidly as an uncoiling spring, and he said quite cheerfully, 'Are you in a hurry, or have you got ten minutes? I need to breathe.'

Debbie said that she could steal ten minutes if he liked, and they strolled along the foreshore together, back towards the village. Their way was impeded a little by mooring ropes and chains and patches of slippery rock, and boats pulled up on the stones, so their progress was of necessity slow.

'Have you ever been sailing?' asked Debbie, idly, just making conversation as she watched the dinghies darting like swallows on the open water beyond the moorings, and the more dignified yachts making their way among them. They made a pretty sight.

'Never. Nothing more exciting than the odd fishing boat, me.'

She glanced at him, suddenly curious.

'Do you have any hobbies?'

'Not got the time for 'em. I go surfing.'

'Malibu, or the ordinary kind?'

'Malibu.'

'You'd probably take to sailing,' said Debbie, after some thought.

'Sailing is a summer thing. My hobbies have to be in the winter.' He grinned at her. 'I plays rugby too, when I get a chance. Or at least, I did – I suppose I may have to pass on that since I done that elbow.'

Debbie refused to be sidetracked. She grinned back at him.

'A coward in a wet suit, huh? Well, you can sail in a wet suit too.'

They walked on in a suddenly companionable silence. Debbie began to feel as if she must have imagined some of the things he had said.

'As a matter of fact, things have been going quite well lately,' she said.

'I saw Mrs Howells the other day, and I thought she looked shattered,' countered Mawgan. 'Why is it I don't never see her in the bar? Everyone else – never her.'

'She's not that interested in drinking in bars, talking about boats.'

'Really? Well, watch it, won't you?'

Debbie frowned at him.

'Do you know, she gave me a similar veiled warning about you, once. What is it with you two?'

To her surprise, he gave her the same answer as Lesley had done all that time ago.

'That's the way it goes. It prob'ly takes one to know one.'

'One what?' asked Debbie, but he refused to say.

They turned round and began to stroll back towards the causeway.

'We did have a bit of a scare earlier this week,' said Debbie, but in fact it had been more than a scare, as she well knew, and he had nearly heard all about it at the time. 'Some silly woman we've acquired for our sins picked up a tummy bug, and said we'd given her food poisoning.'

'It happens. What did you do?'

'We nearly shouted for you,' said Debbie, with a laugh, because they were quite proud of the way that they hadn't needed to. 'Fortunately, the doctor told her not to be so silly. She's going around now saying that it's the septic tank.'

'That's the sort of thing you want to watch, Deborah. Stamp on it, good and quick. You never let people get away with saying things like that.'

'Oh well,' said Debbie, 'nobody really listens. She's a serious contender for the plonker of the week award.'

'You should know your own business best by this time, but if I was you I should whisper into her ear about damaging slander.' As he had done himself, to Tim, but he didn't mention that, and neither did Debbie.

'Oh, I don't think we need to go that far,' she said blithely. 'Everyone else knows her for a prize pillock, she gets on everybody's nerves. She thinks she knows everything, but actually, she's one of the biggest tyros afloat.'

'Don't go falling into the same trap.'

'God, you are in a mood today! What can I say to cheer you up?'

'I could think of something.'

'What, then?'

'Oh no, my bird, it wouldn't be at all the same if I told you,' he teased her, suddenly ablaze with animation again. He kept her laughing all the way back to the Fish, but she left him to walk up the hill alone in an unexpectedly flattened mood.

The Fish was crowded out again, the tables on the forecourt packed, and people sitting along the low wall and spilling out through the doors to the two bars. Mawgan was almost too successful; the Fish appeared to be a gathering point for miles around during the summer, although she supposed it might be easier in the winter. She imagined all the things he had to deal with and worry about, and then working in the restaurant kitchen on top of them, and thought he really shouldn't burn the candle at both ends quite so assiduously. Everybody needed time off, as he had once told her himself. He had been in a really downbeat mood today, and she found that it had rubbed off onto her.

I killed a friend. Will nobody let me try an' forget it?

She was fed up with the catering business, she decided, it was all going sour on her. She couldn't wait for the end of the season.

XVII

Debbie, whose astigmatism on that afternoon had ranged over a wide variety of danger signals had, among her other aberrations, ignored a very specific warning. Ignored it to the point of entirely forgetting to pass it on to Lesley, who might then have relayed it, suitably disguised, to Tim, in which case some of the things that were now about to happen would possibly never have happened at all. It only needed one more ingredient to the mix for the original innocent deception to blow back in their faces like a fractured gas main. The law that decrees that anything that can go wrong, will go wrong, ensured that this last ingredient shouldn't be lacking.

On the evening of the day following Debbie's meeting with Mawgan on the foreshore, Tim gave her a long, cool look when dinner was over and said, 'We're all going into Falmouth tomorrow night for a meal to celebrate Sally's birthday, are you planning to honour us with your company?'

He sounded sour all the time now when he was speaking either to her or to Lesley. Debbie had to make a conscious effort not to tell him so.

'Why not, since I've been invited?' she said, trying to keep it light.

'I thought you might have decided to take the night off again, with your bit of rough down the road,' said Tim.

'My *what?*' Debbie exclaimed, outraged. Tim raised his eyebrows.

'Sunday seems to be your night for ethnic studies,' he said.

'That was a bit unnecessary, wasn't it?' Debbie was furious, not knowing which of his premises to attack first, but retaining by a whisker the sense to realise that the Mawgan angle, to borrow a phrase from Roger, would be a dead duck. 'Once, that's all! I work all the hours you pay me for, and more!' Careful. She bit her lip and hung on to her temper, feeling it slipping out of her grasp. *Bit of rough* indeed!

'Oh, counting are we?' asked Tim. Debbie took a deep breath. She wanted to say *Somebody needs to, for you don't!* Instead, she said, still trying to keep things possible, 'It's a shame Lesley won't be able to come, though. She's going to have to wait in for those Summerskills.' The Summerskills were one of the inherited reservations. They had been a nuisance from the start, for unlike everyone else, they had booked from Sunday to Sunday, and thrown the reservations in that one room completely out of step just when it mattered most. Tim, who she thought might have felt a bit sorry for Lesley, missing a party, spoke dismissively.

'She couldn't have come anyway. That tiresome Rosemary girl hasn't been included in the invitation, or the family just arrived with the kids in No. 4.'

Debbie hesitated, illogically concerned without knowing quite why. She didn't like Rosemary any better than Tim or the other students did, but she felt constrained to say, 'That's a bit pointed, isn't it?'

'Not my decision. It's Sal's birthday.'

Debbie thought that he should have spoken to Sally, who was young and thoughtless but full of enthusiasm, and had invited everyone to her birthday party whom she liked. Fair enough – but Rosemary would be the only one of the students left behind. Sally didn't have to think about the implications of that, but Tim did. She thought that if she was in Rosemary's position she would feel dreadful, the stupid woman didn't know she was a pain in the neck after all. Or maybe she did, and that would only make it worse.

'Shouldn't you say something?' she said, but Tim wouldn't.

Lesley seemed quite philosophical about being left behind.

'I hardly know them anyway,' she said. 'I'll be all right, Mrs Tregear's married daughter is coming in to help with dinner.' Mrs Tregear had two daughters, neither of whom seemed to have names. *My daughter* they already knew worked at the Fish. *My married daughter* had recently returned with *my daughter's husband* and a small child, *my grandson*, from Saudi Arabia. This information seemed unexpectedly exotic, giving a fascinating hint of lives within lives, privately revolving. Roger had remarked that having a Tregear out in the Middle East had probably been a contributing factor to the present unrest in that part of the world, and things should improve now.

What Sally chose to do with her own birthday party, Debbie had to concede in the end, wasn't really their business, and she let it go, not wanting the company of the tiresome Rosemary either.

On that momentous evening, the entire party, about seventeen of them including Tim, Debbie and Roger, squashed themselves into two estate cars, a Mini, and a Ford Escort and left for Falmouth before the Summerskills had arrived, and had an excellent evening. On their return, around a quarter-past ten, Sally's boyfriend noticed that the Fish was still open. 'There's a good half hour of drinking time left, let's go and drink Sal's health!'

'You've done that already,' said Sally, giggling.

'So what? We can do it again. There isn't a law.'

He pulled in abruptly to the side of the road just off the causeway, and the other three cars drew in ahead. Everyone piled out into the road. The idea of finishing the evening in the bar of the Fish met with general approval, and they all headed back along the causeway on foot.

The Fish was crowded, and unusually rowdy. As they approached, Tommy appeared in the doorway to the bars, manhandling a shouting youth in a denim jacket and leather trousers, whom he hurtled out onto the forecourt almost into Tim's arms. In the background, there seemed to be some sort of scuffle going on inside.

'Keep out of the public bar,' said Tim, hurrying his party past. The youth who had nearly knocked him down had thumped back against the wall, limp and breathless. He was grinning as if he was enjoying himself. He turned, and shouted over his shoulder in an ugly voice,

'And tell that fucking murderer he should've stayed locked up!' Tommy aimed a swift cuff at his ear, which he dodged.

'Shut up and bugger off, or I'll fetch the police!' Tommy turned to go back into the bar, and caught sight of Tim, still hesitating outside. 'I should go home if I was you, Mr. Howells, there's a bit of a ruckus in here tonight. Bloody troublemakers from over to Falmouth!'

The rest of the party had already gone inside, too busy talking and laughing among themselves to really notice anything. Tim followed them hurriedly, meaning to suggest that they bought some cans and took them up the hill to Seagulls, but by contrast to the public bar, everything seemed peaceful and ordinary. Even the shouting still going on outside was almost inaudible above the comfortable buzz of talk. The pert girl behind the bar – *my daughter*, presumably – looked excited, and kept glancing over her shoulder as she served them. Contrary to custom, the communicating door between the two bars was closed tonight.

Tim supposed it was all right. Nobody else appeared to be worried. He decided that they wouldn't stay long.

The others had already found themselves a corner and settled into it, and Roger and Debbie and Sally's boyfriend had gone up to the bar to get the first round in. Tim went over to join them.

'Bit of a barney going on in the public bar,' he said, aside to Roger. 'Let's keep it short, we'd better get the girls out of it.'

Roger looked surprised.

'It was only a drunk, wasn't it?' He hadn't heard what Tim had heard. Tim said, 'I expect so,' but he wasn't sure.

'Angwin looks perfectly equal to a drunk, or even two or three,' said Roger unconcernedly. 'I wouldn't fuss, if I was you.'

They carried the drinks back to the table and settled down, but Tim's ears were on the stretch for trouble. He took part in the conversation only sporadically, and was glad for once when that bloody Angwin came into the bar. Angwin, he thought, looked on edge – and the glance that he gave the digital clock up on the wall was swift and calculating. He said something to the barmaid and moved away to take an order.

'Drink up, chaps, I ought to be getting back to poor old Lesley,' he said.

'Oh come on, Tim, it's only ten minutes until closing time!' cried someone. 'Ten minutes isn't going to hurt!'

'What are you having?' Sally's boyfriend got to his feet. 'Come on, it's my round this time, how about a bottle of champers for Sal?'

'I think –' began Tim, and as he spoke there was a sudden crash of breaking glass, and everyone in the room fell abruptly silent.

A large stone had come hurtling in through the open window, and landed in the middle of a cluster of empties. The people sitting round the table had leapt to their feet as it landed and jumped backwards in a hail of flying glass. For an instant, the room was a tableau of startled amazement, and then, before anyone could do anything sensible, a noisy crowd came pouring in through the door.

They were all more or less drunk, and they weren't all of them youngsters, they seemed a motley collection. They bore all the appearance of an organised mob, and they rushed into the bar shouting things such as *Get the fucking murderer, show the bugger what's what, give 'im what's coming to 'im, go get 'im, Gary, show 'im what it's all about!* – the overall theme being well-sprinkled with choice oaths, and throwing anything in their path aside with violence and obvious enjoyment. Women screamed, men shouted, and heavy objects flew in all directions. It was half a fight and half a panic, as a solid phalanx of fishermen and farm-workers came storming in pursuit of the invaders, some of them none too sober themselves, *en route* from the public bar.

The Seagulls party was in an awkward position, hemmed in by chairs and tables into the farthest corner of the bar. Tim, Roger, and several of the other men formed themselves into a protective barrier, but among their womenfolk at least, there was very little screaming.

'What's going on?' asked Sally, round-eyed and bewildered. She was a little pale and looked startled, but she was keeping her head. Over by the door, someone was in hysterics. It was like a scene out of a Wild West film.

The fight was brief, noisy and deliberately destructive, and it was hard to work out who was on which side. It ended with Mawgan, Tommy, and several of the more sober men in the bar overpowering the troublemakers and evicting them rudely onto the forecourt, which was by this time completely deserted. Those who could make a run for it, had, very sensibly, run. Mawgan slammed the door behind them and shot the bolt. He turned, breathless and dishevelled. It was the first time that Debbie had ever seen him flustered.

'Sorry about that, everyone,' he said, in a voice that wasn't as steady as it should have been. 'The police have been sent for, I suggest you all go quietly out by the back way and go home.' He looked at Tim. 'If you go out by the side gate, you can get back up to your place. I'll show you.'

He crossed the room, stepping over the debris, and opened the door that led through from behind the bar counter into the back premises. The occupants of the bar shuffled past him in a bemused silence, only anxious to get away. The woman who had had hysterics was still sobbing convulsively.

Debbie, leaving among the last, hesitated as she passed him.

'Mawgan – '

He looked at her with a cursory glance that hardly seemed to recognise her.

'Go home, Deborah. Keep out of it.'

'But –'

'Please, take her away,' he said to Tim, and Tim was happy to oblige.

'Come on, Deb, you aren't wanted here. You'll only be in the way.'

Tommy showed them the side gate, which allowed them to leave the Fish on the Seagulls side without crossing the forecourt, still the scene of sporadic outbursts of fighting. The cars were still parked under the trees, but the windows of two of them were smashed, and they all had several deep, deliberate scratches on the wings. All the tyres had been slashed with broken glass that lay sparkling on the road beside them. Away along the foreshore there was more shouting and other ugly noises.

Sally spoke out of the darkness, a footnote to the evening. 'This is one birthday I'm certainly not going to forget in a hurry!'

The next day began as it meant to go on, when Mrs Tregear came in through the back door, big with news and saucer-eyed at the thought of the juicy titbit she had for everyone this morning. She found the four members of the staff at breakfast, for these days she started early to get the downstairs rooms done before the guests came down.

'Have you heard the news?' she asked, in a voice pregnant with meaning, and they all looked at her with lustreless early-morning eyes – all except for Roger, that is, who had been for a good enlivening jog at six o'clock and was hungry. He went on solidly with his bacon and eggs.

'There was a big fight at the Fish last night, they broke the place up something awful,' went on Mrs Tregear, with the air of one announcing the outbreak of total nuclear war. 'The police and everything, such a carry on! There's talk of nothing else in the village this morning!'

'We were there,' said Tim, and Mrs Tregear looked disappointed.

'Oh, so you know all about it, then.'

'Yes,' said Debbie. She hadn't slept at all well, and she looked pale and heavy-eyed. Unlike Roger, she had no appetite at all for her breakfast. Mrs Tregear was only momentarily thrown out of her stride.

'A gang from over to Falmouth, they were,' she said. 'Young lads mainly, but some among them as ought to have known better. They was after Mr Angwin deliberate, shouting out in the public bar about how he killed his own sister's husband, so if there was anyone there as didn't know before, they couldn't help knowing then. Tommy couldn't shut them up, and Denise was scared out of her life, poor little thing! In the end Mr Angwin told them to get out.'

'Which they obviously didn't,' said Tim. He didn't want to gossip, he had never thought the day would dawn when he would feel sorry for Angwin. Lesley, to whom it was all news, looked at him reproachfully.

'You never said, when you all got back.'

'You were asleep.'

'But this morning – '

'Oh, shut up!'

Mrs Tregear ignored this interchange as if it hadn't taken place.

'Not at first they didn't go, no. Tommy and Mr Angwin threw a couple of them out, but they popped straight back, and then some of the men joined in and helped to throw the rest out – not long before closing time, that was. Mr Angwin threatened them with the police, and there was a lot of nasty abuse!'

'Yes, we heard it,' said Tim. 'They came into the other bar and broke that up, too.'

'In there, were you?' Mrs Tregear hesitated, torn between the delights of hearing an eye-witness account and continuing with the exciting tale herself. 'I expect you left when it was all over like everyone else,' she said, hopefully. Tim said that they had. Debbie fiddled with the teaspoon in her saucer and kept her eyes looking downwards. Mrs Tregear's glance, bright and interested and missing nothing, flickered over her.

'Well then, you know as they went outside, I suppose, but they didn't go away. They started shouting and throwing stones and breaking windows, and then the police come and broke it up and took them off. Real nasty, it was. But after that – ' Her voice dropped, taking on the tone of someone recounting, with relish, the pay-off to a good story. 'After *that*, so Tommy says, Mr Angwin went like a mad beast – never seen anything like it, he said. Started chucking the glasses one by one at the wall, those that weren't already broken, and swearing like a wild thing, and I'll say this for him, he don't usually! It took Tommy and two of the policemen together to stop him, he was that out of it! Well, we all knew as he had a nasty temper on him, but really! Tommy said he thought he was going to have some kind of fit, he was that beside himself!'

Debbie felt herself shaking so that she had trouble in sitting on her chair. It was hardly a breach of probation to throw your own glasses at your own wall, but even so… poor Mawgan! Poor, poor Mawgan!

Lesley stirred, and laid down her knife and fork – she hadn't been eating, but rather sitting in suspended animation during the recital.

'If you ask me, you should all take care,' she said, precisely. 'That unfortunate man is going to surprise you all by jumping out of an upstairs window, or taking an overdose or something, one of these days.'

Mawgan had said that Lesley would throw herself under a bus. Debbie swallowed, but her mouth was dry. Mrs Tregear was staring at Lesley in amazement.

'Oh no, Mrs Howells, not him! Don't you worry, that one's as hard as nails!'

How she could equate that statement with what she had just told them was a mystery. Lesley got up and began to collect the breakfast plates, scraping the largely uneaten meal into the bin.

'All right, have it your own way. But when he's found splattered all over the forecourt of his pub one morning, don't say you weren't warned.'

All the ignored alarm bells of the past few months began to clamour at once, deafening any chance of sensible thought with their own vital, appalling message. *It takes one to know one* – oh God, what shall I do? The neglected seedling of knowledge, struggling for growth in Debbie's subconscious, popped out two leaves and a bud, just like that. A paralysing wave of her own inexperience and ignorance swept over her, just as it had in the blizzard on the moor. Mawgan had even told her himself, she could hear him now saying *I live on Prozac.* Where on earth had her brains been holidaying?

Tim got to his feet in Lesley's wake.

'It was all remarkably unpleasant,' he said. 'I never expected I'd sympathise with Angwin, but even though the heavens fell on him, our guests will still want their breakfast.'

That ended the conversation, rather to Debbie's relief. She wondered if she should go down to the Fish, and if she did, what sort of a reception she would get. They were friends, at least, surely? She couldn't go right now – but at lunch time, maybe, she could slip down. She didn't know how she was going to get through the morning.

Mr Summerskill intercepted Lesley in the hall after breakfast, as she picked her way through the group of students collecting outside the TV lounge for their morning briefing.

'Excuse me, Mrs Howells, may I have a word with you?' he said. Lesley said, 'Of course.'

He was a tall man, she had to tilt her head to see his face and had an uncomfortable feeling of being overborne and intimidated.

'My wife and I have decided to move on,' he said, suavely. 'If you give me my bill for last night's accommodation, then we shall settle up and be on our way.'

Lesley swallowed. She had played this scene before, and it wasn't any better the second time. She felt a familiar shaking behind her knees.

'But –' she said.

Mr Summerskill looked down at her from his imposing height. He had none of the defensive shamefacedness of the Arnotts, he had the confidence of a man who knew that he stood on firm ground. Tim, passing through on his way to his briefing, said as he passed, 'Everything all right, Les?' patted her shoulder, and was gone before she could gather enough sense to stop him. The hall was suddenly empty, just herself and Mr Summerskill. No Mrs Summerskill, she was upstairs packing. If it came to that, no Mr. Howells. Just the two of them.

'I should tell you that I have considerable experience of this game, Mrs Howells,' Mr Summerskill was saying. 'I was in catering myself for many years, and speaking from what I know of the trade, and I am sorry to have to put it like this, the standards you maintain here are totally unacceptable.' He paused, and Lesley had time to think that the worst thing about him was that he was speaking, if anything, more in sorrow than in anger. Kindly, even, if that wasn't a stupid word to use. He went on. 'My wife and I have taken these two weeks to give ourselves a much-needed break, the first summer break that we have been able to take in years. We looked forward to a pleasant time here by the river, and Seagulls had been highly recommended to us by friends who stayed last year, as a quiet and excellently run establishment. We shall be arriving home this evening bitterly disappointed.'

'But –' said Lesley, again. Mr. Summerskill, having made his rhetorical pause, continued without waiting for her to go on.

'Not only do we find the entire place over-run with a gaggle of extremely noisy young people who seem to have taken over entirely, it also seems incredible to me, speaking as a professional, that with your drainage system in such a state as to cause illness among your guests, you should even remain open. And finally, you cannot seriously expect anyone to remain in a place where the standard of the food is so poor that most of your guests choose to go out to dinner.'

Lesley's jaw dropped. She stared at him, a kaleidoscope of highly-charged emotions chasing themselves around inside her head. Words failed her, only one thought stood clearly, head and shoulders above the rest. After Mrs Tregear's breakfast-time revelations in the kitchen, how on earth could she take this terrible multiple problem to poor Angwin? It was symptomatic of her own state of mind that her resentment against Angwin for collapsing on her just when she needed him most was as great as her resentment of Tim's casual desertion.

She had a terrible feeling of loneliness. Her face, she knew, was scarlet, probably the picture of guilt. Faced with Mr. Summerskill, she found nothing at all to say.

'Oh,' was all that she managed.

Fury and indignation filled her mind, but offered no sensible counsel. It was that Rosemary woman, it had to be – she had been talking to the Summerskills in the lounge when the coffee tray went in, and no doubt she had been chagrined by her exclusion from the birthday party – but how could she possibly expend such malice on people who had never hurt her? And last night's dinner... Lesley passed it under swift mental review, and could see nothing wrong with it. It had been perfectly wholesome, a baked collar of bacon with tinned pineapple, apricots and cherries round it and a bit of parsley sauce out of one of those convenient packets to finish it off, and chips and peas to accompany it. At this time of year, surely every guest house in Cornwall used frozen vegetables, not everyone could have the resources of the Fish. Hurt, shame, amazement, shock, she felt them all.

And still no defence came into her head. She would have to say something soon, or he would.

He did. As if he had read her thoughts, he said, 'I see too, in your current brochure that you offer good home cooking. Frozen vegetables and cake-mix sponge may be what you serve in your home, Mrs Howells, but it isn't what most people would understand by the phrase.'

Lesley hung her head, unable to look him in the face. He wasn't being unpleasant, it would have been easier if he had been. He was being reasonable – the look on his face was almost quizzical. She wanted to say that the sponge hadn't been a cake-mix, but where was the point? He had her exactly where he wanted her, and he knew it.

'I'll fetch my husband,' she said.

Tim proved to be a broken reed. For one thing, he was annoyed at being taken from his legitimate business, even though both Debbie and Roger were present to take over, for another, he didn't see why Lesley couldn't manage on her own this time when she had always done so in the past. He thought that she was simply taking advantage of the fact that, for once, he was here on the premises, rubbing his nose in it. Mr Summerskill, calmly in control of the situation, made mincemeat out of both of them without once raising his voice in anger, settled for his night's lodging , which involved Tim and Lesley giving him a rebate on his deposit, and drove away with his wife, victor of the field. Whatever Mawgan had said on the last occasion, Lesley knew when she had met a superior force.

Tim was, quite simply, furious.

'How could you let him get away with it?' he stormed bitterly. 'You know we can't afford to lose a fortnight's booking, whatever were you thinking of?'

'Me!' stormed back Lesley, in a pleased flood of too-long pent up emotions. 'Me! Why does it always have to be *me?* You just stood there and let him walk all over me, and say my cooking was uneatable – you –' She drew a breath and tried to bite back her tears. Tears would only annoy. 'I hate you, Tim Howells!' she shouted, at the top of her voice.

Debbie came flying out of the lounge, shutting the door hurriedly behind her.

'For goodness' sake!' she exclaimed, grabbing them each by an arm. 'Turn it down, everyone can hear you!' She shoved them through the nearest open door into the dining-room. 'What on earth has happened?'

They told her, variously, interrupting each other and blaming each other, every resentment and hurt that either had felt all summer boiling to the surface in one great, rolling scum of mutual abuse.

'You've been whingeing ever since the season started!' Tim accused.

'You never made the least attempt to help me!' sobbed Lesley, beside herself by this time. 'You've sat on your arse and sneered and called me lazy and fat – you've let me do all the worrying while you sailed around in your silly boats, enjoying yourself – if there's ever been anything unpleasant to be done, you've left it for me to do – I hate you, I hate you!'

'And what about you?' shouted back Tim. 'You seem to have completely lost sight of the fact that we're supposed to be running a sailing school, you've carried on all the time as if we were trying to set up in competition with the Fish and that bloody Angwin! You've taken no interest in the guests, you've gone to bed saying that you're tired every bloody night, you've grumbled on top of that that nobody seems to know you properly, and blamed me for it! You've been too tired, you've said, to be a proper wife to me, morning or night, for three months now, and you say *you* hate *me*! If you ask me, this whole thing's gone beyond the point of no return, and I for one have had enough.'

'You're unfair!' screamed Lesley. 'You're hateful! And on top of it all I suppose you're going to make me have it out with that awful woman even though she's one of yours, and deal with her! Of course you are!'

'Why shouldn't I?' bellowed Tim, outshouting her without effort. 'The trouble began in your department, and you're the bloody expert at these things!'

'I'm not, I'm not,' wailed Lesley. She had very little control left now, the last of it was about to fly out of the door.

'Then I should like to know who has been all this time!' roared Tim, at the very top of his voice.

'Angwin!' screamed Lesley, losing her head completely. 'Angwin, Angwin, Angwin!'

There was a sudden shattering silence, worse than all the shouting. Into it, Tim said, in a mildy questioning voice, 'Angwin?'

Lesley sat down at the nearest table, dropped her head onto her folded arms, and began to howl like a dog. Tim stood statue-still.

'Angwin, by God,' he said, but still quietly. 'You've gone behind my back to Angwin with all your mistakes –'

'*Our* mistakes!' Lesley stopped howling for long enough to snap at him.

'– setting me up to look like a fool, making yourself out to be the great I-know-everything. And all the time...' Words appeared to fail him. 'Angwin!' he repeated bitterly, and stopped speaking.

Debbie had all this time stood as if nailed to the floor by the window. Had she been able to get away without pushing past them, she would have done so, but short of climbing out through the casement, she had no hope. Anyway, she couldn't now, in all fairness, leave Lesley to take the blame for something that she had done.

'It wasn't Lesley,' she said. 'It was me.'

He turned to her, still quiet. From red he had gone to deathly white.

'You, my old friend?' he said. 'Well, how thoughtful. I take that really kindly in you, Deb. Not content with displaying my supposed shortcomings to a man who had already shown that he'd do me down if he could, you encouraged my wife to deceive me. Now that's *real* friendship, Deb. I appreciate it.'

'Don't, Tim,' pleaded Debbie. Lesley didn't help matters by putting in, 'She did do it out of friendship Tim – and so did he. I swear he did.'

'*Angwin* did it out of friendship?' asked Tim, in theatrical amazement. 'Pull the other one, Lesley, it's got bells on! Angwin did it, as anyone with half a brain can see, because he enjoyed helping my wife to make a bloody fool out of me!'

'No!' protested Lesley, scrambling to her feet and running to him. 'No, Tim, no!' She tried to fling her arms round him, but he pushed her away. Her action had reactivated the full force of his anger, he spoke in a spitting-cat voice that made both his hearers flinch.

'My God, I might have known! All that damned phoney charm! But *you*, Lesley, my own wife! I can't believe it!'

Lesley had caught her funny-bone on the back of a chair when he had flung her aside, it was the final straw.

'Then don't believe it!' she snapped. 'Or do believe it, if you feel better that way, I don't care any more! And now, get out of my way please, I've got work to do, if you've got all day to stand here chattering!' She pushed him with a force that made him stagger, reached the door, and was through it in a flash. Debbie made to follow, but Tim stepped in front of her.

'Oh no, you don't,' he said. 'We still have something to discuss, Deborah Nankervis.'

Debbie stopped.

'You're so selfish!' she exclaimed. 'What did you expect Les to do? *You* wouldn't help her – you wouldn't even listen to her half the time. She's right, you did leave her to deal with everything, and so she went for help where she knew she could ask for it. Help for you, Tim, as well as for her. Where would you have been, if she hadn't, not just once but over and over again? You didn't even seem to care!'

Tim latched onto one phrase in this somewhat unwise speech.

'Where she knew she could ask for it?' he repeated. 'She *knew?* How did she *know* that bloody Angwin would help her?'

'Don't call him that!' raged Debbie, suddenly losing control along with everyone else. 'She knew she could ask because I saved his bloody *life!* I asked, Tim Howells, me, me, me! *And not once did he ever let us down – let* you *down!*'

Tim stared at her. Debbie went on, furiously.

'He told us what to say. He told us what to do. Once, he even came up here and said and did it for us. Not because we asked him to, oh no! Because he thought that Les shouldn't be left to handle unpleasantness on her own. And he was right! He was right, Tim, and if you weren't completely selfish –'

'You're starting to repeat yourself,' said Tim.

'Only because I can't think of anything *bad* enough!' raged Debbie.

'Get out,' said Tim, and stood aside from the door. 'Get out – right out! If you're wise, you won't let me see you again today! Just get out, and stay out!'

'All right, I bloody *will!*' said Debbie, and ran past him across the hall and out through the open front door. She ran down the drive as if her feet had wings to them and out into the lane.

She realised then, for the first time, that she had tears streaming down her face – she, who never cried at all – and that she felt sick, shaken, and ready to out-howl Lesley. In this state, after what she knew had happened the previous night, she mustn't follow her first impulse and run straight to Mawgan, he already had more than enough on his plate. In any case, she knew very well that her visits to the Fish under normal circumstances had caused a great deal of gossip, if she went to the Fish hysterical she would probably fuse the village grapevine! No, this time she was on her own. She turned and walked in the opposite direction, on up the hill through the woods.

She walked in a daze. Cars went past her in both directions but she didn't see them. Her eyes were blinded with tears, her heart heavy with shame. She knew that however much of a selfish pig Tim had been – and he had been, she would stick to that – neither she nor Lesley had had any right to expose him to Mawgan behind his back. Only, it had been so easy. Mawgan had put all his knowledge and experience at their entire disposal, and they had used it again and again. So easy. So easy to lose a friend. So easy to wreck a marriage.

A white Volvo estate came up the hill behind her, a Malibu board lashed to the roof rack and Bob Marley blasting out of its open windows. It passed her at a brisk pace, stopped in a squeal of brakes and a shower of small stones a hundred yards ahead, and reversed madly back towards her.

'Deborah!' said Mawgan, practically falling out into the road in his haste. 'Deborah, whatever's happened?'

She ran straight into his arms and was caught and held tightly.

'We had a dreadful row,' she sobbed into the front of his shirt. 'Tim, Lesley and me. Over you.'

'Over *me*? I do seem to be a walking disaster area, don't I?' He cradled her in his arms until her sobs began to abate and then walked her over to the car. 'In you get. Take your time, you can tell me about it as we go along.'

The car moved off again. Debbie sat there with reggae music pouring around her, and dried her eyes.

'I'm sorry,' she said at last. 'I never meant to bother you. I purposely went the other way.'

'Stupid,' he said. She stole a quick look at him, he looked as if he hadn't slept but you couldn't read anything from that. No doubt she looked as bad.

'Where are we going?' she asked, after a minute or two.'

'I'm going to Poldhu. I don't know about you.'

'A day off?' asked Debbie, in surprise, for apart from the fact that he appeared to work seven days a week at the Fish, there must be a monumental mess to clear up this morning.

He made a wry face.

'Yeah. My staff threw me out, they said I was more of a liability than an asset, and push off.' He hesitated. 'I expect you heard about my performance last night? Yes, I thought you might. After all, you employ the matriarch of the Tregear clan, don't you?'

'I was really sorry. As a matter of fact, so's Tim.'

'Good of him.'

'Don't be like that.' She stole a sideways look at him. 'I take it, then, surf's up?'

'I don't much care if it is or isn't. I might just jump off the headland. From the sounds of things, you better come with me.'

'With or without a parachute?' asked Debbie.

'Oh, without – definitely without.'

Debbie thought about her day so far, thought about a day on the beach with Mawgan, thought about jumping off headlands – or out of windows, for that matter. It occurred to her that it might be wise to stay with him.

'All right, then.'

They continued along the lanes, if not in companionable silence, at least companionably. The CD player in the car continued to pour out music and the sun shone overhead, and things began to slip back into perspective. Debbie told Mawgan more or less what had happened, in so far as she understood it. It helped immensely to be able to pour it all out, but when she had come to the end she said, 'And I called Tim selfish!'

He laughed aloud at that.

'We're all selfish, that's why we're all perpetually in the muck. Cheer up Deborah, by this evening it'll've all blown over.'

'I'm not sure that it will.'

'Would it help if I spoke to Howells, or would it simply fan the flames?'

Debbie thought of Tim as she had last seen him in the dining-room, and shuddered.

'No, please don't. At least, not immediately.'

'Tell me when, then.'

'I will.'

To fill a pause, she asked, 'Are you going to be able to open today, do you think?' and then wondered if it was the best question under the circumstances. Mawgan, however, took it calmly.

'Not me. I'm here with you. Tommy won't open lunchtime, I don't suppose, but we should have one of the bars at least up and running by tonight. Who the hell cares anyway? I don't!' He sounded careless, but Debbie was learning fast now. She leaned back in her seat, wishing that she hadn't spoken after all.

She would take today as it came, she decided, as a day on its own, a day stolen from time. Tomorrow – the next day – would be soon enough to take stock. Which she must do, she was walking the edge of a precipice as things were, she was beginning to be certain of it.

So today, just today, would be for them alone.

Cress had known that Gary would do something spectacular. She had pointed him in her brother's direction and deliberately set him alight, much like someone igniting the long fuse on a stick of dynamite. It didn't appear to her to be unethical, even when Mrs. Bennetts told her, between sobs, early on Monday morning, that he had ended up in the cells for it.

'So he won't be able to take you out tonight after all,' she sniffed. 'Them magistrates won't give 'im bail, and what he was doing breaking up a place like that, I don't know, nor ever will! He's a good boy is Gary, not like these football hooligans you hear about. He wouldn't do a thing like that deliberate, and surely his mother should know!'

Cress smiled, a tight, secretive smile that Mrs. Bennetts didn't see, she was weeping too hard. Gary had exploded beautifully. She thought that she would go to St. Erbyn and have a look at the result. She could wheedle one of Gary's mates to take her at least part of the way, and she could hitch the rest or get a bus. She could probably get back in time for her shift at twelve o'clock if she left this early and hurried, and if she didn't, she no longer cared.

The Fish, when she reached it just before ten, had a slightly ruffled look. There was hardboard tacked over the broken panes of glass, and someone – it was Tommy the barman, but she didn't know that – was going round with putty and spare panes, patching things up. Some of the chairs and tables on the forecourt had been damaged in the fight, they were stacked up neatly in a corner until someone had time to attend to them. There was a car parked outside the front door with luggage being loaded into it, perhaps the people had been leaving anyway, but Cress hoped not. She went on up the leaf-hung road to Seagulls. Perhaps the blonde girl would be loading her luggage, too.

She wasn't. She had just come out of the gate and turned up the hill, Cress would know her anywhere. She didn't seem to be in a hurry, just walking with her head down. Cress followed her, keeping just inside the trees, flitting in the shadows.

The car that drove past was just one car among other cars to her, it had no significance until it pulled up so suddenly. She saw the two of them run towards each other and meet. She saw the meeting as it really was, which they didn't, as the total merging of two people in the same way that she and Mike had merged since his death. She knew that Gary hadn't gone far enough.

There was only one thing left to do. Now that Gary had shown her how to be violent, it seemed quite easy. She didn't really want to kill the girl unless she had to, but if she had no job and nowhere to live, perhaps she would just go away.

It was perfectly simple.

XVIII

There was a beautiful rolling surf beating into Poldhu Cove, and the beach was packed to the edge, they had to park along the road and walk to reach the sand. Debbie had dressed to go sailing that morning, as she always did, and had a bikini under her T-shirt and jeans, so that she was reasonably equipped for this unexpected outing; they carried the surfboard down to the sea, laughing together as if it was a normal day off. Debbie, looking her companion over critically, decided that although he could lose a stone with advantage – at least that – he had a solid, rugby-player's physique with a powerful neck and shoulders and measured up reasonably well against most of the other men within her view. He eyed her up too, she noticed, with a bright and interested look and remarked, 'Hey, nice legs, Deborah!' and she didn't think he only meant her legs.

And a normal day off was what it gradually seemed to become. Mawgan was a reasonably competent surfer rather than an expert, he didn't have enough time to do a lot of it, and Debbie had been efficiently taught when she was a young teenager on exotic holidays with her parents but had done very little since. They took turns with the board, managing to swallow a great deal of salt water and doing a lot of laughing, at themselves and at each other, and ended up lying in the shallows watching more skilled performers with the sort of admiration that comes from knowing just how difficult something is. They lunched late, sea washed and content, on pasties and beer at a pleasant pub, sitting on a bench in the sunshine and talking easy nonsense, deriving consolation from each other's company. Time stood still for them, the sun shone for them, the roaring surf made a song for them, and it was only when they drove out along the coast later in the afternoon and found a quiet place where they could lie among the sea pinks and relax together in peace that the subject of the morning's upheaval was mentioned again.

'Will Howells worry about you?' enquired Mawgan, with his eyes closed and looking as deceptively relaxed as a sleeping cat. Debbie had wondered this herself and reached the conclusion that she didn't care very much if he did. She sat up abruptly.

'I shouldn't think so,' she said. 'He said he didn't want to see me again today. It'll have made it very awkward for him – he's got three groups of students all at different stages, and only him and Roger. Serves him right,' she added, after a pause.

'Vindictive little cat!'

Debbie sighed. 'I know it's terribly unforgiving of me.'

'It's a pity, really, that they ever inherited that house,' said Mawgan, after a while.

Debbie had been day-dreaming; recalled thus to the present she looked down at him and found he was looking up at her, a direct and golden stare that for some reason set a pulse beating in her throat.

'Why?' she asked.

'Because without their silly guest house, Howells would have done all right.'

'He would?' The two things, the guest house and the sailing school, were so entwined in Debbie's head that she found it hard to think of them separately.

'Of course he would. When have you ever had any problems with the sailing school? Not once. He knows exactly what to do and how to do it, and all his students think the world of him. I've heard them – if you keep a pub, you hear everything eventually, you'd be surprised.'

Debbie was surprised anyway. She had been so concerned with Lesley's intrusive troubles that Tim's lack of them had escaped her particular notice. She now realised that she had been both blind and prejudiced, and there was no excuse for it since she was – had to be – part of Tim's success.

'It wouldn't have worked though,' she said. 'Without the house, they couldn't have made enough money out of the sailing.'

'Why not? I'll bet a pound to a penny that it's the house that's been *losing* the money. They could've rented a cottage and bought a couple of boats with a bank loan, and worked up gradually. He must've had some sort of redundancy payment to start him off, and great oaks from little acorns grow.'

'I suppose they didn't think of it.'

'Come to that, having inherited the house they could've sold it, and started up with some real capital behind them.'

'They fell in love with the house,' said Debbie. 'Anyway, Lesley wanted a part in it too. She doesn't sail.'

Mawgan sighed, with a touch of despair. 'The classic recipe for disaster – two parts ignorance to one part sentiment. What'd he do before?'

The question took Debbie by surprise, and for a moment or two she simply stared. Then she said, 'He was an engineer. He worked for a local firm – Lawley Engineering, they sponsored my brother Oliver when he sailed round the world. They had to cut back because of labour disputes, and Tim's department just gradually melted away. They make aero engines and things. He worked on new developments, research, that kind of thing There was no more money for it.'

'How in the world does he come to be so dumb, then?' asked Mawgan, in irritation. Debbie gave this serious thought and after a minute, said, 'If you couldn't swim – which I know you can, but just suppose you couldn't for a minute – and you fell into the sea, all your knowledge of catering wouldn't stop you from drowning.'

'True, but I wouldn' have to throw myself into the sea in the first place, would I?'

'You might slip – or get pushed. On the whole, Tim got pushed.'

Talking about him like this made him seem more like Tim again, less the unfamiliar and terrible figure of the morning. She began to feel a little sorry for him, and to wonder how they were all managing. She even began to feel as if she was the rat that had scuttled ashore from the sinking ship. She lay down again and rolled over onto her stomach supporting her chin in her hands, looking down at the sea surging on the rocks below. There was a fishing boat pounding along a short way out, headed for Mullion. She said, slowly, 'Is it silly of me to feel awfully responsible for what happened this morning?'

He didn't answer her directly. 'Feeling responsible for anything that spoils other people's lives is a bugger: believe me, I'm the expert. But ask yourself, if Mrs Howells had asked you not to mention her troubles to me, would you've done it?'

Debbie shook her head. 'Of course not.'

'There you are, then.'

Debbie began to pull at the grass in front of her with one hand, while continuing to support her chin with the other. 'Not really. If I'd never suggested it in the first place – '

'*If*, Deborah, is the longest word in the dictionary, didn't no-one tell you that?'

Debbie turned her head, and their eyes met. She suddenly forgot Lesley and Tim and their troubles. She swallowed, hard.

'Oh,' she said and couldn't have told, a second later, what she had meant it to answer. She lay there and listened to her own heartbeat.

Recognition came all of a piece, quite suddenly and as easily as breathing. She almost laughed, it was so simple. She had never seriously envisaged falling hard and, she rather thought, irrevocably, for the rough-diamond landlord-cum-chef of a country pub who would be the better for easing up on his beer consumption, although she had toyed with the idea in an academic kind of way, and she didn't think anyone else would be expecting it either, but now that it had really happened it was utterly and perfectly right. She realised that she was holding her breath.

'Deborah,' said Mawgan, idly, 'you've got lovely eyes, d'you know that? Grey and beautiful like a storm coming up on the moors… and skin like honey, and hair like spun gold. So where's all the followers?'

'I left them behind in London,' said Debbie, in a voice not quite her own.

'Sorry?'

'No.' She added, inconsequently, 'I colour my eyelashes. And my eyebrows. And I have my hair bleached when the sun doesn't do it for me.'

'I know,' he said outrageously, and grinned at her.

'Swine!' said Debbie, grinning back.

'Personally, I don' bother,' he added. 'But it takes all sorts.'

'Mawgan…' She stopped. The shining world about them seemed to have drawn back, leaving them isolated in the green bowl of the hollow where they lay. Somewhere above them, a lark tumbled singing in the sky, the clear rounded notes of bubbling sound fell about them like a shower of distilled sunshine. The murmur of the surf, of wind over the grass, seemed to fade and left just those pure drops of melody, and the sound of their own breathing.

Oh my God, Debbie thought, clear-sighted at last, here we go, over Niagara…

But they didn't.

Mawgan had closed his eyes against the sunlight, but it could easily have been because he slept for all the evidence to the contrary. He lay relaxed, one knee drawn up and his right arm crooked behind his head, the picture of perfect contentment. Debbie realised that the moment was hers to use, misuse, or ignore as she chose, and felt sweat break out all over her like a rime of ice under the hot sun. Her breathing felt tight.

She reached out and ran the tip of her finger gently along the scars on his elbow, they brought back memories, frightening and even embarrassingly intimate, that had become an integral part of her most precious store over the intervening months, completely without her realisation.

'Does this give you any trouble?' she asked. Her voice sounded as if it belonged to someone else. He opened his eyes again and looked up at her, so he had been wide awake after all.

'It's stopped me manhandling beer barrels, but otherwise, not so as you'd notice.'

'I nearly died when I saw what you'd really done, I spent the whole of the rest of the week imagining horrors.' The probing finger ran gently down his forearm to his wrist, and she watched its progress intently, avoiding his eyes. 'I think I love you, Mawgan.'

Silence. He broke it finally with a faint snort of laughter.

'You *think*?' He brought his arm down and let it rest on the rug between them, but his total relaxation had gone.

'All right, I do love you.' She rubbed her fingers along the fine down of dark hair on the back of his hand. 'Do you remember when you first saw me?'

'Too right, I do. I threw up.'

She giggled, but half-heartedly, raising her eyes to look at his face.

'What were you thinking? Really, not all that punk angel rubbish.'

'Not a lot, as I remember, except for being very glad to see you.'

'And now?'

'You're tickling,' he said, and withdrew his hand. Hazel eyes, serious and watchful, met her own. 'Now, Deborah? Now… I suppose, I think I love you, too.'

'Good,' said Debbie, shaking with relief. 'That's all right then.'

'Is it? Seems like another fine mess to me.'

Debbie wriggled across the rug and lay down close to him with her head in the hollow of his shoulder, feeling the warmth of him through his polo shirt, and he moved slightly so that he could get his arm round her, and they lay there together under the bright sun. Below, the surf roared gently; above, seagulls wheeled in the sunshine, their wings catching the light. The lark had gone.

'I think,' said Mawgan, slowly, 'we're due for a talk, you and me.'

'Make that *over*due,' murmured Debbie.

'I killed a man. You can't get away from that.'

'Did you – really?'

'I was the only one there. If I'd been somewheres else, he'd be still alive. Seems pretty clear to me.'

Debbie said nothing, and after a moment, Mawgan said quietly, 'I went to prison for it. How would your family feel about that?' and the question hovered in the air between them, almost visible.

'I don't know,' said Debbie, after a pause. 'I've thought about it, of course. I came to the conclusion that it couldn't be allowed to matter what they thought, that it was my life. Nothing I do can make my family more split up than it is already, anyway.' The thought of the waiting flat by the marina put bitterness into the words. Mawgan stirred slightly, perhaps recognising it.

'That sounds sad. What about your famous brother? You care what he thinks, I know you do.'

Debbie raised her head.

'Mawgan – you bothered to tell me that you loved me, so what's on your mind? I hope that you're not going to treat me to a grand renunciation scene, like in a sloppy novel! I never did like them, it always seems to me so stupid between consenting adults, and selfish, too, unless there's a really overwhelming reason, which just having gone to prison isn't – and anyway, it would make it really uncomfortable on the drive home.'

'I'm not really into that stuff,' he said. 'Or sloppy novels, come to that.' An edge there. Momentarily, she wondered why.

'Well, thank goodness for that, because neither am I. You had me worried for a moment.' She dropped her head back onto his shoulder. 'Come on then, what's on your mind?'

'How old are you, Deborah?'

'Twenty-four,' said Debbie. 'And I'm no simpering innocent, either, before you make the mistake of thinking I am.'

'Twenty-four...' he repeated, and gave a rather miserable laugh. 'Oh no, Deborah, I wasn't going to make that mistake. I'm crediting you with being grown up, I suppose. If you married me...'

'Mmm,' said Debbie. 'What a good idea! Shall I?'

'Think hard before you decide, I would. You saw what happened last night, and who knows where that all came from, but it shows that there's a lot of bad feeling still around. I wouldn't want that sort of thing to rub off on you. I shouldn't never have started this, but I never thought it'd go this far...' He broke off, troubled.

'We could skip the orange blossom and the satin meringue,' offered Debbie.

'No, my bird, I don' think so.'

'Why not? You're not going to tell me that you're a nice old-fashioned boy, and I'm well past the age of consent. In fact... well, I ought to tell you, I suppose. I have consented. I mean, seriously consented.'

He looked up at her, considering. She could see a little pulse beating under his eye.

'Howells?'

She shook her head. 'No. It was... it was an idea that didn't work out. I'll tell you one day. But it wasn't Tim.' He said nothing, and after a moment or two, she said, 'Anyway, what makes you think I wouldn't be proud to bear your name?'

'I don' think you picked quite the right word there.' Another pause, even longer. 'I might as well say it, I suppose... I'm scared. Again. Do you suppose it means I'm a natural coward?'

'No,' said Debbie. She propped herself on her elbow so that she could see him better. 'No, I don't suppose that. Back there in the snow, anyone would have been scared. Ignorance *is* scary – I know, I was petrified myself and it was much worse for you. But what on earth is there to be scared of this time?'

He took a breath and let it go again, slowly.

'Killing someone is something you don't forget easy,' he said, not looking at her. 'Punishment i'n't prison so much, it's knowing what you done.'

'I can see that,' said Debbie, feeling sick.

'If you can't put it behind you – and I can't – then it goes with you wherever you go. There's no call to make'n worse by...well, by making a girl who loves you miserable, if she's prepared to take the risk. Hair shirts has gone out of fashion, and anyway, I aren't never planning to do it again.'

'Good. That works for me.'

'But there's another side to it. I aren't that popular these days. I used to be. Then I came out of prison and found the sun'd gone in.'

'It takes time to live things down – and effort. Have you really tried? *Really* tried?'

'Maybe not. But what frightens me, Deborah, is that perhaps the sun wouldn't shine on you no more, neither.'

'Isn't that a risk for me, rather than you?' She drew an unsteady breath, feeling happiness as fragile as a cobweb in her hand. 'You said you gave me credit for being grown up.'

'I know I did. And I meant it. You can't make decisions for other people, we all has the right to make our own mistakes. So listen, and if you say one word before I've finished, I promise you I'll never speak to you no more.'

He spoke with such unexpected violence that she was startled. She thought that if she even breathed too hard, the moment would shatter into fragments and be irretrievably lost. She said, very quietly, 'Off you go, then.'

'I told you, didn' I, I've got three sisters,' he said, looking anywhere but at her. 'Marianne, Allison and… well, Cressida. Mum, I should p'r'aps explain, has got a romantic streak wider'n the M5. There's nothing wrong with Marian, Morgan and Alison, but she had to pretty up the spelling to make us different, even Allison has an extra American-style L – we didn't half suffer for it at school. Anna came off first and worst, of course, then when it got to Cress, Dad just let Mum have her head, for fear of what she might think of next.' Cressida had been very much the youngest, he went on, a full ten years younger than himself, seven years younger than Allison, eleven younger than Anna, and possibly because of that she had always been the favourite. Everybody's favourite. She had married the late Michael Stanley before she was twenty. He paused then, as if, the introductions over, he was bracing himself for what must come next. When he spoke again, it was more slowly, choosing his words with care.

'He were a friend of mine, sort of – not my best friend – it aren't that corny, more an acquaintance, and I'd been too long out of England by then to have close friends here anyway. But a friend of sorts, just the same, we went to the same school, tho' I was a couple o' year ahead. She met him through me, and when they married I was happy if they were, but I didn't think much to it. He thought as she was perfect, and anyway, I was pretty involved with the Fish at the time.

'She was too young to be married, really... she'd always been a bit spoiled, being so much the youngest, and she was never...' He paused, frowning. 'Never in the real world with the rest of us, I suppose. She used to make up stories... say she was adopted, things like that. Liked to fantasise about being some princess. Came pretty close to downright lying sometimes, but there weren't no real harm in her, and anyway she grew out of it...' He stopped. 'Well, we all thought as she did.'

'Sounds as if she needed a good dose of the kitchen sink to bring her down to earth,' suggested Debbie, hoping it wouldn't be construed as an interruption. The family was coming alive for her as he spoke: she sensed that, unlike her own, they were − or had been − very close, very loyal and tight-knit together. She got the feeling of hidden laughter behind the bare words, matching her knowledge of him. She thought that, one way or another, Cressida, so much the baby, would have been much-loved, possibly even over-protected, maybe allowed to get away with too much. Mawgan frowned, but more in consideration than denial.

'Could be. You needn't think I haven't thought about it − that, and other things. I have. I've had plenty of time for it.'

'Go on,' said Debbie, after a long pause.

'For some cause, probably all the romantic rubbish she read, and all the daydreaming, she had this idea that marriage was a free ticket to paradise, and when she found it wasn't, she used to come down to the restaurant and complain to me about him. He neglected her, she said, he went out with his friends instead of staying home with her, he played snooker every Friday, rain or shine, until she wanted to scream. I didn't pay no attention, be honest, didn't have time − I just thought she'd shake down when she got used to it. We all thought that if we didn't give her too much sympathy she'd smarten up her ideas and get real. But she didn't.'

He fell silent. Overhead the gulls screamed, filling a pause that went on too long. Debbie waited. She didn't want to prompt him again, and after a time she was rewarded.

'She began to say that he was seeing other women, I don't even know if it were true, but she thought so, or made herself think so, how do I know? She said she wanted children and he wouldn't let her have none. She − I suppose she wrung the last ounce of drama out of it, she always did watch a lot of rubbish on the telly... and she was only a kid!' He spoke with sudden fury. 'Lived in La-la Land, Cress, she always did.

Annoyed some, true enough, but nobody never hurt her if the three of us was around. I suppose I was angry at him, but it didn't go no further'n that. She left him in the end and went back home; that made a real row, things like that don't happen among us Angwins. We was busy at the Fish, but I got my orders to come and help talk sense into her, or even into Mike, and 'though I had the perfect reason not to go, being a sucker, I did. For Cress. To try and put things right for her. If I had a pound for every time I wish I hadn't, I'd be a millionaire.' He drew a breath. 'Don't never interfere in other people's marriages, not unless you want to land yourself in it over your head.

'Time I got there, Mike had come roaring after her, breathing fire and slaughter, and Mum suggested I should take him into the garden and have a man-to-man talk with him – a really crap suggestion, come to think, what did I know? I didn't even have no steady girlfriend, I was far too busy being successful to do more'n play the field. It's no wonder it backfired.' Debbie wondered, with interest, whether he had enjoyed playing the field and would have liked to ask for further details but common sense prevailed. When a man was about to tell you how he killed his brother-in-law, it would be tactless, to put it at its best, to ask questions about past girlfriends.

'Anyway,' Mawgan was saying. 'We did as we was told. We went in the garden, and I asked him what he was playing at, making my little sister unhappy. He just blew up. He said he had loved her when he married her, but she was like a child still, she was like some clinging vine, choking the life out of him. She hated him to step outside the house without her, she wanted him to sit and hold her hand and watch soaps on the telly every evening, she sat around all day and read stupid books while the dust got inches thick on the furniture, so that he was ashamed to take his friends home, and she never so much as sewed the buttons on his shirts. The cooker was an inch deep in grease, and the fridge full of mouldy things dating back to the ice age, while they lived on fish and chips and pizza, and he had to take the washing to the launderette himself on the way to work. He said, on top of all that she grumbled that he never helped her in the house, and what did she do all day, he'd like to know, while he was out earning money for her to spend on more stupid books? And she was jealous as hell, and she wanted to fill the house with babies when she couldn't even look after herself properly. He wanted out, and if she could be honest for two minutes, so did she. You see, I remember every word…'

Another pause, but a more painful one. Now they were coming to it, Debbie thought, and found she was holding her breath. Mawgan drew a breath. He said, 'I got to tell you this, if I don't somebody else will. It aren't true, but he said it. He said if Cress was in love with anyone, if she was even that grown-up, it was with me, and if she was only adopted like she said, why didn't I just sod off and marry her myself if I thought she was so great.'

'Whoo!' said Debbie, really startled now. That, she hadn't expected. She said, cautiously, 'And *is* she – adopted, that is?'

'No of course she isn't. What he was saying was near enough an accusation of incest. It was so stupid I couldn't think of nothing to say. Would you?'

A silence fell, while Debbie first thought about it and then tried not to think about it, and after a while, Mawgan spoke. 'Any sensible person would've backed off then,' he said quietly. 'Not me. I had to shout at him, once I'd my breath back, about this other women he was supposed to have, and then he shouted back at me, hadn't I been listening? We ended up coming to blows – and I know it sounds stupid, but if we hadn't known each other from way back, we wouldn't never have done that.' He paused, giving Debbie time to say, 'Which of you started it?'

'My brief asked me that. He nagged at me until I near enough went crazy, but I don't know, and that's the truth. But at the end, Mike got hold of me and tried to throw me down. He was yelling about how Cress was a lazy slut and spoiled to death and mazed into the bargain… and he hauled off to get space to get at me better, and caught his foot in the grass and… well, he already had me half off-balance, so when he fell, he took me down with him, and because he still had hold of me I landed on top of him, and my weight clunked his head, hard, on the rockery…'

His voice died away. Debbie didn't move, barely breathed.

'It just happened,' he said, at last. 'I swear I didn't do it on purpose. I just knew that he was lying there, and that although he were still breathing then, he were going to die… just like that. It was simple as swatting a fly.'

Debbie said, hardly daring to say it, 'But you didn't kill him. He died, but you didn't kill him.'

'He died because I was there. What's the difference?'

'A lot of difference,' said Debbie. She spoke more strongly. 'You can't be arrested, let alone charged and sent for trial, simply for being there. It was just bad luck. The proper legal term for that is accidental death.'

He said nothing. His eyes were closed, and as she watched, a tear slid quietly out under his eyelashes and ran across his cheek. He put up an angry hand and swiped it away.

'So what happened then?' asked Debbie, after a pause. 'Something did, it has to have. So tell me, you can't leave it there.'

She thought that he wasn't going to, but after a while, he did.

'I got up, and I just stood there… listening to him dying. It was horrible. I couldn't seem to move, I couldn't think, time just stopped, it wouldn't go forward and it couldn't go back… and then I heard a sound, and I looked up, and there, staring over the garden fence, was the kid from next door and one of her mates from school. They'd heard us shouting, and they'd been watching the whole thing. They didn't know Mike was dying, they just thought we'd had a fight. They were sniggering, I remember. Can you believe that? I could move then. I went back to the house and told Dad what had happened, and he rang the police. He had to, did'n' 'e?'

The wind blew, ruffling the sea pinks, and the gulls swooped overhead. The fishing boat had gone out of sight. Debbie, who was never again to feel the same about seagulls, held her breath.

'The inquest made it murder,' said Mawgan, quietly. 'I'd said first off, I thought I'd killed him, but that was just how it came out. But then, what with the incest thing, the police wouldn't let me take it back when I could think straight again. I tried to explain I hadn't meant it zackly, but the two girls – they was only about fourteen – I don't suppose they meant to tell lies, but they'd talked it over together until what really happened had turned into some nightmare. They had plenty to work with, just think 'bout what they must have heard. The charge was only reduced to manslaughter later because they went to pieces in the witness box, one of them had hysterics and the other contradicted herself… and then there was the medical evidence. But Cress wouldn't say… she wouldn't confirm that there was anything she might have said or done that might've explained Mike going for me instead of the other way round. Instead, she went into the witness box and said that she had loved him and I knew it, the whole family knew it. She couldn't think why I should have been so very angry, it was only a lover's tiff, and perhaps I was jealous, she didn't know… the implications was scary on top of the way they two girls twisted everything, there was hardly a dry eye in the house. I got three years, one way and another, and count myself lucky that was all.'

'But surely… surely, she'd said whatever she said to the others? To your family? Surely they would have slapped her down?'

He moved his head slightly in negation.

'Not to the family, no. The press had spoken to her, right at the beginning. She never could tell fact from fiction and they led her on… did you know a thing isn't libel if you only speculate about it? They speculated… And then, I suppose, she felt she couldn't back down openly in court so she just cried, and wouldn't answer, and I don't know if she was trying to help or trying to condemn me, or just trying to put herself in a good light. I don't *know*!' he repeated, huskily, and cleared his throat, too loudly.

Debbie thought, irrelevantly, that that explained his sensitivity to slander, but she was too angry to care right now. It sounded as if, given the muddled evidence, he had got off extremely lightly, and it would be… *interesting* to meet Cressida – but then again, if she did, it might be really murder that time.

'The little cow!' she said, indignantly, before she could stop herself. 'Sorry – shouldn't have said that.' Mum and the two sisters would have known better, of course. *Had* known better, surely, before the finish, but what could they have done? You can't deny what hasn't been said in the open, unless you want to make it look that there something there in the first place. Cressida Stanley, she thought furiously, whether she had acted deliberately or without thinking – and which was worse anyway? – needed a sharp lesson. She had no sympathy for her at all. 'Did she ever apologise?'

'Who, Cress? No. She wrote me in prison and said I'd ruined her life and broke her heart, and that she never wanted to see nor speak to me again. And she hasn't. And that's about it, really.'

Debbie knew that this couldn't be true, and she was determined, now, to get to the bottom of it.

'What about the rest of your family? Did they take the same unreasonable view?' Poor family, they were really stuck on the horns of a horrible dilemma.

'No, of course they didn't. They felt they had to leave town because of all the gossip, and you can imagine what form that took, it got pretty unpleasant after the inquest; even though the press had to shut up then, others didn't – and I suppose they give me the fault for most of that, but we're still on speaking terms. Mike's mum and dad too… they made things… difficult.' Understatement of the year there, probably, Debbie thought, but didn't say. 'You can't *blame* anyone. They said to come home when I was released, but in the end I didn't stay… and they had me there when I was discharged from hospital after our adventure in the snow, and that was worse if anything, but they try, at least. Making the best of a bad job… except Allison. You'll like Allison. She visited me in prison, which was more than Mum and Dad did most of the time, and when they let me out she persuaded me that wrapping my car round a telegraph pole hadn't been a very bright thing to do.'

'Did you? Wrap your car around a telegraph pole? This car?'

'Yes. And no.'

'On purpose?' Did she really want to know the answer to that?

'I don' think so, but I wouldn't take no Bible oath. Anyway, it weren't no great success if it was a suicide attempt, I got some penalty points on my licence and a bill for a new telegraph pole, and I lost my no-claims bonus. Apart from that, no damage, except to the car, which was a messy write-off. None of the family was that amused to find me in the local paper – *again*, so I come back to the Fish, and tried to pick up the pieces by myself – with what success, you've seen.'

'Indifferent, I'd call it,' said Debbie, judiciously. 'Why don't you let other people see a few cracks? Most of them would be glad to help you put it behind you, they're too canny to believe all that incest crap, even Mrs Tregear hasn't said a word about it and believe me, she would have. It's only your attitude, walking around laughing, that they can't swallow.'

'I can't hardly cry in front of them, can I?'

'You might try it for a change.'

'I can't.'

'All right then. Don't. It's only yourself you're hurting, after all. Just don't go pushing yourself too far, will you? Accidental manslaughter I might be able to explain, raving mad is a touchier subject altogether.'

'Oh Deborah, my bird –' His voice broke, and he swallowed hard and for a moment laid his free arm across his eyes. 'Blast you, Deborah, do you always have to cut things down to size? How can I ask you to marry me, anyway? Every decent person that you know would condemn me.'

'The people I know are more decent than you're giving them the credit for,' Debbie told him. She sat up and gathered both his hands into her own. 'Look at me.' She waited until he had done so, and then said, 'Now, repeat after me – Deborah Rachel Nankervis, will you marry me?'

'Deborah Rachel Nankervis, will you marry me?' he repeated obediently, after a small hesitation.

'Yes,' said Debbie. 'Now, that's settled. Easy, wasn't it?'

'Control freak, you!' said Mawgan. 'Wisdom is it, or just innocence?'

'Sheer self-interest, that's why we get on so well together,' said Debbie, instantly. 'Who in their right mind wouldn't want a rich and successful husband?'

'That's putting it a bit high. Overworked and mortgaged up to the neck might be more like it.' He managed a smile. 'Want to change your mind?'

'I'm dreadfully disappointed, of course,' said Debbie, 'but I shall learn to live with it. You can become rich, after all. In fact, you probably will.' She leaned forward then and kissed him gently on the lips, since for once he didn't seem to be going to kiss her, and suddenly found herself seized, rolled onto her back on the rug, and swept helter-skelter into a tangled confusion of sensations and emotions that nearly took them both, speaking metaphorically, straight over the cliff. She managed to struggle free and pushed him away with her hands.

'Mawgan, for God's sake! I don't want to suffer a fate worse than death right here on the cliff top in front of any chance passer-by!'

She had jerked them both back from the edge. He drew away from her, and they looked at each other in silence, and Debbie, Lesley's seed of disquiet by this time a full-flowered plant, found herself thinking, panic stricken, *now what do I do?* realising that she had inadvertently upset the apple-cart and the fruit was rolling all over the grass.

What she had here wasn't a bright and confident man with more than his fair share of charm, and a past to make him more interesting, but something a lot less superficial and very much more complex. An intelligent man who felt himself to be responsible for the death of a friend and buried the mistake from the world under a heap of sparkling trivialities. A person who desperately needed help but fought it off like a fury. Someone whose family, shocked and shamed and no doubt confused, hadn't so much cut him off as stepped a little away from him, at a loss as to what else to do. Superficiality on every front deceiving the whole world, and underneath it, a man who desperately needed to get close to someone and was deeply afraid of finding yet another door slammed in his face. A psychological mess. Her easy phrase about giving himself a breakdown was nothing less than the absolute truth. Unless she did and said the right thing he was just about to do exactly that, go shrieking off into the hinterland here and now on the sunlit cliff top, under the eyes of all the summer visitors.

Debbie aged ten years in ten seconds. It wasn't even a case of *my place or yours?* Either destination would bring the roof down on them. She said the first thing that came into her head.

'Seems like it's us for a dark wood and the back of the car, then.' Her heart was pounding until the blood roared in her ears, a rather unpleasant sensation on the whole.

To her intense relief, his answer was quite ordinary, but even so, she thought, it was a bit like driving with a dodgy fan belt. The crunch might come at any moment.

'Sounds OK to me. Only if you're sure.' It sounded so inappropriately polite, after all the high tension of the last half hour, that Debbie collapsed in a fit of the giggles, and they walked back to the car as if everything was perfectly normal between them, but she did wonder if Mawgan really knew what he was doing, or was simply on auto-pilot, and rather feared the latter. Remembering the telegraph pole incident, she even wondered if she ought to offer to drive, but didn't.

They found the dark wood, but Mawgan said they would pass on the back of the car, if she didn't mind, so they walked into the trees, deep in until there was nothing to be heard but rustling leaves and birds, and nothing to see but tree trunks and undergrowth. There, he stopped and took her gently by the shoulders.

'Deborah, I heard what you said about having already consented, and I appreciate your honesty in telling me, but this is different – isn't it?' She found it suddenly difficult to either look at him or to reply, and he went on. 'You don't have to do it if you don't want to, and I promise you that I won't misunderstand you. I can trust you without the vote of confidence.'

'I want to marry you,' said Debbie, through a throat suddenly painfully stiff.

'And so you shall, my bird, and all the risks that go with me. That wasn't what I meant, and you know it.' He was so close to her that she could see a pulse beating in his throat, hard and fast. She swallowed, trying not to wonder if she was going by the right road.

'What makes you think that I'm such a horrid tease?' she asked him, indignation restoring her temporary loss of poise. 'I love you – I trust you, too – and you need me. Here I am.'

'Deborah, you're a damned fool!' he said, and Debbie, catching a look in his eyes that made all the hairs lift on her arms and the back of her neck, hurriedly dragged him down with her to the ground, trusting to instinct and God.

No, it wasn't passion as she had known it in the past, it was probably not even love in any romantic sense. But it was in no sense brotherly, and it was the key that would turn the lock in the door that would let him back into the human race, the vote of confidence that he so desperately needed, whatever he chose to say. The intimate physical and emotional contact that would, if they were lucky, remove for ever the unseen tag *unclean*. She gave him everything she knew, and he took it with the desperation of a man lost in the dark who suddenly sees light. It was a rough mating, and a frightening one. She was glad that there had been others before him, not least Robin, and then for her that ghost was forever exorcised.

And for him?

A long time later lying on the soft leaves with his dark head cradled in her arms against her breast, she watched him sleeping, exhausted and drained of all emotion, as the light faded under the trees, and wondered exactly what it was that she had done. Turned her entire life upside-down, that was inevitable. She would shock her parents, offend her sister… and alienate her brother, her sister-in-law, her friends? She thought not, but it was one thing to say that you cared nothing for social ostracism, quite another to have to experience it, and she wouldn't win over them all. One friend she would lose straight away would be Tim.

And the village, where she had now chosen to make her life? The people who lived there liked her, as much as they liked any outsider, because of her Cornish name and because she had liked them. What would their attitude be when she announced that she was marrying their black sheep? Would it change – either to her, or to him? And if they banished her into the dark with Mawgan, would he ever handle it?

On the whole she thought that it was unlikely that he would be called upon to try, she found she had more faith in people's kindness. All they needed to do, she thought with a wry smile, was to win over the Tregears and they were home and dry, and after what Lesley said at breakfast, which Mrs T was quite acute enough to add to what had happened at the Fish last night, she had a suspicion that job might be half done already. The public's collective memory was short, they would live it down, maybe only with the passage of time, but eventually.

Some things, you couldn't live down, but the village didn't believe them, did they?

Mrs Tregear never mentioned the word *incest*, and she certainly would have done.

Why not? They were willing to believe the rest.

Because they were there, of course.

Her heart, which had been thumping, began to slow down at the thought. Of course, the village had a ringside seat, they knew exactly, to the last nuance, what the relationship was between Mawgan and his sister, what the opportunities were. And not only the village, his now ex-partner too, and his wife. Had anyone ever asked them?

No. He wasn't charged with incest, why would they?

Just murder, which he hadn't committed.

If they had children, how would they fare at the village school? *Your dad went to prison, na-na-nana-na!*

Best not to think about things like that. She couldn't imagine herself as anybody's mother anyway.

It was getting dark now, just a few red streaks left in a tumble of clouds, black against darkening blue. She wondered what the time was, and if Tim and Lesley thought she had run away for good. Mawgan still slept, with a fierce concentration that seemed bent on making up for lost time, perhaps, she thought compassionately, it was long since he had slept deeply like this. She smoothed his hair, lovingly, feeling its texture through her fingers. It was short and fine, like cats' fur, and he was going to lose it early. Already was, indeed. Heroes of romance, where are you now? This one was archetypal *bloke*, no question.

He stirred in her arms, and spoke in a voice slurred with sleep. 'Deborah, you're laughing. What're you laughing about?'

'Hullo, have you decided to return to the land of the living?' asked Debbie. 'I was beginning to think you'd decided to settle in for the night.'

'What were you laughing at?' he repeated, and opened his eyes. 'It's almost pitch dark! What's the time?'

'I've no idea.'

There was a silence while, she thought, he contemplated their unusual situation and explored its possibilities. Finally, he spoke. 'I'm sorry, Deborah. I shouldn't've done that. I didn't want it to be like that.'

'I rather thought that I asked for it,' said Debbie. With her fingers, she felt delicately along the line of his eyebrows, thick, almost, but not quite, meeting in the middle. *A nasty, vicious temper on him.* She couldn't believe in it. Quick, she would allow, although she had never seen it, quite possibly hell in his kitchen but then, she understood most chefs were: something to do with heat and stress, not nastiness. Vicious was a different concept altogether.

He rolled out of her arms and sat up, although his face was turned in her direction, she couldn't see his expression in the dark.

'Are you joking? It was unforgivable!' His voice was shaking. Oh no, Debbie thought, we're not going there, Mawgan! Get a grip! She said, keeping her voice steady, 'Did you hear me scream? No, you didn't!'

'I bloody near raped you!'

'If that's what you think, you're a lot more innocent than I had you down as.'

'I don't know what's the matter with me – ' he sounded desperate. 'I can't seem to behave like a normal person any more.'

'I'm sure you do know,' said Debbie, keeping calm. She reached out for him. 'Anyway, that isn't true. Most of the time you're completely normal.' She tried to laugh it off, but she could feel it wasn't working. 'Come on Mawgan, ease up, for God's sake!'

'All right then, if I'm completely normal, what about your friends? I never used to care a toss if people liked me or not, but soon as I realised Howells hated my guts, some demon got into me, that I had to try and make it up to him for what I did – to buy him back, I suppose, and his poor little wife... showing off, if you like, and only making things worse. It was me damaged them, not you. We both know it. Is that a normal way to behave?'

'It's certainly not *ab*normal. Actually, I'd call it more insecure.'

He began to laugh, and bit the sound off short. She thought, with a sudden quiver of alarm, that what she had done had breached a dam, and wasn't certain if it was good or bad.

'I was told I could appeal, you know that?' he said 'My brief had never even thought I'd be convicted, let alone imprisoned... but Dad... Dad said...' He stopped, drew a breath and went on. 'He said that Cress had been through enough, that she couldn't go through it again, and I mustn't make her… that the judge had said there was evidence of intent to injure and a motive, as if he was God or something to be always right, and I must take my punishment and not make a fuss to disgrace them all again, just let it be decently buried so that they could all start over… Deborah, how could they? You'd have thought they really believed I meant to hurt him.' His voice broke, running out of control, he caught it back only with an effort. There was no relaxation in him any more, he was taut as a strung bow. 'They let me go down for three years to save her one more day,' he said, 'and you call me *insecure!*'

And it was, although he hadn't said so, most probably his sister's testimony that had sent him down. The little sister that he had loved. But he had missed the point, Debbie thought. It was perfectly possible, given what he had told her, that his father's advice was as much to protect the son as the daughter. They would none of them, Mawgan included, have wanted to run the risk of the stigma of incest being officially added to manslaughter, even if the mud failed to stick in court. She thought she wouldn't say that.

'Don't,' she said, instead. 'Don't, my darling. That's enough, you're tearing yourself to pieces.' There was nothing she could do to help, she knew it. Wondering if it was a wise thing to do, if anything she had done had been wise, she slid her arms round him and laid her cheek against his. 'That's enough, my darling, that's enough. I understand. I love you.'

He might not have heard her. Resentment of injustice, that had been steadily eating him alive for too long, suddenly had to spill over or it would finally burn him away to ash.

'You remember that business in the snow, of course you do,' he said, speaking too fast so that the words fell over one another. 'You know the mess I was in after that, you came to see me… you were almost the only person who did. They did let me back inside the door that time, as a special concession because I couldn't do much for myself and lived on my own… and do you know what happened Deborah, do you? She rang up – Cress did – when I had been there about three days and said that she wanted to come home, and my mother was afraid to tell her I was there. I heard her – later – talking to Dad about it, and he said, *Why should the poor child be shut out of her own home? She's as much right here as he has, when you think what he did.* And Mum said, *How can we send him away when he's hurt? I don't know what to do.*

'So what did *you* do?' asked Debbie, furiously angry, for there was no excuse she could find for that.

'I left, what could I do? I got someone to drive me back to the Fish, and it was my housekeeper there who helped me. She was paid to do it, but at least she was kind. The only one who bothered to check if I was OK was Allison.'

The cute, loveable little sister, Debbie thought cynically, had known that he was home. She had got away with everything so far, so she had done it deliberately, and if opportunity arose, she would undoubtedly do it again. Debbie already loathed her, but never having met her, unlike Kate she saw no reason to fear her. She thought she sounded the ultimate spoilt brat and a turn short of a clove hitch into the bargain. As for Mum and Dad, they must surely have been cruel from bewilderment, unable to see things straight and completely out of their depth. They seemed to have done nothing but wring their hands from start to finish, putting everything on the strong son and protecting the weak daughter, and you just couldn't do that. She was too angry to speak, and into the silence, he made one final, and utterly petrifying revelation.

'They don't go away – the people who shouted outside the house and drove the family out, the ones who stood and jeered on the pavement when I went to court... the ones who cheered when they took me off to prison... they were people I knew, that I thought knew me, and they're still with me now, whenever I'm alone... in the corners of empty rooms and round my bed at night... whispering and pointing at me with bony fingers, peering at me out of little bright eyes with skinny lids... so I just keep busy, and most nights, I sleep with the light on. *Now* do you still want to marry me?'

How could you possibly comfort such distress? Debbie had never felt so much at a loss, even in the snows of February. She could only think how much she wished she could do something.

They slid back down to the ground together, still without speaking, and after a while Debbie became aware that he was crying, the tears hot on her neck. She let it go for a while, and then said, very quietly, 'So how long have you been bottling all that up, Mawgan Angwin?'

'Long enough... and if you *ever* tell anyone about this, I'll never forgive you!' He sniffed unromantically. 'What a plonker.'

Debbie said nothing, tightening her grip, and the minutes ticked by while he got himself under control, and she had time to think sensibly. There was a lot he had still left unsaid, she realised – she had no illusions, for instance, that prison had been *Porridge* or *Birds of a Feather*, particularly with that unspoken slur of incest, and on the whole she hoped that he would never tell her about it. But it was a beginning, at least. For instance, he would probably stop making sick jokes about prison sentences and parole. The next step would be the more delicate business of rehabilitating him in the eyes of other people, so that the sun could shine on him again with wholehearted warmth. To run away, she very well knew, wouldn't be a solution. If she let him run away – and she didn't think he even wanted to – he would never turn the light out at night again.

She had seen that light, she realised, walking on the foreshore with Roger one evening soon after she first arrived. Tim and Lesley, not for either the first or the last time, had been having an argument, and they had escaped to walk together in the moonlight, and that had been for both the first and the last time, poor old Roger.

Mawgan's breathing had steadied, only catching occasionally on a shaking sob, and after a while he said, in a voice that sounded completely his own.

'I'm sorry, Deborah. What a wail of self-pity!'

'Long overdue, if you ask me,' said Debbie.

She wondered if there had been anyone at all, apart from his sister Allison, who had been wholly on his side. What about the other one – what was her name, Anna? Where was she in all this, she hadn't even had a walk-on part in the drama so recently unfolded. As for anyone else, perhaps he had been too recently returned from abroad – or too ambitious – to make close friends, as he had admitted himself. His partner had ducked out, that she did know, had anyone else?

What a bloody awful day this had been, one way and another, but one good thing had come out of it, she was going to marry Mawgan, and hard on that thought she found herself speculating, if a girl married a chef, who did the cooking? Or if she married a publican, did they get a chance to eat at all? There was going to be a lot of adjusting to do.

And all the while, as she lay there and considered all these new ideas, the tension ebbed away and the world resumed its normal orbit. Mawgan had relaxed again, the storm over. Debbie waited.

'I feel as if someone had pushed a very heavy stone off of me,' said Mawgan, at last. 'And really hungry.'

Debbie giggled from sheer relief, she had been wondering if he was ever going to speak again.

'How dreadfully unromantic of you! Me too, hungry I mean. Shall we grope about and find our way back to the car?'

Mawgan sat up.

'If we can find it in the dark, that sounds like a good first move. Let's go.' It was as if nothing had ever happened. Over. Debbie didn't know whether to be relieved or alarmed, but settled for relief as more comfortable.

Finding the car would have been harder if it had been black, said Debbie, when they finally stumbled over it. At least it had shown up in the moonlight. They got back into it and Mawgan switched on the inside light so that they could pick the leaves off each other, which he did with such tenderness, and kissed her thereafter with such love, that Debbie's insides went all jittery.

'Your face is filthy,' she told him, and he laughed quite naturally, as if all was well.

The time, she found to her surprise when she had pulled herself together, was after eleven, their chances of continuing starvation were therefore high.

'If all else fails, I know a good pub where they'll serve me after hours,' said Mawgan, starting up the engine. 'Will you last that long? I'm not at all sure that I shall.' He appeared to have set the drama behind him with a firm hand, his spirits were leaping up again, but Debbie decided after consideration that it was with less brittleness and more natural effervescence than she had yet seen in him. There might yet be a long and thorny path ahead of them, but the future could easily turn out to be a lot of fun.

It was just before midnight when they arrived back, still unfed, in St. Erbyn. The Fish was in darkness except for a light over the outside door, with everybody fast asleep in their beds. Mawgan let them in quietly through the back door with a key, and led her through into the kitchen – the restaurant kitchen, not the original pub kitchen that did the bar lunches – moving around with the ease of one on familiar ground, comprehensively raiding the larder. They sat at the huge steel table to eat, and Debbie, in the intervals between mouthfuls, looked about her and was impressed. Up the hill, she realised, they were playing at catering, on this level, the game was over. Great fridges and stainless steel equipment lurked in every unlit corner of the huge kitchen, where they ate by a single hob light to avoid attracting attention to themselves. The gas stoves were enormous, and even the slicer had been conceived in the grand manner. It was all quite fearsomely antiseptic and clean, too. His workplace. It gave her a peculiar feeling.

'What happens – on a day like today, for instance, when you aren't here?' she asked, suddenly curious. 'Do they just manage without you, I mean? I can't believe that.'

He leaned his elbows on the table, a cup of coffee between his hands, looking at her through a gentle curl of steam.

'We don't do a set menu each night, so we just run one that Jack can handle on his own, and there's a part-timer in the village who comes in to help. He's a good chef, and it doesn't happen often – when I did my elbow must have been the first and last time.' He smiled at her. 'Not perfect, but as you see, the system works.'

'Would you like just to have the restaurant?' Debbie asked. There was a short silence.

'Oh yes,' said Mawgan. 'That was the original idea, didn't I say? The restaurant was mine, everything else was Edward's responsibility.'

'So,' said Debbie, thinking this out as she went. 'Are you a good chef, then?'

'I'm a bloody good chef, yes, Deborah.'

There was another silence. Debbie's eyes roamed round the dark cavern of the kitchen, and her thoughts roamed with them, but round the inside of her head. She spoke casually.

'Then it's a pity you can't just concentrate on this.'

'Life's like that. A bugger.'

Silence again.

'What's that noise?' asked Debbie.

'What noise?' He cocked his head on one side, listening. 'Someone's car alarm going off? They do it all the time, damn things.'

'Must be a very big car.' She dismissed it, intent on the conversation they had been having.

'I can see that you wouldn't want another partner, but haven't you thought about the option of putting in a really good manager for the pub side and the office? Someone you could trust – after all, you'd still be on the premises.'

'Maybe because I've lost the knack of trusting people?'

'You'll kill yourself if you keep on the way you are,' said Debbie, judiciously.

He wasn't listening, she saw.

'That alarm is going on for a long time.' He got to his feet and went over to the window, pushing it open. The sound was much louder. 'I don't think it is a car alarm. It's a fire alarm.'

'Whose?' asked Debbie. 'In the village, somewhere…?' She was suddenly cold.

He slammed the window shut again, heading for the door.

'Could be,' he flung over his shoulder as he went. 'But I think it's the other way. I think it's you.'

'Shit!' Debbie sprang to her feet and raced after him. They left the Fish and headed up the lane via the side gate, running towards the increasing sound of the fire alarm and heading straight into the final scene of a singularly dramatic day.

XIX

Unlike the Fish, Seagulls was very far from quiet. The night was alive with running figures, some of them in their nightclothes, streaming along the drive with Roger urging them on with waving arms, and Tim flying like the wind over the gravel towards the gate.

'Lesley!' he was calling. 'Lesley, is that you? Oh God, *Lesley!*'

There was a curious thickness hanging in the air like fine mist and smelling of October bonfires. Debbie called out, breathlessly.

'It's not Lesley, it's me – Debbie!'

Mawgan had easily outpaced her, she raced behind him and they met Tim head-on, He caught at Debbie urgently, hardly seeming to notice she wasn't on her own.

'Deb, have you seen her? I can't find her – we had another row and she went – I haven't seen her since we all came back –'

He was totally distraught, and she hadn't a clue what he was taking about. She caught at his hands trying to steady him, feeling drained of the power to do so by the demands the day had already made upon her.

'Isn't she in the staff flat?' she asked, and immediately answered herself. 'No, of course you'd know if she was. The boathouse, then? The woods?' The yelling fire alarm was going through her head. She put her hands up to her ears.

'I've called and called,' cried Tim. 'Deb, oh God, where has she gone?' His eyes turned wildly to the house, where Roger was calmly assembling the guests and marching them onto the lawn. 'There's a roaring inferno in the lounge, it must have been going for ages – it'll break loose any minute – I've rung the fire brigade – Deb – '

'Have you checked the whole house?' asked Mawgan, crisp, cool and unruffled, hardly even out of breath. The events of afternoon and evening might never have happened. Oh bless you, thought Debbie, her heart going like a trip hammer. Bless you for the adventurer that you are!

'The house?' Tim's voice rose half an octave at least. 'Why should she be in the house? Everyone is out of the house!'

'Have you checked?' reiterated Mawgan, patiently.

'Oh God – I don't know – she can't be – 'Tim lunged back towards the building and Mawgan caught at his arm.

'Not like that, Howells, for God's sake! Now listen.' It was only the second time Debbie had ever heard him swear. Tim had paused, looking at him wild-eyed. He drew a breath.

'Sorry. I'm listening.'

'We'll both go in. If the fire is in the lounge, it'll have to be through the back, we daren't open the front door – you check downstairs, I'll do upstairs if it's possible. Quickly as you can, and keep low, under the smoke. Don't wait for me when you've done, get straight out again and make sure someone sees you. Deborah – get over there and help Roger look after your guests.'

'Not bloody likely! You don't know your way around!' said Debbie, and ran after them towards the house.

The electricity had gone off some time before, but the emergency lighting was working. The kitchen passage, was dark, hot and swirling with smoke, but not as yet thick smoke. They could hear the fire roaring away to itself in the background, at present at least confined to one room but ready at any moment to break loose and consume everything, the door to the lounge was red hot and beginning to char, the paint blistering, impossible to approach, and in the eerie, roaring silence, the old house creaked and cracked alarmingly as the timbers dried out in the heat. Tim, who had steadied miraculously under the influence of leadership, flew to check the downstairs rooms where it was just about safe to do so, and Mawgan, after only a slight hesitation, made for the back stairs. Debbie, heart thumping with fear and adrenaline, followed him. Mawgan, without looking round, said as he raced upwards, 'You go left, then, I'll take the right. Don't breathe too deeply, keep low.' Eyes in the back of his head, apparently.

It was night outside, but the moon was up and it was possible to see reasonably well between the moonlight and the emergency lights, it was only the urgency and the smoke that made things difficult. Halfway up the stairs, the fire alarm cut out, and as their ears were still ringing in the sudden silence, another sound could be heard above the subdued growling of the fire, a muffled knocking, screaming. The sound of panic.

'Lesley!' called Debbie, scrambling up the last few stairs and pushing through the fire door anyhow in Mawgan's wake. 'That way – along there!' She pointed.

The noise was coming from the bathroom: although the rooms all had ensuite shower rooms there hadn't been room to put in anything larger, so that Lesley's aunt had left the original bathroom as it was for the use of those guests who might prefer a bath; generally this would be those with small children, and Lesley who didn't like the shower in the staff quarters. Now, as they closed with the bathroom door, the muffled knocking resolved itself into the sound of someone hammering frantically on the other side, screaming for help and choking on the smoke all at the same time.

The smoke was much thicker up here, and the heat was terrific. Both Debbie and Mawgan were beginning to cough too. There couldn't be much time left.

'Lesley!' cried Debbie, pitching her voice above the noise that Lesley was making. 'Lesley, we're here!'

'Debbie!' Lesley's voice, muffled by the door, broke on a sob. 'Thank God, oh, thank God! The bloody lock has stuck again – '

Mawgan shoved Debbie out of the way.

'Mrs Howells.' His voice was as calm as if nothing out of the way was happening. 'Mrs Howells, are you sure you're turning the key the right way?'

Pause.

'Who's that?' asked Lesley, in a startled voice.

'Mawgan,' said Debbie. 'It isn't that, Mawgan, the lock sticks sometimes. It's done it before.'

'Oh God!' said Mawgan. 'Don't tell me, that fool Howells didn't do anything about it! Mrs Howells,' he called, raising his voice. 'Stand out of the way of the door, I'm going to break it down.'

'You needn't.' Debbie caught his arm. 'It opens OK from this side. She can pass the key under it.'

There was a scuffling from inside the bathroom, and the key appeared on the carpet at their feet. The smoke, Debbie thought, was getting ever thicker, and she was sure she could hear the fire crackling. It was hotter too, and becoming difficult to breathe properly, but this was no time for giving way to terror. She cupped her hands over her mouth and nose, which helped a little, watching as Mawgan fumbled with the lock. His hands were shaking, she saw, and felt her stomach clench with fear. Then the door opened, and he skidded across the bathroom floor, scooped up the terrified Lesley and flung her, clutching a heap of towels she had gathered from sheer blind instinct, out into the passage.

'Run, both of you!' he yelled. They ran.

The fire escape was at the wrong end of the house, there was only one way out by this time, the way they had come in. Down the back stairs they raced, choking and confused by the smoke, meeting Tim, who had come running up from the kitchen, still desperately searching for his wife, in the passage below. He clutched Lesley and dragged her, scattering towels, to the back door, shouting at Debbie to follow, but Debbie suddenly realised that she was alone and ran back to the foot of the stairs. Her heart was hammering. She could hear the sound of running feet and doors slamming briskly as Mawgan checked for anyone else who might be left behind, at least where he could, and then he appeared at the top of the stairs and saw her, and roared, appropriately enough, 'Get the blazes out of here, Deborah!' as he jumped down the first flight three at a time.

In the event, it was fortunate that she had stayed behind. On the half-landing, he tripped over one of Lesley's scattered towels and finished the descent a great deal faster even than he had intended, hitting the newel-post at the bottom head on, and going slam onto the tiles at her feet. Afterwards, she swore that she heard something snap as he hit.

This time, there was no doubt about the blood, suddenly it seemed to be everywhere. Blood on the newel-post, blood in an elegant curved splat at the foot of the nearest wall, blood trickling along the floor, black in the gradually dimming light. Debbie, completely forgetting to be calm and practical in this emergency, let out a shriek like an express train in a tunnel, which brought Tim racing back. They dragged Mawgan between them, regardless of possible injury, along to the door, there was no time to mess about. Debbie had tears pouring down her face and both of them were coughing so they could hardly breathe.

'We've about ten seconds, I reckon,' gasped Tim, with an effort. 'You push the door wide, I'm stronger than you – ready?' Debbie scrabbled at the handle and wrenched the door open, and they fell through it anyhow, reaching the comparative safety of the outside world just as the door to the lounge fell in, and the fire, breaking free from its half-hour restraint, leapt through and filled the hall with roaring flames, searing heat, and thick choking smoke, fed along the kitchen passage by the sudden blast of fresh air, and all the sprinklers burst into action.

Help waited beyond the door. A couple of the fishermen had come running up from the village to see what they could do, if anything, and were there on the drive as soon as the door opened, and between them they carried Mawgan out onto the lawn and laid him gently down. Roger took one look and ran to the staff quarters for blankets, and Debbie collapsed on her knees beside him on the grass, desperately trying to catch hold of the tail of her self-control. In this, she wasn't helped by Lesley, who took one look at him and let out a hoarse wail.

'Oh God, now he's a dead duck, too!' before breaking into peals of hysterical laughter intermixed with choking, just as the fire engines from Helston came jangling up the drive and all her dreams, and Tim's, went up in a towering pillar of fire behind her.

It was to be an endless night, it had already been more than long enough. Police cars and ambulances arrived hard on the heels of the fire engines, and Mawgan, Debbie and Lesley were whisked off to Truro leaving a scene of Armageddon behind them. Debbie refused to be parted from Mawgan and sat in the ambulance, siren wailing, as they sped along the road, tears pouring down her cheeks and coughing her heart out between lungsful of oxygen administered by a sympathetic ambulance man, and Mawgan just lay there, inert and ghastly, covered in blood. He seemed to have broken his collar-bone, the paramedic told her, soothingly, and knocked himself out when he cut his head open on the newel-post, but head wounds always bled a lot, there was nothing in that. Debbie, terrified that some vengeful deity had cracked his skull for him and he was going to die, took no comfort from this. Remembering the force with which he had cannoned off the post and landed at her feet, she couldn't believe that a broken collar-bone and a bang on the head could possibly be all the damage, but the casualty doctor confirmed it after X-rays.

'A good hard skull,' he told Debbie, with a smile. 'He'll come round soon. We'll tell you when he wakes up.'

Detained overnight for observation along with Lesley, Debbie found it impossible to follow instructions and sleep, in spite of a sleeping pill, and the nurses on the ward were sympathetic, promising to let her know as soon as there was any news. Even so, it seemed a long time, and dawn was already brightening the sky, before one of them tiptoed into the ward and whispered, at last, that he had finally come round.

'Did he say anything?' Debbie whispered back anxiously, because it had been a long time to be unconscious and by this time she was very, very frightened. The nurse smiled at her, reassuring.

'*Is Deb all right?*' she said. 'That's you, isn't it?'

'Deb?' said Debbie, staring. 'He said *Deb?*'

'So they say on the ward. And then he said, *ugh, I can't break a collar-bone in August*, which did sound a bit… well, strange, but you know, he's bound to be confused, he's been out of it for quite a while. There's no need to worry too much.'

But Debbie, her mind at rest, snuggled down onto her pillow and closed her eyes.

'That's my boy,' she said, and then, before she drifted off, added, 'Tell them to handle with care. He has the most unreliable pain threshold of anyone I ever met.'

'I think they already know,' said the nurse, so that she fell asleep on a chuckle.

In the morning, of course, there were the pieces to pick up. Debbie was told she could go home after a check-over, although Lesley was to stay a little longer. She had been to see Lesley, in a room further along the ward, but the visit hadn't been a success.

As soon as she had appeared, Lesley had turned her head away and burst into tears. Debbie touched her shoulder.

'Come on Les – there's no need for this. Everybody's safe.'

Lesley wept harder, twisting away from her.

'I don't know how you can have the face to come near me,' she sobbed. Debbie stared.

'But – '

'Just get out! Get out, get out!'

Two nurses were heading their way, attracted by Lesley's raised voice. Debbie turned to go. She must have looked shaken, because one of them touched her arm, comfortingly.

'Don't worry, she's a bit upset, she's had a bad shock. She'll be better later.'

Would she? There was something here that Debbie didn't understand, wasn't sure she even wanted to understand, but Lesley was setting off into full-scale hysterics. Curtains were being hurriedly drawn round her bed, it was time to leave. She went back out onto the corridor, feeling lost. *Stop the world, I want to get off* – she couldn't remember who had originally said that, but she knew exactly how they had felt as they said it.

Being discharged had raised the problem of how, if she was allowed to leave, she was to get back to St. Erbyn, for she had left after yesterday's row with nothing but what she stood up in, and she was pretty certain that Mawgan had little more than a credit card on him either when they ran out of the Fish, so that washed out any idea of a taxi. She might have taken one anyway and paid on arrival had she been sure that the staff quarters were still standing, but she wasn't. The nurses offered to stand her the price of a phone call, but who would she ring? Seagulls was presumably burnt out, and although Roger had a mobile, if it had survived the conflagration, she had no idea of the number, certainly not of where any of her friends might be. In the end, unable to think of anything better, she accepted the offered change, consulted the directory, and rang Mrs Tregear.

'What a terrible thing!' cried the redoubtable Mrs T as soon as she realised who it was on the phone. 'There's nothing there this morning but a smoking ruin, and lucky nobody was burned alive! How is Mrs Howells?'

Debbie said diplomatically that Lesley was shocked, but recovering, and Mrs Tregear said, 'And Mr Angwin? They say as he saved her life, you and him together.'

Had they? Debbie supposed that they must have. It made her feel sickish.

'I think he's all right. I'm just going to see in a minute, but I've got a problem.'

Mrs Tregear made nothing of problems, with such an exciting event to help to stage-manage. She promised that her daughter's husband would be along as soon as she could get hold of him, it seemed he was in Truro anyway on business. Debbie thanked her, said that she would be waiting just inside the main door, and put the phone down. She had never, to her knowledge, met My Daughter's Husband, but had no doubt that he knew her. Then she set off to find Mawgan, who was on a different ward.

All right had been an overstatement, she realised as soon as she saw him. He had an over-dramatic black eye, his eyeball was bright red, and a surgical dressing decorated that part of his forehead which had made contact with the newel-post. The rest of his face was a nasty greyish yellow that she recognised from another occasion.

'Hi Deb,' he greeted her wearily. 'Isn't this where we came in?'

'I suppose it is.' She managed a smile.

He closed his eyes on a sigh. 'Then do you mind if we go home? I don't think I can stand the show all over again.' He coughed, and winced painfully. 'Bugger! You OK?'

'My chest feels tight and I smell like a bonfire.' She made a face. 'You?'

'I think *unwell* 'bout covers it. You and your bloody lightning!'

'My what?'

'Never strikes the same place twice, you told me. Liar!'

Debbie perched on the side of the bed, hoping she wouldn't leave a dirty mark, and they automatically reached for each other. With his hand safely in hers, she said, 'They're only letting me have a few minutes. I'm going home, for what it's worth, but I'll come in and see you this evening.'

'Home?' he asked. 'No Deb, even if it's still standing, it'll be filthy with smoke, and the smell will hang around for weeks. You can't live there. Ten to one, all the services are off, anyway. Move your stuff into the flat.'

'Flat?'

'My flat. At the Fish. Have a word with Mrs. Solomons, she'll give you the key.'

Debbie sat perfectly still. After a moment, she said, 'Are you sure? I mean… you aren't even there.'

'Got to go somewhere, haven't you?' She nodded. 'Well then. I'll join you before long, anyway.' He closed his eyes. 'If you dig around, you'll find a mobile phone – I think it's on the dresser. Give Dad a ring, will you? The number's in the directory.'

'Under what?' asked Debbie.

'D for Dad. Can you push off now? I love you, but I think I'm going to die…'

She kissed him gently, and went away to await the arrival of My Daughter's Husband with a great deal to think about.

Chel and Oliver didn't listen to Radio Cornwall, so that the first they heard about the fire was when Jerry, Oliver's father, rang soon after Chel had gone downstairs to the craft shop. Since he hadn't started work yet, Oliver actually answered, which was rare.

'Tim Howells rang us just now, and told us the news,' Jerry said, when he had explained. 'It seems Debbie is OK, going home this morning, although they kept her in hospital overnight – she inhaled a bit of smoke – but could you or Cheryl just slip over and check? Would you have the time? Dorothy is very worried about her – well, so am I, come to that.'

Oliver didn't much care if his stepmother worried herself into the grave, but he was attached to his young sister. Driving over to the Helford River and back would take the best part of the morning, even apart from what he might find when he got there, but he answered without hesitation.

'Of course I'll go. How did it happen, for heaven's sake?'

'I don't think Tim knew. He said they got back from a night out in Helston and found the lounge already well alight. No serious casualties, but a couple of uncomfortably close shaves, he said, and nothing left this morning but the staff annexe, which is uninhabitable, and the boathouse. Favourite seems to be that one of the guests who came back early dropped a cigarette down a chair, but there's experts picking through the ashes, so they may know more by the time you get there.' He hesitated. 'Ring me back as soon as you've any news, will you?'

'No problem. I'll just tell Chel where I'm going and I'll be on my way.' He steeled himself to make a very large concession. 'I'll take this bloody mobile with me, so you can find me if you need to.'

'Thanks Oliver. I know you're busy, and I appreciate this.'

'I'll speak to you.'

The first thing he did was to ring the hospital in Truro, but Debbie had left with My Daughter's Husband only five minutes earlier. He then locked the studio and went down to the craft shop to have a word with Chel.

'Bit of trouble in St. Erbyn,' he said. 'They've had a fire, apparently – nobody hurt – but Dad wants me to go and check on Deb. I'll be back later on.'

Chel was in the middle of serving a customer. She stopped wrapping a dish in tissue paper and looked at him with a faint frown on her face.

'A *fire*?' She could feel the familiar cobweb brushing the hairs on her arms, but she didn't know enough to know more than that there was something to know… she gave herself a shake. Thoughts like that led nowhere – nowhere that she wanted to visit, anyway. 'But Deb is OK?'

'Except for inhaling more smoke than is good for her, apparently yes.'

'That's one mercy.' She paused. 'You could check on any undesirables while you're there.'

'Good point. If she brings the subject up, I will.'

'You could bring the subject up yourself.' She knew he wouldn't. 'Let me know what happens. Bring her back with you, if she needs somewhere to go. She can have the sofa bed.'

She watched him through the plate-glass window of the shop as he drove away, and then turned to serve the next customer with a pleasant smile but only half her attention on the job. The fire at the sailing school sat in the back of her mind like a black cloud of smoke, hiding everything. She wished that she could have gone with him.

Debbie asked My Daughter's Husband to drop her at the causeway. She couldn't just turn up with her luggage, she realised, it would be awkward enough if she spoke to this Mrs. Solomons first. The Fish, bereft of its landlord for the second day running, was opening its doors and windows to the morning as usual as she walked into the hallway, and the girl who sat in reception, to her astonishment, immediately leapt to her feet.

'It's you! How's Mr. Angwin?'

'Not seriously hurt, just a bit sorry for himself. Maybe a bit concussed.' Silly to feel awkward, when everyone here must know she had been going around with him for months, but she found it quite difficult to add, 'He told me to ask for Mrs. Solomons, but I don't know who she is.'

'She's the housekeeper. Hang on a moment, I'll buzz her for you.' She turned back to the intercom on her desk, and Debbie fidgeted around in the hall, waiting. The door that led into the kitchen quarters of the restaurant opened unexpectedly, and a head popped round it.

'Good morning. Chef OK?'

This was Tony, the restaurant manager, as she already knew. She said her piece again,

'He'll live. At the moment, he's not sure about that being a good idea.'

Tony grinned at her.

'Poor bugger! I'll tell them in the kitchen, they'll want to know.'

Debbie went back to her aimless, nervous circuit of the hall. It was being borne in on her that whatever the rest of the village might feel, Mawgan's staff held him in some affection. She recalled him saying that they had thrown him out yesterday morning, and realised, for the first time, that there was the same degree of affection – and concern – behind that, too. Interesting.

'Mrs. Solomons is just coming,' said the girl in reception. 'I'm Shirley.'

'Hi, Shirley.' Unsure of her place in the scheme of things, Debbie didn't add, 'I'm Debbie,' as she would normally have done. Shirley probably knew anyway, she told herself, so there was no need.

'Dreadful about the fire, wasn't it?' said Shirley, round-eyed. 'So lucky that nobody was hurt — well except Mr. Angwin, and he isn't *dead*. What will you do, do you think?'

'I've no idea,' said Debbie, realising that it was true. She very probably didn't even have a job any more. She felt tired at the thought of all the complications to come, but fortunately, since Shirley seemed inclined to gossip, the housekeeper came downstairs just then. She, too, asked immediately after Mr. Angwin, and nodded sympathetically as Debbie, for the third time, rehearsed her speech.

'Shirley said you had a message,' said Mrs. Solomons.

'Well… yes.' She shot a glance at Shirley and forced herself not to stand on one leg like an awkward child. 'He said, to ask you for the key of his flat and to move into it.'

'Hey, cool!' said Shirley, before Mrs. Solomons could say anything. 'For always?'

'I think that's the general idea,' said Debbie. They both looked at her. Shirley fumbled under the counter and came up with a key, which Mrs. Solomons took from her.

'You'd better come up,' she said, and led the way back up the stairs. Shirley waved, before turning back to her computer.

At the top, they paused. Mrs. Solomons pointed to the right.

'The guest bedrooms are that way.' She unlocked a door on the left, and pushed it open, standing back for Debbie to precede her. 'And this is the flat.'

The flat took up the whole of this end of the Fish, and had been made by using all the area above the bars, where the original rooms had opened into one another, so it was spacious. On the left, as Debbie went in, was a small galley-style kitchen in medium oak that looked as if it had never been used, and immediately beyond that it opened out into a big room with small-paned casement windows like those of the bars downstairs, overlooking the river to one side and the car park behind the inn on the other. The original roof beams showed in the ceiling. It was, Debbie saw at once, seriously under-furnished for its size, a round wooden table with four chairs round it beneath a hatch from the kitchen, a modern dresser with glass doors to the top half against the back wall between the windows, which appeared to shelter nothing but a few lonely books and a lot of empty space, two red leather armchairs either side of a fireplace with a log-effect electric fire in it, and a television set on a stand. A small coffee table with a low stack of magazines on it completed the tally. Nice curtains, a sort of autumn-leafy pattern, and a paler brown hair cord carpet. No pictures, although there were one or two hooks in the wall where there had been some once, no ornaments, no hearthrug. Nothing personal at all, really. There would be, she saw at once, plenty of room for the furniture from her London flat, in fact it was desperately needed. There was another door to the right of the fireplace, presumably a bedroom.

Mrs. Solomons closed the outer door and followed her into the room.

'I wasn't going to say anything in front of Shirley,' she said. 'This is the best news I've heard for a long time. Are the two of you going to be married?'

'It looks like it.' Debbie met her look candidly. 'Nobody knows but us – and now you – although they may guess. But you won't say anything, will you?'

'Of course not.' She crossed the floor and opened the other door. 'This is the bedroom.' It contained a double bed, with the sort of headboard that incorporates the bedside tables, rather nice, pale natural wood. Nothing else. 'And this is a dressing room, and the bathroom is through it.' The dressing room, at the back of the house, was lined with drawer and cupboard units that included a dressing table. Debbie looked around her thoughtfully.

'I'd call it minimalist,' she said. Mrs. Solomons gave her a strange look.

'He doesn't care,' she said. 'Perhaps now, he will.' She looked at Debbie carefully as if sizing her up, and then decided to continue. 'I don't know what it was like before I got here, I only came when Mr. Angwin took my son on as sous-chef, but according to Tommy, who is the only one of the original staff, his partner and his wife who lived here stripped the place out when they left. It was his sisters that made him get this furniture, went and chose it themselves if rumour doesn't lie.' She gave Debbie a wry smile. 'What you might call the bare necessities. But apparently there wasn't a lot of money floating around after all the trouble.'

The Angwin sisters – the plural surely included Anna, at last – Debbie reckoned, had middle-of-the road tastes, and had gone for reasonable quality rather than quantity, they must have toured the salerooms with an eye to a bargain. The effect they had created was of blandness, but if they had been limited as to means they hadn't done such a bad job. Of course, the place cried out for antiques, but you couldn't ask for perfection on a shoestring. It was the absence of pictures and general knick-knacks that she found worrying, it argued a barrenness of outlook that was scary, and that, she knew, wouldn't be down to them but to him. She looked at Mrs. Solomons with new interest. She had looked after him during the aftermath of the snow incident, he had told her. It was beginning to dawn on her that it was Mrs. Solomons, Tommy, Shirley and the rest who must have kept him sane over the past year. She sat down on the arm of one of the armchairs, rather suddenly, overwhelmed by too much knowledge and too little sleep, and the nagging awareness of her own problems looming in the background.

'You run along and get your things,' said Mrs. Solomons. 'I'll get the sheets changed on the bed, and when you come back, you have a nice hot bath and a good sleep. Things will look better then.' She nodded, brisk but friendly. 'Leave the key with Shirley when you go. Fire regulations.' She smiled as she left, with wry sympathy.

Alone, Debbie sat where she was for a while, looking about her. So this was home, now and in the future. It needed some work on it to bring it up to scratch, but she had the rest of her life in which to do it. Not a lot of room for children, but perhaps they could pinch a room here and there from somewhere else if it ever became necessary. Oliver and Chel would be just up the road, or up the creek if you preferred, how was Oliver going to react to that? He had changed over the past two years, true, but how much? Enough to tolerate living within walking distance of a member of his family? Would he and Mawgan even like each other? They were very alike in some things, but that could cut both ways, they could be the wrong things. She realised that she was putting something off, and got to her feet with a sigh. The mobile phone sat on its charger on the dresser, reproaching her. She picked it up and selected DAD from its directory.

Pip was driving his truck along the narrow lanes around Par, when his mobile rang on the dashboard, he swore and picked it up, illegally clutching it to his ear as he bucketed round a bend.

'Angwin.'

'Mawgan asked me to ring,' said Debbie. 'Did you know he was in hospital?'

'Yes. That pub of his rang this morning.'

He was barking at her. There could be several reasons for that, so Debbie decided simply to carry on and not be intimidated. She heard a horn tooting angrily, and Mawgan's father swore. 'Bloody idiots! Don't know the width of their own cars! You were saying?'

What was she saying? Mawgan had given her no script, just asked her to ring. While she groped for words, the angry voice said, 'Is the boy all right? His mother was worrying.'

Only his mother? Debbie was getting contradictory vibes here. She said, 'Concussion, and he broke his collar-bone. He fell downstairs, did they tell you? The house was burning, and he went in to rescue someone.'

Silence. So long a silence that Debbie began to wonder if he was still there.

'No, they didn't tell us that.' Pause. 'Who am I speaking to now?'

'Oh – sorry! Deborah Nankervis. I'm an instructor at the sailing school that burned down… I was, at least, up to last night.'

'Hmm, bad job all round. Sorry. Bad to lose a business that way, hope it works out. Well, thank you for ringing, Deborah Nankervis. Tell him we're sorry, if you see him.'

He had gone, and only the empty buzzing of the line sounded in her ear. Debbie was about to replace the phone, but hesitated. Were other members of the family in its directory? Allison, for instance? Was it an invasion of privacy to look?

Allison was there. Also Anna, with an international number that Debbie couldn't place closer than *Europe, somewhere*, maybe that explained why she figured so little in the drama. After a moment's hesitation, she called Allison's London number, but all she got was an answer phone. She replaced the mobile on its charger. Time to face up to life outside.

Seagulls was a ruin, the smell of smoke and soot hung around it like a shroud. The house was cordoned off, and there were police and fire service vans parked in the drive, and a policeman on the gate, who stopped her to ask her business.

'Can't go in there, miss. No sightseers, sorry.'

'I just want to get my stuff out.' Debbie pointed to the staff quarters, apparently intact under the trees. 'I don't need to go near the house.'

'Sorry miss, thought you were a gawper.' He smiled at her. 'You'd be surprised at people, makes you think of old Madame Defarge and the guillotine! You can go in, but keep well away to that side, it's not safe by the house.'

Poor Seagulls. Poor Tim, poor Lesley. Debbie picked her way down the drive and opened the kitchen door. She immediately realised that Mawgan had been right, the place was uninhabitable, even here the smell and stain of the smoke was everywhere, acrid and clinging, and water had come in through an open window to flood the floor where the fireman had sprayed to stop the building catching fire. She had been dreaming of that bath, and a change of clothes, now she wondered if she would find any clothes fit to change into.

Tim came out from his bedroom the moment he heard the sound of the door and her footsteps on the floor. He looked shattered.

'Deb! Oh, my dear…'

He must have been here all alone, there was no sign of Roger. Brooding on disaster, Debbie thought miserably, and there had certainly been a surfeit of that.

'Lesley's OK,' she said. 'I expect you know that. She was on the same ward as me, so I saw her this morning.' Saw her, yes. Spoke with her, strictly speaking, no. Tim made an odd, palm-upward gesture with his hands.

'Never mind that, she's made herself history. Is Angwin OK?'

'He will be soon. They're only keeping him because he was knocked right out, and they want to make sure there's no deeper damage, I expect he'll be back tomorrow.' She closed her eyes for a moment, remembering the endless night. 'He broke his collar-bone, and he's not pleased about that.'

'Shit!' said Tim. 'God, I never thought…' She could see him remembering how the two of them had dragged Mawgan unceremoniously across the floor. 'Didn't we make a bit of a mess, manhandling him like we did?'

'I suppose we must have.' Debbie shrugged her shoulders, it seemed unimportant compared to what could have happened had they wasted time proceeding according to the book. She felt nothing but weariness now. 'He'll bounce back. He's tough.' She went through her bedroom door, hoping that he would take this as a signal that the conversation was over, but he didn't. He followed her, and leaned against the doorway, looking in on her.

'Well… good.' He stood there, drooping, a hesitant, unhappy figure.

316

'Look Deb, I didn't mean any of those things I said yesterday morning. You didn't really think I did, did you?'

Debbie made a tired gesture with her hands. None of that mattered any more, and his need for reassurance dragged at her. She sat down suddenly on the edge of her bed.

'No Tim, of course I didn't, it's just this stupid business, that's all. Mawgan did warn me, ages ago quite soon after I got here… but it'll be all right now. I'm sure it will.' And where had that silly platitude come from?

'Too green to be loose,' said Tim, with a grimace. He made a choking sound and came swiftly across the room, dropping on his knees in front of her, burying his face in her lap. 'Deb – oh Deb, I've been all sorts of a fool. And Lesley… Lesley was nearly burnt alive, and that stupid lock was my fault. *My* fault. She asked me –'

More than once, Debbie thought tiredly. Where was the point of all this?

'Don't,' she said. This final call on her sympathy was almost too much. She touched his hair, wiry and fair, so different from the fine dark hair her touch remembered. 'Don't, Tim, please. It's all right. She's safe.'

'Thanks to bloody Angwin!' said Tim, muffled. 'How did I come to be such a fool, Deb? Tell me how?'

Debbie's tired brain was having a struggle to meet this new challenge, her new-found wisdom stretching to breaking-point under the strain.

'I suppose…' she said, 'I suppose we were batting out of our league. All of us, not just you. Arrogant… you wouldn't have expected Mawgan to walk into your old job and just be an engineer, bang, like that, but we all thought we could manage, not just a simple B&B, but pretty comprehensive catering, and with no experience at all. Well, we couldn't, and that's that.'

'That isn't what I mean,' said Tim. He raised his head and looked at her, and for a brief, awful second her heart stood still. 'Debbie,' he said.

'Don't say it Tim – you mustn't say it!' She spoke so fast that she gave herself no time to think properly. 'I'm going to be Mrs Bloody Angwin and stop him jumping out of windows – you and Lesley –'

'Deb, *no!*' To her shocked amazement, he was crying, clutching at her and sobbing into her lap. 'No, Debbie darling, you can't! Not Angwin, *please*, you can't! He's dangerous…'

'Don't be so bloody stupid!' said Debbie. The non-stop, high-level tension of the last twenty-four hours was suddenly too much for her. She got to her feet abruptly, pushing Tim away. 'After all that Lesley's been through –'

'Lesley!' He sat back on his heels and began to laugh, the tears still running down his cheeks. 'Lesley! That's rich, Deb! I told you – Lesley's history!'

She remembered that he had, now that he repeated it. She didn't want to hear why. She couldn't handle it.

'You were worried enough about her last night,' she retorted.

'Only because I felt responsible – you see –' he began to explain. She cut him short.

'I don't see anything.' It was no good, her legs wouldn't support her. She sat down again, lowering herself back onto the bed clutching at the bedhead, like an old woman. 'Do get up, Tim, you look silly down there.' She didn't know if she most wanted to sleep for hours or to howl like a banshee. Perhaps this feeling communicated itself to Tim, for he got to his feet and sat beside her on the bed. Close – too close. She leaned back against the headboard to keep a distance between them. Sleep… yes, she most wanted sleep…

'I'm sorry, Deb.' He spoke gently. 'I shouldn't be bothering you with all this when you're exhausted – yes you are, I can see it in your face. Did you sleep at all last night?'

Sympathy was almost worse than dramatics. Any minute now, she feared he would try to kiss her and comfort her, and she couldn't – she simply couldn't – begin to bear it!

'Tim,' she said. 'Go. Please. I want to pack.'

'Roger's arranged a room up in the village for you,' said Tim. 'I'll show you, help carry your things. Come on, my darling, let's get started then.' He stood up, and reached her suitcase from the top of the wardrobe. Debbie said, stonily, trying to get through to him, 'I don't need a room, but thank you for thinking of it. I'm moving into the Fish. Now will you *please* go! I can't hack this any more!'

Tim dropped the suitcase, swinging round on her with a face of stark amazement, but before he could get a word out there was a step outside, and Roger appeared in the doorway. He must have taken in the situation at a glance, but all he said was, 'Hi Deb. Angwin OK?'

The next time somebody asked that, Debbie thought desperately, she would push them into the river.

'Where's my car?' she snapped, without even saying hullo. It hadn't been outside. There had been a couple of twisted, burnt-out wrecks close to the house, but only the two. All the other cars had presumably been driven away to safety.

'God knows,' said Roger, cheerfully. 'We found your keys on your dressing table, and someone took it off somewhere out of the way. Don't know where, don't know who. Don't worry, it'll turn up. It's conspicuous enough.'

Debbie had elbowed Tim out of the way and begun to throw the contents of her drawers into the case, not noticing, as she did so, that she had pushed a postcard under the lining paper. The piece of paper that fluttered down to the floor, she didn't even see. Tim picked it up and absent-mindedly crumpled it in his fingers, unaware of what he did. The smell of the fire had got in everywhere.

'I need it now,' she said. 'I want to get this stuff down the hill.'

'We'll carry it,' said Roger, as to one soothing a fractious child. He unhooked the picture she had hung on her wall to cheer the place up. 'Got another bag?' He opened the wardrobe and began laying things on the bed.' His presence had a calming effect, and Debbie remembered that there were things she needed to know, she might as well talk about them rather than have hysterics, which she was uneasily aware, were a hovering option.

'What happened last night?' she asked. 'Have we any contingency plans for today? What's happening?'

Tim had sat himself down on the foot of the bed, Roger folded Debbie's shirts and sweaters with competent ease and stacked them for her to pack.

'The village all rallied round, and found beds for everyone. The twat Rosemary and the family in No. 4 had lost everything but their pyjamas, and the others only had the clothes they were wearing, but at least they had their money and things.'

And their lives.

'How did the children take it?'

'I think they enjoyed all the excitement, actually, once they were safely outside.' Roger grinned at her. 'Everyone's OK, Deb, don't worry. We've arranged for everyone to take the day to sort themselves out, and we're all meeting in the Fish tonight to discuss what comes next. A lot of them will want to go home, of course, but they're all insured, so no problem there. Meantime, it's business as usual on the foreshore. We might as well make what cash we can while we can, and there's enough sightseers about, the ghouls! I got some of the others to help me put the boats on the end of the jetty when we'd moved the cars last night, they weren't hurt.'

Debbie admired his poise, but couldn't share it.

'Well, count me out until later, will you? I have to sort myself out, too. Apart from anything else, I'm filthy, and I smell like a garden bonfire.' Roger himself, and Tim, were both enviably clean, she noticed. 'There, that's it. The rest will have to travel the way it came, loose.' Roger picked up her suitcase and a big zipped bag, and Debbie gathered up her lifejacket and the picture and a few odds and ends.

'That all? We've got you a temporary room, with one of the Tregear tribe I'm afraid, but beggars can't be choosers.'

'No need to trouble them,' said Debbie, and was about to explain when Tim interrupted.

'She's moving into the Fish!' he said, speaking for the first time since Roger came onto the scene. He flung the tight ball of paper he was holding away from him, with force. Roger raised an eyebrow.

'Really? Well, I can't say I'm altogether surprised. Come on Tim – bring Debbie's coats and things.'

Loaded, they stepped outside the kitchen door, and there was Oliver coming swiftly towards them down the drive with his shambling step. Debbie dropped everything she held, took to her heels and ran towards him. He caught her and hugged her, and she hugged him back so tightly that he protested.

'Ouch, Deb, let me breathe!'

She had her face buried in his shirt. He smelled, not of bonfires, but of paint and turpentine and a clean scent of shower gel. She burrowed deeper into his arms.

'I see the Mounties have arrived,' observed Roger, appreciatively. He put down the two bags. 'Got a car with you, by any chance?'

'Just outside in the road. The boot's locked. Catch!' Oliver released an arm with difficulty, and tossed the keys of his car to Roger. 'Come on Deb, get your act together.'

'I'm just so glad to see you!' whispered Debbie, almost inaudibly, and began to cry.

She was still crying when Oliver loaded her into his car with her luggage and drove her down the hill to the Fish with Roger in the back

to help: Oliver didn't do serious luggage these days. She was still crying
when they went in through the rear door of the Fish, and Mrs Solomons
met them.

'Upstairs with you, and into that hot bath,' she ordered. 'I've put clean
towels. I'll bring you up a nice warm drink in twenty minutes time, and
I want to find you tucked up in bed.'

'This is my brother,' said Debbie, sniffing. 'And everything I've got
stinks of smoke!' She ended on a wail.

Mrs Solomons looked from Oliver to Debbie to Roger, and decided
that none of the three of them looked likely to be of much help. She took
the crisis into her capable hands.

'Leave it all down here, I'll put it through the machines,' she said. 'You'll
find Mr Angwin's bathrobe behind the bathroom door, put that on and
bundle up the things you're wearing and put them in the passage outside,
you don't want that smell hanging round up there! Take your brother with
you, then, I'll be up in a minute.'

'Capable lady,' commented Oliver, as Debbie took him upstairs. 'Who
is she?'

'Housekeeper,' said Debbie. She didn't feel up to explanations.

The flat had acquired a vase of flowers on the round table, and another,
smaller one, on the mantelpiece. The windows were set wide to the
sunshine and it smelled blessedly fresh and clean. Oliver looked round
him with interest.

'Whose is this then? No – don't tell me. Go and get that bath first, you
smell like a barbecue.'

'Don't go away. Please.'

'I'm not going to. Go on, do as you're told.'

Debbie did. The bath was heaven, she helped herself liberally to
Mawgan's shower-gel and shampoo – he didn't appear to be a bath person
– and then lay inspecting some interesting bruises with a rueful smile on
her face before climbing out, feeling considerably better, to wrap herself
in a towelling bathrobe that would have gone round her twice, emerging
back into the main room looking and feeling like a damp polar bear, to find
Oliver quietly reading the *Caterer & Hotelkeeper* in one of the armchairs.
Her picture, she noticed immediately, was hanging on one of the empty
hooks between the riverside windows. It looked a bit lost there. He looked
up as she appeared, and set the magazine aside.

'That looks better.'

'Smells better, too.' Debbie sat down in the other chair, curling her feet up. 'Sorry I was so wet, I despise myself! I feel much better now.'

'That's good. Do you feel up to telling me who is Mr Angwin whose bathrobe you're wearing, and why you're occupying what is presumably his flat?'

It was unlike Oliver to ask such pertinent questions. She realised that her going to pieces like that must have shaken him, and she sympathised. It had shaken her, too.

'Wait until Mrs Solomons has been back with her warm drink. Then I'll tell you.'

The knock on the door came right on cue, and Mrs Solomons came in with a tray. A savoury smell wafted in with her.

'Hot soup.' She set the tray down on the coffee table, pushing the stack of magazines aside to make room. 'And a nice sandwich to go with it. There's enough for the both of you. You get it down you while you talk to your brother, and then you get your head down for a couple of hours. You'll feel much better after that. There's coffee and milk and sugar in the kitchen if you want it.' She smiled at Oliver. 'You make sure she does as she's told, sir. I'll see to it there's some nice clean, dry clothes ready for when she wakes up.'

She left, and Oliver looked at his sister.

'At least I can tell Dad you're being properly looked after. Now tell me about Mr Angwin.'

'He's the landlord,' said Debbie.

'I gathered he might be. And? Go on, you can eat while you talk. Get it down you while it's still hot.'

'Don't you start,' said Debbie.

The soup was delicious and comforting. They drank it and ate the sandwiches, and afterwards, Oliver made coffee and brought it back to the table. During all this, Debbie talked. And talked. And talked. When she had finished, Oliver said, 'Bloody hell! What a mess.'

'I know. And I don't really know what there is to do to make it better.'

'You've set your heart on him, I take it?'

'Certainly have.'

He looked at her for a long moment, considering. 'Talk to Dad,' he said.

'A bit late for that, isn't it?' asked Debbie, with a touch of bitterness.

'Yes and no. You can't do anything about the fact that he went to prison, that's done. But it does sound as if he shouldn't have, if what he's told you is true. Are you certain it is?'

'Yes. His counsel wanted him to appeal, but the family wouldn't wear it. I think… I don't really know, it's just an impression I got. I think it was because of that unspoken implication about incest… Oliver, until he told me exactly what happened, I thought maybe she was a bit simple – Cressida – but by the time he'd finished, I had her down as a conniving little bitch.'

'She could be both,' said Oliver. He didn't like the sound of the little sister, she had all the hallmarks of a basket case. He wasn't happy about this whole thing, come to that, but it was Deb's life. He said, 'You do realise, both of you, that it's not too late?'

'Too late for what?'

'To appeal, dumbo! You can have the conviction squashed on appeal, even this late in the day, so long as you can provide grounds for it, and then at least he can be the licensee of his own premises.'

'Do you ever miss *anything*?' asked Debbie, surprised.

'Not when it concerns you, no. Who's Thomas Thomas?'

'He's the barman. The bar manager, I suppose.'

'And Mawgan Angwin?'

'Head chef. And Lord High Everything-else. He owns the place.'

'Actually owns it? Not just the manager?'

'Yes. He belonged to a syndicate that came up on the pools, can you believe it?'

'Lucky fellow.' He caught Debbie's eye. 'Then, anyway. And now.'

'Now?'

'Think about it,' Oliver advised. 'Now then, what do you want me to do? I shall have to ring Dad, he'll be waiting for the call. Given all the stories that have been creeping down the grapevine, he's going to ask questions. Do I tell him, mind his own business, or the truth?'

Debbie looked at him helplessly. 'I don't know. What do you think?'

'A very good question. Part of the truth?'

'They're going to have to know sometime, but would it come better from me?'

'I think I'd take less harm in the fall-out. But it's up to you.'

'Could we just… well, prevaricate, sort of, until you've met him?

Then I can use you as a back-up. At the moment you only know what I've told you.'

'That makes sense.' He got to his feet. 'Come on, you've been ordered a siesta. Go get it. I have to go, I've work to do.' He touched her cheek as she stood up too. 'Cheer up. It'll all come out in the wash. We're only a phone call away if you need us.'

Debbie went into the bedroom when he had gone, and stood for a moment, swamped by a feeling of complete unreality. The problems of moving in with someone who wasn't there came in all sizes, large and small. Which side of the bed? He had broken his collar-bone on the left, so perhaps she should sleep on his right, she would be less likely to knock seven bells out of him in the night. They could change round later if necessary. She found she was starting to laugh, and bit her lip, hard, to stop herself. Sleep. Sleep would make it all go away. She crashed onto the bed anyhow, and was asleep almost before she hit the duvet.

Oliver drove home with a great deal on his mind. Chel, seeing him drive back into the square, slipped out of the shop to have a quick word.

'Everything OK?' She knew at once that it was not. 'She's all right, isn't she?'

'She's landed in clover, at least for now. But...'

'The undesirable,' said Chel, immediately.

'Undesirable?' said Oliver. He laughed, not entirely with humour. 'He's not undesirable, Chel, he's incendiary! Just be ready to stand well back when the shit hits the fan, that's all.'

Chel cast a quick glance back at the shop. Lisa, the manageress, was dealing with the only customer they had just then, she waved to Chel cheerily. Chel turned back to Oliver.

'Tell me, but keep it short. I should get back.'

So he did, and she listened, and as she listened, it dawned on her, incredibly, that what she was hearing was the other side of Kate's tale of the quoit, and her blood ran unreasonably cold. Those horrible pictures... the sad, crazy little girl who had painted them... Well, she had known it was all coming her way, hadn't she, when Kate first told her the story? But not like this, not with Debbie so closely involved... and not only Debbie.

It made no sense, but she was suddenly visited with a terrible conviction that if the girl who painted those dreadful pictures ever realised that Debbie was Oliver's sister, she would be dead – and she had no more idea of *why* than she had of how she knew.

XX

Some hours later, rested, clean and generally feeling more like herself, Debbie stepped off the causeway to make her way along the foreshore to what used to be the sailing school. She still felt a little light-headed, an empty sort of feeling that she put down to not knowing what was coming next. She found Roger sitting on the jetty keeping an eye on two of the boats lying on the shingle, the other two being out on hire. He looked as unruffled as ever, enjoying the sunshine. A stiff breeze was blowing the smell of burned building away from the river, it was almost possible to believe that nothing had changed. Debbie climbed up beside him, and they sat there for some minutes without speaking. Then Roger said, 'Feeling better?'

'Yes thank you. God, what an exhibition! I am sorry you had to witness it.'

'Yes, well…' Roger looked at her, sideways. 'Ready for some more, or would you sooner leave it for a bit?'

That there was more, Debbie had woken well aware.

'You'd better tell me. Otherwise it'll only catch me out unawares.'

'That's very true.' He swung his legs for a minute, thinking. 'It was a pretty shitty day, all round.'

'And you don't even know the half of it,' said Debbie, feelingly.

He glanced at her sympathetically.

'Yes, well you were with Angwin, weren't you? Must have been a bit like handling high explosive after what happened… was it only the night before last? It seems like a year ago.'

'Call him Mawgan,' said Debbie. 'I'm sick of all this *Angwin* business, and he's as bad. He never calls Tim anything but Howells.'

'So long as he doesn't call me, Hickling.'

'He doesn't.' And he doesn't call me Deborah as of this morning, either. 'So what went on here, then?' she said.

'After you and Tim had finished slagging each other off in the dining room, the rest of us took our fingers out of our ears and went sailing. I don't think he expected you to disappear as thoroughly as you did.'

'He should have. He was the one who told me he didn't want to see me around.'

'Yes, we all heard.' He grinned at her. 'Poor old Deb. Didn't anyone ever warn you never to get involved in somebody else's domestic?'

Yes, somebody had. Too late.

'Short of climbing out of the window, I didn't have a choice.'

'Point taken. Anyway, the morning was OK, but when we came ashore, of course the Fish was closed for repairs, and there was nowhere for anyone to have lunch – well, apart from the Kosy Kaff and nobody fancied that. I think the smugglers on the wall get to them, and that's before they even try the pasties!'

'I've never been in the Kosy Kaff,' said Debbie.

'You haven't missed anything! So Tim – God, he must be brain-dead! After all the carry on we've had over peeling vegetables and things, Tim suggested that they all got some rolls and ham and stuff in the shop, and Lesley would make them sandwiches. Can you credit it? After the morning?'

'And did she?' asked Debbie, after a moment's respectful silence. Roger shook his head.

'No. She bawled him out pretty comprehensively, so we took everything over to the staff kitchen and did them there. Everyone had a wonderful time picnicking, but of course, Tim and I didn't get back to do the potatoes – that was my fault as much as his. We were having too good a time.'

'Poor Lesley,' said Debbie.

'It was her own fault. She was the one who wouldn't join in. She always is, Deb, there's no arguing with that.'

'I feel too battered to argue, but I want to place it on record that I don't wholly agree.'

'Arguing over it is a dead duck anyway. That song has been sung.' He glanced at the trees and shrubs that half-concealed the burnt-out house, and looked quickly back to the water. 'Bugger, isn't it, Deb?'

'So what happened between Tim and Lesley? Don't make a long story of it Roger, but I want to know.'

'They quarrelled again. Later in the afternoon.' He wasn't looking at her now, apparently scanning the river for their boats. 'He started worrying over where you'd gone, Deb. You know, saying you ought to be back by now, and he never meant you to take him so literally. And Lesley… well, I did tell you, didn't I? You chose not to believe me, but whether you knew it or not, you were one corner of an eternal triangle. She hates your guts, did you realise?'

'But I wasn't! I never made a play for Tim!'

'I know, you were too busy with Angw – sorry, with Mawgan. But I don't think she ever quite cottoned on to that, you know. You see,' he said, with deadly simplicity, 'she so seldom came down with us to the Fish. Even that major bust-up, the one that brought on that solicitor's letter, she thought was all down to Tim being jealous. And to be absolutely fair, it was.'

'She's got to be barking, if she thinks that I –'

'She felt left out,' said Roger. 'All that women's work that you refused to do, and then you went off with her husband. Think about it, Deb, and don't be too swift to condemn.'

'It's unjust of her. It's what I was here for – the sailing.'

'I totally agree, but whoever said that people always had to be just?'

'So what you're saying,' said Debbie, 'is that they had a major row over me?' That certainly explained Lesley's outburst this morning.

'That's about the size of it. And Lesley stormed off leaving the dinner all over the kitchen in its raw state, and Tim said, right, we'll all go and have fish and chips in Helston, and leave her to it. We all went, even that nice little family, made a bit of an outing of it, the kids loved it. He said Les had a migraine, they were all very sorry for her. Most of us stayed on to drink one last Spingo, but the family came back, of course, to get the kids to bed, and Rosemary left just before the rest of us, too, she went on her own and she wasn't having that much of a good time. Tim went back with her. He said he was worried about Les, but I think it was probably you.' He paused. 'The rest of us got back just after the fire alarm went off.'

'What I can't work out,' said Debbie, 'is why Lesley was in the bath at… well it must have been knocking on midnight. I mean, at that time of night, why didn't she simply have a shower back at our own place?'

'That I don't know,' said Roger, but so carefully that Debbie looked at him suspiciously.

'All right, you don't know. But what do you *think*?'

'I *think* she did it on purpose,' said Roger. 'Oh, she didn't know the house was going to go up in flames, of course she didn't. But she *did* know

Tim hadn't mended that lock, and I think she meant to make a great big scene when everyone got back, and make him look a klutz for a change. But that's only an opinion.'

'If you're right, she certainly chose the wrong night.' said Debbie, on a sigh. 'No wonder she wouldn't speak to me this morning. Do you reckon they'll get over it?'

'No,' said Roger, quietly. 'I reckon this is the end of the line for them. For one reason, and one reason only.'

'Yeah,' said Debbie. 'He really thinks he does love me. Oliver always said he was a plonker.'

'For what it's worth, I think he probably does,' said Roger, apologetically. 'I'd go further. I think he always has. And I think she's always known it. But it's not your fault, don't lose sleep over it.'

'I feel awful.'

'Don't,' he repeated. 'You didn't encourage him, I'm a witness to that. And you gave her no real cause for jealousy, and I'm a witness to that, too.'

'Thank you,' said Debbie. He reached across and squeezed her hand.

'Cheer up. Is An – Mawgan going to make an honest woman of you, Deb Nankervis? Or shouldn't I ask.'

'It isn't official. Our families have no idea – except for Oliver. But I did tell Tim, to shut him up as much as anything, so I suppose I can tell you, too. But don't spread it around.'

'So, who do you think you'll be surprising?' asked Roger, smiling at her. 'They've been laying bets down at the Fish – not on *if* so much as *when*. You never answered me when I asked if he was OK, by the way. I chose the wrong moment, I rather think.'

'Yes, he's OK, probably. He'll be back before you know it.'

'This may sound unduly cynical,' said Roger, 'but if he could spin it out a little, it might be not be such a bad thing.'

'Whatever do you mean?'

'Just that his stock is soaring in the village today. I thought you might be interested to know.'

Debbie thought about it. 'That *is* unduly cynical.'

'Well, yes and no. At the risk of sounding as if I'm talking psychobabble, I think the village's attitude to Angwin – sorry – has always been dictated by *Mawgan* himself.'

Debbie remembered what Mrs Tregear had said to her. She nodded slowly.

'Yes, I think you may be right. Aren't people hard on themselves?'

'And at the risk of talking *more* psychobabble, aren't people under stress always? Isn't that part of it?'

Debbie looked at her watch. It was getting on for six, she saw, and interesting though this talk was turning out to be, she had other priorities.

'Has anyone found my car yet? I'm going to Truro to visit him and take him a whole list of things they gave me, before I join you at the Fish tonight, and I should be on my way.'

'Oh yes, I meant to say. You'll find it in the car park at the Fish now. I left the keys with the girl in reception.'

Debbie scrambled to her feet.

'It's been an interesting chat, but I must dash. Tell Tim I'll be there eventually, will you?'

'I'll tell him. And as for the chat, you're welcome. I just hope it helped.'

Had it helped? Debbie asked herself, as she drove through the lanes on her way to Helston to pick up the main road. It had left her with a lot to think about, but she had had that already. She wondered if it would be any use if she tried to talk to Lesley, but abandoned the idea thankfully. Lesley wouldn't listen yet, even if she might later, and it would only make things worse. Roger had absolved her of direct blame, and she was sensible enough to know that he was right, but she knew too that she was as much responsible for the breaking up of her friends' marriage as Mawgan was for the death of Michael Stanley. Had she not been there, it wouldn't have happened. Not then, anyway, or in that particular way. She knew now exactly how he must feel.

He was looking a lot better this evening, she was glad to see, able to sit up and take notice and although still pale, with a more normal pallor. He returned her kiss, this time, as if he meant it.

'You're looking better,' she said.

'You too. This morning you both looked like refugees.'

'Ouch!' said Debbie. 'That bad, was it? Hang on a minute, I'll get a chair.'

When she was settled, he gave her a curious look.

'Dad came in this afternoon. What'd you said to 'im, Deb?'

Debbie cast her mind back.

'Not a lot. I told him what had happened. Why, was he cross?' He had sounded it, certainly. 'I only spoke to him for a minute. I think he must have been driving along.'

'Sounds about par for the course, he'll get done for it one of these days. No… he wasn't cross. It just surprised me he came at all. He said he was checking out a job, but he's never worked this far down even from St Austell. I just wondered.' He almost shrugged his shoulders, and stopped himself in time. Debbie saw the beginning of the movement, and their eyes met on a rueful laugh. 'No,' he said. 'Bad idea.'

'Everyone's been asking after you, and sending kind messages,' said Debbie.

There was a brief silence, during which she tried to read his expression, and failed.

'They looking after you properly?' he asked, after a while.

'Wonderfully. Your housekeeper is a star. She gave us lunch, and treated me like a favourite daughter.'

'Yeah, well…' said Mawgan. He looked moody for a moment, and then added, 'Us?'

'Me and Oliver. I think he had been sent flying to the rescue by Mum and Dad, actually, but I was never so pleased to see anyone.' She wondered if this was the time to tell him what Oliver had said, and decided that it probably wasn't.

'You tell him about me?' asked Mawgan, directly.

'Well, yes. I had to explain how I came to be occupying your space, for one thing. And before you ask, Oliver isn't a person who sits in judgement. He just said he'd like to meet you.'

'That'll be something for us all to look forward to.'

'Don't be like that.' When he said nothing, she cast about for something else to talk about, and remembered Roger's parting message. 'Roger says your stock is soaring in the village, loads of sympathy everywhere. You've never been so popular, you may be surprised to know.'

Mawgan had been sliding into depression, but his irreverent sense of humour caught him out. He gave a snort of laughter, winced and put his free hand to his damaged collar-bone, protectively.

'Oh Deb, please! Don't make me laugh, it hurts. That's a really useful gem of information.'

'Useful…?' asked Debbie cautiously, not trusting him.

'Yes. It solves a big problem – every time I slip in the charts, you can throw me down the stairs.'

Debbie giggled.

'I don't think that's exactly what he meant, but it's an interesting idea.'

Mawgan sobered abruptly. 'So how are things back there? Did any of the house survive?'

'No. It's nothing but a steaming ruin,' said Debbie.

'Poor Howells.' He sounded as if he really meant it. 'What will he do?'

'I don't know. We're meeting later tonight to talk about it. But I think that's got to be it. Only the boathouse and the boats survived, I can't see they'll have the heart to start again just with that, in spite of what you said. They don't have your sort of pragmatism. And I think that Les will want to take the insurance money and run anyway. Tim's finished.'

'Bugger. Well, he won't want my sympathy, but he's got it anyway.'

'At least nobody was killed.' She hesitated. 'I don't suppose you know this, but he saved your life. He came back – I'd never have got you out without him. It was a frighteningly near thing as it was.'

'So that's why my skin feels scorched.' He closed his eyes, she thought he looked suddenly tired. 'I am having a year of it, aren't I? First you, then him… why do you bother?'

'God knows,' said Debbie, sharply. 'Obviously not for your gratitude.' She paused. 'Sorry.'

He reached for her hand, still with his eyes closed.

'Me too. Sorry bird, I'm not at my best tonight.'

'Understandable.'

'Mmm.' Pause. 'Deb…' He had opened his eyes and was looking at her, almost, she thought unexpectedly, as if he was afraid. 'Yesterday afternoon…'

'Don't worry about it,' said Debbie, swiftly. 'Please, we've already talked about it. It's all right.'

'No, it's not. Deb, I don't want you to think me a pig-ignorant Cornish oaf. I don't know what come over me, I aren't usually like that, I promise. I don't see how as I can ever apologise enough.'

'You don't need to apologise at all. I understood.' Better than you do, I'm beginning to think, but she didn't say that. Mawgan looked troubled.

'But I do. And it's going to be weeks before I can make it up to you properly. Oh, *sod* everything!'

'Mawgan. Please, believe me. It's not important.'

'I hurt you.'

'No you didn't.' That was a lie, but she said it anyway. 'Surprised me, maybe. And I'm in your flat, aren't I? Waiting for you?'

'You're some brave woman, then. I don't deserve you.' He had closed his eyes again, hiding his thoughts from her. She could only hope that she had got through to him. 'I can't even think straight…'

'I'll go soon, leave you in peace. I must anyway, Tim will want me there, but I wanted just to see you.'

He opened his eyes again to give her the ghost of a smile.

'You'll know better next time. Deb, I love you. Don't never go away.'

'I won't.'

She thought that he had fallen asleep, and got quietly to her feet to leave, but when she stooped to kiss him gently, he reached up and caught her.

'No you don't, sneaking off like that. Say goodbye properly.'

The kiss, instead of being swift and gentle, lingered pleasantly. Then he placed his forefinger on the end of her nose and said,

'Sleep well in my bed, Deb, keep it warm. I'll be back soon.'

She walked back up the ward in a pleasant daze. Halfway to the door, she passed a woman coming the other way, who gave her a mischievous smile as she went by. Debbie smiled back because she was in a mood to smile at all the world, and it wasn't until she was way down the corridor that led to the door out into the main hospital that a message that had been trying to get through to her brain finally made it to base. She stopped.

She knew that smile. She knew it very well indeed.

She also knew the sturdy build, the round bullet head, the hazel eyes that had sparkled with fun and the fine, straight, dark hair.

Allison? She hesitated, but the small six-bed room where Mawgan was lay round a corner, out of sight. Almost, she turned back, but the claims of her friend and employer, and a feeling that it was fairer to let Mawgan choose his own time and place, sent her on her way.

Mawgan, lying there nursing a splitting headache with his eyes shut, felt the movement of the bed as his sister sat down and opened his eyes with a groan.

'Oh, it's you. What are you doing here?'

'Well, well, well,' said Anna. 'You kept that very dark, little brother!'

'Kept what?'

'Oh, come on! When she walked past me, after that touching leave-taking, she was on a different planet!' She looked at him more closely. 'And you seem to have come back from yours. Who is she? What's her name?'

'Debbie Nankervis,' said Mawgan, seeing no help for it.

'That's a good start. Good name. Who is she?'

'Oh, shut up, Anna, don't you ever give up? She's a sailing instructor.'

'What, at that place that burned down? Is that how you met her?'

'No, as it happens.'

'Where, then?'

'I met her on the moor back in February, if you must know. Anna, I've got a headache, can't you shut up for a second?'

Anna thought. Two and two clicked together to make four.

'Is she the one...? Yes, I can see she is. I love her already!'

'Good, because so do I. If you won't go away, would you like to keep your voice down, please?'

Anna slid off the edge of the bed, and into the chair vacated by Debbie.

'Does anyone else know? In the family, I mean.'

'No. And don't you go telling 'em.'

'I wouldn't dream of it, but I presume you're going to let us in on it one day? If only to invite us to the wedding. There's going to be a wedding, I take it?'

No reply. She watched him pensively for a few minutes. After a while, with his eyes still closed, he said, 'What *are* you doing here, anyway? Aren't you meant to be herding goats up in the Alps, or something?'

'I came over for a holiday.'

'What, all of you? Is Kurt here too, and the brats?'

'Kurt's in Japan, and the brats, as you call them, are up in the mountains with his mother and father. So I just thought I'd come...'

He opened his best eye and squinted at her. She returned the look blandly.

'Oh, really? You just thought you'd come.' The words were heavy with disbelief. Anna said, serious now, 'Are you really fit for this, Mawgan darling? I can come back tomorrow.'

'What, all the way from Launceston? What devotion.'

'Don't try and be sarky, you aren't good at it. And I'm staying with Nan and Grandad.'

'You better tell me,' he said, after a pause for thought. 'What's happened now?' He sounded tired.

'No, it isn't fair. Tomorrow will do.'

'Look, Anna, do you want me to sleep tonight, or lie awake worrying? Spit it out, will you? Tell me the worst!'

'There's not really anything to tell, nothing that you can get your teeth into, that is.' He was watching her properly now, she saw. 'I had this funny letter from Allison.'

'Funny, how?'

'Well, you know Allison, she's always bossing us all around and in charge of everything… but she didn't sound as if she was, any more. She said… she said that Mum and Dad were miserable, being pushed apart by being made to choose all the time between you and Cress, and not necessarily wanting to make the obvious choices, and that Dad is getting really ratty with all the travelling, and Mum hates the house in Launceston and wants to go home. And that she thought Cress was losing the plot completely, and you were only a step or two behind her – and she sounded really pissed off with her job.'

'Nothing new there, then.' He spoke dismissively, and Anna sighed.

'No, I see what you mean. She went to be cabin crew to see the world, and all she's seen is the insides of a lot of aircraft cabins and a lot of airports, mainly exactly the same, she's said so, often. But she has seen the world, too. Well, bits of it anyway. On stopovers and discount holidays and things, she's never sounded so really discontented before.'

'I was talking about all of it. Nothing new anywhere. We've had it all before.'

'But not from Allison,' said Anna. 'She's always been the one to hold us all together.'

'Allison's problem is that what she really wants is out of her reach,' said Mawgan. 'Being cabin crew is a displacement activity, you know that.'

'She should have been a boy,' said Anna.

'Nothing to be done about that. Nothing to be done about any of it that I can see.'

'We-ell.' Anna smiled. 'I think we can stop worrying about you quite so much, you seem to have worked out your own salvation, even if you did break yourself in bits to do it. Is it very painful, poor little brother?'

'Don't try it yourself, that's my advice.' He turned his head carefully, so that he was looking out of the window and not at her. 'Anna, it's Cress's fault. She's the one who's stirring things up all the time. She's the one you want to be chasing, not me. All I want is to get on with my life.'

'I'm not chasing you.' she retorted, indignantly. 'I was sent. Nan wouldn't rest, worrying about you, and you know that's bad for her.'

'Bloody Cress,' said Mawgan, and bit his lip.

'I know, but if she's behaving like a spoilt brat, who made her into one in the first place? We're all to blame.'

Mawgan spoke hesitantly. 'Did you ever wonder if there might be more to it?'

Anna stared.

'What do you mean?'

'I'm not sure… something Deb said when I told her – '

'You *told* her?' interrupted Anna, in amazement. '*You* told her? We all thought you'd shut up like the proverbial clam, and were never going to speak again!'

'Oh, come on. It wasn't that bad.'

'Oh yes, it was. Worse. So what did she say?'

'I can't remember exactly how she put it, but it made me think… this is an awfully hard thing to say, Anna.'

Anna took pity on him. 'That perhaps she wasn't really in the real world? Watched too many soaps? Lost the plot completely? A compulsive liar that doesn't know the truth if it hits her in the eye? Allison and I have been wondering all those things ever since it all happened, so that's not new, either – and if you want to know, so did Mike, long before. But how can we say it to Mum and Dad? We can't, is the short answer to that.'

'There's something else,' said Mawgan, slowly. 'A few weeks ago it were, some woman come to the pub, asking for me. She was worried about Cress, she said, she'd seen her or something, and she thought that Cress was ill. I sent her off to the Blue Crab to check it out for herself, and I said I'd tell Allison what she said.'

'And did you?'

'No. I haven't spoken to her since.'

'Pity, but I don't suppose it would have made any difference. What brought her to you, anyway? I would have thought you'd be the very last person in the world.'

'I think I was the only one of us she could track down. And looking back, I think that's a measure of how fussed she was.'

'Who was she?' asked Anna, frowning. 'Did she say?'

'I think she said she was Kate.'

'Nothing else?'

'No. But I thought she was keeping something back. And I've thought since, I should have made her tell me what it was.'

'What sort of a something?' Anna asked, after a pause.

'How do I know? I let it pass. I froze her out deliberate, if you must know, and now I wish I hadn't.'

'We can find her,' said Anna. 'Maybe Cress has mentioned her at home, if she knows her. I'll get onto it. Don't worry. Look, you've gone the colour of a dirty dishcloth, I'd better go before some nurse attacks me.' She got to her feet. 'I should have kept my big mouth shut. Give my love to Debbie, won't you? What a babe, you lucky man! And I mean it – don't worry. Leave it all to big sister, that's why I'm here.'

She half-expected to find that beautiful blonde girl waiting for her outside the doors, but she didn't. Maybe she hadn't made the connection. Pity, but there was time yet. Anna got into her grandfather's car and set off back to St. Austell. Like many other people who had become, knowingly or unknowingly, embroiled in Cress's affairs, she had a lot to think about.

The Fish was fully operational tonight, both bars back in business and the restaurant full. The incident on Sunday night didn't seem to have noticeably discouraged anybody, in fact, Debbie thought as she went into the lounge bar, there seemed more locals, particularly, in the place than she had ever seen there before. She was stopped three times before she had crossed the floor to join her friends, and each time was loaded with more good wishes to carry back to Mawgan when she saw him. A party of men propping up the bar lifted their glasses to her as she passed, and raised a cheer that made all the summer visitors turn to look at her. She slid into a seat between Roger and Sally, blushing as red as a rose.

'Well, hello,' said Roger, grinning at her. 'Nothing like making an entrance!'

'Shut up!' muttered Debbie. 'What's the matter with them all?'

'Come on, Deb! Hauling Angwin out of a burning building, and then moving publicly into the Fish! What do you expect?'

Tommy came over to their table and placed a full glass in front of her.

'On the house,' he said. 'You try 'n' pay for a drink this evening, and you're banned, maid!' He smiled at her and moved away. Debbie put her hands to her cheeks, feeling her skin burning.

'I thought we'd agreed to drop the Angwin bit,' she said.

'Old habits die hard. I am trying, honest, but *Mawgan* feels like somebody else.'

'Where's Tim?' asked Debbie, belatedly noticing his absence.

'The police wanted a word. He'll be in later. They've finished going through the ashes, so maybe we're going to learn how it started.'

'So we still don't know what's happening.' She looked around the circle. About half the Seagulls guests were there, including the parents of the two children but not the children themselves. Their mother caught her eye and smiled.

'We ended up last night in a house with a couple of children the same age. They all palled up, and now they want to stay. We thought, why not? Our hosts are quite happy to have us, and we've had a bit of a shopping expedition for clothes, and all the essential teddies were saved. We didn't lose the car or anything really valuable. It's probably better for the children not to make a big deal of it and rush off home, we thought.'

Sally laughed. 'They're about the only ones who aren't totally traumatised! Every time I think about last night, I start shaking like a leaf.'

'Know the feeling,' said Debbie.

'Some people have gone home,' said Roger. 'These you see here are the hardy ones, who don't see why their holiday should be spoiled – spoiled any more than it is already, I mean. The village has rallied round a treat, and let's face it, after all that, they *need* a holiday!'

'We came here to learn to sail, most of us,' said Sally's boyfriend. 'We'd still like to do that. The river's still there, if you and Tim and Roger are up for it.'

'I'm up for it,' said Debbie. 'Roger?'

'We'll need to talk with Tim, but in principle, yes, I'm up for it too. All other things being equal.'

Sally yawned, and looked at her watch.

'I don't know about the rest of you, but I'm shattered. I think I'll just crawl away *chez* Tregear and turn in, if you don't mind? We can sort out what we're doing when you two have had a chance to discuss it with Tim and Lesley.'

A murmur of agreement went round the circle. The father of the family said, 'It doesn't really concern us, we didn't book for sailing, but if you're still in business I think the kids might like a few lessons, if you teach them that young. Give them something new to think about.'

There was still no sign of Tim, so Roger said, 'Right. Shall we all meet outside here at eleven-ish, have a cup of coffee, see what we've come up with? Everyone agreed?'

They had all gone. Roger looked at Debbie, and said quietly, 'Deb.'

'What?'

'If Tim decides to pack it in, what will you do?'

'What will *I* do?'

'If you're going to marry Angwin-sorry-Mawgan, you're either going to have to take up catering, which God forbid, after this little lot, or do something else. You're not going to be living in his pocket, be real.'

Debbie sat very still. A spark lit in her mind, flickered, died, but only to a glow.

'What are you saying?'

Roger said, 'If you should have any… ideas, shall we say, remember me.'

She looked up then, and met his eyes, blue and steady. He was smiling at her.

'Don't say anything now. Just if… and when. OK?'

'OK,' said Debbie, and then Tim came in and everything changed.

Debbie had thought he looked dreadful this morning, now he looked ten times worse. He sat down with them, and his hands were shaking so much that he hid them under the table. Roger got up.

'Don't say a word,' he said. 'Stiff drink coming up. I'll be back.'

The glass rattled against Tim's teeth, he could hardly drink. He put it down on the table again, and the liquid jumped around as he did so. He took a breath.

Roger had slid back into his seat. 'So, tell us,' he said. 'What's happened?'

'You remember last night? After you'd gone off in the ambulance, Debbie, and when the fire was under control, everyone was talking – Roger will r-r-remem-mem – oh sh-shit!'

'Take it steady,' said Roger. 'Yes, I remember.' He turned to Debbie. 'When he says everyone, he means the firemen, the police, the guests and – oh, everyone. Yak, yak, yak. How did we think it started, who was the last person in the lounge, all the things you'd expect.'

'And who was?' asked Debbie.

'Nobody really knew. Some of them seemed to think it was Rosemary, but she said she went straight to bed when she came back, and never went into the lounge at all.'

Tim had found his voice.

'We thought it might have been a dropped cigarette end, smouldering away down a chair or something, and Rosemary is one of the very few that still smokes, although it shouldn't have been in the house – Lesley had been in too much of a temper to check round like she usually does – did –'

'And you and Roger?' interrupted Debbie. He flushed.

'Well, yes, I could have done it, if you put it like that, and if I'd known she hadn't. But anyway, the head fireman, or whatever they call him, said no. If that had happened there would have been a lot of smoke, and the smoke detector would have gone off long before the fire got to that stage. We didn't know what to think, because the same goes for an electrical fire, really. But they've been picking over the wreckage all day, and now they're saying… they're saying…' He broke off, rubbing the palms of his hands across his eyes. 'You're not going to believe this, either of you. They're saying it was a petrol fire.'

'But that's impossible!' said Debbie.

'I know, but they can tell these things, God knows how – something about how things burn, and in what direction, I don't know, it's not my field. They told me at the police station, and asked all sorts of other questions… they said we were lucky Lesley's aunt had such good furniture, because if it had been modern foam stuff, Lesley would very likely have died from the fumes before we could get her out – in fact, we wouldn't have got *in*… and he asked why the bathroom door had stuck. And there was a CID man who kept asking what time we all got back, and if anyone had a grudge against us, and about money and everything, and I could see him thinking… and if it turns out to be arson – how *can* it be arson?' He ended on an anguished cry that turned heads in other parts of the bar.

'Hush, keep your voice down.' Debbie said. Foremost in her thoughts was a deep thankfulness that she had been with Mawgan for the entire day and could give him a comprehensive alibi, and immediately on its heels followed a deep pity for Tim. It seemed a completely wrong moment to talk about people's holidays, but Tim went on, despair in his voice, 'And if you think that's enough for one night, try this. All our records went up in the fire, and we have absolutely no idea of who has booked with us, or when they're coming, or where to find them, and the only person who might remember anything at all is Lesley, and she won't speak to any of us!'

Roger put the glass back into his hand.

'Drink,' he ordered. He turned to Debbie. Arson was beyond even thinking about, this second problem at least had the virtue of being accessible. 'What do you think? Sleep on it? We can't do anything tonight anyway. We might have had some ideas by then, if we think about it. I suppose the police will be round our ears before we've finished breakfast, but it doesn't stop us trying to be constructive.'

Debbie thought that there was nothing to be constructive *with*, so where was the point? but Tim had collapsed onto the table. She said the only useful thing that came into her head.

'We'll have to stick around, that's all, ready to do what we can.'

'There won't be any money,' said Roger. 'That won't matter to you, you've got Angwi – sorry, I've said it again. You've got Mawgan behind you, but I can't live on nothing. I'd like to be heroic about it, but a man must be able to eat and run his car.'

'Don't worry,' said Debbie, coming to a sudden decision. Was she mad? Hopefully not. 'That'll be all right. You'll be paid, I guarantee it. And there will be some money from the boats anyway, and the lessons when people want them.'

'No premises though, where will everyone sleep? And the bank will take any money that's going, you can bet your boots.'

'I said, I'll guarantee it. We've got the boathouse, and the boats, and all the sailing school equipment. After the bank holiday, there'll be accommodation available in the area. We'll just have to phone around and do the best we can. And we've got the mobile phones, yours and mine. We'll just have to wing it.'

'*You* can't pay me,' said Roger.

'Yes I can. I owe it to Tim to at least do that much.' She reached out and patted Tim's shoulder. He hadn't even been listening. 'Come on Tim, they've called time, it's time to go.'

'What an exit line!' said Roger, but even he couldn't conjure the vestige of a smile as he spoke.

XXI

Morning came and, as Roger had predicted, brought the police. They were both in and out of uniform, very polite, and almost everywhere. Debbie, breakfasting on fruit juice, muesli and scrambled eggs brought to her by My Daughter, was caught before she left the flat by a burly plain-clothes sergeant, and minutely questioned about the events of Monday, what she had done, whom she had been with, when she had got back. She gave a necessarily edited but essentially accurate account of her day, right up to the time that she and Mawgan had run out of the kitchen, leaving, she now realised, evidence of their presence there on the table, and gone up the hill. He took equally careful notes, and when she had reached the blazing house in her narrative, laid his notebook and pencil down on the table.

'That seems very clear, Miss Nankervis, and if Mr. Angwin confirms what you say, it seems we can cross you both off our list of suspects.'

'You could ask the kitchen staff, too,' she said. 'We left in such a hurry, we didn't clear anything away.' He smiled at her, and she thought that perhaps he had already questioned them. About Mawgan's activities that day? Everyone in the village knew there was bad feeling between him and Tim. And there was the criminal record, too, which wouldn't help. But apparently nothing was further from the sergeant's mind than this.

'Miss Nankervis, while you were working at Seagulls, did you ever hear or see anything that might have led you to think that Mr and Mrs Howells were in financial difficulties?'

'The first year of running a business is always a hard one,' said Debbie. She sipped her coffee, thinking that being grilled by the police was a great deal more uncomfortable, even for the innocent, than most people would believe.

'And you never heard a suggestion, even in fun, that it might be better to burn the place down and collect on the insurance?'

Debbie said, carefully, 'That's a very direct question.'

'Just answer it, Miss Nankervis.'

To say that Debbie was shocked would be to put it mildly. She felt cornered, unsure how to answer. For of course, as she immediately remembered, there had been such a suggestion, she had made it herself. And Tim had asked that silly question about Molotov cocktails of Roger, and at that point, all four of them had been there, although she thought Roger perhaps hadn't heard her contribution. Her hesitation must have spoken volumes, for the sergeant raised a quizzical eyebrow.

'Miss Nankervis?'

If she told the truth, it would sound dreadful. If she told a lie, and Lesley told the truth – as she well might – or even Roger, it would look even worse. She had already hesitated for too long.

'It was a joke,' she said. 'I said it myself. We were all feeling a bit gloomy, and I said it to make us laugh… we *did* laugh.'

He had picked up his pencil again and made a note before he laid it down.

'Mr Howells made no such remark?'

'He made a joke too,' said Debbie.

'Oh yes?'

'He asked Roger – that's Roger Hickling – if he knew how to make a Molotov cocktail. But it was a *joke.*'

'Yes, very funny, I'm sure. He didn't make any remark about, for instance, *an arson job for the insurance?*'

'People say things like that. All the time, they say them. They're…' she stopped.

'Yes, I understand. They're jokes. You know some people with a very black sense of humour, Miss Nankervis.' He looked at her, and she looked back at him. All appetite for breakfast had deserted her.

'About the bathroom door?' he said.

'Oh, that!' She felt on firmer ground here. 'Yes, it kept sticking. We thought perhaps it had the wrong key. Kids, you know? Playing around?'

'Mr. Howells knew this?'

'He was going to see to it.' She heard her own voice, defensive, and winced.

'Mrs Howells says that she asked him to do so, several times. Can you confirm this?'

'I suppose so… once or twice, anyway.'

'But he didn't?'

'He hadn't when the fire broke out – but you can't possibly suppose – oh come on, sergeant!' She was suddenly indignant. 'It didn't *always* stick. And quite often, when it did, you could jiggle it around – nobody could *rely* on it sticking. And anyway, Tim wouldn't! How could he even know she'd have a bath that night, anyway? If Lesley said anything of the kind, it's pure spite!'

He looked at her, and spoke gently. 'Miss Nankervis, aren't you getting a bit ahead of the game here? Nobody has said that Mr Howells did anything at all. We're simply asking questions in order to get at the truth.'

'Sorry,' Debbie felt impelled to say.

'Now. How would you describe your relationship with Mr Howells?'

'Friends,' said Debbie, immediately.

'Just friends? No romantic undertones? Overtones? Pure friendship?'

'Anyone in St. Erbyn will tell you that I've been going out all summer with Mawgan Angwin, who owns this pub. We're going to be married. Does that answer your question adequately, or would you like me to call witnesses?'

'Don't get angry, Miss Nankervis, nobody is accusing you of anything. Mr Howells, how did he regard this friendship of yours, do you think?'

'I can't answer that. You'll have to ask him.'

He appeared to accept this. He rose to his feet, closing his notebook. She would be required to sign a statement, he said, and the police would be obliged if she didn't leave St. Erbyn for the moment. Then he smiled at her, unexpectedly. 'But I imagine you aren't planning to,' he said, and Debbie said shortly that no, she wasn't.

When he had gone, she sat still for a few minutes, wondering if she should telephone her father and ask for his advice, but the reflection that it seemed to be Tim's business rather than hers that had attracted the attention of the police made her decide against it. She and Mawgan had to be in the clear, surely, and with the whole situation so delicately balanced, it might be a mistake to rush in. Instead, she gathered her breakfast things back onto their tray, and wondered what she should do with it. She had never lived anywhere before that had a full complement of cooks, housekeepers, waiters and assorted others, and had no idea how she was expected to behave. She had a feeling that they had no idea either, and that the sooner Mawgan came back to clarify the situation, the happier everyone was going to be. In the end, she left the tray where it was and went in search of Roger.

Once again, she found him on the jetty, where the four Wayfarers were still moored to the far end. He waved when he saw her, and called, 'I thought I'd take these round the point and haul them up by the causeway. Nobody wants to be reminded of this lot.' He gestured towards the sad remains of the house. 'Now you're here, you can give me a hand.'

Debbie joined him, and together they fastened the four boats in a string behind the safety boat, a small rigid inflatable with an outboard, before towing them round to the foreshore by the Fish. The everyday activity was soothing, and Debbie began to feel a little calmer.

'We can stick them back on the jetty tonight, or pull them up on our own foreshore,' Roger said, giving her a hand as she jumped ashore. 'Grab hold then – *heave!*'

But it didn't take that long to haul the four boats up the shingle and lay out the anchors, and they sat on the edge of the causeway with nothing further to do all too soon. Roger spoke first, only after a long silence.

'I take it, the police have given you their third degree, too?'

'Yes. They seem to want to pin it on Tim. Poor Tim.'

'Do you think he would?'

'No. Not with people in the house, children, too. Not at all, come to that.'

'I got a distinct impression that Lesley was in the background, gunning for him. You?'

Debbie nodded, without speaking.

'Spiteful little cow!' said Roger.

After while, Debbie said, 'Do you remember that day Tim made that silly joke about burning the place down?'

'Yes. I had to tell them, Deb. Lesley obviously already had, it would have looked worse…'

'I know. Me too. But it was a *joke!*'

'Somebody did it,' said Roger. 'I don't think there's any doubt about that. And they weren't joking.'

Just for a second, Debbie thought fleetingly of the person who had written her anonymous letters – not Lesley, surely, if she hadn't realised about Mawgan. She hadn't said anything about them, to the police or to anyone else, but it wasn't her sailing school, so *why…?* Anyway, they seemed to have become lost in her move, which was probably the best fate for them. She dismissed them from her mind, and said, quietly, 'Who would do a thing like that? It would take such a lot of hate – '

'Or desperation,' said Roger.

'If there's even a suspicion that Tim or Lesley had a hand in it, the insurance company won't pay out.'

'No. But people before this have taken that risk. Got away with it, too, some of them.'

'You don't *believe…?*'

'Honestly Deb, I don't know what I believe. What I *know* is that this whole thing is a dead duck, and if we stay around, we'll be presiding at a wake.'

'What's the time?'

Roger glanced at his watch.

'Quarter to eleven. We'd better go and sit on the forecourt.' He got to his feet and extended a hand to help her up. 'Did you mean what you said – about seeing I got paid?'

'I wouldn't have said it if I hadn't.'

'I really hate to say yes, but if I'm to stay… you do see, don't you?'

'Roger, don't worry about it. I'll call in the favour one day, maybe.'

For the second time, the flicker of an idea in her own head was reflected on Roger's face. It felt like betrayal, but it was exciting too, and this time, the flicker died to a little more than a glow.

Tim joined them on the forecourt, silent and withdrawn, very pale. The insurance assessor had arrived, he said. He had to go up to the house later, could they manage?

'We'll work it so that we do,' said Debbie. 'Don't worry, Tim.' Stupid remark. He said, in a monotone that sounded unlike him, 'We must put notices in the magazines. The ones we advertised in. The bank has frozen the business account.'

'All right,' said Debbie. 'I'll see to it.'

'I may never be able to pay you back.' He groaned, and rubbed his forehead. 'What a mess, what a bloody mess!'

'Don't worry about it. It won't cost much, anyway.'

'It won't reach the people who booked with Lesley's aunt last year.'

'We'll play them by ear.'

Tim looked up and she saw the desperation in his face.

'Deb... I hate to ask, but I suppose you couldn't...?'

'And I'd hate to say no, so please don't ask me,' said Debbie, but she said it gently. 'I'll help to keep the thing running until we reach the end of the season, Tim, it isn't more than a few weeks, I can do that much. But I can't bail you out. I'm sorry.' She touched his hand. 'Come on, the worst hasn't happened yet.' She thought that he was going to cry. Roger had gone off, tactfully, in search of coffee. 'Tim —' she said.

'Lesley's going home, you know,' he said, and his voice had hardened although the tears still stood in his eyes. 'Her father's coming down for her today; he'll take her straight from the hospital. She says I tried to kill her.'

'What, with the bathroom door? Even the police won't swallow that one!'

He looked at her, apparently unaware that the tears had escaped and were sliding down his face.

'Who did it, Deb? Who'd do a thing like that?'

But she had no more answer for his question than Roger had for her when she asked it.

The problems were really stacking up now, Debbie thought, almost ashamed that her own troubles, minor by comparison, should take precedence in her thoughts over Tim's. If Lesley was going home, a great deal of news and gossip would be going with her. How long would it take to filter through to her own parents? The answer to that was, probably not very long, Lesley would see to that. Whatever form the information took, it wouldn't be good news. She wondered if Lesley had caught on to the real truth yet. Part of her didn't want to know, the other part knew that she needed to. She asked, 'Tim — does Les know about Mawgan and me? Did you tell her?'

He looked at her, hollow-eyed.

'I thought it might make her change her mind,' he said, simply. 'It might have helped, if she had... they wouldn't think I tried to kill her if she stayed with me.'

Thanks, Tim!

'Do you mind?' he asked. 'You told me.'

Yes, to make you go away! Too late now, anyway.

'It doesn't matter.'

Roger came back bearing three cups of coffee on a tray, just as the rest of the party began to appear, straggling onto the forecourt in twos and threes, apparently fully recovered and looking forward to a pleasant day on the river.

So, business as usual. Tim went off after a brief greeting, and Roger and Debbie worked out a plan for the day's lessons. The father of the family offered to take a shift looking after the hiring out of the two spare boats to allow Roger to go on the water to instruct, Sally's boyfriend said he'd man the safety boat, he and Sally ran off, laughing, to launch it. It all seemed unreal to the point of fantasy.

At lunchtime, Debbie slipped upstairs to the flat and tried to ring Oliver, but only got the answering service. Damn Oliver! He was probably there, too, he never picked up the mobile when he was working, and come to think, very seldom when he wasn't. No point leaving a message, she wouldn't be in to take a reply, and she couldn't take a mobile phone on the water. Not in a dinghy full of beginners, and a nice brisk breeze, anyway. She tried ringing her father's office, only to learn that he was in court all afternoon. Ringing her mother, she thought uneasily, wasn't an option. Dorothy Nankervis was a difficult woman at the best of times, and for her, this must be the worst of times. An unhappy woman with her long-standing marriage collapsing around her wouldn't receive the news that Debbie had to tell in a spirit of tolerance and forgiveness, it needed to be filtered through a friendly third party. The confidence wouldn't be helped by the fact that, when she had rung home the evening following the fire, she hadn't so much as breathed Mawgan's name, she had thought then that there was all the time in the world to go carefully. She had never even thought about Lesley precipitating things.

Joke there, by the way. Another of the sergeant's black ones, actually. A friendly third party, ha ha! Oliver, whom her mother disliked to the point of loathing and from whom she received the same in return, or the husband who was maybe about to leave her. Good choice there.

Debbie went back down to the bar, and a jolly lunch with the students. It hadn't occurred to her before that she couldn't confide easily in her mother, and the thought was an uncomfortable one. There was Susan, of course, but she and Tom were off on holiday abroad with their children, she wasn't sure when they were coming back, and whenever it was it would be far, far, too late. She felt very lonely, all her family unavailable and a crisis approaching like a storm to wreck the frail ship of her happiness. The students, happily playing at sailing schools, grated on her painfully.

She made one more try, when they all came ashore at the end of the afternoon, to contact either Oliver or her father, and failed with both. With a feeling of fatality, she went back down to the foreshore to help Roger put the boats away.

'You push off,' he told her. 'I know you want to get off to Truro. There's plenty of people here to help. See you in the bar this evening?'

'I suppose so, but don't wait around for me if you all want to go out.'

'OK. Pick up a couple of yachting magazines while you're out, so we can do those adverts, Tim isn't going to think of it. Do you know the ones?'

For what it was worth, Debbie thought uneasily, as she drove along the increasingly familiar roads. The September issues were already in the bookshops, there was little if any point in advertising in the October issues. There was nearly a month ahead of them when almost anything might happen, and on present form, probably would. Even if Tim wasn't arrested − but she shied away from that thought − it was all going to be a nightmare. She and Roger were only employees, they were free to run if they wanted. Tempting though the idea might look, she knew that neither of them would. She because she was a friend of Tim's, and you didn't run out on your friends, Roger... well, Roger was quietly grinding an axe of his own, and she had a very good idea what it might be. She wondered how much Tim or Lesley had given away to Roger about her circumstances.

Mawgan was looking much improved this evening. When she got there, he was lying on top of his bed wearing the familiar bathrobe, fighting one-handedly with a newspaper. From Debbie's observation as she approached, the newspaper was winning.

'Hi there!' He abandoned the unequal contest to greet her, and Debbie caught the escaping pages before they slid to the floor. 'How's it going? I've had the police round to visit this morning, and they weren't bringing grapes.' There was an edge to his words that made Debbie wonder if they had given him a hard time − obvious suspect, of course, an old lag. 'What's going on back there?'

'Join the club!' She pulled a chair forward and dropped into it. 'What's going on is that somebody torched the place deliberately, can you believe that?'

'Who have you upset?' asked Mawgan, immediately. 'Apart from me, that is, and it *wasn't* me.' Too much emphasis. Yes, they had worked him over all right. She pretended she hadn't noticed.

'Nobody… well, the Svensens possibly, and Mr. Arnott, you remember him? But they wouldn't set fire to the place!'

'Unlikely.'

'Tim seems to be favourite,' said Debbie, reluctantly.

'And did he, do you think?'

Debbie shook her head. 'I can't see it myself, but it really does look as if it has to be between him and Lesley, and she wouldn't have trapped herself after setting the place alight, which rather narrows the field. Only, it just doesn't feel right…'

'Poor old Howells,' said Mawgan.

'I wish you'd call him Tim,' said Debbie. 'He calls you bloody Angwin all the time, and you're just as bad.'

'I never called him bloody Howells. Felt like it, maybe.' He smiled at her. 'Give it up, Deb, we just don't like each other. That doesn't necessarily mean that I think he set fire to his own place, though. I agree with you, it doesn't feel right. He hasn't the brains to think of it, for one thing.'

Debbie decided to ignore that.

'He was with the police almost all of yesterday, but they didn't charge him.'

'Then maybe they won't. Don't worry Deb, the experience won't kill him. It didn't kill me, did it?'

Debbie wanted to say that he was a lot tougher than Tim, but didn't think it would be tactful. Instead, she said, 'We can only wait and see what develops, I suppose. The insurance man was round today, too. If they won't pay out, Lesley's lost her inheritance.'

'What's happening to the business?' he asked, after a pause. 'The season's not over yet, and it's bank holiday this coming weekend.'

'The villagers have been very good.' She said, tiredly and not for the first time, 'We're just having to wing it. We're going to put notices where we can, in the yachting magazines and everything, but we can only hope that people will see them. We don't know who they are, everything got burnt. What else can we do?'

She didn't really expect an answer to what was a purely rhetorical question, and was surprised when Mawgan said, 'Would Howells accept help from me?'

Debbie stared at him.

'You said you wouldn't give him any.'

'That was then.'

'Surely even you can't have any advice to offer on this one!'

'Heavens, no! It's beyond advice. The word I used, if you were listening properly, was *help*.'

'I don't know,' said Debbie. This, she hadn't expected. 'I *think* he'd accept help from the devil himself right at this moment, but he might just rate you rather lower. *Can* you help?'

'Yes,' he said, simply. 'Listen Deb, you mayn't realise this, but I don't advertise for bookings at the Fish, I can't be bothered. To be honest, I wish the rooms weren't there, they're more trouble than they're worth, but since they are… well, I let to passing trade, and the odd party in the restaurant who don't want to drink and drive. Do you hear what I'm saying?'

'You're saying,' said Debbie, slowly, feeling as if a great weight was slipping from her shoulders, 'as each room becomes vacant, it's potentially vacant until the end of the season.'

'That's right. If you want 'em, you can have 'em, they're all yours. There's six of them, three doubles and three twins. There may be the odd advance booking, I leave that to Shirley and Mrs. Solomons, you'd need to check. But I only do breakfast, and they have to eat that in the snug. After that, they're on their own.'

'It's generous of you.'

'Not at all. I'll still get paid, and they'll all have holiday insurance, presumably, so they'll get their deposits back they gave you. And since you booked Saturday to Saturday, I can still let any that aren't taken from Sunday.'

'What about over the holiday?'

'That, I can't tell you until I get back. You'll have to ask Shirley if you need to know before then, but I should think that's a no-go myself. And can you ask Jack or Tony to pick me up after breakfast tomorrow, while you're about it?'

'I can do that,' said Debbie. 'Unless, that is, you have a fixation against women drivers.' Her heart bumped once, hard. Last night had been lonely in the big double bed. She said, 'There's another problem too, Mawgan.' She told him about Lesley. 'I wanted to tell them at home in my own time, my own way, but we can't now. She's got it in for me. She thinks I ruined her marriage. As a matter of fact, I think she's blown a fuse, on the whole I can see why she might.'

'Anna sussed us out last night, too,' said Mawgan, quietly. 'Did you see her? She certainly saw you.' He grinned at her, and she felt suddenly light-headed.

'So what are we going to do?'

'We've two choices. Call the whole thing off, or go out and buy a ring and get engaged properly, get it all over with. My vote goes to the second. So long as you've not got no doubts.'

He had a point, she saw immediately. That would be a very definite statement of intent, and nobody actually had any right to argue with it. Of course, he had never met her mother.

'Take a run at it, you mean, and take them by surprise?'

'There's something very convincing and final about a definite engagement. That's why I've always avoided one.'

'It works for me,' said Debbie, thinking. There was a lot to be said, she realised, for doing it quickly and getting it behind them, and nothing at all to be said for trying to fudge the issue, which was a third alternative.

'Then we'll see about it on the way home tomorrow.'

She looked at him critically. His right eye and the area round it was turning all the colours generated by a mouldering plum.

'I'm not sure you're fit to be seen in a public place. You'll frighten little children.'

'Desperate situations need desperate measures. But you'd better bring me some clean clothes, if I smell like something out of Hell as well, it might just be the last straw. D'you know these people? I don't.'

Debbie turned quickly to look up over her shoulder. Her jaw dropped untidily.

'You rang,' said Chel. 'Twice, apparently. So has your mother, your father, and Susan all the way from Antigua, so we thought we'd better find you. Tim told us you were here, when we finally tracked him down on somebody's mobile, with the help of the pub, thank you very much.'

'Glad they made themselves useful,' said Mawgan, almost automatically. Then he looked at Debbie, a look full of inappropriate mischief. 'So it's too late Deb! The shit has hit the fan. The children of Truro are saved after all.'

'*Why* do you always have to make stupid jokes at the most unsuitable moments?' asked Debbie, on a tremor of indignant laughter. She sobered quickly. 'Lesley got home all right, then.' It was a statement, not a question.

'She certainly did.' Oliver looked at Mawgan in a measuring way, and held out his hand. 'And you, I suppose, are the cause of all the trouble. I'm Debbie's brother. Half-brother. If you can have half a brother.' They clasped hands, warily.

'Half a brain, more like,' said Chel. She sat down on the edge of the bed. Sensitive to atmosphere – sometimes too sensitive for her own peace of mind – she could feel a jumble of emotions in the air around her like bees, not all of them good, but they refused to polarise. She looked at Debbie's Cornishman and liked what she saw, but it was him around whom the emotional bees were buzzing. She smiled at him. 'Hullo. I'm Chel, he's Oliver.'

'Mawgan,' he said, returning the smile.

Oliver had found himself a chair and brought it over. Realising that if they all waited for each other to open the batting, the game would never start, Debbie asked, not really sure she wanted to know, 'What has Lesley said?'

'Remember, we've got it at third, or even fourth hand.' Oliver said. 'It sounds mad to us. She said the plonker Tim tried to kill her, which I don't believe, he wouldn't have the guts for it.'

'Hear, hear!' said Mawgan, in a muted aside that made Debbie send him a dark look.

'It's the reason she gives that I find so hard to swallow,' said Chel. 'She said he did it so he could marry you and get his hands on your money.'

'You've got money?' asked Mawgan, looking at Debbie in surprise. 'I always knew you was a nice girl! But what's this about marrying Howells? I thought you was planning to marry me.'

'I wish you would just shut up,' said Debbie. 'How can anyone talk sensibly with you lying around there, refusing to take anything seriously?'

'Ah, true love!' said Oliver, sentimentally. 'Touching, isn't it Chel?'

'And you can shut up, too,' Chel told him. 'Mind you, Deb, it was a good question. What *is* all this about you marrying Tim?'

'It's news to me, too. I know he thinks he's in love with me, but believe me, it's only a single ticket to marriage. Anyway, he didn't try to kill her. He didn't even know she was in the house.' She paused there, mentally replaying what she had just said, and realised that all three of the others were looking at her gravely. 'I didn't mean that,' she said. 'Not the way it came out, anyway. He didn't set fire to the place either.'

'You don't actually know that,' Oliver pointed out. 'Unless you did it yourself, of course. Did you?'

'She's got an alibi,' said Mawgan. 'To be fair, I think she's right. I don't think he would've done it neither, and I can't stand the bloke.'

'Who's your candidate, then?' asked Oliver with interest.

'I haven't got none. It's one of them mysteries. Aliens?'

'Anyway,' said Chel, after a pause. 'That's all nothing to do with us, although I'm very sorry for them both, losing everything like that, of course. I don't think she was saying that Debbie wanted to marry Tim in any case, just that Tim kidded himself she would. Oh dear, doesn't it all get complicated?'

'It's me that's making the real problem, isn't it?' said Mawgan, and he was no longer laughing. There was no use in denying it.

'There's no getting away from it,' said Oliver, judiciously. 'It'd take a lot of spin to make you look good. Lesley Howells seems to have done a pretty comprehensive demolition job on you, apparently at the same time as insisting that you were the only person who understood what she was up against. Since I seriously *don't* believe a word she says at the moment, I'm not trying to make a lot out of that.'

'Can we get this straight?' said Debbie. She reached out and took a firm hold of Mawgan, suddenly afraid, even at this stage, that he might beat a retreat out of some chivalrous misapprehension. She was relieved when his hand closed round hers, safe and possessive. 'Lesley hasn't told Mum and Dad the same story that I told you?' She wouldn't, of course – couldn't, even. She only knew the popular version.

'It was a bit more highly coloured,' said Chel, diplomatically.

'Oh God, I can just imagine it!' It would have featured a great deal of gratuitous violence involving rockery stones, the gospel according to Mrs Tregear. 'So how did that go down?' she asked, apprehensively.

'Like a lead balloon, I should think,' murmured Mawgan. He realised that Debbie's brother was giving him a strange look; if it hadn't been so unlikely, he would have described it as sympathetic. 'Sorry, I'll just shut up, like the girl said, shall I?'

Oliver said, 'Don't worry about it, anyway. Dad's calling up a transcript of the trial, and if anyone can sort out the wheat from the chaff, he can.'

He caught Mawgan's look of amazement, almost of shock. 'Hasn't Debbie told you what her father does?'

'We haven't discussed families much. Hardly at all, in fact.' He made a face. 'I knew she had one, of course. But mine has gone into a critical mass that's likely to implode at any moment, and we generally found other things to talk about. What does he do?'

'He's a solicitor,' said Chel. 'And a very good one, so don't look like that. Somebody's got to get you out of the mess you're in.'

'And you needn't feel awkward about your family, either,' added Oliver. 'Ours is so at odds with itself, it's got to make yours look like *The Waltons*, and you'd better believe it!'

Debbie said, hesitantly, 'What you said just now – that almost sounded as if Dad hasn't gone into orbit.'

'He said you rang him at the office,' said Oliver. 'He took that as a cry for help, and before I forget to tell you, he said would you do it again tomorrow, he'll be there and waiting for your call. I told him what you told me, I hope you don't mind – either of you.'

'Why, what did you tell him?' Mawgan asked Debbie.

'What you told me,' said Debbie.

'Oh stop – stop!' cried Chel. 'Do you want us all to end up in hysterics? Do *try* to take this a little bit seriously!'

Debbie giggled. 'It's his fault. He carries this aura of levity around with him wherever he goes. It's one of the things I fell in love with. The first thing he ever said to me was a stupid joke, when he was lying on the floor only half-conscious, with the drifts piling up outside and everything scary, and I was a total stranger to him.'

'It must be so dull for people who are just introduced at dinner parties,' observed Oliver.

'Why, how did you two meet?' asked Mawgan, happy to change the subject, and wondering if Debbie's brother realised. On the whole, he thought, the answer to that was *yes*.

'Somebody threw her at me.'

'What, lit'rally?'

'We've the pictures to prove it,' said Chel. 'We'll show you sometime. Now, I think we'd better go. You look as if you've got a really stinking headache.'

'Ssh, don't say that too loud. I want to get out of here tomorrow.'

Oliver had risen to his feet. He looked at his sister.

'Have you had anything to eat yet, young Deb?'

'No. I was going to grab a pizza or something on the way home.'

Mawgan shuddered. 'For goodness' sake, bird – you're living practically on top of a perfectly good restaurant. Row of pretty little AA stars and everything.'

'We'll wait for you outside, and we'll find somewhere together,' said Oliver, and Debbie's heart sank a little. There was a lot more to be said, she knew that, but did she really want to hear it tonight?

Chel and Oliver said goodbye to Mawgan, and on impulse, Chel leaned forward and kissed his cheek. It was the first physical contact she had had with him, and she was about to speak, to say something banal like *take care of yourself*, when all those emotional bees formed themselves into a swarm and settled into a recognisable mass. She drew back in shock, as if they had actually stung her.

'Oh, bugger!' They were all looking at her, she was going to have to say something. Mawgan and Debbie were going to think she was some kind of lunatic, but she still had to say it. She looked wildly to Oliver for help.

'What is it, Chel?' he asked.

The physical bond was broken, the bees had begun to fly again. She reached out and touched the back of Mawgan's hand, and they converged once more.

'I'm sorry, you're going to think I'm mad,' she said. 'You will take care – you *must* take care. There's such *malevolence* directed towards you.' The pretty but horrible pictures from Charlie's studio shimmered at the back of her mind. 'You must take care,' she repeated.

'No prizes for guessing who that might be, then,' said Mawgan, drily, but she knew she hadn't really got through to him. He pulled his hand away.

'Actually, I can think of three candidates,' remarked Oliver, quietly, almost to himself. Chel sent him a sharp look. A warning look? Debbie wondered. He said, more loudly, 'Take notice of her. She's a weirdo, every home should have one.'

Mawgan was rubbing the back of his right hand, where Chel had touched him, against the still fingers of his left.

'We had a woman lived down from us back'long could do that,' he said, so matter-of-factly that the tension broke. 'I never thought much to it, myself.' He had never sounded so Cornish. Debbie looked at him in amazement.

'Just remember,' Chel said. 'I mean it, please. Somebody is watching you, all the time.'

'Ugh!' said Mawgan, expressively. He smiled at her, ruefully. 'I really feel better for that.' But he still wasn't taking it seriously, and she knew that he should.

'Come on, Madame Arcati,' Oliver took his wife by the arm. 'Deb wants to say goodbye, and it's almost chucking-out time. See you outside, Deb.'

They had gone. Mawgan said, 'Do I take any notice?'

'Oliver wasn't laughing,' said Debbie.

'No, he wasn't, was he? So that's the famous Oliver Nankervis.' He looked pensive for a minute, and then laughed, but uncertainly. 'Your family certainly make an impact. Now then, before you dash off, back to real life. Adverts in newspapers, that's what you need, forget about magazines. Tell them the story, ask them to put it somewhere conspicuous, they might even do it for free if you lay it on thick. And give a number where people can ring, can you do that?'

'There's Roger's mobile, and mine.'

'But you're on the water all day.' He thought for a minute. 'Better use the Fish, have all your calls re-routed. In fact, use Shirley, she can e-mail most of the stuff for you. And get someone to make you a large notice to fix to your gate, sending them down there, in case some slip through the net.'

'How can you be so good, when Tim – ?'

'I'm not being good. It's only what I'd hope somebody did for me if the same thing happened. It don't matter whether you like people or not, if you see them sinking in the mire, you at least throw them a rope. And it's my business too, remember – we want people remembering St. Erbyn pleasantly, not thinking what an unhelpful, miserable sort of place it was and never wanting to see it again. Nobody wants their summer holiday ruined.'

'That may be true, but it isn't going to save Tim's business.'

'Deb, you aren't dead until they bury you and stick a big stone on top to keep you down. You remember that, and I'll remember to take care – although how, I don't see. Now you better go, because there's a nurse bearing down on you with a gleam in her eye. See you tomorrow. Early as you like.'

Debbie still hesitated. He had a way of making everything sound so easy, Lesley had complained about it too, she remembered.

'Will Shirley mind? I mean, she doesn't work for us. She works for you.'

'Then I'll ask her. Don't look so worried, Deb. We'll get you through it between us.'

'Is Shirley a Tregear, by any chance?' Debbie asked, and he grinned.

'No, Shirley is a Pengelly. That's the other great St. Erbyn dynasty, but their underground is less well organised. I wouldn't employ a Tregear in my office, believe me. Now, say goodbye nicely before you get thrown out.'

Debbie said goodbye nicely, and enjoyed it, checked with the nurses' station – not earlier than ten o'clock, they said – and went to join Chel and Oliver.

'There's a pub,' she said. 'I asked Mawgan. Just down the road on the right, we can get something there.'

'OK, we'll follow you. Nobody could lose that buttercup of yours.'

The drive was short, allowing little time for discussion, but Chel said, as they moved off in Debbie's wake, 'So, what do you think?'

'I think, if you're going to be the catalyst for the ultimate disintegration of your family unit, it's just as well that the reason should be a good one. But I hope young Deb realises that what goes up, must come down.'

'Mmm.' Chel thought about this as they waited to filter onto a roundabout. 'He was on a bit of a high, wasn't he? Do you think we frightened him, turning up out of the blue?'

Oliver laughed, squeezing out into the traffic.

'We may have had something to do with it, but I don't think there's a lot frightens that one,' he said. 'Probably just as well, since he has to deal with the Dreaded Dot. Where's the buttercup gone?'

'Just turning off, there.'

Oliver turned after his sister.

'Although,' he went on, as if there had been no break in the conversation, 'I think you shook him up a bit.'

'Do you think he thought I was completely out to lunch? I had to say it. It just seemed so important.'

'What's he supposed to do about it?' enquired Oliver, almost echoing Mawgan.

'I don't know – it doesn't seem to work like that, not for me anyway. But perhaps if he just watches his back a bit, it'll be enough.'

'You're loopy, you, do you know that?'

Chel made no response to this insult, knowing that Oliver didn't wholly mean it. By this time they were turning into the car park of a pleasant-looking pub, with enough cars outside it to form a recommendation. It wasn't until they were seated with drinks, waiting for food to be brought, that there was opportunity for further discussion, and it was Debbie, once again, who started it off.

'You said three,' she said, to Oliver.

'Three what?' He looked at her blankly.

'Three candidates for malevolence. The little sister, obviously, that's who Mawgan meant.'

'And Lesley Howells – although she's more lost the plot than malevolent, I suppose.'

'And the third?'

'Look, shall we eat first,' Chel interrupted. 'There's no need to give poor Deb indigestion.'

'I'd sooner know,' said Debbie. 'I'm more likely to get indigestion from wondering than if you come right out and tell me. Dad's behaving like a gentleman, so it's Mum, isn't it?'

'Put it this way,' said Oliver, whose dislike of his stepmother had passed into family legend long ago, 'I wouldn't be in too much of a hurry to ring home. Let the dust settle.'

The Dreaded Dot, he called her. The name had originated with Jerry Nankervis's displaced first wife, and Debbie, although she would have said without hesitation that she loved her mother, also knew that it had been earned. Dot Nankervis could be a very difficult woman, and where Oliver was concerned, seemed to glory in it. Debbie knew that there had been a very nasty row the previous year, and of course, thanks to her ex-boyfriend, she also knew about the flat. She had a dreadful feeling now of things running away out of reach, out of hand, and out of the present into the past.

'She's going to forbid the banns,' she said, with conviction.

'She can't actually do that, take heart,' said Chel, but she spoke sympathetically because her own parents – both of them, not just one – had wanted to do the same when she married Debbie's brother. But Marilyn and Bob had backed down at the eleventh hour. She didn't think that the Dreaded Dot would.

'Look, talk to Dad tomorrow, before you do anything,' Oliver advised her. 'But make quite sure, Deb –' He looked at her with unusual seriousness for him. 'Make quite sure, won't you, that you know exactly what you're doing?'

'You mean, marrying Mawgan may cost me,' said Debbie, not misunderstanding him. 'Well, come to that, *not* marrying him would cost me, too. Cost me more. She can't force me into doing what she wants against my will, unless she wants to lose my respect. And if she does that, what's left of our relationship as mother and daughter?'

'That's it in a nutshell, I couldn't have put it better myself.'

Debbie picked up a beer mat from the table and began to run it, edge on, up and down the polished wood of the table top.

'If I ask you now what you thought of him, you'll think I'm asking for reassurance, which I'm not. But just the same, I want to know.'

'I don't know that we're in a position to judge on such a brief acquaintance. I liked what I saw, which wasn't a lot.' He paused, to pick his words carefully. 'You have to remember, Deb, however simple and straightforward he may have started out, any man who has done and been through what he has done and been through will have been complicated by it, and you need to ask yourself, do you really want to cope with the result?'

'But you did like him?'

Oliver could see how much it mattered to her. He said, almost reluctantly, 'Since you ask, yes. I did. But if you do marry him, you'll have your hands full, that's all I'm saying.'

Chel said, 'I'll tell you one thing, and you needn't cross my palm with silver, it's for free. It may not look like it, just at this minute, but if you get through this sticky patch, he's going to go far – and fast. I think you may be in for a shock.'

'A nice one, I hope,' said Debbie, moodily.

Chel laughed. 'Ever ridden on the big dipper? Just hang on tight and try not to scream too loud!'

'Well thank you, both of you. You've certainly ensured me a nice sleepless night!'

Oliver took the beer mat from her hand and laid it back on the table. He closed his hand over hers, an unusual gesture for him, that made her look up, a question in her eyes.

'Hang in there, Deb,' he said. 'You just have to make your own decision and then make it stick. It's up to you, not your mother, not Dad, not us.

If you want to ride the big dipper, pay the fare. If you don't, if the bare idea gives you vertigo, then stay safe on the ground and keep your money. It's that simple.'

'Are you giving me advice, Oliver? That has to be a first!'

'I'm simply pointing out the facts of life. Nobody gets everything. Look at me, I'm the perfect example. I almost lost everything that I thought mattered, but I've ended up with more than I ever imagined was there to be found.' He smiled at her suddenly, breaking the tension. 'All I've got to do now is sell the bloody pictures!'

Their food arrived then, and the subject dropped. They spoke about uncontroversial topics, Oliver's coming London exhibition, the fast-approaching move from the borrowed studio to the house on the creek, Chel's family, with whom Debbie was on friendly terms. Only once did the subject of Debbie's controversial proposed marriage squeeze into the conversation, when they were nearly ready to leave, dawdling a final few minutes over coffee.

'Candy'll be thrilled, anyway,' said Chel. Candy was her niece, and had shared with Debbie the privilege of being a bridesmaid at her own wedding. 'She's always asking if you're going to get married yet.'

'I promised her she should be a bridesmaid for me, too,' said Debbie. 'I'm surprised she remembers – she can only have been about four!'

'She's not four now, and believe me, Candy remembers *everything*!'

'Her and Annabel, tripping up the aisle behind me… there's a solemn thought!' A cloud crossed Debbie's face. Annabel was her own niece. 'That's if Susan is still speaking to me.'

The thought that if her mother refused to recognise her engagement, her wedding might be as awkward an occasion as Chel's own had been couldn't help but cross her mind. Oliver said, 'Deb, if push comes to shove, you get married down here in St. Erbyn, from our house. And if Susan starts making difficulties, leave her to Chel. She'll come round.'

Her decision, Debbie thought, seemed to be making itself – no, had made itself long since. She said, 'Thank you,' and smiled, but her mother's attitude sat like a shadow at the back of her mind, and as they drove home, Oliver said to Chel, with deep feeling,

'Sodding Dot!'

<h1 style="text-align:center">XXII</h1>

It was almost closing time by the time Debbie parked once more outside the Fish, but the bars were still open and the restaurant, she knew, wouldn't be closing for a long time yet. To her surprise, she found Roger in the bar on his own, or at least, sharing a drink with a few locals, without a student in sight. She went to lean on the bar top beside him.

'What's up? Frightened them all away?'

Tommy came over to take her order. 'Boss doing all right?'

'Take cover,' Debbie advised. 'He'll be back tomorrow morning. I'll just have a bitter lemon, Tommy – a real one, not that diet stuff. Alcohol might be too stimulating after the day we've been having!'

Tommy nodded sympathetically and went to fetch the bottle. When she had her drink, Roger said, answering her question, 'They all took themselves off, they knew we had things to talk about. Come and sit down, there's a table free over there.'

'Where's Tim?' asked Debbie, following him across.

'I don't know. I hoped you'd be back before this.'

'Oliver and Chel came. We had a meal together. I'm sorry, I thought you'd have gone off with the others.'

'It doesn't matter. We can't do anything tonight anyway, but Deb, you do realise that if anything is going to be done it's us that's going to have to do it, don't you? Tim's going to be arrested, if not tomorrow, then the day after, and he can't think properly – doesn't even care, I don't think.'

'But he didn't –' Debbie began, met his eye and stopped.

'Then who did?' asked Roger. 'Look Deb, he had the motive – he and Lesley were going to go bust at any minute – and the opportunity, I told you he came home before us, didn't I? The means was readily available, there's a can for the outboard in the boathouse and none of us can really say how much should be in it. How can anyone believe, realistically, that he *didn't* do it?'

'Do *you* think so?'

'I don't know what I think. But the reason he isn't in here tonight is because Tommy probably wouldn't serve him. There were people in that house, Deb, including two children. He's going to go to prison, and unless you can come up with a better explanation, he probably deserves to.'

Debbie sat very still. She should have expected it, she realised, but it still came as a shock. She had known Tim for years, sailed with him, gone out with him, had fun with him, been like brother and sister with him. He was an integral part of her growing-up years. He had had such dreams with his new wife and his wonderful idea... all come down to this. Ashes, literally. She couldn't believe in it.

'Tim wouldn't,' she said, and for the first time, heard uncertainty in her voice.

'Fortunately it's not for us to decide,' said Roger. 'That will be down to twelve good men and true.'

'Poor Tim.' Poor Lesley, too.

'If there was something we could do to help, we could do it. There isn't. Let's concentrate on what we can do something about, shall we?'

Debbie wished that she had chosen something stronger than bitter lemon. She took a sip.

'We must draft some adverts for the newspapers. Mawgan said he'd ask Shirley to help us.'

It was Roger's turn to be still.

'Did he really?' He took a mouthful of his beer. 'Did he say anything else?'

'He said we could have his bedrooms after the holiday.'

Roger put his glass down, slowly.

'Did he give a reason?'

'He said it wouldn't help anyone if people remembered St. Erbyn for a ruined holiday.'

'God, I do admire that man!' said Roger, but only half in admiration. 'His presence of mind is truly amazing! Deb... look, this probably isn't the time, but can we talk, you and I?'

'We are talking,' said Debbie.

Roger spoke carefully. 'I've said something like this to you before, I seem to remember. Deb, I quite like your Mawgan — I think — but lay aside your rose-coloured spectacles for a moment. He's a very bright boy and he's certainly been around, he knows as much about sailing close to the wind as we do — probably rather more, and one bang on the head isn't going to change that. It can't help but occur to me, sad cynic that I am, that not just over this, but all season long, he's been going to… shall we say unusual lengths?… to preserve the goodwill of Tim's business. Now, I can't help asking myself, why? It certainly isn't because he likes Tim.'

It was like looking down a kaleidoscope, one slight twist and the pattern changed completely. Debbie said, 'What are you trying to say?'

'I'm not quite sure, really. But answer me this, if… say for the sake of argument… someone now wanted to re-invent the sailing school, and do it sensibly this time, would he put up the money, do you think?'

Debbie put down her glass, her mind suddenly seething.

'That's a very good question. The answer is probably *no*, I don't think he has any capital lying around spare. His partner did a bunk when he went to prison, he had to buy him out.'

'Right. Next question, and I'm sorry if you find it a bit personal. Could *you* put up the money, and if so, does he know?'

He hadn't known, at the start of the evening, but by the end of it he had at least had some idea. Debbie recalled, with a jolt, how just before she left, he had stepped up the amount of help he was prepared to give to the point of personal involvement. Up until the moment Chel had mentioned her money, she was pretty sure that Roger was wrong and Mawgan had, in the end, told her the truth… but after it?

Roger was watching her face.

'Ah, I see the penny's dropped at last! *Now* can we talk?'

'They're going to throw us out in a minute.'

'Then we'll go and sit outside. It's plenty warm enough.'

They went out onto the forecourt, and sat in the quiet, breezy darkness. One or two late drinkers coming from the public bar called out goodnight to them as the doors closed behind them. There was the sound of bolts shooting across. Roger said, 'We could do it, you and I, Deb. You know we could.'

'Not that way.'

'No. The right way. If it was part of the Fish complex, Angwin himself would be the licensee, or at least, Tommy would, which comes to the same thing. There'd be no opposition – from him, anyway – to our rebuilding it as a clubhouse. A privately owned sailing club.'

Tim's abandoned dreams crept out of the shadows and paraded themselves in front of them, Debbie almost heard them singing siren songs. She took a deep breath.

'No stupid guest house. We might make a bunkhouse in the old staff quarters… take school parties, or colleges… and on the ground floor, the chandlery that Tim wanted, although God knows where he intended to put it.'

'Showers for visiting yachtsmen. Could you persuade him to do dinners at the Fish? I know he's got the restaurant, but that's a separate thing. But steaks, chips, pasties, that kind of thing? Served in the bar, if people wanted to eat ashore?'

'I can't answer that, we'd need to discuss it with him. But the bar lunches and breakfast don't come from the restaurant, there's another kitchen with different staff, it was part of the original inn. I don't see why he wouldn't.'

'It could work,' said Roger. 'It *would* work!'

'We'd need planning permission. Change of use, all that.'

'And the money would be there? I can't put anything much into it, Deb – mainly my skills and my hard work. I wish I could.'

'The big problem would be, would they sell to me?' said Debbie, without answering the question directly. 'It's Lesley's house. You know how she feels about me.'

'I think it might be the bank's house, actually. Anyway, she needn't know, you could buy it through a nominee. Someone she's never heard of.'

'It seems so disloyal.'

'Deb, I'm sure your bloke has told you that it's a dog-eat-dog world, and if he hasn't, I'm telling you now.'

'It's such a tempting idea…' said Debbie, longingly. 'It feels wicked to even think about it.'

'We wouldn't fall into the pitfalls that Tim and Les did. We'd have Angwin on our side – on our team, in fact. And Deb, there's more. I met this bloke at the sailing club in Helford, he's a Yachtmaster instructor, and he has a boat – in fact, he's said he'll bring it here over the holiday and take some of the strain for us if we want, he can sleep four on board and give them instruction too, unless they're set on dinghies. He's a good bloke. I'm pretty sure he'd come in with us if we made it tempting enough, and bring the boat with him as an asset.'

'There's all sorts of regulations about yachts for instruction purposes.'

'We'll cross that bridge when we come to it. Nobody's looking for now, and it'll be near enough anyway.'

'If we had a proper place to do it, we could give lessons in navigation during the winter. VHF too. Oliver's a Yachtmaster for oceans – he might even come and teach the odd class if it was for me, not Tim. He might even surprise himself, and enjoy it.'

'What about you? You've got your Yachtmaster's ticket haven't you?'

'Offshore. Not oceans. And I'm not an instructor.'

'But you could be. We've got to rebuild, that won't be done in a flash.'

They fell silent.

'Give it a whirl?' asked Roger. In the dark, Debbie nodded.

'Why the hell not?' She held out her hand. 'Put it there, partner.' They shook hands. 'And now,' said Debbie, 'I'm sorry to start our partnership off on such a bum note, but I want to skive off tomorrow morning. I'm collecting the wreckage from the hospital and bringing it home.'

'No problem. I'll set them all drafting suitable adverts, that'll keep them out of mischief. We were going to have to take the morning off anyway, to deal with the business problems. Tim won't.'

'I'll do my share after I get back, promise, I should be back by eleven. And we can have Shirley's help then, too.'

'I'll give Carl a ring first thing, tell him we'll take up his offer. That'll do for starters, until you've met him.'

'Perhaps we'll wake up in the morning and think we were mad even to think about it.'

'No we won't.' Roger got to his feet. 'Come on Deb, they're shutting the restaurant, you don't want to be locked out. See you in the morning.'

They parted, and Deb went upstairs to the flat, just slipping in past Tony as he went to close the door. Her decision seemed to have taken itself, thanks to Roger, if she had ever had any serious doubts, that is. She didn't think she had. This was a life, a husband she could love, a job ditto, a totally fulfilling existence. She knew, in her heart, that all her mother would offer on the other side would be bitterness and dissent, and it was no contest. She felt sorry for her, she realised. From her battles with Oliver to her attempted vanquishment of Chel in the past to her present attempt to manipulate Debbie herself, she had always tried to force her own way onto others. Onto her father's first wife, Helen, too? And Susan, had she really escaped? Nobody could behave like that and expect to be happy, nobody could ride roughshod over others and expect to continue to be loved.

But she would make one try, Debbie decided, as she rolled into bed. She would go to Embridge and try to talk to her mother. If that didn't work, and although she hoped it would, really she knew it wouldn't, then her mother would have to make the decision whether to give in or nurse her pride for consolation.

She reached out to the cool, empty, other side of the bed. There was no way she was having that gap in her life for ever.

And Tim. Poor Tim… had he, or hadn't he?

Like Roger, she found she really didn't know.

Cress hadn't expected the building to go up quite so thoroughly, she had thought the fire would be put out fairly quickly, leaving the place uninhabitable, maybe, so that everyone had to go home. She did realise that she had come within a whisker of killing her brother, but that didn't worry her too much. It would have been a pity, the dead can't be made to suffer, but an acceptable mistake. What had shaken her was when the children had run out of the burning house. She hadn't thought about people, let alone children, being inside. She had thought they were all out.

It had been so easy to start the fire. The window had been left carelessly open, and Gary had told her how it was done, when he was boasting one evening. So easy to start it, and then nobody had been able to put it out, and those poor little children had had to run out, screaming, into the night.

So it had all gone wrong, and the blonde girl, far from being driven out, had been driven straight down to the old white inn that straddled the foreshore, and from there, even her own audacity and courage couldn't smoke her out. She was safe within its walls, and while she was there, Cressida knew, her love would keep him safe, too. But there had to be a way.

'Suppose you wanted to make somebody's car come off the road,' she said to Gary's best mate, Tel. Tel hadn't been involved in the Fish incident, he had been in bed with a stomach upset, fortuitously he might have thought, had he known the word. He looked at her askance.

'That's risky stuff. You never know what's going to happen when you start doing things like that.'

'But there's ways?'

'If I know 'em, I ain't telling you,' said Tel. He had a more highly-developed sense of self-preservation than Gary, and he privately thought Cress was a lot more than a sandwich short of a picnic, there was only a squashed tomato and a bent teaspoon in the basket at all. The lesson of what had happened to his friends was a point to keep in mind, too. 'There's been too much going on down that St. Erbyn place, there'll be cops all over, you'd never get away with it. What you done to Gary, and then that bloke torching his place for the insurance – you'd not get me near it, for a start!'

'What?' asked Cress, startled.

'Ha'n't you heard about that? Going bust, they say he was, and did an arson job. Silly bugger! Didn't even bother to get himself an alibi!' Tel knew all about alibis. He'd used a few in his time. He snorted derisively, and swaggered away. Cress stood there on the corner of the street. She had the weirdest feeling, all of a sudden, that life was running on two different levels, the one where she knew that she had thrown the petrol bomb through the open window, and another, which perhaps was more real, where somebody else had done it for perfectly logical reasons of their own. It never even entered her head that the somebody else was being blamed for what she had done. She felt herself to be in a parallel reality, and the busy scene around her shivered and faded.

'Mike.' He was there at once, he was never too far away. 'Mike, what's happening? It all went wrong, and I feel so bad about it. About the children.'

And Mike replied, inside her head, *It's better to fight and lose than never to fight at all. Time is running out, Cressida, Cresssida... run with it... run...*

She felt strange, disembodied. She had failed him but he was calling to her. The failure, the children, the untraceable artist who had eluded her vengeance, they all cried out to her, driving her. Chel was right: at that moment, if she had known of the connection between Debbie and Oliver she would have gone after Tel and somehow made him do what she wanted, built total triumph out of the disaster at one blow for her phantom lover... but she didn't know. She was as inadequate as a schemer as she had been as a wife, and anyway, there had been nobody she knew to tell her. The force drove her, but in quite another direction. She went with it.

Debbie would never know that Tel, whom she was to be lucky enough never to meet, had by his refusal in all probability saved her from serious injury, or even death. She drove to Treliske for the last time on the morning following her talk with Roger, with her mind buzzing with ideas and plans, and the knowledge that Tim would probably be arrested today lying at the back of it like a dark stone at the bottom of an otherwise sunlit pool.

For the two simple reasons that Seagulls had been forbidden ground to him, and that Debbie had always walked down the hill to go with him in his own car, Mawgan had never before set eyes on the yellow Golf.

'Bit bright, isn't it?' he asked, shading his eyes as if from strong sunlight. 'I got a feeling my street-cred aren't going to survive this trip.'

'Get in and stop whingeing,' said Debbie, opening her own door. 'It's this or a long walk.'

'We're not going to slip through the village without no-one seeing us,' he objected, sliding into the seat beside her.

'Did you want to?'

'Think I'd rather. I weren't expecting to arrive back in a mobile sunflower.'

'Oliver calls it a buttercup. What's your problem? Bashful, are we?'

'I'm a shy, retiring person,' said Mawgan, outrageously, as they set off, Debbie driving more carefully than usual, on the long drive back to the river. She grinned at that.

'A liar, too! Do you want to go round the back way, then?'

'No thanks. That'd mean passing the ruins, and I don't think I want to see 'em yet.'

She parted her lips to say, *wimp*! but closed them again. He had probably been surprised and pleased to wake up and find himself without extensive third degree burns – to wake up at all, come to that. She could see his point about the ruins.

'Is Howells off the hook yet? How's it going?'

'Motive, means and opportunity,' Debbie recited. 'He's got them all.' She felt miserable, just talking about it. 'There's no other suspects.'

'Sounds like he might go down for it then,' said Mawgan, quietly. 'Poor old Tim.'

Debbie looked at him in surprise.

'You called him Tim!'

'Did I? Must be fellow-feeling, or something…'

'There were *people* in the house,' said Debbie. 'Little children…'

'Bad.' They went for a little way in silence. 'Try not to cry while you're driving. You can't see properly.'

'How do you know?' asked Debbie, sniffing inelegantly. 'Have you tried it?' And remembered the telegraph pole and wished she had kept her mouth shut. He didn't answer.

'You've stopped calling me Deborah,' said Debbie, after a while.

'You got a problem with that? Did you want me to go on?'

'No… yes… I don't know.'

'I just got tired of keeping you at arm's length,' said Mawgan, looking studiously out of the window. 'Too much effort. Made my arm ache.'

'I'm glad.'

Another mile or two passed under the wheels in silence. Debbie hadn't expected the trip to be quite so awkward, she had rather been looking forward to it. After a while, Mawgan said, 'He saved me – you and him together. That'll go in his favour. And nobody else but me was hurt.'

'But if he didn't do it –'

'If they can't prove he did it, that'll go in his favour, too. He might even get off, if it helps – with a good lawyer. I read somewheres that motive, means and opportunity, on their own, aren't a case. It takes an eye-witness for that, or a bit of forensic stuff.'

'You said he'd go down.'

'I said he might go down.'

'So what do you really think?' asked Debbie. She changed gear untidily, and the car jerked forward. Mawgan gave a grunt of protest.

'Ouch!'

'Sorry. What do you think?'

'I think he will go down. But he might not. Come on, Deb, how do I know? It all comes back to the same old question, doesn't it? If he didn't do it, then who did?'

'There isn't anybody else.'

'I rest my case. And so will the prosecution. After that, it's up to the jury, and to be fair, the children don't make it look good.'

'That's why you think…?'

'That's why I think.'

'He won't speak to me,' said Debbie, desolately, for this fact had become apparent this morning.

'Sensible fellow,' said Mawgan.

'*Sensible?*' Debbie had been hurt, and it showed in her voice. Mawgan shifted, uncomfortably, trying unsuccessfully to find a position that didn't make his collar-bone ache.

'Deb, get real here. If he has a solicitor, and I hope he has by this time, he'll have been advised not to. It isn't personal.'

'Advised…?'

'His wife says he tried to kill her so's he could run off with you for your money, according to your sister-in-law. Think about it.'

'But nobody can believe that!'

'You'd be surprised what people can believe. Particularly the police. It's part of their job to believe the unbelievable, it's always happening for one thing.'

Five minutes went by. They were nearly at Helston. Debbie said, as if the words were being forced out of her,

'Mawgan… is prison very hard?'

He laughed for answer, a short, unamused bark of laughter that was like a knife in her heart. The silence that followed was more uncomfortable than Debbie would have believed possible. After a mile or so of twisting lane, Mawgan said, mildly, 'Deb, do you think you could stop driving as if you got your petrol down under? I'm sure I can feel the ends grating together.'

'Sorry,' she muttered.

'Just thought I'd mention it.'

She tried to concentrate, but it was difficult. Mawgan said, 'Listen bird, if you're going to spend the rest of your life with me, you're going to have to harden up. It's not going to go away.'

'I just hate to think of him… he's such an innocent.'

'Your brother called him a plonker,' Mawgan remarked.

'Yes, well, Oliver is like you. He doesn't suffer fools gladly. Not that I'm saying Tim is a fool,' she added, hurriedly.

'I hope he suffered me, then.'

Debbie found a genuine laugh, it felt like the first for a year.

'He said, if I married you, I would have my hands full. And Chel said it would be like riding the big dipper at the fair.'

'Do I take that as a vote for, or against?'

'For, I think. Did you like them?'

'They care about you. That's a plus.'

Debbie said, carefully, 'Chel worked in catering too, you know. She had a job at one of the big harbour side hotels, back home in Embridge.'

'Did she?' He didn't follow it up, and she was wise enough to let it go as if it was simply casual conversation.

'And Oliver paints wonderful pictures full of ships and sea and gulls and things.' She pulled in to let a tractor go past, and after that she had to concentrate on driving, as the lanes became narrower, twistier, and infested with crawling cars driven by worried-looking people, more at home on the great motorways of Britain.

Their progress down the village street didn't go unnoticed, but was recognised by the odd friendly salute or even wave as they drove past. They reached their destination without either of them having made any comment on this, and walked together to the rear door: Debbie fancied that the atmosphere inside the Fish shifted up a gear the instant that he walked through, as if the place had simply been ticking over without him. Shirley practically jumped to attention, and Tony immediately appeared at the door to the restaurant. She took his things upstairs and then left him to it, and went to find Roger and her own problems, he wasn't the only one with matters to attend to. She wasn't certain that he even saw her go and could only hope he would have the sense not to get too involved.

Roger was sitting at one of the forecourt tables with a stranger for company, they had their heads close together and coffee at their elbows. Sheets of paper, weighted down by an ashtray, decorated the surface of the table. They both looked up as Debbie's shadow fell across them. The stranger rose politely to his feet.

'You must be Debbie. Carl Colenso.' He held out his hand, and Debbie took it, liking what she saw. He was a similar physical type to Mawgan, which immediately stood in his favour, but taller, and took better care of himself. He had thick, close-growing dark hair that looked as if it might curl, given the chance, blue eyes. Mid to late twenties, good-looking. The name, Colenso, was as Cornish as her own or Mawgan's. Good so far, the locals would like that.

'Carl came over to give us a hand,' said Roger. 'He's a free-lance journalist, he knows the ropes.' He gathered up a handful of papers and handed them to Debbie. 'Read that. If we can get the major dailies to run it with our advert, that should get some response. Want some coffee?'

'In a minute. I've got to make a phone call first.' She ran her eye over the crumpled sheets. Carl Colenso knew his business. He wrote readably, making a human-interest story without sentiment, and keeping to the facts. She decided that she approved of him. 'That looks OK. Can you give me a minute? We can talk properly then.' They exchanged smiles and Debbie walked down to the foreshore, taking her mobile from her pocket as she went. Standing on the edge of the water, she called up her father's office. While she waited to be put through to him, she noted, and again approved, the big Feeling sloop moored alongside the end of the Seagulls jetty where the final section was a floating pontoon and the water was deep. Nice boat. Did he live on it, she wondered? He looked the kind who might. His boat would make a very nice asset, if he agreed to come in with them.

'Debbie!' said Jerry's voice, in her ear. 'I've been waiting for your call. How are you, my darling?'

'In the shit, apparently, from what Oliver was saying,' said Debbie. 'Dad – it's not as bad as Lesley makes out, truly it isn't.' She heard the shake in her voice, and was surprised. She had thought she could handle this one coolly, but apparently not.

'I know. I've got the transcript here in my hand, have you seen a copy? I think the technical term is a fit-up. It might be ticklish getting him out of it. Is it that serious between you, that we should try?'

'Yes, Dad, I'm afraid it is. Oliver said Mum has taken it badly.'

'Debbie, I don't have to tell you that your mother can be an extremely difficult woman.'

'I thought it might be best if I came home to see her,' said Debbie. 'See you, too. There's a lot I need to talk about. It can't be before the holiday, but I should be able to steal a day when it's over.'

'I think you should know that Oliver has given your man a conditional green light. Cheryl too. They rang late last night, I believe they had dinner with you?'

'Yes, they did.'

'I don't think we can discuss it on the phone, Deb darling. Let me know when you can get away, and come to the office here. There's things I need to talk about too.'

'I'll do that. Love you, Dad.'

'Love you too, Deb. Chin up!'

One thing you could say for a solicitor, Debbie thought, as she crunched back over the shingle, they didn't get hysterical over nothing. Her father had his own opinion, obviously, but he could be trusted to keep an open mind until they had talked. She felt better for the brief conversation, but there were breakers ahead, she couldn't kid herself that there weren't. The coming bank holiday would only be the first of them.

A tsunami might have been a better description, certainly for the bank holiday. Some sort of major cataclysm, anyway, Debbie decided, looking back on it from a more peaceful date as yet in the future. It had so much going against it that Tim's problems, about which they could do nothing anyway, temporarily faded into the background. As predicted, he had been arrested and charged with arson, and although he was now out on bail, there would be no help from him. Also as predicted, there would be no insurance payout, the holiday itself ground everything to a halt and nobody knew what was likely to happen next, or even who was technically in charge of the disaster. It was simpler to shelve it for now. Debbie and Roger, ably seconded by Carl Colenso, just soldiered on until someone should instruct them to stop.

It wasn't simply the problem that they didn't know who their guests were, they didn't know how they were arranged either, so the logistics were impossible. If there were any families involved, it would begin to get really complicated, and it was reasonable to suppose, on a bank holiday, that there would be. Most people in the village, although willing to co-operate in this emergency as far as they could, had only one spare room, if they had one at all, and over the holiday, most of them not even that, their own friends and families were coming. The standard of some of the rooms that were available left something to be desired, and the papers, contacted by the combined efforts of Carl and Shirley, were mainly co-operative, but bore disappointingly little fruit. Shirley took two phone calls on the day that the story first appeared, both of whom elected to cancel, everyone else was apparently too busy packing to have time for reading.

'You should have put it on the sports page,' Mawgan suggested, with what Debbie considered to be out-of-place flippancy. 'Blokes at least always find time to read that.'

'That mightn't have been a bad idea,' said Debbie. 'Why didn't you have it earlier?' She sounded cross, but Mawgan, faced with running a pub and a restaurant over a bank holiday with the head chef incapacitated by a broken collar-bone and lingering concussion, had too many problems of his own to have time for hers. They shared the same bed at night, which at present had to be more friendly than romantic, and was therefore frustrating, but apart from that it seemed to Debbie that they barely met. The only virtue, she decided moodily, was that they were both of them too busy to quarrel. He had, she was certain, lied himself out of hospital in order to be at the Fish during its busiest time, and that, she was beginning to be certain, wasn't even the whole story. She was trying to find a tactful moment to ask if he had ever discussed with his GP the concept that he might have left prison clinically depressed, but so far, one hadn't materialised. Tactful moments, Mawgan, and August bank holiday were demonstrably mutually exclusive. To put it bluntly, he was being bloody difficult – not for the first time since she had known him – and she was often quite glad that she had a job to escape to.

Without Shirley, it would have been even worse: Shirley, said Roger, was a star. The notice fixed to the gate at Seagulls directed everyone down to the Fish, and it was Shirley who, along with her normal work, was going to receive the first waves of shock, bewilderment or indignation. Although Debbie, Roger and Carl weren't far away, they couldn't sit around on the pub forecourt waiting for people, there was too much to be done. An accident due to negligence, said Debbie, shuddering at the thought, was all they needed at this precise moment. Every single piece of gear on the boats that might cause trouble had to be checked, then checked again. When you were down, you were vulnerable; it would be too easy to progress from that to down and out. Moreover, she was uneasily aware somewhere in the back of her mind that, if you believed Tim to be innocent, the inference that someone else was out to get them was unavoidable.

'It simply doesn't work,' she said, taking a brief break on the edge of the lawn to check the situation. 'There's a potential twenty people, twenty-two I suppose, if Lesley had planned extra beds in the family rooms and only she knows that, of which four are known to have cancelled. You can take another four, Carl, and I'm sorry about this but you might have to take a family with children. Mawgan's lending us some bed linen, and you're OK for catering, you said. That leaves us with either twelve or fourteen people, including two stop-overs from last week which account for four, and five double rooms scattered all over the village, two of which are already taken, and at least one of which I wouldn't want to sleep in myself. Some of them may well be children too young to be on their own. We can't use the staff quarters because the house isn't safe, the power is off, and everything smells foul. The Fish is full up. Suggestions?'

'Pray that some of them go straight home again?' said Roger, but Carl shook his head.

'They won't do that. Not having come all this way, and certainly not tonight. It's not your fault, you've done all you can. They'll have to sort themselves out.'

'They may not like that.' Debbie clapped a hand to her pocket, and drew out her mobile. 'Hi, Shirley!' She spoke for a few minutes and then put the phone away. 'Family. Two adults, two teenagers, hadn't booked a family room. Shirley's giving them tea. She says they're a bit surprised.'

'Nice way of putting it. That's two rooms gone, straight off.'

'If one doesn't mind sleeping in the saloon with me, I could squeeze in five,' Carl offered. 'Mind you they'd have to get on with each other.'

'Once the actual weekend is over, it'll ease up a bit.' Debbie suddenly realised that she was beginning to enjoy herself. It must be Blitz syndrome, she thought, or, and here was a solemn thought, was she a control freak like her mother? She had never noticed it about herself before, but come to think, Mawgan had accused her of it. It wouldn't really be surprising, nor did the characteristic have to be used for bullying people. She got to her feet. 'One of us had better go and speak to them, and I suppose it has to be me. Keep up the good work, you two.'

Shirley stopped her as she walked through.

'Mr. Angwin went upstairs a few minutes ago. He said to tell you if you came in.'

'OK, I'll go up in a minute. Are those my people?' She gestured to a group in the little lounge area, sitting round a tea table and looking, on the whole, as if they were enjoying the excitement. Nice looking couple and two boys, about fifteen and sixteen. They would enjoy the Feeling, she thought, but it wouldn't do to be precipitate. There could be some littlies yet. The father rose to greet her as she approached.

'Mrs Howells?' He held out his hand. 'I see you've been having a bit of trouble.'

'Debbie Nankervis, I'm the chief instructor.' She and Roger had agreed on this for the sake of convenience, he had said it was only fair. She shook his hand. 'I'm afraid Mr and Mrs Howells have had to take time out to deal with things.' She smiled as she said it, in so beguiling a way that all four of them automatically smiled back. 'We're trying to do our best to save your holiday, if that's what you would like. Only it might be a bit make-do and mend over the bank holiday itself, there's a terrible shortage of accommodation. I'm sorry we couldn't let you know, all our records got burned.'

'Hey, cool!' said one of the boys, his eyes sparkling at the unexpected adventure, and she gave him a friendly grin.

'Rather hot, actually. Did you book with us this year, or with Mrs Howells' aunt last year?'

'We've been coming every year for the past three years.' Mother smiled. What a lot of smiles, Debbie thought, how nice if everyone was like this. 'Mr and Mrs Forbes – Wendy and Angus – and these are Robert and Philip.' Hand shakings all round. 'We booked for the whole fortnight, they've got permission from school. It's the only time Angus could get.'

They could move into the Fish next weekend, maybe even before. That was half a problem solved.

'I can't really do anything now, we've several options and we shall have to wait and see who else arrives.' Smile again. 'Why don't you go out in the sunshine and have a look round, and come back here around six? We should have a better idea then of what we're doing.'

'As a matter of interest,' said Angus Forbes. 'Chief instructor in what?'

'Sailing. It was turning into a sailing school. Didn't Mrs Howells say when she wrote?'

'Only that Mrs Latter had died, and she and her husband were taking over.'

Debbie had caught a gleam in the boys' eyes. She was almost sure that she was going to hand them over to Carl for their first week and give them the holiday of their lives, but there was still the chance that she might not be able to. Smile, she would have faceache by the end of the day.

'I'll see you again later on, then. Have a lovely afternoon, and don't worry. We'll fix you up.'

Relieved to take the smile off her face, she left them and went upstairs. She found Mawgan sprawled in one of the armchairs with his eyes closed, but he opened them when she stood beside him.

'Hullo, you look a bit more cheerful. Having a good time?'

'Actually, yes, I am.' She sat in the other armchair. 'You, on the other hand, look bushed, so do I take it that you aren't?'

'I don't think I'm fit for August bank holiday. I don't suppose you'd like to put the kettle on?'

'I can manage that.' She came back in a few minutes with two mugs of coffee, setting one of them on the table beside him. 'I can see now why you said the guest house was a mistake. We'll be much better off without it.'

'We?' He had levered himself up in the chair and looked a bit more alert. 'What's with the *we*, Deb?'

'Roger and I had this idea. Would you like to hear it?'

'Very much.' Roger had been right, he had it worked out already, she could see. She told him anyway, and he listened with interest.

'That sounds more like it. Mind you, it's always easier to start with a blank page, to be fair. Can you do it? That's a prime piece of waterside property, with a house already on it, it won't go for peanuts, and then you've got to rebuild. Although I might be able to swing something for you there. We shall have to see.'

'There's trustees I need to sound out, but I don't think it'll be a problem. I thought I'd go to Embridge quite soon, talk to my father. About that, and… other things. If he thinks he can help you, will you let him?'

'I'll talk it over with him, yes.'

Bloody little sister! Debbie thought, viciously. Making up damaging lies, and then, oh-so-cleverly not telling them outright, so that they couldn't be denied! She probably saw it all on the telly, silly, destructive little witch!

'What's the matter, bird? You looked quite murderous just then.'

'Just thoughts, don't worry about them.'

Mawgan picked up his mug, but sat without drinking, his eyes unfocussed, lost in thoughts of his own.

'Deb… this is just an idea, you understand. Something you said the other day… I think I'm being the sucker and taking the bait, but your sister-in-law… what exactly did she do in that hotel?'

'Head receptionist, trainee manageress, something like that.'

He said nothing for a while, but she could see that he was thinking deeply. She drank her own coffee, and waited.

'I think I told you,' he said, at last. 'I didn't want the pub, I don't really want it now. It's the restaurant I was after.' He spoke dreamily, sounding quite different from his usual practical self. 'It's such a perfect position, right down by the water. I wanted to turn it into somewhere that people came to from all over… and then I end up, half my time is taken up running a bloody pub!'

'*Could* you?' asked Debbie.

'You bet your sweet life, I could!'

'Modest, with it, too!' she smiled at him.

'No point in underestimating yourself, Deb, you never get nowhere that way. Look at you, you're finding out just what you can do, are you going to lie about it?'

Debbie's mobile rang again before she had to reply to that leading question.

'OK Shirley, I'll be right down.' She switched off and sat for a minute, meeting his eyes. 'What I'm discovering in myself is a frightening gift for organisation,' she said. 'Right, Chef, I must go organise. Take a couple of Paracetamol, have a lie down, before you fall down. Told you I was bossy! See you later.'

She ran down the stairs to greet another two lots of bemused Seagulls' guests assembled in reception, and as she ran, an odd thought came into her head.

Tim and Lesley were being left behind while the rest of them moved on, caught fast in the toils of their own troubles, stopped in their tracks. Herself and Mawgan, Roger, Chel and Oliver, Carl too, were the ones going on into the future that they had dreamed. It would be nice to think that for them, as well, the gates of opportunity would open, but she didn't think it would be for the two of them together, even if it happened for them separately. Lesley maybe, when she had recovered from her breakdown. Tim, poor Tim, would go to prison and find out for himself how it felt to be sent there for something that he hadn't done.

Unless, against all sense, he had done it.

She still couldn't believe it.

XXIII

Debbie took her day's grace when most of the holiday crowds had begun to disperse, leaving behind her an orderly programme and a happy collection of guests. The Forbes family, delighted with their unexpected treat, had enjoyed their time with Carl on the Feeling, and had now been replaced with two young couples, there had been no very young children. Lesley's aunt, on the whole, had gone for older families, and as it happened, most of the people who had appeared, wondering what on earth was going on, in the lounge of the Fish had been Tim and Lesley's own bookings. The quartet of young people, who had now gone onto the Feeling when the Forbes family moved into the Fish at the end of the week, had happily gone off for their first week to fend for themselves, and turned up every morning with smiles on their faces to enjoy themselves in the dinghies. The rest had been accommodated around the village, and the dodgy room hadn't even been needed, so altogether, everyone had reason to congratulate themselves. Carl was settling in to be part of the team, and things were running well. Mawgan, too, was almost back by this time to his normal insouciant self, and had returned one-handedly to his kitchen, saying that he had slacked around for long enough, keeping on the part-timer to lift and carry for him. Debbie, who had never seen him in his chef's whites before, was beginning to believe that he meant what he said. She couldn't help hearing things, living in the Fish as she now did, and she knew, in a way that she hadn't known before, exactly how much he probably owed her for that episode in the snow. Without her, even if he had lived, he might well have lost his arm, and with it, very possibly, a whole, unsuspectedly burning ambition. The restaurant in Milan where he had charge of the kitchen, as Tony, not Mawgan, had told her, had earned itself a Michelin star under his leadership, no mean achievement for a British chef in an Italian restaurant.

'Love the fancy trousers,' she said, standing back to admire him. 'Pity the sling and the Frankenstein scar spoil the effect. Isn't it amazing, the things you don't imagine about people?'

'You've given me a few surprises, too,' he told her. He kissed her on the end of her nose. 'See you later, don't drink too much. I wish I had your job in the evenings!'

'It's a lucky thing I don't have yours,' said Debbie. 'I don't think my *Coq au Vin à la Deb* would exactly go down a storm.'

'You must give me the recipe.' Then, before she could frame a retort, he had gone.

But on the morning that she rose alone in the grey dawn for her trip along the coast to Dorset, she had a dreary feeling that before the day was out she might have learned the price of all this fun and laughter and love, and of the bright future that she and Roger had envisaged. There had been an incident the previous week that she couldn't dislodge from her mind, it had thrown a disquieting new light on the situation, so that what had seemed quite clear and well-defined had changed entirely like one of those confusing pictograms that turn into something else as you look at them closely.

It had all been innocent enough, of that she was almost certain now, the change had taken place within her own mind. It had been evening, and she and Roger had been sitting, together with the two young couples and a scattering of their other students, on the forecourt of the Fish, discussing the day's activities and planning for tomorrow's. She counted them off in her head, herself and Roger of course, Philip and Betty, Richard and Angie, another couple, Bill and Silvana – nice people, all of them, good fun and enjoying themselves, even Italian Silvana who had problems with the language and struggled with technical terms. Then there was Ivan and his girlfriend Kay, and Kay's older sister Hannah, who, she thought now, was probably not quite so nice – but that was subjective, and possibly unfair. There had been a couple of others a little older, about a dozen of them altogether, crowded around one of the wooden tables. Roger and Phil had just got up to fetch a fresh round of drinks. The Feeling, with the Forbes family and Carl, had been still at sea at the time.

'Hey, look who's here!' had cried Roger, and looking round, Debbie had seen Mawgan coming from the bar, a pint in his hand. She waved.

'Come and join us!' The invitation was unnecessary, she had already suggested earlier that he should do so, without much hope that he would. He looked less of a mess in that the bruises were beginning to fade, but the fresh scar on his forehead, he had complained, required a bolt through the neck to carry it off properly. He had, so far, kept away from the general public in the bars, claiming that it was no part of a landlord's duty to frighten the punters. His arrival caused a certain amount of interest.

'Good God!' said Richard. 'Whatever happened to you?'

Mawgan came to stand behind Debbie's chair, the backs of his fingers that held the glass gently and deliberately brushed her cheek making a tingle on her skin. She put up her hand to touch his.

'Fell downstairs,' he explained, briefly.

'You should be more careful,' Betty advised him, smiling. Roger, gathering up empties to return to the bar, grinned.

'He was in a bit of a hurry. The house was on fire at the time,' he said. 'Sit down.' He pulled out the chair beside Debbie on which he had been sitting himself, and indicated the glass. 'Another one of those?'

'Why not?' Mawgan took the chair. 'Tommy knows which. Thanks.'

Angie looked at him with interest.

'Are you the elusive Tim Howells, then? We've been wondering when he'd turn up.'

This subject was a delicate one, round which Debbie and Roger had managed, so far, to skate without disaster. Mawgan said, lazily, 'Do I look like a Tim Howells?'

'Actually, yes.' Angie looked him over critically. 'Sort of dark and squarish and could be Welsh. But you sound like a Cornishman, so I take it you aren't him.'

'Mawgan,' said Mawgan, which in the context of being Welsh or not being Welsh, hardly helped. He had put the glass down on the table, and his hand had found Debbie's, fingers entwined. He grinned at her, wickedly. 'Deb's bit of rough.'

Debbie jumped. The use of Tim's derogatory phrase shook her. She had already realised that more must have passed between Tim and Mawgan than she had ever witnessed, but surely Tim wouldn't have said that to his face? Or − and this was a new thought − had Mawgan said it himself? He was perfectly capable of it, and it did, in all fairness, sound more like him than Tim. The *ethnic studies* gibe that had followed was more Tim's style. The idea that they had discussed her − quarrelled over her even − was uncomfortable.

The others were introducing themselves. The conversation, thankfully, was moving on.

'Are you another sailing type, then?' Ivan was asking. 'Breaking a collarbone must have put a crimp in your style!' He smiled sympathetically, but Mawgan denied any interest in boats.

'You all know more about it than I do,' he said. 'Although I believe Deb has plans to alter that.' They all laughed. He slotted in well, Debbie saw, used to mixing with people in his working life, and at ease with them. She hadn't realised, until this moment, that it was an issue, for because of Tim's feud with him, she had never seen him… against her own background? *Ouch*!

Regional accents were cool these days. She was immediately ashamed of the thought, but it had come into her head unsought. 'He goes surfing,' she said.

'Not totally a wash-out then.' Bill grinned. 'Bit of a Cornish thing, isn't it?'

'We've the beaches and the surf for it.'

They discussed surfing for a few minutes, and then Phil and Roger came back with the fresh round of drinks, and the interruption broke the thread. When Roger had fetched himself another chair, Betty looked at Mawgan curiously.

'So, do you live locally, then, Mawgan?' she asked.

Mawgan had finished his first pint — if it was the first — and started on the next. He wasn't fooled for a minute, even if Debbie wanted to be. So far, in this company, he was the outsider.

'Right now, it's fair to say nobody lives more local'n me,' he said.

Betty looked as if she knew she was being teased, but wasn't certain how. Roger came to her rescue.

'It's his pub,' he said.

Hannah spoke for the first time. Her tone was confrontational.

'You're not the licensee,' she said, sharply.

'No.'

'Why not?' If the question was rude, she covered it by smiling. Debbie felt herself tense, and caught Roger's eye. Mawgan answered, easily, 'Oh, I'm just the man as keeps the books and pays the wages. Tommy runs the bars. I'm the chef for the restaurant.'

Hannah's mouth opened. She said, unforgivably, 'Oh! I don't think I ever met a chef socially before!'

Debbie's lips parted, then she intercepted a slight shake of the head from Roger, and closed them again. Mawgan said, glossing over any offence, intentional or merely tactless, with unexpected social dexterity, 'Not a lot of people have, so aren't you the lucky one? We keep very unsocial hours.'

'It always seems a funny job for a man to do – cooking.' Hannah spoke with a challenge in her voice, but Mawgan only laughed.

'Now you sound like my dad.'

Hannah laughed too, but looked suddenly uncomfortable. Perhaps, thought Debbie, she hadn't intended the remark quite as it came out – or then again, perhaps she had. She had the first, faint, intimation of the line her mother's objections might take, and her heart sank. How could an attitude so outdated be so… well, *real?*

Silvana said, plaintively, 'I do not understand.'

Bill put his arm round her shoulders.

'Don't worry about it, sweet. It's not important.' He gave Mawgan a look that had in it a certain amount of friendliness. 'She's foreign, poor child. She lives in a perpetual state of confusion! They do things different in Milan!'

Mawgan said, with deceptive idleness, 'So they do. I lived there two years, it's definitely not like St. Erbyn.'

He had their attention now, all right.

'*Parlate italiano?*' Silvana demanded, eagerly.

'*Sí.*'

'*Allora parli alcuno!*' she commanded. '*Sono stato un molto tempo dalla sede.*'

'*Che cosa lo desiderate dire?*' He smiled at her. Debbie's jaw had dropped, she realised, she closed her mouth. Silvana waved a graceful hand at the Fish, gleaming white behind them in the fading dusk.

'*Hanno detto che questo e il vostro?*'

'*Sí.* Excuse us one moment,' said Mawgan, to the company at large, and launched out into the unfamiliar language. Really with a Cornish accent? Debbie wasn't in a position to judge. He stopped to hunt for a word occasionally, and Silvana prompted him, her eyes sparkling. Debbie watched with interest; she wasn't alone. It would have been interesting to know what was said, exactly, as at one point Silvana put her hand over her mouth and rolled her eyes expressively. Hannah had turned a dull red, but it had to be from a guilty conscience, she understood no more than the rest of them – except Bill, possibly. She looked, Debbie was glad to see, discomfited. Finally, Silvana broke off with a peal of laughter.

'Yes, you speak Italian,' she said. She turned to Debbie. 'This is one bad man, Debb*ee*! You take care!'

Debbie looked at him suspiciously.

'What have you been saying?'

'Nothing,' he said, airily.

'You took an awful long time to say *nothing*!' She giggled, catching Silvana's eye. Suddenly, the group had coalesced, the threads of the original conversation were picked up as if there had been no interruption, no stranger suddenly thrust into their midst. They had accepted Mawgan as one of themselves, someone important to Debbie, who was in her turn important to them. Only Hannah still looked a little shame-faced, as if she wished she had kept her mouth shut and not pushed so hard.

Mawgan left when Bill and Richard began to collect orders for the next round, saying that he was going to chill out quietly in front of the News upstairs. When he had said goodnight and gone, Betty looked at Debbie, bright-eyed.

'Well, that was a surprise!' she said.

'It was?' Debbie was feeling her way, no longer sure of herself. Angie laughed.

'We all had you and Roger down as an item. We had no idea there was a random Italian-speaking Cornishman in the equation!'

Roger grinned.

'I should be so lucky! I did have hopes at one time, but they only lasted about half an hour. That's the way the cookie crumbles.'

'Oh, come on!' said Debbie.

'True.' He looked at her ruefully. 'You came out of the house with Les, and I looked and I thought, yippee, it's my lucky day! And then, probably not as much as half an hour later actually, *he* walked out of that door over there and I knew it was back to the drawing board.'

'You're making that up! We hardly knew each other!'

'Is that so? Well, all I can say is, he was taking a rise out of you in the way you only do to someone you know – and like – very well indeed. And you were beetroot-coloured and mumbling like an idiot.' He turned to the others. 'I ask you, ladies and gentlemen of the jury, what would you have thought? A clear case?'

There was a murmur of general agreement. Roger looked at Debbie, thoughtful now.

'It's amazing really,' he said.

'What is?' asked Debbie, indignantly. 'That he should fancy me?'

'No. How different Mawgan is from *bloody Angwin*. You're perceptive, aren't you, Deb?'

'From *who*?' Phil demanded, but fortunately, before Roger had to explain, Bill came out of the pub.

'There's a table free in the bar if anyone's interested. It's getting a bit chilly out here.'

Debbie followed the others inside, wondering if Roger had meant what he said, or was just teasing her. She had, she now recollected, given him a quick once-over too, at that moment when they had met. Within... yes, half an hour, she had forgotten it, and never thought about it since. Well, well. Had Mawgan made up his mind that far back? She must remember to ask him sometime.

He hadn't made good his escape, she saw, but had been cornered at the bar by a clique of the locals, and that was at least the third, possibly the fourth or fifth, pint he had sunk tonight. His body language, she thought, was interesting; he didn't want to be there, but he was putting up a good show for the benefit of the customers. He didn't usually drink in the bar at all that she had ever noticed, but perhaps tonight, since he wasn't working... she hoped he would call a halt at this one, alcohol was supposed to be off-limits for the present, after that bang on the head.

How little you knew about people, when you thought you knew everything. Tonight had been very instructive. Indeed, the whole of the past week had been a steep learning curve, it wasn't until you lived with a person that you really got to know them – although she supposed that must cut both ways.

Hannah followed the direction of her eyes.

'He's too old for you,' she said, with a shake of her head. 'Poor old Roger!'

'Excuse me?' Debbie wasn't too fond of Hannah this evening. She heard her own voice, sharp.

'Why, how old is he? How old are *you*, come to that?' Angie was smiling, making a joke of it.

'I'm twenty-five in a couple of weeks.' And Mawgan? She had no idea.

'And him?' said Hannah, pushing for a reaction.

'About the same as my brother, I suppose...'

'Which is?'

'Oh, give it up, Hannah!' Kay sounded impatient. 'Does it matter?' It was becoming obvious, Debbie thought, why Hannah was reduced to holidaying with her sister, no chance she'd get a boyfriend of her own, the cow! Poor old Ivan, rather than poor old Roger!

'It's a perfectly reasonable question,' Hannah argued.

'But hardly your business!'

'Stop it, you two, please,' said Ivan, in the tired voice of someone who had seen it all before, too often.

Angie stepped in with a deft turn of the subject, and the unexpectedly confrontational moment passed. Debbie concluded that for some reason, Hannah didn't like her and wondered why. Because she had a life? Hannah obviously didn't, poor thing – or maybe she thought that Mawgan was the right age for *her*. She wouldn't, after all, be the first of their students who had fancied her chances.

Oliver was thirty-two, but that didn't help. Debbie, thinking back over all the things that Mawgan had told her, discovered an equation that might work. His sister Cressida had married at nineteen, and the marriage had lasted two years – roughly, anyway. Mawgan had been given a three-year sentence for Michael Stanley's death, that made five years, give or take a few months… and she knew that he was ten years Cressida's senior. So that made him what? Thirty-three now? Maybe thirty-four? It would depend at what time of year he – and Cressida – had been born. Say, for the sake of argument, he was eight-and-a-half years older than her, *was* that too old? No, it wasn't. It was just right.

Had she got a hang-up over Oliver, as Lesley had said? Was she really looking for his equivalent? An older man?

Betty caught her eye, and smiled at her, with sympathy.

'Going to have a thick head in the morning, your lovely man,' she observed.

'It'll go well with the concussion,' said Debbie. She looked pensive.

'Men!' said Betty sympathetically. 'Can't live without them, can't live with them! Keep your head down and leave the aspirin in a conspicuous place, that's my advice as one who's been there.'

'I'll remember,' said Debbie.

The next time she glanced across to the bar he had gone.

She went upstairs shortly after, making her excuses to the others who all grinned at her knowingly – although if they thought she was about to make mad, passionate love with a man with a newly broken collarbone, they had never tried – and found Mawgan, not watching the News, which was over by this time, but brooding stormily over a whisky glass with the bottle on the table beside him. He wasn't exactly drunk, but had had enough to be unpredictable. Debbie perched herself on the arm of his chair, on his uninjured side, and refrained from reminding him that he shouldn't be drinking at all.

'Well?' she said, for want of anything better.

'Is it?' He didn't look at her. 'What is it with people? They freeze me out for eighteen months with all that *Mr. Angwin* business, and now, suddenly, we're all friends again, back on first name terms? Well, it don't work!'

Debbie, who had thought it might be Hannah's social *gaffe* at the bottom of this, was almost relieved.

'It does, you know,' she said.

'Really? Explain it, then.'

Careful. Debbie thought for a minute.

'First of all, you have to remember that they don't know the whole truth.'

'Whatever that is,' muttered Mawgan, but at least it showed he was listening. Debbie drew a breath.

'It's all about something Roger said, I think,' she said. '*You've* dictated their attitude to you, yourself. Mrs. Tregear said something the same. They didn't know what to think. They liked you, before it all happened, so it was confusing for them, and you didn't help them, so they followed your lead and backed off. I think, actually, now I come to think about it, they might have been a bit hurt.'

'They could have had a bit more faith, couldn't they?'

'Perhaps they did,' said Debbie. 'It's you that set the terms. They couldn't get near you.'

'I didn't want 'em near. I didn't want *no-one* near.'

'Then where's your grouse?'

He was silent. She removed the now-empty whisky glass from his hand and set it on the mantelpiece.

'People don't like to be shut out,' she said.

Mawgan said, as if it was a personal affront, 'So what's changed, suddenly.'

'Their perception of you, of course.' Debbie spoke calmly, although her heart was thumping. 'You went into a burning house to rescue Lesley. They're all relieved that they can recognise you again and want to let bygones be bygones. Just don't blow it now.'

Mawgan said nothing for a while, and when he did speak it was to change the subject – not necessarily for the better.

'Who's the skinny woman with the constipated outlook?'

'Oh… Hannah.' Debbie pulled a face. 'She's got a chip on her shoulder. Can't get a man, probably.' She spoke dismissively. Mawgan smothered a laugh, to her relief.

'Mi-*ow*!'

'You don't need to take any notice of her.'

'I didn't. So long as you didn't, neither.'

'Why should I?' Before he could answer that question, she added. 'And *you* were showing off to cut her down to size, Mawgan Angwin. So don't give *me* a hard time!'

'I'd have been well stuffed if the girl was German, wouldn't I?' he said, but the accompanying grin was only a ghost of itself. He picked up her hand and held it against his cheek. 'D'you really know what you're doing, Deb?'

'Yes.'

'I love you more'n I thought I ever would anyone… but I don't live in your world, nor you in mine, neither.'

'We'll build our own world. It'll be fine.'

'I hope you're right.'

'Come to bed,' said Debbie, gently. 'You're drunk. Are you always Mawgan the Miserable when you've had a few?'

He laughed out loud at that. 'Stick around, and you'll find out.'

He came to bed without argument, but it was a long time before Debbie, at least slept, lying close to him, wakeful, as the hours ticked by. There was far too much to think about for sleep, but through all the questions, turning and tumbling through her tired mind, Debbie was sure of one thing. The flame of love burned clear. She hoped that it was the same for him, and dared not ask.

At least the alcohol seemed to have chased away the horrors, he had fallen asleep easily which, even with her beside him, wasn't always necessarily the case. She wondered if he habitually drank, and if so, if that was why.

In the morning, that late-night exchange might never have happened, Debbie wasn't even wholly certain that Mawgan recalled it. There was a subtle shift in attitude, from the locals, the staff, and from Mawgan himself, as if some invisible boundary had been crossed, some unseen defences breached, and that was all. It was never discussed between them again.

But that was over a week ago, and it was useless to start thinking about it now, when it was time to leave and face the music at home. Mawgan hadn't stirred when she got up, and looking down at his sleeping face she thought about how many hopes were tied up in him, and for a moment even wondered, treacherously, whether she was releasing the substance for the shadow. It suddenly seemed to her a huge step to take, to maybe leave so much behind to *build their own world*, and what a pretentious concept that sounded now!

But there wasn't any substance, she told herself as she went out to her car. Measured against Chel's, for instance, their family life had always been a major disaster area, could anything really make it worse? They weren't even properly related to each other. Oliver's mother was the world-famous sculptress Helen Macken, still very much alive but almost totally alienated from him: Susan's father, an investment broker named Henry Worthington, had been buried the day before she was born. She herself was a hybrid between the two of them. That could have made a real family of them, but in fact it never had. She had tried to persuade herself when she was a little girl, but the grown-up Debbie was well aware that the family unit was riddled with dichotomies and inequalities, and worse, with bitter resentments.

Her own trust fund was a case in point. Henry Worthington had been a wealthy man, he had left her mother a wealthy woman in her own right. He had also set up a substantial trust for his unborn child, and her own trust fund was Jerry Nankervis's way of balancing the scales. He had done the same for Oliver, and the fact that Oliver had refused to touch it didn't alter the fact that Susan had always felt somehow excluded, as if Jerry, the only father she had ever known, was less her father than he was theirs.

Debbie, negotiating the deserted early-morning streets of Truro more or less on auto-pilot, knew that her sister's bitterness had even deeper roots than this. Oliver was the boy, the only one, but he wasn't her mother's son. Dot's disappointment at having only daughters had made Susan feel inferior, and had fuelled a life-long feud between her and Oliver that, as far as their sister could see, would have no end. Debbie herself, so much the younger and the daughter of both parents, had no such hang-ups, but looking back now from this strange, unaccustomed viewpoint, she found herself wondering why not. Her childhood had been against a background of arguments and rows, most of which had centred around Oliver, a much-older brother whose charismatic personality had ensured her own devotion, and from whose disruptive influence her mother and sister had conspired to keep her as far apart as possible, mostly, at least in the early years, with indifferent success.

Thinking about this brought her, almost without making a conscious link, to another little sister. Had the young Cressida Angwin idolised her own much-older brother in the same way? She was about Debbie's age or possibly a little younger as Debbie knew, and Mawgan was probably not more than a year older than Oliver, as she had already worked out: the comparison was easy to draw. How would she feel herself if, for instance, Oliver was somehow responsible for Mawgan's death? A cold feeling crept over her that had nothing to do with the September coolness of the dawn. It would tear her all ways, she knew, and she was a stable person. What would something like that do to somebody who wasn't? Someone who hadn't been toughened by a dysfunctional family life, to whom the world had always been protective, indulgent and kind? It didn't bear thinking about. Mawgan, although not the most sensitive plant that grew on the planet, was quite bright enough to have worked that out. His family too, and the fact that she suspected they had always been close would have hurt every one of them just that little bit more. No wonder they had, as Mawgan had said so picturesquely, gone into a critical mass.

Driving away from the problem seemed to be bringing it into focus, and as it came into focus she found herself drawing another comparison. Oliver had refused to follow in his father's footsteps and become the third generation of Nankervises to enter the family firm. Mawgan, the same. When they had a chance to really know each other, she thought, they would either hate each other or become soul mates, it was a toss-up which. It was, too, another of Susan's resentments that Oliver had rejected what she would have given anything to have. Susan had wanted to go into law, but Dot had laughed at her and said it was only because she wanted Jerry's attention. A university education was wasted on a woman, and anyway, she wasn't a Nankervis so it wouldn't be the same. She had shunted Susan into a safe, boring marriage to safe, boring Tom Casson and that had been that. None of this had ever been important to the much-younger Debbie, but it suddenly assumed importance now. Dot had always been one to laugh at you and say, no, you don't want to do that, it's a silly idea. Do this instead, do it my way. What would she- or Susan, come to that – make of Debbie's own new-found ambition to run a sailing school?

Debbie thought, with a sinking sensation in her stomach, that nobody had ever stood up to her mother and got away with it, even Oliver couldn't be said to have won the battle, he had simply walked away leaving the field littered with the bodies of everybody else. Chel had come nearest, although she probably didn't realise it herself, but then, there was something invincible about Chel, although Debbie couldn't identify from whence it came. *An inner spring on which her spirit fed* was the nearest she could come to it, and even in her own head that sounded over the top. She couldn't be manipulated, was what it came down to in plain English.

But I'm trying to manipulate *her* – Mum, that is, Debbie thought suddenly. I'm trying to manipulate Mawgan too, telling him about her background like that – *do this, do it my way*. I'm just like Mum, and to be honest, so is Susan. There's not a pin to choose between the three of us. I'm doing it because it's so obvious to me that it's the best way for everyone, but is it really? Is this how Mum reasons it out? Is this how she's thinking about me, at this very moment perhaps?

Cornwall was behind her now, and she felt her mind turning, like a compass needle to the north, to what might lie ahead of her. Not just her mother, what was it her father had said? *It might be ticklish getting him out of it.* If the conviction remained on Mawgan's record, it would follow him round all his life, and he hadn't deserved that. He was bright, talented and ambitious, he didn't need it, like a tin can on the tail of a dog, clattering and rattling behind him and holding him back.

Problems, problems. There was Tim, too, and nothing anyone could do about that, not even her father, it was up to the police. It wasn't her affair, either. *Don't manipulate.*

The only thing that anyone had come up with in his defence was *I don't think he would have,* and if she was honest, not one of them could really be sure. Not one of them had realised how close he and Lesley had sailed to the edge of their world, no wonder they had been so stressed, so at odds with each other. She had refused to help them – she felt guilty about that, but she knew that even if she had known, she would have given the same answer. You didn't throw your good money after someone else's bad, but had her refusal tipped him into arson? She had put the idea into his head herself… or perhaps it had always been there. Perhaps it had never been there. Perhaps.

If not Tim, then who? It occurred to her that, if it had been the Fish that had gone up in flames, there would have been an immediate answer to that, but it hadn't been the Fish, it had been Seagulls, and that was the closest that anyone would ever come to the truth.

She drove into her familiar home town at breakfast time, after a four hour drive, and went straight to her father's office, where he waited for her. He looked at her critically.

'Have you had any breakfast? You look like a waif!'

'I left home at five,' said Debbie.

'Sit down. I'll rustle up some coffee and send someone out for a bacon roll and some fruit, will that do you?'

'Sounds wonderful!'

He left the room and she sat down in the comfortable client chair. She felt as if she was still driving along, and rubbed at her eyes. Five o'clock was too early for anyone to get up. When her father came back, she was yawning.

'Coffee's on its way,' he said. 'I told Michelle to make it strong. Now then,' he sat down behind his desk, pulling a pile of papers towards him. 'Where would you like to start?'

With the bacon roll was the answer that came immediately into Debbie's head, and with it came the realisation that she was already feeling better. A childish conviction that her father would make everything all right again was already brightening the horizon.

'Perhaps we should start with Mawgan,' she said. 'He's what it's all about, after all.'

Jerry pulled a folder out of the pile and opened it.

'Mawgan Garfield Angwin, Chef, convicted at Bodmin Crown Court three years ago of the manslaughter of Michael Ronald Stanley. Served two years of a three-year prison sentence, and was released on parole just over a year ago. Good behaviour since.'

'That sounds like the one.' It had a very bleak, unfriendly sound put like that, she couldn't help seeing her parents' point of view. Jerry looked at her with kindness.

'It's just words, Debbie. It's what lies behind them that is so interesting in this case.'

The coffee arrived then, hot and strong enough to wake the dead. Debbie took a first, grateful sip.

'You said it sounded like a fit-up, on the phone.'

'He was convicted on the evidence of two eye-witnesses, Amy Strong, aged fifteen, whose parents occupied the house next door to his parents' home, and her friend Angela Bartlett, aged fourteen. Those two girls are seventeen or eighteen years old today, and judging from what you read here in the transcript, it might be interesting to talk to them now. There's no guarantee, of course, that either of them can be induced to tell the truth, but it's practically certain they didn't tell it at the trial. Angela Bartlett broke down in tears, and Amy Strong said, first of all, that Mawgan Angwin hit Michael Stanley over the head with a rock as he lay on the ground. *Lay on his back*, that point was established by counsel for the defence. When it was pointed out that the medical evidence proved Michael Stanley died from a blow to the back of the head, she said no, Mawgan Angwin had bashed his head *on* the rock, not *with* the rock, that was what she meant to say. He shouldn't have been convicted on that evidence, his counsel demolished it then and there. There was a similar discrepancy in his own evidence. Apparently he said at first "I killed him," but later retracted it, and said he hadn't meant exactly that.'

I didn't mean it. For a moment, Debbie was back in the cottage and the snow. She bit her lip. Her father went on speaking.

'Because of the rumours of an incestuous relationship, which, although they never came to court, were quite well known, the police were disinclined to accept this; they don't like sex offenders even where, as in this instance, the evidence is only hearsay. But what shored it all up again and sent him to prison was the evidence of his sister.' He looked at a sheet of paper in his hand. 'Cressida Linda Stanley.' He put the folder down. 'She seems to have really had it in for him, her evidence as to motive couldn't have been scripted better by a professional. Do you know what she said?'

'Mawgan told me, yes – some of it.'

'So you can understand why he didn't appeal at the time. Although she put nothing into actual words, and shied away from direct questions by crying her eyes out, the inference was such that the jury chose to convict on the evidence of Amy Strong, even though they obviously didn't like little sister very much. It was, however, quite apparent that for whatever reason, little sister was determined to bring him down, and this affected the final outcome. The charge was murder, but the judge reduced it to manslaughter. The feeling you're left with is that everyone concerned was hedging their bets and the one thing that didn't come out at the trial was the truth.'

Michelle came in with the bacon roll on a plate, and an apple, and tactfully disappeared again.

'Eat,' said Jerry, to his daughter.

Debbie obediently took a mouthful, but it didn't taste quite as good as it should have done. She said, through it, 'So what do we do?'

'The only way to get the conviction quashed is to produce good grounds for doing so. That means, in effect, that as Amy Strong and Angela Bartlett may have committed perjury, indeed, almost certainly did, they must be brought to admit it. However, conspiring to pervert the cause of justice is, in itself, a crime. The two girls were legally minors at the time, but they did send a probably innocent man to prison. They may not want to admit it. If they could be brought to retract, the appeal would probably go through without any reference to Cressida Stanley, your young man's own evidence then being proved to be true, and consequently there being no case to answer.'

'So what do we do?' asked Debbie, again.

'I can't do anything without his instructions.'

'He said he'd be willing to talk to you.'

'Then that must be the starting point.'

Debbie finished the roll and started on the apple.

'Dad… I'm going to marry him, whether he appeals or not. I ought to make that quite clear. There aren't any provisos, no ifs, or buts. If you and Mum won't agree, Oliver says I can be married in St. Erbyn, from his and Chel's house. I'd sooner it wasn't like that.'

Jerry spoke quietly. 'Debbie, I think you must make up your mind to it that, if you do marry this man, you'll be doing it without your mother's blessing or approval.'

'I think I already realise that's on the cards.' Debbie laid down the half-eaten apple. Spelling it out in so many words made her feel sickish. 'Can't you talk her round, Dad? I'd so much rather…'

'I don't think she would be prepared to listen to me. More, many people will feel that she's quite right to take that attitude.'

'But *you* don't feel like that?' said Debbie, urgently.

Jerry was silent, picking his words with care. When he did speak, it was with his eyes fixed on a pen he twirled between his fingers. 'I'm not sure how I feel, Deb, and that's the truth. I can't be happy about you marrying a man who comes from a background where making a fight of it seems a normal thing to do, whatever the rights and wrongs of the outcome.'

'I don't think it was quite like that.'

'Well, maybe it wasn't. We'll hope so. I'll talk with him, anyway.' The unspoken words, *and we'll see* hung in the air. Jerry laid down the pen. 'There's another reason why I'm not the best one to plead your cause. I'm leaving her, Debbie – leaving your mother. In fact, I already have. I told her last year, when she tried to make trouble with Oliver and Cheryl, who already had more than enough to cope with, that if she hurt any of my children just once more, I would go. Now, I don't know why I waited so long. It isn't about you, you're the only one who can live your life. The problem lies with her, and it's taken too long for me to admit it. I hope this doesn't come as too much of a shock.'

Debbie wanted to say, I knew about the flat, Dad, but couldn't. It would betray a confidence and lose a friend his job. She swallowed.

'He didn't even *do* it,' she said, miserably.

'It's not only that, Deb.' Jerry looked at her with compassion. 'It's who he is and what he is, and not only what he did or didn't do, but what he does. Your mother can be a very foolish, stubborn woman, she won't see that a man who runs a pub, or cooks in a restaurant for a living, is not defined by those activities as anything less than someone like me, who makes a living from the law, or Susan's Tom, who is an accountant. He's in good company, she feels exactly the same about Cheryl.'

'Those things don't matter,' said Debbie, but Hannah came into her head as she spoke. It had mattered to Hannah, so why not others?

'No. But she feels that they do.'

Debbie said, slowly, 'I never saw her like that... small-minded and snobbish... silly. I wish I wasn't now.'

'She has a great many sterling virtues too,' said Jerry, dryly. Debbie said, uncertainly this time, 'She's my mother. I love her. Doesn't she love me?'

Jerry wanted to say yes, of course she does, but honesty prevented him.

Dorothy loved herself and her social position, she would love Debbie too only if she did as she was told. His silence spoke for itself.

'I'll go and see her.' said Debbie.

'Yes, I think you have to. But don't expect anything.' Just to be hurt. His heart bled for her, this daughter so close to his heart and so far, this time, beyond his help.

'When I get married,' said Debbie, through a throat that was trying to close up on her, 'will you be there?'

'Of course.' He got up, and walked round the desk to gather her into his arms. 'Of course I will. Footing the bill and giving you away, making an embarrassing speech at the reception, and proud as a king to see my daughter, looking like a princess on such an important day in her life. But I think it will be from Oliver's house.'

Debbie hugged him back, without speaking. After a while, he patted her shoulder and took his arms away, returning to sit behind the desk. He said, as if the last two minutes had never taken place, 'I'll get down to see you both as soon as I can, maybe next week, I shall have to look at the diary.' He smiled at her. 'I shall look forward to meeting Mawgan Garfield Angwin. He sounds an interesting man. He's certainly lived, as they say, in interesting times.'

'Suppose you hate him?' She was suddenly apprehensive.

Jerry looked at his daughter carefully. She was so incandescent with love, whether she realised it or not, that he thought she might quite possibly glow in the dark. He remembered that glow from a long way back. He didn't think he was likely to hate anybody who could make her look that way, but of course, you never knew. It was true that the man who married his beloved daughter with his wholehearted approval was going to have to be a little more than run-of-the-mill.

'So long as he doesn't beat you, I shall manage to tolerate him.' He smiled at her, and she smiled back, but still uncertain, sensing equivocation.

'I don't think he'd ever find the time,' she said. 'Dad, there's something else – I want to re-open the sailing school and run it – run it differently, without the mistakes we made this season. Have you got time to talk about it with me?'

Half an hour later they were still discussing it when Michelle put her head round the door.

'Your client is here, Mr. Nankervis. Will you be long, shall I ask him to wait?'

'Damn!' Jerry glanced at his watch. 'Look Deb, I'm going to have to see this man, it's important. How about lunch with your old Dad?'

'Sounds good to me. When? Where? I'll need to head off back before too long.'

'Come back here at one, I'll get Michelle to book us a table somewhere. And Deb – don't take what your mother may say too much to heart.'

Easy to say, he thought, as he watched her go out of the door with a cheerful wave. Full of her plans – sound plans too, on the face of it – lit up with love, off to face Dot's intransigent ill will. He wished he could go with her, but it wouldn't help, it would simply make things worse. He had tried to warn her, he could do no more. He put Debbie's affairs aside with an effort, and pulled his client's file towards him. He hoped that her love would armour her, and that the man was worth the distress she was going to feel.

Easy to say, Debbie thought, but how could you not take what your own mother said to heart? She got into her cheerful yellow car and drove out to the exclusive area of town where her parents – no, just her mother now – had their home.

It looked like the same old home, but yet it wasn't, there was a subtle change that Debbie supposed was probably in her own mind, because of what she knew. She parked outside the front door and, running up the steps, let herself in as she had always done. Dorothy Nankervis came out of the drawing room to meet her. Her face was stone.

'So you've come at last, have you? And what have you to say for yourself, madam?'

Debbie stopped in her tracks as if she had run into a wall. It felt as if she had.

'Mum! Please don't be like that – I've come to talk to you.'

'The only thing I want to hear from you is that you've seen sense about this infatuation of yours, and come home to be among the people where you belong.'

'Can't we even talk about it? You don't know – '

'I know everything I need to know, thank you. Well?'

The wall was real. It was built of bitterness. It was impassable. Debbie said, 'You mustn't judge by what Lesley says, she doesn't know the truth.'

'The truth.' Dot looked at her with hard eyes. 'Yes, the truth. He's been to prison, this man?'

'Yes – but – '

'A convicted criminal then. And he works in a public house. In the kitchen, I understand.'

Debbie made an effort to be reasonable, she was always glad to remember that.

'Come on, Mum,' she said, coaxingly. 'He doesn't *work* in a pub, he owns it. Doesn't that make it better? And he's the head chef, not a washer-up. That must count for something, surely.'

'I see. After Oliver's cheap little shop girl, we're now to accept a publican with a prison record into the family. And kindly don't keep calling me by that common *Mum*. It's easy to see the kind of company you've been keeping.'

Debbie, who had called her mother *Mum* for longer than she could remember, opened her mouth to protest, and closed it again. Where was the use?

'What would you like me to call you?' Her voice was shaking, she realised. Anger? Tension? Good old-fashioned fear? She had seen her mother like this with Oliver, never with herself. 'Mother?'

'*Mother* is a term used by children who wish to dominate their parents,' said Dot. Susan still called her *Mummy*, but nothing was going to coerce Debbie into doing so, she had outgrown that years ago. She said, 'Can't we be reasonable? Look, shall we sit down quietly and talk about it? Please?'

'This is my home, it is my privilege to invite you in, not yours to take your welcome for granted. And I haven't invited you in, Deborah. I'm waiting for your assurance.'

'It's been my home for years –'

'At this moment, your *home* is on licensed premises with a convicted killer. If you wish to call this house home instead, then I shall be happy to welcome you back. But *as well* is not an option.'

'You're being totally unreasonable –'

'I'm ashamed of you, Deborah! First leading Tim Howells on to desert his wife, and now getting yourself mixed up with rubbish! Have you no consideration for your family, no standards? Your father has a certain standing to maintain, although he seems to have little respect for it, and so do I. Your doings down there in Cornwall have become the talk of the town! And I suppose, in extenuation, you are going to tell me that *Oliver* approves! Well, he has a taste for trash himself, so save your breath!'

Debbie's anger hit in one blinding, destructive flash, as unexpected to herself as it was to her mother. She heard herself saying, 'If that's your attitude, then it doesn't matter what I call you, you're not the Mum I know! *Mrs. Nankervis* will do fine!' She drew a breath. 'I'm going, I don't have to listen to this. You know where you'll find me if you want to apologise. Meantime, don't bother to come to the wedding, you won't be asked!'

She turned then, and stumbled to the door. With her hand on the latch, she heard her mother's voice behind her, coldly furious, 'I wouldn't come to your wedding to a convicted criminal if you ask on your knees, Deborah. The day you marry that man is the day you forfeit the right to call yourself a child of mine. And you can get your junk out of the garage today, or it goes to the tip tomorrow!'

Debbie sat in her car. She was shaking so much that she was afraid to start the engine. She couldn't accept that her mother had believed all that nonsense Lesley had talked about herself and Tim, she couldn't believe that she had called Chel *trash*, and Mawgan, whom she didn't even know, *rubbish*. She wished she hadn't said what she did, and almost was going back to try to patch things up, but her mother's face, staring at her through the hall window, prevented her. There was no forgiveness in that face, no sorrow, no affection. She knew that a bond had been broken that would never mend, and she didn't know what to do.

Hardly able to control her hands, Debbie started up, put her car into gear, and drove unsteadily down the drive and out of the gate. She had no idea where she meant to go. She was as unsafe on the road as if she had been drinking.

It must have been some totally unrecognised homing instinct that took her to the Casson house, because there she was, on the drive, with no idea of how she came to be there, and there was Susan, suntanned from her holiday in Antigua, coming across the lawn with a bunch of roses in her hand. Susan was quite different from Debbie or Oliver, not loose-limbed and beautiful, but sturdy and compact, pretty in a pleasing, everyday way. She had brown hair and brown eyes, and a bossy manner that hid a bewildered insecurity from everyone, including herself. She could be abrasive, and sometimes acerbic, but above all, she always seemed capable and reliable, and she was kind, even if her kindness was sometimes misdirected. Debbie was used to having her in the background, the older sister who always knew what to do. She was so pleased to see her that she was out of the car in a flash, running over the grass to meet her, and Susan dropped the roses and held out her arms to receive her.

'Deb! What's wrong?'

'I think I've just been disowned,' said Debbie, on wail.

Susan took her round to the back of the house and sat her down in a long patio chair on a terrace that had a distant view across the roofs of the town to the sea and was scattered with bright children's toys. She brought her a stiff drink and a little glass bowl of crisps, and a large, friendly Labrador came and lay beside her, panting. Debbie began to stop shaking. When she reached the stage of picking at crisps, Susan said, 'Better now?'

'Yes. Sorry. I think it must have been shock.'

'But what happened?'

Debbie told her, and Susan listened. At the end of the recital, Susan said, 'Deb, I realise that you've been busy with your own doings down in Cornwall, but surely even you could see that this was the very worst moment to choose to try and talk to Mummy? She's in pieces over Daddy walking out, she really didn't need it from you, too.'

'But don't you see, I had to say something. I wanted to put things straight, tell her the truth. Half of what you've heard isn't even remotely true.'

'The truth is still that you want to marry a man who's been in prison, and that none of us have ever met. Oh, except Oliver, of course. I mustn't forget that.' Susan sighed. 'Deb, you can be really dumb! Must you always charge in like the cavalry?'

It was somehow comforting to be lectured in this way by Susan, restoring things to their proper perspective, but Debbie felt impelled to enter an objection.

'Do you honestly think it would have been any different next week? Next month? Come on, Suse! We both know what Mum can be like, we've seen it all our lives with Oliver.'

'Oliver always wound her up. If he'd done what she wanted —'

'But don't you see? That's the whole point. She used to shout at Oliver because he stood up to her, but I never thought she'd shout at me just for trying to explain. And I can surely do what I want with my own life at my age. I'm hardly a child! She was *horrible*, she wouldn't even pretend to listen, and I don't care what's happened, there was no need for that.' She heard her voice rising, and stopped abruptly, biting at her lip.

Susan, who had been much younger than Debbie was now when

her own confrontation with her mother had taken place, and who had backed down and done as she was told, had no answer for this. Instead, she found herself wondering, possibly for the first time, exactly *why* she had backed down. Mummy hadn't been unkind to her, or anything… and then she remembered that she had. That remark about her not really being a Nankervis had been cruel, she could still feel the sting of it now. She said nothing, however.

Deb was looking better, she thought, looking at her critically. White, but she had stopped shaking and probably wasn't going to burst into tears. She suggested lunch. Debbie sat up with a jerk.

'Oh goodness, I'm meant to be meeting Dad! Suse, I don't think I can face it, not lunch out. Having to behave in public… I'm not sure I trust myself not to disgrace him and weep all over the tablecloth.'

Susan got calmly to her feet.

'I'll ring his office. He can come here. There's bound to be something in the fridge.'

Debbie lay back, her eyes closed, feeling the warmth of the sun on her face and on her bare arms and ankles. She heard Susan's sandals clacking across the flags of the terrace, and then silence closed in. She realised that, as much as anything, she felt bereaved and tears prickled behind her eyes. She had grown up with her mother, she knew well enough that from this morning's unpleasant little scene there would be no going back. Her mother never did a U-turn, never had, never would. The mistake, Debbie thought miserably, was probably in allowing it to take place in the first instance, but there had been very little alternative, in spite of what Susan had said. She could have written, which would have produced the same response. She could have postponed confrontation, which would have only made things worse. Or she could have given in, which was unthinkable. She lay still, feeling the sun and mourning.

Susan came back.

'He'll be half an hour. He doesn't mind. He said to tell you it didn't matter what you did, it would have happened anyway.'

Debbie said, not opening her eyes, 'It seems you're the only one of us she's still speaking to.' The words squeezed past a lump in her throat.

'Dissolution of the family, is that what you're thinking? No, you'll all regroup on the other side of this, you see. It's she who will be the loser.' She hesitated. 'And I hope, not me.'

'You?' Debbie's eyes flew open.

'I've never really been one of you, have I?' She tried to speak lightly, but the bitterness broke through.

'No way!' Debbie sat up abruptly. 'Of course you're one of us! And by the way, I want Annabel as a bridesmaid, and if not you, who else is going to take on the role of bride's mother?'

'Cheryl would do it,' said Susan.

'I've no doubt she would, but she isn't my sister. Come to that, I could do it myself, but I want *you* to help me.' She made a rueful face. 'There's some very organising blood in us, Suse. Let's turn it to good use.' She tried to avoid it, but there was a very slight emphasis on the word *good*.

'Oh Deb...' said Susan.

Jerry arrived on time, concerned but not surprised, and Susan made a salad that they ate on the terrace. He was relieved to find his girls on good terms, you never quite knew with Susan, she could be nearly as difficult as Dot when she set her mind to it. Not today, though. Today, she was all Henry Worthington's daughter and Dot might have had nothing to do with her conception. She supported him nobly in his efforts to cheer up Debbie, although he wasn't so sure that they succeeded. Helen had known what she was talking about when she christened her successor the Dreaded Dot.

Debbie told them what her mother had said about her goods and chattels, presently stored in the garage at what had been her home.

'It's not as if there's masses of it,' said Susan, almost as if it didn't matter.

'No, there isn't.' Debbie's London flat had been part-furnished. 'But what there is, is the best I could afford at the time – and all my books, and CDs and clothes and china... there's no way I can get it out today!' She felt her self-control slipping again, and took a gulp of water – iced, spring, trust Susan.

'Don't worry, she won't tip it,' said Susan. 'She just said that to get a rise out of you.'

Jerry wasn't so sure. He knew what Dot was capable of. He looked at Susan.

'There isn't more than a van load – a sofa and a chest of drawers and a bookcase, and a couple of other things, not big. And boxes. Isn't there someone at the yacht club with a Transit, or something?'

'I can think of a couple. I can't organise anything before tomorrow, though.'

'I'll have a word with your mother. A professional word.' He looked at Debbie. 'I expect it may all have to come down to Cornwall on Saturday or Sunday. Will that suit?'

The two busiest days at the Fish. Debbie sighed. She felt vaguely steam-rollered, but relieved too. She would have hated to lose all her possessions, and in such a way, and Mawgan would just have to put up with it. The cold feeling in the pit of her stomach was probably still just the residue of shock, as she had said to Susan, but there was something so final about being despatched back to Cornwall bag and baggage. She swallowed another gulp of designer water.

'Do you have to drive back today, Deb?' Susan asked, as the meal came to an end.. 'I'm not sure you should, after you've been so upset. What do you think, Daddy?'

'I ought to,' said Debbie. 'I want to, I've got to work tomorrow. Please – I just want to get back.' To Mawgan. To her life. To her new friends. Away from here, where nothing would ever be the same again.

'You're welcome to stay the night here, you know,' said Susan.

'Don't pester her, Susan.' Jerry was watching Debbie carefully. 'She'll be OK.'

'I could go with her,' said Susan. 'I could hire a car to get back tomorrow. I just think it's a long way to go on her own under the circumstances.'

'There's no need, Suse – it's dear of you, but I shall be fine.' *Do this, do it my way.* She felt trapped, casting around for escape. She wanted to be on her own, quite suddenly, more than anything in the world. Alone, and headed west. Headed for where her home would be from now on.

'Then phone us, as soon as you get there,' Susan ordered. 'We shall want to know you're safe.'

'I shall be safe.'

She left when Jerry left, afraid that Susan might yet detain her. Her sister had been a star, but she never knew when to walk away. She got into her car and waved goodbye, and headed off for home at last with four long hours in which to be alone with her thoughts.

Susan, left alone on the drive, turned back to her house in thoughtful mood. She had known Debbie all her life, and she wasn't deceived for a minute. She imagined her, driving all that long way, arriving back in St. Erbyn tired out and unhappy, and walking into an empty flat, as presumably she would if this Mawgan was the chef for his own restaurant. Well, he would just have to get himself organised. She went into the house, picked up the phone, and rang Directory Enquiries.

After the experience of the fire, Debbie should have known that shock was something that tended to catch up on you later on, and in fact, the shock of being disowned by her mother without even a hearing caught up with her round about Honiton, when she found tears, unheralded and unexpected, pouring down her face. She wiped them away as she drove, a black mood of despair like fog around her. It was such a huge step she was taking, across some invisible line that separated past from future. Suppose it all went hideously wrong? There would be no going back, the boats were all burning behind her. Suddenly, it seemed a huge undertaking to marry out of her background, out of her world… terrifying. Suppose his family hated her and thought her a stuck-up cow?

'I'm frightened,' said Debbie, aloud, to her car. 'This could all go horribly pear-shaped.' And sniffed, and dashed once more at her streaming eyes.

It wasn't a good journey. Accidents on the road, a lorry stuck under a bridge, and a sudden flurry of heavy rain on the moor held her up, and it was after eight when she arrived back at the Fish. Driving into the rain-soaked car park, she thought that she had never been so glad to see the old building crouching over the muddy causeway. The rain wasn't heavy here, it was just a thin, fine mizzle, but depressing. She went in through the rear door and up the stairs to the lonely flat with a leaden heart, and let herself in.

It wasn't a lonely flat. Mawgan was there. He was dressed for work, but sitting in one of the armchairs, idly turning the pages of a magazine. He looked up as she came in.

'Hullo, my bird. All right?'

She was so surprised, so overwhelmingly pleased to see him there that she just dropped her bag and her keys where she stood and ran to him, falling on her knees and burying her face in his lap. They stayed like that for a while, Debbie crying her heart out, and Mawgan just gently stroking her hair, until, as suddenly as they had come, the tears stopped. Debbie raised her head, sniffing.

'D'you want to tell me about it?' he asked.

'I'm sorry, what a greeting! It's just been a bad day. Long drive. You know.'

He didn't believe her, she saw, in fact she had a feeling that he knew what had happened, but how could he? She put up a hand to brush away a tear that didn't seem to have gone away with the others.

'Come here. There's room in this chair for both of us, if you sit still.' He held out his hand to her. Snuggled against him in the big chair she began to feel better. He said, quietly,

'Deb, I know you've had a bad day, but I want to point something out to you that I think you don't quite realise.'

'What?' asked Debbie, muffled, into his shoulder.

'Don't you dare leave mascara all over me,' he remarked. 'You'll get me had up by the Health & Safety. Come on, stop crying bird. Nothing's so bad as all that.'

'What did you want to point out?' She rubbed a hand under her eyes. 'I think I cried it all off long ago, you needn't worry.'

Mawgan spoke carefully. 'You and your brother, in your different ways, have made out that your family is completely at odds with itself, and none of you cares about the others.'

'It's true – to a great extent, anyway. Of course we care a little bit – some of us, for some of us.'

'Well, I think you're wrong. I think you're all a great deal closer than any of you realise.'

'So what makes you so clever?' Debbie asked, more sharply than she meant. It had been a long day.

'Think about it. At the barest hint of you being in trouble, your brother and sister-in-law was over here in a flash. That isn't *not* caring, Deb. That's caring.'

'Oliver's different.'

'Oh no, he's not. I know about Oliver, him and me come out the same mould, or hadn't you noticed? And it isn't just him, anyway. I've had them all after me today, and that isn't not caring, neither.'

'I beg your pardon?' Debbie raised her head, and he looked into her face seriously, tightening his arm round her.

'Your sister phoned, around half-past three, I think it was, and give me the runaround. She's a fierce one, isn't she? When she and Allison get together, run for your life!'

'*Susan* phoned?'

'Ordering me to be here for you when you got back. She told me what had happened – some, anyway, and I totally agreed with her as it happens. You needed me here.' He kissed her tear-stained face tenderly. 'Come on Deb, things are never as bad as they seem.'

'*You* can say that?'

'Well, maybe some things are,' he conceded, and then went on. 'Then just after six, your father rang, too. He was less fierce than your sister, but the message was the same. You'd taken a battering because of me, and so it was up to me to look after you. And he hoped I meant to do it properly. Real heavy father stuff.'

'Poor Mawgan!' He could feel the tension going out of her, and relaxed his arm.

'Deb, your family is OK. A bit unusual, maybe, but OK. I think you may find that all this is bringing you together.'

'But not my mother. She didn't ring.'

'No,' he said quietly.

Debbie lay still in the curve of his arm, thinking. It came into her head, against her will, that all her life her mother had been like a stone in your shoe, making the family limp along, angry with itself and struggling. Aggressive, pushy, domineering, forcing them all into positions that they didn't want to take up, each of them in their own way trying to find a bearable way to progress. Susan had done what she was told for the sake of peace. Oliver had fought like a tiger for his integrity, she herself had quietly slid out from under and gone her own way. Their father? That, she didn't know. She hardly knew Oliver's mother, but she did know that the marriage had broken up because of her own, although exactly why was another question.

'Oh God,' she said, in sudden pain, and buried her face against him.

After a while, Mawgan said gently,

'Listen bird, I'm sorry, but I got to go. Will you be all right on your own? Roger is down in the bar, leading Shirl astray, shall I send them up here?'

'No, I'm OK.' She sat up, carefully. 'I think I'll have a shower, and then I might ring Chel. Have a bit of a girlie chat. Oh – and Mawgan,' she hesitated.

'Why do I get the feeling I aren't going to like what's coming next?'

he asked, but he was smiling at her with mischief in his eyes in the way she loved, and her heart lightened.

'It's not that bad. Just that, there's probably a vanload of my furniture and things arriving over the weekend, and I don't even know exactly when. She was going to send it all to the tip – ' Her voice broke. Mawgan pushed her gently off his knee and stood up.

'We could do with some more furniture,' he said cheerfully. 'Not to worry, Deb, we'll cope – or somebody will, not me exactly, not right now.' He kissed her nose, lightly. 'I'll send you up some dinner when there's a moment. You go and get that shower, your face looks as if you've gone six rounds with Frank Bruno.'

'And I love you, too.'

On her own, she went into the bathroom and peered at herself in the mirror, and what she saw made her very glad that she hadn't let him send her Roger and Shirley for company. A shower made her feel better, she put on a clean nightdress and Mawgan's bathrobe, the last more for comfort than warmth, and went to find her mobile. Talking to Chel would make her feel better still, because to Chel, who knew the family right down to its grimy underbelly, she could talk freely without feeling she was betraying them.

Chel already knew most of it, she found. Oliver's father, she said, had rung earlier, and Oliver had hit the roof first and bounced off the walls afterwards, she had had the greatest difficulty in preventing him from leaping into his car and heading straight off to St. Erbyn. He had gone out for a walk now to cool down, so they could say what they liked.

They talked for a while about what had happened, and Debbie began to feel better. To Chel, she confided the disloyal thought that had come to her as she lay in Mawgan's arms – arm, rather, and Chel said, 'Yes, I think you're probably right. But do remember, Deb, people can't help the way they are. Oliver's godmother says she was always frighteningly single-minded and hated not to get her own way, but she never worked out if she was being consciously destructive, or just doing things for people's own good as she saw it.'

'That's a frightening concept.' Debbie hesitated. 'Chel – Susan can be a bit like that too, although nowhere near as bad, obviously – and I've been having this awful feeling lately that maybe I am, too. I've caught myself out being really bossy and manipulative – it's scary. I don't want to be like that. She's caused so much harm.'

'Deb, you aren't like that. Come on, get real here!'

'Yes I am. Look at your wedding –'

'Now stop, right there! If we're to take that as an example, where would it have been without you? It was all set to be the non-event of the year before you walked in and pulled it all together at the eleventh hour, and nobody has ever felt anything but really grateful to you, once they got over the shock.'

'Yes, but – '

'But, nothing. It was going to be a total disaster, and it wasn't. You didn't *hurt* anybody. Just surprised them a bit. And I'll tell you something else. Something Helen said to me.' She paused. Debbie waited. She didn't know Helen well enough, she would have thought, for her to have an opinion. Chel said, quietly, 'She said, *Deb builds bridges*. And then she said words to the effect of, I wish she was my daughter, and just for the record, my family think the world of you. Candy thinks you're wonderful.'

'Oh Chel, don't, I've cried myself sick already today!'

'Don't be! What's to cry about? You can't win them all, Deb. You're going to win the really important things, and that's what matters. So cheer up. Look, Oliver's just crashed through the door, do you want a word with him, too? He'll be comprehensively rude about your mother, but it might brace you up a bit.'

Talking to Oliver was like a blast of fresh air. He was extremely forthright on the subject of her mother's behaviour, and told her, without apology, to take not a blind bit of notice, as the only person the Dreaded Dot had hurt, ultimately, was herself. It wasn't that simple, of course, but when she had finished speaking to him she found she did feel that she might live through the day after all, and come out in a brighter tomorrow.

A knock on the door announced one of the restaurant waiters with a tray and the promised dinner, and she suddenly found that she was starving, she had had no appetite for lunch and it was a long time since a bacon roll and half an apple in her father's office. It looked delicious, she realised. Scallops wrapped in pancetta on a sorrel salad, followed by something lurking under a metal dome that looked as if it could be *Coq au Vin*, which was wicked of him, although its relationship to her own concoction of the same name was of the most tenuous kind. It nestled on a bed of saffron rice, and was accompanied by little peas cooked with smoky bacon and shallots, and a spoonful of creamed leeks. To finish off, there was a cold lemon soufflé, and a bottle of chilled sparkling wine accompanied it. It was a good thing she lived an active life, she thought, as she ate every last wonderful mouthful, otherwise she would be as fat as a pig before very long.

She went to bed immediately she had finished, too tired to wait up for Mawgan, he wouldn't be up much before midnight anyway. Lying there, feeling herself unwind, she thought that the day had had tremendous highs as well as frightening lows, and as she dropped almost instantly into sleep, she remembered the lovely thing that Helen had said about her.

Deb builds bridges...

XXIV

Anna had no problem in tracking down Kate. Cress hadn't made a secret to her family of where she was staying during her time in Trelewan, it was only that she had hidden from Kate the name of her family, and that had been almost accidental. Quite simply, Kate had never asked. Grandad was able to unravel the mystery the moment that Anna mentioned it.

'Don't know why you want to speak with her, though,' he said. 'Cress said she was a right little B.'

'She stayed there long enough, if so,' remarked Anna. Garfie Angwin was nobody's fool, and he had his own opinions, mainly kept to himself, about his youngest grandchild. Her carryings-on, he rather thought, had been responsible for his beloved wife's stroke, the boy had always been her favourite. He gave a snort.

'Outstayed her welcome, most like. What you hoping to prove, young Anna?'

'I'm not really sure, but Mawgan thought she had something to tell us. She went to see him you know – this Kate did.'

'Did she, now.' He looked at her with knit brows. 'Seems a queer thing for her to do. Why did'n she tell him, then?'

'I think the answer to that is obvious,' said Anna, and sighed. Living out in Switzerland, as she did, she had been to a certain extent isolated from the family's troubles, being right in the middle of them as she was now had come as a shock. Not because she hadn't *known*, of course she had. She simply hadn't *felt* in quite the same way, being desperately sorry at one remove wasn't at all the same. One thing she really wanted to do, except that she had promised not to, was to tell her grandparents, particularly her Nan, about Debbie Nankervis. They all of them so desperately needed some good news.

'You thinking of going to see 'n then?' Garfie asked.

'I thought I might. Can I use the car?'

'If you think it'll do any good. Can't see the point myself.'

'Somebody has got to do something,' Anna pointed out. 'We can't go on like this.'

'Don't see how as it can help. Best leave well alone, 'f you ask me.'

Anna hadn't asked him, she thought, as she drove the old Ford westward, and somebody did have to do something. She couldn't see anything else offering itself as a suggestion. It must have been something pretty convincing to send this Kate in search of Mawgan, of all people. Knowing what it was might be the first step on the road back to being a normal family again, and if it wasn't they would be no worse off. Being worse off wasn't an option, she had already realised that.

Finding Trelewan was easy, it was on the map. Locating The Quoit was simply a matter of asking in the post office. Anna drove there and parked on the gravel outside. It was a run-down looking place, she thought, and gloomy with all those bushes and things. She felt it would be greatly improved if somebody ran amok with a chain saw and let the sunlight in.

Kate was coming along the path from the studio, carrying two empty mugs. She had been having a cup of tea with Charlie, and she wasn't pleased to see yet another visitor hesitating on her doorstep, she didn't know why the silly people didn't book somewhere instead of wandering in on the off chance. They didn't even have the VACANCIES sign up. Then Anna heard her step on the gravel and turned, and Kate knew at once whom she must be. She wasn't like Cress so much, but she was the living spit of the brother.

'You must be Allison,' she said.

'Anna, actually. Marianne.' She made a face at the fancy name, and held out her hand. Kate, not knowing what else to do, shifted the two mugs into one hand and took the one offered to her.

'You'd better come in,' she said.

She led the way into the kitchen, not sure whether her unexpected visitor was welcome or not. The things she hadn't been able to tell the brother were like cobwebs in her head, she couldn't sweep them out. She drew out a chair at the kitchen table.

'Sit down. Would you like some tea, or something?'

'No thanks.' Anna took the offered seat. 'You must guess why I've come.'

Kate sat down on the chair opposite, the two mugs in front of her on the table.

'It's about Cress, I suppose. She's been long gone from here. I can't tell you anything you don't know.'

'Mawgan thought you could,' said Anna, directly.

'I told him what I went there to say. That I thought she was ill, and someone should look after her.' Kate heard the defensive note in her own voice, and wished she could control it. Even now, she felt guilty over Cress. 'He sent me to a café in Falmouth where she worked. I saw her there, she was all right then. He obviously wasn't interested, anyway.'

Anna asked the question that Mawgan hadn't asked.

'What made you think that she was ill?' Come to that, what made you think he wasn't interested? She might ask that one later, maybe. Or on second thoughts, perhaps she didn't want to know.

Kate hesitated.

'If I tell you, perhaps you'll think I made it up.'

'Perhaps I will. But perhaps I won't. Come on, there must have been a reason.'

How did you tell someone – a stranger – that you thought her sister bayed at the moon? Kate thought that you couldn't, but Anna was waiting. She had to say something.

'She behaved in a very peculiar way.'

'Peculiar, how? Come on, Kate, you went all the way to St. Erbyn to speak to Mawgan, of all people. There must have been a good reason. He said himself that he thought it was the measure of your anxiety. So, was it?'

Perhaps it was the use of her name that disarmed her. Perhaps it was the obvious truth in what Anna had said. Or perhaps it was the relief of realising that both the cool, unfriendly brother and this more approachable sister cared what happened to Cress after all. Kate said, in a rush, 'I saw her, up on the cliff. She was walking along, sort of twisting her hands and talking. There was nobody there, but she was talking as if there was. Then, when I spoke to her, she didn't even know me.'

'People do talk to themselves,' said Anna, but sounded unconvinced. Kate shook her head. She was gathering momentum now she had jumped the first hurdle.

'Not like that. Not *waiting for answers*. And then answering again.'

There. It was Anna's responsibility now. She felt relieved. But Anna hadn't finished.

'Maybe she *didn't* know you.'

'You mean, she'd forgotten me? No, that's not possible. She lived with us here for six months. I haven't changed. Even the clothes I was wearing, she must have seen dozens of times before.'

'You could have told that to Mawgan. He would have listened. He would have done something.'

Kate began to play with the two mugs on the table, switching them round and setting them handle-to-handle, then the opposite way. She didn't look at Anna.

'He said he'd speak to your sister, but he didn't, did he?'

The way that she spoke made Anna certain that she was turning the tables in the immemorial manner of people who know themselves to be in the wrong. She was convinced suddenly that she had only heard half a tale.

'You'd better tell me the rest,' she said.

'You'll hate me,' said Kate, with conviction.

'Don't bet on it. I know whose side I'm on.'

'I thought that it sounded as if she set her brother up to kill her husband.'

Kate began to turn one of the mugs round and round, studying the pattern on it carefully. Anna said, calmly, 'I think you're right. She didn't actually care very much about her marriage, it was obviously on the rocks anyway. Only, I don't see how she would have expected it to end in him dying. I think that was a genuine shock to her, just as it was to the rest of us. What she wanted, or Allison and I think anyway, was to have them fighting over her, like in one of those silly books she read, it was the drama she wanted to be the centre of, she seemed to think it would justify her behaviour somehow. She was always a bit loosely wrapped, Cress.' She paused. 'She found herself in the middle of a bigger drama than she had ever dreamed of, and to be honest, she played it to the hilt. She was always like that. What I think is, it all got out of hand and she didn't know how to stop it, so she just went along with it, like a leaf in a flood. Then afterwards, she couldn't face him and that's what it's all been about.'

'Yes,' said Kate, and she told Anna the story of the quoit.

'She was lying on it, hugging it, you know, as if it was a person? Kissing it, practically having sex with it, it was gross. And I was so angry with her over Charlie that I…' She stopped.

'Charlie?'

So Kate told her what she had told to Chel, and then Anna went away. She had neither absolved nor condemned, but she had looked very shocked, and Kate had no idea whether it was at her own behaviour or Cress's. It never occurred to her that she maybe shouldn't have confided her fears to Cress's sister so hard on the heels of Anna's condemnation of Cress's play-acting.

Anna drove back the way she had come, not sure if she had learned anything to help or not. She had certainly learned something she would be happier not knowing. Even more certainly, she had learned something that Mawgan, quite conclusively, shouldn't ever know, and she was grateful to Kate for not telling him. The problem of Cress, however, remained. She could, of course, still be merely playing to the gallery, but there was something about Kate's story of the quoit that made Anna wonder. Making love to a stone was strange behaviour, even for Cress, but maybe Kate had got it wrong. Maybe it was all to do with this Charlie, that sounded more like Cress. Anna could remember her throwing herself about in an abandonment of grief over all kinds of imagined slights and disappointments, all her life. Not knowing Kate, of course, was harder to explain away, but if Kate had chucked her out, maybe she simply hadn't *wanted* to know her.

It could all be rationalised away, and she really did want to rationalise it, but something niggled at her, and wouldn't let her. Cress had gone her length with spoiled brat behaviour, if the rest of the family were to be believed, and she had drained all their reserves of love and patience, but she was still the little sister that Anna, Mawgan and Allison had looked after and defended all her life. If there was any chance at all that she was ill or in trouble, then Anna knew that she must check it out. When all was said and done, Mike was dead, however it had actually come about, and he had still been her husband at the time. It was only early afternoon, she drove the car to Falmouth.

She knew about the Blue Crab café and she found it easily enough. At this time of day, it wasn't exactly busy and Susie had time to speak to her.

'Cress? No, she's gone. Good job too, she was about as much use as a dose of 'flu!'

'Gone?' Anna echoed. Nobody in the family had mentioned that Cress had moved on.

'Yeah.' Susie snorted. 'Took one look at the holiday crowds and gave in her notice. Went off with some man.'

This, too, was news to Anna. She looked, and felt, bewildered.

'What – somebody she had just met? Who?'

Susie flicked a cloth at a nearby table, knocking a few crumbs from its grubby surface to the floor. She sniffed.

'From what she said, it was somebody she knew from way back. She said he come and asked her to go with him, and her family didn't care what happened to her so she thought she'd go.' She looked at Anna, a challenge in her eyes. 'Said they preferred her brother, what killed her husband. You can't blame her, if so.'

'What was he like – this man? Did you ever see him?'

'No,' said Susie. The door opened and a family came in, heading for one of the window tables. ''scuse me, I got work to do.' She flounced away to take the order, but when she came back she saw to her annoyance that Cress's sister was still standing there. 'Look, I can't tell you nothing. Let me get on.'

'His name,' said Anna. 'Did she tell you his name? Where she went? *Anything?*' If it was someone her family knew, they could trace her, make sure she was all right.

'No, she never said. I think it was some friend of her husband.' Susie scowled. 'Look, I don't know no more, and I can't do with you wasting my time, I've had more'n enough doing her work as well as my own all summer. You could ask Mrs Pascoe, where she had a room.'

Anna got Mrs. Pascoe's address from her by the simple expedient of refusing to go until she had it, and left with her mind in confusion. It was perfectly possible, given Cress, that she had thrown herself into the arms of some new protector, but it was unlike her not to rub the family's nose in the mess. Of course, she might have decided to add to their worries by letting them all sweat for a bit, not knowing where she was, that would be like her, or at least, like the person she seemed to have become since her marriage. Almost, she didn't bother to check with Cress's ex-landlady, but then she thought she might as well.

Mrs Pascoe had nothing to add. Cress had packed her things, paid her rent up to date, and gone off. She hadn't said where. No, she didn't have any friends, except that Gary and he was on remand, breaking up some pub or other when he'd had a few too many, him and his mates.

Anna didn't make the connection. Nobody had told the family about the incident at the Fish.

It was an irony that was doomed to exist unappreciated that if it had been Allison, and not Anna, who had been the recipient of Kate's confidence, she might have taken it more seriously, asked different questions, come nearer, perhaps, to the truth. But Mawgan hadn't passed on the message to Allison, it was Anna in whom he had confided, and Anna hadn't been around at home to witness Cress's increasingly unreasonable behaviour. Being told isn't at all the same thing.

Anna went back to her grandparents' house and told her grandad that Cress had gone off with some friend of Mike's, behaving in her usual spoiled-brat way. She added that she seemed to have gone her length when she was staying with Kate and Charlie, and she didn't blame Kate for kicking her out. Garfie had an understandable down on his youngest grandchild, and accepted this without question. Neither of them had the least idea that they had inadvertently concealed a clue that might, just might, have saved an innocent man from trial, neither did they have any conception of what Cress might actually have done, they were simply glad that she seemed to be sorting herself out at last. A friend of Mike's sounded all right, even likely, Cress was very pretty and appealing, she made men want to protect her. The following day, Anna caught the train for Launceston to spend the last few days of her holiday with her parents, and this version of the truth travelled with her.

It seemed to her, when she told them, that her parents, too, were almost relieved at the news. Cally said, 'If he's a friend of Mike's, he'll be good to her. She'll be in touch when she's settled, I daresay.'

Pip grunted.

'Perhaps now she's something more to think about, she'll stop making her brother's life a misery.'

Cally looked at him in surprise. She had thought that he favoured Cress in the dispute, but it seemed she had been wrong. Or maybe it was simply that, like herself, he hadn't known which way to go. She was treacherously aware of relief that the situation seemed to be resolving itself at last.

'Allison'll be home at the weekend to see you,' she said, to Anna. 'Maybe we can get Mawgan to come up, spend time with us for a change, be a family.' She didn't realise what she had implied. 'Sunday lunch would be nice. What do you think?'

'He works on Sundays,' said Anna. 'And I don't suppose he can drive yet… of course, he could get someone to drive him.' Her eyes gleamed. This might be a way of forcing Mawgan's hand. She didn't make the mistake of thinking he was deliberately hiding his new girlfriend from the family, it was simply a matter of timing and opportunity, and she would like dearly to have it all sorted out and everyone happy again before she returned to Kurt and her twin boys. 'I'll give him a ring, and see, shall I? It's only roast dinners they do on Sunday, his sidekick can handle that for once. Anyway, I can't see he'd be much use carving, or heaving heavy roasting pans around. More of a liability, really.' She went off to make the call, and Pip and Cally looked at each other.

'She'll be all right,' said Pip. 'Don't worry, Cally, she's one as always finds someone to look after her. She'll be in touch when she's ready. And it'll maybe be good to have Mawgan around for a change without her marching in and upsetting us all.'

He wasn't a demonstrative man, but he put his arms round his wife and held her, without speaking, for what was, for him, a very long time.

'How're you fixed on Sunday, Deb?' asked Mawgan, finding her in the bar in her lunch hour. 'Only Anna rang up, she wants me to go over for lunch, and there's nothing stopping me except getting there.' Unconsciously, he echoed Anna's opinion. 'I'm damn-all use here, that's for sure. It might be a good opportunity for you to meet them. Allison'll be home as well.'

Debbie was still feeling a bit tender on the subject of families, but a week had passed by this time and the sun was still in the heavens, the world hadn't come to an end. The hurt would always be there, like a thorn sticking in somewhere, but there was so much to think about that quite often she didn't even feel it for hours on end. Mawgan's family had to be faced sometime.

'I'll have a word with Roger. It's a bit pie-in-the-sky, we've no idea of numbers again, and Carl has taken the Feeling back up-river, he's his own work to do. We know four definites from answers to our adverts, but the rest is a matter of luck.'

'It'll be dropping off a bit now, anyway. Everything is. Second week in

September, schools gone back, weather getting cooler – it'll all be over in a couple of weeks. How d'you feel about that?'

'I've got used to the idea, I think.' Debbie looked thoughtful. 'The bank say we can only continue to run the boats and use the boathouse and equipment until the end of this month, and as we're working for them now, effectively, that's it. After that, it's up to them how they deal with any bookings, not our problem.'

'Time to take stock, then.' He smiled at her. 'We can spend some time on ourselves, there's a thing! I only open the restaurant three nights a week and lunchtime Sundays in the winter.'

'Sounds wonderful!'

He looked at her critically.

'You said that as if you really meant it. You're looking tired, Deb.'

'So're you. We need a day off.'

'Roast beef with the family, then? Anna and Allison are doing the cooking, heaven help us.'

'Oh, what the hell! Why not? I can do the same for Roger. Are they expecting me?'

'Anna will be. The rest will be assuming I shall need to get there somehow, and take what turns up.'

'Haven't you told them?' She stared at him, wide-eyed.

'Not yet, no. I was waiting for a suitable moment. This is probably it.' He hesitated. 'We never did get that ring, Oliver and Chel arrived and the moment sort of passed. Shall we do it now?'

'What – right now, this minute?' She was laughing. He glanced at his watch.

'Why not? We can make it to Helston and back in the time, even with you driving.'

'Roger –'

'Roger will manage. What were you doing this afternoon, anyway?'

'It's maintenance afternoon. I suppose he can manage, really. We're only using two boats, but it does seem an awful lot to ask, with Sunday too.'

'Go and tell him then. I'll be in the office.'

The season was coming to an end, yes, thought Debbie, as she wandered out into the sunshine to find Roger and the week's intake of students. She was beginning to feel, though, as if she had been caught up in a great rushing wind. Her father's visit had begun it. He had come down and stayed overnight, and she had had dinner with him in the restaurant when he arrived, and Mawgan had come and joined them for coffee and liqueurs. Her father had enjoyed his meal, and been disposed to approve of a candidate for his daughter's hand with so much potential. They had talked properly the next morning, although Debbie hadn't been there and only knew roughly what had been said. In the afternoon, she had gone with him to visit the bank and had a long, serious consultation with a senior manager. He had driven home in the evening, leaving her with his qualified blessing.

'I know I can't stop you, my darling,' he had told her. 'I like your Mawgan Angwin, I think he'll be good to you, I think you'll have a good life together so long as you don't expect it to be an easy one. But I'm not sure we can get rid of this conviction, and that, you may both have to accept. But we'll see. He's given me the go-ahead to try, but not if it's going to involve the little sister.'

'He's too kind to her,' Debbie had said. Jerry shook his head.

'No, Debbie, he's scared stiff of her, and I don't blame him. Things are not so bad that they couldn't have been worse, and you'd better believe that. And to a certain extent, your young man *is* guilty, and he's well aware of it. I hope you realise you will have to live with that.' He gave her a serious look, and then patted her shoulder is if to comfort her. 'But I won't cut you off without the proverbial shilling, don't worry.' He had kissed her goodbye and gone, leaving her with plenty to think about. And no, Jerry thought as he drove home, he wasn't happy about this, no father would be. He couldn't help thinking, what he hadn't put into words, *what about when he loses his temper with* you? and knowing that to oppose her on such insubstantial grounds would achieve nothing but deadlock. Anyway, if you believed there had been no real case to answer – as he did – there could be no sensible objection either, but no father could be expected to like it, however pleasant the man involved. As he was, of course. Jerry, who had made a monumental mess of his own life, didn't feel qualified to interfere in that of his daughter, so it had to be left in the lap of the gods. He hoped that he could trust them.

But Debbie wasn't to know this, and there were other things occupying her mind. Chel and Oliver were moving into the house by the creek at the end of the month, and having them living so close was going to be a whole new experience – for all of them, come to think – and now there was to be even more. She wondered what Mawgan's family would make of her, and she of them, much as she wondered what Oliver and her father really made of him. They were both being nice about it, but they couldn't really be happy about the conviction. Well, she wasn't herself – and come to that, neither was Mawgan.

She found herself, and not for the first time, wondering about Tim as she crossed the forecourt to join the cheerful group under the red and white umbrella. Tim had been so hard on Mawgan, but it seemed overkill on the part of fate to land the same situation on his plate. Tim had surely made sufficient restitution when he rescued Mawgan from the burning house. Fate, though, was seldom kind, if sometimes fearsomely just. Poor Tim. She felt, even more than usual, that life had moved on and left him adrift.

Roger was quite happy about being deserted for the afternoon, and didn't even mind about Sunday.

'There'll not be more than a couple of boatloads. I can do the talk in the boathouse in the morning, and take them out in two lots in the afternoon,' he said, cheerfully enough. 'We'd do that anyway, it only means there'll be maybe four in a boat instead of two for once. No problem.'

'You must be beginning to think I'll be a terrible partner. Always taking days off.'

'You've got problems to sort out. All I've got is the job to do. I can't grumble, I get paid.'

'Roger, you're a star. We need to have a proper project meeting before you go home, there's so much to discuss.'

He raised his eyebrows.

'Going to be a goer, you think?'

'Looks very much as if it might.'

Roger released a long, happy sigh.

'That's terrific, Deb! I keep telling myself not to believe in it, it's bound to be a dead duck.'

'Don't count your chickens, or even your dead ducks, but keep your job options fluid.' She got up, ready to leave. 'See you tonight.'

'Last night dinner in town, remember.'

'I'll be back.'

It was unusual to be out with Mawgan on a weekday afternoon. The last time, she remembered, had been the day of the fire, almost a month ago now, but they seemed to have moved into another universe since then, and she trusted that today's outing would end more auspiciously.

'Hey,' she said, suddenly remembering something she had meant to take up with him before. 'You never told me your name was *Garfield*. Garfield is a striped cat in a cartoon strip.'

'Cute and cuddly though,' said Mawgan. 'You never asked me.'

'I think I assumed something more commonplace, like Geoffrey or George.'

'Garfield is a family name. It's my grandad's, too. You find it around, down here.'

'Your family is very dynastic, isn't it? Just like the Tregears, or the Pengellys. Is it a Cornwall thing, do you think?'

'I never thought about it. Maybe it is. People don't stray far from their roots, they get like that I suppose.'

'You strayed, but you came back.'

'You too, Miss Nankervis.'

'Oh… yes, I suppose I have.' She thought about it. 'Oliver and Chel have even met some of our relations, we never even knew we had them. Isn't that strange?'

'Very strange – mind that tractor, you have seen it, haven't you?'

'God, you have got bad nerves!' Debbie slid into a handy field gate and let the tractor past. 'Keep on with the Prozac!' Prozac, she now knew, hadn't quite been another of his black jokes, she had found it in the bathroom, which had answered one question, although she had never seen him take it; he claimed that the last thing you needed to be when in charge of a professional kitchen was spaced out on happytabs. The kitchen staff, Debbie suspected, might not have agreed, and she intended to raise the subject once the season was over. On the credit side though, she realised suddenly, he didn't make black jokes like that any more.

They chose a ring at a jeweller down Meneage Street, a solitaire diamond of moderate size but excellent quality and Debbie averted her eyes from the price tag and hoped the Fish could stand it. As they drove home, with the ring safely in its box in the glove compartment, Mawgan said, out of the blue, 'I've been thinking.'

'Oh yes? About anything in particular?'

'Things in general, really. You're right, I can't go on the way I have been. Apart from anything else, it wouldn't be fair to you.'

422

'We're talking your business here, I take it?'

'Businesses,' he corrected her. True, she thought. She hadn't considered it before, but the restaurant staff called him *Chef*, to the staff of the pub, he was *Mr Angwin*. The two halves were separate entities. They had always been intended to be, and they had stayed that way. She had asked him why the locals called him *Mawgan* these days, as did Tommy, but he had remained *Mr Angwin* to the pub staff, and he had answered, quite simply, 'Because I'm one of them. Their choice.' She had needed to give the answer some thought, but it made sense in the end. She said, now, 'So? What have you thought?'

'Your sister-in-law… Chel. And now I come to think about it, you talk about *Garfield*, how did she come by a name like that?'

'Cheryl. Oliver couldn't be bothered with it, a bit like you calling me Deb. But don't worry, I won't do the same to you.'

'Morgue? No, please don't.'

'What about Chel?' asked Debbie, after a pause.

'Has she the experience to manage the Fish? It's not rocket science, exactly, but I wouldn't want to be having to worry about it all the time.'

'Only Chel can tell you that. Or possibly, I suppose, the manager of the Queens Hotel in Embridge. His name is MacDonald,' she added, helpfully. And then thought *Shut up, don't manipulate!*

'But she was working to become management?'

'So I always understood. I know she'd been through all the different areas – chambermaid, bar staff, waitress, probably even the kitchen – as well as being in reception, because her sister Tracy told me.'

'She knows her way around then.'

'You should talk to her,' said Debbie. 'One thing I can tell you, for sure, is that you could trust her with your disreputable secrets. I'm sure you have some.'

'Me?'

'Don't come the innocent with me, Mawgan Angwin. I wasn't born yesterday.'

'Actually, I haven't many. Are you disappointed?' he said, apologetically.

'It's that word *many* that I like.'

A silence fell between them, but a comfortable one.

'Will your family like me, do you think?' asked Debbie, suddenly.

'Worried about them, bird? They don't bite.' She knew he was looking at her, but kept her eyes on the road.

'I suppose it's always a bit of an ordeal, meeting somebody's family when you're going to be part of it – suppose they don't want you to be, it's always a possibility.' She wished she hadn't said that, the moment she spoke. Her mother had been like that with him, although not exactly to his face. She really must try to be more – or maybe less would be better – sensitive. Mawgan remained relaxed.

'You'll know, come Sunday,' he said.

So, here Sunday was, and here she was, driving the buttercup/sunflower along the A30 towards family lunch with the Angwins, with Mawgan's ring, for the first time, on her finger, and him beside her, apparently untroubled by doubts of any kind, except about his sisters' cooking.

'You are *so* élitist!' she accused, not for the first time.

'I've seen what they can do,' he reminded her, and although she didn't turn her head to see, she heard the grin in his voice. 'Still, so long as the menu don't involve Yorkshire pudding, we might get away with it.'

'God knows what you'll make of my cooking, then, if you're so hard on theirs!'

'Your'n might be better,' he suggested. Debbie blanched at the thought.

'Good heavens, I hope not!' He was teasing her on purpose, she realised, to take her mind off the coming meeting. 'I'm not nervous,' she assured him. 'You don't have to humour me.'

'Then don't you grip the wheel until your knuckles turns white,' he said, and they both laughed.

She wasn't nervous, Debbie thought, or at least, she wouldn't have been if it hadn't been for all the terrible troubles in his family. As it was, she had no idea where he stood, let alone herself, and her own experience of family life, particularly just recently, was no comfort.

'Tell me about your sisters,' she invited. 'You never talk about them, it's like making an expedition into a jungle to look for some undiscovered tribe. You can't blame me for being just a little apprehensive.'

'We gave up on the lurking-in-bushes-with-a-blowpipe thing a few years back, here in Cornwall,' he assured her, and she knew that the irrepressible grin had appeared again. 'The missionaries told us that it weren't nice.'

'Be sensible, please.'

'You've seen Anna already,' he said. 'Allison is more like Mum, I suppose.'

'Oh, very helpful – and I didn't mean what they looked like – what are they *like*? What makes them tick?'

'An atomic clock, I wouldn't be surprised.' She took her eyes off the road for a second to glare at him, making him laugh. 'OK, OK, I surrender! Anna is married and lives abroad, she's got two kids – boys – twins. About four, I haven't seen them since they were babies, so don't ask me. Kurt is some high-powered whiz-kid in computers, goes all over the world, so I haven't seen a lot of her these past few years, neither, but from the little I saw the other night she's still the same bossy big sister she always was.' There was affection in his voice, Debbie recognised. Anna, then, was probably all right. She had looked fun, the quick glimpse of her that Debbie had seen. Very like Mawgan, to be fair.

'And Allison?'

'Allison… oh, Allison is the brains of the family. Very bright, very clever, very frustrated.'

'Frustrated?' asked Debbie, after a pause.

'Yeah…' He drew the word out as if he was thinking. 'One thing the missionaries haven't quite stamped out yet, is sexism. She should've been the boy, not me.'

'I would dispute that – quite forcefully, actually,' said Debbie, and he laughed.

'Glad about that.'

'Tell me, then,' said Debbie, after a pause. 'I've got to meet them all. If there are any hidden pitfalls, tell me where they are.'

'Allison would've liked to slip into my working boots when I stepped out of 'em. Best she could hope for was a job typing letters in the office. So she went to be an airline hostess and that's about it.'

'*Tell me the old, old story,*' said Debbie, almost to herself, but it wasn't Allison in her thoughts so much as Susan.

Neither of them mentioned Cressida, naturally enough, and the conversation, such as it had been, seemed to have come to an end.

Talking about them almost made Debbie believe that she was no longer nervous, but the moment she pulled into the kerb outside the house in Launceston, she knew that even if she had managed to convince him, she had failed with herself. It was a big, solidly-built semi-detached house with a small front garden, in a street of others the same, prosperous but not rich, she classified it to herself, and immediately despised herself.

Bossiness in herself she could handle, she decided, snobbishness, no. The one, you probably couldn't help if you inherited it, but snobbishness was learned. There were two cars already parked in the drive, a sporty little Mazda, and a pristine but elderly Ford. Mawgan looked at them critically.

'Sorry Deb, it looks as if the clans have gathered. That's Grandad's car. Anna, I'll strangle you when I get my hands on you! I just hope you remembered to lay in the champagne.'

'What's that thing they say about sheep and lambs?' asked Debbie. She walked round the car to join him on the pavement, and he took her arm and escorted her through the gates.

The moment the front door closed behind them, Debbie recognised that she had walked into a home. Not anything that even faintly resembled the beautiful, expensively furnished but essentially soulless house in which she had grown up, but a real home. Nothing was luxurious or costly, although all of it was good, and some of it was even slightly shabby, but everything she saw looked well-loved, well-used, and at ease with itself. The hall ran straight through the house from front to back, and smelled of roasting meat, and the sound of laughter came from an open door on the left at the back of the house. Mawgan sniffed the air suspiciously.

'They haven't burnt nothing yet, then,' he remarked, and at the sound of his voice, his sisters appeared at the open door, flushed and aproned, one of them carrying a wooden spoon, smiling a welcome. Anna gave Debbie a comprehensive look and a wicked smile.

'Hullo, we nearly met the other night at the hospital. I'm Anna.' She kissed Debbie, a real, sisterly kiss that surprised her, and went to put her arms around her brother. 'Mawgan – darling – lovely to see you standing upright! You brought her, I hoped you would.'

'It would have served you right if I'd got Mrs Solomons to drive me,' said Mawgan, returning her hug. 'Ouch – watch what you're doing! That hurt!'

Allison came out more quietly. She had the same colouring as the other two, and was recognisably their sister, but was of a taller, slenderer build, darker eyes and her hair had more body and wave to it. She was more sophisticated, Debbie recognised, cast in a finer mould. She found herself wondering which side of the family the little sister had favoured. She found that Allison was looking at her with the same interest.

'Well, hullooo....' said Allison, and smiled. It was useless, Debbie realised, to hold back, the Angwins were irresistible, and anyway, she didn't particularly need to resist them. She smiled back, and Allison, as Anna had done, kissed her cheek but more reservedly. It was Allison, too, who spotted the ring, she took Debbie's hand and looked at it thoughtfully.

'Is this your own fiancée, or have you borrowed her from someone else?' she enquired.

'Mine. All mine,' said Mawgan, in a cat-at-the-cream voice that sparked an instant reaction in his sisters.

'My God, you're some brave!' said Allison, looking at Debbie with round eyes, and Anna punched her brother lightly on his uninjured shoulder. The three of them were teasing, sparring round her, so at ease, so much friends with each other, that Debbie felt a spasm of… jealousy? Her own home had never rung with so much spontaneous mirth. The sound of something sizzling on a hot stove, accompanied by a scorching smell, interrupted them.

'Hadn't you better go and see to that?' asked Mawgan. 'Something's boiling over, from the sounds of it. Where are the rest of the tribe, in the garden?' He grinned at Debbie as he said that, including her in the teasing.

Anna gave a shriek and dived back into the kitchen and Allison said, 'You had better go and break the news to them, and I'll see if there's something in the cupboard more suitable for the occasion than Spanish plonk.' She smiled at Debbie then. 'He'll tell us your name one day, if you stay around long enough. Off you go.'

'Debbie Nankervis,' Mawgan threw over his shoulder as he went to the far door. 'Come on Deb, leave the witches to their cauldron, it's probably time to throw in the toads. No, don't you dare!' as Allison threatened him with the spoon. 'Anna's already set my recovery back three weeks!' Still laughing, he scooped Debbie with him and took her out onto a stone patio where the senior members of his family were enjoying the sunshine.

It was a peaceful scene. The back garden, Debbie noticed almost automatically, was beautiful, somebody loved gardening, but there was notably no rockery. The four people who had looked round at the sound of the outside door were a more daunting sight. An elderly couple sitting together on a swinging seat must be the grandparents, he held her hand, Debbie saw, and she had obviously had a fairly major stroke. The one who had to be the father had laid down the racing pages of the Sunday paper on his knee and was looking at his son and the strange girl with an expression hard to read. The last of the quartet, a graceful, dark-haired, dark-eyed woman, was recognisably the mother of Allison, although the older two had taken almost entirely after their father and come to that, their grandfather, both of whom were simply an older Mawgan with progressively less hair. Her expression was easier to read, Debbie thought she had never seen anybody whose heart was so obviously in her eyes. She felt Mawgan's mood change the moment he set foot on the stone.

'Hi,' he said.

'Son.' Pip gave a nod in his direction. Cally left her chair and went to kiss her son, but Debbie noticed, it wasn't a close embrace, and although her fingers did brush gently over the new scar above his right eye, she made no comment. It was left to Grandad to ask, 'Who's the young lady, Mawgan boy?' while Nan nodded and smiled.

Mawgan introduced her, and Pip gave her a sharp look.

'Deborah Nankervis who rang me? Is that who you are, from that sailing school?'

'Yes,' said Debbie, wondering what he would say, in view of Mawgan's remark about sexism, if she added that she intended to rebuild it and run it herself. She was good at people, she had always thought, but she couldn't get the measure of these four. There was an atmosphere, not unpleasant, but wary, as if none of them knew quite how they should be behaving.

'I owe you thanks,' said Pip. He nodded to her, too. 'Kind of you.'

'Sit down, dear,' Cally patted the chair beside her. 'So kind of you to bring Mawgan over, I hope it hasn't spoiled your Sunday.'

Debbie sat, and smiled at Nan who was smiling at her. A grey mongrel dog of the lurcher persuasion came and lay on her feet. There was something about her at present, she thought, that made dogs seem to want to comfort her. Garfie made some remark about the warm weather for September, and Debbie made some commonplace reply. The moment when Mawgan might have mentioned their engagement had somehow passed. There was nothing more to say about the weather. The dog thumped his tail against Debbie's ankle, she realised that he was the only one with whom she felt entirely at ease, and as of this moment, that included Mawgan.

The conversation, if that was what it could be called, might have run into serious trouble at that point, but right on cue, a shriek came from the open kitchen window.

'Anna, what have you *done*?'

'It's all right,' Anna's voice protested. 'I'll take a whisk –'

'You can't do that! You've killed it!' There was a sound of horrified laughter, and Anna protesting that no, she hadn't, she was sure it only needed some more milk or something.

'Mawgan will know, he thinks he knows it all! Make him be useful for a change.' More laughter, bubbling up the scale, genuinely amused. A door slammed. Allison appeared round the side of the house, giggling.

'Anna's done something terrible to the custard,' she said. 'Come and help – quick – '

Mawgan, Debbie thought, was pleased to have the excuse to go. He let Allison tow him out of sight round the corner. There was the sound of muted voices in the kitchen, and then Mawgan's, strong and clear.

'No Anna, you can't, you've scrambled it. Give it the dog and start again!' And Allison, 'Teach you to show off, I told you custard powder was good enough!' More laughter, fits of it, the three of them striking sparks from each other again the instant they were together. The dog, hearing the word *dog*, gave Debbie an apologetic look and loped off around the corner, she was sorry to see him go. She turned to say something pleasant to Mawgan's mother about the garden, in order to break a listening silence, and received a shock. Cally was sitting there with her eyes closed, and tears trickling gently down her face. She made no attempt to wipe them away.

'Mrs. Angwin –' Debbie said, and then, in face of such inconsolable grief, stopped. Pip set his paper aside on a wooden table, crumpling it.

'It's the way things used to be,' he said. 'There's not been a lot of laughter in this house just lately, girl. It gets to you.'

Debbie sat still, her hands in her lap, and the sunlight caught the diamond on her finger and struck rainbow reflections on the wall of the house. Pip said, without seeming to have noticed it,

'You marrying the boy then, Deborah Nankervis?'

'Yes,' said Debbie.

He grunted. 'Your family know about the trouble, do they?'

'Yes,' said Debbie, again. She had all their attention now. She wondered how much you could say to strangers, particularly strangers who kept such a distance, and then decided that it was surely time somebody said something, and preferably something positive, and she wasn't thinking just of the present stand-off. 'My father is a solicitor. He says there probably wasn't a case to answer, and the conviction can be dismissed on appeal. He thinks the two girls lied, and that would be enough.'

'Oh, *they* lied, but what was the truth?' said Pip, and a silence fell, broken only by Mawgan's grandmother, who made an inarticulate sound that was eloquent of some emotion that Debbie thought was distress. She said, steadily, 'And if that turns out to be a dead end, it doesn't make any difference. We'll still be married. It isn't, after all, as if he did anything desperate, is it?'

The silence this time stretched out into what felt like infinity. Then Pip said, as if surprised, 'Nobody never said that before.'

'My father said it straight away,' said Debbie. 'And he's not just any old solicitor, he's a very high-profile solicitor.'

Pip looked at her in a measuring way, and said, as if testing her, 'Boy was always a handful. Some full of himself, wouldn't do what he should, can't get my head round a man wanting to be a cook. Seems unnatural.'

Debbie smiled, trying to relax but feeling herself tense as a spring.

'At least he didn't want to be a hairdresser. There's yet something to be thankful for.'

Pip almost smiled back. 'I only had the one son. Now there's nobody to leave the business to when I go, seems like a shame.'

The others were all listening, not contributing but hearing every word, spoken or unspoken. Debbie felt her heart start thumping in the way that it did when she knew she was about to do or say something that she might later regret. *Don't manipulate.* Then, immediately on top of that thought came another. *Deb builds bridges.* If ever a bridge needed to be built, it was surely here and now, and the foundation stones were there, safely stacked in her own experience and in what Mawgan had told her on the way here. When she spoke, she was surprised to hear her voice so steady.

'Yes, it's a shame, but you mustn't hold it against him. You can't make people do what you want just because of a family business, if what *they* want is something quite different. That isn't fair.' She paused. 'My father had the same problem with my brother, he's an only son too. Dad wanted him to study law, be a solicitor in the family firm *his* father started.' It was a perfect parallel. They were all listening closely, she saw. 'Oliver would have made a terrible solicitor, and I don't know, but maybe, Mawgan wouldn't have made a very good builder if his heart wasn't in it, but I don't know if you realise this, he's a really talented chef, just as Oliver has turned out to be a really talented artist. The *really* sad thing is that my parents had more than one child. My sister would have made a brilliant solicitor, or even a barrister, and she was just dismissed as unimportant simply because she was a girl.' She found both Pip and Garfie looking at her intently, and smiled, although she was almost too scared. This was manipulation, big time! 'Maybe you should think about *Angwin & Daughter* instead of *Angwin & Son*.'

'Girls don't do labouring work. I served my apprenticeship and worked up.' Pip sounded as if he was giving out the eleventh commandment.

'My sister-in-law did hotel management,' said Debbie. 'She worked in every department, learning how it was done, but she never intended to be a chambermaid, for instance, or a waitress. Of course, you need to know the nuts and bolts, how things should be done, but surely it takes more than brawn to run a successful business. You know that –' she purposely included Garfie in her accusation, '– both of you.'

'Anna's married,' said Pip. 'Gone to live abroad, and that's the boy's doing too.' He sounded uncertain, as if new ideas were hammering their way in. Debbie chose to ignore this provocative red herring.

'Allison isn't married. Mawgan says she's the really clever one, and if she's brighter than him, believe me, she's going some.'

'Girls do marry.'

'So did you,' Debbie pointed out.

'She's an air hostess,' said Garfie. *Girlie job* was implicit in his tone, and a resentment, too, that all three of his grandchildren had broken away so finally from their roots. They must, Debbie thought, have inherited this pioneering spirit from their mother, and she looked at Cally with sudden interest. Once again, she had the sense to make no comment, leaving the silence, this time, to speak for itself.

Cally had stopped crying. She reached out and touched Debbie's arm.

'Come and let me show you the garden.'

By this time, Debbie would have given anything to be beamed up to another planet, and she leapt on the suggestion with relief. The grandmother heaved herself to her feet and came along with them, holding onto Debbie's arm for support. The three of them went slowly down the steps onto the lawn, leaving the two men sitting silently behind them. They walked, at Nan's slow pace, along the borders for a while, Cally pointing out various plants and Debbie admiring, and then Cally said, in almost the same breath as some excellent advice on keeping slugs from delphiniums, 'They always used to be like that, you know – the three of them. Laughing and joking and carrying on. The house was always full of happiness when they were children. Today is the first time…' She spoke almost absently, half to herself. 'I'm sorry I was so silly.' That was more direct. Debbie said carefully, 'Cressida – she was very much the youngest?'

'Too much the youngest – and always a stranger. You know? Not like the others.' She wouldn't, maybe even couldn't, put it more clearly.

'It happens,' said Debbie. 'Heredity is an odd thing.'

'Are your family much alike? You said you had a brother and a sister. Are you close?'

'My family isn't a good example. My father isn't my sister's father, and my mother isn't my brother's mother. I'm beginning to wonder if we're closer than I always thought we were, though.' No use in not saying it, they were going to find out anyway. 'My parents' marriage broke up recently. It seems to have had an odd effect.'

'That's sad,' Cally said, and Nan pressed her arm sympathetically.

'Well… yes and no. You get people in families sometimes who just don't fit, and push the whole thing out of shape… my mother was a bit like that. Wanted everything her way, and every*one* too, you know? It doesn't work. You can't do that to people – not in any way, not even if you mean it kindly or think it's for the best, it's still wanting your own way. You only make things hard for people.'

She wasn't even thinking of Cressida as she spoke, and was startled when Nan dragged her to a stop, saying, with an effort, 'Who sent you?' and answered herself with a single word. 'God!'

'Come on, Mother.' Cally took her other arm and the three of them moved forward. On the patio, Pip and Garfie had moved close together and were talking hard. After a while, Cally said, quietly, 'Mawgan was always the cockiest, being the only boy. Full of himself, like Pip says, always in the middle of things. When he come down, he come down hard.'

And had gone on doing it, Debbie thought. The telegraph pole, the chair, the stairs. Could you get a psychological urge towards self-destruction and not know it? Lesley had certainly thought so.

'He'd changed when he come out of prison,' said Cally, and a world of grief echoed in the words. 'He works too hard, and when he isn't working, he drinks too much. And he keeps all his old friends at arm's length and nobody can get near him. Except you. How did you get so close?'

Debbie said, without thinking, 'I suppose his defences were down. After all, we were snowed in together.'

This time, they both stopped.

'That was you?' said Cally, and suddenly flung her arms round her, hugging her so hard that she had difficulty breathing. There was no doubt of the genuine feeling behind that hug. 'Oh Debbie, you dear girl, how can we ever thank you?'

Nan hugged her too. 'Lovely girl… welcome,' she said.

'I just happened to be there,' said Debbie, and Nan said forcefully, for the second time, 'God!'

They walked slowly on. The dog emerged from the kitchen, licking his lips, and came to join them, padding along one pace to the rear. You would have to work hard to get total disaster with the Angwins, Debbie realised. Laughter would always be one pace behind like the dog, it wasn't just Mawgan, they were all the same. Except possibly his mother. She suspected things went deeper with Cally, and of course, there was no way of telling about the absent Cressida.

'It's a lovely garden,' she said idly

'It takes up the time,' said Cally. She looked up at the house, looming high above them. 'I hate this house. I hate this town, it's not its fault, I just don't belong here! I want to go home.' She spoke so forcefully, and so unexpectedly, that both her companions turned to look at her.

'Then go,' said Debbie. Might as well make a clean sweep while she was at it.

They had reached the steps up to the patio, and Cally called out, 'Pip – Father – do you know who this is? She's that girl who was up on the moor, back'long!'

Both of them turned.

'I always wondered who you might be,' said Pip, speaking slowly. 'You saved the boy's life, they tell me.'

'Twice,' said Mawgan, reappearing fortuitously round the corner of the house. 'She makes a habit of it – she helped drag me out of the burning house, too. Nice to think she feels it's worth it.' For once, he wasn't making a joke.

'Three times!' said Cally, with conviction.

It was a moment too full of emotion, and it created the most acute discomfort. The family were equal to it: Mawgan defused it, in true Angwin style.

'Those two've managed not to ruin the lunch, and want somebody to carve. Please don't leave either of them run loose with a carving knife, let's stay ahead while we're winning!' It wasn't the best joke in the world, but it made them smile. The moment passed.

The bridge was complete. Wobbly still, it would need some shoring up and probably a coat of paint or six, Debbie decided, but all at once they were not just a group of people hideously ill-at-ease with each other, but three generations of the same family. Pip, getting to his feet to go to the rescue of the joint, almost slapped his son jovially on the shoulder in passing, stopped and looked at his palm, and they both laughed, genuine laughter.

'No, maybe not. We've not been very welcoming to your girl, son, find her a glass of wine. There's some in the kitchen, I know, the girls opened it earlier. I'll send it out.'

Allison brought it, on a tray in five glasses, and a glass of orange for her grandmother. She manoeuvred herself into a seat beside Debbie, leaving Mawgan to their mother and grandparents, and raised her glass.

'Here's to you, miracle worker! How did you make them all smile again?'

'By being bossy and interfering,' said Debbie.

'My kind of girl!'

'Here's to us, then!' They clinked glasses and drank. Allison said, 'So what do you make of us all? Are we what you expected?'

'What, when I know your brother? I didn't know *what* to expect!'

'Mmm, see your point. Are you living together?'

'No choice. My place burned down, remember?'

Allison hitched up her skirt to let the sun reach her legs, which were sturdy but shapely, and already enviably brown. She sipped her wine thoughtfully. 'You must think that we're horrible.'

Debbie looked at her in astonishment. 'Why ever should I do that?'

'From where you're sitting, it must look as if we've all been rough on Mawgan.'

Since this was true, Debbie hesitated before she spoke. 'It must have been difficult,' she offered. Allison made a face.

'Nightmare city! I mean – well, Mawgan didn't – couldn't even – deny what had happened, and that was bad enough, but Cress… well, she was the injured party, wasn't she? In anybody's book? What do you do?'

The reasoning behind this was so convoluted that Debbie didn't even try to unravel it. She said, cautiously, 'Mawgan seems to think that the marriage had bitten the dust anyway.'

'Oh, I'm sure it had. But she was still his wife, and I don't suppose she wished him dead… that's the sort of thing that destroys families. And local feeling ran so high…'

'Did it really drive you out?' asked Debbie, quietly, and Allison shook her head slightly, but as if she didn't quite mean it.

'Oh, our friends stood by us… but other people… they behaved as if he was a murderer, which he wasn't – isn't. She talked to the press, you see – they sought her out. That's when it all got out of hand. Nobody could live with it… the shame of it… but it came with us anyway. We brought it.'

'You should go back. People forget.'

'It'll never be over. The family – all of us – will still have to take sides. Whenever she chooses to come home… and how can we side with *him*?'

'Who do you *want* to side with?' asked Debbie, pertinently, but Allison shook her head again, more firmly this time.

'You're too clever, you.' She sipped her wine thoughtfully, and Debbie did the same. She had a sudden clear and rather horrifying view of what devastation the death of Michael Stanley, and its cause, had wrought in this friendly, ordinary, obviously very close family and thought of her own, for the first time, with a feeling that things *could* be worse, and that for some people they were. People who didn't even deserve it, like the Angwins. If you never had such happiness, it couldn't be destroyed. Working out a compromise, as now maybe they could, would only paper over the crack, nothing could ever be as it was before. Cress, absent or present, had seen to that, and they would all always feel… well, guilt. For various things.

'I used to go to the prison,' said Allison, unexpectedly. 'On visiting days, you know?'

'Pretty grim?' asked Debbie, sympathetically. It didn't feel as if they were talking about Mawgan at all.

'Bloody awful,' said Allison. She took a mouthful of wine, her eyes fixed on a distant place that, Debbie thought, she didn't much wish to revisit. 'Mawgan was always so outgoing… but he shut right down, I think he did it to survive. He wasn't really there at all, not the brother I knew. I don't think… I don't think anyone can ever put that kind of experience behind them – not any of it. Do you?'

'God knows,' said Debbie.

'Then I hope He does something about it.'

There was a silence, full of unspoken thoughts. When Allison spoke again it was idly, with a complete change of subject.

'Will you work in the Fish when you're married?' she asked.

'No. I'm hoping your dad will build me a sailing school.' Debbie spoke on impulse, then realised that she meant it. Allison laughed.

'Cool! How does big brother take that for an idea?'

'Philosophically. He has to, we need his input. He's the local expert.'

'Strange, isn't it?' mused Allison. 'You never see your own relatives as experts in anything. You've got a brother, too, haven't you? Is he an expert in something?'

'Oliver? He's an artist, I'm no judge of *expert*. People who should know seem to think so.'

Allison said, still musingly, 'Oliver Nankervis. That's a name I feel I should know.'

'You will know it. Two of them in one family, how shall we live with it?'

'Two?'

'Don't under-estimate your own brother.'

'Never did I think to see this day,' said Allison. She took another sip. 'Just so long as Cress doesn't roll up and spoil it.' Such bitterness. Debbie was startled.

'Is she likely to?'

'She has a gift for it. Destructive little bitch! But Anna seems to think she's gone off with someone, so perhaps we're safe for today.'

'If you want to be, you're safe for any day,' Debbie pointed out.

'Well yes… and then again, no. Like I told you, it's hard to take sides within the family. Cress is so – so useless, we all feel guilty about her, I suppose. Mawgan is the strong one.' She looked gloomy.

'Not that strong. Believe me. Not invincible.'

'Nobody's that,' said Allison.

Anna came to the door into the house at that moment, and announced that lunch was practically on the table and would they all please come inside and get themselves around it *pronto*, so that was the end of confidences.

It was a cheerful meal. Roast pork, with all the trimmings. The sisters had done an excellent job, in spite of their brother's apprehension.

'We thought about beef, but we didn't dare risk the Yorkshire pudding,' Anna confessed. 'Not with our resident restaurant critic sitting here.' She was sitting beside him, and had insisted on cutting up his meat for him with big-sisterly efficiency. 'Just like for the twins,' she had said affectionately.

'So when's the wedding to be?' Garfie was the one to ask, choosing an easy subject with unexpected social skill.

'And where?' asked Cally, smiling.

They had it all arranged between them by the time the apple pie and custard arrived – correctly made custard this time, with unscrambled eggs. Mawgan said it had to be January or February, March only at a push, and Debbie said it very likely had to be in St. Erbyn, from Chel and Oliver's house. The family were thrilled to hear it would probably take place in Cornwall, and then took over, busily vociferous. It was as if a great wave of relief to be standing on common ground again had swept through the house.

'Can you use the Fish for the reception?' Anna asked. 'How many people, have you thought yet? Is it big enough?'

Debbie hadn't really considered a reception. She looked at Mawgan.

'At least you could rely on the caterers,' he said, on the whole unhelpfully.

'And will you have a proper white wedding, with bridesmaids?' asked Cally, and so it went on, with Anna and Mawgan vetoing with one voice a sentimental suggestion from Cally that the twins might be page boys.

The apple pie was simply a smear on the serving plate. Garfie knocked on the table with his spoon, calling for silence.

'Enough of this!' he said, rising to his feet. 'The girl will think we're savages.' The family obediently fell silent, looking up at him. He spoke carefully. 'I a'n't one for making speeches,' he said. 'There 'tis, as head of the family, I should make one now. We've been through some bad times, we don't need telling. Maybe as we've made mistakes, done foolish things, wrong things even. Maybe we'll do 'em again, although I hope as they'll not be the same ones.'

Debbie thought she heard Anna murmur, under her breath, 'Amen!' and a moment later, seeing her smiling face, thought she must have dreamed it. But Garfie was still speaking.

'Today 'as been a good time. Almost like the old times… like as if a breath of fresh air blown through, and we all know why. This young lady as Mawgan 'as brought into the family, we owes her, we owes her for today, and it happens we owes her for yesterday too.' He paused, and a murmur ran round the family circle. 'And we owes her too because there's going to be a tomorrow. Please God, a better tomorrow.' He picked up his glass. 'Raise your glasses for Debbie, and for Mawgan too. Good luck to 'em, I say!' And so did the family, wholeheartedly, while Debbie covered a rosy blush with her hands, and Mawgan put his good arm around her shoulders and kissed her soundly, to family cheers.

Deaths, particularly tragic, unnecessary deaths that get classified as manslaughter can divide families, weddings can bring them together, as Garfie had been wise enough to know. They had arrived in Launceston unnoticed, but Debbie and Mawgan left in the late afternoon with the entire clan assembled on the pavement, still talking and laughing, hugging and kissing, not wanting to say goodbye. It occurred to Debbie, oddly, that it was almost as if the whole lot of them had finished serving a sentence, not just Mawgan. There might be a reaction later, of course, but they would never sink so low or be so divided again. The fragile bridge would hold, she knew it. She hadn't fully realised how much damage the absent little sister had done until today.

Cally put her arms round her and gave her a special hug on parting.

'Take care of him,' she whispered, and Debbie whispered back,

'Certainly will, you can put money on it.'

They drove away, everyone waving.

'You survived the jungle OK, then,' said Mawgan, as they drove onto the A30 to head west. 'So, what do you think? Do we all pass the test?'

'I liked them, they're lovely people,' said Debbie, meaning it. 'More important, did I pass it?'

'You? Top of the class, I wouldn't wonder.' He smiled at her, with love. 'You were amazing. Like the rest of them, I should thank you.'

'Thank me? What for?'

'I thought it was going to be a difficult lunch, to be honest. I thought we'd be well home by this time.'

'You swine!' exclaimed Debbie. 'And there was you lecturing me about *my* knuckles!'

'Would it've helped, if I'd told you?'

'Well… no,' she had to admit.

'What did you say to them all, while I was in the kitchen? It felt like coming out into a different world.'

'Oh… this and that. About you, and about my family a bit.'

He looked at her as if he knew she was holding something back, but he didn't press it. They drove on in a silence that was, on the whole, contented.

Strange about families, Debbie thought, as she drove. Today, away from the Fish and among his own people, she had seen an entirely different Mawgan. Something to do with not being the big bad boss, but just one of the rank and file for a change, she supposed, but more than that. Against the family background, he had actually been another person, maybe it was something to do with the way they saw him themselves. She herself, she was almost sure, underwent the same metamorphosis when her father, or even Oliver and Chel, was around, she could measure that against Mawgan's attitude to her when they were there. Would they all meld together and become familiar, or did this double-persona thing last for ever and ever? Perhaps that was what *familiar* had originally meant. She would never see him in quite the same way, she realised, after this day spent in the heart of his family. The super-competent landlord of the Fish, the talented chef of his own restaurant, would for evermore be linked with the – yes, in spite of everything, the *much-loved* grandson, son and brother whom she had met for the first time today.

'Penny for them,' said Mawgan, watching her.

'Oh…' said Debbie. 'I was just thinking about families.'

'Scary subject!' The nearer they got to St. Erbyn, the more he was reverting back to his more… less?… *familiar* self. She decided not to tell him exactly what she had been thinking.

'They do love you, you know,' she said instead.

'I never thought they didn't.' He didn't sound certain, however. *Bloody* little sister! She said,

'It was a very interesting day, taken by and large.' and left it at that.

XXV

Nothing about life comes in tidy packages. The happy-ever-after of Cress's favourite reading is just that, fiction. In reality, there are always loose ends hanging out, and generally, they never get tidied away. Most often, life has a way of going on and leaving the loose ends hanging there, and the only finality is the funeral at the very end, leaving the questions still unresolved. In this particular instance, there were so many tendrils floating in the breeze, you could have woven a rug from them, Debbie thought. It would have been comforting to be able to write *The End* and move tidily on to the next volume, it couldn't be done. There were a lot of things that couldn't be done.

Take her mother, for instance. She had deliberately chosen to set herself outside the family palisade, and the only one to whom she would now speak was Susan. That was her loss, but also her choice, she had dismissed the Nankervises wholesale, and it was as if they had never been. That seemed to Debbie, when she thought about it in the dark small hours of the night, not just wasteful, but wicked. Her mother had broken up a marriage to get Jerry for herself, that was part of family lore, even if Dot herself denied it, and said the marriage had come to a natural end from Helen Macken's ambition. Although none of them, except Jerry and possibly Oliver's godmother, knew the ins and outs, it was fairly obvious that there was a lot more to it than that, and that both Helen and Oliver, if not Jerry too, had been very much hurt by whatever it was that had taken place. Debbie didn't like to think of her mother as wicked, but she couldn't help wondering what Helen Macken was feeling now that what had been wrested from her had been so comprehensively thrown away. And for what? Some curious sort of pride, rooted in snobbery and watered by spite? She wanted to go on loving Dot, but just at the moment, she was finding it very hard. She had written a letter, apologising for what she had said, and saying that she really hoped her mother would come to the wedding when it took place, but there had been no reply. Nothing to be done about that.

Then there was Tim, back in Embridge now with his parents, awaiting trial. There seemed very little doubt that he would be found guilty, and that Lesley's wonderful inheritance was gone, literally, up in smoke. Sometimes, the evidence seemed so irrefutable that Debbie almost believed it. He hadn't been in touch, and neither had she, his dream, and Lesley's, would go on without them. Nothing to be done about that, either.

As for the little sister, Cressida, she had vanished into the blue with her new man, and not even a postcard had arrived to say that she was all right. Since her family had done their best to be supportive to her, that seemed to Debbie to be the final straw. Even Mawgan, who had of all people no reason to feel kindly towards her, had stepped aside for her, again and again, to his own distress. To leave them to worry was cruel. It would hurt every one of them to a greater or lesser degree, and sometimes she wondered if that was exactly what the spoiled little brat had in mind. Unless and until she chose to get in touch, nor was there anything to be done about that, making a perfect set of three unsolvable conundrums.

Or was that quite true.

On the last Sunday in September, Chel dropped by the Fish unexpectedly. It was almost the end of the month and the last week in the life of the old sailing school, and the only guests for Seagulls were a middle-aged couple from Lesley's aunt's bookings, quite happy to occupy a room at the Fish instead and to spend their days driving around, and so no responsibility of Debbie's. Roger had gone home, promising to keep in touch; Carl Colenso had left his mobile number. If anyone came for the sailing after this week, it was down to the bank to sort them out.

'What are we going to call our new venture?' Roger had asked, on his last night. He and Debbie were sitting together in the bar, making plans.

'The Phoenix Sailing School?' she suggested, off the top of her head, laughing at its quite unplanned aptness.

'Good name,' said Roger, considering. Debbie, who hadn't said it seriously, thought again. It was a good name, he was right, it had a good ring to it, and it was easy to remember.

'There'll be lots to do, just as soon as we can get at it. Will you come back?'

'Soon as you say. And you get that Yachtmaster Instructor – we can look around for another boat. Do Competent Crew and more advanced courses.' The dream was escalating far beyond Tim's horizon. Debbie grinned at him.

'I know a good name for that, too.'

'Dead Duck!' they said, speaking together, and the people in the bar turned to look at them indulgently as they fell about laughing.

But there was no Roger around now with whom to talk things over, and Debbie was at a loose end, even lonely. Being on her own gave her too much time to think, about Tim's problems, about Lesley's, and about her mother's, all apparently insoluble and to a great degree self-inflicted too, which made it even sadder. About little sister Cress, she preferred not to think at all, it made her too angry. After the excitement and the high pressure and constant companionship of the summer, it would be too easy to join Mawgan in being depressed, and the Fish still had a week to run on summer opening times. She was glad, therefore, when her sister-in-law dropped in on her way back from a quick visit to Mr and Mrs Horsefall, now preparing to leave the house by the creek. She struggled up from reception carrying a large, oblong parcel wrapped in brown paper, and Debbie, alerted by Shirley on the intercom, met her at the door to the flat.

'What on earth is that?'

'Engagement present.' Chel leaned it against the wall, thankfully. 'Oliver told me to bring it over, get it out of the way. What are you doing? Organising a car boot sale?' She looked at the muddle on the floor in amazement.

'Unpacking all those boxes,' said Debbie. It had been something to do. The boxes had sat in the corner of the room since they had arrived from Embridge, she had been too busy to attend to them. Now there was suddenly more than enough time. 'Is that what it looks as if it is?' She eyed the oblong parcel.

'What do you think?' asked Chel. Debbie opened her eyes wide.

'Pretty generous engagement present! What did you tell me those pictures were going to sell for?'

'Don't go there,' advised Chel, shuddering. 'Unwrap it instead. Have a look. You and I will have to hang it anyway, we can't expect your one-armed bandit downstairs to do it. It weighs a ton, he must have framed it in lead piping. How is he – the bandit?'

'Nearly good as new. He's physically very fit, and I finally got him to admit to the depression and do what he was told to do months ago, so he's been easier to live with lately, too. I don't think even Tim could really justify calling him *bloody Angwin* these days.'

'Yeah. Oliver said he hoped you'd noticed, or something very like it, when we first met him.'

'Difficult *not* to notice, to be fair, once I was living with him.'

'Tell me about it! Oliver and me are world experts, remember.'

'Don't remind me!'

Debbie heaved the picture onto her sofa, which was now helping to furnish the flat together with her chest of drawers between the windows, and a presently empty bookcase against the wall by the fireplace. It wasn't as heavy as it must have felt after humping it all the way from the car park, but heavy enough. She began to tear off the paper. Chel perched on the arm of one of the armchairs to watch.

'And pub life generally? All it's cracked up to be?'

Debbie shuddered dramatically, her hands full of corrugated paper.

'It's a whole new world! I'm thinking of passing the long, dark, winter days writing a definitive horror story – *The Day the Beer Lorry Came* – followed by its even more horrible sequel, *The Day the Beer Lorry* Didn't *Come.* Eat your heart out, Stephen King!' The last of the paper fell away and she stood back. 'Oh, wow!'

The picture was portrait layout, and Oliver had framed it, not in lead piping but in limed wood. It was of a line of boats, Greek caiques from the looks of them, brightly coloured in reds and blues and yellows, moored beneath a tangle of undergrowth that had been laid on not with a brush, but with a knife. The smoothly applied, contrasting water was clear turquoise, shading in the shallow foreground to the colour of sand behind old glass, and fish swam among anchor ropes, sea-urchins tiptoed among the painted pebbles, weeds swayed in an unseen current. There was no sky visible, but it was full of sunlight and shadows on the glittering sea, you could almost feel the warmth of a clear summer's day. The signature, *Nankervis,* and the date were tucked away in the corner.

'How many thousands?' asked Debbie, awed.

'Best not to ask.'

'We'll have to insure it, and although I don't know what the Fish insurance covers, I'm certain it won't be *that.* We need to know.'

'Ask Oliver then. I don't even want to think about it, it's surreal.'

'Then we'd better get it up on the wall, where it'll be safe.'

There was already a hook up there, fortunately a fairly hefty one. They hoisted the picture up between them, standing on two of the dining chairs, straightened it, and stood back to admire it. The sparely furnished room she had first seen, Debbie realised, was becoming positively homelike. The picture gave it focus and character. Chel looked around her.

'Come on, I'll give you a hand. Let's finish the job.'

'OK. If you let me do the same for you next week.'

'I'm counting on it!' confessed Chel. They set to work, and as they worked, naturally enough, they talked. There was certainly enough to talk about.

'All going well, is it?' Chel asked, and just stopped herself saying *apart from your mother.* She bit her lip, but Debbie seemed not to notice anything. She stood up with a pile of books in her arms, her face sober.

'Well, I don't think Dad is a hundred per-cent happy, but he's putting a good face on it. It isn't that he doesn't like Mawgan, I think he does… but happy ever after isn't exactly an option, is it?'

'It never is,' said Chel. She sat back on her heels and put the cups she was holding down on the floor. 'All your father wants is what's best for you, but at least he appreciates that it's for you to decide what that is. How did *you* get on with *his* family?'

'I liked them. They're very genuine people, and it's been hard on them. All they want is to just get on with life and have it all sorted out – which isn't going to happen quickly.'

'And little sister?'

'Little hellcat! I've never met her.'

'No… I don't think I have, either, or not to be aware of it.' Chel spoke without thinking. Debbie stared at her.

'You? Why should you have met her?'

'Oh… she lived in Trelewan for a while, with some friends of ours who let rooms. Long before you met Mawgan. Before we met Kate and Charlie, come to that – but I suppose I might have seen her round the village and not known.'

'How odd.' Debbie went over to the bookcase with her books and began to arrange them on a shelf. 'I mean, when you think about it – you nearly met Cressida, and if I hadn't been an idiot and set off with that dreadful

444

weather forecast, Mawgan would probably have been dead… almost as if it was all *meant*, somehow.'

'Life is all ifs and buts like that.' Chel took out some more cups and saucers, carefully. 'If I hadn't been going out with a journalist, if I hadn't been living in Embridge… that's how people do meet. And surely he wouldn't have actually *died*. Someone would have missed him.'

'Nobody knew where he was,' said Debbie. A book slipped out of her hand, and she bent to pick it up. 'He just lit out – didn't say where he was going, or anything. Just getting away – the only people who knew he was there were the people at the farm, and they might not have bothered. He was a stranger to them. Although I think they did know who he was…' She felt cold. The book went on the shelf upside-down. She reversed it.

'Well, it's all in the past anyway,' said Chel, comfortingly. 'We're looking forward to getting to know him properly after next week, and actually, even Oliver thinks it's going to be great having you so close. So stop brooding about what didn't happen.' She scrambled to her feet. 'Where do you want this china?'

Debbie only had her own personal things to unpack, it didn't take long. Books arranged in the bookcase, china in the glass-fronted top of the dresser, clothes in the cupboard and drawers that Mawgan – or rather, Mrs Solomons – had cleared for her. Her television set was already in the bedroom, her few pictures on the walls. They were left at the end with a miscellaneous heap of oddments, a pile of CDs and videos, a couple of cut-glass vases.

'Shove them in the bottom of the dresser,' said Chel. 'If there's room. Is there room?' She looked around with satisfaction. 'He's not going to know the place when he next comes in. It looks positively civilised.'

Debbie knelt down and opened the bottom cupboard. There were one or two things already in it, but not a lot, Mawgan wasn't one for a lot of personal possessions, he didn't leave himself enough time to make use of them, although that, Debbie had resolved, was going to change. There were a couple of ornamental objects, a little horse in antiqued bronze and a modern majolica pot that looked as if Allison might have picked them up on her travels, which she pulled out to go on the mantelpiece, a pile of catalogues of catering equipment that from their dates must have been there forgotten for quite a long time, and a photograph, lying on its face. She picked that up idly and turned it over.

'Oh, shit!' said Debbie.

They were all there, all four of them, head and shoulders. Anna, Mawgan and Allison must have been in their late teens or early twenties when it was taken, they were grouped together with Mawgan in the middle, and the little sister, Cressida, in front of him, leaning back against him. She must have been standing on something, Debbie decided, aged around nine or ten, pretty as a picture, with the same dark hair and eyes as her mother and Allison, small and dainty and obviously laughing, childishly pleased with herself and with life. The other three were all smiling too, the mischievous family smile. They were full of life, enjoying themselves, and at ease with each other. It was quite obvious, even in the photograph, that the child was safe and loved, protected by the three older siblings.

Chel had come to look over her shoulder. They knelt together on the carpet, looking at the photograph of the happy family.

'Isn't life a bugger sometimes?' said Debbie, sadly. 'I've thought about her so much, but do you know, this is the first time I've ever seen her? Michael Stanley, in a way, brought what happened to him on himself... but Mawgan will always feel himself responsible – and the reason this obviously loved little girl turned on him like that and threw tantrums at the bare idea of an appeal is that if it was allowed, that left *her* sharing the blame. As she should ... yet they all look so happy here. It's a good thing we don't know what's in store for us.'

Chel said nothing. She reached out and took the picture from her sister-in-law's hand and held it, running her fingers across the surface.

Yes... it hadn't been her imagination. The three older ones were warm under her touching fingers, vital and alive, but when she laid her palm over the child's picture it felt cold... cold... Words floated into her mind... *Full fathom five thy father lies, of his bones are coral made...* she could hear the ripple of water, the hum of a deep current around hidden rocks...

'What's wrong?' asked Debbie, suddenly aware of her stillness. Chel said, 'I think she's dead.'

'*Dead?* She can't be! She went off with some man, Anna said.'

'I think she drowned. I don't know when, or where, and I can't tell you how.'

'How can you possibly know?' Debbie sounded angry. Chel shook her head.

'I can't tell you. I just know, when I looked at that picture, I knew that

446

she was dead, and when I touch it, I can feel it. And I'll tell you something else. That feeling of hate has gone – you remember, I said about it that night in the hospital? I thought then, it must have come from her.' She shivered, although the room was warm.

Debbie stared at her.

'You can't possibly tell that! It's impossible.'

'I know. But I can.' She handed the picture back to Debbie. 'Put it away. Right at the back. She's safe there.' It was an odd thing to say. Debbie did as she was told, and then got to her feet. She wanted to do something – anything – very badly indeed. The happy, constructive afternoon had turned suddenly chill.

'I'm going to make some tea.' She turned on her heel and headed for the kitchen. Chel shoved the CDs and videos into the half-empty cupboard and sat back on her heels. She was trembling. There were other things, that she hadn't told to Debbie. The presence of a man, unseen and, she thought, unreal too, something conjured, not a true spirit. A phantom of the mind… he had loomed above the child in the picture like a dark cloud, there was no protection from that. Not while you lived.

Debbie came back, a mug of tea in each hand. She sat down on the sofa, and Chel got to her feet and took one of the armchairs. They sipped their tea in silence for a minute.

'How can you do that?' asked Debbie, after a while. She sounded calmer, more accepting. 'Are you clairvoyant, or something?'

'I'd like to think not, but I think I probably am. One of my mother's aunts was, too. There've been some strange things that happened… Debbie, I'm sorry. You'd never have known, if I hadn't… I'm sorry.'

'I don't actually *know* now, do I? There isn't even a body, who'd believe me? Or you, come to that. What do I do? Tell me what to do, you started this!'

'I don't think there's anything you can do.'

Thinking about it, neither did Debbie. Chel believed in what she said, that was obvious, and she had a creepy feeling that she believed it too. Even so, there was no way that she could, for instance, say it to Mawgan. Even thinking about it made her head spin. She said, 'It doesn't seem right to say nothing, but I can see what you mean.'

'The thing is,' said Chel, thinking it out, 'unless they've actually asked you themselves, people don't believe you – you've only to think about all those people who predict plane crashes, or say they know where Lord Lucan is – it's a standing joke. An insult, almost. And Mawgan – when I said that to him that night in the hospital. He was too polite to say *bullshit* but you could see him thinking it. On the other hand, even the police ask clairvoyants for help sometimes, and in among all the debris, there's quite often the odd nugget of truth. It comes back to this – I think it does, anyway. You can only tell people if they ask. If they ever start asking where she can have gone, then you could, I suppose, suggest they consult a clairvoyant, if they're that kind of people. Are they? Mawgan certainly isn't.'

'His mother might be.' Debbie sat still, thinking in her turn. 'Would I send her to you?'

'I don't think so. For the sake of credibility, I think it has to be someone else.'

'There's a lot of charlatans around, aren't there?'

'That's why I said, someone else. I might be one, for all you know – for all I really know, too. But I can tell you a couple of people who I'm pretty sure aren't, if it ever comes up.'

'This conversation can't be happening!'

'Or of course,' said Chel, with simple practicality, 'her body may turn up.' She paused. 'But on the whole, if I was you, I'd rather hope not.'

'Why not? It would settle everything…' She met Chel's eyes, and her voice faltered. 'Oh shit!' If Cress's body was found, where would that leave Mawgan? She felt her colour fade.

'Come on, Deb. He *didn't* kill her, so nobody can prove that he did.'

'Tim probably didn't set fire to Seagulls. Where has that got him?'

'It won't happen, Deb. *Deb*! Come back!' Chel spoke sharply.

Debbie pulled herself together, but only with an effort. She thought of the Angwins, struggling to balance son against daughter, brother against sister and not take sides until they nearly pulled themselves apart. She thought of the childish, laughing face in the photograph. Quite suddenly, her sudden fear, all her resentment and fury against Cressida Stanley, dissolved in a totally unexpected tide of pity. She was so young, so immature. So unfit for the self-inflicted tragedy that had been her portion in life. So much a fool to herself. So completely unfortunate.

'I think she sucked them dry,' she said, thinking it out as she spoke. 'They've nothing left to give her now. She took so much from them, that in the end, they're relieved to believe that she's just gone off with someone and is maybe happy.'

'Then perhaps,' said Chel, 'it would be cruel anyway to disillusion them. Leave them to think that and have some peace.'

Debbie said, quietly, 'Poor kid.'

'Yes,' said Chel.

Neither of them had ever met her, but they sat together and sipped their tea, and thought about Cress with compassion.

This time, not even Kate had been there to see her. Cress had walked up to the quoit in the dusk and stood there, with the stone under her feet, feeling the chilly September evening breeze on her cheek. It was nearly autumn, she could smell it in the air. She was perfectly calm, following her own particular star. There was a star in the sky now, she fixed her eyes on it.

'Mike?'

The breeze whispered among the brambles, *Cressida, Cresssida…*

'I couldn't do it. She was too strong. She beat me back, every time she beat me back. She loved him…' It was an admission, she realised, that she hadn't loved Mike, not that way. She had been in love with love, but the blonde girl, Debbie, had had the real thing. She said, 'Mike…' pleadingly. 'Mike, I need you.' Not *I love you.*

And then she saw him. He was standing below her on the very edge of the coast path, beckoning. She heard his voice in the wind. *It's time. It doesn't matter. It's time now… come…*

'Time for what?' asked Cressida.

To move on….

She walked slowly down the little hill, and he held out his arms to her. She began to run. As she ran, he seemed to move away, out over the cliff, to hang suspended against the night sky.

Cressida… come…

She ran, on winged feet, straight towards his open embrace.

Her body fell, without a sound, and the deep sea that washed the foot of the cliffs took her into its arms, and held her, so that she vanished, without trace, to be held in the dark current until she was unrecognisable, gone for ever. The sea around Cornwall's coasts will often give up its victims, but not Cressida. Not ever. She died, and she was never to know what a catalyst for good she had been to those she had wished to harm, nor how much harm she had done to a man she never knew.

For her, at least, that was *The End*. For the others, the play would go on. That's how life goes.

www.ingramcontent.com/pod-product-compliance
Lightning Source LLC
Chambersburg PA
CBHW060303100726
47907CB00002B/263